Jilly Cooper is a journalist, writer and media superstar. The author of many number one bestselling novels, including *Riders, Rivals, Polo, The Man Who Made Husbands Jealous, Appassionata, Score!, Pandora* and *Wicked!*, she lives in Gloucestershire with her husband, Leo, her rescue greyhound, Feather, and five cats. She was appointed OBE in the 2004 Queen's Birthday Honours List for her contribution to literature.

Find out more about Jilly Cooper and her novels by visiting her website: www.jillycooper.co.uk

By Jilly Cooper

FICTION	Wicked!
	Pandora
	The Rutshire Chronicles:
	Riders
	Rivals
	Polo
	The Man Who Made Husbands Jealous
	Appassionata
	Score!
NON-FICTION	Animals in War
	Class
	How to Survive Christmas
	Hotfoot to Zabriskie Point (with Patrick Lichfield)
	Intelligent and Loyal
	Jolly Marsupial
	Jolly Super
	Jolly Superlative
	Jolly Super Too
	Super Cooper
	Super Jilly
	Super Men and Super Women
	The Common Years
	Turn Right at the Spotted Dog
	Work and Wedlock
	Angels Rush In
	Araminta's Wedding
CHILDREN'S BOOKS	Little Mabel
	Little Mabel's Great Escape
	Little Mabel Saves the Day
	Little Mabel Wins
ROMANCE	Bella
	Emily
	Harriet
	Imogen
	Lisa & Co
	Octavia
	Prudence
ANTHOLOGIES	The British in Love
	Violets and Vinegar

Appassionata
JILLY COOPER

CORGI BOOKS

TRANSWORLD PUBLISHERS
61–63 Uxbridge Road, London W5 5SA
a division of The Random House Group Ltd
www.booksattransworld.co.uk

APPASSIONATA
A CORGI BOOK : 9780552156387

First published in Great Britain
in 1996 by Bantam Press
a division of Transworld Publishers
Corgi edition published 1997
Corgi edition reissued 2007

Addresses for Random House Group Ltd companies outside
the UK can be found at: www.randomhouse.co.uk
The Random House Group Ltd Reg. No. 954009

Typeset in 10/11pt New Baskerville by
Phoenix Typesetting, Burley-in-Wharfedale, West Yorkshire.

8 10 9

Penguin Random House is committed to a sustainable future for
our business, our readers and our planet. This book is made from
Forest Stewardship Council® certified paper.

Printed and bound in Great Britain by Clays Ltd, Elcograf S.p.A.

To the Royal Scottish National Orchestra
because they make great music
and I love them all.

ACKNOWLEDGEMENTS

I felt desolate when I finished *Appassionata*, because I'd grown so fond of everyone who'd helped me. I was constantly touched and amazed that musicians who work such punishing hours often for totally inadequate reward should not only be the merriest and the funniest people in the world, but also the most generous with their time.

I must therefore start with a huge thank you to my guardian angels: benign bassoonist Chris Gale, his wife Jacoba, ace cook and viola player, and another viola player, Ian Pillow, who writes Classic FM magazine's wonderfully funny column 'Pillow Talk', all of whom are from the Bournemouth Symphony Orchestra; fair Annie Tennant, Education Officer of the City of Birmingham Symphony Orchestra; Jack Rothstein, super violinist, soloist, leader and conductor, his wife Linn Hendry, another ace cook and a pianist who specializes in violin repertoire and, finally, brilliant violinist Marat Bisengaliev and his wife Steena, sublime first flute at the English Northern Philharmonia. These eight muses gave me inspiration, encouragement, endless introductions and marvellous hospitality. They never minded being bombarded with silly questions:

'Could you bonk a *small* woman on a Glockenspiel?' 'Would tearstains devalue a Strad?' in the middle of the night, and if they didn't know the answer, they always knew someone who did. I cannot thank them enough.

I would also like to thank two great orchestras. The Bournemouth Symphony Orchestra, whose managing director, Anthony Woodcock, very kindly allowed me to spend a fantastic week in Poole, talking to both musicians and management, sitting in on rehearsals, touring the South of England, listening to marvellous concerts. Everyone helped me, but I would like to say a special thank you to: Marion Aston, Kevin Banks, Andy Barclay, Nigel Beale, Philip Borg-Wheeler, Andrew Burn, Johnathan Carney, John Charles, Stuart Collins, David Gill, Stuart Green, Christopher Guy, Helen Harris, Anna Hawkins, Karen Jones, Edward Kay, Jayne Litton, Janet Male, Peter Rendle, Nick Simmonds, Verity Smith, Louise Wright and Peter Witham.

The red lion's share of my gratitude, however, must go to the Royal Scottish National Orchestra. In 1992 I wistfully asked my friend Ian Maclay, who now runs the BBC Concert Orchestra, if he knew a band brave enough to take me on tour abroad. Within twenty-four hours, he had elicited an invitation to tour Spain from Paul Hughes, who must be the nicest man in classical music, and who had just taken over the RSNO as managing director. Thus followed one of the best weeks of my life, as the orchestra roared through five cities bringing the very formal Spanish audiences yelling in delight to their feet. Walter Weller, darkly urbane and charismatic, was the conductor. John Lill, adored by musicians and public alike, was the soloist, reducing us to tears of joy by his piano playing and tears of laughter with his outrageous jokes at the parties afterwards. Jacqueline Noltingk ensured everything ran miraculously smoothly.

In May 1995, I joined the RSNO for a second tour, this

time of Switzerland. Once again they played gloriously to packed houses and their '*music in my heart I bore, Long after it was heard no more*'. Again everyone was sweet to me, but the following were of particular value to my story: Kenneth Blackwood, Helen Brew, Valerie Carlaw, William Chandler, John Clark, John Cushing, Pamella Dow, Morrison and Sally Dunbar, Claire Dunn, Jeremy Fletcher, Charles Floyd, Brian Forshaw, Martin Gibson, John Gracie, John Grant, David Hair, John Harrington, Philip Hore, Duncan Johnstone, Fiona McPherson, Evgeny Minkov, Angela Moore, Jacqueline Noltingk, Joseph Pacewicz, Edwin Paling, Miranda Phythian-Adams, Kevin Price, Stephane Rancourt, Michael Rigg, Alistair Sinclair, Ian Smith, Justine Watts, Stephen West.

One of my heroes in *Appassionata* is a young pianist, so I am deeply indebted for their advice to great soloists: Philip Fowke, Janina Fialkowska, Alan Kogosowsky. I am also grateful to Philip MacKenzie, conductor and moving force behind the west country Amadeus Chorus and Orchestra and his bassoonist wife, Charlotte, who suggested I play the narrator in *Peter and the Wolf* at the Colston Hall in 1992 so I could experience the utter terror of performing as a soloist with an orchestra.

My other more gilded hero is a brass player. Here again marvellous anecdotes and many ideas came from David McClenaghan and John Logan, first and third horn of the RSNO; Martin Hobbs, second horn of the BSO; Lance Green, first trombone, RSNO; Danny Longstaff, second trombone of the CBSO; and, above all, the legendary Tony Turnstall, former principal horn of the Royal Opera House Orchestra, Covent Garden.

My main heroine becomes a conductor, so I was immensely grateful for help from Sir Simon Rattle, Andrew Litton, Jean Paul Casadesus, Stephen Barlow, Ross Pople, Denys Darlow, Michael Burbidge, Olivier Dohnányi and, above all, André Previn. André, that most droll and beguiling of raconteurs and companions, allowed me to sit in on rehearsals and recording sessions with the mighty London Symphony Orchestra, and talked to me for many hours about both conducting and playing the piano. I must especially thank dear Bill Holland and Harriet Capaldi of Warner Classics for producing the most beautiful CD, titled *Appassionata*, from a selection of the music featured in the book. On the recording side, I must also thank Erik Smith, Steve Long and Mike Hatch for patiently answering my questions, as did distinguished composers Orlando Gough and Geoffrey Burgon, my neighbour in Gloucestershire.

On the musical administration side, I'd like to thank Philippa Sherwood and Andrew Jowett of Symphony Hall, Birmingham, and Christopher Bishop, late of the RSNO, and the Philharmonia for all their help and wonderful hospitality; Ian Killik of the English Northern Philharmonia; Lynn Calvin of the Musicians' Union; Libby Macnamara of the Association of British Orchestras; Charles Beare, world expert on string instruments; Sonia Copeland; Chris Steward; Alison Taylor; Ellyn Kusman, Rosamund Leitch of the Wagner Society; Diggory Seacome, timpanist supremo and mover and shaker of the Cotswold Symphony Orchestra.

All the artists' agents in *Appassionata* are perfectly horrid, and bear absolutely no resemblance to darling Sir Ian Hunter, Chairman of Harold Holt or Trudy Wright of Harrison Parrott, both of whom advised and royally entertained me.

During my research I spent a lovely morning at the English National Ballet, where Amanda Gilliland and Jane Haworth were as beautiful as they were informative. I also spent fascinating days at the Royal Academy of Music and the Royal College of Music, watching Professor Colin Metters and the venerable George Hurst assessing student conductors, practising their skills on respective college orchestras. One of the pieces was Bartók's *Violin Concerto*, which Mia Biakella, the soloist, played quite beautifully. I am also grateful to Huw Humphreys, a young conductor, who, after his début at the Holywell Music Rooms in Oxford in 1994, gave me invaluable insight into pre-concert nerves and the problems of galvanizing musicians.

On a plane to Lapland in 1993, I sat next to a delightful bassoon teacher, who told me piano competitions were frightfully bent with large lady judges often receiving grand pianos as bribes. After that I naturally included a piano competition in the book.

I then spent a splendidly inspiring week at the Leeds Piano Competition, where I saw no sign of pianos changing hands, and must thank the competition's founder, Fanny Waterman, and Mary Bailey, from the sponsors, Harveys of Bristol; organizer Liz Arnold; Romilly Meagen of the BBC and Roisin Grimley from Ireland. It was also a great thrill to spend time with the brilliant young British contestant Leon Macaulay, who, immediately after the result, touchingly apologized for only coming second: 'It would have been so much better for your book if I had won.'

I also made friends with Mark Anderson, the handsome American contestant who came third, and he and his wife, beautiful pianist Tamriko Siprashvili, delighted us with piano duets when they came to stay in Gloucestershire.

In August 1994, I spent exciting days at the International World Power Competition. Sulamita Aronovsky was the indefatigable organizer, and I must thank Ann Fuller, Samantha Day, Irish judge John O'Conor and American judge Herbert Stessin for their marvellous observations. Joe Lewis looked after me backstage. Another brilliant British contestant, Paul Lewis, came second, and again spent many hours talking to me.

I must also thank Leonard Pearcey and Ruth Cubbin for twice inviting me to Radio 2's excellent Young Musician of the Year Award. Many musicians helped me with the background material and stories for the book, they include Robin Brightman of the LSO; Richard Hewitt of the NEP; John Hill; Erich Gruenberg; Alberto Portugheis, Elizabeth Drew, Stuart Elsmore, Alistair Beattie, Alexa Butterworth, Mats Lidstrom, Angela Moore, Rodney Friend, former leader of the LSO; Norman Jones, former principal cellist to the Philharmonia; Raymond Cohen, former leader of the Royal Philharmonic and Hannah Roberts.

The music press were also fantastic. Malcolm Hayes of the *Daily Telegraph* and Mike Tumelty of the *Glasgow Herald* held my hand on the tour of Spain; David Fingleton looked after me at the Leeds and took me to endless lovely concerts, as did dear Lesley Garner, super columnist, and Mel Cooper, of Classic FM, who opened his great generous heart and his address book to me on endless occasions. John Julius Norwich invited me to a gorgeous lunch in the country. Norman Lebrecht of the *Daily Telegraph*, author of *The Maestro Myth*, nobly tracked down the legend of the chandelier in Buenos Aires Opera House. Keith Clarke, editor of *Classical Music* magazine and doughty fighter of musicians' causes; Nicholas Kenyon, controller of Radio 3; Professor George Pratt, Peter Barker, and Ron Hall all gave me wonderful support. My old friend and *Sunday Times* colleague, Peter Watson, wrote a terrific biography of Nureyev, which was a constant inspiration when I was inventing my explosive dancer, Alexei Nemerovsky.

All my friends in fact entered into the spirit of the book. Alan Titchmarsh thought up the title *Appassionata*. My piano tuner, Marcus Constance, dreamt up a devilish plot for sabotaging a grand piano in the middle of a competition. Lord Marchwood took me up in an air balloon over France with General Sir Peter de la Billière. Musicians have many ailments. Joanne Murphy advised me on physiotherapy, Dr Joe Cobbe, Dr Graham Hall and Staff Nurse Sue Workman on asthma. John Hunt introduced me to Anthony Norcliffe who knew all about mending brass players' teeth.

On the non-musical front, Patrick Despard of Arcona was fiendishly imaginative about the splendours and skulduggeries of property developing. Toby Trustram-Eve was brilliant on computers, as were Andrew Parker-Bowles on racing; Peter Clarkson and Jean Alice Cook on nuns' names and practices; Susie Layton on decor; Sue Jacobs of Leicestershire Social Services and Deborah Fowler in her book, *A Guide to Adoption,* on adoption. Other friends who came up with ideas include: Susannah and Bill Franklyn; Anthony Rubinstein; George and Dang Humphreys; John Woods; Roger and Rowena and Harry Luard; Francis Willey; Mary and Anthony Abrahams, Graham Hamilton, Michael Leworthy and John Conway of the Archduke Wine Bar.

I'd like to thank Jack and Patricia Godsell for their beautiful Toadsmoor Lake which was a magical source of inspiration, and Dr Ueli Habegger who finally located the island on Lake Lucerne where the ghost horn player can sometimes be heard at dusk.

As well as Spain and Switzerland, my research took me in 1994 to Prague and on to Pardubice where British jockey, owner and trainer Charlie Mann exceeded all expectation by coming second in the Czech Grand National on It's a Snip, and, later in 1995, came first. I must particularly thank Lord Patrick Beresford and Baroness Dory Friesen for masterminding this brilliant trip for Abercrombie and Kent, and thank Sir Derek Hodgson, Queeks Carleton-Paget and Liza Butler for being such beguiling travelling companions.

Many people wrote offering advice and anecdotes. Many numbers went down in my telephone book. Sadly I never followed them up, as in the end I had to get down and write the book.

If researching *Appassionata* was a joy, writing it was an absolute nightmare, because an orchestra consists of so many characters, and mine were continually getting out of control, particularly in their behaviour. In fact Paul Hughes, Ian Pillow and Linn Rothstein, who most heroically read through the manuscript for mistakes, said they had never come across an orchestra who behaved quite so badly as my Rutminster Symphony Orchestra. Nor in fact had I. The high jinks and bad behaviour in the book are totally invented and I would stress that *Appassionata* is a work of fiction. Any resemblance to any living person or organization is wholly unintentional and purely coincidental.

I never got to Bogotá, where the first chapters are set, but Annie Senior and Peter Gibbs-Kennet gave me graphic descriptions and I was much indebted to both the *Lonely Planet Guide to Colombia* and *The Fruit Palace*, a stunning travel book by Charles Nicholl.

Nor would the book have probably been completed if Sharon Young of British Airways hadn't tracked down a folder of early notes I'd left at Glasgow Airport.

I am truly sorry if I've left people out, but if I'd listed everyone who'd helped me, these acknowledgements would be longer than the book.

While writing *Appassionata*, I was gently followed to Prague and Switzerland and all over England by a BBC2 crew from Bookmark, headed by Basil Comely. Occasionally I found it difficult to get to grips with brass players' love lives or seduction techniques in conductors' dressing-rooms with a BBC crew breathing down my neck, but otherwise they couldn't have been more tactful, kind and fun to work with.

My publishers, Paul Scherer, Mark Barty-King, Patrick Janson-Smith of Transworld, as usual, have been impeccable, constantly encouraging and reassuringly rock solid at a time of book trade turbulence. I have also had wonderful editorial help from the glorious Diane Pearson and from Broo Doherty, who grew cross-eyed as she ploughed through 1403 pages of manuscript, crammed with musical references. She was, however, so charming and so enthusiastic about the book that I accepted (nearly) all the changes she suggested.

I am also eternally lucky in having the best, most delightfully insouciant agent in London, Desmond Elliott and his assistant Nathan Mayatt, who spent so much time photostatting and despatching.

For the first time, the huge manuscript was typed on computers. The real heroines of *Appassionata* are therefore my friends: Annette Xuereb-Brennan, Anna Gibbs-Kennet and Pippa Moores, who completed the job on new machines in an amazing five weeks. They worked long into the night, deciphering my deplorable handwriting, punctuating, correcting spelling and pointing out howlers. I cannot express sufficient gratitude to them nor to Ann Mills, my equally heroic cleaner, who somehow cleared up the mess while picking her way delicately through rising tower blocks of manuscript until the house looked rather like Hong Kong.

Sadly, my dear friend and PA, Jane Watts, who supervised so much of the photostatting and collation of the book, and who had given me so much love and support over the past six years, left in November. With huge luck, her place was soon taken by Pippa Moores, who arrived to oversee the move into computers, and stayed to become my new assistant.

My family, *comme toujours*, were staunchness personified. Leo, Felix and Emily hardly saw me for eighteen months, but gave endless cheer and comfort. So did my dogs Barbara and Hero, and four cats, Agnes, Sewage, Rattle and Tilson-Thomas, who provided sweet, silent companionship and protection in the gazebo, even at the dead of night.

Dear gallant Barbara (Gertrude the mongrel in my last four books) seemed determined to cling on to life if only to see me safely into port. She died a few days after I finished writing, leaving the world unbearably the poorer.

Finally, I would like to thank musicians everywhere for the joy they bring, and to beg the public, the Government and the local authorities to give them the support and funding they so desperately need, because a twenty-first century without orchestras would be very bleak indeed.

THE CAST

CANON AIRLIE   Non-executive director of the Rutminster Symphony Orchestra (RSO), a silly old fossil, constantly campaigning for better behaviour.

ALBERTO   The unsalubrious landlord of the Red Parrot Hotel, Bogotá.

AMBROSE   Principal guest conductor, RSO, known as the 'fat controller' – a bitchy old queen.

ANATOLE   A tempestuously talented Russian contestant in the Appleton Piano Competition.

SISTER ANGELICA   A beautiful nun.

ASTRID   Boris Levitsky's stunning Scandinavian au pair.

LADY BADDINGHAM   Much admired ex-wife of Tony Baddingham, the fiendish ex-chairman of Corinium Television.

BENNY BASANOVICH   A very tiresome Russian-French pianist who can only play fortissimo.

BARRY THE BASS   Principal Bass, RSO.

MRS BATESON   A music lover who befriends Marcus Campbell-Black.

JAMES BENSON   A very expensive private doctor.

BIANCA   An adorable Colombian orphan.

MRS BODKIN   Rupert Campbell-Black's ancient housekeeper.

17

ROSALIE BRANDON	A bossyboots attached to the London office of Shepherd Denston, the music agents.
MILES BRIAN-KNOWLES	Detested deputy-managing director of the RSO, a snake in furry caterpillar's clothing, who is after Mark Carling's job.
DAVIE BUCKLE	A beaming bruiser and RSO timpanist.
EDDIE CAMPBELL-BLACK	Rupert's father, an unreformed rake, just emerged from a fifth marriage and raring to go.
RUPERT CAMPBELL-BLACK	Ex-world show-jumping champion, now one of the world's leading owner-trainers. Still Mecca for most women.
TAGGIE CAMPBELL-BLACK	Rupert's wife – an angel and the apple of his once roving eye.
MARCUS CAMPBELL-BLACK	Rupert's son by his first marriage. A pianist whose path to the top is only impeded by asthma and nerves, both chiefly induced by his father.
TABITHA CAMPBELL-BLACK	A ravishing tearaway. Rupert's daughter, also by his first wife.
CANDY	A comely rank-and-file RSO viola player.
LINDY CARDEW	The mettlesome wife of Rutminster's planning officer.
MARK CARLING	Beleaguered managing director of the RSO.
HAN CHAI	A very young Korean contestant in the Appleton Piano Competition.

18

TONY CHARLTON	The indefatigable and perennially cheerful stage manager of the RSO. Known as 'Charlton Handsome'.
MISS CHATTERTON	Marcus Campbell-Black's piano teacher, known as 'Chatterbox'.
LADY CHISLEDON	A lusty old trout and member of the RSO board.
CHRISSIE	An obsequious Northern Television minion.
CLARE	Another very pretty RSO rank-and-file viola player, also the orchestra Sloane.
CLARISSA	Principal Cello, RSO.
CLIVE	Rannaldini's sinister black-leather-clad henchman.
THE BISHOP OF COTCHESTER	Another silly old fossil.
CRYSTELLE	A bullying beautician from Parker and Parker's department store.
OLD CYRIL	Fourth Horn, RSO. Heavy drinker. One-time great player.
HOWARD DENSTON	Wideboy partner in Shepherd Denston, the toughest music agents in New York.
HOWIE DENSTON	Howard's son, a mega-manipulator, who runs the London office.
NICHOLAS DIGBY	The harassed orchestra manager, or 'fixer' of the RSO, who has the unenviable task of getting the right number of players on and off the platform. Known as 'Knickers'.

MRS DIGGORY	Heroic cleaner of the Celtic Mafia's Bordello.
DIZZY	Rupert Campbell-Black's head groom.
DMITRI	A lyrical and lachrymose cellist, later Principal Cello of the RSO.
BLUE DONOVAN	Second Horn of the RSO – blue-eyed Irishman of great charm, who covers for Viking O'Neill, both on the platform and in life. Founder member of Viking's gang, known as the 'Celtic Mafia'.
DIXIE DOUGLAS	A Glaswegian hunk, whose light duties as an RSO trombone player leave him rather too much time to hell-raise and troublemake. Another member of the Celtic Mafia.
MRS EDWARDS	Helen Campbell-Black's underworked cleaner.
ELDRED	A beleaguered Principal Clarinet.
ERNESTO	A bribable Italian judge at the Appleton Piano Competition.
FRANCIS FAIRCHILD	Second Desk First Violin of the RSO nicknamed the 'Good Loser' because he's always mislaying his possessions.
LIONEL FIELDING	Leader of the RSO. A vainglorious narcissist.
HUGO DE GINÈSTRE	The charming, chivalrous, French-Canadian Co-leader of the RSO.
GISELA	Sir Rodney Macintosh's cherishing housekeeper.

ROWENA GODBOLD Charismatic blonde First Horn of the Cotchester Chamber Orchestra (CCO), the RSO's deadly rivals.

PABLO GONZALES An ancient Spanish pianist of great renown.

HELEN GORDON (formerly CAMPBELL-BLACK) Rupert's first wife, now married to his old *chef d'équipe*, Malise Gordon. A legendary beauty and devoted mother of Marcus and less so of Tabitha.

GILBERT GREENFORD A caring beard from the Arts Council. Mark Carling's cross.

GWYNNETH A caftanned barrel from the Arts Council, Gilbert Greenford's 'partner' and another of Mark Carling's crosses.

RANDY HAMILTON Third Trumpet from a brass-band and Army background. Another Celtic Mafia hell-raiser.

HERMIONE HAREFIELD World-famous diva and Rannaldini's mistress, who brings out the Crippen in all of us.

DIRTY HARRY A bass player who never washes.

LYSANDER HAWKLEY Rupert Campbell-Black's jockey, the man who made husbands jealous.

HARVEY THE HEAVY George Hungerford's chauffeur and minder.

OLD HENRY Oldest member of the RSO, once auditioned successfully for Toscanini, now rank-and-file First Violin.

ANTHEA HISLOP A pianist, mostly employed for her sex appeal.

GEORGE HUNGERFORD	An extremely successful property developer.
MOTHER MARIA IMMACULATA	A radiant Reverend Mother.
FAT ISOBEL	A very large viola player.
JISON	A dodgy local car dealer.
BRUCE KENNEDY	American pianist and judge at the Appleton Piano Competition.
KEVIN	A social worker.
MARIA KUSAK	A violin soloist, also employed for her sex appeal.
LORD LEATHERHEAD	Chairman of the RSO and crashing bore on the subject of bottled water.
BORIS LEVITSKY	A glamorous Russian conductor/composer. A bear with a very sore heart as a result of his wife Rachel's suicide.
LILI	A bribable German judge in the Appleton Piano Competition.
LINCOLN	Fifth Horn of the RSO.
HILARY LLOYD	Second Clarinet of the RSO. An utter bitch known as the 'Swan of Purley' because she's very refined and having an *affaire* with the leader. Hell-bent on becoming First Clarinet.
SIR RODNEY MACINTOSH	Musical Director and Principal Conductor of the RSO. Absolute sweetie and sly old fox, who lets others do the worrying.

GEORGIE MAGUIRE	World-famous singer and song writer.
CARL MATTHESON	Homespun American contestant in the Appleton Piano Competition.
JUNO MEADOWS	Second Flute of the RSO. Tiny and tantalizingly pretty, known as the 'Steel Elf'.
MARY MELVILLE	Principal Second Violin of the RSO. A doting mother known as 'Mary-the-Mother-of-Justin'.
SISTER MERCEDES	A very butch nun.
QUINTON MITCHELL	Third Horn of the RSO who wants to be First Horn.
SALVADOR MOLINARI	A naughty Colombian playboy.
MILITANT MOLL	A fiercely feminist rank-and-file viola player of the RSO.
ALEXEI NEMEROVSKY	Principal dancer of the Cossak Russe Ballet Company, known as 'The Treat from Moscow'.
NELLIE NICOLSON	Third Desk cellist of the RSO known as 'Nellie the Nympho'.
NINION	Second Oboe. Militant Moll's exceedingly hen-pecked boyfriend.
NORIKO	An adorably pretty Japanese; rank-and-file First Violin of the RSO.
DECLAN O'HARA	Irish television presenter and megastar. Managing director of Venturer Television.

DEIRDRE O'NEILL	Irish judge at the Appleton Piano Competition, fond of a drop, known as 'Deirdre of the Drowned Sorrows'.
VICTOR (VIKING) O'NEILL	First Horn and hero of the orchestra because of his great glamour, glorious sound and rebellious attitude. The Godfather of the Celtic Mafia.
SIMON PAINSHAW	First Oboe of the RSO. A walking *Grove's Dictionary* who spends his time brooding on his reeds.
PEGGY PARKER	Owner of Parker and Parker department store in Rutminster High Street. A bossy boots and overbearing member of the RSO board.
ROGER 'SONNY' PARKER	Her frightful son, a composer of even more frightful modern music.
MISS PARROTT	The rather heavenly RSO harpist.
JULIAN PELLAFACINI	The highly respected leader of the New World Symphony Orchestra.
LUISA PELLAFACINI	His lovely bosomy wife.
NATALIA PHILIPOVA	An apparently untalented Czechoslovak pianist.
PETER PLUMPTON	First Flute of the RSO.
MISS PRIDDOCK	Mark Carling's secretary, beloved of Old Cyril. An unfazed old trout.
ROBERTO RANNALDINI	Mega-Maestro and arch fiend, currently musical director of the New World Symphony Orchestra.
KITTY RANNALDINI	His third wife, in love with Lysander Hawkley.

24

JACK RODWAY A randy receiver.

SISTER ROSE A sympathetic nurse at Northladen General Hospital.

ABIGAIL ROSEN American violinist, nicknamed 'L'Appassionata' whose dazzling talent and tigerish beauty have taken the world by storm.

THE RUTSHIRE BUTCHER A very critical critic.

SANDRA Christopher Shepherd's secretary.

FLORA SEYMOUR Wild child, pilgrim soul and daughter of Georgie Maguire. Destroyed by a teenage *affaire* with Rannaldini, now concentrating on the viola.

CHRISTOPHER SHEPHERD Abigail Rosen's agent, a control freak, who provides the respectable front of Shepherd Denston.

MISS SMALLWOOD Secretary, Cotchester Music Club.

STEVE SMITHSON Second Bassoon of the RSO and representative of the Musicians' Union. Muscular right arm from throwing the book at people.

DAME EDITH SPINK A distinguished composer and Musical Director of the Cotchester Chamber Orchestra.

TOMMY STAINFORTH Principal Percussion of the RSO.

MRS DICK STANDISH A skittish sponsor's wife.

DENNIS STRICKLAND Principal Viola of the RSO, known as 'El Creepo'.

BILL THACKERY	Second Desk, First Violin of the RSO. Better at cricket than the violin. Jolly good sort.
JAMES VEREKER	A television presenter.
WALTER	A benevolent bass.
SERENA WESTWARD	Head of Artists and Repertoire at Megagram Records.
CLAUDE 'CHERUB' WILSON	Third Percussion of the RSO. Very dumb blond and orchestra mascot.
XAVIER	A Colombian orphan.

THE ANIMALS

BOGOTÁ A black labrador puppy.

JOHN DRUMMOND Miss Priddock's cat, office mouser to the RSO.

GERTRUDE Taggie Campbell-Black's mongrel.

JENNIFER One of Lady Baddingham's yellow labradors.

NIMROD Rupert Campbell-Black's lurcher.

MR NUGENT Viking O'Neill's black collie.

PENSCOMBE PRIDE Rupert Campbell-Black's favourite and finest horse.

SHOSTAKOVICH Rodney Macintosh's grey Persian cat.

SIBELIUS AND SCRIABIN Abigail Rosen's black-and-white kittens. Like magpies, the two of them bring joy.

TIPPETT Dame Edith Spink's pug.

TREVOR Flora Seymour's rescued mongrel.

FIRST VIOLINS

1 LIONEL FIELDING
2 HUGO DE GINESTRE
3 BILL THACKERY
4 FRANCIS 'THE GOOD LOSER'
11 OLD HENRY
12 NORIKO

SECOND VIOLINS

1 MARY-THE-MOTHER-OF-JUSTIN
12 LITTLE JENNY

VIOLAS

1 EL CREEPO
2 SALLY BRIGGS
7 MILITANT MOLL
8 FAT ISOBEL
9 CLARE
10 CANDY

CELLOS

1 CLARISSA
3 NELLIE THE NYMPHO

BASSES

1 BARRY THE BASS
5 DIRTY HARRY
6 EL SQUEAKO

FLUTES

1 PETER PLUMPTON
2 JUNO THE STEEL ELF

OBOES

1 SIMON PAINSHAW
2 NINION

CLARINETS

1 ELDRED
2 HILARY LLOYD

TRUMPETS

PERCUSSION

HORNS

CLARINETS

FLUTES

HARP

SECOND VIOLINS

FIRST VIOLINS

MINSTER
Orchestra

BASSOON
1 Jerry the Joker
2 Steve Smithson

HORNS
1 Viking O'Neill
2 Blue Donovan
3 Quinton Mitchell
4 Old Cyril.
5 Lincoln the Bumper

TRUMPETS
1 Carmine Jones
3 Randy Hamilton

TROMBONES
1 Dixie Douglas

TIMPANI
Davie Buckle

PERCUSSION
1 Tommy Stainforth
3 Cherub Wilson

HARP
Miss Parrott

Managing Director	Mark Carling
General Manager	Miles Brian-Knowles
Orchestra Manager	Knickers Digby
Stage Manager	Charlton Handsome

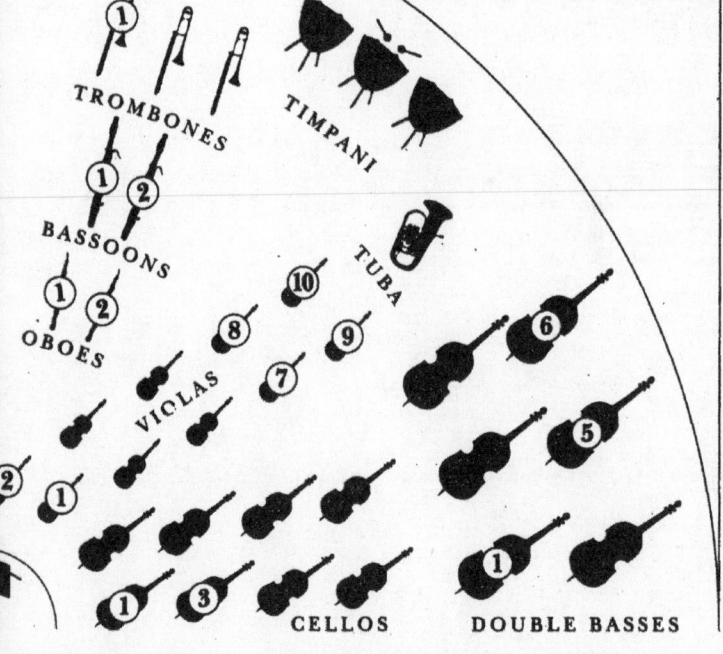

Appassionata

OVERTURE

ONE

In the second week of April, Taggie Campbell-Black crossed the world and fell head over heels in love for the second time in her life. The flight to Bogotá, delayed by engine trouble at Caracas, took fifteen hours. Taggie, who'd hardly eaten or slept since Rupert broke the news of their journey, could only manage half a glass of champagne. Nor, being very dyslexic, was she able to lose herself in Danielle Steel or Catherine Cookson, nor even concentrate on Robbie Coltrane camping it up as a nun on the in-flight movie. She could only clutch Rupert's hand, praying over and over again: Please God let it happen.

By contrast Rupert, concealing equal nerves behind his habitual deadpan langour, had drunk far too much as he sat thumbing through a glossary at the back of a Bogotá guide book.

'I now know the Colombian for stupid bugger, prick, jerk, double bed, air-conditioning, rum and cocaine, so we should be OK.'

At El Dorado Airport, the policemen fingered their guns. Seeing an affluent-looking gringo, the taxi-driver turned off his meter. As they drove past interminable whore-houses and dives blaring forth music, past sky-scrapers next to crumbling shacks, Rupert's hangover was assaulted as much by the shroud of black diesel fumes that blanketed the city as by the furiously honking almost static rush-hour traffic. There was rubbish everywhere. On every pavement, pimps with dead eyes, drug pushers carrying suitcases bulging with notes, tarts in tight dresses pushed aside beggars on crutches and stepped over grubby sloe-eyed children playing in the gutter. How could anything good come out of such a hell-hole?

As Taggie couldn't bear to wait a second longer, they drove straight to the convent. Now, quivering like a dog in a thunderstorm, she was panicking about her clothes.

'D'you think I should have stopped off at the hotel and changed into something more motherly?'

Rupert glanced sideways. No-one filled a body stocking like Taggie or had better, longer legs for a miniskirt.

'You look like a plain-clothes angel.'

'My skirt isn't too short?'

'Never, never.' Rupert put a hand on her thigh.

By the time they reached the convent, a sanctuary amid the squalor, appalling poverty and brutal crime of the slums, the fare cost almost more than the flight. The Angelus was ringing in the little bell-tower. The setting sun, finding a gap in the dark lowering mountains of the Andes, had turned the square white walls a flaming orange. A battered Virgin Mary looked down from a niche as Rupert knocked on the blistered bottle-green front door. But no-one answered.

'We should have rung first to check they were in,' said Taggie, who, despite the stifling heat of the evening, was trembling even more uncontrollably. She looked about to faint.

'I can't imagine they're out at some rave-up.' Gently Rupert smoothed the black circles beneath her terrified eyes. 'It'll be OK, sweetheart.'

He clouted the door again.

Now that he was in Cocaine City, Rupert had never more longed for a line to put him in carnival mood to carry him through the interview ahead. His longing increased a moment later when the door was unlocked and creaked open a few inches and he had a sudden vision that Robbie Coltrane had got in on the act again.

A massive nun, like a superannuated orang-utan, with tiny suspicious eyes disappearing in fat, a beard and hairy warts bristling disapproval, demanded what they wanted. She then insisted on seeing their passports, and looked as though she would infinitely rather have frisked Taggie than Rupert, before grudgingly allowing them in.

By contrast the Mother Superior, Maria Immaculata, was femininity and charm itself. She had a round, almost childish face, like a three-quarters moon, smiling, slanting brown eyes and a cherished olive complexion set off by a very white linen wimple. As she moved forward with a rustle of black silk, the pale hand she held out to Rupert and Taggie was soft and slightly greasy from a recent application of hand cream. Mother Maria Immaculata believed you brought more comfort to the poor and suffering if you looked attractive.

It was the same in her office. Crimson bougainvillaea rioted round the windows outside. Frescoes and wood carvings decorated the white walls of her office. On her shiny dark desk, which seemed to breathe beeswax, beside a silver vase of blue hibiscus flowers, lay the report of Rupert's and Taggie's marriage drawn up by English social workers.

But Maria Immaculata did not set much store by gringo gobbledygook. More importantly, Rupert and Taggie had come with an excellent recommendation from the Cardinal, who was a friend of Declan O'Hara, Rupert's partner, whose television interviews were transmitted world-wide. Even the Pope, who was evidently writing a book, and might want to promote it on Declan's programme one day, had put in a good word.

Anyway, Maria Immaculata preferred to make up her own mind.

And then Sister Mercedes, who acted as the convent Rottweiler, had helped matters greatly by bringing in this beautiful couple – the man as blond, tall, handsome and proud as El Dorado himself, and his wife as deathly pale, slender and quivering as a eucalyptus tree in an earthquake, and whose eyes were as silver-grey as the eucalyptus leaves themselves.

Taggie was clutching a litre of duty-free brandy, a vast bottle of *Joy*, a British Airways teddy bear wearing goggles and a flying jacket, and a white silk tasselled shawl decorated with brilliantly coloured birds of paradise.

'For you,' she stammered, dropping them on Mother Immaculata's desk and nearly knocking over the vase of hibiscus, if Rupert with his lightning reflexes hadn't whisked it to the safety of a side table.

'I h-h-ho-pe you don't m-m-m-ind us barging in, straight from the airport, but we were so longing—' Taggie's voice faltered.

Timeo Danaeos, thought Sister Mercedes grimly. She spent her life pouring cold water on the romantic enthusiams of Maria Immaculata, who was now lovingly fingering the white shawl.

'Dear child, you shouldn't have spoiled us.'

'They will do for a raffle,' said Sister Mercedes firmly.

Maria Immaculata sighed.

'Perhaps you could arrange some tea, Sister Mercedes. Sit down.' She smiled at Rupert and Taggie and pointed at two very hard straight-backed wooden chairs. 'You must be tired after such a journey.'

'Not when you've been travelling as long as we have,' said Rupert, thinking of the wretched years of miscarriages and painful tests and operations, the trailing from one specialist to another, not to mention the humiliation of the endless KGB-style interrogations by social workers.

'Are you capable of satisfying your young wife, Mr

Campbell-Black?' or 'Would you be prepared to take on an older child, one perhaps that was coloured, abused or mentally and physically handicapped?'

To which Rupert had snapped back: 'No – Taggie's got enough problem children with me.'

'You're too old at forty-four, Mr Campbell-Black. By the time he or she is a teenager, you'll be nearly sixty. I'm afraid if you want a baby, you and Mrs Campbell-Black will have to go abroad.'

Rupert gritted his teeth at the memory.

Looking at the two of them, Maria Immaculata felt that beneath his cool, Rupert was the far more apprehensive. Probably because his background, which involved a disastrous first marriage, a string of *affaires*, one illegitimate daughter – the English social workers had hinted there might be others – was much more likely to scupper the adoption. He had, however, been an excellent father to his two teenage children and appeared to have a very happy marriage to this beautiful wife.

And who would not, thought Maria Immaculata, admiring Taggie's sweet face, now that the sun curiously peering through the bougainvillaea had added a glow to her blanched cheeks.

The hand not clutching Rupert's was now rammed between her slender thighs to stop them shaking. It was also noticeable how she winced every time the crying of a baby in the orphanage could be heard over the wistful chant of women's voices coming from the chapel.

Over herbal tea so disgusting Rupert suspected it had been made from Sister Mercedes' beard shavings, it was agreed Taggie should spend the next three weeks helping in the orphanage to indicate her suitability as a mother. Rupert would drop her off and collect her in the evenings. There was no way Sister Mercedes was going to let him loose among her novices.

As a rule, couples were never shown their prospective baby at a first interview. But Maria Immaculata was so charmed by Taggie trying so heroically to hide her longing, that she reached for the telephone and gabbled a few sentences. Sister Mercedes pursed her thick lips – it was all going too fast. Rupert, who'd picked up some Spanish on the international show-jumping circuit, went very still. What if they produced a hideous baby, Taggie had such high expectations.

'You may find you cannot love the baby we have chosen for you,' said Maria Immaculata as though reading his thoughts. 'But our babies are like gold to us, and we, in turn, may decide you are not the right parents to have one, but we thought—'

There was a knock on the door and a beautiful young nun in a snow-white habit, whose dark eyes widened in wonder as she saw Rupert, came in bearing a tiny bundle hidden in a lace shawl.

'This is Sister Angelica, who runs the nursery,' said Maria Immaculata.

I wouldn't mind taking that home, thought Rupert irrationally.

'We thought Mr and Mrs Campbell-Black might like a glimpse of baby Bianca,' went on Maria Immaculata.

This time the hibiscus really did go flying, as Taggie leapt up and stumbled forward, drawing back the shawl and gazing down in wonder at the little crumpled face.

'Oh look,' she whispered. 'Oh, may I hold her? Oh Rupert, oh look,' she gasped, taking the fragile body in her arms.

As if it were the Christchild itself, thought Sister Angelica.

Taggie gazed and gazed.

'Look at her tiny nose and her perfect ears, and her long fingers and she's got little fingernails already and eyelashes and her skin's like ivory. Oh Rupert, was anything ever so adorable?' Taggie's gruff voice broke, and her tears splashed down onto Bianca's face waking her, so the baby blinked and opened big shiny black eyes.

'Oh thank you, she's so beautiful,' sobbed Taggie.

It was as instinctive as one of his brood mares nuzzling and suckling a new-born foal. Suddenly Rupert didn't need that cocaine hit after all.

Seeing the look of pride and triumph on his face, Maria Immaculata mopped her eyes. Sister Angelica was openly crying as she dabbed *Joy* behind her ears. Only Sister Mercedes looked as though her big end had gone.

'There, I mustn't monopolize her, you must hold her,' Taggie turned to Rupert.

But Rupert was only happy because Taggie was over-joyed. To him, Bianca was just a blob. In fact the only baby he'd ever liked had been his daughter Tabitha.

Perhaps Bianca sensed this, because when she was handed over to him she went absolutely rigid, screamed, and even regurgitated milk over his blazer, until Sister Angelica, laughing, removed her.

Meanwhile a dazed Taggie was hugging Maria Immaculata. 'I know it's only the beginning and she's not remotely ours yet, but thank you,' she mumbled. Then, turning to a still, stony faced Sister Mercedes, she settled just for clasping her hand.

'You've all been so kind, oh may I hold her again?'

'Would you like to give Bianca her bottle?' asked Maria Immaculata, then, ignoring Sister Mercedes – to hell with the raffle – added: 'I think this calls for a glass of brandy all round. I do hope you'll be comfortable in the hotel Sister Mercedes has chosen for you. It is very convenient, only three kilometres from the convent.'

To Rupert, the Red Parrot was Sister Mercedes' revenge – a two-storey, cockroach-ridden version of the hair shirt. Having acceded to Rupert's demands for double beds and air-conditioning over the telephone, the landlord, Alberto, whose tight, grease-stained grey vest displayed tufts of stinking, black armpit hair, showed them into a room where the double bed wouldn't have accommodated two anorexic midgets. The air-conditioning consisted of wire netting over the window, an electric fan which distributed the dust and the swarms of insects, and a gap along the top of the walls to let in the blare of the television sets in neighbouring rooms. Outside the rickety balcony was about to collapse beneath the weight of two parched lemon trees in terracotta tubs, and traffic roared both ways up and down what had been described as a 'quiet one-way street'. It was only when Taggie looked round for water to relieve the parched lemon trees, that they realized the nearest bathroom was twenty yards down the corridor.

Seeing that Rupert was about to blow his top, Taggie said soothingly that Alberto couldn't be that bad.

'Did you see those sweet little hamsters running round his office?'

Rupert hadn't got the heart to tell her they were on tonight's menu along with another Colombian delicacy: giant fried ants.

'The only consolation,' he said, crushing a second cockroach underfoot, 'is that the Press will never dream of looking for us here. Tomorrow we'll move somewhere else.'

'I don't think we can. Alberto just told me he's Sister Mercedes' brother.'

But they were so tired and relieved they fell asleep wrapped in each other's arms in one tiny bed.

The next morning, Taggie, shrugging off any jet lag, was back at the convent, blissfully happy to be looking after Bianca and helping Sister Angelica with the other orphans. Having dropped her off, Rupert returned to the Red Parrot and spent half the morning on the telephone checking up on all his horses, including his best one, Penscombe Pride, who had happily recovered from a nasty fall in the Rutminster Gold Cup.

Rupert also tried to cheer up his favourite jockey, Lysander Hawkley, who was suicidal because his old horse Arthur had collapsed and died within a whisker of winning the Gold Cup, and because the girl he loved,

Kitty Rannaldini, was showing no signs of leaving her fiendish husband.

'No Arthur and no Kitty, Rupert, I don't think I can stand it.'

Afterwards Rupert visited the Ministry of Foreign Affairs in Bogotá. As a former government minister, he wanted to see how many strings he could pull, and how much red tape he would have to cut through to enable them to take Bianca back to England.

He lunched with a polo friend, a sleek, charming playboy called Salvador Molinari, who offered him a cocaine deal.

'You know so many reech people, Rupert.'

The deal would have sorted out all Rupert's problems at Lloyds. Regretfully, he refused.

'I've got to behave myself, Sal, until we've got Bianca safely home.'

Later, in the Avenida Jiminex, Rupert bought some cheap emeralds from a dealer for Taggie, his daughters, Perdita and Tabitha, and Dizzy, his head groom. In Bogotá, beside the dark-haired, dark-eyed Colombians, Rupert was as flashily conspicuous as a kingfisher. Leaving the dealers, he was stopped by a policeman, pretending to be doing an official search, who then tried to make off with Rupert's Rolex and his wallet. Being still high from a cocaine hit at the dealers', Rupert knocked the policeman across the street, leaving him minus two front teeth, and went off and bought a gun and a money belt.

On the way to pick up Taggie, the taxi broke down. Having asked Rupert to give him a push, the driver proceeded to drive off with Rupert's briefcase, containing the emeralds and all the adoption papers and medical reports, stamped both in Petty France and by the Ministry in Bogotá.

As Rupert proceeded to shoot the taxi's tyres out with his new gun, two more policemen smoking joints on the pavement, totally ignored the incident. Retrieving his briefcase, finding excellent use for all the Colombian swear words he'd learnt on the flight over, Rupert went off and hired a bullet-proof Mercedes, which made him half an hour late picking up Taggie, which in turn resulted in a sharp dressing-down from Sister Mercedes.

Taggie, she said, had been worried and Rupert had missed a chance to bath and feed Bianca. Rupert tried not to look relieved. As the old monster waddled off to fetch Taggie, he reflected that in a battle with his bullet-proof Mercedes, Sister Mercedes would win hands down.

Taggie reeled out in manic mood.

'Oh Rupert, she's so sweet, she's wearing one of the dresses we brought, and she drank all her bottles, and Sister Angelica said she cried much less today, and I'm sure she smiled at me, although it was probably wind. And Sister Mercedes was really friendly and sat next to me at lunch.'

'Mercedes Bent,' said Rupert.

After a surprisingly good dinner at the Red Parrot, of shell-fish stew and mango-and-guava ice cream, enhanced by a bottle of Chilean Riesling, they were just drinking to little Bianca, when Taggie turned green and lurched upstairs. Glued to the only lavatory on the landing, Niagara at both ends, she threw up and up and up into a bucket until she was only producing yellow froth and specks of blood. A local doctor, summoned by a demented Rupert, said it was only altitude sickness and prescribed rest.

In the morning, when Mother Immaculata popped in with a bunch of roses from the convent garden and a bottle of water flavoured with lemon-juice and sugar, she was happy to report back to the nuns that never had she seen a husband more devoted or worried than Rupert.

By the evening Taggie was delirious, raging with fever,

too ill to be moved as various doctors supplied by Salvador trooped in and out. Trusting none of them, Rupert was onto James Benson, his doctor in Gloucestershire.

'I don't give a fuck if it's three o'clock in the morning, I want you out here.'

'Give it another twenty-four hours, altitude sickness often takes this form.'

'You've given her the wrong jabs, you overpaid clown.'

Upstairs, he could hear Taggie screaming. 'I'll ring back.'

Red-hot pokers were gouging out Taggie's brain, she was being bombed by massive cockroaches, the blades of the electric fan crept nearer and nearer like the Pit and the Pendulum. It was getting hotter by the minute, not a breath of wind moved the gum trees outside, the rains were expected any day.

In her more lucid moments, Taggie screamed for Bianca. 'Don't take her away, I hate you, I hate you.' She was pummelling at Rupert's chest.

Then at three in the morning, Colombian time, as he was changing her soaking nightgown, he thought he was hallucinating too, and that Taggie had turned into his first wife, Helen, whose slender body had been covered with freckles. Then he realized it was a rash, and was on to the hospital in a flash, yelling at them. Twenty minutes later, an old man arrived, yawning, with his suit over his pyjamas.

'Just shut up and leave me alone with your wife.'

He was out in five minutes. He had given Taggie a jab to sedate her and curb the itching. When the blisters developed she would need calamine.

'And you got me out of bed for this,' he glared at Rupert.

'What is it, for Christ's sake?'

'Virulitis.'

A little Spanish is a dangerous thing. Rupert went ashen.

'Smallpox,' he whispered. 'Oh God, don't let her die.'

'Chicken pox,' grunted the doctor.

'Are you sure?'

'Quite; pretty uncomfortable in older patients. Now keep her quiet and stop her scratching. Pity to spoil such a lovely face.'

Dizzy with relief, Rupert belted back to the bedroom, only to find Taggie sobbing her heart out.

'Angel, you're going to be OK.' Rupert took her burning body in his arms. 'But you mustn't scratch.'

'The doctor says I c-c-can't see Bianca for a fortnight or go near the convent in case I give the babies chicken pox. They'll think I'm not healthy enough to be a mother, they'll give her to someone else. Oh Rupert, I can't bear it.'

'I'll sit with her, I'll go every day, I promise.'

Despite Sister Mercedes' furious chuntering, Maria Immaculata was most understanding. Of course Rupert could take Taggie's place. His was the side of the marriage of which she was unsure. It would be good to study him at close range.

TWO

As Sister Mercedes grimly predicted, Rupert caused havoc among the nuns. Anyone would have thought a high-ranking archangel, if not the Messiah, had rolled up as they made endless excuses to pop into the orphanage to gaze in wonder at this edgy, sunlit stranger, whose cold eyes were bluer than Mary's robes, and whose hair brighter gold than any medieval fresco. He also appeared to be poring over endless medieval scrolls.

Soon pale lips were being reddened by geranium petals, habits bleached to new whiteness, eyelashes darkened by olive oil from the kitchen, and beards and moustaches disappearing for the first time in years. Even Maria Immaculata discreetly wafting *Joy*, insisted on giving Rupert religious instruction, while the parish priest, who was as gay as a Meadow Brown after summer rain, bicycled over to preach a fierce sermon on the vanity of vanities.

The medieval scrolls were, in fact, reports on Rupert's racehorses, his television company, and his various enterprises faxed out to the Red Parrot from England.

Other faxes read more like an illiterate serial in a woman's magazine as Lysander, Rupert's jockey, who was even more dyslexic than Taggie, joyfully chronicled the escape of his great love, Kitty Rannaldini, from her fiendish husband's clutches.

Kitty had evidently made her getaway on The Prince of Darkness, Rannaldini's most valuable and vicious racehorse and managed to stay on his back until she reached Lysander's cottage. The horse had carried on into the village and trampled all over the vicar's crown imperials. Rannaldini, even more incensed than the vicar, had retreated to New York to take over the New World Symphony Orchestra, vowing vengeance.

'*and the besst news,*' wrote Lysander, '*is that kittys having my baby in the ortum so Biacna will hav sum ass to kik. Sorry yoov got to babysitt at least yoo can OD on snow or dope. botaga is sposed to hav the best grarse in the werld.*'

Aware of Sister Mercedes' massive disapproving shadow blocking out his light, Rupert hastily scrumpled up the fax.

Despite being the object of every other nun's adulation, Rupert often wondered how he endured those long days at the convent. There were only Sister Angelica and two novices to look after twenty babies in the orphanage, which was part of the old chapel and had high windows out of which you couldn't see. The din was fearful and when the rains came, to the incessant crying of babies, was added a machine-gun rattle on the corrugated roof.

Rupert was also exhausted. Having come to the end of a punishing racing season, masterminded the entire trip to Bogotá and worried himself into a frazzle over Taggie's illness, he was woken all through the night by calls from Tokyo, Kentucky and the Middle East. Like Bogotá, the bloodstock market never slept.

But, although Rupert ran one of the most successful National Hunt yards in the country, he was coming to the depressing conclusion that if he were going to beat Lloyd's and the recession, keep the estate going and support all his children, including Bianca, he would have to switch to the flat full time. Rupert had always been a hands-on boss, but, as he gazed at the sleeping baby, he thought how nice it would have been if he could have started handing over the running of the estate to his son, Marcus. But Marcus was a wimp, only interested in playing the piano.

Bianca was very sweet, Rupert decided, and far prettier than the other babies, but she slept most of the day, and Rupert had finished his faxes by ten o'clock. With plenty of time on his hands, he soon noticed a nearby cot where an older child, with a terrible squint and a dark magenta birthmark down the side of his brown face, sat slumped, gazing at the white-washed wall, the picture of desolation. But when Rupert stretched out a hand to smooth back the child's hopelessly matted hair, he cringed away in terror, whimpering like a kicked puppy.

'Poor little sod, what happened to him?'

'Beaten up and left for dead by his Indian parents,' said Sister Angelica angrily. 'They regard birthmark as sign of devil. We call him Xavier,' she went on, 'but it's him who needs saving. He show no desire to walk or talk, the doctor think he's seriously backwards.'

When Xavier was two, next month, he was destined for the state orphanage, which meant he'd almost certainly never be adopted.

'Even then he'll be lucky,' Sister Angelica added bitterly. 'All over Bogotá, you must have seen the posters, advertising funerals. Always the government have purges. In Chile, unwanted children are left to die in concrete bunker, here, they shoot any kid hanging round street, because it make the place untidy.'

Outside the convent, knee deep in mud, a little grave-yard lurked like a crocodile. Rupert shivered and, noticing Sister Angelica had tears in her eyes, put an arm round her shoulder. Sister Angelica, who'd been plunging rose thorns into her flesh at night to curb her immoral thoughts about Rupert, jumped away, but not before a glowering Sister Mercedes appeared in the doorway.

'You're wanted in the kitchen, Sister.'

Rupert was so bored, he started playing with Xavier, bringing him toys and sweets. At first Xavier shrank from him, but gradually interest sparked in the boy's hopelessly crossed eyes. The next thing was to improve Xav's appearance. He shouldn't be wearing girl's clothes. Rupert returned next day with a blue checked shirt and blue jeans to replace the flowing white nightgown. It was then he realized how pitifully thin Xav was. The trousers, which had to be rolled up at the ankle, were meant for a one year old.

It took two hours, four tantrums and two bars of chocolate to untangle and wash his hair. The screams were so terrible that Rupert had to remove him from the dormitory. The novices were in raptures over Xav's lustrous black curls. Sister Mercedes looked thunderous. She had spent her life in the prison of being ugly; what right had Rupert to raise Xavier's hopes of escape?

The days slid by, the rains continued. They'd have to build an ark soon. Taggie made heroic efforts not to scratch her spots which were crusting over and beginning to drop off. Every night she bombarded Rupert with questions about Bianca, poring over the polaroids he brought her, but beyond telling her Bianca had drunk all her bottles, put on a couple of ounces, cooed and slept, there was little of interest to report. Instead, he found himself talking about Xav who was still shoving him away one moment, clinging and tearful the next.

'I took him a teddy bear this morning, he totally ignored me and it all day. He still hasn't forgiven me for untangling his hair but when I went he yelled his head off.'

This had upset Rupert more than he cared to admit.

*   *   *

But the next morning when he arrived at the convent, Xav babbled with incomprehensible joy, frantically waving his little hands, trying to express himself.

'He's happy,' smiled Sister Angelica. 'He refused to be parted from the bear even in the bath.'

As Bianca was asleep, Rupert gathered up a purring Xavier and carried him across to the delapidated convent school where Sister Angelica, to the counterpoint of rain dripping into several buckets, was telling the children the legend of El Dorado, the Indian ruler, who had coated himself in gold dust before bathing. In homage, his subjects had tossed gold and precious stones, mostly emeralds, into the lake after him. Later the name El Dorado was given to an equally legendary region of fabulous riches.

Many of the Spanish Conquistadores, explained Sister Angelica, men who looked like Senor Campbell-Black, blushing slightly, she pointed at Rupert, had died from shipwreck and starvation when they sailed across the oceans in search of the riches of the lake. Many more Colombian Indians, she pointed to Xav, had been butchered in the process.

'The pursuit of gold,' she added gravely, as she shut the book, 'will never bring happiness. The only El Dorado is found in your hearts.'

Rupert, who'd always pursued gold relentlessly, and who had been wondering what Sister Angelica's legs were like beneath her white robes, raised a sceptical eyebrow.

Wandering out of the classroom, he passed a pile of wooden madonnas, roughly carved in the convent workshop, waiting to be sold in the market. Examining one he was startled to find it opening to reveal a hollowed inside. Jesus, what a country: even the nuns were smuggling coke. As no-one was looking, he slid the madonna into his inside pocket.

Having lunched yet again on rice and herbal tea, any minute he'd turn into a bouquet garni, Rupert realized it had stopped raining. Salvador had invited him out to his house in the country to try out a couple of horses. Suddenly desire to escape from Bogotá poverty and squalor became too much for him. As Sister Mercedes was out, no doubt terrorizing the poor, Rupert persuaded Sister Angelica to let him take Xavier along too, strapping him into the child seat in the back of the Mercedes.

After the rain, every blade of grass and leaf of jungle tree glittered in the sunlight like distilled emeralds. Xav gazed in wonder at towering dark grey mountains, brimming rivers, rainbows arched like limbo-dancing Josephs. He was even more excited by the fat piebald cows and the sleek horses, knee deep in the lush, rolling savannah round Salvador's beautiful white colonial house.

Salvador, who was sleeker than a Brylcreemed otter, was seriously rich. A Monet, a Picasso and a Modigliani hung on the drawing-room walls. Suntanned girls in bikinis decorated the swimming-pool. Sweeps of orchids grew everywhere like bluebells.

'You like?' he asked Rupert proudly.

'Of course, it's beautiful.'

'You should come in on that cocaine deal.'

'I have to keep my nose clean rather than running,' said Rupert, unhitching Xav from the child seat. 'I've got a lot of dependants. Anyway, I can't cope with this country, everything's crooked, the police, the government, the customs men, even the nuns. How d'you live with it?'

Salvador shrugged. 'We have a popular song in Colombia, if you dance with the devil, you must know the right steps.'

He was appalled by Xav.

'You said you were adopting lovely little girl.'

'We are. Just brought Xav along for the ride.'

Salvador lifted Xav's chin, looking in distaste at the

crossed eyes and the purple birthmark lit up by the sun, and shook his head.

'How old is he?'

'Nearly two.'

'Better buy him a pair of crutches for his second birthday, then he can beg in the street. He hasn't a chance once the nuns kick him out. Pity someone didn't give him a karate chop at birth.'

After that Rupert decided not to buy any of Salvador's horses. But if he hadn't resolved to switch to the flat, he would have been sorely tempted by a dark chestnut mare. Leaving a trail of silver spray, he let her have her head across the drenched green savannah, forgetting everything in the dull thud of hooves and the feel of a fit, beautiful horse beneath him. He was away for so long Xav had worked himself into a frenzy.

'Little runt seems quite attached to you,' said Salvador in surprise. 'Probably the only good thing that'll ever happen to him.'

'Come on then.' Leaning down, Rupert lifted Xav up in front of him and set off again.

He expected terror as he broke into a canter and then a gallop, but was amazed to hear screams of delighted crowing laughter, and the faster he went, the more Xav laughed.

Red-Indian blood coming out, thought Rupert, reflecting bitterly and briefly once again on his son Marcus who was terrrified of everything, particularly horses.

As they returned to the house for tea and rum punches, three Borzois swarmed out to meet them. Rupert missed his dogs terribly. He had been very upset to find a drowned puppy in the gutter outside the hotel that morning. He'd probably grown so attached to Xav, he told himself firmly, because he regarded him as a surrogate dog. And he was a brave little boy; when one of the girls in bikinis took him for a swim in the pool, after an initial look of panic in Rupert's direction, he screamed with delight again.

'He's a sweet kid,' admitted Salvador, as Xavier tucked into one of Colombia's more disgusting delicacies, cheese dipped in hot chocolate. 'But he's still too bloody ugly.'

On the way home, Rupert was held up by horrific traffic jams, a solid blockade of lorries belching out fumes, a bus had overturned tipping glass over the road, and a van was being checked by the police. Xav, however, slept through the whole thing. With a pang Rupert noticed the beauty of his left profile now his black combed curls fell over his forehead and his birthmark was hidden.

As Rupert walked into the convent, he was confronted by a jibbering Sister Mercedes, who snatched Xav away like a female gorilla scooping up her baby. How dare Rupert kidnap one of the children? He had seriously jeopardized his chances of adopting Bianca. How dare he raise expectations, she shouted, as a terrified Xav screamed and sobbed as he was dragged away.

Rupert flipped, all thought of behaving well for Bianca's sake forgotten. Sister Mercedes' squawks, in fact, were purely academic. There was no real likelihood of Rupert and Taggie being turned down. All the official documents were now stamped and, in private chats with Maria Immaculata, Rupert had agreed to donate a large sum to repair the school. He had also had enough of Sister Mercedes.

'If you don't shut your trap, you disgusting old monster,' he yelled, producing the hollowed-out madonna from his inside pocket, 'I'll tell the Cardinal exactly what you've been up to, although he's probably in it as well.' And he stalked out, dislodging most of the flaking green paint from the front door as he slammed it behind him.

* * *

Back at the Red Parrot, surrounded by polaroids of Bianca, Taggie had not realized how late Rupert was. She had been wrestling with a letter to her stepson, Marcus, wishing him good luck in a recital (how on earth did one spell that?) he was giving at college next week. She also begged him to come down to Penscombe soon to *'hopfully meat yor nu sisster'*.

Taggie's desire to bear Rupert's child had been intensified because she knew how much he wanted a son to run the estate. This, in turn, would have taken the pressure off Marcus. Saying Rupert got on brilliantly with Marcus had been the only time, in fact, she had lied to the social workers. She was equally ashamed that the moment Rupert walked in she shoved her letter under a cushion and launched into a flood of chat to distract him.

'Dr Mendoza says I'm not infectious any more.' Taggie was about to suggest they popped back to the convent for half an hour when she noticed the bleak expression on Rupert's face, and stammered that she couldn't wait to see Bianca tomorrow morning.

Fortunately Rupert was distracted by the telephone. It was Declan O'Hara, Taggie's father and Rupert's partner at Venturer Television, ringing from Gloucestershire. With his usual courtesy Declan asked after Bianca, Taggie's chicken pox and then the hotel.

'Even fleas boycott this place,' snapped Rupert. 'Get on with it, Declan, what d'you really want?'

'As you're in Bogotá, could you nip over to Buenos Aires tomorrow?'

'It's about two thousand miles, some nip,' protested Rupert, taking a large glass of whisky from Taggie. 'Didn't they teach you any geography at school?'

'I want you to go and see Abigail Rosen.'

'Who's she?'

'About the greatest fiddler in the world, and the hottest property in classical music,' said Declan reverently. 'They call her L'Appassionata. I want to do a two-hour special on her, but her agents, Shepherd Denston, who are even greater fiddlers than she is, won't answer my telephone calls. You're so gifted at doing deals.'

'Blarney wouldn't get you anywhere if I wasn't desperate to get out of this cesspit. And I don't know anything about music.'

'Bullshit your way through. I'll fax out Abby Rosen's c.v. There'll be tickets for you and Taggie at the box-office.'

Rupert promptly rang and squared the trip with Mother Maria, who, delighted that someone had taken on Sister Mercedes, was more than accommodating.

'It will do you good to have a break, enjoy yourselves. I would give the world to hear L'Appassionata.'

'At least we can get out of this dump for twenty-four hours,' said Rupert jubilantly. 'Your father wants us to chat up some female Nigel Kennedy. You'll love BA.'

Taggie was so desperate to catch another glimpse of Bianca, Rupert agreed they could pop in to the convent on the way to the airport. Stopping off at a toyshop, waiting for Taggie, Rupert glanced at a cutting which Lysander had just faxed out from *The Scorpion*. This claimed that Rupert was giving sanctuary to Lysander and Kitty Rannaldini, now that she'd left her husband, and weaved in an old quote from Rupert, that Kitty was well shot of 'an *arriviste* wop like Rannaldini'. Political correctness was never Rupert's forte.

Taggie by now had settled for a pink fluffy rabbit and a musical box.

'We better move it,' said Rupert, adding a red racing car for Xavier to the pile.

But one look at Bianca was too much for Taggie.

'Oh Rupert, d'you mind terribly if I don't come to BA?'

Rupert did mind – terribly, particularly when he thought of his battles with bureaucracy, and his heroic devotion to duty while she had chicken pox. The off-white suit he was wearing was the only thing in his wardrobe that didn't reek of sick. It was also the first time in seven years of marriage that Taggie had admitted that she wanted to be with anyone else more than him. But he was not going to show it.

'Why should I mind?' he said icily. 'Best-looking women in the world live in BA. Thanks for the pink ticket.'

Not even caring that Sister Angelica was witnessing such a scene, not bothering to kiss a horrified mouthing Taggie, ignoring the anguished bellows of Xavier, Rupert stalked out of the convent, nearly dislodging the battered virgin from her niche as he banged the door.

THREE

Rupert's mood didn't lighten until he reached Buenos Aires, a city where he had often played polo and which he had always loved. As he joined the crazy traffic hurtling along the wide streets, elegant regal houses gazed down unperturbed over the half-moon spectacles of their balconies. Even with a chill in the air and the trees in the lush parks already turning, the merry inhabitants appeared to be holding drinks parties on the pavement outside every café. After Bogotá it felt blissfully safe. For the first time in weeks, Rupert left off his money belt.

L'Appassionata posters were everywhere, showing off Abigail Rosen's rippling dark curls and hypnotic eyes, like the leader of some dodgy religious sect.

As her latest CD of Paganini's *Caprices* had just topped the classical charts, her face also dominated the window of every record shop, and she certainly caused mayhem round the opera house. Huge crowds, frantic for returns, rioted and smashed windows. Motorists, driven frantic by traffic jams, anticipated the concert with a fortissimo tantivy on their horns.

Rupert was delighted to flog Taggie's ticket for nearly a grand, but was completely thrown on entering the opera house to see Rannaldini's pale, sinister face glaring down from posters in the foyer. Declan had foxily omitted to tell Rupert that the New World Symphony Orchestra was touring South America, and Rannaldini, as their very new musical director, had flown down to BA to conduct them and Abigail Rosen in the Brahms concerto.

Rupert felt a rare wave of shame. He and Rannaldini had last met at the Rutminster Cup when all their horses had fallen, and Rupert had been venting hysterical rage on Lysander in front of the entire jockeys' changing-room for throwing the race: rage, which had turned out to be totally misplaced, as a post mortem had revealed Lysander's old horse had, in fact, died of a massive heart attack. As Kitty Rannaldini and Lysander were now happily shacked up in one of Rupert's cottages, the '*arriviste* wop', who regarded Lysander as a complete dolt, would, no doubt, suspect Rupert of masterminding the entire *coup*.

Rupert could have done without complications like this if he were going to sign up Abigail Rosen. She was probably under Rannaldini's forked thumb by now.

The five-minute bell put an end to his brooding. He had never seen a hall so packed. People were tumbling out of boxes, sitting in the aisles and on the edge of the stage, standing four deep along the back and virtually swinging from the chandelier which hovered overhead like some vast lurex air balloon.

The orchestra were already on stage tuning up. The only man in the place blonder than Rupert was the leader of the orchestra, Julian Pellafacini, an albino with a deathly pale skin, almost white hair curling over his collar and bloodshot eyes hidden behind tinted spectacles. Julian was such a brilliant musician, sat so straight in his chair at the front of the first violins and had such a sweet, noble expression on his thin bony face as he smiled reassuringly round at the other musicians, that their only desire was to play their hearts out for him.

But, beneath his air of calm as he chatted idly to the co-leader beside him, Julian was deeply apprehensive that Rannaldini would destroy his beloved orchestra. Now, for example, he was making them even more nervous by deliberately keeping them waiting.

The merry chatter in the audience grew louder as the glamorous bejewelled women tried to identify Rupert. Rupert, however, was scowling at a tall, self-important man with a leonine head and a glossy dark beard, emphasizing firm red lips, who was thanking the row in front in a loud booming voice for letting him in.

Rupert loathed beards and he thought the man looked like one of those ghastly Mormon fathers, photographed in colour magazines surrounded by hoards of adoring wives and children, and probably fiddling with the lot of them. He was affectedly dressed in a frock-coat with a scarf at the neck secured with a big pearl tie-pin. Rupert shuddered. By strange coincidence the man was now smugly and noisily informing the admiring redhead on his right that he was Christopher Shepherd, Abigail Rosen's agent, and showing her a haughty, head-tossing picture of his artist on the front of *Time* magazine.

Halting in mid-shudder, Rupert was about to tap Christopher Shepherd on the shoulder and make his number, when the orchestra rose to their feet and in swept Rannaldini to demented applause. For a second, he glared round at his new orchestra and raised his baton. Then the down-beat dropped like a hawk, introducing the first doom-laden octaves of the overture to Verdi's *The Force of Destiny*.

Rupert was tone-deaf and bored to tears by music, but he'd had plenty of practice in being bored and deafened in the last fortnight, and he had to admire the way Rannaldini drew his orchestra together. He might be small but he controlled every note, every nuance, every silence. There were also some ravishingly pretty girls in the orchestra, their split black skirts showing a lot of leg, their eyes going down to their music then up to Rannaldini as they bowed and blew with all their might.

Rannaldini, despite his icy exterior, was in a blazing temper. He had not only been vilely humiliated by Kitty leaving him, he had also been vastly inconvenienced. In one swoop, he had lost his whipping boy and his skivvy, who had tolerated his endless ex-wives, children and mistresses, run his four houses and masterminded his multifaceted career with incredible efficiency.

Since Kitty had walked, or rather galloped, The Prince of Darkness out of his life, Rannaldini had gone through three PAs in New York. The fourth, on the verge of a nervous breakdown, had booked him into the BA Hilton, where his *maîtresse en titre*, the great diva, Hermione Harefield, from whom he was trying to distance himself, was staying, instead of the Plaza in the suite next to Abigail Rosen. Even worse, the new PA had failed to order a white gardenia for his buttonhole, and, worst of all, she had forgotten to pack his tail-coat. Rannaldini had been reduced to pinching one off the Hilton's very reluctant head waiter, which was far too big, and every time he raised his arm he got a whiff of minestrone.

Rapturous applause greeted the end of the overture, but it was nothing to the uproar of stamping, cheering and wolf-whistles that detonated the hall when Abigail Rosen erupted onto the platform. Rannaldini gave her several lengths' start and speedily jumped onto his rostrum to disguise the fact that she topped him by at least three inches. He then waited impatiently, baton tapping, as she shook hands with the albino leader, then bowed and smiled at the orchestra before bowing and smiling at the audience.

Her straight, thick black brows above the tigerish yellow eyes, her hooked nose, huge drooping red mouth, wide jaw, thick dark curly hair, only just restrained by a black velvet bow and marvellous sinewy body, made her look almost masculine. But Rupert had never seen such a sexy girl. Her wonderful long legs were shown off by the briefest black-velvet shorts, while a fuschia-red sleeveless body stocking, emphasized strong white arms, a broad rib cage and high, full breasts.

Totally over the top, yet flaunting the fact that she'd earned them, were the huge diamonds that flashed on the bracelet on her left ankle, as though ice flakes had drifted down from the great chandelier overhead.

And she certainly detonated her fiddle. The Brahms concerto is so difficult it was originally described as having been written against the violin. After a very emotional beginning with a heaving ocean of sound, the orchestra plays on for three minutes before the soloist comes in.

During this agonizing wait, Abigail seemed to quiver like a mustang trapped in the starting gates. And when she picked up her bow, even Rupert had never heard anyone play with such raw passion and vitality, her fingers flickering like flames, her bow gouging out sound like a trowel digging for treasure. She played with total concentration and a wild threatening energy, and gave wonderful flourishes of the bow at the end of every important phrase, as she prowled around the stage, scent wafting from her hot body.

There was also something infinitely touching, when she wasn't playing, in the way she rested her head like a weary child on her two-million-dollar Stradavarius, and so spontaneous when she swung round and grinned at the first oboe, who'd gone quite puce in the face playing the ravishing opening to the slow movement.

Several times, however, she turned to scowl at Rannaldini, his stillness a total contrast to her incessant movement. With his sinister pallor, midnight-black eyes and cloak-like tail-coat, he was a dead ringer for Dracula. Rupert was glad Abigail kept making a cross of bow and fiddle to ward off the bastard's unrelenting evil.

She had now taken up the first oboe's luminous, hauntingly beautiful tune. Glancing sideways Rupert saw that tears were trickling down the wrinkles of the old woman beside him.

'*Mon dieu, oh mon dieu.*'

As Rupert passed her his handkerchief, his thoughts wandered to Xavier, poor little sod, what chance did he have? Rupert had read that lasers could cure a squint and work wonders with birthmarks. But he mustn't think like that. Taggie couldn't cope with two children, particularly one so retarded he couldn't even walk.

The orchestra were into the last movement now – a manic, joyous gypsy dance with terrifying cross-rhythms. Rupert could see the white glisten of Abigail's armpits, the dark tendrils glued to her damp forehead. God, she was glorious. There couldn't be a man in the audience who didn't want to screw the ass off her.

She was plainly into some horse race with Rannaldini, faster and faster, neither willing to give in, both her bow and his baton a blur. The faster they went the more the great chandelier trembled and shot out glittering rainbows of light.

And at the end when the bellows of applause and the storm of bravoes nearly took off both roof and chandelier, Rupert noticed that although Abigail collapsed into the arms of the albino leader and reached out to shake hands with the principals of the various sections of the orchestra, she snatched her fingers away when Rannaldini tried to kiss them.

This was followed by an insult more pointed, when a pretty little girl in a pink-striped party dress presented her with a bunch of red roses and she promptly handed one to the First Oboe who had played so exquisitely.

'*Viva L'Appassionata,*' roared the audience, until she came back and played a Paganini *Caprice* as an encore.

The orchestra, who could temporarily forgive a hard time in rehearsal if the concert was a success, were looking happier and, in homage to Abby, the string players rattled their bows on the backs of the chairs in front, until Julian led them off for the interval.

The only person, surprisingly, who seemed put out was Christopher Shepherd, who'd been making furious notes on the back of his programme, and who promptly disappeared backstage to see his illustrious client.

Deciding also to give Mahler's *Fourth* in the second half a miss, Rupert followed him, defusing the heavy security on the stage door with a good wad of the dollars he'd been paid for Taggie's ticket. Hearing Rannaldini's screams and seeing smoke coming out of the conductor's room, Rupert nipped behind a double bass case and nearly bumped into Rannaldini's mistress, Hermione Harefield, who was waiting to sing the soprano solo in the Mahler. She was wearing a white dress, which looked as though a swan had forgotten to blow dry its feathers, and was making it impossible for a make-up girl to touch up her lipstick as she screeched: 'Abigail Rosen and I had a no-encore agreement.'

'Shut up you stupeed beetch,' snarled Rannaldini. 'We haven't got all night.'

And off they went. Hermione got her revenge by making the slowest entrance in musical history, trapping Rannaldini like a car behind a hay wain on a narrow road.

The crowd, who had turned up backstage to congratulate Abigail and get their programmes signed, were disappointed when Christopher Shepherd went grimly into her dressing-room and locked the door.

The manager of the opera house was almost in tears over the vast fees he was having to fork out for Abby, Rannaldini and Hermione. They cost more than the box-office receipts for the whole evening, he moaned, and he hadn't paid the orchestra yet, nor the marketing people.

'Rannaldini ees impossible,' he told Rupert bitterly. 'He finded out how much L'Appassionata get, and refuse to come out of his room until he get more. He complain about her having too much publicity. Then when I arrange press conference he storm out, because someone ask heem if his wife is coming back. Wise lady to stay away.

'Hermione is just as 'orrible,' the manager went on, 'she see proof of programme and posters, then wait until they are printed to complain they are not OK.'

The poor man was only too happy to accept a further wad of green backs in return for secreting Rupert in the dressing-room next to Abigail's. On the adjoining balcony Rupert could hear everything that was going on between her and Christopher Shepherd.

Howard Denston and Christopher Shepherd were the most successful agents in New York. Power brokers, they moved conductors, soloists and even entire orchestras around the world like chess pieces. Known as Pimp and Circumspect, they complemented each other perfectly. Howard Denston (also known as Shepherd's Crook) was a beguiling wideboy from the Bronx who pulled off the shadier deals and lent on unwilling debtors. Totally amoral, he was only turned on by the big deal. Christopher Shepherd, radiating integrity and Old Testament authority, provided the agency's respectable front.

Christopher had orchestrated Abby's career from the start, settling fees, monitoring her promotion, providing encouragement and advice. Abby tended to play what he told her to, because unlike most agents, he was musical, playing the piano and possessing a fine tenor voice. Having starred in many amateur productions, he saw himself very much as Rodolfo in *La Bohème*. Hence the frock-coat and the pearl tie-pin.

Christopher had a parental attitude to his artists. He was aware of the insularity of soloists, the insecurity of conductors. He knew that this resulted in huge egos that needed the public far more than the public needed them, and that they responded as much to bullying as encouragement.

The instant he locked the door of Abby's dressing-room, she lived up to her L'Appassionata nickname. Dropping the red roses she was putting in the basin, she bounded forward, flinging her arms round his neck, writhing against him, covering his face, that wasn't obscured by dark brown beard, with kisses.

'Was I OK? Was I really OK? Omigod, I've missed you. How long can you stay on in the UK? Did you like the encore? I need you, oh Christo, I want you so bad.' She started to fumble with the pearl pin, then changed her mind. 'No, let's go back to the Plaza, I can't be bothered to change.'

Abby had a clear, carrying voice, which had shed most of its Bronx accent and which squeaked endearingly when she got excited. Christopher, however, was in no mood to be charmed.

'Don't be ridiculous.' Repelled by her trembling, burning sweatdrenched body, which had once excited him so unbearably, he prised off her hands and shoved her away. 'How in hell can you expect to be taken seriously, right, when you come onto the platform dressed as a hooker? Those hot pants are *so* tacky.'

Pulling up a chair and like Rodolfo sitting on it back to front, as if to protect himself from further sexual assault, he asked: 'Where are those gowns Beth bought for you?'

'They're too hot.' Abby would have added too middle-aged and too frumpy, but she didn't want to insult Christopher's wife.

'And why in hell are you wearing that even tackier diamond bangle round your ankle? We all know you're coining it. Dressed like that, you're an insult to Brahms and a brilliant conductor.'

Abby was already prowling round the little room but at the reference to Rannaldini her contrition evaporated.

'He's a monster,' she howled. 'He screwed me on every tempo, dragging or pushing me on. I nearly unravelled in the last movement.'

'Has it entered your thick head that he might be right? He only happens to be the greatest interpreter in the world.'

'Only because he makes the most bucks. That's all you care about. He's an asshole.'

'Don't be obnoxious,' exploded Christopher. 'Why must you always telegraph the fact you come from the gutter, and how dare you snatch your hand away when he was gracious enough to kiss it.'

'Bloody Judas kiss, right? The orchestra detest him, and he's only been with them a few days. They were really complimentary,' she added wistfully. 'Julian Pellaficini said I reminded him of David Oistrakh and he's played the concerto loads of times himself.'

Christopher looked at her pityingly.

'Don't kid yourself your exquisite sound had anything to do with the ecstatic smiles on the musicians' faces. They only rattled their bows so joyfully because your ostentatious and unauthorized little encore pushed them into overtime. And all that posturing and writhing is so unnecessary. Give the audience an orgasm if you must, but please don't have one yourself.'

'That's because you're not giving them to me any more,' said Abby sulkily.

Like a neglected wife, finding comfort in a child, she picked up her Strad and dusted it down, before putting it lovingly in its case, and tucking it up in a periwinkle-blue silk scarf.

'Thank you, little fiddle.' She dropped a kiss on its curved scroll, then turned defiantly towards Christopher. 'I'm not playing for that son-of-a-bitch again.'

'Sure you are.' Christopher opened the fridge. 'You're gonna record all the Mozart concertos with him and the New World Symphony Orchestra, for starters.'

'Like hell I am. Fix me a vodka.'

'You're staying sober.' Christopher poured her a glass of Perrier. 'C'mon, you don't want to catch cold. Get showered and changed. And at dinner you will turn on what little charm you have. "Thank you for making music with me, Maestro, I was only acting up because you're so awesome, Maestro. I'm sorry I broke the no-encore agreement, Miss Harefield." You cannot afford to make enemies.'

'Because you want to sign them both up,' hissed Abby. 'All right, I'm sorry.' She was near to tears now. 'I just want us to be alone.'

But as she peeled off her fuchsia-red body stocking, Christopher reached for her dressing-gown. The size of her breasts no longer turned him on, only her enormous royalties.

'Please kiss me,' begged Abby, 'perlease.'

'We haven't got time.' He was now flipping through her good-luck cards to see if they were from anyone important.

'I've got a feeling Beth suspects us,' he added.

On her way to the shower, Abby halted in horror.

'Oh no, she's been like a mom to me.'

'Well, you haven't behaved like a daughter to Beth,' said Christopher brutally.

'How did she find out? Oh my God, this is awful.'

'People are talking.'

The corniest way of dumping a woman in the world, thought Rupert scornfully. Christopher was even more of a tosser than he looked. Rupert needed a large drink, and he had heard enough.

Emerging from the Artists' Bar ten minutes later, he found Hermione coming off the platform still screeching. Not only had Abby got higher billing, but her applause had lasted four times as long. Seeing Rupert, however, Hermione halted in mid-screech like a child spying a tube of Smarties.

'Rupert Campbell-Black, you've come all the way from Penscombe to hear me sing.'

'I have too,' lied Rupert. 'You were sensational.'

'Then you must join us for dinner. Just Rannaldini, me and Christopher Shepherd. He's charming, and Abigail Rosen, she's a spoilt brat, but we don't have to bother with her.

'There's an official reception first at the British Embassy, I must look in because they'd be so disappointed,' she added, as they were both nearly sent flying by musicians, already changed, charging out to find the nearest bar. 'But you can come too,' she shouted over the stampede. 'Then we're going on to dinner at Wellington's.'

The official reception, like all the diplomatic parties Rupert had ever been to, was held in a large, high-ceilinged room with sculptured yellow flower arrangements on shiny leggy furniture and frightful oils of elder statesmen on eau-de-nil walls. As April signalled the start of the Argentine autumn, the central heating was on at full blast.

Having spent many years on the show-jumping circuit and as a Tory minister, Rupert discovered he knew plenty of people. Most of the guests, however, knew no-one, so they gravitated to the evening's two celebrities. Hermione, who was now wearing a wonderbra and a purple Chanel suit, was livid that the crowd round Abby was so much larger.

Abby had changed into a very short halter-necked dress in oyster-coloured silk, which clung lasciviously to her marvellous body. Her hair, freed from its black velvet ribbon, rippled in Pre-Raphaelite abundance over her shoulders. She was still clutching her dark red roses, whose long stems dripped onto her skirt, moulding it between her thighs. She was also wearing high heels which enabled her to see over the crowd to where Christopher was having a competition with Hermione to see who could crinkle their eyes at one another the more engagingly.

Rupert, half-listening to the ancient Italian Ambassador, who like all ambassadors seemed to have once had an *affaire* with his mother, was tall enough to watch Abby over the crowd. She looked wild, vulnerable and on the brink of tears, as she made heroic attempts to scintillate on the Perrier Christopher had forced on her, politely signing programmes and answering silly questions about how she got such a lovely shine on her fiddle. When the fifteenth person asked how she managed to memorize so many notes, she finally flipped and snapped back: 'By learning them.'

As Christopher was still arched over Hermione, about to free fall down her cleavage, Abby slid out of the group of admirers, across the room, and onto the balcony where Julian Pellafacini had commandeered a bottle of Beaujolais and was quietly getting drunk. Easily the most diplomatic person in the room, who had spent his entire career keeping the peace between troublesome conductors and temperamental players, Julian had suffered this afternoon the almost unique humiliation of being bawled out three times by Rannaldini in front of the orchestra.

Emptying Abby's Perrier over the balcony, he filled up her glass with red wine. After the stifling room, it was blissfully cool. Abby breathed in a smell of damp earth, moulding leaves and the distant reek of bonfires. The full moon was untangling itself from the trees, a round gold ball for Orion's dogs to play with.

'Where's Rannaldini?' she asked.

'Taking a conference call from Japan, or so he says.'

With his blond hair even whiter in the moonlight, and his long pale kindly face, Julian looked like the ghost of Abraham Lincoln who'd had a premonition he was about to be assassinated.

'Rannaldini was so god-damned charming when he was guesting,' he said bitterly, 'that the orchestra, particularly the young players, were knocked out when he got the job. Now they're shell-shocked – like a bride waking up on the first morning of her honeymoon to find her handsome young groom's turned into a werewolf.

'Rannaldini met the Second Flute outside the elevator this evening. "Allo leetle girl," he purred, "I 'aven't made you cry yet 'ave I?"' Julian shuddered and filled up his glass.

'He's a lousy conductor,' said Abby scornfully. 'He only gets edge-of-seat performances because no-one knows what he's going to do next. If you hadn't held the first violins back in the last movement, I'd have come off the rails.'

When she told Julian about the proposed record deal with Rannaldini and the New World he was delighted.

'The orchestra would love it, they thought you were terrific.'

'Christopher didn't,' sighed Abby.

'Then you need a new agent,' said Julian angrily. 'Christopher once tried to get me on his books. I'd probably be as famous as Zukerman or Perlman but I found him,' he chose his words carefully out of kindness, 'too – er – forceful.'

'I've grown accustomed to his force,' sighed Abby.

She jumped as the french windows opened, but it was only a waitress after Abby's autograph.

'We'll trade it for another bottle of red wine,' Julian emptied the remains into Abby's glass. 'Where are you going next?'

'England,' said Abby unenthusiastically.

'Christ, I'd love to work there. If I were single, I'd take the next plane. But the workload's insane. You have to work twice as hard for half the money. I'd never see Luisa and the kids. But my dream is to end up in the Cotswolds, leading some West Country orchestra.'

'I'll join you. Are you coming to dinner?'

Julian shook his head.

'I've got to rally the troops, stop them topping themselves or getting so drunk they don't make the plane tomorrow.'

The orchestra was off to Rio in the morning.

'But let's keep in touch, I don't want Christopher to stamp out that individuality.'

Looking up at the sky Abby noticed a drifting fleece of white cloud had put a great ring of mother-of-pearl edged with rust around the moon.

'That moon's got exactly the same round-eyed, round-faced pseudo-innocence as Hermione,' said Abby, putting Julian's card in her bag. 'God, she's hell.'

'Hell,' agreed Julian. 'The number of times I've seen her jab another soloist in the foot with her high heel to steal a bow.'

Through the french windows, Abby could see her agent putting his empty glass of Perrier on a tray and picking up a full one.

He'll dump me for Hermione just as effortlessly, thought Abby in panic. Hermione, who talked too much to drink a lot, was merely bending over the silver tray to check her reflection.

'Placido is one of the only top-flight singers like me,' she was telling Christopher, 'who doesn't have an agent, but his wife is very supportive. If my partner Bobby wasn't so busy running the London Met—'

Despite having Christopher's full attention, she was miffed that at the other end of the room Rupert was being happily propositioned by the ravishing wife of the Chilean Ambassador, and that Julian Pellafacini, who should also have been paying court, was out on the balcony with that sluttish Abby. Despite the tropical heating, Hermione gave a theatrical shiver.

'Could you possibly close those windows, Christopher, I daren't catch cold. As Placido's always saying, one's voice is a gift from God, one has a responsibility.'

But Christopher had already crossed the room.

'Come inside at once,' he ordered Abby furiously.

'You're supposed to be working, and you're putting Hermione in an awful draught. How can you be so selfish?'

'I figured you were keeping her warm with all that hot air,' replied Abby.

Julian laughed. Christopher glared at him. The moment he'd signed up Rannaldini, he'd make sure Julian got the boot – particularly as now he was wearing one of Abby's red roses in his buttonhole.

Grabbing Abby's arm, Christopher frogmarched her across the room.

'The French Ambassador's wife wants a word about a charity gala.'

'I don't want to talk to her, right?'

'You ought to do more for charity.'

'I do a great deal too much for Help the Agent.'

Christopher turned purple.

'What has got into you?'

'You – you've been so mean.'

'You've got to learn to take criticism,' hissed Christopher. 'Aaah, Madame Ambassador!'

Seeing Christopher belting back to Hermione a second later, Rupert decided to take the bullshitter by the horns. Trapping Christopher against a large yucca plant, he introduced himself as the chairman of Venturer Television.

'Why won't you answer Declan's calls?'

'No point,' said Christopher dismissively. 'Abigail's diary hasn't got a window in the next three years.'

'She talked to *Time*. Declan's the best interviewer in the world. Only take a day. Declan could come to you.'

'We'd be talking six figures,' said Christopher grandly. Then, at Rupert's look of disbelief, added: 'Every thirty seconds someone buys one of Abby's records, OK? We can get those kind of bucks anywhere, and 20 per cent of any overseas sales.'

'Declan sells worldwide.'

'So does Abigail. She was in New Mexico yesterday, she's off to the UK tomorrow, then Paris, Berlin, Prague, Budapest, Moscow, Tokyo, then back for a charity gala in New York.'

'Declan could meet her in any of those—'

'Hermione my dear, your drink needs freshening,' and Christopher was gone leaving an enraged Rupert in mid-sentence.

Christopher controlled Abby's media appearances. He knew there must always be something exciting on the horizon to tempt the record stores, but he had no intention of letting Declan loose on her. The publicity would have been sensational. But Abby was much too impulsive and unguarded, particularly after a few drinks. With a grand inquisitor, like Declan, she could easily break down and dump about her long *affaire* with Christopher and her guilt about Beth.

72

FOUR

Outside a taxi was waiting to take them to Wellington's. Having installed himself in the front and Abby and Hermione quivering with animosity in the back, Christopher was enraged when Rupert sauntered down the embassy steps and jumped in beside Abby.

'Hi,' he kissed her cheek, 'my name's Rupert Campbell-Black. Hermione invited me along.'

'Rupert comes from my neck of the woods,' said Hermione reverently.

Christopher knew exactly whose neck he wanted to wring.

In the dim light, Abby was instantly aware of a flawlessly carved profile, only softened by a beautiful curling mouth, and an iron-hard thigh rammed against hers, because Hermione's bottom had taken up so much of the back seat.

'And you deserved every one of those red roses, darling,' murmured Rupert, making a V-sign at Christopher's rigidly disapproving back. 'Where's Signor Ravioli?'

Hermione laughed heartily. 'You mustn't tease him, Rupert, he's taking a conference call from Tokyo and meeting us at Wellington's.'

Rannaldini, in fact, was not ringing Japan but pleasuring the Second Flute in the conductor's room, and then dispatching her to do his packing at the Hilton. He looked as smooth as hell when he arrived at the restaurant having changed into an ivory silk shirt and a black blazer, with a huge wolf coat slung around his shoulders. But the smug post-coital smile was promptly wiped off his face when he saw Rupert and there was a dangerous moment beneath a large portrait of the Duke of Wellington wearing too much lipstick, when they met face to blue-spotted tie, because Rupert was so much the taller.

'You know Rupert, don't you Rannaldini?' gushed Hermione.

'No, but we have my trainer, Jake Lovell, in common,' said Rannaldini silkily, 'who is about to oust Rupert as leading trainer and who was a very great friend of Rupert's ex-wife.'

Not a flicker in Rupert's face betrayed how much he wanted to hit Rannaldini across the room.

'And we also have Lysander Hawkley in common,' he drawled, 'who's an even closer friend of your present wife, Rannaldini. I gather she's taken up race-riding, and was last seen hurtling across country on The Prince of Darkness – perhaps Jake Lovell could give her a job, although I hear she's expecting Lysander's baby.'

Seeing the murder in Rannaldini's deadly-nightshade-black eyes, Christopher said hastily: 'Shall we go straight in?'

Dinner, as a result, was incredibly acrimonious; scenes from the Battle of Waterloo depicted on the dining-room walls were nothing to the barrage of *sotto voce* bitchery flashing between Rupert and Rannaldini.

Christopher placed himself between Hermione and Abby but just as he was ushering Rannaldini bossily to Abby's other side, Rupert nipped in and pinched the seat. Not having eaten all day, he was more than a little drunk. He was fed up with Christopher for snubbing him and leaving him to pay for the taxi, so decided to irritate both him and Rannaldini by flirting with Abby.

Stung by Christopher's earlier rejection but believing she had a night ahead and a week in the UK with him Abby had taken one incredulous look at Rupert, who was even more beautiful in the relentless overhead light, and was only too happy to flirt back.

'Great entrance this evening,' Rupert told her softly. 'You and Rannaldini looked like Snow White and the single dwarf.'

Abby laughed. 'He is single if his wife's just left him.'

'Couldn't happen to a nastier man.' Rupert unfolded her Union Jack napkin, casually caressing her thighs, as he laid it across them.

'Why does Rannaldini detest you so much?' asked Abby. 'I've just heard him telling Christopher you were the beegest sheet unhung.'

'I didn't know one hung sheets any more,' Rupert smiled blandly at Abby. 'Mrs Bodkin, our ancient house-keeper, likes to hang them out in the wind, but I thought you Americans used massive tumble dryers.'

Abby burst out laughing.

'You still haven't explained why he hates you.'

'His wife, whom he bullied and cuckolded shame-lessly, has just run off with one of my jockeys. He thinks I orchestrated it.'

'Did you?'

Rupert shook his head. 'You should see my jockey, he's so pretty everyone wants to ride him.'

'Why d'you hate Rannaldini?'

'He can't stop flaunting the fact that his trainer is the little sheet who ran off with my first wife.'

'Did she marry him?'

'No, someone else.'

'How very complicated,' said Abby losing interest.

She was quite short sitting down, noticed Rupert, her great height was all in her legs. Her pale face was shiny with sweat, black circles hammocked the bags under the tigerish eyes. Beneath her chin and on her collar bone, her Strad had left red marks as though Dracula had been having a good gnaw. Nanny would have recommended a good dose, reflected Rupert. She was far coarser than Taggie, but still hellishly sexy.

The waiters were plonking down carafes of wine. Obscuring Christopher's view with a large vase of red dahlias, Rupert filled up Abby's glass.

'I know you probably hate to talk about work,' he went on, having listened carefully to two Australian pouffs in ecstasies in the gents at the Opera House, 'but I've never heard the Brahms so lyrically played. I wept in the slow movement. The last movement really captured the Hungarian idiom and in the first movement, I never believed passages in tenths could be so clearly executed, but with such a beautiful sound. You must have a very big stretch,' he picked up Abby's rather large, stubby fingers, 'for someone with such a little hand.'

Abby blushed with pleasure. She'd written this guy off as drop-dead handsome beefcake and he really knew about music. Flustered, she snatched her hand away and grabbed a piece of bread.

'No bread, Abigail,' boomed Christopher, glaring through the red dahlias like Moses on the wrong side of the Burning Bush. He knew how soloists could blow up, eating to stave off loneliness in hotel bedrooms.

Biting her huge red cushiony lower lip instead, Abby studied the menu.

'I'll have spaghetti carbonara,' she told the waiter defiantly.

'You will not,' snapped Christopher, ordering Dover sole and radicchio salad for both of them. 'And no sauce tartare,' he added bossily.

'Odd denial from such a tartar,' said Rupert, thickly buttering a large piece of white bread, sprinkling salt on it in the Argentine fashion, and handing it to Abby.

'Rannaldini was going so bloody fast, I nearly had a bet on the last movement. How much would he earn a night for conducting?'

'About one hundred and fifty thousand bucks.'

Rupert was appalled.

'That's more than my best stallion gets for covering a mare. "Con" is the operative word.'

Remembering Abby's c.v., Rupert gazed into her eyes. They were the same pale yellow as the winter jasmine growing round the drawing-room window at Penscombe, but the irises were ringed with black, and the brilliant whites lined with the thickest dark lashes. Rannaldini had compelling hypnotic eyes, too; perhaps it was essential for a maestro.

'I hear you want to conduct.'

'So I don't have to put up with schmucks like tonight.'

'Isn't it enough being a genius at the violin?'

'Genius is never enough,' said Abby haughtily. 'I want power.'

'Nice scent,' Rupert buried his nose in her wrist. 'What's it called – raw ambition? Your poxy agent doesn't want you to come on Declan's programme. You'd enjoy it. Declan's a lovely man, and Edith Spink's on our board. She's a lovely man too.'

'Spink,' squeaked Abby in excitement, 'I just adore her *Warrior Woman Suite*, a genuine talent, Spink, even if slender.'

'I'd hardly call Edith slender. She weighed in at sixteen stone, all of it muscle, at our last board meeting. When she came to my stag-party, she drank everyone else under the table.'

'You're the dopiest guy.' Again Abby burst out laughing, leaning back as the waiter laid a fish knife and fork on either side of her Union Jack table mat.

'Don't you have any control over your life?' taunted Rupert.

Abby shrugged and drained her glass.

'I live on a treadmill. Hotel bedroom, airport, concert

hall, airport, hotel, recording studio, recital, back to the airport. I know the flight schedules better than the Brahms tonight. I've slept in the most beautiful suites in the world, but had no-one to share them with.'

'Lay down your Brahms, and surrender to mine,' said Rupert lightly.

Then he looked deep into her eyes, holding them, letting his own narrow slightly – corny old tricks he hadn't played for years.

'That is a terrible, terrible waste. How did you meet your gaoler?'

'My dad died early. He didn't make any dough, he never verbalized his feelings, but he cried when he listened to Beethoven and I loved him. Mom isn't Jewish, right? But she became more of a Jewish Momma after she married Dad. She was the one who pushed me. She still calls after every concert trying to control my life. Christopher heard me playing and signed me up when I was twelve. He took me out of school in the States, found me a good teacher for a year, then packed me off to the Conservatoires in Paris and Russia.'

Rupert let her run on. It was quite interesting, and he liked looking at her face which had great strength and at her breasts rising out of the halter neck.

'I never had the life of a normal child,' she added finally, 'music was the only thing that mattered.'

'And Christopher,' Rupert plunged his knife into his steak, releasing the blood, 'how long have you been sleeping with him?'

Abby looked up in terror, eyes staring, totally thrown.

'How'd you know? Please don't say *anything*. Christopher's phobic about scandal. His wife's been so darling to me. Mind you, she's a yachneh,' then, at Rupert's raised eyebrows, added dismissively, 'a housewife with large boobs.'

'I've got one of those,' said Rupert approvingly. 'Jolly nice too.'

But Abby was too distraught to laugh. Leaving three-quarters of her sole uneaten, ignoring Christopher's and Hermione's looks of disapproval, she lit a cigarette.

'Christopher never sleeps with her,' she whispered defiantly.

'A husband,' said Rupert idly,' is a man who tells his wife he never sleeps with his mistress, and his mistress he never sleeps with his wife. I used to be like that. I've got a past longer than the Bible.'

'What happened?' The burning glow of Abby's cigarette was jumping round like a firefly in her shaking hand.

'I married an angel,' said Rupert.

Abby's pallor was lard-like now. Beads of sweat kept breaking out on her upper lip and her forehead.

'Why isn't she with you?' she said sullenly.

'She's in Bogotá, we're adopting a baby.'

'How very caring of you,' Hermione could no longer bear to be excluded from Rupert's conversation, 'to take on a disadvantaged youngster,' she added warmly. 'If I wasn't concertizing all year, Bobby, my partner and I have often thought of adopting a little sibling for Cosmo.'

'Cosmo'd probably eat it,' muttered Rupert.

Hermione's son created more havoc than most earthquakes.

'Of course Cosmo is super-gifted,' sighed Hermione. 'He could inhibit a less bright child. He's such a plucky little horseman, too, Rupert, I thought you might give him some riding lessons.'

Rupert laughed at a scowling Rannaldini.

'Lysander'd better do that, he's the brilliant rider.'

Passers-by kept peering in from the street outside, then leaping up and down in ecstasy and pointing as they recognized Abby. In the restaurant, diners kept coming over seeking her autograph, and then noticing Hermione and Rannaldini wanted theirs as well. Hermione kept singing the same doom-laden bars from *The Force of Destiny*.

Rannaldini sipped white wine very slowly and stared covertly at Rupert. Ironically, until Rupert had got involved with Lysander, Rannaldini had always longed to be friends with him, aware how much they had in common.

Both men were extremely successful, intensely competitive, insanely jealous, spoilt and, ultimately, insecure. Both had had mothers who hadn't loved them, and had taken it out on women ever since. Except that Rupert had got lucky with Taggie. Deep down Rannaldini was bitterly ashamed of being unable to sustain a relationship.

Now he couldn't take his eyes off Rupert, searching for grey hairs, red veins, spare tyres, some sign that the peacock feathers were beginning to moult. Maddeningly there was none. He was dying to have a go at Rupert, but didn't want to betray his longing or the white heat of his animosity in front of Christopher.

Christopher was hopping mad. Everything had gone wrong, he loathed not being in control. He'd wanted Abby to be admiring and respectful to Rannaldini so he could do a number on Hermione, but all either woman could do was to drool over that arrogant, mischief-making Brit., who was now giving Abby his card, and writing the fax number of his hotel in Bogotá on the back.

'I hear you've got Benny Basanovich on your books,' Rannaldini interrupted his thoughts.

But Christopher didn't want to talk about Benny. There were many instrumentalists and singers on Shepherd Denston's books who would profit from an introduction to Rannaldini. That was another reason for signing up the great maestro but that could come later. Tonight all he wanted to talk about was Rannaldini.

As Hermione had gone off to the Ladies in a huff because more people were asking for Abby's autograph,

Christopher said softly to Rannaldini, 'I want to put the two most explosive talents in the world together.'

Rannaldini glanced at Abby. She was a spoilt brat, and not his type. But he'd always been turned on by indifference. He'd enjoy taming her, making her jump, reducing her to crawling submission.

He also wanted that Mozart CD deal, because he suspected the New World Orchestra were not going to be the push-over he'd expected. The board had refused him the total hiring and firing rights he'd had with his last orchestra. It would be good to have a mega-record contract to bargain with.

He wanted the deal, but not Christopher as an agent. Christopher, he decided, was an avaricious thug.

'I'll have a dessert if you will, Christopher.' Hermione had returned from the Ladies, face repainted, reeking of *Arpège*.

'Full many a flower is born to blush unseen and waste its sweetness on desserts,' quipped Christopher gallantly, then whispered, 'I want to set you free from Rannaldini, I want Harefield to be an even greater name than Callas.'

Hermione bridled. 'My voice is considered far more lovely than Maria's.'

'I said a *greater* name, Hermione.'

'I'm not interested in money,' lied Hermione. 'My only desire is to bring music to the masses.'

That was a good sign, Christopher thought. She'd just put her hand on his crotch, but he removed it gently with a little squeeze and a tickle of the palm, in case it met Abby's hand coming the other way.

'I get as much of a charge if Solti says: "You're wonderful, Hermione", as to hear builders on scaffolding shouting: "'Allo 'Ermione, loved your last halbum, bort it for the cover, but I loiked the contents".' Hermione's cockney accent was quite frightful. 'It's the little things that matter, like the ambassador, this evening, saying you're even lovelier in the flesh, I hear that so often, I don't know why.'

Abby caught Rupert's eyes and giggled, then picked up Christopher's hand, examining the fingernails, until Christopher snatched it away, asking sharply what she was doing.

'Look for pastry crumbs, you've got fingers in so many pies.'

'Shepherd's pie,' Rupert refilled her glass. Then, dropping his voice, whispered, 'Christopher wouldn't do business with me.'

'He's so grand, he only talks to God.'

'And Rannaldini answers, I suppose.'

Abby nodded. 'Christopher wants me to record all the Mozart concertos with Rannaldini.'

'I wouldn't. A beautiful pianist who was recording Beethoven with him topped herself two weeks ago.'

'What was her name?'

'Rachel Grant.'

'I've heard her play. She was a wonderful musician.'

'And Rannaldini was terrible to his wife Kitty.' For a second Rupert shed his flip manner. 'Don't mess with him, sweetheart, he's evil, he'll break you.'

Hermione, in between mouthfuls of chocolate mousse, was humming *The Force of Destiny* again.

'I had fifteen curtain calls, when I sang Leonora at La Scala. D'you remember, Rannaldini?'

'We could have a ball if you did Declan,' murmured Rupert. He'd had far too much to drink. His message was quite unequivocal.

Gazing into his beautiful, predatory, unsmiling face, which for a second seemed unnervingly like Rannaldini's, Abby thought how impossible it would be to resist him, if he really put on the pressure, and how gorgeous it would be just to take off with him into the Pampas.

Rupert heard himself saying; 'God, I'd love to sleep with you.'

'I don't sleep.' Abby tossed back her black hair.

'Well, have insomnia with me then.'

They both jumped as Rannaldini's mobile rang.

'Si, si, check eet again, by that time I weel be weeth you.'

Switching it off, Rannaldini smiled round the table.

'My Leer ees grounded, so I charter Mexican jet, one cannot be too careful. I am so relieved we all escape calamity.'

'What d'you mean?' snapped Rupert.

'There is legend,' said Rannaldini silkily, 'that once the great chandelier fall when they perform *The Force of Destiny*, keeling many, many people—'

'I can't remember who was playing Alvaro,' interrupted Hermione. 'But they say the Leonora wasn't nearly as good as me.'

'Always eet breeng terrible luck,' continued Rannaldini. 'Tonight chandelier stay put, but who knows where the ill luck will fall. My orchestra were terrified,' he nodded coldly at Abby as if to dismiss any complaints of Julian's. 'That why they look shell-shocked and thees is why I 'ave jet checked three times just een case.'

Rupert felt icicles dripping down his spine. How could he have left darling Taggie by herself in Bogotá? A handful of nuns was no defence, she might be kidnapped, mugged or raped by some junkie. He should have put her in the hotel safe with the adoption papers.

'Your car is waiting, Maestro.' It was the head waiter.

'Are you coming?' Rannaldini turned to Christopher, then added to Abby with a sadistic smirk, 'Christopher hitch a lift weeth me back to New York.'

'I don't understand,' stammered Abby.

Christopher got to his feet.

'I've got a helluva lot on in New York and meetings

first thing,' he said placatingly. 'I'll get over to the UK later in the week.'

'Red Eye flight, Shepherd's delight,' said Abby meditatively.

Then she went beserk.

'You son of a bitch,' she screamed. 'You never intended to stop over here, or come with me to England.' And she hurled her glass of red wine at him so it trickled like blood down his white shirt.

Hermione was suddenly looking very excited. 'Shall we have a quiet drink in my room?' she said, turning to Rupert. But Rupert had gone.

Cursing himself for not stopping to recharge his mobile, Rupert raced for the telephone. He was unable to get a squawk out of the Red Parrot. Terrified some ghastly fate had befallen Taggie, he urged his taxi-driver, who drove like the great Ayrton Senna anyway, to go even faster, overtaking Rannaldini deep in conversation with that smug bastard Christopher on the way.

Once at the airport Rupert managed to commandeer Rannaldini's plane which was revving up on the runway.

Rannaldini had been so gratuitously offensive to the Mexican crew and insulted their honour by insisting on a third security-check, that their swarthy piratical captain was only too happy to accept yet another bribe. I'll be so broke soon, thought Rupert ruefully, I'll have to take up conducting.

Turning round, the Mexican captain alerted flight control, and flew off to Bogotá. Seeing Rannaldini and Christopher foaming on the runway, Rupert flicked them another V-sign. Declan could do his own negotiating in future.

Having fretted himself into a frazzle, Rupert reached the Red Parrot as dawn was breaking despairingly over the poverty of the city.

As Alberto, yawning and still wearing his grey greasy

vest, unlocked the door, Rupert grabbed him by the shoulders.

'Is my wife OK?'

'*Si, si.*'

Relief fuelled Rupert's rage.

'Why the fuck doesn't your telephone work? I suppose you haven't paid the bill, you idle sod.'

Alberto shrugged. 'Possibly small earthquake.'

'Earthquake!' Rupert's fingers bit into Alberto's plump shoulders until he winced.

'Only small one, Meesis Campbell-Black want to be near Bianca, so she sleep at convent.'

Rupert was so thankful he gave the rest of his cash to the beggars already out on the streets.

He found Taggie still in yesterday's jeans and an old black polo-neck. She had spent the night in a chair, with Xavier, still clutching his teddy bear and his racing car, in her arms.

Yesterday Taggie had had a wigging from Maria Immaculata.

'I have seen many couple here seeking babies and you have very good marriage. Your husband love you, but don't abuse his generousness and take in every limping duck. He may be jealous of Bianca – try to put him, if not first, at least equal.'

Taggie was utterly mortified and as desperate to see Rupert as he to see her. Laying Xavier down in the arm-chair, she fell into his arms.

'I've been so worried, I love you, I missed you so, so much,' they cried in unison.

How could he have propositioned Abby, thought Rupert in horror, when all that was true, good and beautiful in the world was in his arms? He was murmuring endearments and was about to kiss her, when Xav woke and started to cry.

'He missed you as much as I did,' said Taggie in a choked voice. 'He cried himself to sleep.'

She stepped back quickly to stop the child falling off the chair. But suddenly incredulous delight sparked in Xavier's little face. Jibbering with joy, he slid to the floor, swayed on his feet, then, like a man in space, took the first wobbling steps of his life towards Rupert, who leapt forward to catch him just before he fell.

Appearing in the doorway a drowsy Sister Angelica crossed herself. 'This is a miracle.'

Taggie burst into tears, she knew she shouldn't push limping ducks on Rupert, but seeing him dropping the proudest kiss in the world on Xav's black curls, and rubbing his face against Xav's cheek, as he normally only did with puppies, she couldn't stop herself.

'I know it's awful after you lost all that money at Lloyd's,' she sobbed, 'and spent fortunes coming out here, and we couldn't afford for him to go to Harrow, but couldn't we possibly take Xav home as well?' She stroked Xav's little hand now barnacled to Rupert's lapel.

'I can't bear to leave him.'

'Are you sure you can cope with two babies?' muttered Rupert when he could trust himself to speak at last. 'They'll be a hell of a lot of work, and a hell of a lot more red tape.'

Sister Angelica was tearfully crossing herself over another miracle.

'D'you think Maria Immaculata will throw Xav in as a job-lot if I restore the chapel as well?' asked Rupert.

'Dar-ling,' giggled Taggie reprovingly.

But Rupert had turned back to Xavier, tossing him screaming with delight in the air.

'Fasten your seat-belt, Xavier Campbell-Black, you're coming to England.'

Rupert's euphoria was complete later in the day, when he found a fax at the Red Parrot from Abby saying she'd like to do the interview with Declan. She'd be back from her tour in three weeks. Could he write to her at her New York apartment, and not say anything to Christopher.

'*I hope you get your baby,*' she had added at the end. '*And he or she makes you and your angelic wife really happy.*'

He *and* she, thought Rupert, jubilantly, and two fingers to *The Force of Destiny*.

her New York apartment and once everything in
Christopher.

'You never let me talk,' she had sobbed to the deaf. And
even as a mother was and even as you mother sexs really happen.

He and she thought Rupert, probably and two
fingers to the force of gravity.

FIVE

Abby, whose tantrums subsided as quickly as they flared
up, was woken at midday by an enraged Christopher,
who, after interminable delays, had finally arrived in
New York, and who immediately chewed her out for last
night's scene. He had dismissed it to Rannaldini as
some schoolgirl crush. But he didn't trust Rannaldini,
and even less Rupert, not to blab about it all over New
York.

'We've got to cool it for Beth's sake.'

'But I need you,' pleaded Abby who was still groggy
from sleeping-pills. 'At least answer my letters.'

'They've got to stop, too,' said Christopher hastily.

He couldn't man his personal fax at all times, and five
letters a week reeking of *Amarige*, Abby's sweet musky
very distinctive scent, and marked personal, were not
easily explained away.

'Sandra's beginning to get suspicious.'

Sandra was Christopher's secretary, a plump, knowing blonde, at whom Abby had shouted too often when
she was desperate to get through to Christopher.

'Why doesn't she send on my fan mail and my clip-
pings? I need some feedback.'

'Because it's all answered in the office. Sandra's

perfected your signature so she can even acknowledge favourable reviews.'

'She'll be forging my cheques soon.'

Christopher lost his temper.

'I cannot understand your attitude. A complete powerhouse at Shepherd Denston is devoted to keeping your particular show on the road, so you can concentrate on music, which was what you said you always wanted, and all you do is winge.'

Howie, Howard Denston's son, who ran the London office, Christopher continued, would meet her at Heathrow, and drive her up to Birmingham where she was playing the Brahms again with the City of Birmingham Symphony Orchestra.

'And, for God's sake, think of the agency's reputation and wear something long and decorous. The Symphony Hall are generously allowing you to sign CDs in the interval. And remember only sign your name, OK? All those personal inscriptions and *"Love from Abigails"* just hold up the queue.'

'You want to excise love from my life. You could fly out to Tokyo. Oh hell,' she screamed, 'there's someone at the door, don't hang up, please don't hang up.'

Outside were four smiling waiters, all avid to have a look at Abby, as they wheeled in a massive breakfast for two: champagne, grapefruit topped with strawberries, silver domes over sausages, bacon and eggs, a T-bone for Christopher, croissants and blackcherry jam, which Abby had ordered yesterday, anticipating she and Christopher would be ravenous after a long night of love.

'I'm sorry,' sobbed Abby, 'you'll have to take it away.'

Rootling around in her bag, she gave them two hundred dollars.

But when she picked up the telephone again, Christopher had gone.

Nor did her spirits rise when she found Buenos Aires

Airport so upended by Rannaldini's fury and his attempts to charter a new aeroplane that her own flight to Heathrow had been grounded by a temporary strike. Abby, who was wearing jeans and a purple T-shirt, had scraped her hair back and hidden her reddened eyes behind huge dark glasses, but she never managed to remain anonymous. A ripple of excitement went round the airport, as the Tannoy started belting out her latest hit. Next minute crowds were mobbing her, yelling 'L'Appassionata, L'Appassionata' and nearly starting a riot. Abby then ended up on the same flight as Hermione, who despite her big black hat and her white Chanel suit, was deeply miffed not to be mobbed as well.

Looking disapprovingly at Abby's ripped shirt and wild hair, from which the purple ribbon had been torn, Hermione said, as they climbed the steps to the plane: 'You come from a different generation, of course, Abigail, who are more concerned with lights and glitter and showbiz. I couldn't bring myself to pose nearly naked on a record sleeve. Our generation were only interested in the music.'

Abby was about to snap back that nothing mattered more than the music, when she gave a gasp of joy. One of the inside first-class seats in the left-hand row had been packed with hundreds and hundreds of scented yellow roses. Christopher hadn't forgotten. He had done this in the early days of their *affaire*, when he occasionally had been unable to travel with her.

Then the Furies moved in as Hermione, too, gave a gasp of joy.

'Who put those lovely rosebuds beside my seat?'

'They're for me.'

'*Mais non,*' an Air France steward shimmied up. '*Elles sont pour Madame Harefield.*'

An ecstatic Hermione then asked the steward, Jean-Claude – 'what a macho name' – to put the roses in water so Abby could have the seat next to her. She then proceeded to read out the accompanying card from

Christopher in which he said he was so jealous of anyone sitting beside Hermione that he felt compelled to fill the seat with flowers.

'I know he'd have made an exception if he'd known you were going to be on this plane, Abigail,' Hermione went on graciously. 'Then he says, let's see, oh yes, *"Meeting you, Dame Hermione,"* actually I'm not a dame **yet**, *"was like a dream come true, I can't wait for our next encounter."*'

A ruse is a ruse is a ruse, thought Abby bleakly.

Hermione must pay excess baggage on her hand luggage, she reflected a second later, as every steward was summoned to stow away squashy fur coats, make-up bags, endless duty-free gifts 'for my partner Bobby and our son Cosmo – I never come home empty-handed', into every available crevice.

'And I expect a nice glass of bubbly and some caviar, Jean-Claude, the moment we take off.'

Abby cuddled her Strad case. It was like travelling with a Renoir. She even took it into the john on flights.

Those are exactly the words he once wrote to me, she thought numbly, as Hermione lovingly replaced Christopher's note in its little envelope.

'By the way I've got a present for you, Abigail.'

Perhaps I've misjudged her, thought Abby, until Hermione handed over a large signed photograph of herself and a tape of her singing Strauss's *Last Four Songs*.

'I was so touched,' went on Hermione smugly, 'that Rupert Campbell-Black flew all the way from Bogotá to hear me in the Mahler.'

'He came to sign me up,' protested Abby. Oh, what was the use? 'I must say for an older guy he's drop-dead gorgeous.'

'Did you notice his beautiful hands?' said Hermione as though it was the discovery of the century.

'Oh, get real,' muttered Abby. 'He's beautiful all over.'

'He has the most beautiful hands.'

Thank God, the plane was taxiing along the runway.

'What's his wife like?' asked Abby.

'Not a woman of substance,' said Hermione firmly. 'That's why he's drawn to, well, more sophisticated and mature women.'

'Like yourself,' said Abby, looking round for her sick-bag.

'Indeed,' Hermione bowed her head. 'Oh splendid, here comes Jean-Claude with the bubbly.'

Just managing not to throttle her, particularly when she continued to sing *The Force of Destiny*, Abby pretended to sleep, brooding on the tyranny of her life, bound like Ixion on the wheel of fortune-making. She had been excruciatingly homesick when she'd been sent away to Paris and Russia. She had never had time for real friendships with other girls, or going out dancing or on dates, dickering over lipsticks, cooking disgusting dinners to impress boyfriends. The grind of touring had just been bearable when Christopher had been with her. Now she only had endless hours in bridal suites to contemplate her isolation.

The final straw, when they finally reached Heathrow, was that Howie wasn't there to meet her. Rosalie Brandon, his deputy, was full of apologies. Benny Basanovich, the agency's star pianist, had thumped a conductor in Frankfurt, and Howie had had to fly off and sort it out.

'He sent you his best, Abby. There's a car waiting to take you up to Birmingham. I promised Howie' (Rosalie looked faintly embarrassed), 'I'd escort Mrs Harefield home to Rutminster. We're all frightfully excited about the possibility of having her as a new client,' she whispered. 'I'll catch up with you tomorrow. You'll love the CBSO.'

Abby slumped in the front seat of the limousine, cruising at ninety up the M1. Outside the spring barley shivered like animal fur, cow parsley tossed on the verges, the white spikes of blossom on the hawthorn hedges rose and fell like Benny Basanovich's fingers, lambs slept beside their mothers, cattle grazed towards the setting sun. Occasionally an adorable little village or a huge house at the end of a long, tree-lined avenue, flashed by.

All life going on without me, thought Abby despairingly.

Inside the car was as coolly air-conditioned as the bottom of the sea.

Birmingham temporarily cheered Abby up. She was deeply impressed by the orchestra and the awesome acoustics of Symphony Hall. Her hero, Simon Rattle, however, was in Vienna and the guest conductor was a charming wily old fox called Sir Rodney Macintosh. Short, balding, very rotund, with twinkling pale blue, bloodshot eyes, and a pink beaming face above a neat white beard, he wore a black smock, purple track-suit bottoms and gymshoes with holes cut out for his corns.

Normally musical director of the Rutminster Symphony Orchestra, Sir Rodney was drawing to the end of a long, distinguished career and knew everyone in the music world.

'How did you get on with Madame Harefield?' was his first question as he gave Abby tickling kisses on both cheeks.

'I thought she was a cow.'

Rodney looked shocked. 'That's very unkind.'

Oh God, I've goofed, thought Abby.

'Very unkind to cows,' said Rodney. 'They're such innocent, sweet-natured animals,' and he roared with such infectious laughter that Abby joined in.

Leading her to her dressing-room, he waddled ahead, chattering all the time.

'Hermione didn't go to a very good charm-school, did

she, darling? If you want a laugh see her sing Leonore in plum-coloured breeches, got a bum on her bigger than Oliver Hardy.

'I hear Rannaldini was conducting in BA' he went on. 'Defininitely top of the Hitler parade, darling, a cold sensualist, driven by lust that never touches the heart. Here's your dressing-room, next to mine, which is frightfully posh and normally belongs to Simon Rattle. Like a peep?'

'Oh yes please,' said Abby, admiring the grand piano draped in tapestries, the sofas, the scores, the big bowl of fruit on a marble table and the photographs of beautiful children in silver frames. She would have a room just like that when she became a conductor.

Her own dressing-room was full of flowers. Christopher, she thought, with a bound of hope. But they were only orange lilies from Howie, '*Sorry babe, catch up with you later*'; red roses and '*Good Luck*' from Rupert; bluebells and freesias from Declan O'Hara, '*When shall we two meet?*' and finally great branches of white lilac pouring forth sweet heady scent, '*In trembling anticipation*' from Rodney.

Abby hugged him. If only she had a grandfather like him.

'I'll pick you up in twenty minutes, darling.'

Abby was very nervous. She'd been up since six practising in her hotel bedroom. Between them, Rannaldini and Christopher had destroyed her confidence. But Rodney was such a tonic. Although he had been known to crunch glacier mints, filched from the leader during the cadenzas of soloists he disliked, he couldn't have been sweeter to Abby.

'You are an artist, dear child, play at whatever tempo you feel correct and we will accompany you. Isn't it splendid?' he added, as he led her into the vast soaring hall. 'Pity about the cherry-red chairs, ghastly colour, but fortunately here they're always covered in bums.'

Unlike Rannaldini, Rodney was also adored by the musicians. Having kissed the leader on both cheeks, he clambered laboriously onto the rostrum, collapsed onto a chair, mopped his brow on a lemon-scented, blue-spotted handkerchief, and beamed round at everybody.

'That's the hard part over. So lovely to be back with my favourite orchestra. You all look so divine and play so wonderfully, it doesn't matter a scrap I can't remember any of your names.'

The orchestra giggled.

'Now I don't need to introduce this ravishing child, she's had a frightful time in BA with Rannaldini so you've got to be particularly nice to her.'

The orchestra gave Abby a friendly round of applause. Artists in their own right, they were not overawed by soloists.

Rodney opened the score and raised his stick.

'Now, please play together, boys and girls, or I won't know where to put my beat.'

Abby's knees would hardly hold her up in the long wait before she came in, but from her first note, magazines and books were put down, crosswords abandoned, tax returns set aside, and the musicians looked at each other in awe as the raw, sad sweetness pierced the tidal waves of orchestral sound.

'Ravishing, my dear,' Rodney called a halt, halfway through the first movement. 'Brass dearies, it'd be nice if the diminuendo could be slightly more pronounced, i.e. shut up a bit.'

Then when a vital bassoon entry was missed: 'Agonizing over ten across, dear boy, it's Laocoon. I always have trouble spelling it, now you can concentrate on Brahms.'

Much of the rehearsal was spent telling them about Princess Diana, whom he'd sat next to last night, 'such a charmer', and nodding off on the rostrum while Abby and the orchestra played on regardless.

'Which orchestra am I playing with?' he asked, being woken by a particularly noisy tutti.

'The CBSO, Maestro,' said the leader grinning.

'Ah yes. Now boys and girls, why are we so happy? Because Uncle Rodney's in charge. Tiddle um, tiddle um, pom pom, it was together when I sang it.'

Rodney lifted his stick again.

He had the weirdest beat, very high and wavery like a slow drunken flash of lightning. The best maestros, like Rannaldini, had a distinct click at the bottom of the down beat, so the orchestra knew exactly when to come in. But when Rodney was on the rostrum, the leader gave a nod to start everyone off, but it was very discreet because the orchestra had such respect for him.

'I may go to sleep in the cadenza,' he warned Abby.

'When shall we wake you up, Sir Rodney?' asked the leader.

'When you hear me snore.'

The orchestra were in stitches, but despite such jokes and the legendary blasé-ness of musicians, they all stood up and cheered Abby at the end, and they were joined by people who'd crept into the seats all over the auditorium.

Abby burst into tears and fled to her dressing-room.

'Rannaldini should be shot,' said the leader furiously.

Rodney mopped Abby up over a cup of Earl Grey tea, insisting she have one of the sticky cream cakes he'd bought in white cardboard boxes for the entire orchestra.

'Don't worry about this evening, we will get ecstatic reviews, because you are breathtakingly beautiful, and because I am old and have a beard. What an easy way to eminence – to grow a beard. If you're free, we might have a little supper after the concert.'

'Won't you be exhausted?' Abby bit into a huge eclair.

'Certainly not, I'll have a good sleep during the Maxwell Davies which comes after the interval. I'm off home to Lucerne in the morning.'

Abby returned to the Hyatt Hotel and followed her usual routine, eating a small bowl of pasta for lunch, which gave her time if necessary to throw it up before the concert, a precaution she'd taken since bad fish had sabotaged her in Tel Aviv. She then lay down but didn't sleep because she kept praying Christopher might call. An hour before she had to leave for the concert, she washed her hair, then warmed up for twenty minutes in her dressing-room, changing and making up during the overture which gave her as little time as possible to be nervous.

In defiance of Christopher she put on a very short sleeveless dress, covered in midnight-blue sequins, which glittered with every movement, and wore her hair loose but pulled off her face with a crimson bow. She also ringed her eyes with black eye-liner, but left off her mascara in case the Brahms made her cry again.

Rodney had the entire orchestra and the audience in fits of laughter when he waddled on to conduct the overture from *Il Seraglio*, and sent one of the cymbals flying with his big belly.

His jaw dropped ten minutes later when he popped in to collect Abby.

'Dear God, child. What a smasher you are. I ought to wave a sword rather than a baton to drive them off.'

'And you look great too,' sighed Abby. 'I love that black-and-silver cummerbund.'

'Madame Harefield,' said Rodney acidly. 'Couldn't think where I'd found one big enough. If that woman were bowling for England, we'd have no difficulty retaining the Ashes . . . Tiddle om pom pom. Don't be nervous. Birmingham's in for a treat.'

Although Rodney dozed off twice in the first movement, he managed to wake up and bring the orchestra in after the cadenza. The audience sat spellbound by the beauty of Abby's sound and the sadness on her face. Abby always felt the last moments of the concerto were the saddest, as the Hungarian gypsy seemed to romp down the hill, her feet, coloured skirts, earrings and dark curls flying, then suddenly to break down like a mechanical toy, and as the whole orchestra went quiet, limp stumbling through the last two bars, before the three final thunderous chords.

Invariably when Abby played, there was a long stunned silence at the end, as though it were intrusive to interrupt such sorrow and depth of emotion. Then the audience went wild, breaking into deafening rioting applause. Rodney turned, his plump hands apart, his head on one side – 'What can I say?' – before enfolding her in a warm, scented bear-hug.

The audience, crazy for an encore, would have gone on clapping for ages. Abby longed to oblige them, then to unwind slowly, savouring her triumph. But Rosalie Brandon, having spent twenty-four hours humouring Hermione, was back in martinet form, waiting in Abby's dressing-room.

'You haven't time for an encore, you've got to sign CDs in the foyer, and then I've arranged for an interview with the *Guardian*, and then we're having supper with the *Independent*.'

Abby loathed Rosalie being present at interviews. It had been the same when she was a kid, and her mother had insisted on staying in the room when the doctor examined her.

'I'm having supper with Sir Rodney,' she said firmly, 'Christopher never stops chewing me out for not brown-nosing conductors.'

Christopher's right, thought Rosalie beadily, Abby was definitely getting above herself.

Rodney, steaming like a pink pig in the conductor's room as he changed into a clean shirt for the second half, gave Abby a jaunty wave as she passed by on her way to the foyer.

'See you later, Abbygator.'

Reading, snatching like a gull, was in the conductor's room as he shot past into a clandestine for the second half, gave Abby a limited view of the back of his bowed silken head.

See you later, Alberich.

SIX

Abby regarded Rodney as far too old and gay to try anything, so she was relieved when he suggested supper in the apartment in which the orchestra put up visiting conductors.

'You've been stared at quite enough,' he announced as he emerged from the conductor's room, wearing a big black cloak and a beatle cap tipped rakishly over one eye. He was clutching a clanking carrier bag, 'Just a few little extras from Tesco's,' and singing a snatch from *La Bohème*. 'Come along Musetta, devourer of all hearts.'

As they toddled across the square arm in arm, passing cafés, boutiques, pigeons huddling in the eaves and a glittering canal, the moon, slimmer than two days ago, but still sporting a rust halo, was sailing through silvery wisps of cloud.

'Ring round the moon means trouble,' sighed Rodney. 'I do hope I don't get a tax bill in the morning.'

The apartment was blissfully warm, with a gas log-fire which Rodney immediately turned on. Looking down from the moss-green walls were portraits of music's giants: Alfred Brendel, André Previn, Rannaldini, Giulini, Jessye Norman, Simon Rattle.

'You'll be up there soon,' said Rodney, pouring her a large glass of Dom Perignon, then sitting down at the big grand piano.

'What's your favourite tune?'

Abby's mind went blank.

Rodney strummed a few chords and began to sing.

> *'I love Abby in the springtime,*
> *I love Abby in the Fall,*
> *I love Abby in the summer when it sizzles,'*

then changing key and putting on a French accent:

> *'Thank 'eavens for Abigail.*
> *For Abigail get beeger every day.*
> *Thank heavens for Abigail.*
> *She's grown up in the most exciting way.'*

He looked so sweet and naughty, Abby kissed him on the top of his shiny bald head.

Having installed her on a dark, gold damask sofa, with the latest copy of *Classical Music*, which had her picture on the front, he toddled off to rustle her up some scrambled eggs. Abby felt herself unwinding for the first time in weeks. Oh, why were all the sweetest guys gay?

When Rodney returned five minutes later, however, he was brandishing the nearly empty bottle, reeking of English Fern, and wearing nothing but a blue-and-white striped butcher's apron. Rodney's down beat may have been wavery, but nothing could have been more emphatic than his upbeat, which was relentlessly lifting the striped apron like a shop blind.

'My lovely child.' Putting the bottle on the mantelpiece, Rodney advanced briskly.

'Omigod,' screamed Abby.

Flight to both doors was cut off, so she took the only possible way out, and went off into peals of laughter.

After a second, Rodney joined in and they collapsed on the sofa, until the tears were running down their cheeks.

'I thought you were gay, because you kissed the leader and you were so sympatico,' said Abby, wiping her eyes.

'Oh my dear, four wives to vouch to the contrary. Oh well, it was worth a try. You shouldn't be so beautiful and so tall. Those stunning breasts at eye-level are beyond all temptation.'

'What happened to your last wife?'

'She died, three years ago, bless her. Wonderful old girl, used to play concertos in her nightie so she could go straight to bed afterwards.'

'You must be so lonely.'

'Not terribly darling, one's always had a few little friends.'

'Well, put on a bathrobe and I'll make the scrambled eggs.'

After that they had a riotous evening, with Rodney regaling her with stories of the Great.

'Henry Wood gave me my first concert after I came out of the Navy, and my first cigar. He was a charmer. You should do a prom, darling. You'd love it.'

'They asked me,' said Abby wistfully, 'Christopher wanted too much money.'

Rodney frowned and topped up his glass of brandy.

'I've heard that concerto so often, but tonight you made me listen to it completely afresh. I felt that strange excitement we all long for. Like the first time I saw David Gower pick up a bat, or the first time I heard Jacqueline du Pré pick up a bow. You have two matchless qualities, the ability to hold an audience captive and a unique sound that can never be mistaken for anyone else's. But you're dreadfully unhappy, aren't you, darling.' Gently he massaged her aching neck.

So Abby told him about Christopher.

'We call him Chris-too-far over here,' observed Rodney. 'He's avaricious, always pushes his artists too hard, gets as much money out of them as quickly as possible before they burn out. You ought to have been allowed to unwind after that exquisite concerto, or at least have tomorrow off, so you can have some fun, and do other things.'

'I want to have a go at conducting.'

'Don't know how ready the world is for women conductors,' mused Rodney. 'Women in power are often unnecessarily brutal to their subordinates. Thatcher crushing her cabinet, who reacted with appalling spite. Musically you're quite good enough, darling, you've got the authority too, but concert tickets tend to be bought by women and queers.' He gave Abby a foxy nudge in the ribs. 'And they prefer a glamorous bloke at the helm, and orchestras are very tricky, you'd only get by if they loved you.'

'What about Edith Spink?' protested Abby.

'Edith's a chap, and she's got her composing, although her last symphony sounded as though a lot of drunken bears were having a saucepan fight.'

'I must go,' Abby leapt to her feet, as she suddenly noticed how old and tired he looked.

As he led her to the door, he begged her to come and stay in his house in Lucerne.

'It's on the lake and quite ravishing, there'll be no passes, scout's honour, and you're going to come and play for my orchestra in Rutminster, ravishing country there too, and my boys and girls would love you.'

'Shall I pack for you?' asked Abby.

Rodney shook his head.

'The sight of you bending over my suitcase,' gently he patted her bottom, 'would be too much for me. Goodnight, my new little friend.' He stood on tiptoe to kiss her cheek.

'You'd have enjoyed it, you know, there's many a good tune played on an old fiddle, and I'm a spring chicken compared to your Stradivarius.'

*   *   *

Returning, still laughing, to the Hyatt Hotel and reality, Abby found an express parcel from Christopher.

Frantic with excitement, hoping for a gold bracelet or even a diamond pin as an act of atonement, Abby ripped it open and found six copies of the CD contract for the Mozart concertos. It was covered in primrose-yellow stickers telling her where to sign. Also enclosed was a brusque note from Christopher ordering her to return the contracts at once. A car would be waiting at Heathrow tomorrow to take her on to a rehearsal and recital at the Wigmore Hall. The next day she would start recording the Bartók concerto with the LSO.

'*If Declan O'Hara or Rupert Campbell-Black try to contact you, I cannot urge you too strongly to resist them,*' ended Christopher. '*That's the one thing that could screw up the Rannaldini deal.*'

I better call Rupert at once, thought Abby.

Five Mozart concertos, music she loved, spoilt for ever by bullying and screaming matches.

Her shoulders, her arms, her back and her neck still ached. In the old days, Christopher had cured her, rubbing in Tiger Balm, a mixture of herbs and menthol, and sooner or later his fingers had crept downwards in pursuit of pleasure. Abby groaned at the memory.

Taking her violin from its case, she cleaned its strings with eau-de-Cologne, then dusted its smooth flanks and delicate neck curving over into the seahorse head.

'It's you and me against the world, little fiddle,' she said sadly. 'If I don't play you well enough, the bank will take you back again. You must have witnessed so much misery in two hundred and eighty years, but have you ever been played by anyone as lonely and unwanted as me?'

But that wasn't true, Rupert had wanted her, and men's hands had trembled when they'd asked her to sign their records this evening. Even Rodney's jovial elephantine pass had made her aware she was desirable.

She was only so isolated, because Christopher, when

he had wanted her had not wanted witnesses, and had driven away all her friends, and even her noisy fat mother. Pacing her room all night, she watched the sky lighten and the city emerge.

Far below she could now see a row of pretty pastel houses, the kind she would have loved to have settled down in, lining the bottle-green, oily waters of the canal, on which floated brightly coloured barges, attached at the centre like the petals of a flower. All round was debris, where bulldozers and cranes were in the process of flattening beautiful old russet buildings, churches, meeting houses and a factory with tall pipes. I'll be bashed down before I have any chance to enjoy life, thought Abby, her eyes following the path of the canal which flowed under roads and bridges, past a man throwing sticks for his shaggy white dog, along a row of dark cypresses, into the mist, keeping its head down, amid the hubbub of the city. The hands of the little red clock-tower merged into one at six-thirty.

Abby flipped. She was enmeshed like Laocoon, she had to break free. First she chucked Rannaldini's contracts out of the window. Blue birds of unhappiness, they wheeled downwards. Then she took the earliest shuttle to Heathrow, and booked herself onto Concorde.

Buoyed up by an excess of champagne, she wept over a piece in the *Independent* about Rachel Grant, the beautiful pianist, who'd been recording the Beethoven concertos with Rannaldini. She had evidently driven over a cliff because she'd seen a picture in *The Scorpion* of her husband sneaking out of the apartment of a former mistress. *What a tragic loss to music,* wrote the reporter.

Abby got stuck back into the champagne.

I'm immortal, she thought drunkenly as they approached New York. I could fly this aeroplane if they asked me and I can fly straight back into Christopher's heart.

Still feeling immortal, she called Christopher on

landing, but was utterly deflated to be told he was out. Sandra, his manipulative blonde secretary, had gone to the dentist. Christopher's mobile had also been switched off. He was probably at a recording session, where they were not popular.

In despair, plunging down from the champagne, Abby took a taxi to her Riverside apartment. Geography was taking over. This was New York, every brick and street number reminded her of once being happy with Christopher. The river looked grey, seal-like and unfriendly, boats were chugging sluggishly upstream like commuters. Someone had left the elevator door open, so she had to hump her bags up five floors.

Letting herself in, Abby gave a sigh of pleasure to see the pale peach walls, the dark peach carpet. Going into the living-room, she was startled to find an empty bottle of champagne, two glasses and a bunch of pale yellow roses, roughly rammed into a vase. Abby's first terrified thought was burglars. Her eyes raced round the walls and furniture checking pictures, ornaments and silver, but everything seemed in place.

Then, as painful as stubbing one's toe on a dog bowl in the dark, she noticed the grey pin-stripe jacket hanging on a chair. What, too, was the crocodile wallet she'd given Christopher doing on the glass table beside the keys she'd lovingly had cut so he could let himself into the apartment? A letter from Rupert had already been opened.

Somehow Abby's buckling legs carried her next door. She had always wanted a beautiful bedroom. Other stars celebrate overnight fame with Ferraris, yachts or Picassos, or a Central Park penthouse. But Abby, as she practised nine hours a day and faced tiny, indifferent audiences in draughty halls, had only dreamt of a bower of bliss.

In the centre of the room was a vast four-poster, richly swagged with crimson velvet, hand-printed with vast blush-pink peonies. Half a dozen white lace pillows reared up like the Himalayas against the wrought-iron bedhead, which had been intricately woven into a pattern of treble and bass clefs; perfect to cling onto when she writhed like an electric eel above and below Christopher.

She had called in a lighting specialist, to cast a flattering rosy glow, so that Christopher, unlike Tithonus, would never grow old.

On the walls was more crimson velvet, on the polished floor rose-patterned rugs, and on the scarlet lacquer bedside tables, where she'd left them ten days ago, were two huge vases of lilies, whose petals were beginning to droop and wrinkle like old limp hands.

The only blot on her bed of crimson joy was Christopher filling his secretary, Sandra, in very non-dental fashion.

The horrified silence was broken by Abby.

'That's why you kept on at me to buy a New York apartment, so you could send me off on tour and hump this fat tramp in comfort,' she yelled. 'Why didn't you use the office carpet, or the back seat of the Volvo like we used to? Does Beth know about Sandra? I figured it was key not to upset Beth.'

Looking round, she noticed the closet doors were open. Sandra had obviously been trying on her clothes. A peacock-blue party dress lay inside out on the floor. A bottle of lemon-and-rosemary oil stood unstoppered by the bed.

'I'm surprised you bother with that stuff, Sandra,' Abby addressed Sandra, almost chattily, 'the only thing Christopher enjoys having massaged is his ego.'

For a frozen moment Christopher panicked – then he wriggled out from underneath Sandra, and wrapping a red towel round his loins, advanced on Abby.

'What the hell are you doing here?' he thundered. 'How *dare* you let the Wigmore Hall down. I hope you weren't photographed coming off the aeroplane, or they'll figure you've accepted another booking.

Shepherd Denston are backing that concert, we stand to lose a lot of money,' he glanced at his watch on the bedside table, 'unless you get back on that aeroplane at once.'

Abby looked at him in bewilderment.

'I cannot believe what I'm hearing.' Holding her hands over her ears, she stumbled out to the kitchen.

Christopher followed her, determined to bluff it out.

How dare she treat with Rupert behind his back; how dare she leave Rosalie in the lurch, and swan off with that old reprobate Rodney Macintosh.

Abby's eyes were rolling, she was as grey with shock as the river outside. Christopher could smell the champagne sour on her breath. He was just reaching the fortissimo climax of his fury, when Abby told him she had chucked Rannaldini's contract out of the window.

'It's now being dumped on by Birmingham pigeons, which is what it deserves. You don't give a fuck about me. I'm just the eternal jackpot on the fruit machine. How many millions of notes have I played to buy this apartment, and you've just desecrated it. Well, you've blown it this time.'

Seizing the carving knife, which Sandra had used to level the bottom of the rose stems, Abby bent back her other hand, almost abstractedly examining the veins, faint as biro marks, on the inside wrist. Then, raising the knife, she made a deep cut, half an inch above her watch-strap.

Seeing her hand hanging like a snowdrop, spurting blood, and the agency's livelihood gushing away, Christopher leapt forward to stop her slashing her right one.

'Not your bowing hand, for Christ's sake.'

SEVEN

Abby was raced to hospital. Micro, neuro and plastic surgeons jetted in from all over the world to save her career. After a seven-hour operation, including a massive blood transfusion, they managed to repair both the tendons and the arteries and suture the nerve sheaths. As the nerves had been severed, she was spared a lot of pain when she came round. That would come later as the nerves grew back pitifully slowly at a millimetre a day.

She was kept heavily sedated with tranquillizers, antibiotics and painkillers pouring in through the drip. Counsellors poured in, too, and physiotherapists to waggle gently the lifeless fingers.

Abby had no movement left. She couldn't cup her hand, move her thumb across to her little finger or open and shut or splay her fingers at all. She would have to wear a splint for months to stop her hand contracting like a vulture's claw, which meant all the muscles would waste.

Abby asked only one question: would she ever play the violin again?

'In time,' said the chief consultant. 'If you persevere with the physio. The nerves will take at least a year to regenerate, then we'll be able to tell more. Whether you'll ever play to concert standard is doubtful. There's too much pressure put on young soloists today.'

Abby was devastated. There were fears for her sanity, as she sobbed uncontrollably for hours on end, or gazed blankly into space.

How could she have deliberately destroyed her God-given talent just to break out of Christopher's boa-constrictor stranglehold, to spite him because he no longer loved her?

Christopher had tried to hush up the story, arrogantly ordering Abby to say nothing, as he passed himself off as the lone boy-scout hero whose tourniquet had saved Abby's life. Unfortunately, the porter in Abby's block had noticed Sandra going in and out. Who could forget those knockers in a hurry?

Christopher had also patronized and ridden roughshod over too many people and wriggled out of paying for too many lunches to have many friends in the Press. The result was a monumental scandal, particularly at such a tragic loss of a unique talent.

'TIGRESS AND CHEATER,' shouted the headlines over huge pictures of a smouldering Abby and a sancti-monius Christopher. Christopher had also lied about the fact that Beth had found out. She had had no idea and was wiped out by such betrayal, which made Abby feel infinitely worse.

Nor were matters helped by Hermione, who was at first irked by the massive coverage, then, when it showed no signs of abating, decided to cash in and fly to New York.

'CARING HERMIONE IN MERCY DASH,' announced *The Scorpion* with a picture of the great diva on the hospital steps clutching a bunch of already drooping roses and her latest CD, label out, as presents for Abby.

Ignoring the fact that after thirty seconds Abby had rung down in hysterics to have her chucked out,

Hermione afterwards told the army of reporters that she had advised Abigail to involve herself in charity work.

'"Think of the poor people of Rwanda," I urged her. "At least you are being looked after by wonderfully caring hospital staff." I hope the sacred message of my latest CD, *Heavenly Hermione*, will bring her spiritual refreshment.'

Abby, who'd had to be given a massive shot of Valium, wasn't remotely cheered up five minutes later when Rupert sauntered in. He was in New York to check out laser surgery for Xav's birthmark, and arrived with a carrier bag over his head.

'What in hell are you doing?' snarled Abby.

'Hiding from Hermione.'

'She's only interested in your beautiful hands, and they're still on show.'

'Actually she's far too busy fighting for access to the make-up department with all those consultants, who are becoming television stars, providing bulletins on your progress.'

He removed the carrier bag and smoothed his hair. He was wearing a love-in-the-mist blue shirt which matched his long blue eyes, which in turn matched the patch of blue sky which was all Abby could see through her window. Part of a sunny outside world, which seemed lost for ever.

'Poor old duck,' said Rupert, remembering the bleak horror of Taggie's miscarriages. 'It must be like losing a baby.'

'Far, far worse,' Abby snapped. 'Like losing a thousand babies. Every time I played a concert, I gave birth.'

Rupert was appalled by her appearance. A forelock of dark hair fell damp and flat to her eyebrows. Her fleshless face was dominated more than ever by the haunted, heavily shadowed yellow eyes. The only plumpness left was in the curve of her lower lip. She had lost twenty pounds. Seeing her huddled, wide-shouldered, long-legged body, Rupert was reminded of some shell-shocked youth fatally wounded in the trenches.

Getting out his fountain-pen, he drew a blue cross on the inside of her right wrist just where it joined her hand.

'This is the place if you want to top yourself properly. You did it too far up the arm, just means the nerves take longer to grow back.'

'Will they?'

'Course they will. I had no feeling for six months after I trapped a nerve at the LA Olympics; Ricky France-Lynch's arm took nearly three years; my son-in-law Luke's hand was pulverized by a polo ball. We all got better.'

He had brought her a bunch of lilies of the valley, and a little silver replica of a head of garlic.

'That's to ward off evil, you're to keep it beside you all the time. Taggie's also made you a tin of fudge. She sent love and said she was dreadfully sorry.'

'Thanks,' said Abby listlessly. 'Did you get your baby?'

'We got two, Xavier and Bianca. Flew them home last week. The grooms had hung a welcome home banner across the gate and balloons all up the drive. Edith Spink brought the Cotchester Chamber Orchestra over in a bus to play "Congratulations". All the dogs had bows, it was great. Xavier couldn't believe his eyes. He's walking all over the place now. And his first word was Daddy, so he's obviously going to be a diplomat.'

Rupert gave a big yawn.

'Sorry, we're not getting much sleep at the moment. Bianca's routine's all out of sync.'

His tearing spirits made Abby feel even more dreadful, particularly as they kept being interrupted by nurses popping in to check Abby's fingers for gangrene and gaze at Rupert.

'They never allow me a second to brood,' groaned Abby. 'And oh God, the counsellor's due at three o'clock.'

'Don't believe in that crap,' said Rupert. 'Only person who can sort you out is yourself. Counsellors are flooding into Penscombe at the moment. There's a ghastly beard with an Adam's apple who's got a crush on Taggie and keeps forecasting disaster because we've adopted a black child. He asked me yesterday whether I was going to teach Xav the customs of his country? Did he want me to give Xav a line of coke for breakfast, I said.'

But Abby wasn't listening, being too wrapped up in her own tragedy.

'I can't do Declan's programme now,' she said sulkily, 'if that's what you've come for.'

Rupert's face softened.

'I came to see you, because I was dead worried and because I like you a lot. Classical music bores the tits off me, reminds me of my first wife, but you made it as exciting,' Rupert cast round, 'as a good Gold Cup.'

Abby started to cry. Rupert took her in his arms.

For a second, Abby clung to him enjoying the muscular warmth, then, as the counsellor came in, she screamed with rage: 'Is there no peace except beyond the grave?'

'Don't talk like that,' chided the counsellor. 'She's doing great,' she added to Rupert.

'I must go,' Rupert got to his feet. 'The only answer,' he ruffled Abby's hair, 'is to become a conductor. That shit Rannaldini needs some competition.'

Shepherd Denston, who were in turmoil, were fast coming to the same conclusion.

'If only Abby'd done the job properly,' grumbled Howard on a conference call to Christopher and young Howie in London, 'she could have become a cult figure like James Dean or Marilyn Monroe.'

'Not enough mileage,' said young Howie. 'She's better alive. We gotta find something for her to do.'

Shepherd Denston needed the money. It was not just the houses on Long Island and the old masters and young mistresses, acquired on the expectation of Abby's massive income. The agency had also extended themselves dangerously, backing concerts throughout Eastern Europe, only to find the newly free populations were hungrier for new cars than culture.

'What a pity that contract with Rannaldini never got signed,' said Howard.

'We better get her Strad back,' said Christopher briskly. 'Can't let it lie idle. Maria needs a decent instrument.'

Maria Kusak was Abby's bitterest rival, one of the agency's rising stars.

'Fact that Abby's pulled through suicide, like coming off drugs, or cracking anorexia, is gonna evoke public sympathy,' said Howie, then groaned as his secretary handed him a fax saying that Benny Basanovich had been so drunk in Munich he'd skipped pages of Prokofiev's *Third Concerto* before falling off the piano-stool.

'The only answer,' said Howard, 'is for her to learn to conduct, while we see if her hand's gonna recover.'

For now though, Abby must leave the limelight until the scandal had died down. Sir Rodney Macintosh, who'd said some uncomfortingly sharp things to Christopher after the accident, gallantly came to the rescue, and offered Abby the use of his house on Lake Lucerne.

'The wild flowers are out of this world, darling, and the mountain air is purer and more exhilarating than Krug.'

Rodney's ancient housekeeper, Gisela, who was used to temperamental artists, would build up Abby's strength. There was every score in the world to work on. She could have a resident physio and a succession of student conductors to teach her the rudiments.

Christopher, everyone decided, must bow out of Abby's life. Another reason why Lucerne was a good idea. Her career, in future, would be handled by the London office and, when he wasn't racing all over Europe to sort out the chaos caused by Benny Basanovich, by Howie Denston.

EIGHT

Clutching her silver clove of garlic, Abby arrived in Lucerne. Rodney met her and, with a series of loud bangs, singing: '*All boys are cheap today, cheaper than yesterday,*' to the tune of 'La Donna e mobile', drove her out to his house along the lake.

Known as Flasher's Folly, it stood on the town side of a wooded peninsula, which seemed to crawl into the lake like a huge furry caterpillar. The house itself was square, black gabled, with a mossy red roof and warm yellow walls smothered in white wisteria. The oak front door was thirty yards from the water's edge. Behind the house was a lawn flanked by honeysuckle, rose colonnades and a water garden fed by two springs. Separating the garden from the mountains was an orchard and a copse of linden trees. Rodney's fourth wife, the one who'd played concertos in her nightie, had plainly been a wonderful gardener.

'We've had some great parties over the years,' Rodney squeezed Abby's shoulder. 'In heatwaves we often bathed starkers in the lake at midnight.'

The entire attic was set aside for Rodney's train sets. He could run ten trains simultaneously along the tracks without any crashes.

'The secret of conducting is to be able to do ten things at once.'

Abby's big bedroom took up most of the second floor and had windows front and back. As well as a four-poster with sprigged white-and-yellow muslin curtains, it contained a piano, a record player, bookshelves packed with every score from Purcell to Gorecki, a stuffed bear wearing a Victorian bishop's mitre and, among other pictures on the pale Parma-violet walls, a portrait of Rodney's second cousin, Myrtle, who'd become a missionary.

Apart from Gisela, the household included Rodney's cat, Shostakovich, a huge, indolent charmer with long grey hair and big orange eyes, who usually lay around in pools of sunlight, but who was currently weaving round Abby's legs, being driven crazy by a heady smell of *coq au vin* from the kitchen.

'Oh wow, how lovely to have a cat.' Ecstatically Abby bent to stroke Shosty, as he was known. But as she gathered him up, her left hand couldn't support him, and he crashed to the floor, flouncing off on fluffy grey plus-fours.

'Lands on his feet like his master,' said Rodney reassuringly.

Like Rupert, he was horrified by Abby's appearance; so tall, thin and pale, a tree stricken by lightning. She touched her left hand constantly, desperate for the return of any feeling.

To distract her he led her to the front window. Outside, the shimmering pale blue lake seemed to merge into the powder-blue mist and the grey-blue sky without any horizon. But gradually snowy white peaks began to appear.

'Look darling, they're all coming out to welcome you. Those are the Riga Mountains and that big crooked peak is Mount Pilatus, named after Pontius Pilate. Legend has it that after he sentenced Christ to death, he came here to suffer for his sins.'

117

Pilate and me, thought Abby bleakly.

'I can think of worse places. It's better than Croydon,' said Rodney.

Woods were now emerging on the opposite shore. 'Now you can see Tribschen,' he went on, pointing to the prettiest white doll's house on a high grassy mound, 'where Cosima lived with Wagner and, before he became a conductor, Hans Richter worked there as Wagner's secretary.'

'Richter,' for a second Abby was roused out of her apathy, 'my hero. He was such a brilliant musician. Orchestras just adored him.'

She didn't add that with his beard, mane of hair, broad shoulders and air of authority, Richter had looked rather like Christopher. Richter, however, had been a devoted husband. A Christopher with honour. But she must forget Christopher. Hopelessly she clutched her silver garlic.

Aware of her misery, Rodney pointed to an island of trees rising out of the water about fifty yards from the shore.

'After a long day of copying out *The Mastersingers*, Richter, a very strong man, used to row across the lake from Tribschen at dusk, embark on that island and practise the French horn, thus starting another legend of a mysterious ghost horn player.'

Leaning out of the window on those early summer evenings, waiting for the stars to come out, Abby often imagined she could hear the first sweet notes of a horn, but they were only owls hooting and the cries of the water birds.

Looking back on her first few months in Lucerne, Abby was appalled that she behaved quite so horribly. Generous, passionate, demanding, workaholic, her last twelve years had been dominated by Christopher and more recently by her Strad, which had now gone back to the bank. Abby missed the Strad even more than

Christopher; her relationship with the violin had been so close, so joyous, so tactile, so successful, it had been like taking a beloved dog back to a rescue kennel. And the heartbreaking beauty of her surroundings only made her loss worse.

The doctors were pleased with her. By October the severed muscles had knit so she now had some movement in her fingers, but she still had no grip and no feeling in her palms or her fingertips.

Her worst problem, however, was her inability to relax. Raging at the slowness of her physical recovery, she plunged into conducting, standing in front of the long gold mirror in her room endlessly waving a baton to records, trying to anticipate the entrances of the various instruments, or giving herself blinding headaches poring over scores long into the night.

Her main difficulty was having to conduct in a vacuum. If only she could have returned from Lucerne with a case of different musicians, set them up like chess pieces, breathed life into them, and rehearsed and rehearsed them until she dropped.

'How can I practise without an orchestra?' she raged at Rodney. 'It's like learning to be a good lay from reading sex books.'

'I could certainly help you with the latter,' said Rodney.

'It isn't a joke.'

So Rodney in his sweetness, for her twenty-sixth birthday on 26 October, rounded up all his musician pals in Lucerne and Geneva, the twenty-strong local choir and four soloists, and arranged for them to spend the weekend at Flasher's Folly.

The plan was for Abby to rehearse *The Messiah* with them on Saturday and Sunday and then give a performance in front of an invited audience on Sunday night. Abby was so excited and terrified, she became utterly impossible. Desperate for evidence that her hand was better, she was also constantly and recklessly testing it.

Rodney only spent about a third of the year in Lucerne and Gisela liked everything to be perfect. On the Friday morning before the concert, gold leaves were tumbling into the lake, but it was so warm she had laid breakfast outside. *Café au lait*, bacon and mushrooms picked at dawn from the orchard, home-made croissants and apricot jam were all served on and in rose-patterned gold-leaf plates, cups and saucers, part of a priceless set of twelve.

Rodney, who was whipping through *The Times* crossword, which was faxed out to him from Rutminster every morning, always had his orange juice out of a heavy glass tumbler, of which he was inordinately proud. Engraved with his name and a picture of a puffing train, it had been presented to him by his orchestra on his seventy-fifth birthday last year.

Gisela, despite being old and rheumaticky, hated to be helped. But Abby was desperate to prove her grip was getting stronger, so the moment breakfast was over, she stacked everything including Rodney's tumbler onto the tray.

'I'll carry it.' In alarm Rodney put down *The Times*.

'I'm OK.'

The next moment, Abby's hand had slipped and everything had smashed into a hundred pieces on the flagstones.

'Why the hell don't you leave things alone?' shouted Rodney.

Too horrified to apologize, Abby stormed upstairs leaving the mess. Within seconds the 'Hallelujah Chorus' was blaring out of her bedroom. And when Rodney stumped angrily upstairs to play with his trains, Abby had ostentatiously banged her windows shut to blot out the sound of shouting, whistling and hooting. Even when Shostakovich appeared mewing at the window Abby screamed at him to go away. He had a maddening habit of sitting on scores, or leaping onto her shoulders like a witch's cat when she was giving her all to some elaborate aria.

At one o'clock, she was playing 'Worthy is the Lamb' so loudly that she didn't hear Gisela's tentative knock, so Gisela let herself in. Always trying to tempt Abby to eat more, she had made her a pale pink smoked salmon soufflé, wild strawberry ice-cream, and had squeezed her a glass of her favourite pink-grapefruit juice. Also on the tray, which she placed on the table by the window, was a bowl of vitamins and a posy of mauve autumn crocuses.

Abby went beserk.

'For Chrissake, how many times do I have to tell you, I'll come down when I want to eat.'

Gisela's kind, rosy face crumpled in dismay.

Upstairs the 8.10 from Zurich ran into the 10.55 from Geneva with a crash, as Rodney toddled downstairs. His station-master's cap, askew over his eye, did nothing to diminish the roaring rage on his face.

'How dare you shout at Gisela like that, you spoilt brat! Everyone is falling over themselves to be nice to you. Gisela and I are going into Lucerne this afternoon and if you're not in a better mood when we get home, you can pack your bags and get out.'

Again, Abby was too distraught to apologize. But after they had gone she sobbed her hopelessly muddled heart out. How could she have been so ungrateful? God would punish her by never allowing her to play the violin again.

'Oh *please*, what gets into me?'

Wearily she picked up her stick and the battered yellow score of *The Messiah*. It was cheating to conduct to a record, and made her lazy and slow to adjust. Rodney's musicians, if he hadn't already told them not to turn up for such an ungrateful cow, would probably play it in a completely different way. She'd have to sing and imagine it in her head.

Handel's original version of *The Messiah* was scored for a very small orchestra and Abby had arranged her room so each instrument was represented by a different object. The bookshelf on her left was the First Violins, the chest of drawers next door the Second Violins. The faded crimson armchair the First Oboe, the trouser press the Second Oboe, the stuffed bear in the mitre seemed appropriately august to play both bassoons.

Rodney's beady Cousin Myrtle, gazing down between the windows, which looked on to the back garden, represented the violas. And Abby's white-and-yellow four-poster, against the right-hand wall, which she hadn't made yet, had to act as the harpsichord.

The Messiah begins with the entire orchestra playing together loudly and gravely for twenty-four bars. Abby glared round the room to see that everyone was paying attention, paused and raised her baton. Rannaldini was said to have a down beat that could halve butter straight from the freezer. Abby was determined to be as incisive. *One*, her stick whistled downwards, *two* to the left, *three* to the right, and *four* in a sweeping quarter-circle back to one.

At bar twenty-five after a diminuendo, the tempo changed and she had to cue in the crimson armchair and the chest of drawers after the first beat of the bar, and then bring in the bookshelf and the trouser press, followed four bars later by the stuffed bear, the four-poster and Rodney's Cousin Myrtle. And all the time she had to sing the tune in a breathless soprano.

Playing away for all their worth, the whole room reached bar ninety-seven, and the first recitative: 'Comfort Ye . . .' Beating eight quavers to the bar with her right hand, Abby exhorted the bookshelf, Cousin Myrtle, the chest of drawers and the four-poster to play slowly and quietly by shaking her left hand, still as rigid as a Dutch doll's, downwards, as though she were drying her nails. Glancing round she nodded to her dark green bathrobe hanging on the door who was standing in as the tenor.

'*Comfort ye, comfo-ort ye-ee, my pee-eeple,*' sang Abby,

quelling Cousin Myrtle with a death-ray glance for coming in too early. As she speeded up the tempo to walking pace for 'Every Valley,' she must remember the bassoons, who dodged about all over the place throughout the aria. Nor did she think the stuffed bear was capable of counting thirty-one bars between twiddles, should she forget to cue him in, but somehow they circumnavigated every '*rough place and crooked straight*', to end with a splendid run of trills from the crimson armchair.

'Well done, everyone,' called Abby. 'Try and be even more together.'

Only the stuffed bear and Cousin Myrtle were looking at her, but in her experience most musicians didn't bother to look much at conductors.

And now for the first chorus, with a ten-bar allegro tutti, before she stretched out both hands to the gold trees in the orchard outside, who were playing the part of the chorus.

'*And the glory, the glory of the Lord,*' sang the alto apple trees.

'Terrific, wonderful,' Abby urged them on. 'Oh wow,' she added as she cued in the plums, the pears and an ancient quince tree, to bring in the basses, sopranos and tenors. It seemed right that such a pretty delicate tree as the pear should sing soprano.

Oh thank God, it was all coming good.

'*And all flesh shall see it together,*' encouraged the apple trees.

Abby worked on frenziedly until the light started fading. She was just about to embark on 'A Trumpet Shall Sound', which required a solo trumpet, when she noticed a candidate had rolled up in the form of Shosty who was back, mewing piteously, rubbing his fur against the window pane. She'd been so foul to him earlier. Putting down her baton, Abby opened the window. Leaping onto her shoulder, Shosty smelt of thyme and marjoram, he must have been hunting at the bottom of the mountain.

For a second he purred round her neck, a grey muffler, louder than any percussion player, then jumped onto the table to lick up the butter that had escaped from the smoked salmon soufflé.

Although her wrist ached dreadfully, a great peace swept over Abby. She'd had such a good afternoon's work. How could she have been so foul to Gisela and Rodney? It was she who needed her rough places planed with the most vicious sandpaper. She'd go into Lucerne tomorrow and buy Gisela that new winter coat she'd been talking about.

Abby wandered over to the front window. The sun had set, leaving the lake a drained vermilion. The snowy mountains opposite had turned dark pink like summer or rather autumn puddings, as they rose out of their gold ruff of woods. To the left she could see the island where Hans Richter had practised his French horn. There were no horns in *The Messiah*. If only some wonderful musician could row over from the island to woo her. She was almost resigned to the loss of Christopher, she no longer jumped with hope each time the telephone rang or the post arrived. But she felt overwhelmed with sadness, like the Marschallin in *Der Rosencavalier*, that something she had so cherished had gone for ever.

She jumped as Shosty, bored by salmon flavoured butter, joined her on the window-ledge, weaving against her. Putting out an idle hand to stroke him, Abby froze, whipping back her hand as though she had had some fearful electric shock; then she put it back, held it there and began to tremble violently. There was no doubt, she could feel the faint tickling of his fur against her palm. Pressing down gently she could feel the hardness of his backbone, and running her hand to the left encountered the ramrod straightness of his tail. Then she rubbed the hopelessly wasted ball of her thumb against him. No feeling there yet, nor in her fingertips. Still shaking, she put her palm down again; she could definitely feel his fur moving.

The next moment, the front door banged.

Gathering up Shosty, she raced downstairs screaming with excitement.

Rodney was standing in the doorway still in his station-master's cap, smiling guiltily. He'd spent far too much money on, among other things, a new train set. Gisela, as though catching the last rays of the sun, was proudly wearing a new red overcoat.

'Oh Rodney, oh Gisela,' screamed Abby.

'Darling, you look happier,' said Rodney, who never harboured grudges.

On the way down the last flight, Abby lost Shosty, who, indignant at being carted in such a noisy and unseemly fashion, wriggled out of her arms and flounced off to the kitchen.

'I can feel, I can feel, I can feel Shosty's fur on my hand,' whooped Abby, going straight into Gisela's arms. 'I'm sorry I've been such a bitch, I was so scared.'

Gisela could feel Abby's face soaked with tears, and her desperate thinness. Her ribs were protruding like an old-fashioned radiator.

'There, there,' she stroked Abby's heaving shoulder, 'you will get best now.'

Putting down his parcels, Rodney took Abby's hand and kissed the palm.

'Can you feel that?'

'I can feel your beard tickling more than Shosty's fur.' Abby was between tears and laughter. 'I'm gonna play the violin again.'

'Richter and Wagner shared half a bottle of champagne when Wagner wrote the last bar of *The Mastersingers*,' said Rodney happily. 'We all deserve a nice bottle of Krug.'

Appassionata

FIRST MOVEMENT

NINE

Abby worked for nearly two more years in Lucerne before moving to London to take a conducting course at the Royal Academy of Music. A solid roan-and-white Edwardian building, the Academy stands in the Marylebone Road, flanked by plane trees. The autumn term had already begun, but London was enjoying a very hot Indian summer. Few members of the Academy's orchestra, red-faced from lugging heavy instruments, noticed the 'Viva L'Appassionata' poster hanging from the flagpole as they scuttled in through the glass front door.

Inside, anticipation had reached fever pitch. Since her attempted suicide, Abby had achieved cult status among students who collected her old records and pinned up her posters, portraying her in her tempestuous gypsy beauty. In a materialistic world, she had sacrificed all for love.

In the foyer, therefore, an unusual number of students, who should have been at their various classes, pretended to read notices about scholarships and forthcoming concerts. Such was the excitement that one half expected the antique fiddles to break out of their glass case and offer Abby their services, or Sir Henry Wood in his red robes to shout 'Bravo' from his portrait in an ante-room.

As the clock edged towards a quarter past ten, and there was no sign of her, the students reluctantly dispersed, except for a tall boy wearing a navy-blue baseball cap to dry his hair flat, and a girl with a dark red bob, who was scornfully reading a letter which had been pinned to the notice-board:

> *Dear Musicians,*
> *Thank you for making music with me so delightfully. I must congratulate the Academy on a super orchestra.*
> *With great pleasure*
> *Hermione Harefield*

'Stupid cowpat,' muttered the girl, and getting out a biro she wrote: *PS. If David, the hunky First Trombone, wants to pop in to the Old Mill, Paradise, he'll be most welcome to a bed for the afternoon.*

'Flo-*rah*, stop it,' chided the boy. 'You're going to be seriously late.'

'Oh, all right.' Grabbing her viola case, Flora hopscotched across the black-and-white checked floor slap into her teacher.

'Why the hell aren't you warming up?' he said furiously. 'I put my head on the block putting you forward for this, don't you dare let me down.'

'Yes Mr French, sorry Mr French, promise to do my best, Mr French.'

Flora scampered off into the Duke's Hall where gold-framed portraits of illustrious former students looked down from paprika-red walls on to a packed audience of students, parents, teachers and talent scouts.

Two friends had kept a seat in the back row for the boy in the baseball cap. Flora sauntered up onto the stage where the Academy orchestra, grumbling about the cold after the sunshine outside, were tuning up, practising difficult solos and runs in different directions like skaters. Both sexes were huddled in sweaters and trousers, wore clumpy shoes or trainers and no make-up. The only way you could distinguish the girls was by their long flowing undyed hair, which was mostly drawn back from high clear foreheads, although a few, in Abby's honour, had turned up with wild Appassionata gypsy curls.

The object today was for this year's student conduc-tors, who sat in a nervous nail-biting row behind the horns, to try out their skills on the Academy orchestra in the first movement of Bartók's *Viola Concerto*.

Flora was playing the solo and she and the musicians had endlessly to repeat the same bits as one conductor after another fumblingly attempted to control the orchestra and were repeatedly taken apart by a genial but highly critical professor, who sat in the second desk of the second violins with a score making notes.

The Bartók concerto is extremely difficult, and with all the stopping and starting, the timpanist, the percus-sion and the brass (including Hermione's hunky trombone player) had very little to do, except count bars between the occasional flurry of notes, which they often missed because the conductors forgot to bring them in.

'You're not keeping the orchestra down enough,' shouted the professor to a sweating Swede, who was flapping on the rostrum as though he were about to fly through the vaulted roof. 'We can't hear Flora.'

'Just as well,' Flora grinned at the Japanese leader, who had a lean beautiful body and a face like a Red Indian. 'It's the cadenza next. I'll need scaffolding and oxygen to reach that top A. What the hell's happened to L'Appassionata?'

To fox any press who had in fact been humiliatingly non-existent, Abby had been smuggled in by a back door. Shivering behind dark glasses, dying of nerves, she was dickering whether to rush out and be sick again.

How could she do justice to such a beautiful piece, particularly when the orchestra were only playing it for the first time?

The soloist, Abby decided, was extremely good. She needed to work on her technique; she ground to a halt twice in the cadenza, and burst out laughing when during a really sad bit she'd caught a friend's eye in the audience, but generally she executed the high notes effortlessly and joyfully and in the lower register the sound was mellow, dark and mysterious.

She was also extremely attractive. Her figure was hidden by baggy black trousers and a thick black cardigan, but she had a clear pale gold skin, merry green eyes, a plump face ending in a pointed chin and her shining bob was the same warm burnt-sienna as her viola.

Above all, she played with total insouciance keeping up a stream of *badinage* with the orchestra, chewing gum and reading her tattered poetry book every time there was a pause. Now she was sitting on the lean thigh of the Japanese leader awaiting the next victim, a plump Greek called Adonis, who had soft white hands and gold teeth to match his gold corduroy shirt. All his friends trooped round behind the brass section to video him conducting.

'Like photographing the captain of the *Titanic*,' murmured Flora, getting to her feet.

Sweat was glistening on her upper lip, a russet lock had fallen away from the tortoiseshell slide. There was a chorus of wolf-whistles as she took off her black cardigan to reveal a dark green T-shirt embroidered with yellow daisies and tucked into a wide leather belt.

'Vy d'you have to distract me viz striptease?' grumbled Adonis. 'Now don't vorry, I vill follow you.'

'I don't vant you following me, I want you with me,' said Flora, raising her viola.

Adonis tried very hard, but the orchestra were all over the place. The genial professor sighed. He was going to have his work cut out with this lot.

That soloist is smart, thought Abby wistfully. Adonis was now going much too fast, but she always caught up.

Glancing sideways, she noticed the boy with the baseball cap. Totally still, really listening, he followed every note Flora played. What a beauty, thought Abby, he's the one who ought to be called Adonis.

A punch-up was narrowly avoided because Adonis skipped another page and missed out the hunky trombonist's last entry yet again.

Abby, who'd been studying the concerto for the last fortnight, couldn't bear to hear it so butchered. But would she do any better? The notes of the score swum meaninglessly before her eyes. Oh God, she hoped she wasn't going to be sick again.

Adonis was followed by Lorenzo, a handsome Italian who made beautiful gestures, but who seemed more interested in ogling Flora and the video cameras.

'This one's got two left hands,' murmured the professor as Lorenzo kept smoothing his hair with his right hand.

'You've occasionally got to beat in time, Lorenzo,' he called out. 'No matter how emotional you feel, you've got to first and foremost be a traffic policeman so the orchestra can follow and know where they are, particularly in a piece with so many changes of tempo.'

'I try again.'

This time extravagant waving and fists clenched to heaven were followed by four bars of total silence.

'Where am I?' Lorenzo smote his noble brow.

'In the Duke's Hall,' giggled Flora.

'You're lost,' said the professor.

'But not forgotten.' Parking her chewing-gum on the side of the rostrum, Flora gave Lorenzo a kiss.

'That is a disgusting habit, Flora,' reproved the professor.

'I don't know what score you studied, Lorenzo, but I don't think it was Bartók's *Viola Concerto*.'

The orchestra grinned. Lorenzo turned scarlet, and started to argue.

'Discuss it with me later,' said the professor firmly. 'We've got time for one more before lunch.'

The rest of the conductors, waiting behind the horns, leapt to their feet like MPs frantic to speak, but the professor had nodded to the back of the hall.

'Here comes Abby,' said Flora, sliding off the leader's knee.

The Japanese boy looked round.

'That is not her.'

'Bet you a tenner.'

'I don't have your kind of money.'

Few of the audience or musicians recognized Abby. She was so thin and wore black jeans, a Black-Watch tartan shirt, dark glasses and no make-up. Her hair was short and curly like the young Paganini. The scarlet pouting lips, the clinging minis, the wild gypsy voluptuousness had all gone.

'Car-worker rather than Carmen,' murmured Flora.

Abby gave nobody any time to give her a cheer. She carried no score, only a baton, as she loped up the hall and jumped up onto the rostrum. As she whipped off her glasses, the orchestra could see the imperiousness in those strange, unblinking yellow eyes, which was belied by the white knuckles and the frantically knocking knees. For a second she was grabbed by utter panic, her mind a snowstorm. How could she have been so stupid as to conduct without a score?

Then she said quietly; 'This is a beautiful piece, let's give it some shape and feeling.'

She suggested some small alterations to the strings and woodwind, then turned to the brass and the percussion. 'I'm afraid you guys don't have much to do, which makes it easier to goof off. I'll try and make things as clear as possible for you. Good luck.'

Her hand, as she raised it, was shaking so crazily even

Bartók couldn't have captured the cross-rhythms, but once she brought it down the entire hall realized who she was, because she was in a class of her own.

The beat of her right hand was knife-edge clear and, although her left hand was a little stiff, she still couldn't splay her fingers or cup her hand, she managed to show the orchestra exactly what she wanted and in addition convey the emotional intensity she needed. The one vestige of the old Abby was the way she swayed to the music like a dancer.

But she had only to glare at the brass to shut them up and she completely enslaved the trombones by bringing them in exactly right and giving them a radiant smile of approval afterwards.

Flora found it nerve-racking having the world's greatest violinist beside her, but she loved the way Abby glanced round to synchronize orchestra and soloist, and swept aside the orchestral sound so Flora could always be heard.

Are these the same musicians? Is this the same piece? thought the professor in rapture, letting Abby run through the entire movement without stopping, and then leading a whooping, cheering, stamping round of applause.

'You have all the marks of a great conductor,' he told Abby. 'You have nerve but not nerves. It will be a joy to teach you.'

Everyone was longing to congratulate her, but they were too shy and so was she, so they all left her and scampered off to lunch.

Abby was just pulling out her music case from underneath her chair to put away her stick when she heard a voice say: 'Excuse me.'

Swinging round, Abby found the soloist and the boy who had been sitting at the end of her row. Standing up he was at least two inches taller than Abby, and when he whipped off his baseball cap, he revealed a beautifully shaped, freckled forehead and hair an even darker red than the girl's. Abby wondered if they were brother and sister. The girl did the talking.

'I know it sounds corny, but we've got every one of your records. That was a fantastic performance. We wondered if we could buy you lunch, just to celebrate.'

Abby longed to accept but she was so near the edge, that she snapped back: 'I'm far too busy to waste time eating.' And then stalked out.

Five minutes later, Flora tracked her down in a distant practice room, trying not to be overheard by the pianist bashing out Liszt's *Dante Sonata* next door. Abby was huddled against the blue velvet curtains, her shoulders shaking.

Flora had long been haunted by a description of a vivisection clinic where the animals had their vocal chords cut on admission so, however bad the pain became, all you could hear was desperate rasping. This was the sound Abby was making now.

'You were seriously good,' stammered Flora. 'In fact the only thing to cry about is how awful we were. Mind you, you were lucky to find somewhere to cry, practice rooms are harder to get here than tickets for your old concerts.'

Looking up, Abby saw the kindness in the girl's eyes belying her flip manner.

'I'm sorry,' she croaked. 'The last time I was on a platform I was playing the Brahms concerto with the CBSO.'

'I know,' said Flora. 'Everyone knows everything about you. Although what a brilliant conductor you'd turned into was certainly hidden in the mists of Lake Lucerne.'

'It was your solo,' gulped Abby, fishing for another tissue.

'I can quite understand that.'

'No, you play real good. You've got a fantastically natural sound, I guess you reminded me of myself.'

'I should do,' admitted Flora, 'having based my style entirely on yours. All our generation has, music schools are churning out more little Abbies than an ecclesiastical property developer!'

Abby's lips twitched.

'At least come and have a drink.'

Outside in the sunshine the boy was leaning against the railings, his nose in the selected piano works of Chopin, making notes with a pencil.

'My name's Flora Seymour, by the way,' announced the girl. 'And this is Marcus Campbell-Black.'

Abby perked up. 'You must be Rupert's son.'

Marcus waited, never knowing if the next bit was going to hurt or not.

'Goodness, you're like him,' Abby admired the long, dark, curling eyelashes and the exquisite bone structure. 'It's *just* like looking at a fabric sample in a different colour.' Except Abby couldn't ever imagine Rupert blushing or being lost for words.

'Rupert came to see me in the hospital and gave me this.' Delving in her jeans pocket Abby produced the silver clove of garlic. 'To ward off evil. Do tell him I take it everywhere and give him my best.'

'He said he'd met you,' said Marcus guardedly.

Round the corner he opened the door of his Aston Martin for her.

'You go in the back,' said Flora, 'then you'll have room for your legs.'

'Georgie Maguire: *New Man*.' Abby picked up a tape on the back seat in excitement. 'This must be her latest. Oh wow! Christopher, my ex and I, "Rock Star" was our sort of big tune. I know it's terrible shmaltz and I shouldn't say so, but I just adore Georgie's music.'

'You should,' said Marcus, starting up the car and ignoring Flora's kick on the ankle. 'Georgie's Flora's mother.'

'Omigod!'

'I'll tell her you're a fan,' said Flora. 'She'll be really pleased, she's a terrific fan of yours.'

Abby looked at Flora with new respect.

'Gee, I'm sorry I was rude earlier.'

Flora shrugged. 'Mum's the same. She can't bear strangers muscling in, particularly when she's coming down after a concert. And she goes ballistic if people drop in at home.'

Abby noticed Marcus wheezing as he drove. Petrol fumes were floating on the hot air and the walk to the car had made him breathless. Reaching into the pocket of his shirt he got out his inhaler and squirted a couple of jets into the back of his throat.

'Marcus is asthmatic,' explained Flora. 'Thank God we can forget about that for a bit.' Pulling the Bartók concerto out of the stereo she threw it in the glove compartment.

'Put it back in its case,' grumbled Marcus. 'And if you must smoke, don't use the floor as an asthtray.'

Flora grinned. 'Don't be a fusspot.' Then, turning round to Abby, continued, 'I can't get over how different you look.'

'I cut my hair and my losses. Which did you think was the worst of those conductors?'

'Adonis by a very swollen head,' announced Flora.

'I can't think how you followed him,' said Marcus.

'If you learn to follow any idiot, you get more dates later,' Flora added scornfully. 'Conductors are so thick. They carry a white stick to tell everyone they're deaf. Marcus has been wonderful,' she added to Abby. 'He's been playing the piano version for me all week.' Leaning across him, she chucked some more chewing-gum out of the window which landed on the shiny dark green flanks of the Bentley drawing up beside them.

'Jesus, when will you learn to behave?' Marcus accelerated away from the Bentley's fist-shaking chauffeur. 'I thought Lorenzo was even more of a talent-free zone than Adonis. He's got no sense of rhythm.'

'He has in bed,' said Flora. 'Look at that sweet Jack Russell. I wish I could have a dog in London.'

'When did you go to bed with Lorenzo?' asked Marcus in surprise.

'Oh last week, some time. He keeps wanting repeats. I quite fancy Toniko, I've never had a Jap.'

'Where did you two meet?' asked Abby, wondering what on earth the relationship was between them.

'We were at school together,' said Flora.

Marcus and Flora were the star pupils at the Academy. Marcus was a great beauty. He had inherited Rupert's Greek profile (so vital in a pianist) and his elegant long-legged, broad-shouldered body. But he also had his mother's glossy dark red hair, freckles and huge startled eyes, which were the same soft acid green as spring moss. Desperately shy, he was, however, unaware of his miraculous looks and, like a fawn or faun, seemed likely to bolt into mythical woods at any moment. In his third year at the Academy, he was destined for a brilliant career as a pianist if he could conquer his asthma and his nerves.

Flora, who was only in her second year, and who was as sexy and self-confident as Marcus was shy and retiring, had a voice even more beautiful than her mother Georgie. She was still taking singing lessons but, despite pressure from her teachers, who liked to feature illustrious ex-pupils in the prospectus, she showed no interest in taking up singing as a career. Instead she was concentrating on the viola.

Her official excuse was that she didn't want to be tagged as Georgie Maguire's daughter.

'I don't have Mum's charisma, nor her ability to project.'

In reality she had been totally wiped out by an *affaire* with Rannaldini when she was sixteen, and had decided singing was too isolated a career. She had deliberately chosen the viola, that lovely but unobtrusive Cinderella of the instruments, because it blended into the orchestral sound like cornflour, was seldom heard on its own and was the butt of endless jokes.

In doing this Flora felt she was putting on a mental hair shirt, submerging her flamboyant personality, in the hope that God would forgive her the *affaire* with Rannaldini and somehow alleviate her suffering.

With their famous parents and their hefty private incomes, Marcus and Flora, in the current economic climate of vanishing grants, could have been the victims of a lot of envy and flak at college. As they were both exceptionally talented, utterly without side, and it was soon realized that Marcus's apparent aloofness was only shyness, any prejudice had swiftly evaporated.

TEN

The quick drink turned into a three-hour session. All the tables outside Marcus's and Flora's favourite Italian restaurant were taken, so they lunched inside demanding a large carafe of red wine prestissimo, and larding the rest of their order for canelloni and ratatouille with musical terminology, which involved a lot of back-chat and giggling with the waiters.

Despite their age differences, Abby was nearly twenty-eight, Flora nineteen, Marcus twenty, they found they had a huge amount in common. As children of the famous, Marcus and Flora understood the pressures and the sacrifices.

'One is never centre stage,' sighed Flora. Like Abby, both Rupert and Georgie had toured extensively and Marcus told Abby how wretched Rupert had been after he gave up show jumping.

A lot of lunch was spent telling Abby how brilliantly she had conducted. Always boastful when she was unsure of new people, with her tongue loosened by unaccustomed drinking on a very empty stomach, she went into an orgy of name-dropping about the famous musicians who had, it seemed, either tried to screw her or screw up her career. Inevitably she eventually launched into a tirade against Rannaldini.

Flora let her run and, although she had downed most of a carafe of red by the time Abby had finished, no flush had invaded her pale cheeks.

'Did you sleep with Rannaldini?' she asked idly.

'Certainly not,' said Abby pompously. 'He came between me and my art.'

Flora kneaded her bread into a pellet and lobbed it at the restaurant cat.

'When I knew him he came between my legs. Whoops, sorry.' Then, at Abby's look of incredulity, continued: 'I had an *affaire* with him when I was still at school.'

'You gotta be joking. What happened?'

'He dumped me, left me behind like an indifferent paperback in the folds of a hotel bed.' Flora waved to the waiter to bring another carafe.

'How long did it last?'

'It's a long, long time from May to September,' sighed Flora. 'Rannaldini's so promiscuous, that being hopelessly, hopelessly hooked on him has all the exclusivity of a widow in the First World War, but it doesn't seem to hurt any less; no safety in numbers.' Her voice was getting faster and faster. 'It's like being alive in your coffin, but no-one hears you scrabbling to get out. I know he's a shit, but not an hour passes when I don't want him.'

She dropped her head like a broken daffodil, then the next moment had stubbed out her cigarette on Marcus's untouched ratatouille.

'Oh Christ, Markie, I'm sorry.' Her head fell sideways onto his shoulder. As he put up a freckled right hand to stroke her cheek, she clutched it.

'Heard the latest viola joke?' said Marcus to cheer her up.

'What?'

'What d'you do with a dead viola player?'

'What?'

'Move him up a desk.'

Flora's mouth lifted slightly.

Marcus had eaten, drunk and talked much less than the others. Occasionally his eyes met Abby's and a shy, helpless smile drifted across his face. He was beautifully dressed in chinos, a dark brown cashmere sweater and a Prussian-blue shirt, which went perfectly with his dark red hair. When he removed his sweater Abby noticed he had a pianist's physique: breadth of shoulder, arms grooved with muscle, and big hands that could stretch a tenth with ease. A gold signet ring bearing the Campbell-Black crest flashed on his left hand, as he practised on the table snatches of Chopin's *Grande Polonaise* which he had to play in a college recital next week.

He's very appealing, thought Abby, through a haze of wine. Perhaps I need a toyboy, particularly one who could simplify difficult repertoire by transcribing it for the piano. He also picked up the check.

'I'll pay you next week, it's the end of the month,' Flora called out as Marcus went over to the till. 'I think I bought the whole of Jigsaw and HMV yesterday morning. Leave it,' she said as Abby got out her purse, 'Marcus gets a massive allowance from Rupert.'

'How did you two meet?'

'As I said we were at school together. I'd been drinking at lunchtime, *comme toujours*. I felt sick during a concert and threw up into Marcus's trumpet. I think that was the moment Rannaldini fell, albeit temporarily, in love with me.'

Out of the window, a horse-chestnut tree, tawny against the palest blue sky, reminded Flora of the same great bell-like trees in Rannaldini's park.

'How was he really?' she asked as she emptied Marcus's untouched second glass of wine into her own.

'Being upstaged by Marcus's father. Rupert had flown out to sign me up for Declan O'Hara's programme.'

Again Abby couldn't resist boasting. 'Rupert came on really strong; if I hadn't been crazy about Christopher, we'd certainly have ended up in bed.'

'I wouldn't tell Marcus that,' interrupted Flora sharply. 'He's bats about his stepmother.'

Abby jumped slightly as Marcus chucked three gold pound coins onto the red-and-white checked table-cloth. As he put a fiver alongside the pile of notes in his wallet, Abby saw a photograph of a very beautiful redhead.

'Is that your partner?' she asked archly. 'D'you go for redheads?'

'No, it's my mother,' said Marcus.

As it was four o'clock there was no point in going back to the Academy so, after Flora had rushed back to fetch her viola, which she'd left under the table, they tottered down the road to Madame Tussauds because Abby had never seen her own waxwork.

'I went to see it as a pilgrimage my first day at college,' confided Flora.

On the top floor, they discovered Rupert's waxwork in red coat, breeches and brown topped boots, gazing moodily into space among the great sporting heroes.

'Hi, Dad,' said Marcus.

Ironically Rupert was next to Jake Lovell who was looking equally unfriendly.

'Isn't that the guy?' asked Abby perplexed.

'Who ran off with Marcus's mother,' said Flora, 'who we don't talk about in Rupert's presence. I'm amazed they don't come alive at night and throttle each other. Hi, Mum.'

There was Georgie Maguire with her long russet hair and sensual smiling face, clutching a microphone among the pop stars. Drifting into Classical Music, they ran slap into Hermione, mouth wide open in song.

'Queen of the nightmare,' stormed Flora, 'ought to be in the chamberpot of horrors.'

Abby liked Flora more and more, particularly when

she removed her chewing-gum and stuck it on Hermione's nose and topped her dark curls with Marcus's baseball cap.

'Flor-ah,' hissed Marcus, retrieving his baseball cap and looking nervously at an ancient dozing assistant.

'Hope to God she doesn't come to life like Hermione's statue in *The Winter's Tale*.' Getting out a Pentel, Flora drew a big black moustache on Hermione's upper lip.

Abby was clutching her sides and Flora was lighting an illicit cigarette. Then the temperature plummeted as though they had just stepped out of a plane in the Arctic Circle, and they found themselves confronting a fearsome, lifelike Rannaldini, brandishing his baton like a dirk. Everything was in place, the gardenia, the trained grey hair, the three inches of dazzling white cuff.

'Waving his wand like the wicked fairy,' said Flora stonily, 'Good afternoon, Maestro.' Drawing heavily on her cigarette, she shoved it between Rannaldini's fingers.

'If I was wearing a pin, we could stick it into him,' said Abby.

By now their giggling had roused the attendant. Marcus hastily distracted him by asking where they could find Abigail Rosen's waxwork. He's got a beautiful voice, thought Abby, a bit like Prince Charles's but with a slight break in it.

The attendant hadn't recognized Abby and, after much head-scratching and consulting of lists, announced that her waxwork had been melted down because she wasn't considered famous enough any more.

'I flew too near the sun,' said Abby tonelessly.

Once they got outside, she crumpled against Marcus.

'I guess I'm an applause-junkie worse than Hermione,' she sobbed into his shoulder. 'I grumbled about the pressures at the time, OK? I complained endlessly about media intrusion, but I just can't get used to not being famous any more, no fan mail, never being in the paper, not even the classical music press, and now this.'

The rush-hour traffic, crawling towards the Westway where a huge setting sun blazed like a stop sign, looked on fascinated. A trio of workmen crammed into the front of a blue van, seeing Abby so tall, slim and wide-shouldered in Marcus's arms, lent out and shouted: 'Fucking poofters.'

'Fucking homophobes,' shouted back Flora, making a V-sign.

'It's only because your agents have deliberately kept you out of the public eye,' she comforted Abby. 'Look how deliriously excited everyone was today. Once the Press twig you're the new Karajan, they'll never leave you alone.'

'And that's as bad a nightmare,' wailed Abby. 'And I miss my Strad. It's now being played by a bitch called Maria Kusak. I know she won't look after it.'

'I expect she'll leave it in restaurants like I do,' said Flora, as they rustled through plane leaves unhinged by the day's great heat. 'Now we could go to the Planetarium which would put everything in perspective and make us realize how infinitely trivial our lives are, but unfortunately it's just shut, so we're going to take you to meet a very glamorous Russian conductor.'

'All Russian conductors are drunk and incompetent,' said Abby ungratefully.

'Boris is often very drunk but he's a good conductor,' said Marcus.

'And a lot of people unaccountably think he's a terrific composer,' added Flora, reflecting that it couldn't have been good for Abby's ego, that all the people pouring out of offices stared at Marcus rather than at her.

But Abby had stopped in her tracks.

'Are you talking about Boris Levitsky who married Rachel Grant?'

Flora nodded.

'That's weird.' Abby was really agitated. 'I read a piece about Rachel's suicide. It really influenced me, right, that she could drive off a cliff, because she'd caught Boris cheating on her. After I cut my wrist,' Abby's voice broke, 'I wanted to write to Boris and tell him I was sure Rachel didn't mean to kill herself. It was just a crazy gesture to wipe out the hurt, with an even greater hurt, anything to make the pain go away.'

'Tell Boris that, I'm sure it would comfort him,' said Marcus.

'Boris was very well known in Russia when I was at the Moscow Conservatoire,' sniffed Abby later, as Marcus edged the Aston Martin through the traffic. 'We all went to his concerts. It was a great scandal when he fell in love with Rachel and defected to the West. She was a marvellous player.'

'I wasn't a fan of hers,' said Flora with rare coldness. 'She was an awful bitch. You couldn't blame Boris for straying. He used to be one of Rannaldini's assistant conductors, and Rachel so detested the influence Rannaldini had on him that she had an *affaire* with Rannaldini out of spite. Took him off me to be exact, that's probably why I hate her.'

'But I thought Boris and Rachel were reconciled,' protested Abby.

'They were,' said Flora, 'but Rannaldini and Boris were after the same job, running the New World Symphony Orchestra in New York. Boris looked as though he was going to get it. He was young, brilliant and back with Rachel. *The Scorpion* caught him coming out of Chloe's, his ex-mistress's, flat. I'm sure Rannaldini tipped them off. Typical shitty thing he would do. Rachel saw the photograph in *The Scorpion* and drove off the road. Hey presto. Rannaldini, crying crocodile tears over the death of the finest pianist of her generation, lands the New York job. Can we get some drink from that off-licence, Marcus?'

'We can't stop here.'

'We'll have to stop somewhere. Boris'll have drunk any drink he's got. Boris was shattered by Rachel's death,' Flora turned back to Abby. 'Particularly because she left him two young children to bring up. Not a great aid to composition. Despite such set-backs, Boris has had loads of women since Rachel died, men get over these things much more quickly than women, because they're in a buyer's market, but he still misses Rachel and feels dreadfully guilty about her. People are always giving him money to write things, then he doesn't deliver. The Rutminster Symphony Orchestra commissioned a requiem to Rachel more than two years ago. An old duck called Sir Rodney Mackintosh—'

'I'm his protégée,' said Abby sniffily, 'I've only been stopping at his house for the past two and a half years.'

I can't be expected to know her entire c.v., thought Flora irritated.

'Rodney's so darling,' added Abby possessively.

'Darling,' agreed Flora. 'So you probably know Rodney felt sorry for Boris, but again Boris has failed to deliver. Everytime he picks up his chewed pencil he thinks about Rachel, starts crying and has to have another huge glass of red wine, and the RSO have to keep rescheduling.'

'Boris was a great conductor,' mused Abby.

'But not especially focused. He's going out with some big boobed Bratislavian bassoonist tonight. So Marcus and I said we'd babysit.'

ELEVEN

'Don't mention Rannaldini,' muttered Flora as, clinking bottles in time to the clanking of the ancient lift, they slowly climbed to the sixth floor, 'or Boris will foam at the mouth.'

Boris was already foaming at the mouth. Hardly concealing his manhood with a Ninja Turtle face towel, he was waving a toothbrush instead of a baton. Having opened the front door, he dived into a nearby bathroom to spit out the toothpaste. He had just had a bath and was trying to dry a pair of boxer shorts with a hair-dryer.

Despite a sallow skin, deep-set eyes almost entirely concealed by puffiness, dark hair like an unclipped poodle and a chunky, rugger player's body, there was an undeniable Byronic smoulder about Boris.

Abby took one look at him, realized she was half an inch taller, kicked off her shoes and bolted to the loo to repair her smudged eyeliner and even put on some lipgloss.

Boris took one look at Abby and decided to give the Bratislavian bassoonist a miss. He and Abby were soon gabbling in Russian about their Moscow days.

'What have you got for us to drink?' asked Flora.

'I cannot drink, I am on vagon.' Then Boris saw the bottles Flora was taking out of an Oddbins carrier bag, 'Oh vell, perhaps I am not.'

Abby was even unfazed by the messiest living-room ever. It was very Russian with crimson and scarlet furniture and gold icons on the midnight-blue walls, but every chair was piled high with clothes. The grand piano buckled under scores, covered in drink rings, and upended silver photograph frames. The dark red velvet cloth on the big table could hardly be seen for hamburger boxes and bottles wafting stale remnants of drink. On the bookshelves were half-eaten apples, overflowing ashtrays, tapes and CDs out of their cases.

While the entire family obviously chucked their shoes and boots in one corner, the rest of the floor was littered with orange peel, pencil sharpenings, tissues and crumpled-up pieces of manuscript paper.

'Oh Boris, you are a slut,' sighed Flora. 'Where are the children – hidden under the rubble?'

'I forget to tell – the kids, they stay with friends.'

'Good thing, they'll get bubonic plague if they stay here.'

Flora removed a curling ham sandwich from the mantelpiece.

'When did you last eat?'

'I verk since midnight last night,' said Boris proudly. 'Nearly twenty hours.'

While Flora chided, Marcus, who was more practical, had found a black dustbin bag in the kitchen and now settled down to clear up the mess.

'Where's the stuff you've just written?'

'I put it in the samovar for safety,' said Boris.

'Is it numbered?' asked Marcus, retrieving it.

'Not that it matters,' Flora, who was opening bottles, murmured to Abby. 'Play it back to front, upside-down, it wouldn't make any difference.' She blew a kiss at Boris.

'Let me see,' said Abby reverently.

Marcus held out a manuscript page covered in a mass of black corrections.

'Looks as though a lot of centipedes have been doing the Highland Fling after a mud bath,' said Flora. 'Why can't you use a rubber instead of crossing out?'

'Because eef my first thought was best, eef I rub it out, it is gone.'

'How can anyone copy that?' grumbled Flora.

'I can,' said Marcus, removing the pages to the safety of his music case.

'Vot does eet sound like?'

'I'll try and play it later when I've tidied up this dump.'

'What a wonderful wife you'll make someone.' Flora lobbed some orange peel at Marcus's black bag and missed. 'If you want to make yourself useful,' she said to Abby, 'go and wash up four glasses. Abby had a dazzling début as a conductor,' she was telling Boris as Abby returned with an assortment of mugs, cups and even a small vase.

'Ear is the only theeng that matter,' said Boris, filling them all up to the top. 'Ear and rhythm, telling the orchestra how and ven to play. A conductor must learn what is possible to ask, then ask the orchestra ten times more. He must also come into a room at any time and command attention.'

'"*You have that in your countenance which I would fain call master,*" or rather maestro,' quoted Flora, settling down to sort out the mountain of newspapers thrown down by the fireplace.

'What piece did you do?' asked Boris.

'Bartók's *Viola Concerto*.'

'Ah,' Boris gave a theatrical sigh and drained his glass. 'Bartók is like me. His last Christmas he could never leave hees flat because he was so ashamed he had no money to tip lift man.'

'Bartók had security till he was eight, then his father

died like mine did,' said Abby, taking a huge gulp of red wine.

'He was Aries like me,' said Flora.

'Like mine, his genius was never recognized.' Boris was near to tears. 'He die in poorness like I shall.'

'If you gave up drink and worked a bit harder, you'd be very rich,' said Flora, tipping a pile of *Guardian*s into Marcus's dustbin bag. 'Oh look, here's your hairbrush, that must have been missing for months.'

Removing it from the pile, Flora sat down on the arm of Boris's chair and started to brush his wild curls.

'My music reflects the chaos of our times.'

'I don't know why you don't save time and programme this flat instead.'

Ignoring her, Boris topped up Abby's glass. 'I am sorry about your wrist. I have all your records. Vil you play again?'

'My physio thinks so, but I still can't grip the neck of a violin and my fingers can't get around the strings.'

'Eet is same, I 'ave music bursting to get out of my head, but I cannot write.'

'It's not the same at all,' reproved Flora. 'You can still move a pencil. Don't be a drama queen.'

'Ouch,' said Boris, as she tugged at a tangle at the back. 'What's got into you?'

'I am sick of an old passion. Christ, you've got chewing-gum here.'

'I wanted to tell you, Boris.' Lowering her voice Abby broke into Russian again, obviously talking about Rachel because soon they were both crying and wiping each other's eyes and pouring out more glasses of red.

'Summit meeting between the super powers,' said Flora drily, as Marcus returned with a second dustbin bag.

Beautiful red-and-blue patterned rugs were beginning to emerge on the floor and a gold-and-blue embroidered shawl on the piano where Marcus was righting the silver-framed photographs of the old days in Moscow: children on toboggans, grannies with swept-up hair, the young Boris with Prokofiev and Shostakovich.

'That vas my Rachel,' Boris pointed to a photograph of a beautiful but disapproving-looking woman. 'She vas a saint.'

'She was a crosspatch,' said Flora, getting a black velvet toggle out of her trouser pocket to tie back Boris's curls. Finally she brushed his wild eyebrows.

'There, Mel Gibson.' She kissed the tip of his nose.

'How many voices are you scoring the *Requiem* for?' asked Abby.

'None,' said Boris flatly. 'The instruments play the voices. The RSO chorus is full of squawking amateurs and Hermione Harefield wanted to sing soprano part. So I stop them all. I 'ate singers.'

Returning to the pile through which she was making slow progress because she kept stopping to read things, Flora was now brandishing an unstamped postcard with a charging bison on the back.

'Why are you writing to Edith Spink?'

'She send tape of concert of my *Berlin Vall Symphony* she did in Vest Country. It sound so 'orrible, I write telling her never to play my vork again. I vondered vot happen to that postcard, geeve it to me.'

'Don't be silly,' Flora tore up the postcard and chucked it into Marcus's black bag. 'Edith's a good egg. When Rannaldini blocked my scholarship to the Academy, she put in a good word. You're stupid to upset her, Boris, she's on your side.'

'Not ven she play my music like that. I shall have to go back to teaching.'

'You can't, you hated teaching,' said Flora sensibly. 'All those staff meetings about handles on lavatory doors, all the fuss when you wanted time off to go to performances, let alone rehearsals. And you can't compose if you have to write lectures. You've got to finish *Rachel's Requiem.*'

'I never meet a deadline or an honest woman,' said Boris sulkily.

'That's bloody rude when I've given you the benefit of my advice. Christ,' Flora pulled out a sheaf of brown envelopes, 'don't you ever pay bills?'

'Not if I can't pay them. I cannot buy my kids clothing, I cannot redecorate my flat. Look at the damp.' Boris pointed to a dark stain above the window.

'You'll be able to paper it with brown envelopes,' said Flora, 'Here's one from the Danish National Ballet – surely you don't owe them any money?'

Opening the envelope Flora triumphantly shook out a cheque for thirty thousand kroners which Boris held up to the light in ecstasy.

'It's for ballet they want me to write about Little Mermaid.'

'That's terrific,' said Abby excitedly. 'You'll get repeats everytime anyone wants to do it and they can sell videos and tapes in the foyer.'

Boris, whose melancholy alternated with raging high spirits, became quite expansive at the prospect of relative riches. Normally he, Flora and Marcus would have played chamber music into the small hours but desisted in deference to Abby.

'What are your plans?' he asked her.

'Take the course at the Academy. I've familiarized myself with loads of scores in Lucerne, now I need practise. I'll take any gig offered.'

Having tidied up as much of the sitting-room as possible, Marcus was wheezing so badly from the dust that he had to retreat to the kitchen, resort to a couple of puffs from his inhaler, and sit down for ten minutes, hunched over the kitchen table to recover his breath. Then he started on supper. There was only a certain amount of his day that he could cope with other people. He needed to be alone now to think about next week's concert.

Finding a lot of eggs of dubious antiquity, some rock-hard Gruyère and some big tomatoes, he decided to make cheese omelettes and tomato salad. There was no vinegar so he used the juice of a wrinkled lime and brought a loaf out of retirement by turning it into garlic bread.

Rubbing the Gruyère up and down the grater until the curls of cheese had over-flowed the bowl, he studied the Chopin, humming and making notes.

'Need a top-up?' It was Abby with a bottle.

Marcus shook his head.

She looked much better than she had earlier. There was a sparkle in her eyes and colour in her cheeks.

'My, that's good,' Abby pinched a bit of tomato out of the salad bowl. 'Who taught you to cook?'

'My stepmother.'

'The divine Taggie,' teased Abby. 'Hermione Harefield said she wasn't a woman of substance.'

'She's the most s-s-ubstantial person I know,' stammered Marcus furiously. 'She's b-b-eautiful and k-kind and she's the only woman who's ever made my father happy. That bitch Hermione's just jealous.'

'I told you to keep your trap shut, Abby,' said Flora, appearing in the doorway.

After supper, leaving the others to drink and gossip, Marcus settled down to play the piano. Boris's flat was on the second floor of a four-sided block which looked out on to a square of garden dominated by a huge golden catalpa.

It was so mild that people in the surrounding flats opened their windows, wrapping their children in duvets, so they could all listen to Marcus until the stars came out, clapping and cheering whenever he stopped and shouting for him to go on.

'Audience don't do zat for me,' grumbled Boris. 'But he is good boy,' he confided to Abby, 'I teach him piano at school. Ven Rachel die he turn up at the house asking what he could do, looking after kids, helping me sort things out. He is gentle, but he is not at all vimp and he play like dream.'

Abby, a bit drunk now, was equally enchanted but also tearful. She must not neglect her physio.

Having dispatched the *Grande Polonnaise* with a great flourish, Marcus got out more music and launched into a modern piece, explosions of crashing notes, interspersed with a sad, haunting tune.

'That's beautiful,' called out Abby. 'What is it?'

'Ees familiar.' Boris looked perplexed.

'Bloody well should be,' said Marcus. 'It's part of the "Dies Irae" from *Rachel's Requiem*. I finished transcribing it last night.'

'I wrote that?' Boris leapt to his feet. 'Play it again. Where's my violin?'

'Under the sofa,' said Flora.

Impatiently Boris tuned up and began to play the main tune with Marcus accompanying. Marcus's copying was dark and clear which made it very easy to read.

Having Jewish blood like Abby, Boris tended to soup up the melody, playing very emotionally with great rhetorical gestures.

'This is very grateful piece,' he told Abby and Flora in delight.

'You mean rewarding,' corrected Flora. 'Yes, it's breathtaking. Like Bartók, *"full of hitherto undreamed of possibilities"*.'

Occasionally stopping to change a note, totally absorbed, they played on.

'Marcus is seriously good,' Abby told Flora. 'Nothing can stop him making it.'

'Let's make some coffee,' Flora led Abby into the kitchen.

'Marcus is happy and relaxed at the moment,' she went on, 'because he's among friends and he's had the odd drink but he's crippled by nerves, throwing up for hours before concerts, and he's already had to cancel two recitals because of asthma attacks, which doesn't help in the music world, which hates unreliability.

'Shall we wash up?' Flora looked unenthusiastically at the supper plates.

But, as the dishwasher was still working overtime, gurgling away cleaning all the silver and china they'd unearthed from the sitting-room, she decided to leave it.

'Nothing ever gets clean that I wash by hand.'

After some rootling around she found a tin of Gold Blend in the breadbin and, unable to find a spoon, shook some coffee into four cups.

'Also,' she added, switching on the kettle, 'Marcus has a terrible hang-up about Rupert, who doesn't see the point of him at all.'

'But Rupert seemed so caring in BA,' said Abby perplexed. 'And when he visited me in the hospital.'

'Rupert's dazzling,' agreed Flora, 'but the brighter the moon, the darker the shadow it casts and it's no fun being son of Superstud. Rupert's always preferred Tabitha, Marcus's younger sister, and he passionately disapproves of his son and heir taking up anything as drippy as the piano, when he should be at home learning how to run the estate.'

'How did it turn out with those kids Rupert adopted?'

'That's the worst part,' sighed Flora. 'I'm afraid there's no milk. Rupert's totally besotted with the boy, Xavier, cured his squint and nearly his birthmark, got him racing round on Lysander's old Shetland pony. Rupert's got the tearaway he's always wanted,' Flora lowered her voice. 'It's crucified Marcus.'

Returning to the living-room, Abby heard a voluptuous explosion of notes, and gave a cry of joy. Marcus was playing Beethoven's *Appassionata Sonata.*

'It's so darling, to play that – well – sort of in my honour.' She went over to the piano.

'Sort of,' Marcus blushed, being a truthful boy. 'Next week I'm also playing it in a recital at college.'

'I'll come along,' said Abby in excitement, making Marcus blush even more darkly. 'Did you know that to understand the *Appassionata*, Beethoven said you have to read *The Tempest*?

> *This music crept by me upon the waters,*
> *Allaying both their fury, and my passion,*
> *With its sweet air.'*

Marcus nodded. 'My stepfather told me, and quoted the same lines. Sorry,' as a flurry of wrong notes resulted, 'I'm no good at talking and playing.'

Abby retreated to the sofa.

'God, my back aches,' said Flora, who was plaiting Boris's hair. 'Three hours of Bartók takes it out of you.'

'I've got some Ibuleve in the bathroom,' said Boris.

A smell of bonfires was still drifting in through the open window. Glancing at his watch Marcus saw it was nearly eleven o'clock. They were still clamouring for more in the flats outside. He'd better stop soon or the kids would never get to bed. He launched into Roger Quilter's *Children's Overture*.

'*There was a lady loved a swine*,' sang Flora, as she returned with the Ibuleve.

That's a stunning voice, too, thought Abby in envy. Goodness they were a talented trio!

Flora slumped between Boris's knees, calmly pulling off her daisy-embroidered T-shirt and using it to cover high, pointed breasts, as Boris began to rub the gel into her shoulders.

And I wonder what *their* relationship is, thought Abby.

Glancing across the room as he launched into 'Baa Baa, Black Sheep' Marcus met Abby's eyes, saw the admiration in them and thought how lovely she looked, her strong, proud face softened by the lamplight. She was much more boyish than he'd expected. Sitting on the sofa, her long legs tucked underneath her, she looked like a model for *Gentleman's Quarterly*.

Marcus's timidity with women had been exacerbated two years ago at the stag-party of Basil Baddington, one of his father's wilder cronies. Rupert, irked by Marcus's apparent lack of interest in girls (after all, he was supposed to produce an heir one day), had organized a hooker.

Marcus had been quite unable to get it up and had been violently sick. Terror, which makes people take deeper breaths, triggered off a violent asthma attack, which could have been fatal. The whole thing was hushed up by Rupert's GP, the admirably unflappable James Benson, who got Marcus onto a nebulizer at the local hospital just in time.

Before he'd lost consciousness, miserably aware of regurgitated wine all down his dress-shirt, Marcus had heard James Benson reproving his father.

'You must be more careful with him, Rupert, you know he's never been strong.'

By mutual agreement neither Taggie nor Marcus's mother had been told of this disaster, but Marcus's relationship with Rupert, always shaky, had inevitably deteriorated.

Reluctant to witness the love he had always craved, so unstintingly lavished on little Xavier, Marcus had avoided Pensombe and concentrated on his career. Girls, except Flora who was more of a pal, were avoided even though they chased him like mad, not least because of his father's bank balance.

Last night after copying out Boris's score until long after midnight, Marcus had collapsed into bed, only to be jolted by a terrifyingly erotic dream about Boris, and woken, sobbing his heart out because it could never be possible.

Having dreaded confronting Boris today, he was ecstatic to find himself suddenly so attracted to Abby. His blue shirt was still stiff from the salt of the tears she'd shed outside Madame Tussauds. All this added radiance to his playing.

'Who did Marcus's mother marry?' asked Abby, thinking of the stepfather who had quoted *The Tempest*.

'Malise Gordon, thirty years older,' replied Flora, writhing half in ecstasy, half in pain under Boris's fingers. 'He's been a brilliant stepfather and really encouraged Marcus, but that doesn't make up for one's own father not giving a toss.'

Flora suddenly shivered. They had been so wrapped up in talking they hadn't realized how cold it had become. As she banged down the big sash window the telephone rang. It was Helen, Marcus's mother, in hysterics. It was a few moments before Boris could get any sense out of her. Malise had had a massive stroke and been rushed to hospital. Marcus must go home at once.

TWELVE

Marcus drove straight home to Warwickshire. He was bitterly ashamed afterwards that his main emotion was despair that he would probably have to duck out of a recital yet again, and disappointment that he would no longer be faced with the terrifying yet magical prospect of Abby in the audience. He wasn't even very worried about Malise who, never having let him down, seemed unlikely to start now.

In fact Malise never regained consciousness. Marcus was devastated. He had loved his stepfather deeply. Kind, formal, old enough to be his grandfather, Malise had always encouraged him. They had played endless duets together; Malise had explained harmony, taken Marcus to concerts and shared with him his 78s of Myra Hess and Denis Matthews and Solomon. He had also provided him with a role model of total integrity and honour.

But Marcus had to surpress his anguish in order to comfort his mother who, having been adored and wrapped in cotton wool by Malise for sixteen years, was quite incapable of coping with funerals, let alone life, on her own.

The Press, of course, had a field-day dredging up the

old story of how Malise as *chef d'équipe* had held the British Show-Jumping Team together during their golden era, and how during the LA Olympics, when Rupert Campbell-Black's great rival, Jake Lovell, had run off with Rupert's wife, Helen, the team had gone on with one man short to win the gold. There was also a lot of guff about how Malise had picked up the pieces, marrying Helen and restoring her self-confidence, which had been shattered by eight years of hell married to Rupert, and a disastrous few weeks with a miserably dispossessed Jake, who couldn't wait to belt back to his wife.

The funeral was rather like a rerun of Madame Tussauds with all the show-jumping greats rolling up to pay their last respects and Rupert and Jake glaring into space.

As a further insult, Jake had brought along his son Isaac, a brilliant young jockey, who had beaten one of Rupert's horses earlier that week. The only thing that could have redressed the balance for Rupert would have been if Marcus could have played Malise's favourite Bach *Prelude* quite beautifully on the Steinway that Helen had insisted on hiring for the service.

But Marcus's asthma always grew worse under stress and, in the panic of overseeing all the last-minute arrangements, he forgot to bring his inhaler. He just managed to help carry the coffin the three hundred yards across the village green to the church before collapsing fighting for breath beside his mother.

Helen was still young enough at forty-four to be described as 'absolutely stunning' rather than 'having been absolutely stunning'. She was far too unnerved at seeing Jake again after all those years, and wondering guiltily if she were wearing too much blusher and eye-shadow on the grounds that Malise would have wanted her to look beautiful, to notice Marcus's plight.

Unfortunately a church filled with flowers and the

fumes from the ancient pew, which had recently been treated for woodworm, made the band round Marcus's chest even tighter.

Rupert's best friend, Billy Lloyd-Foxe, had reduced everyone to tears, including himself, reading the 'Dedication to the Horse', which always brought the house down at the end of the Horse of the Year Show. According to the service sheet Marcus should have been next but, white and sweating, he could only clutch his chest and shake his head, so, after a long agonizingly embarrassed pause, the parson, who had been a family friend for years, twigged what was up and carried on with the service.

Marcus was only aware of the reproach in his mother's eyes.

'I didn't break down, I didn't fail, Malise,' she seemed to be saying and such a public failure would only confirm Rupert's conviction that his son totally lacked big-match temperament.

Marcus had also been incapable of carrying the coffin to the graveside. Staggering back to the beautiful Queen Anne rectory in which Malise had lived all his life, revived by several squirts from his inhaler, he had been able to hand round drinks and sandwiches. There had been a horrible fascination in being introduced by Helen to Jake Lovell. He was amazed his mother could have left his gilded glamorous father for anyone so small and insignificant.

And then Rupert had walked into the room, caught the three of them talking and stalked right out of the house dragging a protesting Taggie and Tabitha with him.

Returning to the kitchen for more sandwiches Marcus had found Malise's big-boned tactless daughter, who'd been brought up in the Old Rectory and whose eyes were now running over the furniture like beetles, wondering what she could claw back.

'The boy's not going to be much support to Helen,' she was saying to Mrs Edwards, Helen's daily. 'Sickly looking fellow. Daddy did so much for him.'

And Marcus had wanted to shout: 'I loved him, too.'

But the funeral was only the beginning of the nightmare. Malise had left his desk and everything else in order. To quote his favourite writer Montaigne, he had been *'booted and spurred and ready to depart'*. He had also hidden his worries from Helen so well that she'd had no idea how badly he'd been hit by Lloyd's. He had made the Old Rectory and its twenty acres over to Helen, but not lived the necessary seven years to avoid estate duties. What little money was left would be eaten up paying the Lloyd's losses.

Helen was so distraught Marcus felt he had to give up his London digs and stay with her at least for the autumn term. Helen managed to justify this sacrifice as not being too great. It would be so much better for Marcus's asthma living in the country and commuting to London for his weekly lessons, and at least it would get him away from that trampy Flora.

Helen was too self-centred to realize how upset Marcus was by Malise's death. She had always lacked the gift of intimacy and been admired rather than liked. Now, for the first time in her life, she felt popular and absolutely amazed by everyone's kindness: the wonderful letters, the solicitous telephone calls, the invitations to stay, the quiches and apple-turnovers left in the porch: *Dear Helen you must eat!*

But once this stream of sympathy dried up and she no longer had the funeral to plan, Helen sunk into apathy. Terrified of becoming addicted she refused to take tranquillizers or sleeping-pills, or even a stiff drink to get her through the increasingly dark winter evenings.

She had never got on with her daughter Tabitha, who was still at boarding-school, who spent all her time at Penscombe with Rupert and Taggie; Marcus and his career therefore became all she had to live for. Marcus felt the millstone of her dark cloying love weighing him down and once again was ashamed of longing so much for all the fun of his London life with Flora, Boris and now Abby. The piano seemed to be his only refuge.

Meanwhile, over in New York, Rannaldini had not been enjoying the domination over the New World Symphony Orchestra he had hoped for, possibly because his musicians were in revolt that he earned a hundred times more in a night than they did in a week. He was still having gruelling battles with the unions and endless lawsuits had been brought by unfairly sacked musicians. There was also the unread pile of unsolicited manuscripts and far too much contemporary music to programme and no Boris to weed out and translate it for him any more.

Two and a half years on, Rannaldini was also still brooding on how he could get his revenge on Rupert, for orchestrating the break-up of his marriage to Kitty and hijacking his plane in BA.

'The elm is a patient tree,' murmured Rannaldini, 'it hateth and waiteth.'

A few days after Malise's death Rannaldini was lunching on oysters and seafood salad in his penthouse flat which was papered with platinum discs and photographs of himself with the famous and which overlooked the tawny autumnal beauty of Central Park.

Picking up *The Times* which was flown out to him every day from London, Rannaldini observed that another wife was standing by her cabinet minister husband. The photograph had been cropped at waist level, but Rannaldini felt sure the wife had a stiletto heel in her husband's Gucci toe-cap and a knee in his groin despite the linked arms and the frenetically smiling faces. Kitty had not stood by him – the bitch.

Turning the pages, easing a piece of squid out of his back teeth, Rannaldini discovered Malise's obituary, a glow job describing his brilliant war, his knowledge of paintings, his work on the flute and his skill as a *chef d'équipe* where he was the only person who could harness the genius of Rupert Campbell-Black.

He is survived by a second wife and one daughter from his first marriage, read Rannaldini, pouring himself another glass of Pouilly-Fumé.

He could remember the exquisite Helen at a school concert, definitely one of Rupert's finest thorough-breds, an earnest intellectual snob, thirty years younger than her upright second husband and in need of a little excitement.

Smiling, Rannaldini took out a piece of dove-grey writing-paper, and picked up his jade-green fountain-pen. He wrote in green ink:

> *My dear Helen, (may I?)*
>
> *Please forgive my presumption but going through some old newspapers which I hadn't had time to read, I found The Times obituary of your husband.*
>
> *What an extraordinary fine-looking, multi-talented man. I had no idea that the M. M. Gordon, who wrote, to my mind, the definitive work on the flute, was married to you. I would so like to have met him.*
>
> *You won't remember but we met briefly when your son accompanied my daughter Natasha when she sang 'Hark, Hark the Lark' at a Bagley Hall concert a few years ago. He showed immense promise. I hope he has taken up the piano as a career.*
>
> *You must be utterly desolate but please comfort yourself. As Voltaire wrote—*

Rannaldini sighed with pleasure. Helen would love Voltaire, but he decided to translate the poem, Americans weren't too hot on French.

> *There are two deaths,*
> *And one is such that all men dread and all abhor.*

The one is to be loved no more,
The other's nothing much.

This is in no way to dismiss the depths of your suffering but at least you are safe in the knowledge you were never betrayed. My young wife left me for a boy her own age two and a half years ago. I cannot say I envy you, but at least Malise's love for you and yours for him is intact and untarnished.

Does Malise have any unpublished work? I would be so interested to read it and assist its publication.

Perhaps when your heart is a little easier you would have lunch with me. I have a jet or a helicopter that could collect you, perhaps when I am next in London, and we could share our sadness.

Yours ever,
Rannaldini.

'Hark, Hark the Lark,' sang Rannaldini as smirking, he sealed the envelope and set the letter aside to be posted in a few weeks' time when the trickle of consoling letters would have dried up and his would have far more impact.

Helen *was* utterly charmed. Rannaldini's letter arrived at the beginning of November at the nadir of her despair. It looked as though she was definitely going to have to sell the Old Rectory and Malise's daughter, whom she had never liked, although she'd taken on Malise's two black labradors which Helen had also never liked, was contesting the will and had laid claim to Malise's prettier pieces because they were family heirlooms.

Of course Helen remembered Rannaldini from the school concert, arriving late and plonking himself next to Hermione Harefield so Helen had been forced to move back a row and sit next to Rupert, who had behaved abominably as usual, whispering to Taggie and even nodding off and snoring in counterpoint to the Mozart concerto Marcus had been playing so beautifully.

Helen was utterly heartbroken over Malise's death but Rannaldini's letter comforted her. She wrote back a charming note, littered with quotations, saying lunch would be delightful. After all, she told herself firmly, Rannaldini might well be able to give Marcus a leg-up in his career.

Marcus, meanwhile, with conspicuous gallantry, had tackled his father about giving Helen an allowance. Rupert had replied that he'd think about it but had gazed out of the window at the reddy-gold leaves cascading down from his towering beeches as fast as his money seemed to be pouring into Lloyd's. Thank God, he hadn't been too badly hit and had never risked the house or any of the land, but he didn't see why the hell he should support Helen. It was sixteen years since she'd buggered off and he'd paid every penny to support Marcus and Tabitha and was still giving them both whacking great allowances.

When he'd first met Helen she had been working for a publisher and always pointing out his literary deficiencies. She could bloody well get a job now.

Privately Rupert was absolutely livid with Helen for asking Jake Lovell back to the house after the funeral. Jake was doing too bloody well as a trainer and Rupert was consumed by all the ancient jealousy that Malise had loved Jake more than him.

To top it, Taggie had enraged Rupert by asking Helen to stay for Christmas, claiming that she and Marcus couldn't be all alone the first year after Malise's death.

'I suppose you're going to serve lame duck at Christmas dinner?' he said nastily.

And Taggie, remembering Sister Angelica's warning about too many limping ducks, felt a cold chill.

THIRTEEN

Rannaldini planned his first telephone call to catch Helen at a particularily low ebb. She had just returned from Evensong at which Malise should have been reading the lesson. The church had always been full of admiring ladies on such occasions. Tonight they had turned up to see how his widow was coping. Not very well it seemed. Afterwards, as Helen emerged into the drizzle of a chill November evening, feeling them all shying away, she had scuttled off, black-scarfed head bowed, slipping on the yellow leaves concealing the slimy paving stones. She was too distraught to pause and to speak a word of comfort to Malise in his cold bed. Tomorrow she would bring him the pinched remnants of the rose garden.

As Marcus had gone to hear Murray Perahia playing at the Wigmore Hall, Helen had a long night ahead, terrified of sleeping alone since the black labradors had departed, even more terrified of waking to the horrors of life without Malise and a new one hundred thousand pound Lloyd's bill.

The telephone was ringing as she came through the door. Malise? An instinctive desperate hope, but it was only a friend who'd been in church bossily summoning her to a dinner party.

'Only ten of us, do you good to get out. Eight for eight-thirty, strictly caszh.'

Helen had never been casual in her life.

'I'm not up to it, Annabel.'

'Course you are, I've asked Meredith Whalen for you. Such a duck and when one gets to our age, I'm afraid one has to put up with gays.'

'Why should some poor gay have to put up with me? I'm sorry, I can't.'

Helen banged down the receiver with such force the roses on the hall table scattered dark red petals all over the flagstones, joining a shoal of leaves which the icy wind had swept in through the still open front door. The drawing-room flowers were dropping. She mustn't let standards slip. The telephone rang again.

'I truly can't, Annabel,' she shrieked hysterically.

'Signora Gordon,' said a deep caressing velvety voice, ''Ow are you. Theese ees Rannaldini 'ere.'

He was so gently solicitous that Helen found herself quite able to accept an invitation to lunch on Wednesday, when Rannaldini's spies had made sure Marcus would be safely at the Academy.

Helen had always prided herself on her homework, but on this occasion she had no need to buy any of Rannaldini's CDs, Malise had collected most of them, admiring their clarity, colour and controlled passion.

Helen also rewatched Rannaldini's famous video of *Don Giovanni* and found it deeply disturbing as the cameras lingered on Hermione Harefield's rosy romping nudity and even more so on the still cold face and beautifully moving hands of Rannaldini himself.

She was horrified that with Malise only two months dead she should be thrown into such a panic at the prospect of lunching with such a fatally glamorous man, or how resentful she felt towards Malise for leaving her too poor to buy a new dress. She couldn't find her newish olive-green cashmere anywhere, wretched Tabitha must have whipped it, which meant she had to fall back on the Saint Laurent black suit she'd worn to Rupert's and Taggie's wedding. At least its white puritan collar would hide the dandruff which had snowed down since Malise's death.

Wednesday morning brought more devastating bills. Helen, who'd been up at first light, spent the morning in tears tidying unnecessarily. She had felt her daily woman's chaperonage when Rannaldini arrived was more important than the gossip Mrs Edwards would later impart round the village.

But as a final straw, Mrs Edwards rolled up, puffing with excited disapproval and brandishing a bad-taste piece in *The Scorpion*. Who would Helen, the most beautiful widow in England, marry now? Suggestions included Pierce Brosnan, Boris Levitsky, Richard Ingrams, Edward Heath, Julian Clary, Lysander's father, David Hawkley – a darkly handsome headmaster who was, as *The Scorpion* pointed out, a dead ringer for Malise; and, horror upon horror: Rannaldini, photographed smouldering on the rostrum.

Helen couldn't stop blushing, as she told Mrs Edwards, that by extraordinary coincidence Signor Rannaldini would be popping in that morning to look at the colonel's unpublished work on the flute.

'I must f-find a f-folder for it,' she stammered, bolting upstairs.

'And I should coco,' muttered Mrs Edwards, taking a hefty slug of the colonel's sloe gin before strategically positioning herself with the Antiquax in the study off the hall. Not that there was much to polish. The poor little soul couldn't stop cleaning since the colonel had passed away.

In front of her dressing-table Helen prayed her blushes would not spread to horrible red blotches on her neck. Starting on her face, she plucked a grey hair from her left eyebrow, and five more from her temples, combing lustreless tendrils over her hair line to hide more dandruff. It would be drifting soon.

Taking her hand-mirror to the window she gasped in horror. With a compass, despair and worry had scratched new lines round her pinched mouth and reddened eyes.

Outside, the garden looked horribly untidy, half the trees stripped, half-showing rain-blackened limbs at awkward dislocated angles as they struggled out of their red-and-yellow rags. Then before her eyes a gust of wind covered the lawn with leaves again. Malise had insisted on sweeping them up at once. The leaves would break her in the end.

Glancing in the mirror she saw that tears had left a blob of mascara on her cheek-bone. As she wiped it away the skin stayed pleated. Helen gave a groan. She couldn't face Rannaldini. Mrs Edwards would have to say she was ill.

But, bang on midday, punctual for the first time in his life, Rannaldini landed his big black helicopter on the lawn sending all the leaves swirling upwards around him as he leapt out; Don Giovanni returning from the eternal bonfire.

'Blimey,' said Mrs Edwards, applying Antiquax on top of Antiquax.

For Rannaldini was stained mahogany from ten days studying scores in the Caribbean sun. Wading through the leaves like a surfer he handed Helen a big bunch of tabasco-red freesias. Then he briefly put his arms round her so she could enjoy the muscular springiness of his body and its sauna-warmth as though he had indeed emerged from hell-fire.

'I know exactly how tired and lonely and cold you feel all the time,' he murmured, then stepping back and staring deep into her eyes. 'But nothing dim you great beauty. No wonder autumn ees in retreat when you upstage heem like this.'

Rannaldini had always been able to lay it on with a

JCB. Blushing redder than the freesias Helen invited him in while she put them in water.

Better than a film star, thought Mrs Edwards, kicking the study door further open as she rubbed Antiquax into the blue damask arm of a chair.

As Helen belted off to find a vase and slap on another layer of *Clinique* foundation, Rannaldini explored the charming drawing-room, with its apricot walls, faded grey silk curtains and glass cases containing Helen's porcelain collection. One would have to break the glass to reach her as well, reflected Rannaldini.

He thought it a particularly beautiful room because of the preponderance of his records and because of a photograph of Tabitha on the piano. Bareback, astride an old grey pony, her hair was in a blond plait and her eyes were as cool and disdainful as Rupert's.

The elm is a patient tree, it hateth and waiteth, thought Rannaldini lasciviously.

Malise had had a good eye for paintings. Rannaldini admired a Cotman and a little Pisarro, but what had possessed him to hang that frightful oil of poplars against a sunset with a cow which looked more like a warthog in the foreground? Then he read the rather obtrusive signature: Helen Gordon.

On a side table was an open poetry book.

Who would have thought my shrivel'd heart
could have recovered greenness? read Rannaldini.

In the desk the green leather blotter wouldn't close round the sheaf of bills. Flipping through them Rannaldini saw that Helen really was in trouble. The Cotman and the Pisarro would soon be off to Sotheby's.

Hearing her footsteps as she returned with the freesias in a saxe-blue jug, he turned back to her painting.

'This is excellent.'

'Oh, how darling of you. Malise liked it. I didn't have much time but perhaps now—' Helen's voice trailed off, then pulling herself together she picked up a file on a side-table.

'You said you'd like to see Malise's unpublished work. Have you really got time?'

'It is huge honour, I will make time,' lied Rannaldini.

Mrs Edwards was polishing the hall table now to have a better look. The Colonel had been a real gentleman, although rather frail towards the end, but this fellow looked as though he had three or four more pints of blood pumping round his veins and that lovely Boris Chevalier accent.

'You help Malise?' asked Rannaldini.

'I made suggestions,' said Helen eagerly.

'How lucky to have someone to share one's life work.'

Rannaldini's deep sigh fluttered the pages as he returned them to the file.

'It's fascinating how the flute was given the cold shoulder by musicians in the nineteenth century,' began Helen earnestly, 'because it lacked sufficient expressive range.'

'May I?' To shut her up, Rannaldini took Malise's flute out of its case, tuned for a second and started to play.

'Prokofiev. Malise played that.' Helen's eyes filled with tears.

'I am sorry. I will stop.'

'No, no, I never dreamt I'd hear it again so soon. Do you play other instruments?'

'Piano, oboe, trumpet, bassoon, violin, teemps.'

'Goodness, with so many accomplishments what made you become a conductor?'

Rannaldini laughed.

'Because at heart every man wants to be a führer. We must go to lunch. I take you home.' Then seeing the apprehension in Helen's eyes, added, 'Don't worry, my secretaries, my gardener, my 'ousekeeper and her 'usband, my driver, Uncle Tom Cobbley and probably his grey mare will all chaperone you.'

As the helicopter circled the Old Rectory before turning south, Helen could see Mrs Edwards belting down the drive twenty minutes early and gave a wail.

'I forgot to put on the alarm, I'm so scared of being burgled.'

Rannaldini smiled at her. It's already too late, my darling.

Orange leaves of beech, saffron flames of larch still flickered in the umber woods as they flew over the little village of Paradise up the River Fleet to Rannaldini's house, Valhalla, lurking pigeon-grey and wrapped in its conspirator's cloak of trees.

Helen had a heady glimpse of tennis-courts, a swimming-pool, the dark serpentine coils of a yew-tree maze, wonderful gardens, horses out in their rugs in fields sloping down to the river and deep in the wood, the watch-tower, where Rannaldini worked and seduced. Valhalla itself, narrow-windowed and brooding had been built before the Reformation.

'I've been reading a fascinating book on the dissolution of the monasteries,' began Helen.

Not wanting another lecture, Rannaldini whisked her down dark passages, past suits of armour, tattered banners and tapestries into a red drawing-room.

'How pretty,' gasped Helen.

'Meredith Whalen decorate it and the kitchen when I was married to Keety. You 'ave such exquisite taste, I pay you to theenk up new colour schemes.'

'Oh, I couldn't take your money.'

'My child,' purred Rannaldini, 'I know you need eet, as I need your help to exorcize bad memory of my life with Keety. Next week I go to Prague for ten days. By the time I return you must think up something wonderful.'

But Helen was crying again.

'Malise and I were going to Prague on 21 November for our anniversary. Malise tried to get tickets for a production of *Don Giovanni* at the Stasis Theatre.

Mozart premièred it there in November 1787, you know, and that was where they made *Amadeus*. But it was sold out.'

'Because I am conducting,' smirked Rannaldini.

'Of course, how stupid of me,' said Helen appalled. 'Since Malise died I don't remember anything.'

'Eet ees shock. It'll come back.' Rannaldini poured her a glass of Pouilly-Fumé. 'You shall come to Prague with me instead.'

'But I can't leave Marcus and I can't afford it,' babbled Helen.

'You will be my guest. I stay in flat. I book you room in nice hotel. I will send you plane ticket and ticket for *Don Giovanni* just for twenty-four hours, you deserve a treat.'

Putting a warm hand on her neck as comforting as a wool scarf just dried on the radiator, he led her down more passages to the big kitchen whose walls were covered in a glossy green paper, populated by jungle animals and birds.

'I certainly couldn't improve on this,' sighed Helen.

'I want eet changed,' said Rannaldini chillingly. 'Keety loved the parrots and the humming-birds. I want eet out. Sit down. I will make your lunch.'

'A bowl of soup will do,' stammered Helen. 'I can't eat at the moment.'

'Then you will start.'

From a next-door office, despite faxes billowing out like smoke, four telephones constantly ringing and the raindrop patter of expensive computors, Rannaldini's secretaries, who'd all read *The Scorpion*, kept finding excuses to pop in and gawp at Helen.

Princess Margaret's office had rung, they said; Domingo wanted advice on an interpretation; Sir Michael Tippett wondered if Rannaldini had had a moment to look at his latest opera; Hermione had rung four times. Rannaldini said he would call them all back later.

As he cooked, checking rice, throwing pink chunks of lobster into sizzling butter, then laying them tenderly on a bed of shallots, tarragon and tomatoes, separating eggs, boiling down fish stock, Helen talked. Her tongue loosened by a second glass of wine, she told him about her money problems, the big house she couldn't afford to keep up, Marcus's asthma and her worries about his friendship with Flora. She was delighted when Rannaldini dismissed Flora as 'an evil little tramp'.

'We will take Marcus to the mountains,' he went on warmly, then his voice thickened like the eggs in the double saucepan. 'How about your daughter?'

'Quite out of control.' Helen didn't want to tell him how incensed she had been about the appropriation of the olive-green cashmere. So she added: 'At half-term Tabitha borrowed my credit card saying she needed some school books, then used it to buy a pair of jeans and spend the afternoon on a sunbed. I cannot stand such vanity and such lies.'

Rannaldini, who was no stranger to lies and would have been quite out of control on a sunbed with Tabitha, expressed his disapproval. Topping a cloud of white rice with butter and putting it in a slower part of the Aga, he gave the lobster sauce a stir, and started chopping up chives for a salad of lettuce hearts.

'How can you do so many things at once?' marvelled Helen.

'I am conductor.'

Helen wandered over to the screen which Kitty, over the years, had lovingly covered with photographs of Rannaldini and the famous.

'Everyone's here,' she cried, thinking what fascinating people she would meet if Rannaldini became her – er – friend.

'Why d'you record in Prague?'

'Because it's ten times cheaper than London or New York. Not speaking ill of your country, Helen, but I am tired of New York. Last time I record a Haydn symphony the shop steward sit watching second 'and go round, four seconds to go, eight bars from the end, he leap on to the stage. "All right, you guys, it's over." I tried to keel him. I had to be pulled off. Eet takes an act of congress and then of God to get rid of musicians over there.

'I am almost broken man,' sighed Rannaldini, belying it by removing his suede jacket to show off his splendid physique. 'But I must not talk any more, I will burn your lunch.'

Putting a white mountain of rice on each emerald-green plate, he spooned over the sizzling lobster mixture, then poured on the buttery sauce, topping it with a dash of cayenne.

'Voila!'

'This is too much,' protested Helen.

'You weel eat every bit, even if I have to feed you.' Rannaldini filled up her glass again.

How wonderfully easy to give dinner parties, if one were living with Rannaldini, mused Helen, and think of the guest list. Her eyes strayed again to Kitty's screen.

'It is quite, quite delicious,' she said in awe.

As he told her his plans for the future Rannaldini's warm eyes never left her face.

'The leaves tumbling down remind me of new leaf I must turn over. I am tired of jetting round world. I must settle down in this lovely house, write music and build up a great orchestra of wonderful musicians, who would not be always chasing engagements and money like the London orchestras or threatening strike action like the guys in New York.'

'You could be another Simon Rattle,' said Helen warmly.

Rannaldini scowled.

'The CBSO is second-rate provincial orchestra,' he said haughtily.

'You can't say that. Malise always felt—'

Fortunately Rannaldini's third secretary popped her

head round the door to say the Princess of Wales was on the line.

'My dear,' Rannaldini took the telphone, 'may I ring you back in one hour.' He'd be leaving for the Albert Hall to conduct *Turangalila* around five o'clock.

Helen was so speechless with admiration that this great Maestro should find time for her she forgot about Simon Rattle.

'Why don't you come with me this evening?' asked Rannaldini, playfully spooning the last of her lobster into her mouth.

'I must get back for Marcus.'

'Eef only I had had a mother like you.'

'Will Hermione Harefield be singing in Prague?' asked Helen. 'This salad is so good.'

'No, she sing in *Aida* in Rome, and elephant run away with her. *Nellie the Elephant pack her trunk and run away with Hermione,*' sang Rannaldini. His face was expressionless but he gave Helen a wicked side-glance and she burst out laughing.

'Poor Hermione. I have to confess,' Helen went on, 'I do have reservations about *Don Giovanni* as an opera. The Don reminds me so much of Rupert,' she gave a shiver, 'and the way he used to get his best friend Billy Lloyd-Foxe to cover for him like Leporello.'

'I know,' Rannaldini slid his hand over hers. 'Jake Lovell talks of you often, how terribly unhappy Rupert made you.'

'How kind of Jake,' said Helen, touched.

'Jake threw you life-belt when you needed it,' said Rannaldini. 'But long term he would have bored you, you are much too bright for him.'

Machiavellian, Rannaldini pressed every organ stop of Helen's vanity.

'That's why he let you go,' he added, knowing perfectly well that Jake had dumped Helen.

'Do you think he's happy with his wife?'

'Jake dream of you often,' lied Rannaldini, selecting a

ripe peach, caressing its downy curves, 'And who would not?' Picking up a knife, he laid bare the gold flesh.

Helen found herself not only sharing the peach with him but, after another glass, agreeing to come to Prague.

Rannaldini's secretary then brought in a pile of fan mail.

'Have you sewn that button on my tail-coat?' he called after her shapely departing back.

'People think being a conductor,' he continued as in dark green ink he scribbled his name on each letter, 'is all helicopters, jets and princesses, but eet consist of worry where you'll stop long enough to get your laundry done.'

'Genius shouldn't have to worry about clean shirts and missing buttons,' said Helen shocked. 'Rupert never bothered to answer fan mail,' she added.

'That appal me,' Rannaldini signed a couple of photographs. 'Eef by writing back to these young people I can lead them on to a lifetime of loving music, it is small thing.'

'What a genuinely good man you are,' Helen suppressed a belch. 'How people have misjudged you.'

'Come for a walk,' said Rannaldini, putting his huge wolf coat round her shoulders. 'How it become you, a leetle lamb in wolf's clothing.'

As they walked up a path behind the house, the low afternoon sun kept parting the clouds, shining through yellow-and-orange leaves, so they glowed like amber and topaz. Rannaldini picked up a red beech leaf and held it against a soft brown wand of ash leaves.

'You must always wear brown with your red hair,' he told her. 'Black is too hard.'

As they passed a monk's graveyard, Helen noticed a little pink flower with bright crimson leaves growing out of the wall.

'What a dear little plant.'

'It ees called Herb Robert, all the year it flower, the monks used the leaves to staunch flow of blood.'

'Herb Roberto,' teased Helen, as they stopped to lean on a mossy gate. 'Such a beautiful name, why don't you use it?'

'My mother, who reject me, call me that.'

'Roberto,' repeated Helen softly.

'Coming from your lips it sound bettair.' Not wanting to frighten her, Rannaldini decided against a kiss.

As they turned for home, a biblical ray appeared through the clouds spotlighting Valhalla and the saffron larches, as though the place was on fire.

'Look Helen, it is omen, my past go up in flames like *Götterdämmerung*. I bring you on this walk,' Rannaldini took her hand, 'because the trees at the top of the wood never turn because they only get sunshine in the evening. Oh Helen, let us have some sunshine in the evening of our lives.'

Helen squeezed his hand, so moved that she couldn't speak.

'Before you come to Prague,' said Rannaldini, 'I must send you my video of *Don Giovanni*.'

Helen, who prided herself on telling the truth, took a deep breath.

'We have the video, Roberto, but I must say, neither Malise nor I thought it was your best effort. The music was delightful but all the sexual innuendo and the nudity seemed to trivialize the production.'

'Go on,' said Rannaldini icily.

'And we both felt that the camera rested on your face too much. Although it's fascinating watching a great conductor at work, it rather distracts from the action.'

'My *Don Giovanni* achieve higher rating than *EastEnders*.'

'It had popular appeal maybe, Roberto,' said Helen earnestly, 'but I think you are capable of greater things.'

'Do you indeed?' Rannaldini gazed fixedly ahead.

Realizing she had goofed, Helen said hastily, 'I guess it's my fault, as I said the Don is so like Rupert.'

'How is Rupert's exquisite wife?' asked Rannaldini silkily.

Helen's face tightened; she was wildly jealous of Taggie. Not only had she made Rupert happy, she was also adored by Marcus and Tabitha, and when he was alive, by Malise.

That'll teach her to slag off my *Don Giovanni*, thought Rannaldini in amusement.

'I expect she's busy chaining herself to some railing to stop lambs and calves being shipped alive to the continent,' said Helen tartly.

The thought of Taggie Campbell-Black being chained to anything excited Rannaldini unbearably.

'Peter Maxwell Davies is on the telephone.' The second secretary greeted Rannaldini and Helen as they entered the house. 'Have you looked at his symphony yet?'

'Put it in my briefcase, I do it tonight,' Rannaldini looked at his watch.

'Do you admire Boris Levitsky's *Berlin Wall Symphony*?' asked Helen, anxious to keep her end up. 'Malise and I were overwhelmed by it.'

'Hopelessly derivative. Boris speak of being divinely inspired by the great composers.' Sneeringly, Rannaldini pretended to pick up a telephone, ''Allo, Beethoven, 'Ow are you? I am ready to receive message, I take it down . . . and out come chopsteeks.'

'That's unfair,' said Helen reprovingly. 'Boris is very dear. He's been so supportive since Malise died, he rings me three or four times a week. I know Marcus would love him as a stepfather,' she added defiantly, and then felt absolutely miserable.

She is very insecure, decided Rannaldini, Malise had restored her confidence and hung a picture-light over her beauty; now it had gone out.

Changing tack, he said gently: 'Many men would like

to be Marcus's stepfather. Eef you didn't like my *Don Giovanni*, I must give you other records and eef you won't come to Albert Hall, Clive, my chauffeur, will drive you home.'

Later that evening, Marcus endured a half-hour moan about bills from a restless, sobered-up Helen. He then pointed to Nielsen's *Flute Concerto* and Mahler's *Resurrection Symphony* lying on the piano.

'If we're that broke, why are you buying that bastard's records?'

Startled, because Marcus was normally so tolerant, hoping Mrs Edwards wouldn't drop her in it, Helen tried a grey lie.

'Rannaldini wrote me a delightful letter, admiring Malise's flute book and sent me the Nielsen and the Mahler because he thought I needed cheering up.' Helen gave a deep sigh.

'Sure, Mum, Rannaldini's still a fiend. He wiped out Flora and he crucified poor Kitty. You ask Lysander.'

'Lysander stole Rannaldini's wife,' said Helen furiously.

'Because Rannaldini was so unfaithful to her. He's randier than Dad's Jack Russells.' Then, as Helen winced, added, 'Small man syndrome. Although for a small man he casts a long shadow, and he's got a repulsive black-leather-clad henchman called Clive, who takes women off the bone for him.'

Helen shuddered.

'Why does he dislike Boris so much? I read it somewhere,' she added hastily.

'Boris is taller,' said Marcus, 'and a million times more talented. Rannaldini only admires musicians who are dead.'

'This article said he could be nice.'

'Only because it's such bliss when the electrodes stop.'

FOURTEEN

Helen was appalled. The last thing she wanted was another promiscuous sadist. When Rannaldini called, she'd just refuse politely. But Rannaldini did not call. Expert at fostering addiction, he knew exactly how to give a blue glimpse of Paradise before slamming the skylight shut. Whizzing off abroad, he left Helen to stew for a fortnight until she was diving for the telephone, snatching letters from the postman and scanning the pallid November skies praying one of the circling rooks would grow into a big black helicopter.

Then, on the morning of the opening night, when she had abandoned all hope, Rannaldini rang blithely from Prague.

'I hope you are coming; a messenger will drop tickets for plane and for *Don Giovanni* within the hour. Clive will meet you at Prague. I book you into charming discreet hotel, L'Esplanade.'

'I didn't know I was expected,' Helen's voice scraped down a blackboard of indignation. 'I can't make it at such short notice.'

'I didn't want to pressure you,' confessed Rannaldini. 'An I wasn't sure of production, but eet come good.'

Then, after a long pause, he whispered, 'I need you, Helen.'

As Helen arrived at Heathrow, a defiant red sun leaving the western sky aflame had just been sucked below the dark horizon like Don Giovanni.

Never had Helen been less prepared for a trip; normally every local legend would have been memorized, every fine church charted. In anticipation of their own proposed trip, Malise had bought her a guide book to Prague. But she had been too superstitious to open it and once she was on the plane she couldn't take in a word. She kept panicking about things, including her wits, she had left behind.

To avoid the Bourbon-breathed attentions of a businessman with hairy nostrils in the next seat, she accepted a copy of *The Times* from the hostess, only to find among the birthdays that international conductor, Rannaldini, was forty-four today – on the cusp of Scorpio and Sagittarius, those two most volatile and darkly virile signs. Rannaldini must want to share his birthday with her and she had brought no present except a first edition of Malise's book on the flute. How awful.

Although fog symbolizing her confusion delayed the plane by nearly two hours, Rannaldini's Leporello, the sinister Clive, his light eyes as unblinking and expressionless as a cobra's, was still waiting. Helen kept as far away from his lean leather-clad body as her seatbelt would allow. She was so thin now, there would be nothing for him to take off the bone.

She was far too uptight to be more than fleetingly aware of empty, ill-lit restaurants, floodlit fortresses and spires, a gleaming river and overcrowded unkempt trees, trying to escape over park railings.

As the Czechs had only recently had mass access to cars, the driving was hair-raising. Clive swore under his breath as somehow avoiding head-on collisions he hurtled Rannaldini's black Mercedes down the narrowest of streets, rattling over the cobbles as if he would bang the heads of the tall lowering houses together.

The hotel, as Rannaldini predicted, was charming, with a crescent of smiling receptionists.

'Take your time, we've missed the first act,' Clive called after her, as an ancient, knowing porter drove the rickety tram of a lift up to the fifth floor.

Seeing her pinched, twitching reflection in the lift mirror, Helen was overwhelmed with longing for Malise; he'd always thought she looked beautiful and would have known exactly how many kopeks to tip the porter.

The next moment she was gasping with joy for her entire room was filled with different coloured freesias, embracing her in their sweet heady scent. Beside a blue glass bowl spilling over with persimmons, peaches and passion-fruit was a bottle of Krug on ice and the bathroom was full of soap and bottles containing every permutation of Balmain's *Jolie Madame*. How darling of Rannaldini to have realized it was her favourite perfume.

More magical still, on the drab beige bedspread lay a long crushed velvet dress in the same soft umber as the drenched ash wand he had picked up in the wood. On the dressing-table was a red leather case from Cartier's and a letter.

> *My darling,*
> *The dress is to go with your beech-leaf hair. In box*
> *is small present to echo the stars I will put back in*
> *your eyes.*
> *In hope,*
> *Rannaldini.*

Collapsing on the bed so hard it nearly broke her back, Helen opened the box. Inside glittered a diamond necklace. The dress was wonderfully becoming, the high neck and long sleeves concealed her jutting collar bones and refugee arms. The ribbed clinging velvet made her look saluki-slender. But what would happen when Rannaldini undressed her and found the skeleton beneath the skin? And how could she not sleep with him after accepting these gifts? She wouldn't mind so much if her bottom hadn't dropped and if she didn't feel so leaden-limbed and out of practice. What would happen if she froze inside as she had done so often with Rupert?

The clasp of the diamonds nearly defeated her shaking hands. She was going home. The telephone rang. Oh, why wasn't it Malise?

'Whenever you're ready,' lisped Clive's voice.

As Helen came out of the lift, he was singing to himself.

> 'Where's my master, Don Giovanni?
> Making love to youth and beauty
> While I stay on sentry duty.'

But there was no admiration in his face. He preferred the more butch male singers from the chorus.

It had been the worst pre-opening week he could remember, he told Helen on the drive to the theatre, Rannaldini's clashes with singers and orchestra had been epic.

'Musicians here are used to working for the state and having the same job for life, so it doesn't matter if they learn the parts or arrive on time. They're very bolshy. All the singers were in tears at the dress rehearsal. Donna Anna said first-night nerves were a doddle compared with Rannaldini's rages.'

I'm the one with the first night nerves, thought Helen. Clive shouldn't discuss his boss like this.

'It's incredible to think,' she said reprovingly, 'Mozart himself conducting the première of *Don*

Giovanni in this very theatre more than two hundred years ago.'

'And Casanova was in the audience and wrote some of the libretto,' leered Clive, thinking Rannaldini would have left both the Don and Casanova standing this week. 'There's the theatre.'

Ahead, romantically and softly lit by old-fashioned street-lamps and hung with window-boxes full of clashing red-and-mauve geraniums, rose a square, peppermint-green building. The foyer was flanked with hefty pillars that would have challenged even Sampson.

'How beautiful,' sighed Helen. 'If only we weren't so late.'

'In Mozart's day it was fashionable to be late and not stay the course,' said Clive as he locked the car doors. 'The Kings and Princes of Prague used to make a quick exit from the royal box down those,' he pointed to an outside staircase, 'so they could rush off to their fancy pieces.'

Helen looked bootfaced. Clive was far too familiar. Then they both jumped at a deafening machine-gun rattle coming from the auditorium: the traditional applause for the conductor at the beginning of the last act.

'Shit,' muttered Clive.

Only by brandishing his identity card as Rannaldini's minion, did he manage to smuggle Helen past the doorman, who had had death threats not to admit latecomers.

'Does Signor Rannaldini know I've arrived?' asked Helen as they belted up the wide spiral staircase.

'No,' lied Clive. 'Once an opera starts Rannaldini cannot be disturbed. He hates to lose the mood. He paces the conductor's room like The Prince of Darkness. Sometimes in the interval he has a shower and changes his shirt in a trance, not realizing it.'

'There are moments when art transcends everything,' panted Helen.

But, as Clive smuggled her into a box overlooking the

pit, the door banged and, in her nervousness, Helen dropped her bag with a clatter. There was a horrified silence. Bows stopped moving, wind and brass players stopped breathing. Rannaldini whipped round in a fury, he was known to scream at late-comers, or worse still, hurl down his baton and storm out.

But, as he caught sight of Helen, huge-eyed in the half-light, diamonds glittering at her graceful neck like the Pleiades, he gave a wonderfully theatrical start and stopped conducting. Donna Elvira languishing on her balcony, Don Giovanni and Leporello swapping clothes in the shadowy garden and all the musicians looked at him incredulously as though a metronome had broken down.

Rannaldini gazed at Helen. Then a smile of such rare sweetness and joy spread across his face that a ripple of laughter went through the orchestra and the nearby boxes and everyone was desperately craning round and leaping to their feet to see the beauty who had stopped the great Maestro in his course.

Hastily Rannaldini pulled himself together.

'I am sorry.' Briefly he turned to the audience then back to the musicians and singers, 'We begin the trio again. *Taci injusti core.*'

The exquisite music started, Don Giovanni resumed his amorous escapades. Helen was overwhelmed. Clearly, even for Rannaldini, there were times when love was much more important than art. Clive was grinning broadly when, during an exuberant tutti, he slid back into the box bearing a bottle of champagne, a glass and a plate of caviar.

'With the Maestro's compliments,' he whispered. 'He was worried this afternoon that you might not have had time to eat.'

The toast was still warm – like Rannaldini's hands. Helen quivered with excitement. Marcus had so misjudged him. She must eat a little but she mustn't crunch too loudly.

In the dim light she admired Mozart's theatre. Gold tiers decorated with plump white cherubs rose up and up to a huge unlit chandelier. Oblong gilt mirrors on the inside of each slate-blue velvet box, huge gold tassels on the midnight-blue curtains on either side of the stage, the musicians' instruments all added to the sub-dued glitter.

Below her, in a pit bigger than one of the Czech Grand National's fearsome ditches, the musicians played as if their lives depended on it.

It was also a mark of Rannaldini's genius that after such an interruption, he immediately got his glamorous cast of unknown singers back on course without any slackening of tension. It was also obvious, except to a daz-zled Helen, that after her arrival both Donna Anna and Donna Elvira sang of the pangs of love with even more tearful conviction. Zerlina, exuding snapping sloe-eyed sexiness in a cherry-red peasant's dress, on the other hand, was glaring at Rannaldini as she defiantly flashed soft white thighs and black stockings, held up by one red and one purple garter, at her stodgy lover, Masetto.

But Helen had only eyes for Rannaldini, bewildered that such energy should come out of such stillness. His hardly moving stick twitched like a cat's tail. His hair, now raven-black with sweat, was the only evidence of expended energy.

They were into the moonlit graveyard now. As Giovanni vaulted over the wall to boast of more con-quests to a terrified Leporello, Helen thought once again, with the anger of too much champagne, how like Rupert he was.

Then she gasped in terror as the gaunt grey statue of the Commendatore on his stone horse came to life and to the doom-laden accompaniment of the trombones uttered the first dreadful greeting to the Don.

'*Your laughter will be silenced before morning.*'

'*Who goes there?*' undaunted by any ghost, Giovanni swung his machine-gun round the tombstones.

As the sepulchral voice rang out again ordering him to leave the dead in peace, Helen's blood ran even colder. The statue looked so like Malise on his death-bed. Malise had rescued her from Rupert, now he seemed to be warning her from the grave to stay away from Rannaldini.

But Helen was most unnerved by the lascivious half-smile on Rannaldini's face as the handsome young Don, still raging and unrepentant, was finally sucked down into a quicksand of leaping flame.

'A-a-a-h!'

It was like watching a great aeroplane crash. The Prussian-blue curtains closed like the gates of hell. There was a stunned pause as the audience realized Rannaldini had scrapped the last moralizing chorus. Then followed a deafening roar of applause. As the lights went up and the vast chandelier glittered like a huge thistle overhead, Helen could see the full beauty of the theatre, its soft blues and golds like a sunlit day at sea. But loveliest to Helen were the tier upon tier of ecstatically cheering people.

Down below the musicians were shaking hands and hugging each other in delight, as the cast trooped onto the stage, elated but slightly bewildered at such an ovation. How pretty the girls were, strong-featured, red-lipped, lusty and displaying such full white breasts as they bent to gather up the carnations raining down.

Rannaldini got the greatest cheer of all. For a man who'd been conducting for two hours forty minutes, who was black under the eyes and whose suntan had faded, he looked magnificent, smaller than any of the men but dwarfing them with his personality. Donna Elvira and Donna Anna, on either side of him, had kicked off their high heels and the audience cheered even louder as he kissed their hands and then reached out for the hand of Zerlina who was sulking down the row.

Then the chorus returned and everyone sang 'Happy

Birthday' in Czech and Donna Elvira presented Rannaldini with pink roses and a bust of Mozart.

Helen was in despair. Surrounded by such youth and vitality, how could he bother with a scraggy wrinkly like herself? Grabbing her bag she frantically applied blusher then jumped as Clive banged on the door.

'Time to congratulate the Maestro.'

As he led her down into the dingy catacombs behind the stage, she was reminded of Dante's *Inferno*, but was reassured by a glimpse of the Commendatore. Having removed his grey make-up and his white wig to reveal a ruddy complexion and wavy yellow hair, he was now putting on bicycle clips and eating a sausage sandwich.

The conductor's room was pandemonium. The screaming matches, the fearful bullying had been forgotten in the euphoria of an historic performance. Cast and musicians alike were pouring in to thank Rannaldini, bringing him hastily written cards with their addresses on. Rannaldini, because he could see Helen working her way down the long queue, and he wanted to create an impression of amiability, bothered for once to shake hands with everyone and promised to return as soon as possible.

Still in his tails, he had only had time to remove his white tie and gardenia. He was burning hot, yet wringing with sweat, as he took Helen in his arms.

'My beautiful child, I 'ave longed for this moment,' he murmured in English, too fast for the Czechs to understand, then *sotto voce* to Clive, 'Get rid of everybody at once.'

'You *will* come on to our party, won't you, Maestro?' pleaded Donna Elvira.

'I bake birthday cake for you,' whispered Donna Anna, pocketing his discarded gardenia.

'I must have shower, I will see you later,' said Rannaldini.

Zerlina said nothing, but her mascara was streaked

with tears as Clive frogmarched her without any gentleness down the passage.

The moment they had gone Rannaldini locked the door.

'That was a most exciting p-p-erformance,' stammered Helen.

Rannaldini smiled evilly.

'You wait till later, my angel.'

Helen blushed. 'It was far more erotic without nudity.'

'I leesten to you,' said Rannaldini gravely.

'Oh, if I was some small help,' Helen was in heaven. 'And the way you control them all with this tiny stick.' She picked up his baton, 'It's a magic wand.'

'I weesh I could transform thees room into a bower of bliss,' said Rannaldini fretfully.

Nothing could have been less seductive than the fluorescent lighting, the ugly brown carpet, the repro desk and hard chair, the fitted cupboards, the pedal dustbin, the fridge and shower behind a dingy beige plastic curtain.

'You should see my room in New York,' Rannaldini hastily kicked a purple garter under the desk.

'But enduring art, not surroundings, are what matters,' said Helen earnestly. 'And thank you so much for this wonderful dress, Roberto, and the flowers, and the caviar and champagne and these beautiful diamonds. But it's not *my* birthday.'

'Don't be silly.' Cutting short her thanks, Rannaldini lifted the diamonds and slowly kissed her collar bone, caressing it with his tongue until she was squirming with desire.

'I must be the one person in the world who didn't know it was your birthday,' she whispered. 'The only thing I brought you was a first edition of Malise's book, but it's at the hotel.'

'That ees the present I want second most in the

world,' said a delighted Rannaldini. 'Now I feel Malise geeve us his blessing.' As he gently fingered her ribs, the ball of his thumb was pressing against the underside of her breast.

'The present I want you to geeve me most ees yourself.'

But, as he moved into the attack, Helen leapt away.

'We can't, people know we're in here, you ought to change, you'll catch your death.'

Rannaldini deliberated. Many women were desperately turned on by a burning, sweating *après*-concert body. Helen was probably too fastidious. The elm is a patient tree. Rannaldini got a bottle of white out of the fridge and filled two glasses.

'Will you wait while I have a shower?'

Embarrassingly aware, a few seconds later, of Rannaldini naked behind the shower curtain, Helen said she would put his roses in water.

'They droop already, unlike me,' Rannaldini shouted over the gush of water. 'I am so pleased you are here. Kiri and Placido say the same. Everyone pours in and kisses you, saying how wonderful it was, then they drift away.'

'None of those young women wanted to drift away this evening.' Helen was unable to keep the edge out of her voice. 'I am sure everyone felt *you* should have played the Don. That boy was much too young for the part.'

'The libretto describe Giovanni as a licentious young nobleman,' protested Rannaldini. 'I am neither young nor noble.'

'Any moment you are going to be ennobled, Sir Roberto,' said Helen archly, then as Rannaldini emerged from the shower, his sleek still brown body as smooth as butterscotch, a big white towel slung around his hips, she caught her breath.

'And after Malise,' she faltered, 'you seem very, very young to me.'

'That is kind.' Rannaldini turned back to the basin to clean his teeth.

'As I was saying, people drift away after a concert theenking you have more important people to see, so you go back to your hotel, hyped up, totally alone, and you ring home and say, "The applause went on for fifteen minutes," and they say, "Yeah, yeah, I've got this ghastly problem with the deesh washer."'

'I'd never bother, I mean, genius should never be bothered with problems like that,' said Helen aghast, totally forgetting how often she moaned to Rupert when he was show-jumping in the old days.

Rannaldini turned, flashing beautiful clean teeth at her.

'Come here my darling, stop playing games.'

'Don't you want to go to your birthday party?'

'Certainly not.' There would be far too many recently pleasured members of the cast wanting repeat feels.

Sliding into a splendid red silk Turnbull and Asser dressing gown, he picked up the bottle and glasses and sang in a rich baritone:

> *You lay your hands in mine, dear*
> *Softly you'll whisper, yes*
> *Tis not so far to go, dear*
> *Your heart is mine, confess.'*

'You sing beautifully,' sighed Helen, taking his hand.

'Come, let me show you Mozart's theatre.'

'Where is everyone?' quavered Helen as he led her up and down steps along pitch-black passages.

'Gone home,' said Rannaldini, who'd tipped the night porter more than he earned in a year. 'Wait 'ere, don't move.' He let go of her hand.

Helen was petrified, the darkness was strangling her. Then she heard footsteps.

'Rannaldini?'

There was no answer.

'Don't play games with me.'

Suddenly she saw a flicker ahead, oh thank God, Rannaldini was lighting candles. Stumbling forward she gave a piercing shriek as she found herself looking up into the livid face of the Commendatore's horse.

'Over here. You must not be so jumpy.' Rannaldini drew her over some cables to where candles were flickering merrily on either side of a vast carved bed hung with turquoise-and-white striped curtains and foaming with white linen sheets and laced pillows.

'Who's this for?'

'Giovanni chase Zerlina round eet in Act One. Let's have some moonlight.' Rannaldini tugged down the moon from Act Two so it shone dimly into the four-poster.

But as he drew her towards the bed, Helen began to tremble violently.

'Come.' Rannaldini stooped to pull her dress over her head. 'It is time for the butterfly to emerge from her chrysalis.'

Helen burst into tears; it was the same trick she had used to halt the Rake's progress of Rupert twenty years ago. Rannaldini, too, was all contrition.

'What ees eet, my darling?'

'Malise was just so like the Commendatore. Tonight's our wedding-anniversary, I feel he was trying to warn me off. All those young women drooling over you this evening. Marcus told me you were dreadfully promiscuous.'

'A good boy to protect his mother,' said Rannaldini smoothly, vowing to sabotage Marcus's piano career at the first opportunity.

'And why didn't you call me for two weeks?'

Rannaldini sunk to his knees, burying his face in her concave belly.

'Because I knew I was unworthy. You are so lovely you would have stopped both Casanova and Giovanni on their road to ruin. I, too, have been wicked. Oh Helen, save me from the flames.'

Rannaldini was gratified to feel tears dropping on his forehead. Gotcha!

Leaping to his feet he pushed her back onto the bed.

'I'm so scared, Rannaldini.'

'Do not be, we play little game.

Behold, your faithful lover
Lives for you alone,'

sang Rannaldini, really straining to reach the top notes.

'*Think no longer on that appalling moment.*
Your father and your husband shall I be.

'You felt safe with Malise,' he went on, 'because he was both father and lover to you, and made you feel like a little girl. Tonight, let us pretend this little girl has sunk into a decline, because she is so sad. Her family is worried so they invite important doctor from London to see her.'

Sitting on the bed, Helen felt a squirming excitement.

'The doctor geeves her medicine,' Rannaldini raised a glass of wine to Helen's lips, stroking her hair with his other hand.

'Now she must undress – ' very slowly he drew the brown dress over her head – 'so the doctor can examine her all over.'

Gently he began to stroke Helen's freckled shoulders and arms.

'She is lovely but much too thin.' Rannaldini peeled off her grey silk petticoat. The next moment her grey silk bra had followed slithering suit.

'Ah, how sweet.' In delight Rannaldini gently massaged her breasts. 'How small they are, but the kind doctor will prescribe injections and a diet to make them full and beautiful again. Look how the nipples shoot out like sycamore buds. The leetle patient is very, very excited,' he went on, 'but she is frightened, her mother is downstairs and the doctor seem to be taking a leetle too long. Now he has peeled off her very clean knickers.'

Helen gave a moan of helpless excitement.

'Look at her little bush, like a damp fox, naughty excited leetle girl.'

Rannaldini's smile was satanic. The concentration in the heavy-lidded eyes was total. His voice was deep, slow, hypnotic.

'Eef the doctor suggest an operation, he would have to shave her so she is even more like leetle girl.'

'That's perverted.' Helen leapt to her feet in agitation.

But Rannaldini's great strength pushed her back.

'Every bit of her body must be explored.' He drew a magnifying glass out from under the pile of pillows. 'See she has sweet little clitoris, quite beeg enough for pleasure, the doctor stroke it to see if it is in good working order. And it is, see how easily he slides his fingers in, one finger, now two, good little girl.'

Helen arched and groaned too excited to care any more, buckling against the relentlessly stabbing fingers, writhing beneath the delicately stroking thumb.

'The doctor is excited, too, he knows with loving he can cure all her seekness.'

Just for a moment his fingers emerged and trailed downwards.

'Shall the doctor examine his little patient in an even more shaming and private place? She will find it so naughty and exciting, she will beg and beg for more.'

'No.' Helen was struggling. 'Please, Rannaldini, no.'

'Another time.' His fingers were stabbing again, her breath was coming faster and faster.

Quickly Rannaldini slid out of his dressing-gown, his body dark gold in the flickering candlelight, his splendid cock raised for the down beat.

'Look, he geeve you standing ovation. This is most awesome steeple you will see in Prague, my darling.'

Helen's 'A-a-a-ah' rivalled the Don's, but hers was of

ecstasy, as Rannaldini blew out the candle, and plunged deep into her and darkness. He had never dreamt he could make her so wildly excited.

'*Nobilmente sed appassionate*,' whispered Rannaldini as he drove on to conquest, and this time the metronome never faltered.

...as Rannaldini sniffed at the candle, and plunged
deep into her, "Oh yes," she had bowed down he..
would deliver heroic wild..
...Someone said someone some... who could have said my...
above quickly arrived, and this time the neighbours
heard them.

FIFTEEN

Helen was woken by such beautiful music she thought
she had fallen asleep with the wireless on at home. Then
she took in the gutted candles, the blue-and-white
striped curtains, and breathed in a feral waft of *Maestro*
clinging to the wolf-coat which Rannaldini had solici-
tously laid over her naked body.

Wriggling into the coat she stumbled across the dimly
lit stage, to find Rannaldini already dressed. He was
holding a score and picking out a tune on the harpsichord. Hearing her, he looked up and smiled.

'I didn't wake you.'

'What time is it?'

Rannaldini glanced at his huge Rolex.

'Quarter past seven.'

'I haven't slept through the night since Malise died.'

'That's because you were so tired and so loved.'

'What's that tune? I know it so well.'

'On a different instrument. I conduct *Missa solemnis*
in Berlin tonight. It is very difficult piece so I flip
through score, that was violin solo from the
"Benedictus".'

'Didn't you sleep?'

'I was too happy. People say it's mistake to get your heart's desire. I'm thoroughly enjoying it.'

Edging through the music-stands he lifted her down from the stage.

'My leetle lamb in wolf's clothing.'

Collapsing against him, hoping he'd make love to her again, she whispered: 'I love you, Roberto.'

'Good,' smirked Rannaldini. 'What is the purpose of the lamb but to feed the wolf?'

Not taking on board what he said, Helen picked up the huge score covered in red-and-blue pencil marks.

'You work so hard.'

'Not so hard as Beethoven. In his own words, "*You must sacrifice all the little things of social life for the sake of your art.*" That's why you must never fret if I don't call you, I am only making love to Beethoven.'

Leading her to the harpsichord he picked out the exquisite tune again.

'The violin ascend to heaven like we did last night. When I conduct Beethoven, I am so proud I am half-German. Because Beethoven had greatest struggle to write the *Missa*, he thought it his greatest work. A friend drop in when he was composing the "Credo", he found poor Beethoven, "*singing, howling and stamping*". Oh Helen, I dream of composing again, you must be my muse.'

Seizing her hands, he gazed deep, deep into her eyes, then he said playfully: 'But muse and genius must be fed. Get dressed and 'ave a shower, my darling, I have to listen to some pianist who beg me to hear her.'

The pianist, dark, plump, very young, was playing Chopin's *Fantasie Impromptu* quite brilliantly when Helen returned to the auditorium. Instantly Rannaldini halted the girl and introduced her.

'This is Natalia Philipova. Now what ees it you want to know, Natalia?'

The girl clasped her hands

'I know I have years of hard work in front of me, Maestro, I am willing to practise eight hours a day and more. All I want to know is if you think I can ever make it as a soloist.'

Rannaldini examined his fingernails.

'Not in a million years,' he said smoothly. 'You will be able to give your friends and your family a lot of pleasure, I advise you to leave eet at that.'

'You were a bit rough on that poor kid,' reproved Helen.

'I save her ten years of wasted time,' said Rannaldini.

They were sitting in a little café in the main square which looked like an Ideal Home Exhibition of best architecture down the ages. They had breakfasted on croissants, damson jam, slivers of cheese, rolled-up slices of ham with cream billowing out of each end like brandy snaps and black expresso laced with cognac.

'Usually I go off my food if I'm attracted to a man,' said Helen, sounding perplexed. 'But when you're around I seem to eat like a labrador.'

'That's because the strict doctor,' Rannaldini ran a leisurely hand up her thigh into her groin, 'has ordered his little patient to start eating again.'

Helen flushed, horrified she should have been so wildly exhilarated by last night's games.

Rannaldini waved for the bill.

'Come. I have one hour to show you Prague. Let us go to Charles Bridge which, thank God, is closed to cars.'

As they walked down to the river Helen gave a cry of joy. On the opposite bank the old city stretched itself luxuriously in the first sunshine of the day. All higgledy piggledly, cupolas, turrets, domes, roofs and spires in soft pink, ochre, peppermint-green and drained turquoise, rose like casually stacked stage-sets. Against the blue skyline was a cathedral with a faded sea-green dome topped with a gold star, next to it stood a tawny castle with crenellated battlements like a child's fort.

'Who lives there?'

'Havel,' said Rannaldini smugly, 'I dine with heem on Thursday.'

But most breathtaking of all was the river itself. Mist was rising filling the great arches of the bridges, curling in wisps over the icy water. The result was a million shifting shadows. The trees and the houses on the bank cast different shadows on the mist and the moving water. The shadows of the mist, wisps themselves, and the swans and ducks gliding in and out of these wisps, cast and received shadows of their own.

'Everywhere Zeus is searching for Leda,' said Rannaldini softly. 'And see how the sooty black statues across the bridge cast the darkest shadows of all.'

Furious not to have mugged up the city and because Malise had always praised her recitations, Helen launched into *The Tempest*.

> *'The cloud-capp'd towers, the gorgeous palaces,*
> *The solemn temples, the great globe itself,*
> *Yea, all which it inherit, shall dissolve*
> *And, like this insubstantial pageant faded,*
> *Leave not a rack behind.'*

'This rake is *not* going to be left behind,' mocked Rannaldini, putting his arm through hers to lead her over the bridge.

'You are getting cold. The Russians may have left Prague, but icy wind still blow straight from Moscow.'

Sixties music was belching out of a loud speaker. The people pouring over the bridge, as if to repudiate any accusation of Communist drabness, wore brilliant collars: violet, turquoise, shocking pink, but their bulky anoraks and strap-under-trousers looked very out of date.

As the mist thinned in the sunshine, the river seemed to be strewn with cobwebs. The statues, on the other hand, were covered in real, frozen cobwebs, which glittered on the sad, strong Slav face of Christ on the cross like a veil of tears.

'I theenk of Prague as Sleeping Beauty that's only just awaked. Two sleeping beauties,' Rannaldini turned and kissed Helen's lips, his dark glasses only an extension of his black impenetrable eyes. 'And last night you awake.

'There's St Christopher.' Moving on, he pointed to more statues. 'And St Cyril and St Barbara, patron saint of miners. Kafka wrote story about bridge, describing her beautiful hands. The statues 'ave to be restored and rebuilt every year.'

'Like a face lift,' said Helen.

'You will never need one,' Rannaldini touched her cheek, 'You have eternal youth.'

They had reached the centre of the bridge. Upstream the river still steamed like a race horse. Downstream it was as smooth and green as *crème de menthe* with a striped pink pleasure launch chugging towards them, and cafés with their umbrellas down on the bank.

'Now we come to Prague's most famous saint, St John of Nepomuk,' said Rannaldini, 'who was the Queen's confessor in fourteenth century. Her husband, King Wenceslas IV, was a thug. The story about him setting out in snow with page boy, wine and pine logs to cheer up some peasant, ees balderdash.' Rannaldini's eyes creased up with malicious laughter. 'This Wenceslas was insanely jealous of his beautiful wife and torture her confessor to reveal her secrets. When Nepomuk refuse, Wenscelas pull out poor man's tongue and chuck him in river.

'But,' Rannaldini pointed to a brass plaque set into the side of the bridge, showing the unfortunate monk being heaved over the side, 'where he land, five bright gold stars spring out of river, and hover there until Nepomuk's dead body was fished out.

'This is spot where he went in.' Picking up Helen's hand, Rannaldini placed it on a jagged gold cross on top of the bridge wall. 'Over centuries lovers come to touch the cross together,' Rannaldini spread his big hand over hers, 'in the hope that their love will last and prosper.'

Burying his face in Helen's neck, he breathed in the last vestiges of *Jolie Madame.*

'Now you know why I breeng you here.'

'What a beautiful story,' sighed Helen, glancing back at the plaque, 'the body of the poor monk is bright gold, too.'

'That is where people have rubbed his body for luck over the centuries.' Rannaldini stretched out his hand, idly caressing the upside-down Nepomuk.

The plaque also showed the Queen making her confession to Nepomuk through a grill. Nearby her cruel handsome husband idly stroked an adoring lurcher. But the tension in his body showed how hard he was listening. How often during her first marriage had Helen lurked on landings and outside rooms trying to overhear Rupert making assignations?

'The King even looks like Rupert,' she was thinking aloud now. 'He's got the same Greek nose and long eyes.'

'He love his dog more than his wife,' teased Rannaldini.

'I nearly cited Rupert's dog Badger as co-respondent,' said Helen bitterly.

'I think you are more in mourning for your first marriage than the second,' mocked Rannaldini.

'My first one nearly destroyed me. I can't go back to that again.'

The mist had almost disappeared. Upstream a flotilla of air balloons hung like teardrops. Artists were setting up easels. A street musician playing 'Lili Marlene' on the accordian was tipped with unusual generosity by Rannaldini.

'We could have done with you in the orchestra last night, my friend.'

'Thank you, Maestro.'

'How good you are to everyone,' sighed Helen.

'One more saint.' Rannaldini led Helen beyond the bridge and down some stone steps to the water's edge on which stood a lone statue of a slim young knight with a lion at his feet and a gold sword glittering in his hand.

'Now listen carefully,' Rannaldini paused in front of the statue. 'St Brunswick save the lion from a cruel and wicked dragon. Consequently the lion became Brunswick's devoted companion and also the symbol of Prague. Brunswick's job was to guard the city.'

'The day the Communist walk in in 1949,' Rannaldini's beautiful voice flowed on like the river, 'Brunswick's gold sword totally vanish. The legend was that it would only return when Prague was freed. The very night Prague was liberated,' suddenly Rannaldini seemed to have difficulty speaking, 'the joyful crowds sweeping over the bridge notice the gold sword was back in place in Brunswick's hand.'

'A miracle,' said Helen shakily.

Rannaldini nodded. Removing his dark glasses he drew Helen into the lichened, blackened arch of the bridge and kissed her.

'Since Keety leave me I have not been able to put my heart into conducting, let alone composing. Last night, with young inexperienced musicians and singers, we produce performance of a lifetime. Later while you sleep, you look so beautiful, I write my first music in fifteen years. I dedicate it to you. You have freed my inspiration and given me back my gold sword so I can protect you.'

'Oh Rannaldini.' Tears were glittering on Helen's face like frozen cobwebs. 'That's the dearest thing anyone's ever told me.'

'Who would have thought my shrivel'd heart
Could have recovered greenness?' murmured Rannaldini, remembering the open poetry book on the table at the Old Rectory.

'That's my favourite poem,' said Helen in amazement. Midges were dancing like mist shadows against the bridge wall. Tourists drifting by gazed down on the beautiful couple.

'I must go.' Reluctantly Rannaldini tore himself away. 'Tonight I will conduct *Missa* just for you, my darling.'

If he had asked her to follow him to the end of the world, let alone Berlin, Helen would have gone.

As they drove back to the hotel, Rannaldini told Helen he was spending Christmas in his house in Tuscany with his children and two of his ex-wives.

''Ow about you?' he asked.

'I shall be staying with Rupert and Taggie and *my* children,' said Helen, showing off how well she, too, got on with her ex.

The temperature dropped perceptibly.

'No doubt you weel have the pleasure of meeting my third wife, Keety and her husband Lysander, Rupert's leetle catamite.'

Helen looked startled.

'I've always thought Rupert and Billy, his best friend, were unnaturally close, but Rupert's always been aggressively heterosexual.'

'Typical homophobic behaviour,' said Rannaldini dismissively.

'Not a very intellectual Christmas for you, my dear. At least you can enjoy the sainted Taggie's cooking.'

SIXTEEN

Helen arrived at Penscombe on Christmas Eve and hadn't been in the house five minutes before Taggie realized what a dreadful mistake it had been to invite her.

She had put Helen in the most charming spare room, overlooking the lake and the valley and newly decorated with powder-blue walls, daffodil-yellow curtains and a violet-and-pink checked counterpane. Flames danced in the grate, and on the bedside table were a flowered tin of shortbread still warm from the oven and Christmas roses in a silver vase.

Helen immediately pointed out that Taggie was so lucky to be able to afford to redecorate and this was the room she'd so often slept in after fearful rows with Rupert. Then, when Taggie stammeringly offered to move her, Helen sighed that all Penscombe reminded her of how unhappy she had been.

Taggie was also desperately worried about Marcus, who had driven his mother over and who looked absolutely wretched, and was already getting on Rupert's nerves.

'Why does he keep saying "Oh, right," when it plainly isn't?'

Unlike Helen, who drooped about not helping at all, Marcus, despite his asthma exacerbated by Rupert's dogs, insisted on carrying in endless baskets of logs, chopping onions until he cried, spending hours peeling potatoes, apples and, most fiddly of all, sweet chestnuts. In return, Taggie had had the ancient yellow toothed piano in the orange drawing-room tuned but every time Marcus tried to practise Rupert's terriers started howling.

Marcus, in turn, was also desperately worried about Helen.

'I'm sure she's having a nervous breakdown,' he confided to Taggie. 'She won't stop crying.'

He felt as ineffectual as the flakes of snow that were drifting down and losing themselves in the rain-drenched lawn and the gleaming wet paving stones.

'They always say the first Christmas is the worst,' said Taggie sympathetically.

What neither of them realized was that Helen was only suicidal because Rannaldini hadn't been in touch since Prague – not a telephone call, not even a Christmas card. She was far too proud to tell anyone that he had dumped her after a one night stand, just because she was spending Christmas with his enemy.

Christmas Day was even more fraught. Among the guests at Penscombe was Rupert's father, a merry old Lothario, just liberated from his fifth marriage.

Having opened and drunk all the miniature bottles in his stocking before breakfast, he spent the day plastered, pinching bottoms and calling Taggie and Helen by each other's names.

Opening presents had also been a nightmare because Helen, who seemed to have been given so little, insisted on watching everyone else open their presents.

'I'm honestly not interested in material possessions,' she kept saying quite untruthfully.

She was in addition appalled that despite Marcus's

entreaties, Rupert had not used Christmas to slip her a large cheque or announce that in future he would be giving her an allowance.

Tabitha was also acting up dreadully. After two and a half years she still carried a torch for Lysander who with Kitty had been invited to Christmas dinner. She was insanely jealous that Xav and Bianca seemed to have been given many more presents than her.

Finally she was enraged because Rupert had only given her a new car, a dark green Golf convertible, for Christmas when she'd wanted a brilliant young event-horse called The Engineer. Rupert, however, had desisted because Tabitha had ploughed all her GSCE exams in the summer and because the asking price of twenty thousand pounds for the horse was too high.

This omission had triggered off a blazing row which was exacerbated by Tabitha's refusal to come to Matins.

'What have I got to thank God for?' she shouted. 'He hasn't given me Lysander or The Engineer and I don't know why you're uptight about my GCSEs – your wife's never passed an exam in her life.' With that, she stormed out banging the door.

Unable to cope with his first wife at any time Rupert spent most of Christmas Day out of the house. Traditionally the grooms had the day off, so he used it as a marvellous excuse to escape with Lysander to the yard to do the horses.

He was in a twitchy mood anyway because there had been a lot of dropped telephone calls since yesterday. Rupert was only too aware of how beautiful and young his wife was, and he suspected Dr Benson's handsome new partner and Kevin, the leftie social worker, who'd overseen Xav and Bianca's adoption, of both being in love with her. Ghastly Kevin had even given Taggie a rose for Christmas which had been planted outside the back door, and which Rupert kicked everytime he passed.

And now Kev had had the temerity to drop in – natch

at drinks time – bringing Colombian wooden dolls for Xav and Bianca. He had been invited to stay on for smoked salmon and champagne by Taggie, desperate to provide Helen, very frosty from being called 'Taggie' and having her bottom pinched by Rupert's father, with some intelligent conversation. Helen, who was now nose to nose on the sofa talking to Kevin about Nepalese folk music, winced in anticipation of the inevitable upheaval as Rupert swept in followed by Xavier and his usual pack of dogs.

Seeing Rupert's bootfaced expression Kevin tried to humour him.

'This little chap's new,' he said, pointing to an adorably floppy black labrador puppy with hooded tobacco-brown eyes and vast paws, who was romping with Rupert's lurcher, Nimrod.

'He's mine,' said Xav, joining both dogs on the floor. 'Daddy gave him to me for Christmas. He's called Bogotá.'

'You never stop nagging me to find Xav a black friend, Kevin,' drawled Rupert. 'And now I have.'

'I didn't mean—' began Kev, his Adam's apple wobbling furiously.

'Of course you didn't,' said Helen in outrage. 'Why must you trivialize everything, Rupert? One simply cannot underestimate the importance of ethnic origins.'

'Why aren't you living in America then?' snapped Rupert.

'Rupert,' said Taggie appalled, which gave Rupert the excuse he needed.

'I know when I'm not wanted,' he said and, gathering up Xav, stalked out of the house.

Running after him, but failing to catch him, Taggie returned to the drawing-room.

'It's so sad,' Helen was saying to Kev, 'that Rupert hasn't got any easier over the years.' Then, turning to Taggie, said, 'I'm afraid I can't cope with scenes like that, I'm going to lie down.'

There should have been eleven for dinner, five women and six men. As well as Lysander and Kitty, Taggie had invited Lysander's father, David Hawkley, who, as a handsome widower and a headmaster, would have been perfect for Helen, but unable to face an English winter he had pushed off to Mykenos. Tab's boyfriend, Damian, whom she tolerated as second best to Lysander, had taken umbrage, after being called a leftie yobbo by Rupert once too often, and ducked out as well. Then, after a mysterious telephone call this morning, Rupert's father Eddie had asked if he could bring a woman friend, which meant they were two women extra.

Pre-dinner drinks were scheduled for seven-thirty. By seven o'clock Taggie had reached screaming pitch. The geese were sizzling enticingly, the Christmas pudding bubbling, the red cabbage, the celery purée, the crème de marron were warming gently in the left of the Aga and the potatoes cut round and as small as olives only needed frying very fast in clarified butter at the last moment.

Bianca, however, had been given a maddening Christmas present – a cordless toy telephone which rang when she pressed a button and which everyone, particularly an increasingly jumpy Helen, kept mistaking for the real thing.

In addition, Taggie had been driven crackers all afternoon listening to the chatter of Mrs Bodkin, Rupert's ancient housekeeper, who was more hindrance than help, and refereeing fights beween dogs and children. These had culminated in a screaming fit from Bianca, because a bored Nimrod had chewed the feet off Kevin's Colombian doll. This had resulted in Taggie shouting at Bianca and dispatching a disapproving Mrs Bodkin to take her up to bed.

And Rupert wasn't even here to write out the place names for her; it would be so humiliating if she spelt them all wrong in front of Helen. She couldn't ask

Marcus as he'd gone off to collect Flora, who, to Helen's irritation, he had invited for moral support.

Taggie was panicking; she hadn't even changed when there was a knock and a plump, smiling face came round the door.

'Oh Kitty,' said Taggie and burst into tears.

'Whatever's the matter?' Kitty dumped brandy butter, winter fruit salad, apple sauce and mince pies down on the kitchen table.

'Everything,' sobbed Taggie. 'Tab's in a screaming strop. Rupert's pushed off to the pub and I don't think he'll ever speak to me again for giving Ann-Marie Christmas week off and asking Helen to stay. And she's been just awful. She hasn't lifted a finger and can't stop looking at everything and saying, "New picture, new carpet, new sofa," and it's years since she b-b-buggered off and Rupert and Lysander have worked so hard and done so well in the last two years, we're entitled to have something new.'

Kitty patted Taggie's heaving shoulders; she'd never seen her friend in such a state.

'I'm sorry,' sniffed Taggie. 'And I've been vile to poor darling Bianca, and I haven't said hallo to you, Arthur, are you having a nice Christmas?'

Arthur nodded. A blond, beaming bruiser just two and a quarter and capable of causing considerable havoc, he was clutching a toy trumpet. Having wriggled out of his blue duffle-coat, he was only interested in finding his hero, Xavier.

'Xavier's not back yet, darling,' said Taggie. 'He's pushed off with his rotten father.'

'Go and change,' said Kitty soothingly. 'Lysander's gone to the pub to get some drink. He'll bring Rupert back. I'll take care of everything.'

'If you could keep an eye on the goose and feed the dogs, and put out a bowl of puppy food for Xav's puppy when he gets back. You do look nice,' Taggie admired Kitty's blue wool dress.

'It's a bit 'ot,' admitted Kitty, 'Lysander gave it to me. I'm ashamed we've had such a lovely day. Arfur and I didn't get up till lunch-time and Lysander came back to bed after he and Rupert had done the 'orses, and you've been slaving away.'

Wearily Taggie climbed the stairs to Bianca's bedroom where there was no lack of ethnic reminders. The yellow walls were covered with posters of Colombian countryside, sweeps of orchids, giant water-lilies and the lake where El Dorado's gold was hidden which looked like a green yolk in a jagged grey eggshell of rock.

Bianca was never angry for long. Now, wearing new red pyjamas covered in reindeer, her dark curls tied on top of her head to keep them dry in the bath, she was bending over a doll's pram putting her new footless doll to bed.

'No, you tut up, Rosie,' she was saying sternly, 'I've been working my ass off all day for you.'

Giving a gasp of horrified laughter, Taggie gathered up Bianca and covered her with kisses.

'Oh my angel, I'm sorry I swore at you. I love you so much.'

With her pale coffee-coloured skin flushed from the bath, her big black eyes and her loving smile, Bianca was the most beautiful child in the world, and had the sweetest nature, although spoilt rotten by everyone.

'Mummy tired, mummy crying,' said Bianca, then reaching over she pressed her new telephone.

'Hallo,' she said, 'I'm afraid Rupert can't take your call at the moment.'

Taggie giggled.

'God knows what he's up to,' she took Bianca's hand. 'Come and talk to me while I get ready.'

But going into her bedroom, Taggie gave another utterly uncharacteristic howl of rage. Half her wardrobe had been pulled off its hangers and dropped on the floor, or on top of Nimrod, who was stretched out on the bed. He now raised a purple see-through shirt with his waving tail. Taggie's tights drawer had been ransacked and the only sheer black pair filched. The pale pink camisole top Rupert had given her for Christmas had vanished, as well as her new pale amethyst satin blazer.

Charging into the bathroom she found her make-up box upended, and shampoo, eye-drops, hair dryer and God knows what else, missing.

'Tabitha,' she screamed up the stairs, 'how fucking dare you?'

'Anything the matter?' Helen appeared out of the bedroom opposite.

Just your bloody daughter, Taggie wanted to shout.

But, clenching her fists, she managed to control herself. 'Sorry, I was yelling at one of the dogs.'

There was a pause. Helen was wearing long black velvet with a scooped neckline showing off jutting collar bones. Deciding to look tragic rather than stunning, she had left off her jewellery except Malise's regimental brooch.

'What a lovely dress,' said Taggie dutifully.

'It's hanging off me,' quavered Helen, 'I've lost over a stone since Malise died.'

Shutting the door firmly behind her, she went on, 'And I don't have enough shoes to let Rupert's damn dogs eat them. I suppose he's not back. No? He was always disappearing like this when I was married to him.'

Going towards the stairs she jumped as the telephone rang.

'Hallo,' piped up Bianca. 'Is that Tabiffa? How fucking, fucking dare you.'

Taggie had no time to do more than wash, tie back her lank hair and put on a peacock-blue dress covered with red poppies, which Rupert loathed but which was the only uncreased thing in her wardrobe.

'Have a drink,' she said going into the drawing-room.

'Oh, champagne,' sighed Helen, 'I wish I could afford it at home.'

She was obviously bored with Kitty who, encased in her blue wool, was getting pinker by the minute.

How could Rannaldini have married and been upset by the departure of such a frump? wondered Helen.

Everyone, except Helen, was cheered up by the arrival of Flora who was wearing a grey silk shirt tucked into black velvet knickerbockers. Her red hair, tied back with a black bow, had all the shine and bounce that Helen's had lost. She was also weighed down with presents: a Body Shop basket for Helen; Beethoven sonatas played by his hero Pablo Gonzales for Marcus; a tape called 'Let's Ride to Music' for Rupert – 'I thought your father would at least know "The Galloping Major"; and a long clinging silver-grey silk jersey cardigan for Taggie.

'Oh bliss,' cried Taggie overjoyed.

'Marcus said your eyes were silver-grey.'

'I'll put it on straightaway. Marcus, darling, can you open another bottle?'

'Isn't this room gorgeous?' Flora looked round, then seeing Helen looking broody and sensing her despair, Flora delved into her carrier bag.

'I forgot. Boris sent you this, Mrs Gordon.'

'How very dear of Boris.'

'It was dear,' said Flora, 'cost most of Boris's last advance from the BBC and it's the first present he's ever wrapped up. "I cannot cope with this chello tape," he kept saying.'

'Open it, Mum,' urged Marcus, but Helen had put it on a side-table.

'Where's Grandpapa?' asked Marcus.

'Gone to collect his mystery guest,' giggled Kitty. 'It's like *What's My Line*? Is she in show business? Does she provide a service?'

'That's probably them,' said Helen, as the dogs barked, but soon the barks turned to wimpers of excitement as Lysander weaved in, beautiful in a dinner-jacket and already drunk.

Having kissed Kitty in delight, hugged Flora, who was an old friend, clapped an arm round Marcus's shoulder and shaken Helen's hand, he proceeded to tell them what a wonderful time he and Rupert had had in the pub, and how much Xav had won on the fruit machine.

Lysander was a beautiful rider and his sympathy with horses had contributed hugely to Rupert's successful transition to the flat.

'Marcus says you've done brilliantly,' Flora told him.

'I did brilliantly at Christmas,' giggled Lysander, 'look what Arthur gave me.' Raising a leg to show off luminous Father Christmas socks, he nearly fell over.

How could Kitty have left Rannaldini for such a silly boy? thought Helen in amazement.

Lysander nearly fell over again when Taggie walked in wearing her new silver cardigan. Like Penscombe streams in the winter sunshine, it glittered so radiantly on her long slim body that no-one noticed her lank hair or her laddered tights.

A second later she was followed by Xav storming in on a new motorized tractor, followed by Bogotá and Nimrod, fighting noisily over a chewstik shoe. Xav had a glossy pudding-basin hair-cut these days. His eyes were speculative, arrogant and almost straight. He had been so happy since he moved to Penscombe that he had acquired all the confidence of a young rajah.

'Where's your father?' asked Taggie through gritted teeth.

'Changing,' said Xavier.

'He's changed.' Rupert sauntered in doing up his cuff-links, and headed straight for Taggie who ducked her head when he tried to kiss her.

'You're an absolute shite,' she hissed.

'I am a shite in wining armour.'

'It is not funny. There are masses of bottles to open and no-one's done the seating plan.'

'Good, I can sit next to you, you are so beautiful.'

'And you are so drunk and late.'

Rupert tried to pull himself together. 'Go and open the red wine,' he ordered Marcus. 'And get some logs. We haven't met.' He nodded at Flora, then seeing Kitty, now scarlet in her blue dress, said, 'Evening, Mrs Hawkley, you're well rugged up.'

Kitty was terrified of Rupert and he, in turn, didn't see the point of her at all, but she kept Lysander on the rails and got him up in the morning, even if she did look like boiled bacon.

'Did you bring me a present?' Xav asked Flora.

'I certainly did, but you've got to share it with Arthur and Bianca,' said Flora, handing him a large box of chocolate willies, which triggered off screams of laughter and excitement.

Only Helen looked disapproving. Typical Flora. What with his ex-wife and his cast-off, she was reminded of Rannaldini at every turn. And now Tabitha had stalked in, ravishing in Taggie's pink camisole top and amethyst blazer, a purple mini round her groin, clean blond hair flopping over her angry blue eyes and flawless skin.

'Lovely jacket,' murmured Flora enviously.

'That's Taggie's,' snapped Rupert.

'So?' Tabitha glared at her father.

'I lent it to her,' mumbled Taggie. Oh, why was she so wet? Unable to face a showdown she fled to the kitchen where Marcus was opening bottles of *Château Latour* and had lit all the candles in the dining-room.

'You are an angel,' sighed Taggie.

At least the little potatoes were a perfect golden brown as she topped them with chopped parsley. The smell of truffle-flavoured goose was too much for the dogs who formed a slavering crescent round Taggie as she edged them out of the oven.

'You're so lucky to be able to escape to the kitchen.' It was Helen's shrill voice again. 'You shouldn't be humping logs, Marcus. Hi, Mrs Bodkin,' Helen embraced her old housekeeper. 'Surely you're not working on Christmas Day. We used to get village girls in in the old days.'

You are definitely going to get this boiling fat in your face in a minute, vowed Taggie. It was twenty-past eight, everything would be ruined if Eddie didn't show up soon.

'Can't wait to see my father's latest bimbo.' Rupert refilled everyone's glasses.

Then, over more barking, a deep voice cried; 'Coo-ee, everyone, we're here.'

'Oh no.' Flora looked at Marcus in horror.

'*Timeo Danaos et prima donna ferentes,*' sighed Marcus.

The next moment, Eddie, wearing a dinner-jacket green with age, and leering like Old Steptoe, walked in with Hermione, who was wrapped in a cranberry-red wool cloak with an ermine-lined hood looking as deeply silly as she did stunning.

'So caring of you to include me in your festivities,' she said, advancing on a flabbergasted Rupert with out-stretched hands.

'I didn't know you knew my father.'

'Eddie and I are old friends,' said Hermione with a roguish twinkle. 'Other dear friends begged me to sing at their Christmas Eve soirée, it was so late when I got to bed and the Christmas Day flights are so hopeless, Eddie persuaded me to fly out tomorrow.'

'Where are you going?' asked Rupert.

'To Rannaldini's, where else? My partner Bobby and little Cosmo are already out there. Rannaldini's taken a Bohemian castle for the festive season, he likes to have all his children and ex-wives around him.'

'Not all,' said Lysander, putting an arm round Kitty.

'Oh, there you are, Kitty,' Hermione ignored Lysander. 'What's happened to my *Merry Widow* contract?'

Sliding out of her red cloak and a red-and-white Hermes scarf, she handed them to Eddie.

'Put them in the hall, dear, and bring in my gifts.'

She was looking wonderful in boned red velvet with a bell skirt which showed off her comparatively small waist and pretty legs. A huge ruby pendant glowed above her big breasts.

I cannot believe this, thought Helen in mounting hysteria, Rannaldini's ex-wife, his cast-off and now his mistress.

Having handed round CDs of her latest hit, 'Santa of the Universe', Hermione was now embracing Taggie before presenting her with a box of last year's crystallized fruits and the salmon-pink gladioli, wrinkled in their Cellophane, which she'd been presented with the night before.

Barely acknowledging Flora, whom she detested, she turned joyfully on Helen.

'How are you? How are you? We met many moons ago with Rannaldini at Bagley Hall.'

'How is he?' whispered Helen.

'Oh, full of beans. He was telling me your late husband—' Hermione bowed her dark head. 'I'm so sorry, we won't discuss it – wrote a wonderful book on the flute. I want you to have an advance copy of "Only for Lovers".'

Helen looked down at the CD case which showed a smirking Rannaldini with his hands on Hermione's bare shoulders.

'Thank you,' she mumbled, then leapt as the telephone rang. Rannaldini must have got the number from Hermione, but Rupert had already picked it up.

'Cun I speak to Tubitha?' he said acidly. 'Can't you ever find a boyfriend who speaks the Queen's English?'

Snatching up the telephone, Tabitha flounced out.

Helen was looking round at the Turner of Cotchester Cathedral against a rain dark sky, at the Landseer of mastiffs and the Stubbs of two chestnut mares under an oak tree.

'That's new,' she said, nodding beadily at the Lucian Freud of a whippet and a rather muscular nude.

'It reminded me of Nimrod,' Rupert smiled down at his lurcher, who was striped black and brown like a bull's eye.

Having romped all day with his new friend Bogotá, Nimrod was stretched out on the sofa, fawn belly speckled with mud, paws in the air, chewstik shoe in his mouth, gazing adoringly up at his master out of one shiny onyx eye.

'What used to hang in its place?' asked Helen perplexed.

'The Ingres, I sold it.'

'How could you?' said Helen appalled.

'I hate big dark lard-like women,' said Rupert, glaring at Hermione, who bored with charming Eddie, came bounding towards him. Rupert was her real prey.

'What happened to that Colombian lad you were thinking of adopting?'

'He's here,' said Rupert, beckoning Xav.

Getting no reaction from the boy's impassive, watchful face, Hermione cooed: 'May I have one of your chocolates?'

As she helped herself, putting her red lips over the knob, Lysander got such giggles he had to hide behind the curtain.

'I bet you don't know what my name is,' Hermione smiled winningly.

'Yes I do,' said Xav.

'Bet you don't.'

'Yes I do. It's Mrs Fat Bum.'

'Rupert's father's brought a bumbo,' murmured Flora, as a shaking Lysander disappeared again.

'Dinner,' announced Taggie.

All Taggie's efforts to make the dining-room look pretty had paid off. The pale scarlet walls and ivy-green curtains were echoed by a centrepiece of snowdrops, holly and Christmas roses. The only lighting reflected in glass and silver came from the flickering fire, fifty white candles and the picture lights over the family portraits.

'That was me,' said Eddie, nodding at a handsome youth in uniform.

'Oh, what a relief,' Helen's voice quavered. 'You've changed nothing here.'

'Except wives,' said Rupert. That'll teach her to be nicer to Taggie, he thought, as Helen brimmed and bit her lip.

Rupert, on the other hand, had taken a shine to Flora and, as there was no seating plan, put her on his left with Hermione as the lesser of three evils on his right, and Helen between her and Eddie, who was on Taggie's right. Marcus, Tabitha, Lysander and Kitty could sort themselves out.

'It's perfect,' he called out to Taggie as he cut into the goose, dropping the first slice into Nimrod's waiting jaws.

'That's far too much for me,' whimpered Helen as he handed her the first plate.

'I'll have it,' said Hermione, piling on most of the little brown potatoes.

Having filled up glasses and handed round the vegetables, Marcus found himself sitting next to Kitty. She might have a face like boiled bacon, but she was so adorable and, having worked for Rannaldini, had lots of gossip about soloists, conductors and helpful agents.

She refused red wine, when he tried to fill up her glass, because she was having another baby.

'Lysander's coming to the ante-natal classes,' she said proudly.

'I love rolling around on the floor with a lot of women,' yelled a jubilant Lysander down the table.

'That goose was something else,' sighed Flora, finally putting her knife and fork together.

'Have some more,' said Taggie.

'Yes please,' said Eddie.

Tabitha didn't even bother to toy with a piece of goose as she read Dick Francis under the table.

Please give me Lysander, she prayed.

Please let Rannaldini call, prayed her mother.

'I think we ought to drink to the cook,' said Eddie, with his mouth full, 'To Helen,' he said, draining his glass.

Everyone, except Helen, howled with laughter.

'I love you,' mouthed Rupert down the table at Taggie.

'I think we ought to drink to absent friends,' Hermione smiled round, 'Bobby and Cosmo.'

'Abby,' said Flora and Marcus.

'And Malise,' said Helen with a sob.

'Of course,' said Rupert, 'Malise!'

After everyone drained their glasses there was an embarrassed pause.

'And I think we ought to drink to absent fiends,' said Flora, as Rupert filled her glass again. 'To Rannaldini!'

SEVENTEEN

The flickering bright blue halo had retreated like a genie into the Christmas pudding. *Château d'Yquem* gleamed topaz in the wine glasses. Gertrude, Taggie's little mongrel, bristled in a green paper admiral's hat on her mistress's lap. Xav, who never seemed to go to bed, was sprawled on his father's knee, tunelessly singing 'Cars in the bright sky look down where He lay' because it made Rupert laugh.

Why doesn't my father love me a millionth as much as that? thought Marcus wistfully. He was so frantic to practise he was beginning to twitch like a junkie. All the pieces he'd been learning seemed to be sliding away. Across the table his mother looked shell-shocked.

'I cannot believe you are forty-four,' Hermione was telling her. 'I hope I'll be as lovely as you when I reach your age.'

'Which is in about two minutes,' said Flora crossly.

'Why don't you take an evening class?' urged Hermione. 'There are courses for antique restoration, archery, ball-room dancing – you might find a new chap there. They've even got a class for understanding teenagers.'

'My father would profit from that,' said Tabitha

acidly, glancing up from Dick Francis. 'Where's Grandpa?' she asked Marcus.

'Ringing my grand-mugger,' said Xav.

'I didn't ask you, smart ass,' snapped Tabitha.

'It's true.' Rupert came to Xavier's defence. 'He proposes to her every Christmas.'

Bored with counselling, Hermione looked sourly at Xav, still on Rupert's knee, which was exactly where Hermione would like to have been. Rupert had always had a strong head, but he had drunk so much during the day, and Xav's eyes were so much improved that it was debatable as to which of them was now squinting the most.

'Very caring to take on a coloured lad,' observed Hermione.

'Piss orf,' drawled Xav in exactly the same bored voice as Rupert.

Lysander got the giggles again.

'Why don't you run along to bed,' suggested Hermione. 'You could play my cradle song tape, or Mummy could read to you.'

'Mummy can't read,' said Xav. 'I'll be reading to her soon.'

'High time you went to boarding-school, young man,' said Hermione irritably. 'Are you going to Harrow?'

'Eventually,' said Rupert forking up Christmas pudding at great speed. 'This is miraculous, Tag.'

'I suppose King Faisal went there,' mused Hermione. 'But I do feel single-sex boarding schools encourage homosexuality.'

'Not nearly so much as women like you,' said Rupert coldly.

Hermione burst into merry laughter.

'You are a tease.' Then, turning to Marcus, she asked pointedly, 'Did you go to Harrow?'

'No, he went to Bagley Hall,' said Taggie quickly, seeing Marcus go scarlet, 'As a day-boy because of his asthma.'

'Have you got a girl friend?' persisted Hermione.

'He's got me,' piped up Flora, noticing how Helen winced.

Hermione also shot Flora a not-much-cop glance and, mistakenly thinking she would endear herself to Rupert by being good with a miserably squirming Marcus, asked: 'How long have you had asthma?'

'All my life, I think.'

'They say it's inherited,' Hermione was determined to keep Rupert's attention.

'Must have skipped a generation, then,' said Rupert, as Eddie returned to the table and pretended to admire Hermione's ruby pendant in order to gaze down her front. 'Marcus gets his heavy breathing from my father.'

God, Rupert's a bitch, thought Flora and, to distract everyone, held her cracker out to Xav. This and subsequent bangs sent all the dogs, including Gertrude, racing out of the room. Xav slid off Rupert's knee in pursuit of his puppy.

Feeling terribly sorry for Marcus, Kitty, who was wearing a paper crown redder than her face, asked him if he'd had some nice presents.

'Marvellous, Dad and Taggie gave me some lightweight tails, one gets so hot in concerts.'

'Now you've got to get some work to try them out,' said Rupert.

'Hasn't he told you,' cried Flora, 'he's too flaming modest, he's got a recital in Cotchester Town Hall on 21 February. You've all got to come.'

Marcus smiled deprecatingly at the excited faces, but his moment of glory was short-lived.

'Talking of special occasions, I'm going on *Desert Island Discs* on Saturday at seven-thirty,' announced Hermione. 'My agent Howie Denston said that at least Sue Lawley and I have lovely legs in common. I hope you'll all tune in.'

'Better alert the monkeys to evacuate the island,' muttered Rupert.

Looking up from the tangerine she was peeling, Taggie hastily asked what records Hermione had chosen.

'All my own – so fascinating to compare the different accompanists – and conductors. Rather exciting – the programme coincides with a special New Year announcement.' She beamed at Rupert.

'Do tell us,' asked Taggie.

'My lips are sealed. But I'm dying to see the inside of Buckingham Palace,' she added roguishly. 'Have you ever wanted a knighthood, Rupert?'

'No.'

'Lady Thatcher offered him one twice,' said Taggie quickly.

'Because I have it on good authority that Rannaldini is going to get his K in the New Year's Honours list.'

'Sir Roberto,' said Flora flatly. 'That should increase his pulling power.'

'He can have one-Knight stands,' said Lysander.

Unable to take the roars of drunken laughter, Helen fled the room. Outside she ignored Nimrod and Bogotá, who were engaged in a furiously, growling tug-of-war over Hermione's Hermes scarf.

Going in search of Helen five minutes later, Taggie found her washing up in the kitchen, rubber-gloved hands whisking round the hot suds, glasses upside down on a tea-towel.

'Poor Mrs Bodkin looks so tired, I thought I'd give her a hand.' The reproach was implicit. 'It's lovely and cool in here, I always find goose a bit rich.'

'I'm sorry,' mumbled Taggie, 'I'll take people upstairs, and then we can have coffee.'

I'm being a bitch, thought Helen miserably, but I can't help it. Taggie's got everything – youth, looks, children, Rupert's love and the beautiful house and garden which was once mine.

Although Lysander beamed drunkenly across the table

at him, Marcus had never felt more *de trop* than when left pretending to drink port with the men, who talked non-stop about horses.

Tomorrow, Lysander and Rupert would hunt until two, then the helicopter would take them and Eddie to Kempton in time for Penscombe Pride's big race at three-thirty.

'He'll walk it,' said Lysander.

Marcus took another surreptitious squirt from his inhaler. The steroids he'd been taking to combat his allergy to dogs and new paint had given him a wretched sore throat.

'Should be a good crowd out tomorrow,' said Eddie. 'Always liked the Boxing Day Meet, mind you hunting's gone to the dogs since so many people who do their own horses come out.'

Fortunately for Marcus, Flora put on 'Let's Ride to Music', and 'The Galloping Major', thundering through the house, soon flushed out the men.

'Boom, boom, boom,' went the regimental drums as screaming with drunken laughter Eddie and Flora, cheek to cheek, clasped hands outstretched, trotted up the hall to 'D'you ken John Peel', followed by Lysander and Kitty, and Rupert and Taggie, then broke into a canter to 'Bonny Dundee' with a pack of dogs barking excitedly behind them.

'Right wheel, halt, dismount,' shouted Rupert as the band swung into *Aida* which had been his and Eddie's old regimental march.

Unfortunately Hermione, returning from a respray upstairs, couldn't resist singing very loudly along, so everyone gave up marching and allowed her to put on 'Santa of the Universe' jumping out of their skins as 'Hark the Herald Angels' filled the house.

'What with my first wife continually hitting the roof and Hermione taking it off, I'm not going to have a slate over my head soon,' grumbled Rupert.

Flora, Rupert, Marcus, Kitty and Tabitha, who'd actually put down Dick Francis, were playing consequences. Taggie, who was too slow at writing to play, was handing out liqueurs. Lysander, an even slower writer, was playing chess with Eddie, who was telling him about Rupert's mother.

'Played chess together during the first dark days of the war when no-one knew if Hitler was going to strike. Wonderful woman, turned me down again this evening – know we'll end up together.'

Hermione, meanwhile, had rather startled Rupert by sinking to the floor at his feet, her dark head in danger of being singed by his cigar. He'd go off piste down her cleavage in a minute.

'Where are we?' he asked

'Woman's name,' said Flora.

Putting down his cigar, Rupert wrote 'Hermione'. Handing his turned-over piece of paper to Tabitha, he touched her hand. The rows over The Engineer had upset him very much, he'd probably buy her the damn horse in the end.

Eddie and Lysander were so drunk they couldn't remember whose move it was.

'Think I should marry her?' Eddie nodded in Hermione's direction.

'God, no,' Lysander turned pale. 'She's awful.'

'Damn fine looking, damn rich, sort out my Lloyd's lorses.'

'Not worth it, anyway she's got a husband.'

'Must be loopy to leave a beautiful woman like that at Christmas.'

'He's gay.'

'Whaddja mean?'

'Queer.'

'Good God.' Eddie's teeth nearly fell out.

Lysander giggled. 'Don't let her get her Santa Claws into you.'

'Ha, ha, ha, ha, Santa Claws, that's good,' Eddie choked on his third glass of port.

'*Good King Wenceslarse looked out*,' sang Hermione on CD and in real life.

I cannot stand it, thought Helen, who was perched on the arm of Marcus's chair. I've seen King Wensceslas' statue on the Charles Bridge, she wanted to shout, and he wasn't good at all, and the stupid story about St Agnes' fountain and the pine logs is garbage. But none of these drunken philistines would be remotely interested unless she told them she had been on the bridge with Rannaldini.

Sensing her anguish, Marcus reached back to retrieve Boris's present.

'Please open it, Mum, it's really nice.'

'Do have a drink,' pleaded Taggie.

Helen shook her head violently, sending tears flying out of her eyes.

The group round the fire had finished the first round of their consequences.

'You start, Tabitha,' said Flora.

Tabitha unrolled her piece of paper. 'Penscombe Pride,' she began, in her flat little voice, then starting to smile, 'met Hermione – on top of the muck heap, Pridie said: Give us a blow job. Hermione said to Pridie: I am about to have my period. Pridie gave her the clap, Hermione gave him a great kick up the ass, and the consequence was . . .' Tabitha burst out laughing.

'Tabitha,' protested Taggie, 'that's enough.'

'Why must you spoil everything?' Tabitha turned on her step-mother like a viper.

About to send her to bed, Rupert heard a clip-clop on the flagstones, and cheers and shouts of laughter greeted a grinning Xav, riding into the drawing-room on Tiny, Lysander's delinquent Shetland pony. Xav had got Tiny's measure completely and punched her on the nose if she ever tried to bite him, but he couldn't stop her lashing out at Hermione, sending the discomfited diva scrambling like a camel to her feet. Having vented her spleen, Tiny proceeded to hoover up the straw from Helen's Body Shop basket, until she encountered a pearl bath drop and curled up her lip.

'Quick, get a camera,' Rupert told Marcus.

But Tabitha had flipped.

'You never let me ride ponies into the house,' she screamed. 'That child is spoilt rotten, he got far more presents than Marcus and I put together. It's bloody unfair, you love him far more than you do us.'

'Bloody, bloody unfair,' beamed Bianca, appearing in the doorway with her telephone. 'Hallo, I'm afraid Tabiffa's in the bath.'

'And she's revoltingly spoilt, too,' yelled Tab. 'I was never allowed down at this hour.' And storming out, she slammed the door shaking every piece of china.

Helen burst into tears.

'Why is everyone always fighting in this house?' she sobbed. 'Why can't you all be nice to each other?'

You could start off by controlling your daughter, thought Flora mouthing, 'Don't worry' at Marcus.

'They should bring back National Service, particularly for women,' said Eddie. 'Checkmate.'

Appalled that Xav and Bianca could have caused such a terrible row, Taggie leapt forward to comfort Helen who was now wailing: 'I can't go on, I can't go on, oh Malise.'

'Take that pony back to the stable at once, Xav,' ordered Rupert.

'*In the bleak mid-winter,*' sang Hermione on the CD, as Mrs Bodkin put her head round the door:

'Telephone for Mrs Gordon.'

'Talk about the ungay Gordon,' grumbled Flora, as Helen shot out of the room, sending Boris's present flying, 'And that's five hundred pounds down the drain, poor Boris. She's a frightful drip,' she added.

Rupert agreed. 'God, I hope you marry Marcus.'

Looking into her eyes, which were the light emerald

of the winter barley rampaging over his fields, he picked up the sadness and remembered the gossip.

'Still hung up on Rannaldini.'

'I guess so, he recurs like malaria.'

'You could do better.'

'And I have to say that when I was at Bagley Hall, you were voted the man to whom we most wanted to lose our virginity.'

Rupert smiled.

'If I wasn't bespoke,' he jerked his head towards Taggie, who was anxiously pouring a glass of Armagnac for Hermione, 'I couldn't think of anything nicer.'

'You *will* go to Marcus's concert, won't you?' pleaded Flora.

But Rupert had been distracted by the return of Helen suddenly looking radiant, tears dried like raindrops in a heatwave. Bewildered by her mood swings, Marcus sloped off to check with Mrs Bodkin who had telephoned.

'He wouldn't give his name, but it was a foreign-sounding gentleman.'

Marcus so hoped it was Boris, who had been screwing up courage to ask Helen out. But when she finally opened his present, the beautiful porcelain nightingale had shattered into a hundred pieces.

Alone in the kitchen Taggie cried and cried. An exhausted Marcus had finally got Helen to bed. Arthur, woken by the din, had been taken home by Lysander and Kitty, who had annexed Flora as well. Tab wasn't in her room and had probably taken refuge with the grooms over the stables. Eddie had passed out on the sofa, leaving his teeth in one of Hermione's crystallized greengages. Taggie had put a duvet over him. Hermione's limo had borne her away to an early flight in the morning.

The dogs had collapsed on their bean bags. The dishwasher swished and swirled round the last consignment of rare glasses and coffee cups. Helen would have been appalled that Taggie hadn't washed them by hand.

Only Rupert and Gertrude, the mongrel, who had taken umbrage over the new puppy and the crackers, and escaped through the cat door, were missing. Nimrod, the lurcher, brought out a rubber cutlet he had been given for Christmas and squeaked it to make Taggie laugh. But she went on crying so he slunk back to his basket.

'I've lost my dog, my husband and the present list. No-one will know what anyone's given anybody,' sobbed Taggie.

She jumped at the crash of the cat door. There was a scampering of claws and in charged Gertrude, wearing Rupert's black tie, and hurled herself on Taggie.

She was followed by Rupert squinting worse than ever. A blond lock of hair had fallen over his forehead, an empty brandy bottle swung between his fingers.

'Gertrude and I have been hiding, we don't want Mrs Fat Bum as a stepmother.'

'She's gone,' sobbed Taggie.

'Angel, what's the matter?'

'I wanted to show I was a better wife than Helen.'

'Oh, darling,' Rupert folded her in his arms. 'I'm sorry I've been such a shit, but I can't stand my first wife, and I loathe Hermione and Marcus gets on my tits and Tabitha's impossible, and all I want to do is screw you stupid.'

'I'm stupid anyway,' said Taggie, but she stopped crying.

'I was such a wreck when I met you,' mumbled Rupert, 'Helen just reminds me how vile I was. You've taught me to love.' He kissed her wedding ring finger. 'You've twisted me straight. I've got a present for you.' Rootling in his pocket he produced a silver locket.

Inside were Daisy France-Lynch miniatures of Xav and Bianca.

Taggie nearly started crying again.

'Oh how lovely, I wish there was room inside for you as well. Oh, thank you.'

'I want a night inside your shining armour,' said Rupert, fumbling with the pearl buttons of her silver cardigan. 'I'm probably past it, but let's go and try.'

'Only if you promise to come to Marcus's concert,' said Taggie.

Unable to sleep, Marcus heard the two of them come to bed, softly laughing. Outside the clouds had rolled away leaving a pale grey sky so crowded with stars the constellations were indistinguishable. He had just made the agonizing decision that he couldn't go back to the Academy next term either. Tab would return to Bagley Hall in a fortnight, he couldn't leave Helen alone in the Old Rectory in this state.

EIGHTEEN

Dame Edith Spink, composer, conductor and musical director of Venturer Television and the Cotchester Chamber Orchestra, had been responsible for Marcus's recital in Cotchester.

Built like Thomas the Tank Engine, she had leant on Cotchester Musical Society of which she was president.

'Boy's extremely talented,' she boomed, glaring at the wilting committee through her monocle, 'and incredibly cheap for one hundred pounds.'

This was a considerable plus because the musical society never had any money.

Marcus had already learnt Chopin's *Grande Polonaise, The Bee's Wedding* and Beethoven's *Appassionata Sonata* for the concert he'd cancelled because of Malise's death so he decided to play them again. The *Appassionata* was fiendishly difficult, but it would be a compliment to Abby, who had dominated his thoughts throughout the long winter in Warwickshire, and who had promised to bring Rodney over from Lucerne for the concert. He would kick off with two Scarlatti sonatas and, then as a compliment to Boris, end the second half with his titanic *Siberian Suite*.

This had dismayed his piano teacher, Miss Chatterton, known at college as 'Chatterbox', when Marcus visited her in her leafy North London suburb the day before the concert.

'Levitsky isn't remotely audience-friendly,' Chatterbox absorbed modern jargon, then flogged it to death. 'The provinces hate contemporary music, particularly if they can't pronounce it. You'll have them leaving in droves. At least end with the Chopin so they've got something to look forward to.'

'The programme's already printed,' sighed Marcus. 'Anyway I can't let Boris down, he's so low.'

Boris's thumping great crush on his mother showed no signs of abating, even though Helen wasn't responding at all. She had hardly thanked Boris for the porcelain nightingale and, claiming she was too busy with Marcus's recital to see him, had thrown herself into the role of supportive mother with a vengeance.

The lovely golden walled cathedral town of Cotchester had been a royalist stronghold in the Civil War. After an appalling journey with wind and rain nearly sweeping him off the motorway, Marcus arrived around teatime at the town hall, a splendid baroque edifice two hundred yards down the High Street from Venturer Television.

His hopes of a peaceful couple of hours rehearsing were shattered by Helen who was standing on the steps pointing in horror at his poster and brandishing a programme.

'How could you bill yourself just as Marcus Black?'

'I don't want to cash in on Dad's name.'

'It's the only thing he's given you.'

'Except a lot of dosh,' protested Marcus, getting his dark suit and his music case out of the Aston.

'And why did you send them that awful photograph?' moaned Helen, 'Your hair was longer than his was.' She pointed disapprovingly at Charles I's statue in the centre of the Market Square.

'He was lucky only getting his head cut off.' Ruefully, Marcus stroked his own short back and sides.

'Looks much better,' said Helen, who, because Rupert was expected, had nagged him all week to have a haircut.

Marcus glared at his reflection in the dark mirror in the foyer.

'Everyone'll see my ears going bright red with nerves.'

'I hope you washed them.'

'Mu-um, they don't have opera glasses at recitals.'

Picking up the programme he gave a shout of laughter for above his name it said, in large letters: *An explosive new talent*, Dame Edith Spunk.

But Helen was in no mood for jokes. Last night the Cotswold Hunt, who seemed to epitomize Rupert's disreputable past, had hired the hall for their annual Hunt Ball.

Apart from a disgusting stench of drink and cigarettes, they had left three broken windows letting in a vicious east wind, a lot of sick in the Ladies, a pair of red knickers and some suspicious-looking stains on the sofa bed in Marcus's dressing-room. Even worse, there were drink rings, cigarette burns, spilt bourbon and candlewax all over the keys of a grand piano on which Marcus was expected to play.

Marcus was delighted. His hands sweated dreadfully before a concert and it would be far easier to grip the keys, particularly the black notes, of which there were thousands in the *F minor Appassionata*, if the piano were sticky and dirty. Alas, Helen then explained virtuously that she had already set to with a flurry of meths and righteous indignation. The keys were now so clean they would slip away from his fingers like minnows.

Soloists have been known to sandpaper down the ivories of concert grands to get a better grip. Rubenstein had even sprayed the keys with hair lacquer. But there was no way Marcus could find lacquer on a late Sunday afternoon.

Just managing not to snap at Helen, he was cheered by the number of cards and presents in his dressing-room, particularly when he found Abby had sent him a beautiful green-leather-bound copy of *The Tempest* postmarked Lucerne. Inside she had written:

> *This music crept by me upon the waters,*
> *Allaying both their fury, and my passion, With its*
> *sweet air.*
> *Good luck, Marcus,*
> *Warmest*
> *L'Appassionata.*

Marcus trembled with excitement as he smelt the faint trace of her scent on the pages.

Next he opened a silver shamrock from Declan O'Hara and a bottle of Moët from Flora's mother, both thanking him for the invitation to the recital, but regretting they would be away.

What invitation? Marcus felt a wave of anger. Helen had obviously been at work again. There were other good luck cards from famous friends of his parents he hadn't seen since he was a child.

As he hung up his suit in the cupboard, he found a pale gold silk dress with an Yves Saint Laurent label, which he hadn't seen before.

Outside, he could hear Helen saying: 'We're expecting Sir Rodney Macintosh, Declan O'Hara, Dame Edith, Boris Levitsky and Georgie Maguire and loads of students and teachers from the Academy. Marcus's father is flying back specially from the yearling sales in Florida. And, oh, I forgot, Abby Rosen's coming, yes the violinist, my son has a bit of a reputation as a lady's man.'

Rushing into the passage before Helen became even more cringe-making, Marcus found her talking to an old biddy in a long grey overcoat, who had the face of a rather overexcited dromedary and a drifting white bun like an icepack on top of her head.

Helen introduced her as Miss Smallwood, the social secretary.

'Our artist,' bleated Miss Smallwood eagerly. 'Are you like your father? Well, perhaps not,' she sounded slightly disappointed. 'I was wondering if you could give a little talk to our members before the concert.'

'A-a-absolutely n-n-not,' stammered Marcus. 'And Mum, Georgie and Declan can't make it.'

All he wanted to do was to get at the piano, slippery keys and all. He found the sound hard and bright in the treble, but after having 'Lydia Pinker' and 'American Pie' bashed out on it all last night, it was very woolly in the bass. He would have to pound the keys to make the left-hand lines in the *Appassionata* clear enough.

Nor, unlike the Cotswold Hunt, could the musical society afford to heat the hall which was getting colder by the minute. Marcus couldn't play if he were cold.

He couldn't play now. Helen, stationing herself bossily round the hall to test the accoustics, kept snapping his concentration.

'I can't hear you from here. You're very faint from here.' Then up in the gallery, where she found a white bra with Tabitha's name-tape inside. 'You really must project more from here.'

He'd reached screaming pitch when the piano tuner rolled up and proceeded to bang out Chopin's *Grande Polonaise* far better than he had, so Marcus retreated to the upright in his dressing-room to run through certain tricky passages only to be interrupted by Helen again.

Venturer Television, BBC Cotchester, *The Times* and *Classical Music* all wanted to interview him. Wasn't it exciting? As he wasn't prepared to give a little talk, she'd arranged a press conference with sandwiches and glasses of wine.

Marcus was aghast.

'I can't, Mum, for Christ's sake. They're only here because of Dad. I have to go into myself before a concert and be completely alone with the music.'

'Uh-uh,' Helen shook her head playfully. 'You're not going to have a moment to feel nervous.'

You mean you're not risking a re-run of the cock-up at Malise's funeral, thought Marcus.

'We're jolly well going to show Rupert this time,' said Helen.

Marcus started to shake and wheeze and took a couple of puffs from his inhaler. He'd already used it too much in the last forty-eight hours. His throat was very sore. He had the beginnings of a rash round his mouth.

Out of the window in the dusk, he could see the great shadow of the cathedral like a warning finger, and the wind pleating the flooded water meadows and lashing the trailing twigs of the weeping willows almost horizontal.

Marcus managed to smile at the Press, but he could hardly remember his date of birth. Only when they asked him which pianists he most admired he had no difficulty in saying Emil Gilels, Myra Hess and Solomon and, among the living, Pablo Gonzales. As he suspected, the Press were only interested in him in relation to Rupert.

But was trying to master that big black brute of a piano all that different to getting the best out of a difficult horse? he wondered. As a child Marcus's worst nightmare had been going into restaurants or to airports with Rupert, who so instantly and effortlessly attracted the limelight. It was ironic that he had chosen a profession entirely dependent on limelight. But it was the only way he could express himself and more recently, the only way he could tell Abby what he felt about her. But it was not to be. As the Press were trailing out, Abby telephoned.

'I'm so sorry, Marcus, but Rodney's been hospitalized with bronchitis. I guess it isn't serious but I daren't leave him. I know you'll be great and see you very soon.'

As Marcus put down the telephone almost weeping with disappointment, Miss Smallwood handed him some drooping crimson flowers.

'Hellebores from Dame Hermione's own garden,' she said reverently. 'Her gardener brought them all the way from Paradise. Dame Hermione wishes you all the luck in the world, but daren't risk a cold in this weather, such a caring person.'

By seven o'clock the hall was filling up with members of the musical society, variations on Miss Smallwood in flat shoes, long coats with triangles of brightly coloured scarves around their necks, all huddling together for warmth. Any hell fires fanned by the Cotswold Hunt Ball had receded long ago.

Two more telephone apologies came from Rupert's friend, Basil Baddingham and the Bishop of Cotchester, who both claimed to be laid low by the same bug. As a note of bathos the hunt saboteurs had got the night wrong and rolled up to wave placards saying: 'Cotswold Butchers' and 'Don't victimize our vixens' and generally hassle the Hunt Ball. Learning Rupert, who'd hunted with the Cotswold all his life, was expected later, they decided to hang around.

As Marcus changed into his dark suit and had fearful difficulty putting cuff-links into his grey-and-white striped shirt, he noticed the coloured windows of Cotchester Cathedral lit up for Evensong.

He should be the one on his knees praying for his hubris in thinking he could play the *Appassionata* and the *Siberian Suite*. Even the Chopin was so clear and linear, it gave you nowhere to hide and the left-hand part was just as challenging as the right.

Having showered and washed her hair, Helen had changed into the gold silk dress and wanted approval.

'You look stunning, Mum.'

'You really think so, and it goes with these shoes?'

'Perfect,' said Marcus dutifully.

241

'I guess I had to have something new. It's your first professional date.'

She has no idea, thought Marcus in despair, as he put on a crocus-yellow tie, bought for him by Flora to jazz up his whole outfit.

'Isn't that rather loud?' began Helen.

There was a rat-tat-tat on the door.

'Fifteen minutes, Mr Black,' cried Miss Smallwood, 'and Lady Baddingham's just arrived,' she added excitedly. 'But she's afraid Dame Edith has been struck down by the same dreaded lurgy as our bishop.'

Marcus fought an hysterical desire to laugh.

Monica Baddingham, Basil's sister-in-law, had caused an uproar last year when she had walked out on her vicious venal husband of nearly twenty-five years' standing and moved in with Dame Edith.

Such was Monica's popularity in the area – she had worked endlessly for charity and been kind to everyone and she seemed so blissfully happy with Dame Edith – that the scandal had blown over. Helen would normally have disapproved violently of such bohemian escapades, but realizing how influential Monica had suddenly become in the music world, she scuttled out to say hallo.

She was less amused by the arrival of a very jocund company from the Academy who conga-ed in led by Flora. In order to drink on the way down they had hired a minibus and had now stationed themselves on the left side of the hall so Marcus's ravishing female fan club could drool over him while he played.

Boris, also on the bus, was in a frightful state of nerves. His hair looked even more electrocuted than usual. He wore a grey track suit, the loose trousers of which kept falling down his chunky body, and his suede feet seemed to curl round each other like bear claws.

'I don't want *Siberian Suite* to be hackled.'

He was longing to sit next to Helen who meanly introduced him to Marcus's teacher, Miss Chatterton, so they could be nervous together.

'Do tell Marcus,' Miss Chatterton begged Helen, 'that the audience will only enjoy it if Marcus smiles and enjoys it, too.'

Not many people, thought Flora in disappointment. It was crucial to have bums on seats, because anyone who contemplated booking Marcus in future would check with Cotchester Musical Society whether he pulled the crowds.

Oh thank God, here was Taggie looking ravishing as always, in a dark red suit and rather tentatively leading Bianca by the hand. They were followed by Kitty, Mrs Bodkin, all Rupert's grooms and estate workers and finally, Tabitha, who might have been very jealous of Marcus if she had not received seventeen Valentines and been danced off her feet at the Hunt Ball.

The sight of Bianca, enchanting in a tartan, smocked wool dress with a white collar and dark green tights, gave Helen a legitimate excuse to express her jealousy of Taggie with a burst of anger.

'Is that wise? It's a long programme?'

Taggie flushed. 'Bianca adores Marcus, she'd have been heartbroken if I'd left her behind. If she starts acting up, I'll take her out, I promise. Hallo, Monica.' Taggie turned in delight to embrace Lady Baddingham, for whose dinner parties she had often cooked before she was married. 'Isn't this exciting? Edith's been so wonderful to arrange all this for Marcus.'

'Edith's hopping mad not to be able to make it,' said Monica, a big-boned handsome woman, whose red veins clashed merrily with her emerald-green coat, 'Is this one of your smalls?'

She beamed down at Bianca. 'Isn't she adorable? You can't start them off at concerts too early.'

Helen could have screamed.

'Where's Rupert?' she snapped.

'He should be here,' Taggie looked at her watch. 'I hope the fog isn't bad.'

'About a hundred and twenty,' said Miss Smallwood

counting heads. 'Not bad for a beastly February evening. It's nearly half-past, we ought to start.'

Marcus was hunched over the table in his dressing-room, panic about an impending asthma attack making him even more breathless. He couldn't let everyone down again. His reflection glittered silver with sweat in the mirror. Then Helen had burst in in a rage.

'Absolutely typical, your bloody father's helicopter's been grounded by fog. He and Lysander rang from the M4. They won't make it before the interval, if at all. So, we're going to start.'

A great calm swept over Marcus. At least Rupert wouldn't be bored witless or sneer at the low turn-out. Quickly he washed the sweat off his face and straightened his tie.

Nerves overwhelmed him again as he fell up the steps to the platform and sidled towards the piano, hangdog as the last person picked in a team.

'Please smile, Marcus,' begged Miss Chatterton.

'Will you nudge me when I'm meant to clap?' Taggie whispered to Monica Baddingham.

With a brief shy nod to acknowledge the rattle of applause, Marcus sat down, fiddled with the height of the piano-stool, gave his fingers a last wipe.

'Hair's too short,' muttered a member of his fan club.

'I like it, more butch,' said another.

'He's utterly gorgeous any way,' sighed a third.

On her right Flora noticed an old man in a beret getting out a score.

For a second Marcus sat clasping his hands to stop them shaking, then one seemed to escape like a white dove above the keys, then it fell in a skirl of bright notes, a weightless shimmer of sound and the Scarlatti was away.

Forgetting the cold, members of the Cotchester Musical Society smiled in relief. The estate workers and the grooms looked at each other in amazement – was this their sweet diffident Marcus?

At the end of the Scarlatti, Marcus got a splendid round of applause, augmented by the whooping, cheering and stamping feet of his friends from college.

'Good boy, Marcus,' piped up Bianca when there was a pause which set everyone laughing and clapping again.

As Marcus came on to play the *Appassionata* he was smiling. The bass was still woolly but suddenly the sound blossomed, producing such thrilling contrasts of loud and soft, of tender and so fierce that the big black piano shook on its legs.

How could such unleashed forces be contained in such a slender, youthful body, wondered the audience, marvelling, too, at every angelic ripple of sound as Marcus captured not only the nobility but also plumbed the extraordinary depths and dramas of the piece.

Part of the intense pleasure for Marcus's friends was to see the almost unearthly happiness on his face. Flora clutched herself in ecstasy and looking round noticed a tear like an icicle glittering on the wrinkled cheek of the old man in the beret.

The middle movement was so beautiful as theme and variations chased each other round the keyboard that the tears sprung in Marcus's eyes, too.

But, as he lingered over the runs and pauses which bridge the second and last movement, he told himself that he must keep something in reserve for the fireworks of the finale.

Allegro non Troppo, Beethoven had warned. He had known the dangers that awaited the unwary pianist, the temptation to show off and run out of puff.

Marcus was usually nervous as the end approached, like the last looming fence in the show-jumping ring. This evening he was utterly confident. But, as he tensed himself to leap into the fray, there was a kerfuffle at the back of the hall.

'You can't go in now,' cried Miss Smallwood.

'I can do what I fucking like,' drawled an all-too-familar voice. 'We've come all the way from America to hear this bloody concert.' And Rupert stalked up the aisle, trailing a red-faced Lysander.

'Daddy,' crowed Bianca.

Rupert proceeded to kiss an enraged Taggie, climb over her to his seat and shove Lysander into the one beyond next to Kitty.

Last time Rupert had been to a concert was at the end of term at Bagley Hall, when the auditorium had been packed to bursting because it was compulsory for all four hundred and fifty pupils, their parents and eighty teachers to attend.

A hundred odd people huddled in the stalls, many of them dingily old and plain, didn't seem a very satisfactory turn-out.

'Not many people here,' he muttered to Taggie.

'Shut up,' she hissed.

'Tut up, Daddy,' reproached Bianca.

Glancing up, Rupert saw Marcus, huddled over the piano staring at him in terror, a baby hare caught in the headlights.

'Carry on, Marcus,' he said sharply. Then, turning to Taggie, demanded, 'Why didn't you bring Xav, and what's she doing out of school?' He glared at Tabitha now engrossed in a new Dick Francis.

From then on it was nightmare. The endless swirling semi-quavers of the last movement escaped in all directions like ants under a jet of boiling water. Marcus's fingers seemed drunk, had changed shape. Icy cold and sweating they scrabbled and missed Helen's clean keys.

Then Rupert's mobile rang and Lysander, who'd been at the brandy on the way down, couldn't stop laughing and loudly said, 'Oouch' when Kitty kicked him on the ankle. Distracted, Marcus played a repeat for the third time, wrong notes clattering down like hailstones.

Surreptitiously, Rupert opened a catalogue to check the prices his yearlings had reached. Forgetting himself, Lysander suddenly said: 'That was a bloody good horse.'

'Tut up, Lysander,' said Bianca reprovingly.

Aware of his father's utter boredom, Marcus lost his place and ground to a halt. There was a dreadful silence. Marcus put his face in his hands.

'Take your time,' called out Monica Baddingham kindly.

Somehow Marcus stumbled through the prestissimo and fled to his dressing-room.

Bolting backstage, Flora found him slumped, white and shaking on the sofa bed, his breath coming in great wheezing gasps.

'I can't go back, not with Dad there.'

'It was wonderful – you were playing better than ever before. You can't let that bastard get to you, you've got to remount and finish the course.'

'Anyone for orange squash or coffee?' Miss Smallwood popped her white bun round the door.

Marcus clenched his fists.

'He needs something stronger.' Flora drew a half-empty brandy bottle out of her pocket.

'He can't have alcohol,' said a horrified Helen who was dripping around like a wet hen.

Flora looked round for a tooth mug.

'He's got to relax. This'll zap the asthma much quicker.'

The Cotchester Musical Society didn't have a licence, so Rupert, who couldn't understand why Taggie was so cross when he'd bust a gut to get there, swept Lysander off to the Bar Sinister, Basil Baddingham's dive in the High Street. Most of Marcus's fan club followed them in wonder. By the time they returned, Marcus had dispatched the Chopin adequately and was now playing *The Bee's Wedding*.

Rupert proceeded to get out his blue silk handkerchief and pretend to be trying to catch the bumble bee, which reduced Lysander to even more helpless laughter.

'Stop it,' hissed Taggie over the applause at the end. 'If Bianca can behave herself, you two bloody well can.'

At the prospect of Boris's *Siberian Suite* many of the audience, including four girls who'd come in off the street mistakenly hoping it might be warmer inside, hadn't bothered to return from the pub.

Cheered by another slug of brandy, ignoring the bewilderment of the audience, Marcus kicked off playing the suite quite beautifully. Boris was in ecstasy, delighted that in sympathy, the rain was rattling the window-panes that weren't broken and the icy gale, whistling through the ones that were, was billowing out of the dark blue curtains at the back of the platform.

Rupert was reduced to shuffling his feet, sighing and reading Taggie's programme. His face, quite expressionless as he clocked the *Marcus Black*, twitched slightly when he spotted the *Dame Edith Spunk*.

Dame Spunk has put up a Black in more senses than one, he thought sourly. After this fiasco, there was no way the society would ever ask Marcus back. And what the hell was Venturer doing advertising in the programme. The musical society were exactly the kind of old trouts who were always complaining about sex and violence, and television going to the dogs.

The penultimate movement, allegro furioso, in which Marcus had to drag his nails up the strings inside the piano to emulate the shrieks of the Siberian gales, dispatched more musical society members into the night. Even if television was going to the dogs, it was preferable to this din, which you couldn't even nod off to.

Crash, crash, deliberately bringing down rows of notes at a time, Marcus's whole arm was now moving up the piano.

'I'm bored, can we go?' Rupert whispered to a seething Taggie.

'Lucky things,' he sighed enviously, as two more bids scuttled out.

Boris was in despair; soon there would be no-one left to hackle his music. Seeing his father asleep, Marcus lost his place and stopped, and too embarrassed to bow he fled to his dressing-room.

Fortunately the remaining audience, thinking he had finished and blissful it was over, clapped, cheered and stamped their feet to get Marcus and their circulation back, so he returned to take a couple of bows. Monica Baddingham, whose ringing voice was used to calling to labradors across open spaces, then shouted, 'Bravo' several times and announced that the composer was in the audience, so everyone clapped Boris, too.

Dreading Helen's reproaches, Marcus was relieved to pass her on the pay telephone on his way back to his dressing-room.

With trembling hands he put his encore piece, Schumann's *Dreaming*, back in his case with the other music and wondered miserably if he'd ever have the guts to play in public again.

The poor professional, however, must always smile after a concert so people may be fooled into thinking it wasn't too bad.

His friends, crowding in accepting glasses of white, were kind because they loved him.

'How was the piano?' asked Flora.

'Terrible.'

'What was wrong with it?'

'Too many wrong notes.'

And his friends giggled in relief that he didn't seem too cast down.

'You were dazzling until your bloody father arrived,' grumbled Flora. 'Abby'll be livid she missed it.'

'You were terrific,' Tagggie hugged him. 'We're all dying of pride. Bianca loved it.'

'Good boy, Marcus,' said Bianca, as he gathered her up into his arms.

'Hallo, darling, you were good. Sorry about the ghastly cock-ups,' he added to Taggie.

Taggie was too loyal to say she was sorry about Rupert, who had been side-tracked, talking to Monica Baddingham, an old chum whom he hadn't seen since she had shacked up with Dame Edith. He was amazed how good she looked, and even more so when she insisted Marcus had played very well.

'I've got to whizz home and tuck Edith up with a hot toddy, but I'll drop him a line. Have you got his address?'

'He's living with Helen. That's most of the trouble. How much would he have made this evening?'

'Oh, about a hundred pounds, plus expenses.'

And he's been practising for this concert for months, thought Rupert darkly.

He was overwhelmed by the greyness of the whole occasion. Wandering backstage, he was enraged to find himself at the back of a queue of more old biddies, who wanted their programmes signed, particularly when one, not realizing he was no longer her MP, gave him an earful about the poor dustbin delivery in the area.

He was so fed up that he took it out on Marcus when he finally reached him.

'At least you got round this time. Monica's just told me how much they paid you. I think you should consider another career, something more lucrative, like nursing.'

Marcus's friends, on the way out, laughed in embarrassment.

'Rupert,' reproached Taggie, seeing the brave smile slipping on Marcus's face. 'He's only joking,' she whispered. Then, relieving Marcus of a sleeping Bianca, added defiantly, 'Everyone else thought you were marvellous.'

As they all drifted away, Marcus could see Helen was off the telephone and steeled himself to face her bitter disappointment. To his amazement, she was very chipper.

'I've just been talking to the *Evening Standard*, they want to run a big story tomorrow.'

Marcus had very regretfully refused to go out on the toot with the bus load from the Academy, because he'd promised to have dinner with his mother. Now she suddenly cried off.

'Janey Lloyd-Foxe is having – er – marriage problems. I promised I'd pop in and see her, so you go out with your friends.'

But as Marcus ran outside, he saw the minibus lurching off down the middle of the High Street.

The musical society were pointedly turning off lights and locking doors. Wearily Marcus returned to his dressing-room. He ought to change, his shirt was still ringing wet. His neck was stiff, his arms and elbows were sore, his back ached as he slumped in the lone chair close to tears. Next month he would be twenty-one and going nowhere. He was roused by a knock on the door and an old man staggered in on crutches. Long white hair trailed out from under his black beret and he was wearing a black belted mac and dark glasses.

'I am not too late?'

Oh Christ, thought Marcus.

'Of course not.' He leapt to his feet. 'Would you like a chair?'

'Please.'

'And a glass of wine?'

'Please.' But when Marcus poured it, the old man put the glass shakily on a nearby table and took both Marcus's pale, strong beautifully-shaped hands in his own which were covered in liver spots and as bent and as arthritic as oak twigs. The contrast could not have been more marked.

For a second the old man gazed at them. Then to Marcus's horror, he dropped a kiss on each palm. Letting them drop, he took a sip of wine.

'Those are the hands of a great pianist whom one day the world will know.'

'Really?' stammered Marcus. Perhaps the old poofter was harmless, after all.

'Really. I 'ave never 'ear *Appassionata* play like that, so beautiful, so eentense.'

'I had a memory lapse.'

'Stupid jargon. You stop. So? Eef one takes reesks one makes meestakes. You work 'ard on piece, no?'

Marcus nodded.

'You will always have to. Eef you have no originality, it is easy to reach perfection. The Levitsky piece is beautiful, too. But next time put the Chopin at the end so the audience stay because they have some bon-bons to look forward to.'

'My piano teacher said the same.'

'I don't take pupils any more,' went on the old man, 'but eef you feel like a week in Spain, I have lovely house, you would be very welcome. I would be 'appy to geeve you lessons.'

In what? wondered Marcus. He never knew what to do when men made advances, the old ones in particular were much harder to turn down; it seemed so rude. He was also sure he'd seen this man before.

'You're seriously kind,' he mumbled, 'but my step-father died and basically I have to look after my mother.'

'She will recover.' The old man creaked to his feet, then holding his sticks with one hand, he got a card out of his pocket.

'Don't forget. The invitation is always there. But I may not be much longer.'

'Thank you.' Marcus pocketed the card.

Then to his intense embarrassment, the old man raised a hand and started stroking his cheek.

'You have beautiful face which help in our profession.'

Marcus just managed not to leap away in horror. Thank God there was a knock on the door. He never thought he'd be so pleased to see Miss Smallwood, who was anxious to pay him and get off home. She even gave him a fiver for petrol, about enough to get the Aston round the statue of Charles I and back. Only when he'd thanked her and signed the receipt and was letting himself out of a side-door did he bother to glance at the card. He gave a gasp and rushed under a street-light. It couldn't be. It couldn't. It was, too. The card said: PABLO GONZALES.

With a whoop of joy, Marcus swung twice round the street-light, then, fighting for breath, tore up a side-street to see if he could catch the old man, his hero, his utter God. But, like the minibus, the huge Bentley had swept off down the High Street towards London.

The only media reference the next day was that as Rupert had been leaving his son Marcus's concert, he and Lysander Hawkley (the man who made husbands jealous, now married to Kitty Rannaldini, etc.) had got into a fight with the hunt saboteurs.

NINETEEN

Taggie was of such a forgiving nature that Rupert was amazed the following morning when she still only snapped back in monosyllables and crashed his bacon and eggs down in front of him at breakfast.

'What *is* the matter?'

'You should have switched off your mobile.'

'Not when someone was trying to tell me my best three year old's been kicked. She's as lame as a cat this morning. That's more important than some tin-pot concert.'

'Not to Marcus, it wasn't.'

'Tut up, Daddy,' beamed Bianca.

'And you can belt up, you cheeky monkey,' Rupert turned on her.

'Stop being horrible to *all* your children, you great bully,' shouted Taggie, and Rupert stalked out, kicking Kevin's rose even harder on the way.

Rupert was as skilled as Stalin at sustaining cold war. But it was such a beautiful day, and the robins and blackbirds were singing. Yellow celandine and coltsfoot exploded on the verges and after yesterday's downpour, all the little streams, hurtling into his lake had set it glittering like a tiara on the brow of the valley.

Best of all, the vet had reassured Rupert his filly would be fit for the One Thousand Guineas. Returning from lunching with an owner, remembering that Kitty was taking Xav, Bianca and Arthur to a children's party, Rupert felt suddenly springlike and decided to slope home early.

A great orange sun was filling his rear mirror and warming the lichened trunks of his chestnut avenue as he roared up the drive.

Ringing Taggie to tell her he would check things were all right in the yard, and then be in and she was to get upstairs and out of all her clothes, was met with an extremely icy response. Taggie then hung up. Storming into the kitchen, Rupert found his wife still fully dressed, her face pink and shiny, as she took the skin off a just-boiled ham.

'Why are you still sulking?'

'I am not sulking, I'm angry. The only thing I really hate, hate, hate about you is the way you're so vile to Marcus. It *was* a good concert. The people who know about music gave him a standing ovation.'

'All five of them. They were just relieved such a bloody awful din was over.'

'You're be-e-e-e-estly,' screamed Taggie. 'See pigs jolly well can fly.'

Grabbing the ham, she hurled it at Rupert, who ducked so it crashed into the dresser behind him, breaking two coronation mugs, and smashing the glass on a framed photograph of Gertrude the mongrel, who led the stampede of dogs from the room.

Rupert couldn't stop laughing which made Taggie crosser than ever.

'Get out of my life,' she shrieked.

Having cleared up, chuntering like a squirrel the while, washed the ham, and sprinkled the fat with breadcrumbs, Taggie had cooled down, and went in search of Rupert. She had been turning out the attic and nearly filled up a skip with the contents.

By the time she had searched the house, the huge gold sun had deepened to scarlet, and was flaming the puddles in the yard. Then she saw Rupert, on top of the skip. He was sitting on an ancient sofa, whose springs had gone, sharing a packet of crisps with Nimrod the lurcher, and reading *Horse and Hound.*

As Taggie burst out laughing, Rupert leapt down, pulling her into his arms, nuzzling at her neck.

'Let's go to bed.'

'Not until you promise to be nicer to Marcus.'

'That's blackmail.'

'I mean it, and we ought to give a twenty-first birthday party for him next month.'

'And then he can invite all his ghastly bearded musical friends. Oh all right, you can see how badly I want to go to bed with you.'

'And you'll be nice at the party.'

'I promise, and if you don't come upstairs, I'll take you here and now in front of all the lads.' Rupert started to pull Taggie's jersey over her head, so she scuttled protesting inside.

Marcus, however, quashed the idea. Helen, he said, was still in mourning and not up to a party. Privately, after the horrors of Christmas and his début concert, he couldn't face a family get-together.

Rupert was relieved he didn't have to cough up, but, again pestered by Taggie, gave Marcus a beautiful Munnings of one of Eddie's old steeplechasers, Pylon Peggoty, who'd won a lot of races. Rupert had been trying to track the painting down for years. Marcus wasn't wild about horses, they gave him asthma, but he was deeply touched, knowing Rupert would have given anything to keep the painting.

Flora, who was broke, but always incredibly generous,

had gone busking for three days, and bought Marcus Pablo Gonzales' recording of all Chopin's piano music. Marcus listened till he was cross-eared. Abby sent him a crate of champagne, and said they were all missing him in London. While she was in Lucerne with Rodney she'd discovered a fantastic nineteenth-century composer called Winifred Trapp, who'd written among other things a wonderful piano concerto.

'Perhaps you'll play it, if I can get a record company interested.'

Helen was delighted Marcus got so many presents, it made her feel less guilty about standing him up again on the night of his birthday. Marcus didn't mind. On the strength of the cheques he'd been given, he had just bought a second-hand Steinway on the never-never and was dying to try it out. It had arrived late that afternoon after Helen had gone out, and, big, black and shiny, was now dominating the charming porcelain-crammed drawing-room at the Old Rectory, like a bull trying to be good in a china shop. Marcus hoped Helen wouldn't be too upset by the intrusion.

She'd been so strange lately, ringing up and pleading he came home for supper, sobbing that she couldn't stand another evening on her own, then he would find a brief note when he arrived, saying that she'd had to go out, after all, leaving him nothing for supper.

Having heated up a tin of tomato soup, and noticed some surprisingly sexy underwear, gold satin french knickers, with a matching bra and suspender belt, clinging to the side of the tumble dryer when he put in his shirts, Marcus settled down to the Bach *Preludes*. The Steinway was magical, unlike the brute at Cotchester where every note had been like lifting a ton of coal.

He so wished Malise was still alive. Helen pretended to be interested in music, but he and Malise had really been able to dissect pieces together and Malise's detached, kindly criticism had been such a help and a comfort. Marcus hoped he was OK in heaven, he had been such a courteous man, but strangely shy underneath. Perhaps he was playing duets up there with Boris's wife, Rachel.

Miss Chatterbox used to tell Marcus that he must practise as though he was performing, even if it were only for the cat. Tonight, to make up a little for letting him down at the funeral, Marcus played for Malise.

About midnight, he started to worry. Outside he could hear the foxes barking. The central heating had gone off, so he put a hot-water bottle in Helen's bed and turned on her bedside light. She was only saying yesterday how she dreaded sleeping in a big empty bed, reaching out in the night to find Malise wasn't there.

To his relief he heard the front door bang. He had never seen his mother look so beautiful. She was wearing a dress of crushed tobacco-brown velvet, which caressed her wonderfully slender figure and brought out the red-gold highlights of her sleek bobbed hair, which seemed to gleam with health for the first time in months. She wore no lipstick, so her slender oval face was dominated by her huge hazel eyes. Marcus didn't recognize the necklace of amethysts which ringed her throat as softly flattering as violets, nor the long dark fur coat slung around her shoulders, nor the flat, but beautifully cut dark brown shoes, which set off her perfect ankles. Helen had arched insteps and always preferred high heels.

She was so spaced out, she didn't even notice the new piano. As she hugged Marcus, she reeked of a musky feral scent she had never worn before. Why was he so instantly and disturbingly transported back to that end-of-term concert at Bagley Hall? Then Helen, who drank very little, amazed him by suggesting they open a bottle of Malise's ancient Sancerre.

'For your birthday,' she said tenderly. 'I can't believe it's twenty-one years since I first held you in my arms. You've brought me so much joy.'

But as soon as he'd fetched the bottle, which was covered in cobwebs and in no need of being chilled, from the cellar and poured it out, Helen raised her glass, and said she must share her great happiness with him.

'Oh Markie, I'm going to marry Rannaldini in Chelsea Register Office tomorrow.'

'You what?'

Then it all came spilling out, the weekend in Prague, the cancelled evenings, her almost suicidal misery at Christmas, and all because Rannaldini had backed off, not sure if he was capable of making a commitment.

Marcus was utterly aghast. Mrs Edwards had dropped some heavy hints that a foreign gentleman had been calling. But Marcus assumed it was Boris. Boris would be heartbroken.

And of course, that explained the kissed-off lipstick, the new fur coat, the amethysts and the flat shoes so she wouldn't be taller than Rannaldini. Her other great love, Jake Lovell, had been small.

She even smelt of Rannaldini, the same disturbing scent that he had wafted round the hall years ago when he had arrived so late for the school concert.

In despair, Marcus begged his mother not to go ahead with the wedding.

'Malise has only been dead five months, Mum. Rannaldini's a monster. You don't know him. Actually he's worse than a monster. He's a cold-blooded sadist who wiped out Rachel, and Flora and made Kitty's life a nightmare.'

'You haven't heard his side,' said Helen, who was in a pontificating mood, to justify the white heat of extreme sexual passion and the joyous expectation of becoming mega-rich again. Rannaldini, she explained, was so caring. He was going to put on a concert to raise thousands for her branch of the NSPCC, which would attract maximum attention now that he had been awarded his knighthood.

'He's specially composed an elegy for sad children. It's so beautiful. And he'll buy you your Steinway outright, and help Tabitha in her eventing career. I believe in redemption,' Helen smiled mistily. 'Rannaldini came into my life and saved me when I'd reached an all-time low.'

'So you've settled for an all-time gigolo, Lady Rannaldini,' said Marcus savagely.

'Don't be obnoxious, you sound just like your father.'

'You were nearly destroyed by Dad's philandering.'

'And look what happened when Daddy met the right woman?' reproved Helen, though even now she had a slight edge to her voice. 'You never stop telling me how blissfully happy Taggie's made him.'

'At least warn Dad, it's only fair,' begged Marcus.

'No, no, he'll do something horrible to sabotage it. I deserve some happiness, Markie, I've been so desolate since Malise died.'

If Helen hadn't wept and begged, Marcus would never have gone to the wedding, but he could never bear to see his mother cry.

Earlier that same day, Tabitha had had another blazing row over the telephone with Rupert because he still refused to buy her The Engineer.

'You shouldn't tangle with inferior regiments,' Rupert had snapped, and Tabitha had hung up on him.

Late the following afternoon, Taggie, in an attempt to heal the breach, had rung Bagley Hall to find out if Tabitha would be coming home for the weekend, only to be told that Tabitha's mother had taken Tab out of school for a very special occasion. Her housemistress had been very mysterious and refused to let on what it was.

In a rage – how the hell was Tabitha going to pass any exams if she was always being yanked out of school – Rupert telephoned Helen in Warwickshire. Getting no answer, he rang Bagley Hall and left a furious message that Tabitha must ring him the moment she got back.

Tabitha finally telephoned so early the following morning, Rupert was still asleep.

'Where the bloody hell have you been?'

'In London. At Mum's wedding, since you ask.'

'Wedding!' thundered Rupert.

'Yes, at Chelsea Register Office. She really looked gorgeous in pale crimson silk like the Tailor of Gloucester, a big dark crimson hat and some gorgeous garnets. I thought you'd be pleased – she won't need to ask you for money any more. And you'll never guess who she's married.'

'Who, for Christ's sake?'

'Rannaldini. He's really, really nice.'

For once Rupert was silenced.

'Are you there, Daddy? We all had lunch at the Ritz afterwards.'

'We?' said Rupert ominously.

'Marcus and Jake Lovell were witnesses. Gosh, he's attractive,' said Tabitha blithely. 'And Rannaldini's going to buy Marcus a Steinway as a joining-the-family present, and guess what? He's bought me The Engineer – so nice to have a father who loves me again – and Jake Lovell's going to train him. Mum's going to adore being Lady Rannaldini.'

Rupert went ballistic, particularly when he saw the exclusive in the *Telegraph*.

'*One of the bonuses of marrying the most beautiful woman in the world,*' Rannaldini was quoted as saying, '*is that I acquire two beautiful step children, Marcus and Tabitha. As a musician and an owner, I intend to help and guide them in their chosen careers. Malise was a brilliant horseman, a flautist, and a wonderful stepfather. I hope they won't feel his loss too much any more. They have both been delightfully welcoming.*'

As well as a picture of the happy couple, there were also photographs of Rannaldini smiling at Tabitha with his arm possessively round her shoulders and, worst of all, of Marcus beside Jake.

The telephone rang. Rupert dived on it.

'How about your ex marrying Rannaldini?' said *The Scorpion*.

Kitty read out the *Telegraph* piece to Lysander.

'Wowee, game and first set to Rannaldini,' he said in horror.

'He'll break her,' shivered Kitty.

Helen had been dreadfully patronizing to her at Christmas, but she couldn't wish such a fate on anyone.

Kitty jumped as the telephone rang. It was Rupert. Had she got Rannaldini's telephone number in London?

He was so appalled and enraged at the thought of Rannaldini getting his filthy hands on Tabitha that he rang up at once. Helen and Rannaldini were still in bed, later to fly to Milan, where Rannaldini was conducting *Don Carlos* at the Scala. Poor Marcus picked up the telephone.

'Why the fuck didn't you stop it?'

'I t-t-tried,' stammered Marcus.

'Like hell – and why the fuck didn't you warn me? Have you considered what that paedophile might do to Tab? Your mother's a whore, she might as well have married the devil.'

Marcus lost his temper.

'She did that the first time round. No-one could have made her more miserable than you did.'

'She's a parasite,' howled Rupert. 'She's always been greedy, never bothered to earn a penny in her life. Now she's sold out to the highest bidder, and you'll never make it either, you're a parasite, too. Don't expect to get another penny out of me. Go and sponge off Rannaldini.'

'I don't want your bloody money,' yelled Marcus, 'I'll get there on my own.'

And he slammed down the telephone. He was struggling for breath, desperately delving in his pocket for his inhaler, when Rannaldini came smirking out of the bedroom. He was wearing the blue-and-green Paisley dressing-gown which Marcus and Tabitha had clubbed together to give Malise for his seventy-fifth birthday, a month before he died.

'What's the matter, dearest boy?' crooned Rannaldini.

He's the Erl-King, thought Marcus in terror.

'You bastard,' he gasped. 'How dare you tell the papers I've been welcoming, you know I was dead against the wedding, and only came to it because of Mum. If you hurt a hair of her head, I'll kill you. I don't want any of your bloody money or your Steinway either.'

Somehow he got himself to Flora's digs without collapsing, and then had to cope with Flora, for once dropping her guard and sobbing wildly that there was no hope of her getting Rannaldini back any more.

Rupert was so incensed, he proceeded to cancel both Marcus's and Tab's allowances, and write them out of his will.

'It's Tabitha Rannaldini's after,' wept Flora. 'That's what's driving Rupert crazy.'

The only thing that cheered Flora up was the new Dame Hermione's fury over the marriage.

'Talk about caterwauling for her demon lover.'

Helen, oblivious of the devastation she had created, returned from her weekend in Milan more in love than ever, and reprimanded Marcus for being horrid.

'Roberto so longs for everyone to be friends.'

As Rannaldini already had five houses, she also felt magnanimously that she should put the Old Rectory on the market, because it had such unhappy associations for her, and hand half the proceeds over to Malise's daughter.

'It's such a good time to sell in the spring when the tulips, the appleblossom and the crown imperials are all out.'

The final straw for Marcus came when he wanted to listen to Myra Hess playing the *Appassionata* on Monday evening, and discovered Helen, in a flurry of tidying, had chucked out all Malise's old 78s. Marcus was on to her at Rannaldini's London flat in a trice.

'How could you? They're irreplaceable.'

'Don't be silly. They're all on CD now – Rannaldini's getting them for you as a surprise.'

'I want the 78s. Malise left them to me.'

'Darling, be reasonable, they were only cluttering up the place.'

'Like me,' shouted Marcus, slamming down the telephone.

Outside the window, white daffodils lit up the garden and the dark yew hedges, a little unkempt now, which Malise had planted to divide it. Did Malise's ghost, astride his old hunter, jump them in the moonlight? Would the new owners cut them down?

Marcus, who had lived here since he was four years old, was now not only penniless, but soon to be homeless. He was surveying the wreckage of his life, when the telephone rang. He couldn't cope with a reproachful Helen, but it was Abby jibbering with excitement.

'I've got my first gig, conducting the Rutminster Symphony Orchestra. Rodney and Howie squared it for me. Only one problem, right? I've gotta learn the repertoire in a fortnight. Will you help me?' There was a pause. 'You don't sound very excited for me, Marcus.'

'Mum's just married Rannaldini.'

'I read it. Not the ideal stepfather – I'm really sorry. But think of the doors he'll open for you, and at least it'll get your mom off your back, and you can come back to the Academy. It's poor Flora who's been blown out of the water. God, I'm scared about this gig.'

Appassionata

SECOND MOVEMENT

TWENTY

Abby was as driven as a conductor as she had been as a violinist. Sweeping into the Old Rectory, she hardly noticed how ill Marcus was looking.

It was ironic that one of the pieces he had to help her learn was *Ein Heldenleben*, a Hero's Life, Richard Strauss's tone poem, which included a portrait of Pauline, Strauss's capricious, demanding wife. Abby was a lot like Pauline, thought Marcus. She interrupted him for help whether he was practising or just firing off hundreds of letters to orchestra managers, concert halls and music clubs in a desperate attempt to get work. She had also commandeered Marcus's CD player and would drag him out of bed in the middle of the night to listen to some rival violinist as she sobbed: 'I'm better than that, aren't I?'

This would have been the ideal moment for Marcus to have made a move. But he was haunted by his failure with Rupert's hooker, so each time he bottled out, lying for hours afterwards twitching with desire.

He was also heartbroken that he couldn't afford to stay on at the Academy. When Rannaldini and Helen returned from their extended honeymoon, he would have to move into a tiny room in Ealing. He could pay the rent and keep up the instalments on the Steinway, on which fourteen-thousand pounds was still owing, only if he took half a dozen pupils a day. By the time he'd paid off his college debts, the bank had started bouncing cheques. He had torn up all his credit cards. The only card in his pocket was Pablo Gonzales's, but meeting him now seemed like a dream. Marcus didn't have the bottle to write to him. His asthma was awful, he couldn't walk twenty yards without stopping to rest.

If Abby was exhausting, she was also expensive. Seeing such a large, beautiful house (and this was only Marcus's mother's place. Flora had already told her about the glories of Penscombe), Abby assumed Marcus was just another trust-fund baby, and Marcus was too proud to tell her otherwise. As she had lived with Rodney, now she would live with Marcus. She was not grasping, her records had left her very well provided for, just thoughtless. Having worked for twelve hours sustained only by Granny Smiths and black coffee, she would emerge at dinner time.

'I'm exhausted and absolutely starved.'

If dinner wasn't ready, she would insist they took her scores out to the nearest restaurant where, having wolfed down a couple of baskets of bread, she often found she wasn't hungry when the two courses she'd ordered arrived, and Marcus, being his father's son, picked up the bill.

Back at the Old Rectory her mess spread from room to room, and had to be hurriedly tidied away by Marcus each time a buyer arrived to look at the house.

As the concert approached, Abby grew more histrionic, dickering over what to wear on the night – 'I gotta look dignified and drop-dead gorgeous' – and having screaming matches with Howie Denston, her agent.

The new Lady Rannaldini, thought Marcus, would go

bananas when she saw the telephone bill, but that was Sir Roberto's problem.

Mrs Edwards was in her ... ment.

'Lady Rannaldini's res...nce,' she would announce as journalists started ringing up, so they simply assumed Abby was Rannaldini's protégée.

To keep the tabloids at bay, Howie installed bouncers. As a result the more enterprising reporters disguised themselves as prospective buyers. The man from the *Telegraph* got so into the part he even put in a bid for the Old Rectory, and was furious to be gazumped later in the week by a girl from the *Independent*.

Marcus took two days off to hold Abby's hand. For a start, he drove her down to Rutminster.

'How far is it?'

'Malise and I always reckoned it was Beethoven's *Ninth* to Rutminster and *The Creation* to Cotchester.'

'It would have been far quicker in the Aston,' said Abby petulantly.

As a last-ditch measure, to appease the bank manager, Marcus, the day before, had sold his beloved Aston and bought a third-hand, mustard-yellow Maestro, which Abby didn't feel had sufficient gravitas. She was not even amused by jokes about taking the Maestro down in the Maestro. The next two days were going to be lean on laughs, thought Marcus with a sigh. Still, it was a beautiful day, with primroses fizzing along the bright green verges like sherbert and the cottage gardens still full of daffodils.

After a steep climb, Marcus stopped the car.

'Get your head out of Richard Strauss for a sec and look at that.'

Abby gasped with joy for down below in a bowl of wooded hills softened by opal-blue mist, rising from the same River Fleet that flowed through Cotchester, lay the ancient town of Rutminster. There was the racecourse where Rupert's horses battled with Rannaldini's to win the famous Rutminster Cup. There was the cathedral, its spire soaring into the air like a litter prong trying to catch the tiny, paper-white clouds hurtling across the the bright blue sky. Along the river bank, weeping willows rinsed their blond hair in the glittering aquamarine water.

'There's the Herbert Parker Hall, where the gig is,' said Marcus, pointing out a hulking Victorian monstrosity standing in its own park to the west of the town.

'How awesome,' sighed Abby, oblivious of the hideous proportions and the ox-blood walls which clashed vilely with the faded russet of the rest of the High Street.

'Who *was* Herbert Parker?' she asked.

'Oh, some nineteenth-century haberdasher who made his pile and then built one. His descendants own Parker and Parker, the department store in the High Street. That Queen Anne house, overlooking the river to the east of the town, is the Old Bell Hotel where you're staying.

'What you can't see is the secret passage from H.P. Hall, as it's known, to the Shaven Crown in the High Street. You'll be sent flying during the break by stampeding musicians. Goodness, they've got portaloos, they must be expecting huge crowds.'

Dropping into the valley, they entered thick woods. Through the first faint blur of hawthorn and larch, gleamed a lake, reminding Abby of Lucerne and the ghost horn player. Then she jumped at the sight of her own photograph smouldering down from a large oak tree. From then on, there were 'L'Appassionata' posters everywhere.

'Oh Marcus,' her voice quivered, 'I feel as if I'm coming home.'

Even though the concert wasn't until the following night, Rutminster swarmed with Press. Megagram, Abby's record producers, were reissuing all her old records and had spent a lot of money promoting the concert. The tickets could have been sold five times over. Big screens had been put up in the park, so disappointed punters could watch from outside for a tenner.

Double cherries lining the path up to H.P. Hall were still in bud.

'We thought of forcing them out with a blowlamp in your honour,' said Mark Carling, the extremely harassed managing director of the Rutminster Symphony Orchestra who came rushing out to shake Abby's hand.

He had thinning mousy hair, and tired red-rimmed eyes peering furtively through granny spectacles which seemed too small for his big, worried face. Desperately shy, he found the social side of running an orchestra a torment.

'I'm in the middle of a rather sticky conversation with the Arts Council, who tend to call the shots. I hope you'll forgive me, if my secretary, Miss Priddock, shows you round. Miss Priddock's very much the power behind the throne,' he said, scuttling off in relief.

Miss Priddock had once been pretty and for a brief period Sir Rodney's. Plump, mono-bosomed and given to pussy-cat bows, she looked as though she pulled on her blue-rinsed hair like a tea cosy each morning. She lived in the Close with John Drummond, a large, self-important black cat with a white shirt-front which made him look as if he were wearing tails. Drummond, who accompanied Miss Priddock to work and doubled up as office mouser, was known as the 'purr behind the throne'.

Seeing the imperceptible toss of Abby's head that she was being abandoned to a secretary, Miss Priddock mentally branded Abby 'a madam' and said they had never had a concert like this before. Poor Mr Carling was run off his feet.

'He's lucky to have you,' said Marcus, sensing ruffled feathers. 'You must be seriously busy.'

'I deal with everything,' said Miss Priddock, ushering them into a palatial foyer, whose peeling burnt-sienna walls were almost entirely hidden by L'Appassionata publicity material.

'Light bulbs, blocked toilets, computers breaking down,' she went on, 'they run to me. I'm also Clare Rayner to the entire orchestra. If they're homesick, got marital problems, can't pay their mortgage or the gas bill, they end up in my office. I can't do much, but I'm a good listener.'

And a conceited old bag, thought Abby, as led by John Drummond, his black tail erect, Miss Priddock swept them along the inevitable labyrinths where under naked light bulbs, groups of musicians pretended not to stare.

'This is the band room,' added Miss Priddock, 'where the musicians relax, and this is the hospitality room where we entertain sponsors and friends of the orchestra.'

'And this is the instrument room.' Flinging open the door, Miss Priddock surprised a couple in flagrante. Abby caught a quick glimpse of a girl spread-eagled naked on the glockenspiel, her long silver-blond hair trailing like a River Fleet willow. Beside her stood an equally blond man with wicked slitty dark eyes and broad bare shoulders tapering to a narrow waist. Unbuttoning his jeans with one hand, he had the other rammed between the girl's legs.

Miss Priddock didn't turn a blue-rinsed hair.

'Buck up, Viking,' she said briskly, 'rehearsal begins in ten minutes,' and almost dotingly closed the door.

'Who was that?' asked Abby, flabbergasted.

'Viking O'Neill, First Horn and Juno Meadows, Second Flute.'

'Don't musicians get fired for that kind of behaviour?'

'Not Viking,' said Miss Priddock firmly.

'He's got two horrendous horn solos in *Oberon* and *Ein Heldenleben*,' said Abby. 'I hope he's up to it.'

'Viking's up to everything,' said Miss Priddock skittishly. 'The platform's through that door.'

With a shiver of excitement, Abby could see the stage set up with chairs and music-stands, and hear the glorious heady din of musicians all practising different passages from the *Oberon* overture.

'And here's your dressing-room. It's Sir Rodney's normally, but he vacates it for guest conductors.'

On a low marble table, Abby was touched to find a huge bunch of white hyacinths and narcissi and a note from Rodney telling her not to seduce all his orchestra before he saw her tomorrow night.

The room, befitting him, had an extremely comfortable double bed, only thinly disguised as a sofa by a few embroidered cushions, a massive bath, a buckling wine rack, a store cupboard filled with large glasses, tumblers, tins of caviar, foie gras and artichoke hearts. On the walls were photographs of Gisela and Shosty outside Flasher's Folly, of Rodney's late wife playing in her nightie and of Rodney and the orchestra out in the park under the turning trees on the occasion of his seventy-fifth birthday. In the wardrobe, Abby found a set of his tails and breathed in a waft of *English Fern*.

'Oh, I wish he were here.'

Miss Priddock's face softened.

'We all do. I'm afraid Lionel Fielding, our leader, is away guesting with some northern orchestra,' she gave a more-fool-them sniff. 'But his co-leader,' the warmth returned to Miss Priddock's voice, 'a most delightful French Canadian, Hugo de Ginèstre, will do everything to smooth your path.'

Hugo was very smooth, as he swept in, all fire and flourish, brandishing his bow like d'Artagnan. Like d'Artagnan, too, he had a glossy moustache, a neat beard, cavalier curls just beginning to recede from a noble forehead, and big soulful dark eyes, which kept suddenly twinkling with merriment. The Musketeer image was further accentuated by a dark brown velvet jacket and a floppy white silk shirt, tucked into black cords which were, in turn, tucked into boots.

Kissing Abby's hand and then both her cheeks, he said how honoured the RSO were to welcome such a great musician.

Marcus, who was feeling exhausted and spare-prickish, looked at his watch.

'I'll take what you don't need and check in at the Old Bell,' he said.

'Don't be long, I need you –' suddenly Abby looked vulnerable, and Marcus's heart leapt then fell as she added – 'to help me if I get stuck.'

'*Courage, mon enfant*,' said Hugo, as he led her into the auditorium.

Gripping the brass rail of the rostrum to disguise her shaking hands, Abby looked down at the RSO spread out before her. Many of them were paunchy, most of them pale and drawn, after a long winter of late nights, long hours' teaching, playing other dates to make ends meet, not seeing the sun and gazing at black dots.

A handful were brown from skiing, some of the girls were young and very pretty, the men handsome, but on the whole they needed an iron over their faces and their clothes. Their gleaming instruments – gold, silver, conker-brown, burnt-umber and black – looked in much better shape. But together, they had the power of a wolf-pack. They looked at Abby curiously but coolly, poised to co-operate or gang up.

Then Abby smiled.

'It's great to be here with you guys. Today we'll concentrate on *Oberon* and *Ein Heldenleben*.'

By ill luck, *Oberon* would start with a solo from the First Horn, who was now dressed in black jeans and a 'Spoilt Bastard' T-shirt, and laughing his head off. Blushing, Abby looked up at him and nodded. Viking sat there, his horn to his mouth, but not making any sound. Abby nodded again. 'When you're ready, First Horn.'

'I'm ready, Maestro.'

There was another long, agonizing pause; the orchestra grinned into their instruments.

'I think he's waiting for you to give him the upbeat, Maestro,' whispered Hugo.

'Oh shit, I never thought of that.' Abby whipped her stick up and then down and they were on their way. She was dying of nerves. But expecting one of Rodney's bimbos (the last one had got lost in the New World), the RSO were staggered how good she was. Thanks to Marcus she was embedded in the music, giving every important cue, detecting wrong notes from the babble of sound. Musicians detest stopping and starting, and Abby luckily also had the ability to shout out or sing instructions on the wing.

Simon Painshaw, First Oboe, had carrot-coloured dreadlocks and screwed up his thin face when he played as though he was drinking vile medicine out of a straw.

'That was fantastic,' Abby called to him after a particularly beautiful solo, 'but three bars after twenty-nine, you should have played A flat.'

Blushing beetroot like an unattractive winter salad at the unaccustomed praise, Simon mumbled that his part said A.

'Then yours is a misprint.'

The musicians looked at each other in awe.

The brass players, when they got excited, made enough din to strip the rest of the paint off the foyer. Abby managed to shut them up.

'I gather that the RSO brass section are the wonder of the West Country,' she beamed across at them. 'But it would be kinda fun occasionally to hear what the rest of the orchestra can do.'

The brass section shuffled their feet sulkily but they forgave Abby when she overheated, and whipped off her dark blue jersey, mistakenly taking her white T-shirt with it, to display a pair of stunning breasts.

Hugo was also a joy, playing with panache, never

taking his soulful dark eyes off her, clapping his hands to shush any chatter, pleased that Abby consulted him throughout.

And the First Horn was more than adequate. After the ridiculously delayed start, Abby nearly dropped her baton, because he played with a radiance and purity completely at variance with his distinctly *louche* appearance. He was also the most outrageously attractive man Abby had ever seen, lounging high up at the back of the orchestra, his French horn, like the sun in his arms, matching his streaked gold hair. His dark brown eyes seemed permanently narrowed as if he were taking aim before firing one of Cupid's arrows. He had a pale narrow face darkened by stubble, a snub nose, and his big mocking lips somehow managed to compose themselves round the mouth piece of his instrument This was an eighteenth-century horn with a pretty painted bell made of gold leaf, beaten very thin and giving it enormous range.

He's the ghost horn player, thought Abby in wonder.

'You do very well,' said Hugo, as he and Abby had a cup of tea in the conductor's room.

'You gave me so much help,' said Abby, 'and the orchestra sure take their lead from you.'

'And I from you,' said Hugo, who was having a little bet with himself that it would be under ten seconds.

'There are some very interesting players,' mused Abby.

Six seconds, thought Hugo.

'Particularly First Oboe, and – er – First Horn. A wonderful primitive sound. Why's he called Viking?'

'He wore an eyepatch to his audition to hide a black eye given to him by a jealous husband,' said Hugo, gratified to have won his bet, but disappointed that Abby had reacted like all the rest.

'When Victor, that's his real name, first came here,' he went on, 'he reminded everyone of a Viking blowing a conch in a flat-bottomed boat before nipping ashore for a spot of rape and pillage.'

'Does he,' Abby removed her Earl Grey tea-bag, then added super-casually, 'have a particular partner?'

'Well, he's slept with most of the girls in the orchestra.' Getting up Hugo tested Rodney's bed. 'He only has to say, "Hallo, sweetheart," in that peat-soft Irish voice to some pretty new cellist. Next minute she's horizontal in the car-park.

'Horn players,' Hugo rearranged the cushions up one end, 'live on the edge. First Horn and First Oboe are the riskiest instruments to play because they're so heard and so exposed. Viking's the hero of the orchestra, because he stands up to visiting conductors and the management.

'The management, on the other hand, think the sun shines out of Viking's brass' – rising from the bed Hugo prowled round the room – 'because he pulls in the punters. If he isn't playing, they ask for their money back.'

Hugo opened Rodney's food cupboard, examining tins and jars with rapt Gallic interest. Abby, who hadn't had any breakfast, dipped a piece of shortbread in her tea.

'How old is he?'

'Twenty-eight.'

'Same age as me. No disrespect to the RSO, but why hasn't he been snapped up by one of the London orchestras, or made a fortune as a soloist?'

'Viking's lazy and unambitious.' Squatting down Hugo whistled over the vintages of the wines in the rack. 'He prefers hell-raising with his friends, they're known as the Celtic Mafia, and playing football on Sundays. There was a mass walk-out when the management tried to introduce Sunday afternoon concerts.

'Anyway, why should anyone want to work in London?' asked Hugo. 'Have you ever tried carrying a double bass on the tube? You can get to work in ten minutes here and park, and you have a salary even if it's a pathetic one. You get a chance to rehearse before a concert and the audiences are loyal. I like it when people stop me in Rutminster High Street and say, "That was a great concert, Hugo." The countryside is marvellous and the cottages are very cheap.'

'You make it sound so attractive,' said Abby wistfully.

Hugo laughed – dashing d'Artagnan again.

'And the pickings are good. There are many, many single women in the country. Others have husbands who go to London in the week.'

'I don't approve of married men having *affaires*,' said Abby primly.

'Nor do I,' said Hugo. 'I'm divorced.'

Out of the window Abby could see extras running up the path to take part in *Ein Heldenleben*, which required a much bigger orchestra than *Oberon*.

'Has Viking ever been married?' she asked.

Hugo shook his head, too polite to snap that he'd been quizzed so often about Viking that he was thinking of making a tape.

'But there is evidence he is taking life more seriously. Recently he left the ramshackle house on the edge of the Blackmere Lake, which he shares with the Celtic Mafia, and moved in with Juno Meadows, Second Flute, who lives,' Hugo's dark eyes gleamed with laughter, 'in a converted squash court.'

'Does she have long blond hair?'

'That's the one, *ravissante* in a doll-like way.' Hugo tested the bed again, wondering what Abby was doing this evening. He had a terrific strike-rate with girls disappointed by Viking.

'Juno,' he added wickedly, 'is so refined, she insists on eating bananas sideways.'

Abby burst out laughing.

'And,' continued Hugo, 'despite being a hypochondriac, who rings in sick with a dislocated eyelash, she is very tough. The orchestra call her the Steel Elf. She refused to sleep with Viking till he moved in. He nearly went mad. Now she's pushing him to get a better job. That's why he was playing at Covent Garden last night. He's already picking up her mortgage. But all the orchestra, including Viking, he's a gambling man, are having bets as to how long it will last.

'I 'ave to say I love the bloke, and we all forgive him, because he's such a marvellous musician.' Hugo looked at his watch. 'We better get back, here endeth the first lesson.'

'Omigod,' said Abby appalled, 'I forgot you had that horrendously difficult violin solo coming up. I should have left you in peace.'

'Probably stopped me worrying,' said Hugo philosophically.

What a pity, thought Abby, that he was at least three inches shorter than she was.

The tattered, bottle-green curtains had been pulled back as far as possible to accommodate the increased orchestra. Viking had four extra freelance horns in his section. There were two gold harps soaring like a king and a queen and an exciting array of percussion including a snare drum, which made a sinister relentless rattle, and cymbals gleaming like Ben Hur's chariot wheels.

Irritated there were more players on stage, the orchestra were involved in their usual grumbles about over-crowding, music-stands and chairs in the wrong place, lighting and heating. Tomorrow they would have to cope with television cables and cameras. As Abby mounted the rostrum, she noticed Juno Meadows, Viking's girlfriend, to the left, smugly aware of taking up hardly any room at all. Feeling disappointed Viking was taken – why the hell was she lusting after profligate horn players? – Abby was now in a didactic mood.

'*Ein Heldenleben*,' she told the players, who'd heard it all before, 'means a hero's life.'

She was interrupted by the arrival of a very fat, very pretty blonde, who sent several music-stands flying and waved frantically at Viking before plonking herself down beside a furious Steel Elf.

'Who the hell booked Fat Rosie?' muttered Hugo. 'You only need thin musicians for Strauss.'

'A hero's life,' went on Abby, 'could be described as kinda autobiographical. It was written when Strauss was only thirty-four.'

'Must have been bloody arrogant,' said Viking, applying the Second Horn's strawberry-flavoured lipsalve to his big mouth.

'Just like you,' said the Second Horn, retrieving it.

'Quiet please.' Hugo clapped his hands.

'In this piece,' continued Abby, 'Strauss paints a savage picture of the critics who attacked his music. They are portrayed by the woodwind, scraping, squeaking and playing out of tune.'

'Juno won't have to try,' sneered the First Trumpet, who had a cruel red-brick face.

'Who said that?' Viking was on his feet.

'Don't rise.' The Second Horn pulled him back by his 'Spoilt Bastard' T-shirt.

'Only joking,' grinned the First Trumpet unrepentantly. 'Sorry Juno.'

The orchestra, particularly the prettier girls, who entirely agreed with the First Trumpet, smirked into their music-stands.

'Strauss also portrayed his tempestuous relationship with his wife, Pauline,' went on Abby, 'who was a coquette and very capricious.'

The First Trombone, who had a complexion like red rock, very blue bloodshot eyes and hair the colour of wet sand, rather like a South of France travel poster, put down his copy of *Playboy*.

'You mean she was an absolute bitch,' he said.

The orchestra giggled. Abby decided to ignore him.

'As I am sure you all know, Pauline is portrayed by the leader of the orchestra.' Abby smiled fondly at Hugo.

'Hope you're going to wear a pretty frock, Hugo, dearie,' shouted the First Trombone.

'And Strauss even portrays himself in the closing pages on the French horn.' Abby smiled up at Viking, who put down *Auto Express* and smiled back.

'After a terrific battle,' concluded Abby, 'when the brass and percussion can really play fortissimo, the work ends with the hero and his wife reconciling their differences in one of the loveliest tunes ever written, with the solo violin singing and sobbing and the solo horn – er – weaving round her like a great purring panther.'

'Grrrrrr,' growled Viking.

'Show us your tits again,' shouted the First Trombone.

Abby blushed crimson.

'Let's get started.'

It was like hanging onto the coat-tails of a hurricane, thought Abby, as she opened her raised arms, and whipped the orchestra to a frenzy in the battlescenes, then quietened them for the love duet. Here, she felt Hugo, although a dashing and technically faultless player, lacked passion. If only she could have taken his place, providing Viking with a player up to his weight. As she sang along with them, she realized how unendurable life would be until she could play again. She hadn't done any physio for weeks.

Confronted by genius, however, Abby was always generous. Passing Viking on her way out as he put his horn back in a battered case, lined with crushed purple velvet, she stammered: 'You were terrific, I'm not just bullshitting.'

'It's like being a racing driver or a test pilot,' said

Viking. 'You just got to believe you'll come out the other end.'

Hugo's right, thought Abby, he does have the sexiest peat-soft voice in the world, and he was a good three inches taller than she was.

TWENTY-ONE

Hugo took her to the Shaven Crown for lunch. The record shop in the High Street had a display of her CDs and a coloured cardboard cut-out taken from an old photograph when she'd been all wild-haired and smouldering.

'D'you think people will recognize me?' she asked Hugo in alarm.

'Of course, the explosive element is still there, the lovely body, the lovely face.'

Was her face lovely? he wondered. The nose was too big, the eyelids, the bottom lip, even the jaw too heavy and yet and yet.

'Genuflect to our benefactress,' he added sourly, as they passed a big department store, draped in banners saying: 'Parker and Parker Welcomes Abigail Rosen.'

There were even windows devoted to men in tails and women in spangled evening dresses playing instruments.

'You'll meet Peggy Parker tomorrow night,' said Hugo. 'She's as squat and brick red in the face as the Herbert Parker Hall. She loves to patronize the arts, patronize being the operative word. And she's not very keen on Rodney because he remembers her when she was a junior in the underwear department with a tape measure hanging from her neck, and he was always nipping in to buy lingerie for his various popsies. That was before Peggy married the boss. She's now on the RSO board and a Force to be Reckoned With, because she pumps in a lot of dosh.'

'I hope she doesn't force the orchestra into those awful dresses,' shuddered Abby.

The Shaven Crown had a thatched roof kept in place by a wire hairnet and pale pink walls. Inside it was already packed with musicians and full of inglenooks, black beams, barmaids in medieval dresses and a long-suffering landlord, who wore a monk's habit when the antics of the RSO became too much for him.

Huge orange logs in the fireplace gave the impression of having smouldered for centuries. Having installed Abby in an alcove on a black bench which said, 'Leader's Chair' in gold letters, Hugo went off to order.

Abby was soon distracted by shouts of laughter. Edging along the bench, peering through a pair of hanging lutes, she saw Viking surrounded by cronies including his Second Horn who had bright blue eyes, and the First Trombone who'd acted up during the rehearsal.

'Absolutely flagrante,' Viking was saying.

'What happened?' asked the First Trombone, draining his pint of beer.

'I had a bit of a day,' began Viking, 'I had lunch with Thin Rosie, went back to her place and did the business, came out and on my way to the Garden bumped into Fat Rosie, so I went back to her place and catered for her.'

'That's why she was looking so cheerful this morning,' said the Second Horn, glancing up from the *Independent*.

'Then I gave my considerable all to *Tristan and Isolde*,' went on Viking. 'Three hours of it. I kept falling asleep, Jesus, I was tired. I josst managed to drive home to

Rutminster, fell into bed, josst dropped off, when I was woken by an imperious tap on the shoulder. Her indoors saying: "Haven't you forgotten something?"' Then over the howls of laughter, added, 'That's why I had to re-accommodate her on the glockenspiel this morning, and in barges Priddock, John Drommond and L'Appassionata.'

As Hugo crossed the bar with his bottle of red wine, Viking leant round to see who he was lunching with, and seeing Abby, without any embarrassment, raised his glass to her.

'All the girls behind the bar want your autograph,' said Hugo, 'and Bernie the landlord wants a photograph taken with you.'

She still loves the recognition, he thought as he filled up their glasses.

'I shouldn't drink.'

'Yes you should, to celebrate, and eat. Two steak-and-kidney pies are on the way.'

'That's the nucleus of the Celtic Mafia, the wild men of the orchestra,' said Hugo, after another roar of laughter from Viking's table.

'That's Blue Donovan, reading the *Independent*. The quiet one, a seriously good guy and usually broke because he sends so much money back to his family in Derry. Always falling asleep because he plays most nights in a jazz club.'

'Very attractive,' mused Abby.

'Very. Blue covers for Viking musically and in real life. Beneath the sang-froid, Viking's pretty neurotic. First Horn has to have iron in his soul.'

'Oh wow, this looks great,' cried Abby as a steak-and-kidney pie with gold pastry billowing out of the little dish, a baked potato and broccoli were put in front of her. 'I'm starved.'

'Can we have some mustard, Debbie?' called out Hugo.

'French or English?' asked the pretty barmaid.

Abby smiled sideways under her lashes at Hugo: 'I always prefer French.'

Feeling encouraged Hugo continued his run down on the Celtic Mafia.

'Sitting next to Blue is the First Trombone, Dixie Douglas. A brawny fearless Glaswegian, Dixie comes from northern brass band stock – lips of steel – his light duties as a trombone player give him rather too much time to booze, letch and mischief-make. You want to watch him, Abby. He's trouble.'

'He already has been,' said Abby. 'This is so good. I shouldn't eat the pastry, but I'm gonna.'

'Finally, the man with a moustache, who looks like a sandy-haired Clark Gable, is Randy Hamilton, Third Trumpet, another fearless hell-raiser from a barrack-room background. Randy's energies when not boozing and womanizing are spent improving his golf handicap and loathing the First Trumpet, Charles Jones, nick-named "Carmine" Jones because he goes bright red during solos.

'Carmine, you may have noticed, had a go at Juno this morning, just to wind up Viking, because he hates the Celtic Mafia, and he's been trying to get Juno into bed ever since she joined the orchestra, and he's livid Viking got in there first. He always moves in on any pretty girl that comes on trial. "If you sleep with me, darling, I'll put in a good word, along with my dick." He's a very, very nasty piece of work.

'Both Randy and Dixie are married with wives living in Scotland, whom they go back to sometimes at week-ends. Otherwise they live in a house on the lake known as The Bordello, with Blue and until recently, Viking. That's about it really.'

'Thank you, Hugo,' said Abby earnestly, half-watching a pretty waitress carrying a tray of shepherd's pie across to the Celtic Mafia. 'It's crucial for conductors to learn as much as possible about their musicians.'

'Yeah, yeah.' Smiling slightly, Hugo undid an oblong pat of butter and dropped it on his potato.

'When did you leave Canada?' asked Abby.

Hugo started to tell her, but immediately lost Abby, because a large black collie had jumped onto the bench seat between Viking and Blue, had a red paper napkin tucked into his collar, and started wolfing his own dish of shepherd's pie, plumey tail wagging as he carefully ate round the cooler edges first.

'Who's that?' asked Abby in amazement.

'Mr Nugent.'

'Goddamn silly name.'

'The fur on the top of his head was too heavy, and kept falling into a middle parting which, together with a slightly unctuous manner, gives him the appearance of a Victorian grocer, hence Mr Nugent. Viking's had him since he was a pup.'

Filling up an oblivious Abby's glass, Hugo edged his corduroy thigh within a millimetre of hers.

'Nugent often sleeps in Viking's car, which adds to the general stench and mess. He also rounds up the Celtic Mafia after hours, and always gets first place for the horn section in the tea queue during the break.'

Abby didn't even feel Hugo's thigh against hers, because Viking had strolled over to the bar to buy another round. She noticed his leather jacket was cut short to emphasize a high jutting bottom and long, muscular legs.

'He's in good shape,' she turned to Hugo. 'Does he work out?'

'Only how to get his next lay. That's how he gets his exercise.'

Mr Nugent crawled across the floor to reach his master's heels.

'Surely dogs aren't allowed in here?' exclaimed Abby.

'They're not, but when Bernie banned Nugent, the entire Celtic Mafia defected to the Old Bell and the bar-takings halved, so Nugent was allowed back again. The bottom line is that Juno can't stand dogs, that's what's going to cause a rift between her and Viking. Talk of the Devil,' he added as Juno walked in.

She was wearing a fluffy pale pink track suit. Her blond hair was tied back with a pale pink ribbon. Her face was delicately flushed like a wild rose to match. She couldn't have been prettier.

Having kissed Viking on the mouth, refused a drink and asked if there was any room for a little one, she plonked herself between Blue and Viking.

'What have you been up to?' said Dixie snidely. 'Aerobing or jogging, yoga-ing or yoghurt-ing or aromatheraping?'

Like the rest of the Celtic Mafia, Dixie was torn between jealousy of Viking for having pulled her, and jealousy of Juno for annexing Viking.

'I've been to the gym,' said Juno, 'and I went to see my bank manager. He gave me a glass of sherry.'

'Mine gives me bounced cheques,' said Randy gloomily.

'And I bought our tea, someone has to.' Although Juno had a squeaky little voice like a mouse orchestra, her bluey-green eyes were as cold as distilled fiord water.

'Nice track suit,' said Blue the peacemaker.

'I got it from the Children's Department of Parker and Parker, and I got us two chops,' said Juno, looking disapprovingly at the refilled pints of beer.

Dixie ruffled Nugent's black fur. 'Good thing the old boy stocked up on that shepherd's pie.'

'Dogs only need one meal a day,' snapped Juno. 'We ought to go back. I need to pick up a grapefruit and some cottage cheese.'

'Wow, you are going to have a blow-out,' mocked Randy.

'Viking's eating habits are shocking.' Juno pursed her pretty lips, then her eyes widened as Marcus rushed through the door. Even deathly pale, black under the eyes and wheezing frantically, he was beautiful.

'Abby darling,' he panted, 'I'm desperately sorry, I crashed out on my hotel bed for five minutes, next thing I knew it was a quarter to two. Are you OK?'

'Don't I look it?' said Abby warmly. 'It's been wonderful having someone to discuss the finer points of repertoire.'

And what have I been fucking doing for the last two weeks? thought Marcus.

Feeling she had been a little harsh, Abby added to Hugo: 'Marcus is a marvellous pianist.'

'We could use you in the Tchaikovsky tomorrow night,' grumbled Hugo.

'Who's playing?' said Marcus.

'Some crumpet of Rodney's, called Anthea Hislop, known as "Hisloppy" – she's so slapdash.' Hugo grinned at Abby. 'With two of you on the same night, the orchestra was going to paste "Ban the Bimbo" posters all over H.P. Hall.' Then, seeing Abby's expression of outrage, hurriedly added, 'But you're no bimbo, sweetheart. She did great today,' he told Marcus.

'I want to find some truly revolutionary way to do the Tchaikovsky,' said Abby earnestly.

'Get the horns to come in in tune at the beginning, instead of splat-two-three,' suggested Hugo, 'and you could try to make Hisloppy play occasionally at the same tempo as the orchestra.'

TWENTY-TWO

The run-up to the concert was distinctly fraught. Anthea Hislop turned out to be as curvacious as she was catastrophic as a pianist. This resulted in several spats with Abby which enlivened the rehearsal, but put Abby into the deepest gloom. As Anthea was one of Shepherd Denston's most successful artists, Howie Denston insisted on motoring down from London to take her, Abby, Marcus and Mike Carling, the RSO managing director out to dinner.

Marcus thought that after Rannaldini, Howie was the most dreadful man he had ever met. Allegedly the most cut-throat agent in London, he was short and plump with a white oily face, little black eyes, black hair which fell in a kiss-curl over his low forehead, and very long arms from lugging potted plants to ingratiate himself with large lady artistes. He plainly didn't give a stuff about music and, like his father, was only turned on by the deal.

Howie's only redeeming feature during a very sticky evening, when Abby and Anthea completely ignored each other, was that when he wasn't jabbering into his mobile, he was talking incessantly about himself, which at least kept the conversation going.

'I have ab-so-lute-ly no private life. I exist only for my clients. My mobile is never switched off.'

He clearly thought it was a huge concession to travel out of London, and seemed to expect wild boars covered in woad to ramraid the restaurant at any second.

Mark Carling, who hardly ate anything, left after the main course to look after a wife who had shingles. Seeing the bill was imminent, Howie jumped thankfully into a hovering limousine and steamed back to London for a breakfast meeting with his most illustrious client, Hermione Harefield.

Howie owned a five-bedroomed house on the canal at Maida Vale and earned at least four hundred thousand pounds year. He was not a day over twenty-three.

Anthea, bored because there was no-one to vamp, disappeared shortly afterwards. Whereupon Marcus lost his temper.

'Your agent is the most revolting little man I've ever met. He's pig-ignorant and he's a bloody shirt-lifter.'

'Marcus,' said Abby appalled, 'what has got into you? I'm the one who's got the big date, right? I don't want to hear this kinda shit. Howie's an absolute powerhouse.'

'Power bungalow you mean, revolting little man.'

Marcus's attitude didn't change when he was woken by a call from Howie at six o'clock the following morning.

'Hi, Pretty Boy, for God's sake, keep the *Daily Mail* from Abby.'

Hermione's rage at Rannaldini marrying Helen had been exacerbated by a piece in *The Scorpion* about Abby staying at Helen's house, and therefore being Rannaldini's protégée. In revenge Hermione had given an interview to Lynda Lee-Potter. *How Abby Rosen slashed her wrists because her lover filled my aeroplane seat with yellow roses.*

'Fucking Hermione,' yelled Marcus. 'How dare she.'

'These dames are all the same.'

'Hermione's not a bit like Abby, she's your client, you should bloody well control her.'

But Hermione was a more important client, as was Anthea. Abby might easily bomb this evening.

'Got to go, Tiger, see you at the press conference, don't forget, keep the *Mail* from Abby.'

Abby was too busy rehearsing to see the *Mail*, but the rest of the media pouring into Rutminster had read the piece. They had all promised not to question Abby about Christopher or her attempted suicide, but within seconds Beattie Johnson from *The Scorpion* was on her feet.

'If Christopher Shepherd caused you so much grief, aren't you getting your own back on him and men in general by becoming a conductor, so you can boss them around?'

Abby had immediately burst into tears and stormed out, leaving the place in an uproar.

At least the programme looked splendid with a lovely new picture of Abby on the front, and, even more lovely to the RSO, eighty pages of expensive advertisements for banks, cars, credit cards, clothes, jewellery and make-up.

It was also a lovely mild night. The birds were still singing, the sun had just set in an orange-and-pink glow, but to combat any symbolism, the moon was rising out of the Blackmere Woods as Abby arrived. She was gratified not to be able to see an inch of the park round the H.P. Hall for spectators with rugs and picnics.

There was an explosion of flash bulbs, police held back the cheering, excited crowds and there, to Abby's joy and relief, was Rodney, smiling, rubicund, and waiting at the front door with his silver-and-black cummerbund embedded in his vast belly to the width of a snake belt.

'Good evening, Maestro,' he raised her hand to his lips. 'Don't let them see how frightened you are,' he whispered. 'You look utterly sensational.'

Abby's short hair was brushed straight back from a lily pale face. Her only make-up was eye-liner round the hypnotic eyes, which seemed to glow like tourmaline. The Maharishi effect was heightened by midnight-blue silk trousers and a long collarless matching jacket, which buttoned up to her neck. She wore no jewellery, the only note of frivolity was the *diamanté* buckles twinkling on her black suede pumps. In her pocket, warding off evil, was Rupert's silver garlic.

'They haven't had a turn out like this since Pavarotti in Hyde Park,' Rodney led her into the conductor's room. 'Oh, darling, I'm so proud.'

'They've only come to see if I've got two heads,' said Abby, as Mark Carling barged in.

'You look wonderful, Maestro. What the hell are we going to do, Rodney? We've got about two hundred too many Press and nowhere to seat them.'

'Put up a few fences,' suggested Abby, through desperately chattering teeth, 'that's what they like sitting on best.'

She started to run through *Oberon* in her head, moving her hands to the music. Viking's opening solo followed by the strings, then that spine-chilling shimmy downwards on the flutes, then blank. She simply couldn't remember what came next.

In panic she turned to Rodney.

'I guess I better use a score.'

'Darling child, it'll come back, relax.' He shoved a glass of champagne into her hand. 'Take the edge off your nerves.'

Next, they were interrupted by Howie, who'd nipped for a second out of Anthea's dressing-room.

'Good luck, kid, you look to die for.'

'Sorry about the press conference.'

'Forget it. Fact that you survived heartbreak and a suicide attempt creates public sympathy.'

'Get out, Howie,' said Rodney icily.

There was another knock. It was Hugo, sleek and glamorous in tails. He had sent two dozen red roses, '*To the unbimbo*', at the Old Bell, which had made Abby laugh, now he said, 'Are you ready, beautiful Maestro?'

Abby nodded, quite unable to speak.

'Good luck.' Hugo sauntered out onto the platform, fiddle aloft to great cheers. He was very popular.

'Good luck.' Marcus gave Abby a quick kiss. He was so nervous for her, he was going to stay outside in the park.

The auditorium was fuller than in Buenos Aires. Many of the audience and all the Press were poised for the public humiliation that so often accompanies a dramatic change of career.

For a second, Abby paused, panic stricken, on the edge of the platform, then turning she saw a smiling Rodney; his pink, bald head gleaming under the naked light bulb, as he blew her a kiss. Abby touched her silver garlic, then she was on her way, sweeping into the light, to an impassioned bellow of applause, which was taken up by the crowds in the park. She shook hands with Hugo.

'*Courage, mon amie.*'

Then Abby forced herself to smile and bow to the audience, listening to the manic rattle of palm on palm which was so near in sound to a firing-squad.

'Kerist, she's gorgeous,' said Blue.

'Shades of Imran Khan,' agreed Viking, 'or something that Edwina Mountbatten wouldn't have been able to resist.'

Abby noticed the Steel Elf, enchanting in black silk with her blond hair piled up, and then she looked up at Viking, who smiled at her, wonderfully confident. At her nod, he put his horn to his lips.

Abby gripped her stick, the upbeat rose and fell like a wand in fairyland, and as if by magic, the notes floated out from the midgy dark green depths of Oberon's forest. Then she remembered nothing until an avalanche of applause crashed over her, bringing her back to earth.

Throughout the overture she had been completely in charge, yet able to become the music, her beautiful body undulating like seaweed in the dark blue silk. The orchestra, noticing the cruel scar on her left wrist every time she raised her arm, realized how important the evening was to her and had played as though their lives depended on it.

The Tchaikovsky was less successful. The mood was set by the First and Second Violins who had to rise and stand back, muttering 'Bloody concerto' as Abby's rostrum was shoved forward, and the Steinway was wheeled onto the centre of the stage by the stage-hands in their dinner jackets.

Once the music-stands and chairs were rearranged, Hugo struck an A on the piano and the orchestra half-heartedly pretended to re-tune. They loathed concertos. Soloists stole the limelight and, particularly in the case of pianists, obscured half the orchestra, and made conditions even more cramped.

Most of them, however, found it difficult to keep a straight face, as Anthea swept onto the platform in a kingfisher blue-and-gold brocade dress, strewn with tassels that appeared to have been tugged off the sofa in her suite at the Old Bell. She then attacked the piano with the fury of a secretary who'd been asked to stay late and type a fifteen-page report on an old Remington whose ribbon had run out. The only drama was whether one of her large blue-veined breasts would fly out of her soft furnishings and whack the principal of the second violins in the eye.

'That is the worst pianist I've ever heard,' Abby shouted as she stormed back to the conductor's room afterwards.

'Hush darling.' A very sheepish Rodney put his hand

over her mouth. '*Mea culpa, mea culpa,* I must have been drunk or very tired when I hired her; probably both.'

'She played the whole thing in boxing gloves.' Furiously Abby tore Rodney's hand away.

'None of the audience will have noticed, and those who did will have marvelled at your restraint. Listen, they're still clapping.'

Rodney handed her a glass of champagne.

'I don't want a drink, I need my wits for *Heldenleben*. Come in.'

It was a distraught Mark Carling.

'Thank you Maestro, you were magnificent.' Then, turning to Rodney, he groaned, 'That soloist was dreadful, dreadful. How could we have booked her?'

'You must have had a tip-off,' said Rodney blandly, 'and you know how the Arts Council love women. Anyway, she was called back five times; she can't have been that bad.'

'Only because they wanted to look down her dress,' snapped Abby. 'Anyone with binoculars could have seen her pubes.'

It is customary, even after the most terrible performance, for the management to visit a soloist and tell them they have been wonderful. Mark, a man of integrity, was in despair.

'What can I say to her without perjuring myself, Rodney? Particularly with that creep Howie taping every word as evidence.'

'Follow me,' Rodney winked at Abby. 'Back in a tick, darling heart.'

Hair dripping with sweat, aching all over, Abby was dying for a quick shower to clear her head before the Strauss, but curious, she lingered as Rodney flung open the door of Anthea's dressing-room, then pausing in the doorway, opened his arms.

'Anthea, my darling,' he boomed, 'magnificent is *not* the word.'

'Very clever,' muttered Mark in admiration, 'must remember that one.' *Magnificent*, he tapped it into his pocket computer, *is not the word.*

As Anthea was temporarily tied up with Rodney, Howie felt it safe to sidle out and pay court to Abby for a second.

He was going to have his work cut out at the party later. Anthea and Hermione would want his full-time attention, so would Abby, and after hearing *Oberon*, Howie was determined to sign up Viking, who was a really hot man. Probably straight but Howie wouldn't mind getting his jaw broken finding out.

The audience were flowing back now. The piano had gone, and there was nothing to distract them from Abby and a vastly enlarged orchestra. The Tchaikovsky had done her no favours with the critics. She had forty minutes to redeem herself.

Everything was going wonderfully. *Ein Heldenleben* was drawing to a close. The woodwind had made horribly crabby and discordant critics. The brass had been so loud and exuberant in the battlescenes they must have roused Strauss in his musicians' heaven. The drums had thundered continuously. The four cymbals had clashed in perfect unison to mark the end of hostilities, and Don Juan's horn call, the warrior returning from the wars in search of dalliance, had echoed joyfully through the park.

Abby's hair was sopping, her face lurexed with sweat under the hot lights. She could see the shadow of her hands moving on the bare lectern. Somehow, she must hush the huge orchestra to make the pianissimo contrast of the love duet all the more touching. The cor anglais was now gracefully paddling like a swan. Throughout the piece, Abby had felt like a pilot, faced by a massive dashboard of dials and switches. Her aeroplane had survived the thunder and lightning of a great storm; she was now bringing its precious cargo of musicians safely in to land.

Then, as she cued in the horns, nothing happened. She tried again, nothing. She gasped in horror. Cramp gripped her right hand, which had never let her down in three years, totally immobilizing it. After a three-hour rehearsal this morning, then three-hours practising in front of the mirror, followed by all the tension of the performance, it had finally seized up.

For a few seconds, the orchestra cruised on automatic pilot. Realizing something was wrong, the cor anglais kept paddling, Hugo was poised to take over, when Abby grabbed her right elbow with her left hand, yanking it through the motions, one, two down, three to the left, short four and five back and six up to the centre, and one, two down, to re-establish the tempo.

The pain was so excruciating she thought she'd black out. But there was only one more discordant outburst from the orchestra to go as the weathercock shrieked, the wind howled, the enemies trumpeted, then the hero's theme was back, with the horns, basses and cellos leaping nobly and majestically up the scale, and they were into the love duet.

On the big screens outside, the vast crowds could see Hugo's sleek, dark head cocked to listen, and Viking never taking his narrowed eyes off Abby's face, which was now shining with tears, as she cajoled them through the last few bars. And as suddenly as it had gripped her, the cramp melted away, soothed as much by the solo violin's exquisite lullaby as by the unearthly beauty of Viking's dark, tender reply.

Lifting both arms, she was back on course, bringing the great aeroplane down, down through the blue and landing without a bump on the runway. She felt so relieved, she almost forgot to bring in Carmine Jones and his trumpets to echo the hero's theme fortissimo. Then a mighty crash from the wind and brass faded into the final peaceful, reassuring chord – the hero finally triumphant, bringing the H.P. Hall and the park outside yelling to their feet.

Marcus leant against the rough trunk of a big horse-chestnut tree, clutching himself; his debts, lack of recognition, loneliness, unrequited love, Rupert's animosity, all totally forgotten. He had never heard anything so wonderful in his life, particularly as the gruesome butchering of the Tchaikovsky had nearly broken his heart. Oh darling, darling Abby, and darling St Cecilia or Polyhymnia, or Euterpe, or whoever guides the fortunes of musicians, prayed Marcus, make the same thing happen to me.

After the sixth call-back, Miss Priddock braved the stage with a huge bunch of red roses and, employing her old trick, an exhausted tearful, ecstatic Abby broke the cellophane with a stab of her baton, and handed a rose to Viking and one to Hugo who was near enough to kiss her.

The next time she returned with a beaming Rodney, who got a great roar of delighted recognition and immediately hushed the audience.

'My lords, ladies, gentlemen, musicians, we have just heard a masterpiece about a hero overcoming his enemies, most beautifully played.' He winked at his orchestra, triggering off a volley of 'bravoes'.

'But tonight we're speaking about a heroine,' he shushed more cheers, 'who, in the last three years, has battled with dreadful pain, adversity, self-doubt, only to emerge tonight into a new career, as triumphant as she looks beautiful.' One final time he raised his hand for quiet. 'I am proud of the RSO, but the night is Abigail Rosen's. Ladies and gentlemen, a star is reborn.'

TWENTY-THREE

As she fled back to her dressing-room, it was like the old days. People pressed themselves against the wall to let her pass, cheering her, others reached out to shake her hands, for others it was just enough to touch her for luck.

Howie was in raptures, fluttering round her, taking credit for everything. Anthea was a has-been, she didn't even get the limo to take her back to London. Instead, it swept Abby on to a party at the sort of shabby grand house much featured in British mini-series before the stylist moves in. It belonged to Lord Leatherhead, the chairman of the orchestra.

'Don't get him on to bottled water, for God's sake,' Hugo had warned her. 'He's changed his family motto to "Springs Eternal".'

As the limo clanked over a cattle-grid, Abby caught a glimpse of a llama and a couple of yaks blinking in the headlights.

Having insisted on showering and changing first, she had arrived so late that she was relieved to see Mr Nugent still there, plumey tail waving as he paid court to the house springer spaniels, who were more interested in finishing up abandoned plates of moussaka and spitting out the aubergine.

Howie was delighted that although Megagram had bankrolled the party, half the record producers in Europe seemed to have crashed it, climbing in through large Georgian windows or bribing the kitchen staff. He was less amused that half the agents in Europe had done the same thing, and were now circling Abby like jackals.

'The fuckers, the fuckers, why didn't Megagram put bouncers on the door? But they're gonna have to fight to keep you, Tiger,' he told Abby. 'You stick with me, I'll field any difficult questions.'

Orchestras aren't generally invited to parties, being a large number to cater for, but tonight a representative selection of the glamorous and well-behaved had been allowed in to impress potential sponsors.

Old Henry, the oldest member of the orchestra, a rank-and-file fiddle player who could tell you whether Heifetz had started up bow or down bow in 1942, but hadn't heard of Abby before yesterday, came over and kissed her hand.

'It's not often I know why I became a musician.'

Abby longed to talk to him, but he was immediately sent flying by Dame Edith Spink. Massive and monacled, with the solid waistless figure of a cooling tower, Edith promptly whipped the dark red carnation out of her dinner-jacket and presented it to Abby.

'Bloody good show, particularly the Strauss. That Anthea needs her bottom spanking.' Dame Edith looked as though she'd quite like to oblige. 'But you kept your nerve; made the RSO play out of their boots, which I have to say they've grown much too big for. You must come and guest with my boys and girls at Cotchester. You were lucky to have Hugo. *Heldenleben* really sorts the leaders out from the leaders. That little squirt Lionel Fielding would have made the most ghastly cock-up.'

'I love your work,' stammered Abby. 'We all OD'd on *The Persuaders* at college. I'd just adore to discuss conducting with you some time.'

'Come to lunch,' said Edith. Then proudly, almost shyly, as though she were drawing forward a boat by its splendid figure-head, she reached for the handsome, high-complexioned woman behind her. 'Have you met my partner, Lady Baddingham?'

The Press were everywhere, snapping everyone, desperate for a new angle on Abby's triumph.

'Who's the latest boyfriend?' asked a subtly smiling journalist.

'That has nothing to do with my conducting,' said Abby haughtily. 'My goal is for people to judge me as an artist, not a woman.'

'Mm, of course,' said the journalist, taking in Abby's tight leather trousers, and clinging yellow bodystocking.

On cue, Anthea wiggled past, hotly pursued by Randy Hamilton.

'Does Anthea feel the same?'

'No-one could regard Anthea as an artist,' snapped Abby.

Howie, meanwhile, had buttonholed Viking.

'I work twenty-four hours a day,' he was saying. 'I am married to my clients, but I could find a window in my schedule to buy you lunch. How about *Le Manoir aux Quat' Saisons* next week?'

The Celtic Mafia were getting drunk.

'That's the most important agent in London, you've just told to piss off,' Blue reproved Viking.

'Time is fleeting,' said Viking, holding out his glass to a waitress. 'And artists' agents very long winded. D'you think Rodney's bonked Abigail?'

'Aye,' said Dixie. 'She stopped at his place long enough.'

'Who's the boy with dark red hair? Pretty as a picture, never takes his eyes off her.'

'That's Marcus Campbell-Black,' said the Steel Elf warmly. 'He's lovely looking.'

'That explains it,' said Dixie. 'Must be picking up her bills.'

'Not after this evening,' said Viking.

The musical press, determined to refute Strauss's unflattering portrait of critics, were falling over themselves to praise both Abby's conducting and her newly reissued records, which they'd mostly slagged off in the past as being over-emotional and teetering on sentimentality.

Now, as they poured double cream over their chocolate roulade, they were bracketing her with Jacqueline du Pré, praising her passion, her lyricism, her wondrous lack of inhibition.

Furious to be out-cleavaged by Anthea, every valley should *not* be exalted, Hermione had tonight done up two buttons of her yellow Chanel suit. In her pocket, however, was a promising note from Rannaldini:

> *Carissima,*
> *Our love was too important to be ruined by marriage.*
> *I needed another Kitty to run my life and free me to*
> *embrace you again.*

Rannaldini was little Cosmo's father, reflected Hermione, perhaps she should forgive him. Fortunately Abby hadn't seen the Lynda Lee-Potter piece and, in a mood of euphoria, kissed Hermione on both cheeks, and allowed them both to be photographed arm in arm by *Hello!*.

This didn't stop Hermione telling the *Telegraph* how much she admired the RSO for giving amateurs a chance to conduct.

'It was the same when Edward Heath did *Cockaigne* with the Bournemouth Symphony Orchestra. They were so supportive to him, and ordinary folk in the audience loved feeling they could have got up and done the same thing. Music should be brought to the people, my next open-air concert . . . By the way d'you happen to know the name of the First Horn?'

'OK, darling,' shouted Rodney, teetering on a sofa to see over Abby's ring of admirers, 'just off to look at the conservatory.' Climbing down, he linked arms with a voluptuous brunette wearing a lot of fuchsia-pink lipstick.

On their way, they had to go through Lord Leatherhead's office, where, on another sofa, Rodney noticed his Third Trumpet, pleasuring a blonde, and, patting him on his broad, bobbing Glaswegian bottom, called out: 'Keep to the left, keep to the left, you never know who you may meet coming the other way.' Then, bending down to ascertain the identity of the blonde, added, 'Hallo, Anthea darling, so glad my boys are taking care of you.'

'Patrick Leatherhead ought to put some of your brass section in his wildlife park,' said the brunette as she and Rodney reached the conservatory.

Terrified of being interrogated about his mother's marriage by Dame Edith, Lady Baddingham, the Press or, even worse, Hermione, Marcus lurked behind a huge bamboo plant expecting the Viet Cong to attack at any moment. Peering through the leaves, he could see Abby still surrounded by admirers, the ringed moon before bad weather again. He was agonizingly aware of his own desperate poverty and Abby's leap back to fame. She would vanish from his life now.

'Hallo, darling boy.' It was Rodney, wiping off fuchsia-pink lipstick. 'Hasn't Abby done well?'

'Marvellously.'

'Been a bit like rescuing a blackbird with a broken wing,' observed Rodney. 'However fond you get of the thing as you nurse it back to health, you've got to set it free, and just hope it survives *and* comes back.'

Marcus gave a start. The old buffer was more perceptive than he'd thought.

'I'm away for ten days,' added Rodney. 'But give me a ring when I get back and come and play for me. Must go and have a word with darling Norma Major.'

Abby was dying on her feet, drunk, because she hadn't eaten since breakfast, running only on adrenalin. The good thing about fame was you never talked to yourself at parties, the bad thing was you tended only to talk to the people who wanted to boast they'd met you, the interesting ones were usually too shy.

Peggy Parker, a non-executive director of the RSO and chairman of Parker and Parker in the High Street, had wanted to meet Abby all evening.

'Ay must thank ye-ou, Abigail for a most enjoyable concert. Your outfit was spot-on, very tasteful and under-stated as befitted the occasion.'

Clad in thousands of silver sequins, weighed down by make-up, fat-nosed, little-eyed, Mrs Parker looked like a hippo who'd spent an afternoon at Estée Lauder. Pinioning Abby against a suit of armour, similar to the corsets which somehow induced curves in her massive bulk, she launched into the offensive.

'But next time you return to Rutminster, Abigail, I hope you will feature one of our evening ge-owns on the podium. Ay even thought of creatin' a new colour for you, a light cerise, called Podium Pink. Ay can see you in cerise.'

And I'll see you in hell, thought Abby, fingering her silver garlic.

She felt boarded up, like the Canterville Ghost. Behind Mrs Parker, Howie was hopping from foot to foot, desperate to whisk her off to impress someone else. She would have liked to talk to the First Flute, Peter Plumpton, who had played so exquisitely in the slow movement of the Tchaikovsky, or to have picked over the concert with Hugo. But Hugo was a political animal and having chatted up all the record producers, was now deeply engrossed with Dame Edith. Anyway Abby really only wanted to talk to Viking. She could see his blond head against the peacock-blue wallpaper, but he had been besieged as she had all evening, and she was leaving first thing in the morning. And oh hell, Hugo had shaken off Dame Edith and was moving in on the left.

Then, miraculously, as if magnetized by her longing, Viking looked round, stared for a fraction longer than was polite, and then smiled. Abby felt her exhaustion and depression vanish as her cramp had during the concert. Almost imperceptibly Viking jerked his head towards a door on the right marked 'Private'.

'Must go to the bathroom,' mumbled Abby. 'Great to meet you, Mrs Parker.'

She found Viking in a library, reading a book on fly fishing, Mr Nugent stretched out on a dark green damask sofa behind him.

'Well done,' he said softly. 'That's one concert I'd have done for nothing,' which is the greatest compliment a musician can pay.

Abby flushed. 'You were terrific, too.'

Viking noticed how tired she looked, but how the clinging gold body-stocking brought out the blazing yellow of her eyes, and how enticingly it clung to her breasts and flat midriff, and how his hand itched to follow it inside the black leather trousers down between her legs.

'Nigel Dempster just told me you don't want to be regarded as a woman,' he said mockingly.

'Not if it means the Press only concentrating on my sex life.'

'Sure, sure. What happened just before the love duet?'

'Cramp, my stick hand gave out.'

Viking picked it up idly, shooting a thousand volts through her.

'Poor little hand, probably jealous of all the attention the left one's been getting. I've got a mentally handicapped sister in Doblin. She's otterly gorgeous, but everyone makes such a foss of her, her brothers and sisters sometimes feel very neglected.'

He picked up Abby's other hand, subtly drawing her nearer as he examined the scar.

'How's this one coming on?'

'I don't know,' Abby snatched both hands away. 'I can't talk about it.' Although she wanted to terribly.

'Mosst have been hell watching Hugo,' said Viking gently.

'Hell,' confessed Abby. 'His technique's to die for and he has a beautiful sound, OK? But he lacks drama, right? I kept thinking how outrageously I'd have acted up at the beginning, and then how passionately and tenderly I'd have abdicated at the end.'

'Abby-dicated,' murmured Viking.

Embarrassed, close to tears, she glanced up at him, noticing the dark blur of beard on the hard, lean jaw, the big laughing lips, slightly reddened and bruised from having been pressed so long against his mouthpiece (oh lucky, lucky mouthpiece), the wide nostrils of his snub nose, the fan of dark gold eyelashes, above the long, speculative eyes that were slowly searching her face.

'Oh yes, sweetheart,' he said softly.

Abby jumped as Mr Nugent shot off the sofa and out of the door.

'Where's he gone?'

'Must've heard your heart beating. Nugent's terrified of thunder.'

'It wasn't!' said Abby confused and indignant. 'How

can you assume? That's ridiculous.' Panic made her ungracious. 'Anyway, they say you're just a stud.'

'Sure, that's why I'm stoddying you.'

He had such an untroubled smile, so utterly confident of approval. Abby wondered if the silver locket round his neck contained a picture of Juno.

'Bad luck getting trapped by Mrs Parker,' said Viking. 'She puts such a strain on her corsets. Blue and I thought of getting up a petition to Save the Whalebone.'

Abby laughed, relieved yet disappointed at the shift in subject. 'Must be kinda fun playing for the RSO,' she said, hearing tarzan howls coming from next door.

'Kinda,' Viking mimicked her. 'You don't earn any money. The difference is if you're a bank manager and you're caught holding hands with a cosstomer, you're fired. Here, if the Second Bassoon is caught bonking a fifteen year old in the H.P. car-park—'

'Or the instrument room,' said Abby drily.

'Or the instrument room indeed. Rodney will just say, "Which car? Where is she? I want part of the action."'

'Who's taking my name in vain? My two favourite people.' Rodney put his arms round both their shoulders.

Hell, hell, hell, thought Abby.

'Am I pushing myself too hard?' Rodney frowned at himself in the looking-glass opposite.

'What have you been up to?' said Abby, noticing fuchsia-pink lipstick all over his shirt.

Pressed against his belly, Abby and Viking stared at each other.

'Oh, there you are, Rodney, at last I've caught up with you.'

It was Mark Carling looking distraught, closely followed by Nugent licking his lips.

'Can I pin you down on repertoire? You know we're planning a Haydn/Stravinsky festival for next March. The Rite of Spring hasn't been taken . . . I was just wondering.'

'Darling boy, I couldn't do the first fucking bar of that, you know I'm useless at those big orchestral thingies. Juno darling, you get prettier by the second.'

It was the Steel Elf.

'Oh, there you are, Victor,' said Juno coolly. 'Get off the settee, Nugent.'

As Nugent slid off the sofa, Viking slid out of Rodney's embrace.

'You're tired, sweetheart.' His voice was gentle and solicitous.

'A little.'

'I'll take you home.'

As he put an arm round Juno's shoulders, she looked as tiny and delicate as one of Oberon's fairies.

''Night, Mark. Congratulations, Maestro,' Viking nodded at Abby. 'See you when you get back, Rodney.'

Watching him dropping a kiss on Juno's hair as they went out, Abby felt as though she'd been kicked in the gut.

'Why does he wear that goddamn locket round his neck?'

'It contains the mingled earths of Northern and Southern Ireland,' said Rodney.

'I wondered if I could introduce you to some of our sponsors, Abby?' asked Mark diffidently.

The next moment, shouting, 'Call you in the morning, Viking,' Howie erupted into the room.

'Where in hell did you get to?' he reproved Abby. 'You gotta meet Sir Larry Lockton of Lockton Records. They've just had a massive injection of Japanese dough.'

But everything was suddenly too much for Abby.

'All I want you to do,' she begged Howie tearfully, 'is to tell Christopher I did well this evening.' And she fled from the room.

Marcus finally tracked her down in the spare room where people had dumped their belongings. She had taken someone's violin from its case and had it under her chin. Her right hand was wielding the bow, but the fingers of her left hand, with all the pathos of a crushed daddy-long-legs, were impotently scrabbling at the strings. She was crying helplessly.

Horrified, Marcus ran to her.

'Abby darling, please don't. You did brilliantly this evening.'

'I don't give a damn about conducting. All I want to do is play the violin again. And you can fuck off, and get out of my hair.'

'Pissed,' commiserated Dixie, coming out of another spare room as Marcus stumbled down the stairs. 'My wife's the same. Drink always gets women like that.'

Rodney took Abby back to the Old Bell.

In the morning, she discovered Marcus had gone.

TWENTY-FOUR

Abby's reviews were sensational. MIGHTY LIKE A ROSEN, wrote the *Observer*, ABBY INTERNATIONAL., said the *Telegraph*. Even the Rutshire Butcher, a local malcontent, who strung and strung up for *The Times*, who had a terrifying influence over the Arts Council and who usually flayed the orchestra alive, was extraordinarily complimentary and compared Abby to Lester Piggott galvanizing a seaside donkey into winning the Derby.

The RSO grumbled that it was always the same, if a concert was bad, the orchestra got slated, if good the conductor was praised, but in reality they were euphoric, and so were the management. The takings, plus an unexpected one hundred thousand pound legacy from some local philanthropist, went a long way to wiping out the massive overdraft run up by Rodney overpaying his famous friends.

Despite the accolades, Abby felt very flat and restless after the concert. She was also ashamed of being vile to Marcus, but when she rang the Old Rectory, Mrs Edwards, in high excitement, revealed that Marcus had moved out and not left an address.

Back at H.P. Hall, however, Mark Carling had received a fax from Boris's agent: Boris wanted to duck out of conducting the Modern Music series, because he was still wrestling with *Rachel's Requiem*, which would now have to be rescheduled yet again.

As a result, Howie and Mark engaged in a little horse trading. Abby would be allowed to cut her teeth on the Modern Music series, and Howie would let the RSO have Shepherd Denston soloists and singers at a discount. Megagram were delighted. Abby's reissued records were racing up the classical charts. The orchestra was thrilled. The Modern Music series, known as 'Squeakygate', and only put on to suck up to the Arts Council, was anathema, and now they could at least relieve the boredom by lusting after Abby. Abby was equally thrilled and, already getting above herself, talking to Flora in grandiose fashion about being the next Giulini.

Temporarily she decided to stay at the Old Bell, and was put in the Lord Byron Suite overlooking the river. There was a facsimile of '*So, we'll go no more a roving*' on the wall, and a painting of Byron in a turban, looking as dark and explosive as Abby herself.

With concerts most Saturdays, the orchestral weekend fell on Sunday and Monday. Arriving on her first Tuesday, Abby found the dark red H.P. Hall rising out of a ruff of white cherry blossom.

Standing on a flat roof, letting down rolls of different brands of lavatory paper to test which was the longest, were Miss Priddock, assorted secretaries and John Drummond the cat, who fancied himself in an Andrex ad.

This was yet another economy measure, along with stopping the orchestra using the management telephones, reducing the wattage of the light bulbs, and not replacing musicians when they resigned.

On the way to the dressing-room, Abby passed the sanctimonious and detested general manager of the orchestra, Miles Brian-Knowles, inevitably known as 'Brown-Nose'. Miles had thatched mousy hair, a complexion like luncheon meat, caused by frequent outbreaks of acne, a permanently pursed mouth and eyes so close together they could see through the same keyhole. A born-again Christian, who held prayer meetings with selected members of the orchestra, Miles always wore shirts with a high white collar giving him an ecclesiastical look, and softly soled shoes, enabling him to spy out bad behaviour and then sneak to Peggy Parker. He'd achieved Olympic-level at sucking up to his superiors hence the nickname. He was now having a row with Viking.

'You were not at your great-aunt's funeral,' he was saying in an aggrieved fluting curate's voice. 'I saw you with my own eyes playing on television for the London Met.'

'Indeed you did not,' Viking was saying indignantly. 'That was my twin brother Danny, he's a far finer player than me.'

'Why wasn't he burying your great-aunt?'

'Danny has no sense of duty.' Viking raised his eyes piously to heaven.

'I do not believe you, Viking. You did not apply for a letter releasing you to play for the London Met. You could be sacked for this. And please don't bring that dog in here.' He glared at Mr Nugent who sat listening with his head on one side.

Viking's spreading his wings, thought Abby, Covent Garden last month, the Festival Hall this. Juno's pressurizing is beginning to work.

In the auditorium the orchestra were re-assembling, discussing rooms they'd wallpapered or plants they'd bought over the weekend. A violinist was cutting his nails. Two women viola players were trying to organize a dinner party.

Abby was given a desultory clap when she came in. In return she thanked the RSO for a wonderful concert, and said how happy she was to see them again.

'Now let's have an A, Simon,' she asked the First Oboe.

Because it was April Fool's Day, Simon Painshaw, with a completely straight face, played A flat.

'Everyone transpose half a tone up,' said Abby, who had absolute pitch and knew it was April Fool's Day, and brought her stick down.

Caught on the hop, the orchestra burst out laughing and gave her a proper round of applause.

The morning was spent sifting through repertoire, struggling with a lot of swearing through a horror by a member of the Lesser Avant-Garde of Bulgaria, full of grunts and shrieks as though a tom-cat was being gang-raped by elderly badgers. They then moved on to an appalling serenade for solo triangle, cow bells and tom-toms with extended catawauls on the strings, written by someone called Roger Parker.

Viking immediately took out a final reminder from British Telecom and on the back drew a bucket, and wrote '*crap*' on the side, then handed it down the row. Abby, of the same mind, called a halt after five minutes.

'We're not programming this garbage.'

'Maestro,' Dixie Douglas, the troublemaking First Trombone, put down page three of the *Sun* and raised a large red hand. 'I would respectfully submit that this is a work of towering genius.'

The orchestra laughed.

Dixie then explained that the 'garbage' entitled 'Eternal Triangle', had been composed by 'Sonny' Parker, Peggy's ghastly son, the RSO's composer-in-residence.

It was hoped Mrs Parker would give a quarter of a million pounds towards the orchestra's centenary celebrations next year.

'A concert has been planned for her sixtieth birthday,' concluded Dixie, 'in the gre-ounds of her 'uge house.'

'I don't care,' said Abby mutinously. 'It's still garbage.'

The orchestra exchanged delighted glances. A run-in

between L'Appassionata and Nosy Parker had distinct possibilities.

Later Abby had a cup of coffee with Mark Carling who was beginning to meet her eyes and joke with her.

'"Magnificent" is not the word you'd use about this office,' he gazed round at the chaos.

Mark was a sweet man, who loved music with a passion and who had previously been very happy running an early music group in London.

'Hugo says you did awfully well today,' he told Abby. 'It's lovely to see the orchestra happy. They do tend to grumble a lot. But I believe they have a tough life for very little money. I try to think of that when they barge in here and behave horribly.

'I envy you winning their confidence so quickly,' he added wistfully. 'When I go into the band room, they part like the Red Sea.'

'I guess they think a lot of you.' Abby tried to sound convincing.

'They'd forgive me if I were able to give them rises,' sighed Mark. 'The malaise is general. Orchestras everywhere are finding that with audiences plummetting, reduced Arts Council and local government funding and sponsorship being harder to come by, there's less and less money to spare.'

Abby was too wrapped up in the next week, digesting the arcane repertoire and imparting her findings to the orchestra, to notice how bad things were financially. Not only had Rodney overspent dreadfully, but the obscure music chosen by Mark to appease the Arts Council had not pulled in the crowds. Recordings, television and film work had dried up. There had been no more proms since Rodney fell asleep on the rostrum during *Daphnis and Chloé* and, for the first time in years, the orchestra had not been invited to take part in the next county's prestigious Cotchester Festival.

On her second Tuesday morning Abby got an ecstatic letter from Rodney. The Swiss were going to name a train after him.

'Just imagine the darling boy chugging through the mountains, we can all go for rides on him and gaze at the wild flowers.'

Running into the General Office in excitement to break the news, Abby found Miles Brian-Knowles tearing out his thatched hair. Herman, the kindly German guest conductor, known as 'Vun Two Vun Two', who had been standing in for Rodney for a month, was that evening doing the hellishly difficult *Missa Solemnis*.

The stage had already been extended, losing three hundred stall seats to accommodate the soloists and the Valkyrie might of the Rutminster Choir. And now Herman was sitting sobbing in Miles's chair saying: 'I am not a Nazi. If the orchestra won't apologize I'm going home.'

Meanwhile, in the auditorium, the orchestra were playing silly buggers and singing: *'He was Her-man, and he did us wrong.'*

'Herman's paid five grand a concert to stand up and be electrifying,' grumbled Viking to Blue. 'He's got no right to bore us and be incompetent.'

Hugo, who had another very difficult solo in the *Missa*, had retired to the leader's room to practise in case Herman was coaxed back.

Stupid Kraut, thought Abby hubristically, hasn't a clue how to handle musicians.

Even more dramatically, at lunch-time Mark Carling resigned. The Arts Council, after all he had done to please them, had slashed the RSO grant by 4 per cent, so now with inflation running at 3 per cent, they would be plunged into debt again. Having no money meant Mark couldn't plan ahead and would have to scrap big productions like *Fidelio* scheduled for later in the year. The final straw was an enraged letter about the music put on to please the Arts Council.

Dear Sir,
If you continue to programme this drivel, I shall
cancel my subscription.

Disasters come in threes. About to fly from Lucerne to
take over the baton later in the week from poor harassed
Herman, Rodney suffered a massive heart attack. The
orchestra were shattered. Forgetting how Rodney had
led them into debt and borrowed money off them, they
only remembered his wonderful anecdotes about the
famous, his kindnesses, rigging up a big screen so they
could watch Wimbledon and the way he swept them all
out to dinner when he was in funds.

'Rodney avoided tax, but not attacks,' said Viking,
who'd gone very white. 'He'll be OK,' he added to a
distraught Abby.

'I must go to him.'

'I'll drive you to the airport.'

'Your car wouldn't make the outskirts of Rutminster,'
said Hugo scornfully. 'I'll take her.'

'Well, take him my St Christopher for luck,' said
Viking.

As the RSO were now facing a mega-crisis of cash and
morale, an emergency board meeting was called. With
Mark Carling gone, the executive directors included
Miles Brian-Knowles, who acted ever-so humble at
board meetings because he wanted Mark Carling's job,
and Harry Hopcraft, the financial director, who was
within a year of retirement, and against any innovation
particularly if it involved spending money.

Among the non-executive directors were the chairman, Lord Leatherhead, who was tone deaf but who
had been fond of an aunt who played the tuba; Lady
Chisleden, a stuffy old trout, whose reputation for
virtue had been somewhat tarnished a few years ago,
by rumours that she had been seen pleasuring
Rannaldini's ancient gardener during the famous

Valhalla orgy; Peggy Parker, who referred to the orchestra as 'we' and who never missed a concert; various bankers, brewers and building society supremos (the three Bs which keep orchestras going), and Canon Airlie, a Handel freak, known as the unloose canon because like Mrs Parker, he was always inveighing against hooliganism.

Finally, there were two directors from the orchestra: Simon Painshaw, Principal Oboe, who was a walking Grove's Dictionary if given the chance, and the Principal Viola, Dennis Strickland, known as 'El Creepo', because he was always brushing against breasts.

These directorships, which lasted two years were supposed to be chosen from the best people to fight the orchestra's corner. But such was the distrust of management, that Simon and El Creepo had been the only people last time to put their names forward.

The boardroom itself looked across to the russet spires and roofs of Rutminster. The ruby blur on the horse-chestnuts in the park was turning buff as the green leaves pushed out of each sticky bud. The spring sunshine, however, cruelly highlighted the faded dusty brown velvet curtains with the hems coming down, the worn blue carpet, the peeling blue-and-fawn wallpaper, the Paisley design concealing the damp patches. On the walls were also an oil of Herbert Parker, who looked like Bach after a short back and sides, an aerial view of Rutminster showing the concert hall, some framed programmes from the early days, and a photograph of a drooling Peggy Parker shaking hands with the Duchess of Kent. The room however, was dominated by Rodney's portrait over the fireplace. Ruskin Spear had brilliantly captured his Falstaffian merriment. Any moment, you expected him to wink.

Canon Airlie opened the meeting with prayers for his recovery. Miles really shut his eyes and said the loudest Amen.

Miss Priddock, who was taking the minutes, burst into

tears and was comforted by a swig of brandy from one of the brewers' miniatures. Lord Leatherhead then suggested they offer Abby Rodney's job.

'She's got a high profile, she'll pull in the sponsors and the advertisers. She'll attract fat record contracts – we were all impressed by the way Megagram chipped in – and she's played with many of the top conductors, so she'll pull in the big names.'

'She's also a fine musician,' chipped in Lady Chisleden. 'I don't want to speak ill of the ill, but Rodney hated learning new pieces. Abby will bring in a younger audience. Ours is getting a bit hoary.'

'And the orchestra like her,' said Harry Hopcraft, the financial director. 'I haven't heard such laughter coming from rehearsals since Rodney fell off the rostrum. And she's cheap.'

Howie Denston (who'd been on the telephone before Rodney reached intensive care) had offered most reasonable terms.

'Look how well Dame Edith has done at Cotchester,' said Peggy Parker. 'The English have always thrived with a woman at the helm. Think of Boudicca, Elizabeth I, Victoria—' She waited expectantly.

Miles didn't fail her.

'And of yourself, heading your great Parker and Parker empire.'

Peggy Parker bowed graciously.

'With respect though, Mr Chairman,' continued Miles in his fluting voice, 'I feel Abigail Rosen is too young and inexperienced.'

El Creepo, who liked Abby because she was beautiful and had praised his solos, said that Simon Rattle and Toscanini had taken over when they were even younger.

'Auditioning'll take months,' urged Harry Hopcraft. 'And think of the air fares and the hotel bills.'

'We ought to consider the alternatives,' persisted Miles. 'What about Olaf?'

'Talks far too much in rehearsals and bores the

orchestra,' said Simon, whose solos Abby had also praised.

'What about Vladimir?'

'Liable to turn nasty,' said El Creepo. 'Uses us to familiarize himself with obscure repertoire, then rushes off to record it with other orchestras.'

'What about Hans?' asked Lady Chisleden. 'Such a charmer.'

'Said he wanted to live in the area and get to know us then pushed off on the first plane back to Switzerland after every concert, and he's always drunk on the rostrum.'

'Sheraton's miserable in Germany,' added Simon, 'but it would take six months to extricate him. Rannaldini's restless in New York, but we could never afford him and Boris Levitsky.'

'Is dishy,' said Lady Chisleden eagerly.

'But totally unreliable,' snapped Peggy Parker.

'None of them is as famous as Abby,' said Lord Leatherhead. 'We must have someone who can haul audiences away from the television.'

Miles cracked his knuckles.

'What about Ambrose?' he suggested in desperation.

Everyone shuddered. Ambrose, the principal guest conductor, known as the 'Fat Controller', was a bitchy old queen who'd been guesting for three months in San Fransisco. ('Coals to Newcastle,' said Viking.)

'Ambrose is bound to block Abby's appointment when he returns,' said Lady Chisleden. 'He loathes women.'

'All the more important to engage Abigail at once,' insisted Peggy Parker, envisaging a whole series of concerts in which Abby dazzled in a different Parker and Parker evening ge-own, and blissfully unaware of Abby's comments about her son's composition.

'Don't you think we should consult the orchestra?' said Simon Painshaw, examining his red dreadlocks for split ends.

'Heavens no,' said Harry Hopcroft. 'They'll disagree on principle.'

Miles's was the only dissenting voice: he was even more fed up when, over Earl Grey and digestive biscuits, the board showed no inclination to appoint him as managing director.

Everyone agreed with Lord Leatherhead that they needed a new broom with a City background, who could capitalize on Abby's marketability.

'He must be musical,' urged Lady Chisleden.

'And able to give the orchestra spiritual guidance,' urged Canon Airlie.

Lord Leatherhead said he and one of the bankers had someone in mind.

'Will you approach him then, my Lord,' said Peggy Parker.

And I'll never suck up to you again, you old monster, thought Miles furiously.

Glancing out of the window, Lord Leatherhead saw Abby, back from Lucerne, leaping out of a taxi, running up the path, as lithe and graceful as the white cherry blossom tossing in the April breeze. As a treat, the board decided to call her in and offer her the job.

'I'd like to hear how Rodney is, too,' said Lady Chisleden.

There was a rip in Abby's jeans, a smudge on her forehead and her dark curls stood on end.

She had had a frightening and exhausting three days and had only come back because she had exchanged a few comforting words with Rodney, who had urged her to carry on with Squeakygate.

'He was so darling,' she said, as Miss Priddock bustled in with a fresh pot of tea. 'He sent you all his love, particularly you, Miss Priddock, and said please don't worry. He said he'd get much better much quicker if they added some Krug to his drip, and at one moment, he looked round at all the tubes,' Abby gave a sob, 'and then said, "Darling girl, I'm not frightened of death, it's just getting there that worries me"'

When they offered her the job, she burst into tears for a second time, and hugged everyone including El Creepo. Her delight and her impassioned promise that she would work her heart out for Rodney's orchestra, until he could take over again, touched them all.

'The problem with modern orchestras,' she went on, 'is that conductors are so busy jetting round the world, they never have time to learn the repertoire or get to know the orchestra. I want to live in Rutminster and become part of the community. Thank you all for giving me this wonderful chance. Can I sign the contract as soon as possible, in case you change your minds?'.

'Who is going to tell the orchestra?' asked El Creepo nervously, after she'd gone.

'Oh, tell them after the contract's signed,' said Harry Hopcroft. 'We don't want them putting their oar in.'

TWENTY-FIVE

Having been nearly flattened by musicians charging out of rehearsal to the Shaven Crown, Abby floated off to ring Howie, who gave her a bollocking for over-enthusiasm.

'If you hadn't rolled over we could have screwed another grand a concert out of them. I'm only going to draw up the contract for a year, right? To see how you get on.'

Privately he was convinced the RSO would have folded long before then.

As everyone had gone home, Abby stole into the auditorium which seemed filled with the ghosts of former players. Herbert Parker's haberdasher's gold crest of interwoven thimbles, needles and cotton reels glittered on the faded dark green velvet curtains. Even the gold cherubs decorating the fronts of the boxes seemed to be tooting their long trumpets to welcome her.

'*My band, my own band,*' sang Abby, waltzing down the aisle in ecstasy. '*I'm gonna make you the greatest band in the world.*'

Leaping onto the rostrum, she was singing

Beethoven's *Fifth Symphony*: '*De, de, de, dum, de, de, de, dum, de, de, de, dum*', at the top of her voice and conducting with wild flourishes, when someone started playing the First Violin part. Whipping round, Abby nearly died of embarrassment to find Hugo who'd been working late.

'How was Rodney? Better it would seem.'

'I figure he'll pull through,' Abby leapt down from the rostrum, 'he's determined to ride in his new train. Thank you so much for driving me to the airport.'

Something's happened to her, she's glowing, thought Hugo in disquiet, and it's nothing to do with Rodney. God, he hoped Viking hadn't got there first.

'You look like the cat that's got the cream. You must be in love.'

'Oh I am,' Abby whirled round the platform.

Bugger Viking, thought Hugo.

'In love with a whole big orchestra, right? Promise, promise you won't tell anyone.'

'Sure, sure.'

'You are looking,' Abby paused in mid-whirl, nearly falling over, 'at your new boss.'

'What!' No cymbal crash could have been louder.

'The Board's just appointed me musical director.'

Hugo was enchanted, particularly because it had nothing to do with Viking, and suggested dinner at a discreet out-of-town restaurant, the Heavenly Host, in Paradise.

The sunny day had turned into a beautiful evening with the first green leaves spotlit by the falling sun against a navy-blue sky. Lambs were racing in the fields, cricketers in sweaters were practising in the nets. Hugo pointed out various pretty thatched cottages belonging to members of the orchestra, including his own, which was smothered in clematis montana with a front garden filled with grape hyacinths and primroses.

'This is where you should get a place. I come home in

the evening, see cows in the fields, and stop thinking "Bloody orchestra". We can have a night-cap there later if you're not too tired.'

'I'd just love to,' said Abby.

Hugo was such a gentleman, he'd never try anything unless she wanted it. But, looking at his beautifully manicured hands on the wheel and his powerful thighs in those lemon cords, she thought perhaps she did.

Hugo would be the perfect man, kind, sophisticated, utterly honourable, with whom to celebrate the end of three years' celibacy.

'That's Rannaldini's house,' Hugo halted, putting a caressing hand round her left shoulder and pulling her across the same powerful thighs, so that out of the side-window, she could see Valhalla, towering and tasselled with emerald-green larches.

'How can he leave such a fantastic place to work in New York?'

As they arrived at the restaurant, Hugo pointed out a pilgrimage of frogs laboriously crawling across Paradise High Street on their way to the River Fleet.

'Just like the RSO, no matter who they're bonking, how much they've drunk, whatever mischief they're up to, oversleeping or missing the bus, some inner clock tells them the time and somehow they always make the gig.'

'That's so dear,' said Abby in a choked voice. 'And this is so gorgeous,' she cried as they went into the restaurant.

Angels reclining on clouds and twanging gold harps had been painted on the walls. Pretty waitresses, in flowing white robes and haloes, handed out scrolls instead of menus. Vases of lilies stood on each celestial blue table.

Being mid-week, the restaurant was pretty empty. Hugo felt free to talk and, over a celebratory bottle of Moët, he told Abby about the Berlin Wall existing between the musicians and the management, who were known as the 'Fourth Reich'.

'The management think the orchestra are a bunch of capricious, male-dominated, backbiting, money-grubbing hooligans. The orchestra think management is inefficient, lazy, uppity, tone deaf, overpaid and spends its time drinking coffee and taking three-hour lunches.'

The candlelight gave a warmth to Hugo's sallow skin, his dark eyes gleamed with laughter.

'The only time the orchestra venture onto the top floor is to ask for days off or more money, or make private telephone calls. In fact the orchestra's attitude to management,' Hugo picked up the menu, 'was summed up this afternoon by the chairman of the Players' Committee telling the Press about Mark Carling's resignation.'

'What did he say?' asked Abby fascinated.

'He said: "I feel great joy and sadness. Joy that Mr Carling is leaving, but sadness that it won't be for another three months."'

'That's obnoxious,' Abby was shocked rigid.

'And that,' sighed Hugo, 'after all Mark's done for the orchestra. Poor guy was so upset, he's walked out, and we'll have to put up with that dickhead Miles Brown-Nose until they appoint another managing director.

'But with an average RSO salary of fifteen thousand pounds and most of them forced to take teaching jobs and freelance work to pay the mortgage,' said Hugo fairly, 'it's not surprising they're tired, tetchy and demoralized.

'They're all spoilt,' he went on. 'They've been the best player in their school, in the local youth orchestra, probably at college. Parental hopes centred on them, so on the one hand you're dealing with eighty-six Pavarottis who all think they can play the concerto better than the soloist. On the other hand they've been soured by being told how to play Beethoven's *Fourth Symphony* every week by a different idiot, who earns more in an evening than they all do put together in a month. The hall is terrible,' he went on, 'a blackbird on the first day of spring would sound dire in there, and there's no money to repair it.'

'Are you ready to order, Monsieur de Ginèstre?' an angelic waitress put down a plate of little pies, filled with salmon mousse and scrambled eggs, and topped up Abby's glass.

Hugo, who had hardly touched his, because he had been talking so much, ordered garlic mushrooms for himself and Abby as a first course. After a lot of French *chat du jour* with the manager, they agreed on boeuf bourguignonne, new potatoes and haricot verts as a main course.

'Musicians love food,' said Hugo. 'The best thing about a concert is eating afterwards. Tomorrow night,' he put a leisurely hand on Abby's jeaned thigh, 'I will cook for you.'

Abby, who hadn't eaten all day, was trying not to wolf all the little pies.

'Go on about the orchestra, I guess I better know the worst.'

'The main problem,' Hugo was studying the wine list with intensity, 'is that there isn't room in the area for two orchestras. And the Arts Council are dying to close one down. There's only fifty miles between us and the Cotchester Chamber Orchestra, who are smaller and much better run by Dame Edith Spink. And they've got the backing of Venturer Television. As a result they're pinching more and more of our dates, and more of our sponsors.

'They specialize in early music when they are not programming Dame Edith's junk. They've done fifteen CDs in the last seven months, and they've got some really good musicians. The RSO used to be a terrific orchestra, specializing in heavyweight nineteenth-century music.'

'And will be again,' interrupted Abby firmly. 'But first I gotta fire some of the musicians. Juno Meadows for a start, she's awful, and there are some dreadful string players, and an old boy in Viking's section, who should have been pensioned off years ago, as should that old bass player, with the hearing-aid, for Christ's sake. And the First Clarinet's a basket case.'

'His wife keeps threatening to leave him, normally he's a good player,' protested Hugo.

She doesn't miss a trick, he thought.

'Omigod,' Abby gave a moan of greed as a huge cloud-shaped plate of mushrooms, dripping in garlic butter and parsley, was placed on the blue table-cloth for them to share.

'Tuck in,' said Hugo.

Abby, however, was reluctant to be distracted. Dunking a piece of bread in the butter, she said: 'Most of that lot will have to go.'

'Well, that's a good thing,' Hugo popped a mushroom into her mouth, 'because there'll probably be a mass exodus once they hear you've been appointed. Then you can slot in your own people.'

'Will they be very hostile?' said Abby in alarm.

'They won't like working for a woman.'

'But there are lots of women in the orchestra.'

'That's different, they're in subordinate positions. Mary Melville, Principal Second Violin and Clarissa, Principal Cello, are the only section leaders.'

'But they've been darling, so far,' Abby felt champagne, garlic mushrooms and too many pies churning unpleasantly round and took a slug of water.

'That's because no-one takes Squeakygate seriously,' confessed Hugo. 'They loved Rodney, but they still winged about him. Now he's gone, they'll canonize him.

Orchestras see the fronts of conductors so they only fall in love with their departing backs.

'You must be tough with them, Abby, or they'll walk all over you, and you *must* keep your distance. You're a very attractive woman, but once one of them gets you into bed, the rest will be wildly jealous and lose any respect for you. And don't think they'll keep it a secret. You can't be a member of the Celtic Mafia unless you report back on every conquest.'

Sidling down the heavenly blue velvet banquette, Hugo slid an arm round Abby, and pressed his lips to hers.

Abby was so startled, she kissed him back, a glorious exchange of garlic butter: her first French French kiss. Sitting down, Hugo was the same height as her.

'I can't wait to show you my cottage,' he whispered.

'I haven't showered since this morning,' stammered Abby, then kicked herself for being so *gauche*. Frenchmen were supposed to relish unwashed women, like camembert.

'I've just had a jacuzzi installed,' Hugo seemed to read her mind.

'I thought you said I mustn't screw any members of the orchestra,' chided Abby, who was nevertheless getting wildy excited.

'I did,' Hugo's eyes were no longer soulful, but smiling wickedly - d'Artagnan of the flashing rapier again.

'Quite frankly I can't stand playing second fiddle to Lionel Fielding any more, he's back the day after tomorrow and he's such a wanker, so I'm off to lead the CCO. Edith and I were bashing out the nuts and bolts after your début concert. I gave my notice in this afternoon,' he added triumphantly. 'I'm no longer a member of your orchestra, my darling, so there's nothing to keep us apart.'

And he lunged back into the attack.

Abby was so enraged that her great ally was abandoning her in her hour of need, that she leapt to her feet, and emptied the plate of mushrooms and butter all over Hugo's yellow cords.

Then she shouted across to the manager: 'If you bring in the boeuf bourguignonne, I'll empty that over the son-of-a-bitch, too.'

And she stalked out.

TWENTY-SIX

Abby's spirits were scarcely raised the following morning when she went into the general office to study the wall chart of future engagements. It was like a wallflower's dance programme. There should have been bookings two years ahead. The RSO hardly knew what they were doing in the autumn.

A moment later, Miss Priddock rushed in brandishing the *Rutminster Echo* as if there'd been a death in the family.

RUTMINSTER ABBY, shrieked the huge headline.

Someone, probably Hugo, incensed by the destruction of his yellow cords, had leaked the story of her appointment.

'*Some achieve greatness, some have greatness thrust upon them,*' wrote the Rutshire Butcher, arguing that Abby was an example of the John Major Syndrome. '*You push someone young and inexperienced into a position of huge responsibility and then you pray like hell,*' which didn't make Abby any happier.

The orchestra, with predictable artistic caprice, were absolutely livid. They had not been consulted. Abby hadn't worked her way up as a conductor. She had no track record.

'It's a nice day, let's go on strike,' said Randy Hamilton, who'd had a big win on the Grand National and wanted to play golf with Dixie.

The rest of the orchestra were too strapped for cash to strike and plotted rebellion. It had been a lark having Abby poncing around with Squeakygate, but there was no way they were having her as musical director, planning the repertoire and taking over all Rodney's concerts. They vowed to break her in a month.

'Poor Princesse Lointaine,' sighed Viking, when she gave him back his St Christopher. 'The honeymoon's over before you even had time for a wedding night.'

Instantly the orchestra started making her life a misery, turning rehearsals into the worst kind of blackboard jungle, barracking her, anwering back, carrying on when she told them to stop, passing notes, farting, burping and in her first concert as musical director, totally ignoring her and playing the Dvořák *Cello Concerto* and Beethoven's *Fourth Symphony* exactly as they had always played them. Abby felt as effectual as a tiny child trying to flag down a passing helicopter.

At this initial concert, she first fully appreciated the deficiencies of the hall. The acoustics were frightful. The whole building trembled every time the express to Paddington went by. Every fire engine, back-firing car and tolling cathedral clock could be heard. Rain poured through the roof. Now she realized why they'd installed portaloos for her début concert. Only the most deafening tutti could drown the clanking of chains in the Ladies.

Nor did Abby get any support from Lionel Fielding, the leader, and Hugo's reason for leaving, when he returned. He should have acted as a buffer between her and the orchestra, but accustomed to being a big fish and finding a far greater violinist had been appointed over him, he flew back in a rage that he had not been consulted.

Lionel was a very vain man, whose romantic good looks were marred by a petulant expression. Although he spent more time blow-drying his flowing ebony locks in the leader's room than practising his solos, he wasn't above launching into a Paganini *Caprice* before concerts just to unnerve less experienced string players.

He loved all the little marks of respect owed a leader, musicians standing up for him, being asked to dinner with the board and to parties after concerts. And since he had been guesting with a northern orchestra, who had a very lush leader's room, with an en suite bathroom, a sofa, fridge and coffee machine, he was very discontented with the chair in a large cupboard provided by the RSO, and determined to replace it with something grander.

Known as the 'Incredible Sulk' because of his black moods, Lionel had a sweet wife, Miriam, who used to play Second Oboe. Lionel, however, had insisted she return home to look after their three children – 'I will not have latch-key kids' – leaving him free to pursue the Second Clarinet, Hilary Lloyd.

Nicknamed the 'Swan of Purley', because she was the leader's mistress, Hilary Lloyd was an organizing bitch in her late twenties, who ran the RSO conker competition and terrorized any young pretty girl in the orchestra, by raising her eyebrows and sighing every time they played a wrong note. She also put in industrial earplugs in protest against the din of the brass section and to unnerve her section leader, a gentle old boy called Eldred whose job she wanted.

A school sneak, Hilary never forgot a birthday nor an insult. The players tended to suck up to her because as leader's pet, she could make life very difficult, particularly in a time of recession. She had a very inflated idea of herself and would suddenly yell out, 'Lionel, the First Violins ought to be more pianissimo,' in the middle of a rehearsal, which was completely out of order.

Hilary's best friend was ostensibly Juno Meadows, but they enjoyed a spiky relationship, Hilary envying Juno's fragile beauty and her acquisition of Viking, and Juno envious of Hilary's minor public-school background and her acquisition of Lionel, who as leader, outranked Viking. Much of their conversation revolved round whether Juno would reform Viking, or Lionel leave Miriam. Hilary prided herself on being better at sex, cooking and cherishing than Miriam. She would set her alarm for 3 a.m. so she could listen to Lionel playing the *Kreutzer Sonata* on the World Service.

Hilary had a cottage outside Rutminster which Lionel visited on the way to and from work, but unlike Viking he didn't pay the mortgage, having a large one of his own already. As a result Hilary was very tight with money, never buying a drink and always taking the manilla envelope round to collect for leaving presents, so no-one would realize she hadn't put in any money.

The departing Hugo had been much-loved, and Hilary collected enough money to buy him some new yellow cords, a pair of waterproof trousers and a symbolic gym slip and hockey stick, because he was defecting to join the Headmistress's team in Cotchester.

His leaving party, in Close Encounters Wine Bar near the cathedral, was extremely wild. Viking and Dixie brought the house down with a touching rendition of 'The Lost Cords'. Canon Airlie, taking a midnight stroll with his Welsh terrier, Trigger, was appalled to see a shrieking schoolgirl with only a hockey stick for protection being chased across the Close by the Celtic Mafia and a large barking black dog. The schoolgirl was then stripped of her gym slip and thrown into the River Fleet. Rushing to her rescue, the Canon nearly suffered a coronary on being confronted by a thick hairy chest and worse, as Hugo emerged laughing uproariously, bellowing French expletives, from the foam.

*   *   *

Abby had not been invited to the party – 'You're management now, duckie ' – but heard the sounds of revelry as she leant wistfully out of the Lord Byron Suite, breathing in the smell of white lilac and newly mown grass, and praying that one day she would be accepted.

But no-one could accuse Abby of cowardice. Her first job was to sort out the RSO.

'I know you're all desperately underpaid and hung-over,' she told them with a smile the following morning.

The orchestra, green to the gills, did not smile back.

'And I'm going to push for more bucks for you,' went on Abby. 'But not until you play better. You've got sloppy and lazy and there are too many players not pulling their weight: faking or being protected by their colleagues.'

She then produced the bombshell that she wanted the entire orchestra to re-audition behind a screen and in front of a listening panel in the American fashion.

'So no bias against women, foreigners, young or old, black or white, can creep in. This won't mean mass sack-ings, we can't afford it.' Abby smiled again at the orchestra who glared back stonily. 'I just want to locate the bad apples.'

'We could start with you,' shouted the bullying, brick-red faced First Trumpet, Carmine Jones.

Miles Brian-Knowles, the general manager, who was already cross with Abby because she claimed she was too busy to meet and charm any sponsors, was absolutely furious.

'You can't sack anyone, it's not just the money, the unions won't let us, and any musician fed up with working in London is far too expensive.'

The board, however, supported Abby, as did one of her few fans, the stage manager, Tony Charlton, known as 'Charlton Handsome'. Charlton was a larky boy, who looked almost as good in jeans as Viking, and resented the fact that the Celtic Mafia creamed off the prettiest groupies after concerts.

'They're a lot of prima donnas, Abby, you stick to your guns,' he encouraged her as he rehung the dusty brown velvet curtains across the board room to provide a screen, and turned the big mahogany table sideways. He then lined up chairs on the far side for a listening panel, which would consist of Abby, Miles, relevant section leaders when they weren't auditioning themselves, and Miss Priddock with a list of numbers for each member of the orchestra to be ticked off 'Yes' or 'No' after they'd played.

Most stretched of all by the event was Nicholas Digby, the incredibly harassed orchestral manager. Nicholas had an anguished face, ginger hair falling like Saluki's ears on either side of a very bald cranium and looked rather like Mr Pinch in *Martin Chuzzlewit*. One of his many jobs, along with providing complimentary tickets, and seeing the soloists' dressing-rooms were all right, was getting the correct number of musicians on and off the stage for every concert. He had a nervous break-down every winter finding extras when the RSO were laid low with flu.

He now had the thankless task of feeding members of the orchestra one by one into the board room and attempting to preserve their anonymity by stopping them speaking.

'Leave off your aftershave, and stump in in Doc Martens,' Dixie advised Randy. 'And they'll assume you're a woman and pass you automatically.'

Sections varied in size in the RSO. Lionel, as well as leading the orchestra, presided over thirteen first violins. Peter Plumpton, First Flute, on the other hand, only had the Steel Elf and an occasional piccolo player to boss. Section leaders, or principals as they were known, were responsible for the various problems within the section, stopping personality clashes, deciding who should sit where and next to whom, generally improving the sound.

They also tended to shield bad players. Barry, the Principal Bass, a grey-haired giant with a gypsy's face, who came from a rock band, had an old boy, known as 'El Squeako', in his section. El Squeako, who relied on his double bass to hold him up, had a hearing-aid which frequently let off eldritch squeaks during the most intimate pianissimo, reducing the entire orchestra to hysterical giggles. Somehow El Squeako had to be nursed past the listening panel.

It was a matter of pride for Viking to get all his section through. His only worry was Old Cyril, the Fourth Horn, whose lips and teeth had gone so he couldn't centre the notes any more, and who drank too much out of nerves and despair.

Once a great player and friend of Dennis Brain, Old Cyril always wore a tie and a jacket to rehearsals, sat up straight, was polite to everyone, loved his garden and Miss Priddock for the thirty years he had been with the orchestra.

Viking knew he ought to take the old boy aside and tell him he was holding the section back, but Cyril had looked after Viking when he joined the orchestra eight years ago. He would never survive if he were fired and had to eke out an existence teaching, and Viking wasn't going to dump him now. Cyril, however, hadn't helped himself by downing beer after beer in the Shaven Crown on the day of the auditions.

By lunch-time, Abby had reached screaming pitch. Why in hell had she started the beastly thing? If she heard another *Mozart* concerto murdered, she'd go ballistic. She'd forgotten, too, how terrifying auditions were for players. With throats constricting, fingers stiffening, tongues tying, and breath shortening to nothing, it was worse than ironing someone else's silk shirt.

Number Thirty-Nine, who'd just come in, played

exquisitely for three minutes before launching into a flurry of wrong notes and bursting into tears.

Appalled, Abby jumped up, pushing the brown velvet curtains apart, to find Little Jenny, the round-faced baby of the orchestra who sat at the back of the Second Violins.

'You did great,' Abby put her arm round Jenny's heaving shoulders. 'We all thought you were a far more experienced player. Of course you're through. Go and have a large drink.'

'It was your idea to audition everyone,' said Lionel nastily as Abby flopped back into her chair.

'We better all go to lunch and cool down,' said Miles primly.

Abby, who was not remotely hungry, went in search of Jenny's section leader, Mary Melville, known as 'Mary-the-Mother-of-Justin', because she was absolutely bats about her baby son. Abby wanted to tell Mary how good Jenny had been and that she ought to play at a desk nearer the front.

The band room acted as a sitting-room where musicians dumped their instruments, ate their packed lunches and relaxed when they weren't needed in a piece of music. As well as low sofas, chairs and tables, there was a ping-pong table, a notice-board and a small bar at the far end, providing bacon sandwiches, hot dogs and soft drinks, tea and coffee.

The room fell silent as Abby entered.

'I'm looking for Mary.'

'Gone shopping,' said Clarissa, Principal Cello, who apologized for speaking with her mouth full and, to everyone else's horror, invited a pathetically grateful Abby to join her for a cup of coffee.

Clarissa, like Charlton Handsome, was another of Abby's supporters. She admired her as a great player and, as the mother of three with a husband out of work, Clarissa was always too worried about paying the mortgage and the school fees and scurrying from teaching jobs to cabal and bitch with the rest of the orchestra.

Slumping down on one of the uncomfortable olive-green sofas, trying to ignore the hostility all around, Abby was amazed to see Viking, who normally went to the Shaven Crown at lunch-time with the Celtic Mafia, unenthusiastically eating cottage cheese between two pieces of Ryvita.

Beside him the Steel Elf was looking at colour charts.

'This room is terrible,' she glared up at walls painted a vile shade of hen's diarrhoea green. 'Why don't we all pitch in and rag and drag it a nice peach one weekend?'

'Needs some decent pictures,' said Viking, not looking up from *Viz*.

'Perhaps we should commission a portrait of our new musical director,' said Hilary, who had her back to Abby.

'Won't be here long enough,' said Juno bitchily.

'Ignore them,' whispered Clarissa, returning from the bar with two cups of coffee.

'Thanks,' whispered back Abby. 'What's Viking doing here?'

'Dixie has a tenner on at 100-1 that Juno will kick Viking out before the end of April,' murmured Clarissa, picking up the black tights she was darning, 'so it's in his interest to lead Viking astray.

'On Sunday, Viking was supposed to be putting up shelves. Dixie lured him out to the pub and Viking didn't get back till midnight. Madam was hopping,' Clarissa lowered her voice even further, 'and has refused to sleep with Viking unless he stops drinking and carousing, and he has.'

'My God, for how long?'

'About forty-eight hours.'

Viking, meanwhile, was trying to look as though he was enjoying cauliflower florets and Vegemite sandwiches.

'What did you put in for Nugent?'

'Nothing, I keep saying dogs should only be fed once a day. With the warmer weather, he can soon sleep outside. What d'you think of that colour for our bedroom, Victor?'

'Onspeakable. Nugent will not sleep outside,' he handed Nugent half his sandwich, which Nugent promptly spat out, regarding it as no substitute for his own shepherd's pie at the pub.

'Any chocolate biscuits?' asked Viking.

Juno cut a grapefruit in half and handed one part to Viking with a plastic spoon and a napkin. 'Here's your dessert.'

'Some achieve grapefruit, some have grapefruit thrust upon them,' sighed Viking. 'Oh Christ.'

Old Cyril had come in, cannoning off both sides of the band room door before collapsing hiccuping on a sofa, gazing out unseeingly at the chestnut candles tossing in the park.

He was followed by Mary-the-Mother-of-Justin, angelic face flushed with excitement over the photos she had just picked up from Boots.

'This is Justin.' She brandished a photograph of a gorgeous two year old in front of Abby and Clarissa.

'Gorgeous,' sighed Abby. 'And that's darling of you and him.'

'I expect my husband'll put that one in his wallet,' Mary said happily.

'You don't have a photograph of me in your wallet, Victor,' nagged Juno.

'Haven't got a wallet,' said Viking, who was returning from the bar with a cup of black coffee for Cyril and a Penguin for Nugent.

'Haven't got any money either.'

Neither Covent Garden nor the London Met had yet paid him and Juno's mortgage was eating into his salary.

Hearing guffaws from the window, he swung round. It was Dixie and Randy grinning and red faced from the pub.

'We've bought you a box of After Eights, Victoria dear, to round off your slap-up meal.'

Viking auditioned in the middle of the afternoon, and he mobbed the whole thing up. Somehow he had persuaded the pianist to play a piece of music more suited to a strip club. The listening panel pursed their lips and looked even more disapproving when, after a couple of bars from the French horn, a lacy black bra flew over the brown velvet curtains, followed in leisurely succession by fishnet stockings, scarlet satin garters and, finally, a purple G-string, which landed on the shiny board-room table in front of Abby.

Abby's cries of 'This is obnoxious,' were then drowned by Don Juan's horn call, before Viking launched into the love duet from *Ein Heldenleben*, establishing no doubt as to his identity.

Sauntering out, he left a note on his chair: '*Please leave this seat as you would find it*,' for Randy Hamilton, who laughed so much he could hardly play.

'Fuck,' Randy said, after the tenth wrong note.

'Shut up, you are not allowed to speak,' hissed a sweating Nicholas, who was supposed to be calling out players' numbers to the listening panel as he fed them in.

'Fuck,' said Randy for a second time, so distracting Nicholas, that Blue, plus horn, was able to slide into the board room unnoticed, and hide in a big cupboard in the corner.

Thus, when a swaying Cyril was posted in by Viking, and Nicholas had called out his number, fifty-five, Blue put his horn to his lips and played the horn solo from *A Midsummer Night's Dream* so beautifully, the panel halted him after a couple of minutes.

'That's fine,' Abby turned to Miss Priddock. 'Put a "yes" to Number Fifty-Five.'

'Definitely,' agreed Lionel and Miles.

The next moment, to their horror, a beaming Cyril staggered through the curtains, solemnly shook hands with them all, blew a kiss to Miss Priddock and tottered out.

Miles and Lionel and Abby were all furious, but not so cross as Quinton Mitchell, Viking's Third Horn, who threatened to sneak to the panel about Blue's playing instead of Cyril.

'I have to sit next to the drunken old bugger.'

'If you breathe a word,' Viking seized Quinton's lapels, 'I'll tell Mrs Mitchell exactly who you were op to at Hugo's leaving party.'

'Fifty-Six,' shouted Nicholas.

The piano started playing, a few seconds later a flute joined in.

Lionel and Miles stared fixedly at their notes. Abby felt as though steel nails were being drilled through her head. A wave of vindictiveness overwhelmed her.

'That's enough warming up,' she shouted a few minutes later. 'We're pushed for time, right, can you get started.'

There was a pause, then a furious squeaky little voice said: 'I've just played the slow movement of Poulenc's *Flute Sonata.*'

Abby shook off Miles's restraining hand.

'Can you come through?'

Anger made Juno look even more enchanting, putting a rare warmth in her cold eyes.

'It's no good, Juno,' said an unrepentant Abby. 'I guess you'd better look for another job, you're just not up to it.'

'I was good enough for your predecessor,' hissed Juno and stormed out.

'That was very unwise,' smirked Lionel.

'Wonderfully lyrical,' he murmured mistily a minute later, as Hilary, whom he'd coached between bonks last night, started paddling laboriously through the slow movement of Mozart's *Clarinet Concerto.*

She was interrupted, however, by Viking, barging in without knocking, all slitty eyes and blazing Irish rage.

'How dare you sack Juno?' he yelled at Abby.

'S-s-she's useless, she must have slept with someone to get that job.'

'She's sleeping with me, and if she goes, I go.'

And in barged Blue.

'If Viking goes, I go.'

And in marched Dixie and Randy.

'And if Viking and Blue go, we go,' they chorused.

'Woof, woof, woof,' barked Mr Nugent, bringing up the rear.

'You fucking band of brothers, I don't understand you guys,' yelled back Abby. 'I guessed love was blind, but I never figured it was deaf as well. I don't know why you're being so supportive,' she added to Nugent. 'Juno'll have you out in a trice.'

Miles, who disapproved of swearing and dogs, looked very shocked.

As a result, the Steel Elf was reinstated but Abby had made herself an implacable enemy.

TWENTY-SEVEN

Poor Abby had such good intentions. But being musical director of the RSO continued to be an absolute nightmare. After one particularly rowdy rehearsal towards the end of April, during which Viking had peremptorily summoned the entire brass section out into the car-park to push his ancient BMW because he was late for the dentist, Abby received a summons from the manager.

Finding Lord Leatherhead and Miles, who'd given her even less support than Lionel, awaiting her, Abby steeled herself for a wigging. Instead, they told her they had found a new managing director.

'It's George Hungerford,' said Lord Leatherhead in tones of awe. 'We've been very, very lucky.'

Abby had no idea who George Hungerford was, and was even less impressed when they told her he was one of the few property developers who had managed to increase his fortune during the recession.

A rough, tough Yorkshireman, who in his youth had sung bass in the great Huddersfield Choral Society, George had always fancied running an orchestra, and reckoned he could sort out the RSO in one or two days a month with his hands tied behind his back. He would take over at the beginning of May.

All the female musicians and the secretaries on the top floor were wildly excited that he was also between marriages. 'Gorgeous George' as they already called him, could also be relied on to take L'Appassionata down a peg. Blood in the aisles was joyfully predicted.

Abby was too worried about next week's concert and her even more revolutionary plans to re-audition the entire and often frightful Rutminster Choir before the German Requiem in June, really to take in George's appointment.

Wrestling with the complexities of the last movement of Sibelius's *Fifth Symphony*, she had only fallen into bed at five o'clock by which time the dawn chorus, who sang infinitely better than the Rutminster Choir, had started. She was woken by a maid coming in to clean the room at nine-thirty. Leaping out of bed, she frantically tugged on yesterday's sweaty clothes. Racing down the High Street, she reached the auditorium at seven minutes to ten, only to find the place deserted. Unlike American orchestras, British players had a maddening habit of scuttling in at the last moment. As a final insult, Viking wandered in yawning at half-past ten.

'Sorry I'm late,' he smiled unrepentantly at Abby. 'I was having a helicopter lesson and I couldn't find anywhere to park. Hi, sweetheart.' He paused on the way to kiss the Steel Elf.

Incensed because the French horns start the *Fifth Symphony*, Abby proceeded to dock half an hour off Viking's pay, which triggered off the orchestra. She had vowed to be accommodating today and as a joke had even circulated a photostat of a dictionary definition of the word, pianissimo, to all the brass section to stop them drowning everyone else. But they had merely made paper darts and thrown them back at her.

Lionel the leader, who should have supported Abby, made no attempt to hush the chat that rose like a fountain whenever there was a pause. Now he asked if he might have a word. Abby jumped down from the rostrum, acutely conscious of her scruffy appearance and dirty hair beside Lionel's coiffeured glamour. Even his breath smelt of peppermint, as he said: 'Look, we've recorded this symphony with Rodney and Ambrose. If you want to get through it, just sit on top of the orchestra and coast.'

'And leave you in charge, no, thank you,' snapped Abby.

Lionel and Hilary exchanged told-you-so shrugs.

Two minutes later Abby called a halt.

'Excuse me, flutes, you were dragging a little.'

'You amaze me,' Juno lowered her long blond eyelashes, 'we were only following you.'

Ignoring the jibe, Abby tried to inspire them by telling them of Sibelius's emotions when he wrote the symphony, but they all started yawning.

'As you know the last movement ends with the six huge hammer blows of the God Thor,' persisted Abby.

'My back's thore after all those semi-quavers,' said a voice from the back of the violas.

'Cut out the programme notes and get on with it,' shouted Randy.

Dixie got out a porn mag.

Abby's messianic streak emerged five minutes later when the horns launched into a glorious swinging tune.

'This is a great euphoric affirmation of hope,' she said earnestly, 'which Sibelius wrote after he discovered that he wasn't dying of cancer, after all, so I want you horns to play as though the sun was bursting through dark clouds and . . .'

Viking let her run on for a minute, before looking up.

'You mean you want it louder,' he drawled.

The orchestra cracked up.

'No, I do not,' screamed Abby. 'I want you to play with more passion, and build up to a splendid sforzando.'

'It says fortissimo in my score.'

'Oh for God's sake, let's get on.'

Nellie Nicholson, the orchestra nymphomaniac, was a third desk cellist whose cello was nicknamed 'Lucky' by the male musicians. Five minutes later she came in loudly in one of the long pauses between the final hammer blows.

'Sorry, sorry, Abby,' she called out apologetically. 'A fly landed on my score and I played it by mistake.'

Again the orchestra cracked up.

Abby totally lost her cool.

'What in hell's the matter with you guys?'

'You are,' piped up a voice from the back of the violas.

Abby couldn't detect the offender who was hidden by Fat Isobel, who was even larger than Fat Rosie. Fat Isobel had a big jaw, and always looked as though she'd cleaned the grill pan with her hair. Despite this, on last year's tour of the Oman, lots of Arabs had seriously tried to buy Isobel. Leaping down, barging between the second violins and violas, somehow circumnavigating Fat Isobel, Abby found Clare, the orchestra Sloane, and Candy, her best friend, from Australia, both ravishing blondes, playing battleships and discussing their sex life.

'You will not hide behind Isobel,' stormed Abby.

As she yanked their music-stand into view, the viola part of Sibelius's *Fifth* fluttered to the floor.

'Excuse me, Maestro,' Steve Smithson, the RSO's union rep, was beside her in a trice, breathing fire. 'It's Mr Charlton and the stage hands' job to move the music-stands. If you observe Rule 223,' he brandished the book under her nose.

For a second he and Abby glared at each other. Behind him Abby could see Nicholas, the orchestra manager, bald head bobbing like a buoy at sea, as he hopped from one foot to another in the wings, terrified at the prospect of a walk-out before the concert.

Wearily, Abby climbed back onto the rostrum.

'Let's play the last page again, and no-one is to come in between hammer blows.'

'With respect, Maestro,' said Lionel silkily, 'it's half-past eleven,' and was nearly knocked sideways by junior members of the various sections and a barking Mr Nugent racing out to be first in the tea queue.

Abby slumped in the conductor's room, burning face in her hands. Having had no time to put on a deodorant, she could smell last night's sweat, now sour with fear. Dipping a towel in cold water, she rubbed it under her armpits, then groaned as she glanced in the mirror, the rust jersey was far too hot and clashed with her hectic red cheeks, her hair rose like Strewel Peter. She knew the orchestra were trying to goad her into resigning. She mustn't be beaten.

Outside she could hear the cuckoo. Beyond the park, over the palest green rolling fields of barley, she could see the Blackmere Woods and knew what she must do. Splashing her face with cold water, she picked up her stick with resolve.

The second half went better. The horns and trumpets were swinging joyfully like monkeys in the jungle through the glorious heroic tune. The bows of the string players were a blur, they were going so fast.

But, as Abby paused to improve the ensemble playing of the Second Violins, little Claude 'Cherub' Wilson put up his hand.

Cherub, Second Percussion, had blond curls and blue eyes and hardly looked old enough to be playing in a primary-school band.

All the orchestra adored him. Miss Priddock baked him cakes. Even the Celtic Mafia allowed him to travel in their car to concerts to act as Court Jester. He was now sitting in the percussion seat behind Viking.

'Scuse me, Miss Rosen.'

'Yes Cherub,' Abby's face softened.

'You know that bit in the first movement?'

Abby picked up the score and patiently started to leaf back through the pages.

'Which bit, Cherub?'

'The bit when the horns come in an' the trumpets an' the strings.'

'There are a lot of bits like that.'

Cherub leant forward, consulting Viking's score.

'I found it a minute ago, it goes, la, la, la, la, la, la, la,' he sung in a shrill falsetto, 'or maybe it's *la*, la, *la*, la, la, la.'

The orchestra were clutching their sides.

'Don't laugh at Cherub,' snapped Abby. 'I know that bit,' she flipped more pages. 'Here it is. But you're not even playing,' she cried in outrage, then realizing she'd been hoodwinked, 'in fact there's no percussion in this symphony.'

'I know,' Cherub beamed at her. 'But it's a nice bit, isn't it? We do like nice bits you know; can you play it again?'

'No, we flaming can't,' Abby contemplated hurling her score at him, but she couldn't throw that far.

Quivering with rage, she clutched the brass rail, counting to ten, deciding to give them one more chance.

'During the break,' she leafed forward to the last movement, 'I looked out at the Blackmere Woods, and realized how all the different greens contribute to the beauty of the spring, merging together like a great orchestra.'

Cynical, bored, impatient, menacing, the RSO spread out below her.

'I like to think of you, Eldred and Hilary, and your clarinets providing the acid yellow of the poplars, right, and the trombones,' Abby smiled at Dixie, 'like the stinging saffron of the great oaks, and the flutes, the lovely eerie silver of the whitebeams. Barry's basses splendid dark evergreens, and of course the horns, Viking and Blue and co., soaring like beech trees topped with radiant dancing pale green.'

'I don't want Nugent lifting his leg on me,' grumbled Viking.

But Abby was in her stride. Looking round at the rapt faces, she thought: I've got them at last.

'I could find trees to illustrate the wonder of the trumpets and the bassoons,' she smiled forgivingly at Steve Smithson, the union rep, 'but all I want to say is that like the spring the sound of your individual instruments can blend together to create the beauty of Sibelius—'

But, as she paused to wipe away a tear, Dixie Douglas let out a long and hellish fart.

Immediately Hilary leapt to her feet, flapping her score in horror.

'Lionel, *do* something.'

And Abby flipped. She was screaming so hysterically at Dixie, that she didn't hear the door opening at the back of the hall, or notice the laughter freezing on the faces of the players.

Hearing voices, however, she swung round.

'Get out, get OUT, how many times have I told you, visitors are not allowed in the hall during rehearsals.'

'Unless they wear gas masks,' said Viking.

But the visitors came on. Abby swung round again, with the words: 'Didn't you fucking hear me?' dying on her lips. For it was the chairman, a smirking Miles and a handsome, belligerent stranger.

'Sorry to interrupt you, Abby,' said Lord Leatherhead heartily, 'but I just wanted to introduce you all to your new – er – chief executive, George Hungerford.'

All the orchestra clapped in delight.

Surreptitiously, from behind the bulk of Fat Isobel, Candy got out a huge red brush, powdered her nose, then handed the brush to Clare.

George Hungerford had a square jaw, a broken

nose, a mouth set like a trap and tired, hard, turned down eyes behind horn-rimmed spectacles. He looked as tough as a limestone cliff and about as unscalable. He had thick hair, which was cropped very close to his head and the colour and strokeable texture of a bullrush. His dark grey suit was well cut to set off flat, broad shoulders, but also to disguise a spreading midriff.

'He looks like a bouncer,' murmured Randy Hamilton.

'And we all know who we want him to chuck out,' murmured back Dixie.

George then mounted the stage and told the orchestra in a broad Yorkshire accent, how much he was looking forward to working with them. As he talked, his eyes moved solemnly over each player as though he was memorizing their faces for some future conjuring trick.

He didn't envisage any great problems, he said.

'Running an orchestra's like running any other business. If it doesn't make a profit, you make changes. I'd like to look at what you're all up to before I make any decisions.' Then he added without a flicker of a smile, 'And I hope you all play a bloody sight better this evening.'

'Why the hell's George Hungerford interested in us?' Viking asked Blue. 'His usual form is bribing planning officers and knee-capping little old sitting-tenants.'

'I'd lie down in front of his bulldozer any day,' sighed Candy.

'Looks ruthless,' said Hilary, with a sniff.

'He is, too,' giggled Clare, the orchestra Sloane. 'His wife was called Ruth. They split up last year. I read all about it in the *News of the World*. Ruth ran off with one of his even richer rivals. She's very beautiful in a Weybridge, skirt-on-the-knee, matching accessory way. Those classical types always screw like stoats beneath the Elizabeth Arden exterior.'

'You should know,' said Hilary bitchily.

Abby slunk back to the Old Bell, mortified that George's first impression should have been of a sweaty, shaggy, screaming virago. Tonight she would wow him.

As if in anticipation, two cardboard boxes of ge-owns were awaiting her from Parker's; horrors in mauve, lime-green, jaundice-yellow and the most shocking pink, encrusted with rhinestones, sequins and *diamanté*, over-busy with cowled necklines, floating panels and kick pleats.

Accompanying them was a handwritten, bullying note, urging Abby to make George's first night special with an evening gown fitting the occasion in every sense. Mrs Parker had somehow got hold of Abby's measurements.

Incensed at being dictated to, Abby didn't even try them on, merely washing her hair and dressing in the flowing indigo trouser suit she'd worn at her début concert.

She wished she had a friend in the orchestra with whom to discuss George. He had seemed so forceful because he'd made no attempt to ingratiate himself. He had certainly electrified the women in the orchestra. Parker's sold out of scented body lotion by closing time, and scuffles broke out in the changing room, as the prettiest girls fought for a glimpse in the communal mirror as they applied blusher and knotted coloured ribbons in their hair.

Hilary was livid, on George's first night, that Eldred and not she was playing the clarinet solo in the *Mother Goose* Suite.

'That dress is much too low, Nellie,' she snapped. 'You know we can't show bare arms or cleavages.'

'Some of us haven't got cleavages to show,' said Nellie, rudely as she sprayed *Anais Anais* behind her knees. 'George Hungerford won't know I haven't got plunging permission.'

'With all the different floral scents wafting from the

orchestra,' giggled Candy to Clare, 'Abby's going to get her image of a spring meadow, if not a wood.'

Abby was desperate for everything to go well, but, alas, the concert was a disaster. Some joker had slotted a page from Dixie's porn mag into the middle of her *Mother Goose* score. Scrumpling it up in a rage, she chucked it over her shoulder, where it landed in the massive, corsetted lap of Mrs Parker, who was already spitting because no ge-own had been worn.

The hall was half-empty and the pouring rain, which had discouraged random ticket buyers, dripped through the roof on Abby's head, but failed to extinguish the fire in a local bakery, so the first movement of Sibelius was ruined by clanging fire-engines. Worst of all, one of Miss Priddock's programme sellers, over-excited by the arrival of George Hungerford, charged back and forth to the Ladies throughout, and when a chain wouldn't pull, started furiously clanking in syncopation to the heroic swinging tune in the horns, reducing the RSO to more fits of laughter.

'Delhi Belly Variations,' murmured Viking to Blue as he emptied water out of his horn.

But at last they reached the six wonderfully dramatic hammer blows, which test any conductor, because an audience can often assume the whole thing's finished and start clapping too early.

Abby's pauses were the longest and most dramatic ever heard in the H.P. Hall, but during the penultimate silence, the chain in the Ladies clanked again. Dixie Douglas promptly corpsed and came in a beat too soon. Forgetting herself, an incensed Abby raised two very public fingers at him and, running off the platform, locked herself in the conductor's room, refusing to acknowledge any of the applause. She needed a show-down with George so she could pour out her grievances, but when she finally unlocked the door the place was deserted, and the caretaker was locking up.

Escaping through a side-door, Abby found the rain had stopped, and breathed in a lovely smell of wet earth and the lilies of the valley which Old Cyril had planted under Miss Priddock's window.

During concerts, the orchestral car-park was jam-packed with small used cars, vans, old Volvos with different coloured doors, Morris Minors and Viking's ancient BMW with the 'Hit Me, I Need the Money' sticker in the back. It was now deserted except for a blue Rolls Royce and one of George Hungerford's heavies in a chauffeur's uniform and a state of shock.

'Fort we'd never escape wivout injury,' he patted the Rolls' bonnet, 'but it was empty in five minutes. Vroom, vroom, vroom. No-one 'it us. Never seen driving like it.'

'Glad they do something well.'

'It was a grite concert. Don't know how you remember all them notes.'

'Thanks,' said Abby. 'Where's your boss?'

The chauffeur nodded up to the chairman's office, where George Hungerford, puffing at a cigar, blotted out light from the window, as he paced back and forth, talking and talking.

Probably about me, thought Abby wearily.

As she entered her hotel, a yawning receptionist handed her a big bunch of wild garlic.

'A child has just delivered this.'

Imagining some kind of voodoo, Abby was about to chuck the starry white flowers into the street, when she found a note, which she ripped open with trembling hands. She read:

Dear Miss Rosen,
Sorry I upset you,
love
Cherub Wilson.

It was the first kindness anyone had shown her in weeks.

Abby started to cry helplessly. She must get a grip on herself.

Her honeymoon with the Rutshire Butcher it seemed was also over. His review of the concert was headlined: FLUSHED WITH SUCCESS – '*The lavatory chain*,' he wrote, '*was the only thing that played at the correct tempo in Sibelius's* Fifth Symphony.'

TWENTY-EIGHT

Fortunately George Hungerford disappeared in his helicopter the following morning, no doubt looking for properties to develop. He also had several acres in central Manchester to think about. After a slight blip in the recession, the developer's cranes were flying again.

In the afternoon, the RSO, who were supposed to provide music for nine counties and who had at least two away fixtures a week, were due to set off to Starhampton in the West Country. Two coaches had been laid on for the hundred-mile journey. The first coach, which included non-smokers and non-drinkers, a bridge four who played regularly together and a high-minded group, headed by Hilary, who sang madrigals, was known as 'Pond Life'. The second, which included drinkers, smokers and brass players was known as 'Moulin Rouge'.

The Musicians' Union is one of the few unions virtually untouched by Thatcher's reforms. Steve Smithson set out on every trip armed with a tape measure (because any gig over seven miles away entitled the musicians to a meal allowance), a stop watch so they got sufficient breaks the other end and a thermometer to make sure the hall, cathedral or school in which they were playing reached the required seventy degrees.

Before an away fixture there was always an argy-bargy between Steve and Nicholas, the orchestra manager, who was known to the musicians as 'Knickers'.

Orchestras are sustained by silly jokes. When poor Nicholas was unhappy and stressed out, which was most of the time, they all chorused 'Knickers Down', or 'Knickers in a Twist'. Today Knickers had caught Steve trying to persuade the bus drivers to leave at one and dawdle, instead of one-thirty, so that the musicians could claim for a lunch allowance.

It was now twenty-nine minutes past one and Knickers stood beside the artists' entrance of H.P. Hall, ticking off names in a tartan notebook as musicians clambered aboard the two coaches.

By one-thirty only Little Jenny was missing. As she played at the back of the second violins, it wouldn't be a major crisis if she didn't show up. So the buses set off, splashing down the High Street out into the angelic springtime, stopping to pick up Simon Painshaw from his bachelor pad in the Close and Hilary from her thatched cottage, and Barry, the Principal Bass, from his converted barn, with his beautiful new second wife running barefoot across the lawn to kiss him goodbye.

After yesterday's downpour, cricket pitches under water glittered in the sunshine and puddles reflected thundery grey sky, pale green trees and clashing pink hawthorns.

It was an incontrovertible fact that however capable the RSO were of pulling rabbits out of hats and playing superbly when they reached their destination, many of them behaved like hyperactive children before and afterwards.

Usually Viking drove to concerts in his battered BMW, which had been fitted with a hooter that played Don Juan's horn call. Into the car he would cram Juno, Blue, Randy, Dixie and Cherub, so they could all apply for a petrol allowance, or on occasion, a train fare.

But, at the last moment, Juno had cried off with flu.

Finding a replacement at such short notice had added to Knickers' problems.

As it was also Viking's birthday, he and the Celtic Mafia decided to travel on Moulin Rouge. Viking, who'd been blasting his lip away moonlighting with a local jazz band, hadn't been to bed and was drunk when he got onto the coach. Freed from Juno's beady chaperonage, he was soon pouncing on every girl in sight.

'That guy's got no stop button,' observed Candy, who was sitting beside her friend Clare, who was flipping through *Hello!* and *Tatler* recognizing all her friends.

'When he's plastered he'll bonk anything,' Clare lowered her voice, 'Juno gave him a Black & Decker for his birthday, such an affront to his manhood. I think he's miserable.'

'Then why does he leap to her defence whenever Appassionata has a go at her?'

'Must be elf-obsessed,' giggled Candy. 'Oh, there's you,' she peered at *Tatler*. 'That ball gown's great.'

From the back of the coach came shouts of laughter and the snatch of a rugger song, followed by Cherub's high-pitched giggle which set everyone off. Blue sat slightly apart sipping malt whisky, immersed in Alan Clark's *Diaries*. Randy and Dixie were obviously determined to catch up with Viking, who was now snogging an overjoyed Nellie the Nympho.

In the Pond Life coach in front, as they drove through the outskirts of Bath, the madrigal group could be seen making silly faces.

'*April is in my mistress' face and July in her eyes,*' sang Lionel in a light tenor as he gazed at a simpering Hilary.

Also in the group was Simon Painshaw, his red dreadlocks flying as he tossed his head in time to the music, and Molly Armitage, a rank-and-file viola player. Known as 'Militant Moll', Molly had short spiky hair, an aggrieved face, a triangular figure, with narrow, twitching shoulders falling to massive hips, and thought everything degraded women. She was having an *affaire* with Ninion, Second Oboe, who was half her size and normally very meek. Molly, however, had so fired him up that he had become very assertive and wanted to oust Simon as First Oboe. Militant Moll also wanted Ninion to leave his wife and take her name.

'*Fa, la, la, la, la, la,*' sang Militant Moll, gazing into Ninion's blinking fieldmouse eyes.

'*Lardi, da, da, da, da, da,*' giggled Nellie, buttoning up her dress as she collapsed behind Candy and Clare. 'That Hilary is such a bitch. Look at her vamping Lionel in her pie-frill collar. She gave me another bollocking about my cleavage last night. "You are not allowed to show flesh, Nell, we are all supposed to look black at distance."'

Nellie caught Hilary's mincing whine to perfection.

'I'll black her eye. You wait till she sees what I'm wearing tonight, the slit up my skirt meets my plunge head-on. I wonder how long it'll be before L'Appassionata is shoehorned into one of Nosy Parker's ghastly ge-owns.'

'Wonder how long it will be before Gorgeous George shoehorns her out of the job,' said Clare. 'You can't get away with V-signs on the platform, even if it's only at Dixie.'

'Taking my name in vain as usual. Any of you girls want a drink?'

Dixie armed with paper cups and a bottle of Southern Comfort, was swaying above them. His normally red face and neck were now as brown as a builder's from so much free time playing golf and reading the *Sun* on the flat roof of H.P. Hall.

'There you are again,' Candy had found another picture of Clare, this time at a wedding in *Hello!*.

'And there's my wicked brother and there's Mummy,' cried Clare.

Dixie glanced at *Hello!*.

'I wouldn't mind getting orf with Mummah myself,' he mocked, as he handed paper cups to both girls.

Clare giggled. Despite that gha-a-a-astly accent, she thought Dixie frightfully attractive.

Dixie also had the 'hots' for Clare. Despite those awful corduroy culottes and the matelot jersey tugged down to cover a big bum, and an Alice band holding her brains in, Clare was a natural blonde with lovely skin and slender ankles.

'I'll fix Lady Clare,' Dixie muttered to Randy on his return. 'I'll wipe Daddy's smile off his face in *Hello!*.'

As Candy emerged from the coach loo, which was shaped like an upended coffin, Viking, ready for new sport, called out: 'That's a gorgeous T-shirt.'

'On special offer in Parker's this week,' said Candy.

'All my offers are special,' retorted Viking, pulling her onto his knee.

Abby, who still hadn't had time to buy a car, hired one to drive to Starhampton. Popping into the hall to pick up a black satin trouser suit from the conductor's room, she found Little Jenny in floods, her round face red from the hairdresser, her brown hair a mass of Pre-Raphaelite curls.

'They kept me under the dryer so long I missed the bus. Knickers'll murder me.'

'No, he won't, hop in,' said Abby. 'You can remind me to drive on the left. Have you had any lunch? There are sandwiches in the glove compartment.'

It soon became clear that Jenny was thrilled not to be going on the coaches.

'If you ride in Pond Life, Hilary and Molly sneer at you. It's all right going there on Moulin Rouge, at least you can smoke, but it's terrifying coming back, all the guys pounce on you.'

'Who does?' asked Abby.

'El Creepo and Carmine Jones,' Jenny bit into an egg-and-cress sandwich. 'They both told me I'd get the job if I went to bed with them,' she shuddered.

'That's gross,' said Abby in horror. 'Who else?'

'The Celtic Mafia. They all think they're God's gift. All brass players are chauvinist pigs and homophobic. They despise Simon because he's gay and Ninion because he's gentle. Dixie and Randy are the worst. The other day,' Jenny went absolutely scarlet, 'the coach was driving past a sewage farm, and Dixie looked round at me, and shouted, "Close your legs, woman." I was so embarrassed. That's George Hungerford's new place.'

Up an avenue of limes, Abby could see a large red Georgian house, big enough to be a school or a mental home. No doubt George would convert it, flog it and move on.

'The changing rooms are a nightmare,' went on Jenny, tucking into cucumber-and-tunafish. 'Every time you take your clothes off, you feel the scorn. I know I'm overweight, but they make you feel like an outcast. And none of them seem interested in learning to play better. They accuse me of being a creep if I take my music home, or if I practise during the break. And they're so awful to conductors.'

'Don't I know it,' sighed Abby, desperate for reassurance.

'Oh, they don't like you because they hate taking orders from a woman. I think it's mean,' said Jenny, and having finished all the sandwiches, she fell asleep.

As Abby drove towards the slowly sinking sun, the countryside changed. White houses with grey roofs replaced the thatched cottages. The verges became banks filled with anemones and violets. Fields, divided by winding streams lined by osiers, rose into rounded hills. Wild garlic was taking over from fading bluebells. She must thank Cherub for his flowers, and she must fight on and restore some idealism to the RSO and protect people like Simon, Ninion and poor Little Jenny.

She arrived at Starhampton Town Hall as the instruments were being unloaded from a huge grey van with 'Rutminster Symphony Orchestra' written in red letters on the side. Barry was worried about a missing double bass which had already been unloaded. Carmine Jones was having a row with Charlton Handsome, the stage manager, whom he claimed had dented his trumpet.

'You'll bloody well have to pay for it.'

Viking was on Knickers's mobile calling Juno.

'Hi Shweetheart, howsh Nugent?'

As Abby followed the winding passages backstage, she could see through a door marked 'Ladies of the Orchestra', musicians hanging up black dresses from Next, Monsoon and Laura Ashley, and taking instruments out of cases, which also contained dusters, Lockets for sore throats, Ibuleve for aching backs, apples, fruit drinks in oblong cartons and pictures of husbands, boyfriends and children.

Having driven here with Abby, Jenny was delighted to find herself an unaccustomed centre of attention.

'What was she like?'

'OK, she shared her sandwiches with me. I think she's lonely and wanted someone to talk to.'

After a quick rehearsal and dash into Starhampton for something to eat (and in the Celtic Mafia's case to drink), the orchestra emerged transformed and mysteriously glamorous in their tails and black dresses to face a packed hall.

Both Hilary and Peggy Parker had a fit when they saw Nellie's slit skirt fall open to reveal a red suspender belt and black fishnet stockings. Peggy Parker's piggy little eyes were soon distracted by Francis Fairchild who played on the second desk of the First Violins. A wonderful musician, Francis was known as the 'Good Loser', because he was always mislaying his possessions. Tonight he had lost his black shoes, and padded onto the platform with black socks tugged over his brown shoes.

The Magic Flute overture fizzed along. The provinces were crazy about Mozart, and the audience were looking forward to his *Second Horn Concerto*. But just as Abby was returning to the platform, she heard crashes and shouting coming from the Green Room.

Rushing in, she found Lionel, Nicholas, Miles, Charlton Handsome, the Pond Life driver and two stage hands in dinner-jackets trying to restrain Viking, who was plainly out of his skull. Seeing Abby, he shook them off.

'Maestro,' mockingly he bowed, his slitty eyes going in all directions as he swayed in front of her, 'let me play, I know I can play the concert.'

The scores of Haydn's *Trumpet Concerto* were kept stacked in the van for any emergency. The sneering bully boy, Carmine Jones, despite his dented trumpet, would be more than happy to play it. Quinton Mitchell, the Third Horn, who badly wanted Viking's job, was equally happy to stand in for him and play the Mozart. But Abby hadn't mugged up the Haydn, and despite his disruptive behaviour, she still carried a flickering flashlight for Viking.

'OK, if you figure you can do it, go ahead.'

It was a terrifying gamble, drink stops tongues and fingers co-ordinating. Throughout the concerto, over her left shoulder, Abby was aware of Viking swaying like a white poplar in a high wind. But he played flawlessly as though the shade of his hero Dennis Brain was lovingly guiding his breath and his long fingers. Perhaps it was his sadness over Juno, thought Abby wistfully, which made the middle movement unbearably poignant.

Having glassily acknowledged the roars of applause, however, Viking staggered back to the band room and passed out.

Elgar's *Second Symphony* was a success after the break, particularly with the orchestra, because Abby was so carried away by the melancholy nostalgic music that she slowed down again, and pushed the orchestra into over-time, which put poor Knickers in a twist once more.

As there were some excellent chip shops and Indian restaurants in Starhampton, Knickers was also worried he might lose several musicians. But the quickest dressers in the world, within seconds, the orchestra were back in their clothes, tails back in plastic hangers, crushed velvet dresses shoved into carrier bags, and the instruments stowed away in the van.

Francis the Good Loser was chucked out of the Pond Life coach for trying to smuggle on a take-away curry.

'Let him go and stink out Moulin Rouge,' shouted Randy Hamilton. 'We'll all go and mob up Pond Life.'

So clanking bottles, carrying bags of chips and camp-followed by Clare, Candy, Nellie and Jenny and four percussion players, the Celtic Mafia changed buses.

Having had a good sleep in Elgar's *Second Symphony* during which Quinton did stand in for him, Viking had woken up and was raring to go.

'It's my birthday, I can behave *exactly* as I like.'

He then remembered the birthday cake Miss Priddock had baked for him and tried to cut it on its silver cardboard disc with Blue's penknife. As the coach moved off through the empty streets of Starhampton, however, he upended it spreading cream and chocolate butter-icing all over the floor of the bus to the noisy cheers of his supporters.

The bridge four looked on stonily, particularly when Viking bore a pretty thoroughly over-excited married piccolo player off to the back of the bus. The madrigal group decided to ignore such infantile behaviour.

Militant Moll got out her song book.

'We better call in the pest-control officer,' she said sourly to Hilary, who'd just given Nellie yet another lecture on being improperly dressed.

'In the final analysis, I prefer Byrd to Gibbons,' Ninion was telling Simon Painshaw.

'Unfair to gibbons,' shouted Randy, making monkey faces and scratching himself under the arms.

The Celtic Mafia corpsed again. Lionel cleared his throat.

'*Come away, come sweet love, the golden morning breaks,*' he sang to a dimpling Hilary.

'*All the earth, all the air of love and pleasure speaks,*' sang Ninion, blushing as he gazed up at Militant Moll's granite jaw.

A rival singsong, however, was soon in full swing at the back of the bus.

'*If forty whores in purple drawers were walking down the Strand,*' bellowed Randy and Dixie. '*Do you suppose, the walrus said, that we could raise a stand?*'

Dixie had Clare on his knee. Her big bum felt nice and warm, as he stroked her slender ankles.

'Just ignore them and keep going,' hissed Hilary.

'*My bonny lass she smileth*

When she my heart beguileth,' sang Simon, casting nervous glances at the back of the bus.

'*Fa, la, la, la, la, la,*' screeched Hilary.

'*Bloody sight too far, la, la, la, la, la,*' sang Dixie, chucking Clare's velvet Alice band into the passing pale green woods.

'*I doubt it, said the carpenter, but wouldn't it be grand,*' sang Randy, pulling Candy onto his knee.

'That's enough,' snapped Lionel, but to no avail.

'*And all the time, the dirty swine was coming in his hand,*' chorused the Celtic Mafia.

'Disgusting. Do something, Lionel.' Hilary had gone pink with rage.

Afraid to confront the Celtic Mafia head-on, slipping on chocolate butter-icing and cream, Lionel strode down the bus to lodge a complaint with Knickers who was far too busy sitting on top of the driver, urging him on like Ben Hur. If the coach reached H.P. Hall later than twelve-thirty they would be into the next day, and by union rules, the musicians would be entitled to an extra free day later in the year.

'You're the leader, Lionel, you sort it out,' said

Knickers firmly, then to the driver: 'Left here, then we can short-cut to Bath.'

Nellie the Nympho had other plans. Installing herself in the right-hand seat, just behind the driver, she un-buttoned her pink cardigan, enough for Blue still immersed in Alan Clark, to rub Ibuleve into her shoulders.

'*As it fell upon a day in the Merry Month of May,*' sang the Madrigal Group with gritted-teethed desperation.

'*The love juice running down my index finger,*' hollered back Dixie.

'*The way we used to come, and how we lingered,*' sang Randy in harmony.

'*Oh, how the smell of you clings,*' joined in Viking, finally letting go of the ecstatic piccolo player.

'*These foolish things remind me of you,*' sang Randy, smiling into Candy's eyes.

'Rather like being an air hostess,' giggled Cherub, as he slid down the gangway carrying paper refills of whisky to Blue and Nellie, who, by this time, had undone most of her buttons. In his rear mirror, the bus driver could see her splendid breasts wriggling as she writhed under Blue's expert fingers. The bus was definitely slowing down.

May 1st was nearly over. Anxious to win his bet, Dixie was geeing up Viking.

'Why don't you ring Juno?' He handed him Knickers's mobile.

'Hi, schweetheart,' said Viking a couple of minutes later, after punching out three wrong numbers. 'Howsh Nugent?'

'The bitch hung up on me,' he said furiously.

Abby, who had been coerced into attending some mayoral reception, caught up with the coaches, around eleven forty-five. She'd been thinking of ways to make Little Jenny happier and, looking into the coach, was horrified to see Viking, whisky bottle raised to his lips like a conch, coming down the gangway, well, like a Viking, and pulling a girl into his arms. Abby nearly ran into a stone wall, the girl had long brown Pre-Raphaelite curls.

Drawing level, Abby peered in. Definitely Jenny. She must be rescued at all costs. Crawling along behind the coach, ignoring Cherub and Lincoln, Viking's Fifth Horn, who recognized her and started waving like children, Abby waited for the next pee break.

Spitting with righteous indignation, she fought her way into the bus, seized Jenny's hand and catching her off balance, dragged her out into the balmy night, where huge moths were bombing the bus's headlamps.

'What d'you do that for?' said an aggrieved Jenny, shoving her left breast inside her bra.

'Viking's a beast, an animal. I'm so sorry, Jenny, I should have insisted I drove you back home.'

'I didn't mean Viking,' squeaked Jenny. 'I've wanted to snog him ever since I joined the orchestra.' And with that she shot back into the bus.

But by this time Jenny's innings were over. Seeing Fat Isobel stampeding him like a rhino, Viking looked up the coach and saw Hilary.

'Come here, crosspatch.'

As his beautiful mouth came down on hers, Hilary pretended to fight him off, but she was secretly delighted. Just wait until she told Juno.

Fat Isobel, however, was still bearing down.

'Come on,' said Viking, pulling Hilary down the steps to the vertical coffin-shaped lavatory, where he found Militant Moll on the way out.

'Sweet Moll Malone,' taunted Viking, pushing her back into the coffin, 'come and be degraded.'

Although Moll fought him off, she was also delighted. Just wait till *she* told Juno. Then she discovered Viking had Hilary in tow and had locked the coffin door on all three of them. Furious banging followed.

'Whatever did Viking do to you?' said Lionel furiously when at last Hilary emerged with her feathers ruffled.

'I'm not going to tell you, but he's got to apologize. I can't wait to ring Juno.'

Slightly too long afterwards, Militant Moll emerged looking equally ruffled.

'I've been sexually harassed,' she hissed at Ninion. 'Why didn't you come and rescue me?'

Hilary had just finished wising up Juno, when the coach doors opened to let her out at her cottage.

'See you in about twenty minutes,' she whispered to Lionel, who, for appearance's sake, had parked his car at H. P. Hall.

Clarissa and Mary-the-Mother-of-Justin were so tired they had slept through the whole journey. Mary's head was resting on Clarissa's shoulder.

'Pretty thing,' murmured Viking, stopping in his tracks to admire Mary's madonna face and bending down, kissed her on the lips. For a second, Mary smiled, then opening her eyes, and realizing it wasn't Johnno, her husband, she clouted Viking across the face. Sliding to the floor, he passed out cold.

As Randy, Dixie, Blue and Little Cherub carried Viking, like another coffin, to the door of Juno's converted squash court, singing the 'Death March' from Saul, Mr Nugent started howling, and in the darkened bedroom above, the net curtains twitched furiously.

'*Oh, how the smell of you clings,*' sang Randy.

'*Fa, la, la, la, la, la,*' sang Cherub, giggling hysterically and trampling on a lot of pink tulips.

The cathedral clock tolled the half-hour.

'*Ding-dong, ding-dong, ding-dong,*' sang the rest of the bus to wind up Knickers. They would reach H.P. Hall after twelve-thirty and get their free day.

Down below a ding-dong of a different kind was taking place. As Randy played the 'Last Post', waking up the entire street, and Nugent's howls increased, a furious Juno, who'd been given a blow by blow account by Hilary, greeted Viking with a rolling pin.

Viking didn't make it until the break the following afternoon, staggering in, looking greener than the band room, followed by an exuberant Mr Nugent.

'Behold El Parco,' shouted Randy.

'There's a special offer for rolling pins in Parker's basement,' yelled Dixie.

'But all Viking's offers are special,' said Blue drily.

'All right, all right.' Wearily Viking held up a shaking hand. 'Will anyone I've got to apologize to, please line up.'

'You can start off with me,' said an angry, north-country voice, and everyone nearly dropped their cups of tea as George Hungerford stalked in. 'If you ever behave like that again, you're fired.'

'How the hell did he become a section leader?' George asked Lord Leatherhead later.

'Rodney thought it might make him more responsible, but I'm afraid Viking's a lawlessness unto himself.'

369

TWENTY-NINE

As soon as the rehearsal was over George bore Abby off for a pep talk.

'There's a light bulb out there,' he added grimly, as he frogmarched her up the aisle, 'and this curtain was hanging off its rail the first time I came down. This is an unloved hall.'

'It's an unlovable hall,' snapped Abby. 'We need a new one or at least a couple of million to restore it, right? Not to mention the chairs that all squeak and the music-stands which clunk.'

She was still listing imperfections when they reached George's office which had already been re–wallpapered in brushed suede in a rather startling ginger, and re-carpeted in shaggy off-white. It was also now humming with smart computers. The Stock Exchange Index on the television screen showed that George Hungerford shares were up ten pence. The news of his appointment to the RSO couldn't have reached the City yet, thought Abby sourly.

The three-piece suite in shabby Liberty print had gone too, replaced by squashy pale brown leather sofas and chairs. A big oak desk dominated the room and on nearby tables like doll's houses, stood exquisitely made

Perspex models of domestic properties and office blocks, which George was currently developing.

On the walls a Keith Vaughan and an Edward Burra of rugged Northern landscapes and a Lowry of a bleak school playground mingled uneasily with aerial views of buildings and a huge map of the British Isles with various property sites ringed.

George had clearly found himself a nice base in the West Country. John Drummond, washing his black fur on the window-sill as he eyed up the brushed suede as a potential scratching-board, and a green vase of Old Cyril's lilies of the valley, beside the four telephones on the oak desk provided the only cosy note.

Having dispatched a swooning Miss Priddock to make tea and peremptorily ordering Miles's secretary to hold all calls, George launched into a list of Abby's imperfections.

The trumpets in the first movement of Elgar's *Second Symphony* had come in two bars too early, and the whole thing had been ten minutes too long.

Immediately Abby was on the defensive.

'Rattle and Previn have both taken longer.'

'I don't bluddy care. It pushed the orchestra into overtime, I want the leader's ass off his seat by nine-thirty. Same thing this afternoon, your little masterclass on the 'Dance of the Seven Veils' again pushed them into overtime.'

'And I know whose head I'd like on a platter,' muttered Abby, particularly when George said he wanted her to attend the receptions after every concert, so she could chat up sponsors and council members.

'That's your job,' grumbled Abby. 'My job is to improve the orchestra.'

'Haven't made a great success of it so far,' said George bluntly. 'And you won't have an orchestra at all if we go on losing money like this.'

He then ordered her to turn up at tonight's party.

'You're still a celeb, there's no price put on the buzz

folk get from meeting you. Sponsors need more than their names on the programme, they want their clients to meet the stars. And you can put on a dress. I gather you haven't been out of trousers since you've been here. Your legs are probably the only hidden asset this orchestra possesses.'

Removing his spectacles, he made his eyes redder by rubbing them. He looked very tired, but Abby refused to be mollified.

'I don't have the time to socialize.'

'Uh-uh,' countered George. 'You're coming to this do, and you'll chat up tonight's sponsor, Dick Standish. He runs Standish Oil. He's bringing another potential sponsor, Paul Nathan, CEO of Panacea Pharmaceuticals.'

'We can't be sponsored by drug companies. They do such horrific things to animals.' Protectively Abby stroked John Drummond, who purred in loud agreement.

'Don't be fatuous,' said George irritably. 'There wouldn't have been any Michelangelo without the Medicis.'

Swiftly changing the subject before she could argue, he added: 'And you ought to know your orchestra by now. Americans are supposed to be good at names. First Flute, Second Trombone's far too impersonal.'

Then, as Abby opened her mouth to protest, he continued, 'It has far more effect when you're bawling people out, if you use the correct name.'

'Right, Godfrey,' said Abby briskly, then as Miss Priddock came in with a tray weighed down by rainbow cake and daisy-patterned porcelain, 'No, I haven't time for a cup of tea, thanks, Miss Prism.'

The party was held in a blue-and-white striped tent outside the hall. The section leaders had been invited to mingle with the Great and the Good, but were far more interested in stuffing their faces with as much food and drink as fast as possible.

An eager-looking matron in chewstik-pink polyester immediately collared Davie Buckle, the timpanist. Davie's face was as round and as blank as a satellite dish, and he wiled away long bars of rest playing patience on top of his kettle drums.

'What d'you do?' asked the matron skittishly.

'I'm a basher.' Davie grabbed two glasses of white and thrust one into her hand.

'What's a be-asher?'

'I play the drums,' said Davie, seizing a fistful of prawns in batter.

'How exciting. I'd love to do that if I had the time. Percussion looks so easy.'

Accustomed to such inanities, Davie didn't rise.

'Why don't you have any time?' he asked.

'Well, I have to look after Dick. My husband,' she added by way of explanation, 'he sponsored tonight's concert, he's in oil.'

'What is he? A bleeding sardine?' asked Davie and choked on his drink, because Abby had just stalked in looking absolutely sensational in a red body, no bra and the minutest wrap-over skirt.

'I said a dress, not you oonderwear,' said George furiously.

Peggy Parker was even crosser. She was livid about Abby's plans to audition the choir and her suggestion that Peggy and several of her more august cronies, including Lindy Cardew, the wife of Rutminster's planning officer, who all screeched like hungry seagulls, should stand down.

Nor had Peggy been charmed by the scrumpled-up photograph of Charlene, 44-22-35, playing the 'Flowers of the Field' on a slit-kilted Scotsman without the aid of bagpipes, which had landed in her lap in the middle of *Mother Goose* two nights ago.

She now ambushed Abby on her way to the bar.

'Why d'you persist in rejecting my ge-owns. As musical director you should be projecting an image of femininity, graciousness and dignity.'

Abby was about to snap back that weighed down with Peggy Parker's rhinestones, she'd hardly be able to lift her stick, but opting for tact, mumbled that she didn't feel confident enough as a conductor to draw attention to herself so dramatically.

Mrs Parker swelled like a bullfrog.

'You clearly feel confident enough to dispense with most of the choir.'

'Must get a drink and circulate,' Abby cut across her in mid-flow. 'George only invited me this evening to brown-nose sponsors.'

And she was gone leaving Peggy Parker, furiously mouthing and appropriately pegged to the damp grass by four-inch scarlet heels.

The party was spilling out of the tent. Emerging into a starry evening lit by chestnut candles, Abby was waylaid.

'Hi Abby, I'm Jison.'

Jison turned out to be a dodgy local car-dealer. After three-quarters of a bottle of Sancerre and a long look at Abby's legs, he agreed to put ten thousand pounds into sponsoring *Messiah*, which the orchestra was performing in Cotchester Cathedral at the end of November, and which would later be transmitted on Christmas Eve.

'Grite to drive one of the Ferraris up the aisle,' Jason said excitedly.

'Great,' agreed Abby absent-mindedly because Viking had walked in.

He had skipped the rest of the afternoon's rehearsal. It was late-night shopping and Blue had discovered him and Nugent fast asleep in one of the four-posters in Parker and Parker's bedding department just in time for the concert. Whiter after yesterday's excesses than his crumpled evening shirt, he was still surrounded by admiring women. Glancing at Abby, however, he raised his glass of red and wandered over.

'You look glorious, sweetheart.'

Totally thrown by a compliment, Abby became ungracious.

'Can't say the same for you. Why in hell d'you drink so much?'

Viking laughed, making his bloodshot eyes narrower than ever.

'If you're as charming as I am, you get your glass filled up more often.'

To prove this, as he emptied his, waitresses converged from all sides to fill it up again.

'This is Jason,' Abby introduced the beadily hovering car-dealer. 'I thought you'd given up drink anyway,' she added reprovingly.

'Not any more, Juno's thrown me out.'

'How come?' asked Abby, trying desperately not to show how thrilled she was.

'Juno wasn't entirely pleased with the state in which I returned. The Prima Donna had been on the mobilé to her. And I left Nugent with her.' Glancing down, he ran his fingers through the dog's silky fur. 'I hoped if they spent some time together, they might make friends.

'Alas, Nugent escaped in disgosst and rolled and in disgosst at the state in which he returned home, Juno went out and bought a kennel and chained him up in the garden. I was also in the dog house when I got home, so I crawled out and joined Nugent, but he was a bit smelly, so we decided to walk home to The Bordello.'

Abby couldn't help laughing.

'But aren't you miserable it's over?' she asked.

'Not at all. Thanks, sweetheart.' Gathering up a hand-ful of sausage rolls from yet another lingering waitress, Viking fed them to Nugent.

'Nugent certainly looks pleased.'

'He is. Blue gave him a bath this morning.'

In fact the only casualty, went on Viking, was his BMW which had finally packed up.

'You should invest in one of my Ferraris,' said Jason, patronizingly. 'Then you could really pull the birds.'

Viking replied with considerable hauteur, that he could pull the birds when he was riding a tricycle, and threw a goat-cheese ball at Lionel, who, after a quick bonk in the leader's room, had waited until the party filled up to smuggle in Hilary, who had not been invited.

Why is Viking's arrogance to die for and Lionel's so repulsive? wondered Abby as she watched Lionel licking his teeth, fluffing up his ebony locks, squaring his shoulders as, with head erect, he awaited his stampede of fans.

He was delighted at first to be clobbered by Mrs Dick Standish but less amused when she asked him what was his daytime job.

'You may see us looking glamorous in our tails,' he said petulantly, 'but you don't realize how much practising, rehearsing, travelling and admin goes into each concert.'

'At least you have job satisfaction.'

'Not so as you'd know it,' said Hilary glaring over at Abby, then bristling with disapproval, as Clare, who'd been smuggled in by Dixie, bounded up to them.

'I say, Romeo and Juno have split up.'

'That's very stale buns,' said Hilary crushingly.

'But seriously exciting. Viking seems to be getting on rather well with our musical director, perhaps she'll be the next swastika on his fuselage.'

Abby was trying not to feel wildly elated that Viking had stayed beside her so long. He was just telling her about a cottage by the lake, when she was accosted by a little bearded man in sandals with a pasty face and a straggling pony-tail, who immediately introduced himself as

Peggy Parker's son, Roger – 'But everyone calls me Sonny,' – the composer of the *Eternal Triangle Suite*. Had Abby fixed a date for the première?

Abby said she wasn't sure. With George's arrival, the schedule was all up in the air.

'Is anyone recording your stuff?' she asked him.

As Sonny shook his head, his pony-tail flew like a horse irritably swatting at flies.

'After all the popular, easily digested fare around, people tend to find my music gritty and complex, but I am philosophical. *The Marriage of Figaro* was a disaster when it was first programmed.'

'I was so moved,' he went on earnestly, 'to hear the toilets flushing during the Sibelius two nights ago, particularly in the last bars, that I have commenced a new work for full orchestra. I plan to provide sound effects of a rumbling train, pneumatic drills, people coughing, rustling toffee papers, cars back-firing,' he ticked off the list with black-nailed fingers, 'and finally a chorus of flushing toilets.'

Abby burst out laughing.

'You must include the snoring of the Rutshire Butcher then.'

But, receiving a sharp kick on the ankle from Viking, she realized Sonny was utterly serious.

'My goal is to prove great music can overcome any interruption.'

'I look forward to hearing it,' mumbled Abby.

Sonny was droning on, and Abby was praying he'd leave her and Viking alone, when Blue came over.

'Who are all these spivs in sharp suits wandering around H.P. Hall sticking penknives into the brick-work?' he said in a low voice.

'George Hungerford's henchmen,' answered Viking.

'I think so, too.'

'George Hungerford seems very able,' said Sonny pompously.

'More like Cain, if you ask me,' said Viking.

Abby was screwing up courage to ask Viking to show her the cottage by the lake when Mrs Standish rushed up.

'Such fun to be a woman conductor, you did fritefly well.'

'Why, thank you.'

'My husband's tonight's sponsor.'

'Oh, wow!' Abby remembered George's brief. 'That's so good of him, we're so grateful.'

'I just wanted to know,' Mrs Standish went pinker than her dress, as she turned to Viking, 'how you musician chappies address a female maestro?'

'We call her "mattress",' said Viking idly, then seeing Abby's lips tighten, he added softly, 'because we're all dying to lie on top of her.'

Abby tried and failed to look affronted.

'I'm afraid my chariot of fire's grounded' went on Viking, 'but I'll walk you back to the Old Bell if you like.' He ran a finger down Abby's arm, setting her heart hammering.

'I'll give you a lift, Abby,' said Jason proprietorially. 'We can discuss things over a spot of dinner.'

Miserably remembering Hugo's warning about getting involved with a member of the orchestra and George's insistence that she chatted up sponsors, Abby accepted Jason's invitation.

Popping into the Ladies on her way out she noticed someone had already scribbled joyfully on the walls: MR NUGENT ROLLS OK.

She could have wept, and even more so as Jason held open the door of his red Ferrari for her.

'I'm definitely going to sponsor that *Messiah*. Who wrote it by the way?'

Nor did George Hungerford seem very impressed when she told him she had found a sponsor the following day.

'Looks like a wide boy, better get it in writing.'

He then announced he had axed Mahler's *Symphony*

of a Thousand at the end of next season because it was too expensive.

'That's defeatist,' said Abby furiously.

'We can't afford the extras.'

'If the orchestra were up to full strength,' said Abby shirtily, 'we wouldn't have to spend so much on extras.'

She took a deep breath. 'The musicians must have more money, to stop the exodus. Barry's threatening to leave because he can't pay the mortgage on the barn and the Child Support Agency.

'Clarissa's also looking around. She's a really good player,' pleaded Abby. 'She's gone for an audition with the LSO this afternoon, because she's having sleepless nights worrying about the school fees.'

George watched John Drummond stretching luxuriously in his out-tray.

'I have absolutely no sympathy with people who send their kids to pooblic school,' he said coldly.

'That's rich, revoltingly rich,' exploded Abby, 'from someone who's just bought a property up the road, which makes Buckingham Palace look like a rabbit hutch.'

'We are not talking about me,' George glared at her. 'I didn't go to pooblic school, never did me any harm.'

'I wouldn't put it to the vote.'

'Anyway, I'm not a musician.'

'That's quite obvious. How can you replace the *Symphony of a Thousand* with Boléro, and Tchaik *Five.*'

'Because you've reduced the choir to such a state of disarray,' snapped George, 'that I don't imagine they can possible re-assemble by next season. Anyway Tchaik *Five* has a beautiful solo for Viking.'

Abby raised her fists to heaven. 'Oh, we mustn't forget Viking.'

'There are worse things – Viking pulls in the punters. This orchestra is an endangered species, we need more booms on seats, more recordings, more touring, more Gala evenings.'

This brought him to Mrs Parker's birthday concert at the end of July which coincided with the centenary of the store.

'A treat in store?' asked Abby sarcastically.

'No,' replied George, booting Drummond up the backside for attacking the brushed suede. The concert, he went on, was to be held in the grounds of Rutminster Towers, Peggy Parker's neo-Gothic excrescence above the town.

'You better provide umbrellas and clothes pegs to hold down the music in case of wind and rain,' taunted Abby.

'Mrs Parker has chosen the music,' said George heavily. '*William Tell*, Liszt's *First Piano Concerto*, *The Polovtsian Dances*.'

'Omigod, why doesn't Mrs Parker sing 'Lady in Red' to crown a really intellectual evening.'

Abby was goading George; she could see a muscle going in his clenched jaw, his squared-off nails whitening as he clutched the oak table, but he said quite mildly, 'In case the Arts Council regard the repertoire as insufficiently adventurous, we're going to programme Sonny Parker's *Eternal Triangle Suite* after the interval.'

'Jesus!'

'As the function will attract a lot of media attention,' went on George quickly, 'Mrs Parker would like you to be appropriately dressed. She will give an extra one hundred thousand pounds to the orchestra if,' George didn't quite meet Abby's already furious eyes, 'Parker and Parker are allowed to dress and restyle you from top to toe. New gown, new make-up, new hair-do, jewels. You'll enjoy it.'

'I will *not*!'

Seeing the fury on Abby's face, George busied himself lining up paperweights and files on his desk.

'And it's bluddy good pooblicity for the orchestra. Parker's are planning a massive promotion. All the nationals'll cover it. The *Telegraph* are planning a huge feature on the new re-vamped Abigail.'

'So you've already agreed,' Abby was outraged.

'With your permission,' said George placatingly. 'We need the money, Abby, you're a beautiful yoong lady and we all know you'll look chumpian.'

Abby, who'd been feeling her age in the last month, was so startled that, like Viking yesterday, George had actually paid her a compliment, that she rolled over and reluctantly agreed.

'The messing-up of a maestro,' she said gloomily.

The instant he got her consent, George reverted to normal belligerence, and said brusquely that that would be all.

'Last night's concert was better,' he opened the door for her. 'But the symphony was still too long. Miss Priddock's been handling complaints from people who missed their last trains and buses all morning.'

In a rage Abby went back to the conductor's room and leafing through the *Eroica* pencilled in a huge 'No' beside every repeat sign, which meant a lot of work for the library, who had to change all the parts before the evening.

During the Brahms *Second Piano Concerto* in the first half, Abby noticed Viking smiling at a pretty redhead in the audience, and pointing to his watch to suggest a rendez-vous after the concert. Abby then proceeded to knock a quarter of an hour off the *Eroica* giving heart attacks to several ancient bass players, and everyone got their last trains.

For an orchestra whose hobby was grumbling, the RSO were delighted with George Hungerford. Socially maladroit, he was deficient in small talk, but he asked the right questions and listened carefully to all the answers, aware that a grievance aired is usually a grievance forgotten. He also recognized individual players in the building and then put up their photographs in the foyer, on the premise that the public ought to recognize them, too, and he invited them back to drinks at his splendid new house.

George would generate work, the RSO decided, and get them out of trouble. He certainly generated too much work for Miss Priddock and very tactfully provided her with an EA (an executive assistant, so Miss Priddock felt upgraded, too). The EA turned out to be a ravishing bimbo called Jessica who'd just returned with an all-over tan from the Seychelles. Nothing could more successfully have demolished the Berlin Wall between musicians and management, as male players, who hadn't visited the top floor in years, plied Jessica with flowers, chocolates and invitations like love-sick schoolboys. El Creepo even got stuck up the tallest horse-chestnut tree in the park the day it was rumoured Jessica was sunbathing topless on the flat roof.

'Isn't George a ball of fire?' exclaimed a besotted Miss Priddock, as she handed Abby her mail.

'Fire's the operative word,' said Abby gloomily. 'He'll have me out of here the second my contract ends.'

Desperately tired and unhappy, she was grateful to have three weeks' break at the end of June, while Ambrose, the Fat Controller, who was back from San Francisco, took over as guest conductor. But she dreaded the caballing when he, Miles and Lionel got together.

THIRTY

Abby found it impossible to recharge her batteries while staying at the Old Bell. She was too conscious of the RSO festering at the other end of town. Too proud to call Howie and say she wanted out, she decided to think positively and look at the cottage by the lake of which Viking had spoken. Longing to capture the fun and friendship of her days at the Academy, she telephoned Flora, who was uncharacteristically listless. Wiped out by Helen's marriage to Rannaldini, she had found herself increasingly marking time and unable to concentrate at college.

'And I've got another year to go.'

'There's a viola vacancy at the RSO,' said Abby. 'Why don't you audition for it? Don't say you know me, right? Then you could come and share a cottage with me down here.'

'God, I'd like that, I'm fed up with London, particularly in this heat.'

'How's Marcus?' asked Abby carefully, reluctant to confess how much she missed him.

'I hardly see him, he's so busy writing letters, taking in pupils and fending off their frightful mothers. He hasn't got any time to practise, let alone come out in the evenings.'

'Mothers are far too old for Marcus, goddamn cradle-snatchers.' Abby was predictably outraged. 'He'd find lots of teaching work down here, he could start with any soloist booked by the RSO. Perhaps he'd like to share this cottage as well.'

There was a long pause.

'He might,' said Flora. 'I'm sorry, Abby, but you were such a bitch to him.'

'I know, I was so uptight that night, I don't know what got into me. I really miss him.'

'Well, you'd better ring him then.'

'Why don't you get him to drive you down to the audition, then we can go and see the cottage afterwards.'

'They weren't at all enthusiastic at college,' grumbled Flora, as Marcus turned off the M4. 'Just because I'm missing a day's rehearsal for the end-of-term concert. You'd have thought my career was more important.'

'They probably can't forgive you for not becoming a singer.'

'That's what they tell me every day,' sighed Flora. 'What d'you think about sharing a cottage with Abby?'

'I don't know. It would be nice to have somewhere I could practise. I started playing Rachmaninov's *Second Sonata* at eleven o'clock last night and people on both sides started banging on the walls, but I'm not sure I can cope with Abby's ego.'

In his shirt pocket was a letter which he already knew by heart.

> *Darling Markie,*
> *Please forgive me, I'm sorry I chewed you out.*
> *I miss you so much – both as a friend and as an*
> *advisor. We used to have such fun discussing*
> *repertoire . . .*

Fun for her thought Marcus wryly, remembering the hysterics, the endless demands and the interrupted nights.

Along the Gloucestershire lanes, he noticed the trees were losing the tender green of early summer. The hedgerows were festooned with wilting dog-roses. Buttercups and dog daisies shrivelled amidst the newly mown hay.

'Heaven after London,' sighed Flora. 'Maybe we could cope with Abby's ego if there were two of us. You could do the night shift.'

'I practise at night. Jesus, it's hot.'

Marcus looked terribly white and had lost a lot of weight.

'Let's get an ice-cream and a bottle of wine,' suggested Flora. Then, looking down at her sawn off T-shirt, frayed Bermudas and dusty bare feet, wondered, 'Do you think I look smart enough for an audition?'

'Frankly, no. We've got time to nip into Bath and buy you something.'

'Do I really want this job if I've got to tart up?'

'Yes, you need some fun.' Marcus took his hand off the wheel and stroked her cheek.

'How's your mother?' asked Flora.

'OK.'

Flora's second question was more difficult.

'How's Rannaldini getting on with Tabitha?'

'She's in America for a year working in some racing yard.'

Marcus didn't tell Flora, Helen had caught Rannaldini leering at Tabitha undressing through a two-way mirror.

'I've got a new viola joke,' he said to distract her. 'How many viola players does it take to wallpaper a room?'

'How many?'

'Three – if you slice them thinly.'

* * *

Candidates at auditions are judged 70 per cent on their playing, 30 per cent on their ability to fit into the relevant section. The right attitude was needed, a core of hardness to cope with the cut and thrust of orchestral life. You couldn't be too sweet or likely to cry if you were shouted at. Neither shrinking violets nor violists were encouraged.

Auditions could be very acrimonious. The leader of the orchestra could favour one candidate, the section leader another, the musical director or a member of the board another. Steve Smithson opposed anyone from abroad on principle. But no-one felt remotely enthusiastic that morning about the colourless bunch struggling through solos from Telemann's *Viola Concerto*. They seemed to encapsulate all the jokes about the dumbness and dreariness of viola players.

The board-room clock edged towards five past one.

'Flora Seymour's late,' said Miles, looking at the last name on the list.

'Give her another five minutes,' said El Creepo, the section leader, who dreaded the prospect of re-advertising the job.

'If she can't turn up on time there's no point in employing her,' said Lionel, who was longing to share a bottle of chilled white wine in the long grass with Hilary.

They were the only people left except the accompanist who was thinking of the marmite-and-scrambled-egg sandwiches in tin foil at the bottom of her music case. It was a measure of the lacklustre nature of the morning's performances that none of the other section leaders had bothered to stay for more than a few minutes.

'OK, that's it. Sorry, Flora,' Miles ran a red Pentel through her name.

'Flora's the one who's sorry,' said a clear piercingly distinctive voice. 'I can't even pretend there was a pile-up on the motorway. We stopped in Bath to buy suitable clothes to be auditioned in, and I forgot the time. I'm really sorry.'

Miles was the first one to speak.

'It's absolutely no problem at all.'

'Can I get you a glass of water or a cup of tea before you start?' asked Lionel.

'Would you like five minutes to freshen up and unwind?' said El Creepo.

There was nearly a pile-up on Rutminster High Street as word got round and musicians on their way to the Shaven Crown did a speeded-up U-turn worthy of Benny Hill. Flora proceeded to play with such insouciance and *joie de vivre* in every note that the board room soon filled up.

Apart from Cherub, who crawled under people's legs and chairs and ended up to his horror, practically sitting on the Fat Controller's knee, latecomers had to lurk in the passage.

Flora's new coffee-coloured silk shirt fell so charmingly over her wrists as she romped through the first movement of the Walton *Concerto*, and her short fawn suede skirt clung so enticingly to her dancing hips that afterwards even Simon Painshaw and the Fat Controller were making thumbs-up signs to El Creepo and Miles to offer her the job.

One of the reasons George Hungerford had taken over the RSO was because he loved music. He had been dismayed to find admin was taking up 95 per cent of his time. Leaving H.P. Hall at nearly midnight yesterday he had taken his soaring in-tray home but had fallen asleep at the kitchen table over a large whisky and a forkful of roll mops, and had had to bring the in-tray back untouched this morning.

Coming out of his office, he found the passage crowded with musicians peering in through the board-room door with the rapt attention of a pack of hounds watching *Basil Brush* on television.

Then he recognized his favourite piece of music, Elgar's *In the South* overture. In amazement, as he stood on his toes to see into the jam-packed board room, he realized a young girl with a shiny dark red bob was playing Elgar's transcription of the piece with a fresh and exquisite sound. Her eyes were closed in anguish, her head shaking almost in bewilderment at the dark, sad, liltingly beautiful tune pouring out of her viola.

George felt all the uncontrollable knee-jerk reactions, the sudden catch of breath, hair rising on the back of the neck, tears swamping the eyes. Hastily turning to the window, through which was wafting the sweet lemony smell of lime flowers, so no-one could see how moved he was, he was overwhelmed by the emptiness of his life since Ruth had left him. He was brought back to earth by a most unusual round of applause.

'That was absolutely beautiful,' said El Creepo, blowing his nose.

'Beautiful,' agreed Lionel, after hastily checking Hilary wasn't within earshot. 'What are you working on at the Academy at the moment?'

'Mostly singing Eve. We're doing *The Creation* as an end-of-term concert.'

'D'you have to strip off?' shouted Dixie from the back.

Flora laughed. 'I'm allowed to keep on my fig-leaf.'

'Going to give us a demo?' asked Dixie.

'That's quite enough,' snapped Lionel. 'Trust you to lower the tone, Dixie.'

'I only wanted Flora to lower her fig-leaf.'

'I would like to ask Miss Seymour,' Miles glared at Dixie, 'why she wants to play in an orchestra, and the RSO in particular.'

For once Flora seemed lost for words as her eyes ran over the men staring at her, then she beamed from ear to ear.

'I guess I'd like some fun.'

Everyone beamed back.

Much too sexy for her own or anyone else's good, thought George.

In the end, the RSO offered Flora six months' trial.

'In case either of us don't like each other,' said El Creepo, 'which is *most* unlikely.'

'I'm afraid we can only offer you thirteen thousand a year,' said Miles apologetically.

'You couldn't make it thirteen and a half?' asked Flora. 'I'll probably have to pay back my grant.' Then, shaken out of her habitual cool, added, 'I can't tell you how pleased I am.'

So were the men in the orchestra. Even the Celtic Mafia charged round in jubilation saying, 'She's got the job, she's got the job.'

Abby was jubilant, too, because she'd set the thing up.

'I've organized chilled French champagne, Scotch salmon, alligator pears and fresh berries,' she told Marcus and Flora, 'We'll have a picnic by the lake and then we'll go and look at the cottage.'

In the third week in June, Abby, Marcus and Flora moved into Woodbine Cottage which lurked like the palest red fox cub, peering out of its woodland undergrowth. It was situated two hundred and fifty yards from the lake, up a rough track, which would become a running stream in wet weather. They would have difficulty getting out if it snowed, but at least they wouldn't be gawped at by locals or tourists wandering round the lake.

The cottage itself was early nineteenth century and quite enchanting. Pale pink roses arched over the rickety front gate, pink geraniums in pots leant out of every window and a stream hurtled under the mossy flagstones that led up to the pale green front door. Clematis, white roses and honeysuckle swarmed up the soft red walls. The front garden was crowded with pinks, snapdragons and tall crimson hollyhocks. Behind the cottage a lawn bounded by ancient apple trees sloped up into soaring woods which protected the cottage from north and east winds. Beyond the front gate, red and white cows grazed in a wild flower meadow rising gently to poplars on the horizon.

'You won't get much sun until midday,' the owner, a sweet widow, told them apologetically.

'Suits us,' said Flora, 'we're not early risers.'

'You will be now you've joined the RSO,' said Abby firmly.

Inside, the cottage, to Abby's delight, had adequate plumbing, a modern kitchen with a Cotswold stone floor and a big scrubbed table. The drawing-room had a huge mirror in which she could practise conducting, and plenty of shelves for scores and books. Upstairs were two largish bedrooms looking over the meadow, a bathroom and an attic bedroom under the eaves.

Marcus was worried the place was so isolated. With every move he had to find a doctor and locate the nearest casualty department. He would have to make doubly sure that he always had spare inhalers and a pre-packed syringe to inject himself.

But the real plus was that, under a spreading chestnut tree, in the top left-hand corner of the back garden, had been built a studio. This had a shower, a loo, a fridge in which he could put his pillows to kill the dust mites, plenty of room for a bed and the Steinway on which he had just managed to keep up the payments.

'My late husband was a sculptor, who liked to work at night,' the sweet widow told Marcus, 'I like to think of another artist living here.'

With a studio, Marcus could also take in private pupils without bothering the others, and retreat to avoid the dust and fluff bound to be created by Abby's and Flora's sloppy housework and the two black-and-white kitten brothers, Sibelius and Scriabin, which Abby had rushed off and acquired from the nearest rescue kennels the moment they moved in.

'Two for joy, they're just like magpies,' said Flora in ecstasy, as the kittens with thunderous purring buried their faces in a plate of boiled chicken.

'Can you imagine poor Schubert moving twenty-four times. I'm exhausted after a day of it,' added Flora.

There was still masses of sorting out, but she wandered off to the kitchen returning with a bottle of Moët and three glasses. Abby raised a disapproving eyebrow. It was only three o'clock.

'I'm not going to make a habit of it,' said Flora airily, 'but it is a special day.'

'We are going to introduce a new regime,' insisted Abby virtuously, 'no pop music, no TV, we'll go for long walks, read aloud and discuss music and ideas in the evening.'

'No television, that's a bit steep,' cried Flora in alarm. 'What about *Men Behaving Badly*, *Blind Date*, and *Keeping Up Appearances*?'

'You'll soon get used to it.' Abby raised her glass. 'To us.'

'We better start making our own wine,' muttered Flora. 'Go and jump on a few elderberries, Marcus.'

'And make our own amusements,' said Marcus, and he and Flora sat down to bash out a four-handed version of Schubert's *Marche Militaire* on the ancient upright in the drawing-room.

'Abby's clearly going to take rural life very seriously,' giggled Flora. 'She's already bought galoshes, gloves, a rain hat and a Dryzabone for country walks.'

'She can count me out,' sighed Marcus, 'I can't do more than forty yards at the moment.'

Wandering out into the back garden, clutching a still purring Scriabin, the browning lawn scratching her bare feet like horsehair, Abby jumped as she heard the glorious horn call from *Don Juan* echoing through the woods. For a second she thought the others, bored of duets, had put on a record. But no-one could mistake that radiance and clarity. It was Viking practising for next week's concert. There it was again, hardly muffled by the leaves.

The Celtic Mafia's Bordello, rented so they could play music and hell-raise as loudly as they liked, lay on the other side of the lake. Perhaps they could start giving Woodbine Cottage dinner parties round the big kitchen table. Was Viking putting out signals playing *Don Juan* on her first day? Perhaps he didn't know she had moved in. She must get some change of address cards printed, she thought with a shiver of excitement.

That night she fell asleep instantly for the first time in months, soothed by the sound of the stream under her window rushing down to join the lake.

Returning to work after her three weeks' break was like going back to prison. Miles and Lionel, who'd chiefly employed Flora to put her nose out of joint, couldn't wait to break the news of her appointment.

'We would have waited for you to OK her,' said Miles smugly, 'but she's so talented, we decided to snap her up.'

'The Academy says she's got a fantastic voice,' even Lionel was looking quite moony, 'which is useful if we ever need an understudy.'

'What's her name?' Abby was idly flipping through her post.

'Flora Seymour,' Miles laughed heartily. 'We all want to see more of Flora.'

'Georgie Maguire's daughter,' said Abby, opening a typed envelope with a London postmark.

'I said Seymour not Maguire.'

'Still Georgie's daughter.'

'You sure you've got the right girl?'

'Quite,' said Abby with a malicious smile. 'Flora and I were at the Academy together. She auditioned while I was away on vacation, right? So I couldn't be accused of bias. She's living in the cottage I've bought by the lake.'

'Bought a cottage,' spluttered Lionel. 'You're planning a long stay with the RSO?'

'Sure am,' crowed Abby. 'Get a look of this.'

It was confirmation from Howie Denston that Megagram wanted to record all Fanny Mendelssohn's music and all four of Winifred Trapp's *Harp Concertos* with Abby and the RSO.

'Who's Winifred Trapp?' asked Miles scornfully.

'It's pronounced Vinifred,' said Abby rudely. 'She's a terrific nineteenth-century Swiss composer. She had to stop home and care for her elderly parents, so her *oeuvre* was only performed by family and friends, which meant she used a very small orchestra, which means Jackboot Hungerford can cut down on extras. I discovered her when I was living with Rodney in Lucerne. She makes marvellous use of yodelling and cowbells.'

'Yet another hall-emptier,' snapped Miles, but even he couldn't argue with a fat record contract.

Wandering back to her dressing-room, Abby bumped into Viking and her heart stopped. His lean normally pale face was tanned a warm gold. Sunbathing with his hair drenched in lemon juice had turned it nearly white. He was wearing a sea-green polo shirt and dirty white shorts.

Abby couldn't resist telling him she had heard him last night.

Viking looked alarmed.

'Don't tell anyone you heard me practising – it's terrible for my image.'

On an ego trip, Abby had to break the news about Winifred Trapp and Fanny Mendelssohn.

'It's nearly the hundred and fiftieth anniversary of Fanny's death.'

'Fanniversary,' Viking grinned broadly.

'Must you trivialize everything?'

'I have a theory about obscure repertoire,' said Viking, 'If it's onplayed, there's very good reason. It's

393

either onplayable or onotterably bad. If you record it, however, you get a reputation for brilliance and innovation because there's nothing to compare it with.'

'You would have an utterly defeatist attitude.' Abby flounced off in a fury.

To save money, it was decided to run a joint Mendelssohn and Trapp series in the late autumn, then Megagram could perhaps be leant on to pay for the rehearsals. There was just time to slot this change of repertoire into next season's smart brochure, which had a picture of Abby on the front.

George had also effected a saving of thirty thousand pounds a year by sacking the marketing manager, who'd kept coming up with fatuous ideas about laser beams and back projections and the orchestra playing in their national costumes to prove how international they were.

Abby returned from her holiday to find Clarissa had left as threatened – not to London – but to join Hugo and the CCO. Abby felt betrayed and as though she had lost an ally. But she wasted no time in bringing in a new Principal Cellist, called Dimitri, who refused to be parted from his cello because it was the only possession he had managed to smuggle out of a Russian Labour Camp. Speaking precious little English he had difficulty getting a job and was as thin as a skeleton. But after spending a couple of nights in the attic bedroom at Woodbine Cottage and playing chamber music with Flora and Marcus, he soon regained his confidence. Although he cried everytime the orchestra played *The Great Gate of Kiev*, he added wonderful gravitas and a great deep Russian sound to the cello section. As a result, Dimitri adored Abby and was horrified by the orchestra's deep disrespect for her.

Despite Miles's and Lionel's belief that it would put Abby's nose out of joint to employ Flora, Abby liked pretty women in the orchestra, as long as they played well. She had therefore spiced up the back of the violins with an enchanting Japanese girl called Noriko. Noriko couldn't pronounce her 'L's and kept everyone in stitches ordering River and Bacon at the Shaven Crown and suggesting the Steel Elf, who was having trouble paying her mortgage since Viking moved out, 'should take in a roger'.

Viking and Juno were both too proud to make it up, but romance-watchers had noticed Juno definitely making big bluey-green eyes at George Hungerford.

'That would be a dangerous liaison,' said Dixie gloomily, 'she would have us all out in a trice.'

Flora's first rehearsal with the RSO at the beginning of July was greeted with a chorus of wolf-whistles. She had tied back her newly washed hair with a grey ribbon, she wore no make-up on her gold freckled skin. Her legs in grey linen shorts were almost chunky. But there was an undeniable sexuality about her, perhaps because she was totally lacking in new-girl nerves. Used to playing solo at college, she attacked every piece with vigour, and if she came in too early, or played a wrong note, she burst out laughing, thus giving confidence to other new-comers like Jenny and Noriko who were too shy of scorn even to practise in public.

Flora took Foxie, her puppet-fox mascot, everywhere with her, reducing the nearby players to fits of giggles by making him conduct with her pencil, or putting his paws over his ears and shaking his head at moments of discord or stress. Flora also chattered to everyone and was absurdly generous.

In her second week when they were waiting for Abby who'd been delayed by some management wrangle, Flora plied her own section and the surrounding players with lemon sherbets. They were about to rehearse the *Valse des Fleurs*, which required a harpist, and even contained an important harp cadenza.

Harpists are often regarded as something of a joke in

orchestras. But, if the RSO laughed at Miss Parrott, they also loved and admired her. A middle-aged spinster with piled-up strawberry-pink hair, she always wore high heels and very bright colours: 'If you're in the shop window for a long tayme you tend to fade so Ay like to look colourful,' and rose above the orchestra as dignified as her gold harp, which she plucked at with long red fingers.

Miss Parrott looked on and missed nothing, passing the time when she wasn't playing knitting brightly coloured scarves for her favourites in the orchestra. Blue and Viking had two each. She always had a beta blocker and a glass of sherry before concerts, and liked to play her harp beside the flutes, complaining bitterly if ever she were relegated to the back of the Second Violins.

Although Miss Parrott claimed: 'My feet are danglin' from the shelf,' she had no shortage of male admirers to mend plugs and tyres for her and carry her harp in and out of concert halls. Finally she was an inveterate moonlighter and, that very evening, after she'd dispatched *Valse des Fleurs* in the first half at Rutminster, would be belting over to Cotchester to play Debussy's *Dances Sacres et Profanes* with the CCO.

Having finished her lemon sherbet, she asked Flora if she could have another one.

'Goodness, Miss Parrott,' piped up Cherub, 'you've got a big suck.'

'If you were ten years older, and Ay were ten years younger, Ay'd show you, young man,' said Miss Parrott calmly.

Shouts of laughter greeted this as poor Cherub went as red as his bass drum.

As a new girl, Flora had been placed behind Fat Isobel, beside Militant Moll and in front of Juno and Hilary, none of whom were at all enthusiastic about her arrival.

Viking, who usually claimed *droit de seigneur* over any

pretty girl who joined the orchestra, had noticed Flora's bitten nails at the audition and the occasional flicker of desolation on her face, and didn't believe she was as bonny and blithe as she appeared.

Writing: *'Will you have a drink with me after this?'* on a paper dart, he chucked it in her direction.

Alas, the dart flew over Flora's head and fluttered down onto the massive bosom of Fat Isobel who, still disappointed at being passed up during Viking's erotic bonanza on the bus to Starhampton, swung round nodding frantically in acceptance.

'Jesus, I'll have to empty Oddbins,' muttered an appalled Viking.

'Isobel's got lovely skin,' protested Miss Parrott kindly.

'Pity there's so much of it,' sighed Viking.

The rest of the Celtic Mafia were still crying with laughter when Abby arrived.

'Quiet please, let's get started,' she said briskly. 'Where are Clare and Dixie?'

'Still in the pub,' said Juno primly.

'Shall I go and get them?' piped up Flora eager to escape for a quick one.

'Noriko can go,' said Abby, adding pointedly, *'she doesn't drink.'*

She couldn't help feeling wildly jealous that Flora had been accepted so easily and had this gift of making people love her. Everyone wanted to play chamber music with her, the telephone rang the whole time at the cottage, her pigeon hole at H.P. Hall was filled with notes.

I must start playing the violin again, thought Abby fretfully, so people want to play chamber music with me.

'It's only because Flora's new,' Abby overheard Juno saying bitchily to Hilary. 'They'll soon get bored of her.'

THIRTY-ONE

Rutminster was gripped by a heatwave. Plans for holding Piggy Parker's sixtieth-birthday concert inside or providing the orchestra with a canopy were shelved as the ground cracked, the huge domed trees in the grounds of Rutminster Towers shed their first yellow leaves and Mrs Parker repeatedly cursed her mother for conceiving her in a Ramsgate boarding-house in October rather than in September – which meant her birthday fell at the end of July, by which time the roses had gone over.

Short of glueing back every petal, the only answer was to bus in furiously clashing bedding plants from Parker's Horticultural Emporium. Lorry-loads of electric-blue hydrangeas and scarlet petunias were racing armies of caterers up the drive, as the orchestra struggled in for an early rehearsal and to check the timing of the fireworks in *William Tell*, before the heat became too punishing.

Rutminster Towers itself stood in all its neo-Gothic glory, surrounded by a formal garden and parkland, overlooking the River Fleet. A platform for orchestra and choir had been set up on the river's edge. Bronzed workmen putting up a large red-and-white striped VIP tent eyed Flora as she paddled and splashed water over a panting Mr Nugent.

Mrs Parker was frantic everything should go well. As a year ago, a pleasure launch of Hoorays playing pop music and drunkenly yelling 'Hellair' had disrupted *Panis Angelicus*, she was personally prepared to dam the river with her vast bulk to stop anyone sailing upstream during the concert.

She had, however, graciously invited the ladies of the orchestra to hang their dresses in the Long Gallery.

'Is that a genuine Picasso?' asked Nellie, as she peered in awe into the le-ounge.

'No, no,' giggled Candy, 'look on the back. It says "Do Not Freeze, This Side Up".'

'Admiring my Picarso,' said a loud voice behind them. 'It was a silver wedding-gift from my late hubby.'

'She's even matched her grand piano exactly to the panelling,' Clare told Dixie as she returned from the house, 'and every piece of ghastly furniture is for sale.'

'You don't think an old bag like Piggy Porker would pass up an opportunity for commercial gain,' said Dixie. 'You could probably buy that oak tree for twenty grand.'

'I'll pay Sonny twenty grand to stay away,' said Clare. 'He's been so preoccupied with his première he even forgot to buy Mumsy a birthday card.'

Today was also the birthday of Ninion, Second Oboe and oppressed partner of Militant Moll.

'Just proves what utter crap astrology is,' sneered Carmine Jones getting his trumpet out of its case, 'when a thug like Piggy Porker and a wimp like Ninion have birthdays on the same day.'

Ninion ignored the crack, but his hands shook as he read his and Mrs Parker's horoscope in the *Rutminster Echo*, which was part owned by Mrs Parker anyway, and which said it would be a good day for fireworks.

Underneath his mild blinking, field-mouse exterior, Ninion was hopping mad. Second Oboe often doubles up as cor anglais, but Knickers and Abby had humiliatingly not thought he was good enough to play the long ravishing cor anglais solo in *William Tell*, and brought in Carmine Jones's wife, Catherine, as an extra.

Militant Moll should have been pleased a woman had been given the job. Instead she berated Ninion for not standing up for his rights.

'You are quite capable of playing that solo, Nin. Why d'you let people push you around? Catherine Jones is a drip not to have left Carmine years ago.'

Moll was taking Ninion to a woman composers' workshop in Bath as a birthday treat. Ninion brooded; he was fed up with women.

The surrounding fields were silvered with dew as the orchestra tuned up, but no breeze ruffled the forget-me-nots languishing on the river-bank. As Flora returned a dripping Nugent to Viking, she breathed in a heady scent. At first she thought it came from a nearby lime tree. Then she realized it was Blue's aftershave, which he never wore normally, and that he had put on a ravishing new duck-egg-blue shirt. Blue was so handsome, quiet and dependable, but there was a sadness about him. Flora wondered if he were gay and secretly in love with Viking. He never had any women around.

'God, it's baking,' said Viking, who was sharing his breakfast of a pork pie and a Kit-Kat with Mr Nugent. 'Oh, go away,' he snapped at Fat Isobel, who'd been panting after him like a St Bernard since he'd taken her out for a drink.

Flora looked up at the house. 'How the hell did Piggy Porker get permission to build such an excrescence in such a beautiful park?' she asked

'Every councillor has his price,' explained Viking contemptuously. 'All the fat cats on Rutminster Council, who you'll see guzzling champagne this evening probably received a nice nest-egg in a Swiss bank or holiday home in Barbados. I wonder if Alan Cardew, the planning officer, would enjoy knowing that his wife Lindy is currently being knocked off by Carmine Jones.'

'How could she? He's loathsome. Imagine that brick-red sneering face kissing you.'

'That's why Lindy was so livid when Abby sacked her from the choir. She can't pretend to be sloping off to choir practice any more.'

'All right, let's get started,' Abby had arrived, looking deathly pale after a sleepless night wondering whether to do a runner rather than be made over by Peggy's beauticians. She was wearing a dark red vest and black bicycle shorts, and her lips tightened as she saw Flora gossiping with Viking.

The orchestra quickly whizzed through *William Tell*. Catherine Jones wasn't turning up until the concert, so Ninion had to deputize for her, which made him crosser than ever. The fireworks would be let off after the trumpet fanfare during the rousing finale, which everyone knew because it had once been *The Lone Ranger*'s signature tune.

Fortunately the electrician who'd spent the morning hammering Roman candles, rockets and Catherine wheels onto posts liked music and knew exactly when to start the display.

'Miss Rosen, we're ready for you. I'm Crystelle by the way,' called out a Parker beautician, who hovered, smiling like a crocodile. Her make-up was so thick you could have chucked rocks at it.

For a second Abby stared down at her, terrified and proud, Sidney Carton at the scaffold. Then she gathered up her sticks and her scores.

'Please don't ruin her, she's so beautiful,' called out Flora as Crystelle frogmarched Abby back to the house.

'You need your eyes tested, Flora,' said Carmine Jones nastily.

'And you need a face transplant,' shouted Flora.

The orchestra roared with laughter; singly most of them were too frightened to take on Carmine, whose face was now engorged with rage like a slice of black pudding.

It was now time for Sonny to take a last rehearsal of his *Eternal Triangle* for orchestra, cow bells and yodeller. A little man with a very large ego, Sonny (or rather Mumsy) had paid for several extra rehearsals. Many contemporary composers prefer to be programmed with other twentieth-century music. Not Sonny.

'I'm not frightened of comparison with the great masters.'

Crash, bang, plink, plonk, went the orchestra. Sonny, a hopeless conductor, looked as though he were swimming through deep water and occasionally spearing a jelly fish.

Nor did he know anything about music, but fancying Viking, whose body was turning dark gold above his dirty white shorts, called out: 'Four bars after twenty, Horns, marked gestopft. Could you play it on your own?'

'Gestopft' means putting the right hand up the bell of the horn to produce a muted buzzing sound. Viking, however, muttered to his section, 'OK lads, play flat out.'

The next moment five horns blared out making two nearby pigeons and the rest of the orchestra jump out of their skins.

'For goodness' sake,' spluttered Hilary, who hadn't imagined she'd need her industrial ear plugs in the open air.

Sonny, however, was in raptures.

'Splendid, Viking, splendid.' He thrust forward a circle formed by his first finger and thumb.

'Nor does the silly bugger realize that the trumpet's been transposed into the wrong key by the copyist for the last three rehearsals,' said Viking scornfully.

'He's been too busy jogging so he can rush up onto

the platform in time to catch the applause,' said Blue, shaking water out of his tuning slide.

Sonny had also been active organizing a claque of comely youths from the soft-furnishing department to provide a standing ovation.

'Now, really clap your hands, boys, shout, "Bravo" and stamp your feet.'

Sonny's favourite, however, was rumoured to be a plump young man with soft brown curls in all the right places, who was going to dress in lederhosen and provide the yodelling tonight.

At ten o'clock, by which time the temperature had soared into the nineties, the orchestra were released, many of them to sunbathe so they would look good in their summer uniform of white dinner-jackets, or for women, dresses in a single colour, whose skirts must fall at least nine inches below the knee.

As Rutshire was playing Yorkshire on the cricket ground next to the cathedral, Old Henry and Old Cyril found a couple of deckchairs. As he opened a can of beer, Old Cyril thanked God for the millionth time that Viking and Blue had carried him through his audition.

Having spent the morning on the telephone shouting at his builder who had omitted to put a staircase in a new office block: 'Now, that's one I really can't lie about, George,' George Hungerford had also hoped to slope off to the cricket ground to cheer on his home county.

Coming out of his office, however, he had found Eldred, the First Clarinet, in tears. They were so badly in debt that his wife had left him.

'You better tell me about it,' sighed George, going back into his office.

Carmine Jones's face grew even redder as he pleasured Lindy Cardew, wife of Rutminster's planning officer, on her peach nylon sheets.

'I'll get you back into the choir, Lindy, if it kills me.'

Poor Catherine Jones had no time to practise her cor anglais, she had been far too busy washing and ironing Carmine's dress-shirt and getting suspicious-looking grass stains out of his white tuxedo, and sobbing over the primrose-yellow taffeta dress with huge puffed sleeves which had been fashionable the year the Princess of Wales had married Prince Charles, the same year she had married Carmine. Apart from a black polyester shift to wear to winter concerts, she had not had a new dress since then.

Tonight's outfit had to be one colour. Cutting the orange firebird made of sequins from the yellow taffeta bodice as she shoved baked beans down fractious children, Catherine had jagged a large hole in the bodice. At this rate, she wouldn't have time to wash her hair. As Carmine was pathologically stingy he had ordered Catherine to come home immediately after *William Tell* to relieve the babysitter and not even stay for drinks in the interval. Catherine fingered a large bruise on her left cheek and hoped make-up would hide it.

The soloist in Liszt's *Piano Concerto* that evening was Benny Basanovich, a half-French, half-Russian pig, who could only play loudly. He therefore chose pieces (and women, said Viking) where he could bang away. Good looking in a brutal fashion, Benny had thick black ram's curls falling to his shoulders, a hooked nose, slanting eyes beneath thick brown eyebrows and a big, light red mouth. A Shepherd Denston artist, he'd always been wildly jealous of Abby because she was more famous than him, but he got much more work than he deserved because Howie fancied him.

After a brief telephone call to Lionel, both men decided that Lionel would follow Benny and bring in the orchestra as necessary, and that everyone would ignore Abby.

* * *

By two o'clock, the beauticians had Abby corsetted, dressed, made-up and coiffeured. She was then subjected to an interview and a long photographic shoot with the *Daily Telegraph*, followed by a press conference and photo-call in the burning heat.

'Can't I even take off my panty hose?' pleaded Abby.

'Certainly not, Luvlilegs have taken a full-page ad in the programme,' said Crystelle, shutting up such subversion with a huge powder-puff slap in Abby's face. 'Always remember to brush powder upwards, it raises the hairs on your face and gives you a far livelier expression.'

'Don't you look a poppet,' cried Peggy Parker in ecstasy. 'What a transformation.'

Peggy herself, already made-up and wearing a white kimono over her massive corseted bulk, looked like an all-in wrestler. On the window-sill, as more dark blue lines were drawn under her lashes, Abby noticed a gift-wrapped present.

'*To Abigail Rosen, Thank you indeed for a very pleasant concert, sincerely, Peggy Parker,*' said the accompanying card.

There was one for Benny, too.

Out of the window Abby could see a beautiful sunken garden, crammed with red, white and blue rock plants. She wanted to dive into the lily pond in the centre, crack open her aching head and never wake again. Catching sight of a dreadful drag queen in the mirror, she gave a moan of anguish. But Abby had never lacked courage, one hundred thousand pounds for the RSO was worth twelve hours of humiliation.

The sweet heady smell of honeysuckle and tobacco plants grew stronger with the coming of night, mingling with the hundred different 'fragrances' of Mrs Parker's invited guests who had paid one hundred and fifty pounds for their tickets and hospitality throughout the evening, and who were now noisily spilling out of the VIP tent. Most of the women had streaked hair and wore a lot of make-up which looked better as the light faded. They enjoyed a concert, they knew the tunes from Classic FM and it was such fun to look at each other's jewels and clothes and see who'd been asked.

They all longed for a word with George Hungerford, whose manly, attractively rumpled face was always looking out from the financial pages, but sadly he was being monopolized by their husbands, hoping perhaps that some of his huge success might rub off on them.

George, in fact, was in a foul temper. He had somehow mopped up Eldred and persuaded him to play, but he was fed up with being bossed around by Peggy Parker. He had also just had a frightful row with Benny, who had refused to come out of his dressing-room and give a 'very pleasant' concert to anyone unless he was paid cash up front.

The orchestra were nearly all in their seats. Miss Parrott had availed herself of Peggy Parker's offer of ge-owns at trade. A symphony of harebell-blue tulle with a mauve-blue beehive to match, she smiled across at Dimitri, the Principal Cellist, who started the concert.

Knickers was in a terrible twist, again, running around in his shirt sleeves, livid that he'd had to hand over his white dinner-jacket to Francis the Good Loser, who'd brought tails by mistake. Francis had also forgotten his black socks, and rectified the mistake by smothering his ankles with Old Henry's black boot polish.

Catherine Jones was late. As a Second Oboe wasn't needed in *William Tell*, Ninion propped up the bar and festered. He wasn't going to help them out if Cathie didn't show up.

At half-past seven on the dot, Mrs Parker, resplendant in a diamond tiara and red bustier with matching organdie skirt, swept down the hill in a white open-topped Bentley. Beside her, a third of her size, but radiating equal complacency, sat Sonny in a white silk tunic. With his lank dark hair loose round his silly beaky face, he looked like a parrot peering out of its baize cloth.

Dismounting from their triumphal car, Mrs Parker and Sonny were clapped onto the rostrum by the audience led by Sonny's claque from soft furnishing.

They were followed by Abby. Clad in an electric-blue lurex shirtwaister which fell to mid-calf, she was shod in electric-blue shoes, whose four-inch heels kept falling into the cracks in the ground. Due to the tightness of her skirt it took her three goes to climb onto the platform. She was bowed down by vast rubies at her neck, ears and wrists. Her hair was bouffant, lacquered and blonded, her make-up thick as a raddled old tart in the early evening sunshine.

The orchestra, ably led by Lionel, were clutching their sides.

Flora was torn by horror and helpless laughter. Oh poor Abby. Marcus who loved Abby was absolutely furious; he wanted to punch Mrs Parker and George on the nose. He was also having increasing trouble breathing because of the heat, dust and pollen, and because the chauffeurs were keeping their engines going to enjoy the air-conditioning as they waited in the car-park.

Viking who had not forgotten the beauty of Abby's figure in a red body-stocking was equally appalled.

'Jesus,' he muttered to Blue, 'she looks like Michael Heseltine in drag.'

'Joan of Arc burnt at the stake did not do more for France than I have for this orchestra,' hissed Abby to the First Violins as she passed.

'Throw a few faggots round the base then,' murmured Lionel to Bill Thackery, the co-leader.

'Plenty of those around,' said Bill, who was very

straight, glaring at Sonny's claque dominating the third row.

'Well done Abby, you look chumpion,' lied George.

Having countenanced this transformation, he had to support it publicly, but was secretly horrified.

Mrs Parker and Sonny had already mounted the platform. Vast and tiny, a telephone box beside a small snowman, they were joined by an electric-blue beanpole, and the photographers went berserk.

'Peggy's done it again, have to hand it to her, the gal's got style,' chorused her friends.

At a distance, Abby had a certain splendour like the Statue of Liberty.

Mrs Parker then introduced the 'new look' Parker and Parker had especially created for Abigail Rosen.

'Abigail's *coiffeure* has been softly styled and high-lightened by Guiseppe.'

Clap, clap, clap, clap, went the audience.

'*Maquillage,*' Mrs Parker had been practising her French, 'by Crystelle, rubies by Precious, armpits – ' Mrs Parker allowed herself a little joke – 'by Braun.'

'Hope Militant Moll's listening,' muttered Candy.

'Abigail's ge-own is designed by myself, do a twirl, Abigail, you will all notice the kick-pleat.'

Clap, clap, clap, clap.

'This is terrible,' groaned Viking.

'Foxie's going to write a new book of martyrs starting with Abby,' said Flora.

Surreptitiously getting her puppet fox from underneath her chair, she made him wave at Abby, who continued to gaze, grimly into space, not a smile lifting her blood-red lips.

'Those in the front rows,' vulpine Mrs Parker leered round, 'will notice Abigail is wearing *Peggy*, my new in-house fragrance.'

'I'm wearing Piggy,' stage whispered Clare, reducing the entire viola section to hysterics, which were fortunately drowned by the orchestra playing, 'Happy Birthday, Peggy.'

Mrs Parker nodded graciously.

'Thenk you, thenk you.' Then, turning graciously to Abby, 'and now, Maestro, will you make music.'

THIRTY-TWO

Ninion, still brooding, propped up the bar. He had drunk a litre of cider and a large gin and tonic as a chaser. He should have been playing that solo. Then he had a brainwave. Pushing his way through the crowds he reached the electrician who was doing the fireworks.

'It's my birthday,' he began pathetically. 'My parents were so poor we could never afford fireworks at home.'

Touched by this tale, the electrician, who wanted to get drunk with his mates, accepted a tenner and handed the job over to Ninion.

The only person who looked worse than Abby was Cathie Jones. Her tired red-rimmed eyes were as worried as an Alsatian's above a muzzle. Scurf from nerves encrusted the prematurely grey roots of her lank coppery hair. Her tights were mostly darn, her make-up thicker than Abby's to cover the bruise on her cheek. She was so thin that the ghastly primrose dress looked like a hand-me-down from a much older sister. A cheap brooch, covering the hole she had torn this afternoon, resembled an outsize nipple.

'What a dog,' said Quinton Mitchell, Third Horn, in disgust. 'No wonder Carmine's humping Lindy Cardew.'

Blue swung round to land Quinton one, but just in time Abby raised her baton, an exercise in weightlifting as her ruby bracelet glittered in the fading sunlight.

Dimitri was just about to draw his bow across the strings, when a loud voice said; 'If you're into harcheology, Turkey is definitely *the* place, thank you very, very much.'

It was Lindy Cardew coming in late, blowing discreet kisses at Carmine.

'That's 'im,' she whispered to her friend. 'You just wait till he blows 'is trumpet.'

Abby shot Lindy an absolutely filthy look, not lost on any of the audience, and brought down her stick.

Buoyed up by a beta-blocker and several swigs of sherry from Miss Parrott's hip-flask, Dimitri and his four cellos brought tears to everyone's eyes with the beautiful introduction which was followed by the thrilling crashes of the storm. Abby found it almost impossible to conduct in high heels; only the thought that she would land on El Creepo stopped her falling into the orchestra.

It was time for Catherine Jones's cor anglais solo, and the instant she started playing, the mockery faded on people's faces. She looked as though she was sucking some heavenly nectar out of a bent straw, as if an angel's hand had run over her strained, tortured face restoring its former beauty.

Even the waitresses stopped washing up glasses to listen to the langourous, hauntingly lovely tune. No wonder Carmine was jealous. Even Abby looked at peace, her hand rising and falling in slow motion like a dancer's as she smiled down at Cathie.

Such enthusiasm was too much for Ninion. A plague on both you hussies. There was a deafening explosion. For a terrifying moment, people thought it was a bomb, then twenty thousand pounds' worth of fireworks erupted.

Crash, crash, crash, went Roman candles, jumping

jacks, Catherine wheels, spilling out red, white and blue sparks; whoosh went the rockets exploding miles into the air, lost against a fading turquoise sky including the climax which said: HAPPY BIRTHDAY TO PEGGY PARKER in red, white and blue. Cathie's solo, and Peter Plumpton's flute variations were totally obliterated, and there were no fireworks left for Carmine's fanfare and the rousing finale. Piggy Parker was not the only one going ballistic. Blue was on his feet.

'I'm going to strangle that focking electrician.'

As he dived for the edge of the platform, Viking pulled him back: 'Wait for the break and we'll both throttle him.

'I need you to drown Benny,' he added as an after-thought, as a nine-foot Steinway was wheeled on to the usual grumbling from the First and Second Violins. Clare, Candy, Flora, Juno, Nellie, Noriko and Mary-the-Mother-of-Justin, who had all been taken individually aside and told that Benny was playing the concerto just for them, waited expectantly. Cherub, who was playing the famous triangle solo in the third movement, shook with excitement, his triangle swinging from its silver stand like a hangman's noose.

Benny was definitely drunk when he came onto the platform, even the lingering sulphur of the fireworks couldn't disguise the wine fumes. He'd hardly bothered to warm up. He just regards this as a bread-and-butter concert, thought Abby furiously.

Twiddles from the orchestra, followed by rigid-fingered banging from Benny, had the audience, who were all now fanning their sweating faces with their programmes, jumping out of their seats.

Marcus put his head in his hands; how could anyone play so insensitively and so badly? Oh God, give me a chance.

At first, Abby tried to cover up Benny's missed entries and fluffed lines, then she realized that half the orchestra were ignoring her and following Benny.

Others like Dimitri, Blue, Viking and Flora, feeling desperately sorry for Abby, were following her instead. The result was almost more contemporary than Sonny Beam and, as Benny skipped a few bars whenever things got too difficult, everyone was soon jumping around like Tom and Jerry.

'I played the last page three times,' muttered Viking, at the end of the first movement.

'Library gave me the wrong concerto,' said Blue grimly.

Ninion, by this time, had escaped across a little bridge to the opposite bank with another litre of cider and a duck caller. So the slow movement, despite Benny's bashing, was accompanied by furious quacking as though Donald Duck had joined Tom and Jerry.

Further hassle was provided by the mosquitoes, unchecked by the darting swallows, who were now attacking players in droves, particularly the balder heads of older members of the orchestra. Finally a huge dragonfly landed like a helicopter on the baldest head, that of Dimitri.

'Quack, quack, quee-ack,' called Ninion plaintively from the reeds.

Any giggling by the orchestra was then obliterated by Benny crashing into the last movement, interspersed by the silver shimmer of Cherub's triangle. Cherub looked so angelic with his blond curls, pink cheeks and his excited smile, that the audience gazed at him, which made a furious Benny bash louder than ever.

At the end Abby stormed off, catching a four-inch heel in a chair leg, and falling off the platform into George's arms.

'Let me go,' she hissed, enveloped by his strength and solidarity, longing to sob her heart out on one of his wide shoulders.

'The Press want a photograph of you and Benny,' said George.

'I do not share that pianist's interpretation,' said Abby through gritted teeth.

'Nor do I to be honest,' conceded George, who had vowed never to book Benny again. 'But let's just get through this evening.'

Fortunately the audience who'd chatted throughout hadn't noticed a thing wrong and were now looking forward to 'bubbly and nibbles' in the VIP tent.

'What is the matter with Eldred?' asked Quinton as Abby returned and raised the horn section to their feet for a special clap.

'Wife's just left him,' said Blue.

'Is that all? Thought he must be upset he was half a tone sharp in that last solo.'

But Blue had gone leaping into the crowd like a blood-hound in search of the focking electrician.

The setting sun balancing on the horizon gilded the huge trees of the park and softened the ox-blood stone of Rutminster Towers. House martins dived in and out of the eaves feeding their young. In the VIP tent the ice had run out, all Peggy's pals expecting 'bubbly' were disappointed to be fobbed off with mulled Pimm's.

'So looking forward to meeting Abigail,' they all chorused.

'Artists don't like to break the mood in the middle of a concert,' Mrs Parker was telling them sententiously. 'You will all have the chance of a few words later.'

'Hum,' said Flora, who'd been smuggled into the tent by Viking, 'I don't know what sort of mood Abby'll be in.'

'It's a terrible concert,' Viking shook his head. 'Acoustics are always dire outside unless you're up against a brick wall.'

'Like the management,' said Dixie, scooping up half a dozen asparagus rolls.

'Also like the management,' agreed Viking. 'The strings get totally lost.'

'Thank God,' said Dixie.

'I don't know how you lot got in here,' said Miles beadily, 'but if you're going to crash parties and avail yourself of Mrs Parker's hospitality, you can jolly well stop coffee-housing and mingle with her guests.'

'George Hungerford is awfully good at mingling,' observed Flora, as she watched him pressing the flesh, talking to MPs, lawyers, local businessmen, shop owners along the High Street, never stopping long, too shy or too busy to want to get caught, but making each person feel important and welcome:

'You must come to H.P. Hall and hear the orchestra. I'll send you a couple of tickets, we've got some good dos coming up in the autumn.'

'He's sponsor hunting,' said Dixie.

'Up to a point,' said Viking. 'He's also bought fifty acres on Cowslip Hill and wants to build on them, my guess is he's greasing palms.'

Flora was screwing up courage to talk to George. She and Abby had been discussing Marcus's poverty, and his heartbreakingly slow progress, over supper last night.

'If I push him, the management'll resist,' sighed Abby, 'they're still pissed off I smuggled you in.'

'I'll try and introduce him to George,' said Flora. 'The only problem is that Marcus is so shy and unpushy, he'll probably bolt.'

Now Marcus had joined her and Flora could see George getting nearer. Like most of the men he'd removed his dinner-jacket showing a roll of fat over his trouser belt. His evening shirt was transparent with sweat, his square face red and shiny. Why on earth did all the women in the orchestra find him sexy? And oh God, here was Benny, black curls soaked from the shower, cream silk shirt unbuttoned to the waist.

Deciding Flora was the most seductive of all the girls he'd propositioned, Benny sidled up.

'How about a leetle deener at my 'otel, no-one would mees you, if we slope off.'

'Piss off, you disgusting Frog,' said Viking coldly.

Benny was about to land Viking one, but was distracted by the arrival of George, Mrs Parker and Lord Leatherhead, who had been boring Mrs Parker's guests silly rabbiting on about bottled water.

'Good concert, well done, all of you,' he said heartily. 'Peggy, I don't think you've met our latest recruit, Flora Seymour. She plays the viola jolly well.'

Mrs Parker, who was even redder in the face than George, didn't look remotely interested until Lord Leatherhead added that Flora's mother was Georgie Maguire.

Oh hell, thought Flora.

'I'm a large fan of 'ers,' said Mrs Parker in excitement, 'I've got all her records. Perhaps she'd like to visit the store one day. We could find her something really outstandin' for her next concert.'

'That's sweet.' Catching Viking's eye, Flora started to giggle, then seeing George glaring at her, added quickly, 'I wonder if I could possibly introduce a friend of mine, Marcus Campbell-Black.'

Beautiful boy, thought George. Looks as though he was born in a dinner-jacket, she would go for someone like that.

'Are you the son of?' asked Mrs Parker skittishly. 'Very delighted to receive you.'

Marcus winced as her diamonds dug into him.

'I've shot with your father,' brayed Lord Leatherhead. 'A very fine shot.'

'Marcus is a very fine pianist,' piped up Flora. 'No, he is,' she continued ignoring Marcus's hands frantically waving for her to stop. 'He was at the Academy and he plays like an angel. Could he audition for you some time, Mr Hungerford, or we could send you a tape?'

'Good idea,' said Lord Leatherhead.

'Phone me at the office,' said George then, as the warning bells started, 'You lot better get back.'

'I 'ope you will play at one of my soirées at Rutminster Towers, Marcus,' said Mrs Parker graciously, 'or come to afternoon tea under the walnut tree. Perhaps your father would like to look in, too. I'm sure he'd appreciate how much the RSO do for young people.'

Marcus, however, had boiled over. 'I haven't seen any sign of it,' he said furiously, 'or you wouldn't have humiliated darling Abby by forcing her into that seriously hideous dress.' Then seeing the horror and fury particularly on Mrs Parker's face, added, 'You succeeded in making one of the most beautiful women in the world look like a disgusting old slag-heap. You should be bloody well ashamed of yourselves.' And, turning on his heel, he stumbled out of the tent.

'If your friend wants to get to the top as a soloist,' an enraged George turned on Flora, 'I don't think he's going about it the right way.'

The choir had a good screech and the audience a good chat during the *Polovtsian Dances* by which time the sun had set, leaving an orange glow on the horizon, so no-one could read their programmes any more. Not that it mattered during the *pièce de résistance* which was only too easy to resist, Sonny's *Eternal Triangle*.

Crash bang wallop, plinkety plonk, catawaul screech, went the orchestra to an increasing crescendo of shifting bottoms and mutterings as people ducked to avoid a night raid of bats.

'Yodelayayo,' carolled the plump young man in lederhosen.

Abby's electric-blue shoes were killing her, her wrists and shoulders were agony, but that was nothing to the

417

ghastly humiliation ahead, being hawked round Peggy Parker's vulgar friends like one of Tamberlaine's captured war lords.

Amidst the frightful din, she could hear Cherub ringing cowbells, reminding her that tomorrow she was flying out to Lucerne and Rodney for a month, and this nightmare would be over.

There was only a page left. Cherub had finished his last little solo. Then, during a dramatic pause when the orchestra were completely silent for three bars, Lindy Cardew could be heard saying loudly to her friend: 'No, no, no, she hasn't got a black one. She's got a long furred marmalade one.'

Abby flipped. Swinging round she howled: 'Will you flaming well shut up,' which was fortunately drowned out for many of the audience by the final deafening tutti.

Manic that such a frightful din was over, geed up by the claque from soft furnishing who all wanted Cherub's telephone number, the audience gave the piece a great reception, which gave Sonny plenty of time to run on and take his composer's bow.

As Abby came off the stage clutching red-and-white gladioli and royal-blue delphiniums, she was accosted by a BBC crew and a horde of Press asking her about her new image.

Exactly on cue, a mallard, no doubt unnerved earlier by Ninion's duck caller, dumped copiously on Abby's electric-blue bosom, whereupon Abby laughed for the first time in days and said straight to camera: 'Well done, duckie, that's a distinct improvement.'

The next moment, horrified Parker minions charged forward to hurry her into the house and sponge her down. Upstairs Crystelle waited, ready with a respray before Abby met her public: 'The most important part of your evening.'

'I'm terribly sorry, I have to distance myself for a few

minutes after a concert,' said Abby and dived into Mrs Parker's bathroom locking the door.

On the way to the Long Gallery to dump her viola, Flora flexed her aching back and wondered what had become of Marcus. He'd probably cooked all their geese with the management, but how brave and wonderful he had been.

Hearing a kerfuffle, Flora edged forward. Round the corner Blue had got hold of Ninion and hung him by his white dinner-jacket on a row of pegs.

'You snivelling little bastard,' he hissed, glaring into Ninion's terrified blinking eyes, then he hit him very hard across the face with the back of his hand.

'What did you do that for?' bleated Ninion, swinging helplessly.

'Don't you ever do anything like that to Cathie Jones again; you're not fit to lick her boots.'

Blue was about to hit Ninion again when George arrived, clicking his fingers for two heavies, who pulled him off.

'That's enough,' snapped George. 'Throw him in the river to cool him down,' he told the heavies. 'And I want you in my office first thing on Monday morning, Ninion.'

'What was all that about?' whispered Flora to Miss Parrott.

'Brass have a problem when it's humid,' sighed Miss Parrott, righting her mauve beehive in the mirror, then, seeing the sceptical expression on Flora's face, added, 'Blue has rather a soft spot for Cathie Jones. And I think he's upset Carmine, made her go home before the interval.'

Knickers was in a further twist. Retrieving his white dinner-jacket from Francis to wear at the party, he found it covered in black boot polish. Francis would lose his job at this rate.

Benny was even more upset, having decided to plump for second best, he couldn't find Nellie the Nympho anywhere.

'Yodellayayo,' came an ecstatic cry from the shrubbery.

'Someone's dropped a pair of lederhosen,' sniffed Fat Isobel, who was crying because she wouldn't see Viking for a month.

'I'm going to miss you, Lady C,' Dixie was telling Clare in that ghastly Glaswegian accent which had become music to her ears. 'The moors will be purple with heather.'

'Daddy's going up to Scotland for the 12th,' said Clare, 'I could go with him, then we could meet.'

'We certainly could,' said Dixie looking much happier. 'Piss off you disgusting Frog,' he added as Benny slid a too high hand round Clare's waist.

Peter Plumpton, the First Flute, being small always got drunk very quickly.

'Putti, putti, putti,' he cried, as he advanced with an outstretched hand on a group of reconstituted-stone cherubs.

Miss Parrott was sharing a log, a bottle of white and a plate of Dover sole and lobster poached in Sauterne with Dimitri.

'That opening to *William Tell* was the loveliest thing Ay've ever heard,' she was telling him.

'Your solo in Wrist's *Piano Concerto* was perfect,' confided Noriko.

'Three agents have tried to sign me up, I'm going to be the next Evelyn Glennie,' giggled Cherub, squeezing her little hand.

Meanwhile favoured customers, who hadn't heard Abby yelling at Lindy Cardew, were congratulating Peggy Parker, who hadn't either, on the graciousness of the occasion.

'Abigail will be de-own shortly,' promised Mrs Parker regally.

Mrs Parker's bathroom had a dressing-room mirror with lights going round in a semicircle. Watching the moths helplessly smashing their wings and bodies against the burning bulbs, Abby gave a sob. It was just like her and the RSO. Out of the window she could see members of her orchestra chucking the stuff down their throats no doubt laughing themselves sick to see her so humiliated.

She jumped at a banging on the door.

'We're waiting,' called Crystelle.

'Just a sec,' shouted Abby, turning on the shower.

At home having checked her sleeping children and paid the babysitter out of her pathetic housekeeping allowance, Cathie Jones climbed wearily upstairs. She was too tired to eat.

Gazing out of her bedroom at the stars she started to cry, then not wanting to wake the children, fished in her skirt pocket for a tissue and found a piece of paper on which someone had scrawled the words: *'Darling Cathie, Thou art fairer than the evening air, clad in the beauty of a thousand stars.'*

Five minutes later, Abby stalked out into the garden and as usual everyone fell silent. She had changed back into her red vest and bicycle shorts. Her hair was slicked back and still dripping, her make-up totally washed off. There was a long, long pause.

'What the fuck,' snarled George.

Huge, menacing, he bore down on her.

'Get bluddy oopstairs and back into that dress.'

Abby had never seen anyone angrier, except perhaps Mrs Parker.

'What's happened to your beautiful ge-own,' she screeched.

421

'I left it and the shoes on your bed.'

'And what about those rubies.'

'They're on your dressing-table,' said Abby, then waving an ironic hand at the RSO who were now filling their faces with Dover sole and lobster. 'Why should I need rubies, when my orchestra are my jewels.'

THIRTY-THREE

The month of August was traditionally a holiday for the RSO. All in all, Abby got a rotten end-of-term report. An enraged Mrs Parker was threatening to withdraw her promised one hundred thousand pounds, and in cahoots with Miles and a horrified Canon Airlie, who had both heard Abby shouting at Lindy Cardew, were agitating for her dismissal. George fired off a written warning about consistently subversive behaviour, pointing out that Abby had only seven months left on her contract. Abby promptly tore up his letter. She should have spent August relaxing and, in the light of her disastrous conducting career, seriously attempting to play the violin again. The physio and the London specialist both said there was nothing more they could do. The block was in Abby's head. But Abby couldn't bring herself to try, terrified her genius had deserted her, and after her Strad, any violin would be a let-down.

She had hoped to spend August in Lucerne, enjoying Gisela's cooking and having her feathers unruffled by Rodney. He appeared to have made an excellent recovery from his heart attack and was now teaching himself the cello, playing with great vigour and a lot of wrong notes.

In Lucerne, as in England, the heatwave showed no signs of abating and had already singed the woods around the lake, whose level had dropped more than a foot. Two days after her arrival, Abby stretched out in an orange bikini, lake water drying on her darkening gold body.

Despite the heat she and Rodney had just polished off the palest green avocado mousse and an exquisite fish salad, which Gisela had made for lunch, plus a bottle of Pouilly-Fumé. Abby was now misery-eating her way through a bowl of figs, her big white teeth tearing at the scarlet flesh. From the nearby shadow of a blue striped umbrella, Rodney sat drinking Armagnac, puffing at a large cigar, and listening as he had done since she arrived. He was very distressed to see her so unhappy.

'Which of my naughty boys is causing you the most bother?'

'They all hate me,' moaned Abby. 'Dixie, Randy, that vile Carmine, Quinton, El Creepo (beneath his smarmy manner), Davie Buckle, Lionel, Viking most of all.'

'Are you apologizing enough, darling? If you start with the wrong beat, if you show three instead of four, you must say, "It's my fault".'

'That's weakness,' stormed Abby. 'Basically they hate taking orders from a woman, right. And we've got such terrific stuff coming up. I told you about Fanny Mendelssohn and Winifred Trapp.'

'You don't want too much of that.' Rodney tipped his ash on the parched yellow grass.

'Celebrating women in the Arts?' demanded Abby.

'Lot better places to celebrate them.' Then, seeing the outrage on Abby's face, added hurriedly, 'You know I adore your sex, but I don't feel they're at their best composing music.'

'That's because you've never bothered to listen to them. Christ it's hot.' Angrily, Abby peeled off her bikini top. 'And I bet they'd have delivered on time, if any one had really appreciated their music, not like Boris Levitsky. We're recording *Rachel's Requiem* next season and not a squeak out of Boris, and I gotta learn the wretched thing. Wasn't Viking a friend of Boris's?'

Always she returns to Viking, thought Rodney, feeling his cock stir as he glanced at the beautiful breasts only slightly less golden than the rest of her body.

'Not really a friend,' he said 'Viking's spoilt – he and Boris were in spiky competition over who could pull the best girls. Lionel's your main problem. One can't operate if the leader's against one – I'm afraid he'll always be a thorn in your deliciously firm young flesh, darling.'

'Not so young any more,' grumbled Abby. 'I'll be twenty-nine in October.'

'And I'm going to be seventy-nine in October, don't be a silly-billy.'

Abby sat up swinging her legs sideways. 'I wish all men were like you.'

'I'm not that different from the rest of them.' Stretching out a warm hand as though he was testing a peach, Rodney gently fingered her breast.

Abby gasped, amazed at the sudden quivering warmth between her legs.

'I-I see you as the grandfather I never really had,' she stammered.

'Really?' Rodney raised a mocking eyebrow, as his thumb caressed a rapidly hardening nipple.

'Where's Gisela?' whispered Abby.

'Making crab-apple jelly. Artists are oblivious when they are in the process of creation.'

Abby shut her eyes as the languid practised caress continued.

'You're the one turning me to jelly; d'you really want me, Rodney?'

'My child, a slow burn doesn't mean the flame isn't poised to singe the ceiling.'

'Oh Christ,' exploded Abby as, unwelcome as the

bones singing in *Ezekiel*, the white cordless telephone rang.

It was Flora.

'You're not the only one in the doghouse, Abby, Hitler Hungerford says he'll tear up Boris's contract if he doesn't deliver on 1 September, and he wants Boris to pay back the two-thousand-pound advance. Boris is in hysterics, he hasn't got two pence, let alone two grand. I've asked him to stay. I hope you don't mind. Perhaps Marcus and I can prod him into action and at least copy the stuff out for him.'

Abby looked down at Rodney's hand, wrinkled, covered in liverspots, yet making it almost impossible for her to think rationally: 'Boris can sleep in the attic bedroom.' She glanced sideways at Rodney's watch. 'I'll try and get the four o'clock plane.'

Rodney sighed as she switched off the telephone.

'Probably just as well, darling. Tell Boris to give Lionel a long, flashy but not too difficult solo to keep him quiet. Haydn said you could do anything with musicians if you gave them the chance to show off.'

He was sad to see Abby go, but quite relieved. He wanted to learn the cello part of *Don Quixote* and he didn't think he could have coped with a month of such obsessive introspection.

No-one could have been more obsessively introspective than Boris. Abby reached home before he did, and was pleased to see her little faded red-brick cottage peering out of the yellowing woods, the fox cub now seeking refuge from the hunting season.

'You don't think Boris has topped himself,' said a worried Flora. 'We expressed him some cash for his train fare and a taxi.'

Boris arrived with the first stars, having drunk his taxi fare on the train and drenched himself, falling into the lake, on his stumbling walk from the station. His only luggage was a bulging Waitrose carrier bag, of which Flora speedily relieved him.

'Have you brought us some goodies?'

'I vish.'

Inside, frantically scrawled on a mass of manuscript paper were the endless abandoned beginnings of *Rachel's Requiem.*

'I cannot write. I cannot pay back the RSO, I cannot pay Astrid, my lovely au pair, so she has taken the cheeldren to Rachel's parents, who think me murderer anyway, for one month to geeve me peace to write.'

His upended dark curls were streaked with grey, his eyes were black caverns. He was shaking uncontrollably.

But after a very hot bath, and a change into Marcus's sweatshirt and jeans, which now fitted his formerly stocky body, Boris had cheered up enough to tuck into a large steak, French beans and mashed potato, cooked by Marcus, and was soon pouring out his troubles and a great deal of red wine.

'Schumann say: Requiem is a thing one writes for oneself! I shall not leeve long,' Boris coated a piece of steak with mustard, 'I am like Mozart, someone vill have to finish vork for me.'

Flora, who had Scriabin on her knee, removing goose-grass burrs out of his plumy white tail, picked up a spoon and helped herself to some French beans.

'Who could finish it for you?' she asked innocently.

'Edith Spink or perhaps Sonny Parker,' suggested Marcus equally innocently.

'Never,' Boris crashed his hand down on the kitchen table, spilling his half-pint of red wine. 'Ovair my dead buddy.'

'It's going to be dead anyway,' giggled Flora. 'You'll be twanging a harp on a cloud beside Rachel.'

'Flora,' reproved Marcus, mopping up the wine with a piece of kitchen roll. Scriabin's proximity was making his eyes water.

'I listened to John Tavener at the proms last night,'

Flora ignored Boris's scowl. 'It hardly left the note of D. You can be less boring than that.'

'How far have you got?' asked Abby.

'I sketch most of it in the head, but I am so tired vorking sixteen hours a day.' Then, as Flora played an imaginary violin, moaned, 'I am so disappointed and frustrated at non-performance of my vork.'

'How can they perform it, when you don't write anything but rude postcards to Edith Spink?' said Flora, returning to the French beans.

'Are you still not having singers?' asked Marcus, trying to lead the conversation into less thorny paths.

Boris nodded his shaggy head.

'Britten write requiem to his parents wizout singers. I 'ate singers.'

'I hate musicians,' sighed Abby. 'You've licked that spoon Flora. Why don't we dispense with them as well.'

'Then we could have sixty minutes of silence,' said Flora, 'jolly peaceful and much cheaper.'

'The Arts Council would find it very meaningful,' added Marcus.

'You all joke,' grumbled Boris, scooping up the rest of the mashed potato and adding an ounce of butter. 'None of you realize, not Lear, nor Oepidus nor 'Amlet suffer like I do. I'm so vorried I'm written out.'

'Course you're not,' said Flora, 'you'll feel better after a good night's sleep, and no bottles of red under the bed. We'll all help you.'

'Tomorrow I go on vagon,' said Boris, refilling his glass.

Because Marcus stayed at home to practise and give piano lessons while Flora and Abby left the cottage to work, it was assumed that he had the time to shop, cook, unload the dish-washer, transfer dripping underwear from washing-machine to dryer, feed the cats, change duvets, let in plumbers and electricians and often pay for them, too.

Predictably the lion's share of helping Boris fell to him. Thus the following morning, it was Flora who read out the nine sections of the Mass, so Marcus could copy them down and Boris could later tick off each section as he finished it.

'"Dies Irae",' read Flora, who was wandering round the kitchen with Scriabin, a purring black-and-white ruff round her neck.

'That's a joke for a start. Rachel was such a crosspatch she gave Boris months and years of "Irae", always making him smoke outside and not putting salt in any-thing except wounds.'

'Next,' Marcus looked up.

'"Rex Tremendae", what a terrific name for a dog.'

'Got that.'

'"Agnus Dei",' Flora giggled. 'Sounds like Doris Day's sister. Doris was seriously kind to dogs and filled her house and the annexe with strays – I wish we could have a dog.'

'Well, you can't.' Clad only in her bikini, Brahms' *Second Symphony* under her arm, Abby was on her way out to the garden.

'What are you doing?' she asked crossly, as she went through the living-room and found Boris sitting on one of her pale beige Habitat sofas, with manuscript paper, several pencils and erasers on an uncomfortably low table in front of him.

'I'm thinking what to put,' said Boris sulkily. 'It's August and the birds are mute from feeding their young as I am. Zee muse as desert me.'

'We are not a muse,' murmured Flora to Marcus.

'Rodney suggested you wrote a long easy solo for Lionel to keep him quiet,' suggested Abby.

'I 'ate Lionel, little vanker, I will make eet impossibly deeficult.'

Cheered at the prospect of Lionel on the rack, Boris started to scribble down notes, but, having been bawled out by Abby for spilling a sneaked glass of red wine over her new yellow rush-matting, he retreated sulkily to Marcus's studio.

Here he worked feverishly, sometimes stopping to discuss ideas with Marcus, working out details on the piano together, singing phrases which Marcus, who had absolute pitch, could take down like shorthand.

But Marcus's main task was emptying waste-paper baskets of scrumpled-up paper. The progress was desperately slow. Boris spent a lot of time ringing Astrid, ostensibly to check on the children.

'Such a good father,' sighed Abby.

A week later, Boris had struggled to the end of the 'Dies Irae' and 'Rex Tremendae', and Flora and Marcus were copying them out in the garden, helped by the kittens who kept jumping on top of the manuscript paper and shooting their black pens all over the place.

'Probably improving it,' muttered Flora. 'Talk about Slav labour. And how many times do I have to tell you not to clean up after Abby – you're too nice to her.'

They were harvesting in the field beyond the front gate, huge gold blocks rising like ingots out of the platinum-blond grass. But suddenly over the roar of the huge combine, Flora and Marcus heard Boris tapping out a tune on the piano, rising fourths and fifths, tentative but haunting. He was playing it again, changing it slightly, shoving in a few discords, then he played the first version.

Marcus and Flora looked at each other.

'Oh, please don't spoil it,' they said in unison, as Boris introduced an interrupted cadence, and started messing around with the tempo.

'We must tell him,' Flora leapt to her feet.

'He told us not to disturb him.'

'We should before he buggers it up. Write it down. That is the most glorious, glorious tune,' cried Flora, pushing open the door of Marcus's once immaculate studio. 'Play it again.'

Marcus followed, removing Boris's wine glass from the top of the Steinway, which was already covered in drink rings, then scribbling down the notes on a piece of manuscript paper. As he finished he said in ecstasy: 'It's miraculous, Boris.'

Boris shook his head and, retrieving his glass, filled it up.

'It's too good, too little, too nice, too predictable.'

'You're crazy, Boris,' interrupted Abby, who had heard that last version. 'It's so beautiful.'

'Stunning.' Flora picked up the piece of manuscript paper and sang the tune, lifting the hair on the back of everyone's necks.

'That's it, "Rachel's Lament",' said Marcus, sitting down and playing it on the piano.

Abby fingered the curves of Boris's violin, never more longing to join in.

'Please make it a horn solo for Viking,' she begged. 'Viking wouldn't sentimentalize it.'

Boris looked sulky. 'It is too sweet for my Rachel.' And, snatching the page, he tore it into little pieces and stormed off into the wood, not returning until nightfall.

All the same the composition of such a beautiful tune, unleashed something in Boris. The next day, although he grumbled every time the others sang it, he kept working feverishly, sixteen hours on the trot, increasingly encouraged by what he had produced, wading through the rapids, clinging to one stepping-stone after another, until by the last evening of the third week, he had written six out of nine sections.

It was still so hot, they had all the cottage windows open. Abby was upstairs working on the Brahms *Second Symphony* which the RSO were playing their first week back. Flora was copying out the 'Agnus Dei' in the kitchen and also watching a prom production of *Götterdammerung* on television, fulminating because

Brünnhilde had just jumped Siegfried's horse into the funeral pyre.

'Bloody bitch, I'll report her to the RSPCA.'

She had turned down the sound because Marcus, who had a recital in the North of England the next day, was practising Schumann's *Scenes from Childhood*. Even on the old sitting-room upright, it sounded exquisite, and Marcus had hardly had any chance recently to play anything except Boris's stuff.

He's the most talented of all of us, thought Flora guiltily, and he's the one who makes all the sacrifices.

Marcus had reached a little piece called 'By the Fireside', when Boris burst in, tears streaming down his anguished face.

'Rachel play that very last time I see her, she, too, have recital next day,' he sobbed, 'I pull her off piano-stool in middle and we made love.'

Seizing Flora's yellow sarong from the floor, he wiped his eyes and blew his nose.

Marcus leapt up in horror.

'I'll stop, Boris, I'm dreadfully sorry.'

'No, no, go on, play it on Steinway, it ees catharsis.'

Marcus was not very happy with his recital. He drove all the way to a small Lancashire mining town. No-one welcomed him except the caretaker. There were thirty people in the audience who clapped him politely. Afterwards a secretary paid him one hundred pounds. The whole trip cost him almost as much in petrol, as he drove on the following day to see his grandmother in Cheshire, who'd been hit by Lloyd's and her sixth husband, and who never stopped grumbling about the small allowance given to her by Rupert. Marcus stayed a couple of nights trying to cheer her up, but depressing himself, realizing how desperately he missed his father and everyone at Penscombe.

Returning to Woodbine Cottage in the early evening, he found the usual chaos, the washing-up machine was full and unloaded, the sink full of mugs, glasses and plates. In the fridge there was no milk, half a yoghurt, some apricot-and-nut pâté and half a grapefruit. There was also no bread. Tapes and CDs lay out of their cases like loose change on the sitting-room carpet, the plants had wilted, no-one had emptied the dustbin. Finding a squirming sea of maggots when he opened the lid, Marcus closed it quickly. The cats were weaving round his legs, reproachfully, rejecting a bowl of Whiskas covered in flies' eggs.

Marcus wanted to yell at someone but the place was deserted. He had just finished straightening things out and was gasping for breath as he staggered round the house with a watering-can, when the others rolled back from the pub in total euphoria.

'We've had a brilliant few days,' cried Flora. 'Boris has finished except for the orchestration.'

'You did the trick, playing the Schumann the other night.' Boris thumped Marcus on the back so that the watering-can missed a pot of geraniums and spilled all over the sitting-room table. 'That night I dream my Rachel forgive me. I weave *By the Fireside* into "Lachrymosa".'

'And into "Rachel's Lament", which reappears again as the most ravishing solo in the "Libera Me" at the end – it's stunning,' sighed Abby.

'How did you get on, Marcus?' asked Flora, getting a bottle of white wine out of a carrier bag.

'Not brilliant.'

'Many people?'

'Not a lot, but at least they paid me.'

'Ah well, that's good, then.' Flora picked up the corkscrew.

'If you're not too tired,' asked Abby, 'perhaps you could play us what Boris has written.'

They were all so happy, he couldn't shout at them.

No-one could be bothered to stagger over to Marcus's studio, besides he was fed up with the drink rings on the

Steinway, so Flora lit one turquoise candle and one blue and put them in the candleholders on the old upright.

Their soft light flickered on Marcus's face, which gradually grew less pinched and strained as he miraculously deciphered Boris's scrawl, his fingers moving with increasing assurance over the sticky yellow keys.

Meanwhile Flora on the viola and Boris on the fiddle, when he wasn't reaching for his pencil to scribble some change or sobbing his heart out, joined in, harmonizing as they went.

Often the music was dense and hideously discordant, particularly when Boris muddled through Lionel's appallingly demanding solo, muttering happily, 'This'll fix him, zee vanker,' but often some magical tune or cadence would emerge, and Marcus would pause and shake his head in wonder.

'This is incredible, Boris.'

After the beautiful solo of 'Rachel's Lament' had faded softly away, the requiem ended most uncharacteristically with a joyous fanfare.

'And trumpets sound for Rachel on zee uzzer side,' said Boris, wiping his eyes.

The next moment, utterly exhausted, but triumphant, the three of them collapsed in each other's arms.

'You've done it, you've done it.'

'No, you play zee Schumann, Marcus, you deed it,' said Boris. 'After zat I produce in trance like Handel's *Messiah*.'

'Levitsky's Messier,' giggled Flora, 'if we're going to compare handwriting and crossing out.'

As Marcus started to play the 'Lachrymosa' again, really making it sing, Boris raised his glass to Abby who was huddled on the sofa clutching Sibelius.

'I zank you, Abby, for giving us roof over the head.'

'We're The Three Tenants,' announced Flora, shimmering down a glissando with a flourish of her bow. 'Eat your hearts out Placido, Luciano and José.'

Glancing round, Marcus realized Abby's shoulders were shaking: 'What's the matter?' He jumped to his feet.

Abby looked up, her face crumpled and soaked with tears.

'You're all so lucky.' And, dropping Sibelius on the carpet, she ran out into the garden.

'She's pissed, and Boris has been getting too much attention recently. Leave her,' said Flora.

'I cheer her up,' Boris went towards the french windows.

'I think you should have a bath first,' said Flora, 'I don't believe you've touched a bar of soap for a fortnight.'

Putting the kettle on, Marcus realized he hadn't eaten all day. There didn't seem any point starting. When he took out a cup of coffee to Abby in the garden, all the daisies that had shrivelled on the parched yellow lawn seemed to have sprung up in the star-covered sky. Boris was sitting on the old white bench under the greengage tree with his arm round Abby.

'You must guest more,' he was telling her. 'When I conduct the London Met or the New World, the musicians adore me because they 'ate Rannaldini so much. Don't cry, my darling, I vill dedicate *Requiem* to you.'

THIRTY-FOUR

Boris had cracked the *Requiem*, now, as Flora said, he had only to 'add the rough edges'. The next morning, having bathed at length and washed his hair in Marcus's shampoo, and put on yet another pair of Marcus's boxer shorts, he took the draft into the garden, looking handsomer than most dawns as he sat in a deck-chair eating dried apricots.

All great artists sacrifice the emotions and lives of those around them to further the interests of their art. In a mood to be expansive, Boris realized he had pushed Marcus too far.

'You are sad.'

'I'm OK. I wish my father would forgive me and I could see Taggie and Tab and the kids again. I wish my mother wasn't married to that shit Rannaldini and I wish my career wasn't going backwards.'

Boris's face softened. 'I will write a very good piano part into the *Requiem.*'

'Not much point. I was so rude to Old Mother Parker, George Hungerford'll never let me over the RSO threshold again.'

'Markie.' It was Abby calling from the kitchen, looking radiant in a new scarlet bikini. She had also washed her hair and was reeking of *Amarige*. 'I can't open this jar of coffee,' She said as Marcus went inside. 'My grip still isn't right. Isn't it a beautiful day?'

'Forecast says rain,' Marcus said, handing back the jar. Out of the window, he could see huge white clouds gleaming like arctic cliffs in the sunshine, banking up beyond the wood. 'God, we could use it.'

'Oh, Markie,' suddenly Abby looked wildly excited, 'd'you think Boris fancies me?'

It was the question he'd been dreading.

'I'm sure.'

'Oh, darling Markie,' Abby hugged him, giving him the cruel benefit of her hot scented, nearly naked body. 'You're the little brother I never had.'

Hearing the post-van rattling over the dry stones up the lane, Marcus had an excuse to wriggle free before she felt the frantic hammering of his heart.

He was absurdly pleased to get a letter from the musical society in Lancashire.

> *Dear Mr Black,*
> *Yours was the first concert our society has ever had. We all enjoyed it very much indeed. We would like to thank you, and take the opportunity of booking you again next year.*

Boris had a letter from Astrid.

'I haven't ring her since Vendesday because of vork,' said Boris mortified. 'I vill ring her once I get to end of "Sanctus", at least I can pay her now.'

Abby's good mood evaporated when she read a post-card with a photograph of a donkey on the back which had arrived from Viking to Flora, saying how much he was looking forward to seeing her, and that he hoped L'Appassionata had recovered from her strop.

Conscious of a *froideur* despite the heat, Flora decided to make herself scarce. She was fed up with copying black dots. She wanted to buy a new dress and get her hair cut, and tried to persuade Marcus to go into Rutminster with her.

'I ought to practise.'

'And there's still a mass of copying to do,' protested Boris.

'Can I borrow your car, Marcus?' said Flora.

Left alone with Abby and Boris, Marcus felt increasingly claustrophobic as Abby, stretched out on the grass in her bikini and pretended to make notes on the huge score of Brahms' *Second Symphony*.

Boris, flat stomached and lean hipped now he'd lost so much weight, his sallow skin turning a smooth dark brown, pretended to orchestrate the 'Sanctus'.

He's absolutely gorgeous, Abby gazed at Boris through splayed fingers. It was lovely that he was dedicating the *Requiem* to her. Imagine her biog: *Not only was Abigail Rosen the Paganini and the Toscanini of her age, but also Boris Levitsky's Immortal Beloved.* Rodney's caresses had made her aware of how desperately she needed a man.

'Sheet, I 'ave run out of manuscript paper,' Boris glanced down at the laboriously copying Marcus. 'You got any more?'

'This is my last page.'

'And Flora's taken the car,' wailed Abby.

'I wonder who's got some?'

'Certainly not the Celtic Mafia,' said Abby with a sniff, then exchanging a languorous eye-meet with Boris, volunteered, 'I'll call Old Henry.'

Marcus was passionately relieved to escape. The busstop was only half a mile away if he took a short cut through the woods. Twenty yards down the track, he turned round to find Abby hovering at the gate. 'Just wanted to check you've got your inhaler,' she had the grace to blush. 'Please take it slowly.'

Just to make sure I've really gone, thought Marcus bitterly.

I must ring Astrid, thought Boris, as he put down the orchestrated 'Sanctus'. But, on his way to the house, he passed Abby, poring over Lionel's impossibly difficult violin solo which Marcus had just copied out and left on the garden bench.

'God, this is wonderful – if only I could play it.'

'You vill,' said Boris, 'I used to be a teacher, I taught Marcus, I vill help you to play again.

'You take the bow in this hand.' Boris kissed her fingers. 'You take the violin in this one.' He picked up her left hand, examining the palm. 'Such a strong fate line, so much passion.' Slowly he ran his tongue along her heart line.

Abby shivered with excitement, not least because she'd got all the feeling back.

She and Boris were exactly the same height. For a second he gazed at her, then buried his lips in her scented neck below the left jawbone.

'This ees where you put your violin,' he whispered, 'I weel make you bettair.'

As he kissed her lips, he was enchanted by the wild enthusiasm of her response.

Rain brought back the wild flowers, the butterflies and Viking O'Neill to Rutminster. He had enjoyed his time in Dublin. He had recorded the Strauss *Horn Concertos*, played chamber music, romped with his numerous nephews and nieces, gossiped to his mother until four in the morning, looked up old girlfriends and drinking pals. He had also acquired a second-hand BMW convertible into which he had transferred the *Don Juan* horn call.

But by the end of three and a half weeks he had had enough. He lusted after Flora, about whom he'd had a lovely erotic dream last night, but which had faded like a rainbow when he tried to retain it. And then there was Abby.

He had had a letter from Rodney:

Darling boy,
   Beneath that golden exterior you have a heart of gold. Please be kinder to Abby, she is so isolated and sad. Genius should be pruned, but also sunned and fertilized. I suspect she analyses far too much and should let her instincts take over. If you, as leader of the pack, eased up on her a little, the boys and girls would follow suit. Dear me, I miss you all so much.

Viking wondered about being taken over by Abby's instincts. He didn't really fancy her. She was too overbearing, too self-centred, too troublesome, but she irritated him all the time like a sharp piece of apple lodged in his teeth.

The downpour stopped as he approached Rutminster. Pausing in a lane of traffic, he noticed harebells glinting like amethysts in the verge, and meadow browns and common blues dancing ecstatically over the drenched fields. A red admiral had also upended itself on the top of a thistle, avoiding the prickles, as it sucked the sweetness from the mauve flower. With Abby, you'd have to accept prickles and all.

Odd to have a traffic jam on this road, then he realized all the drivers were slowing down to gaze at a beautiful girl at the bus-stop. Her long blond hair and faded denim dress seemed to echo the gold wheat fields and the blue of the sky. With her were a boy and a girl, both very dark haired, pale and sloe-eyed. Must be the child-bride of some rich Arab, thought Viking dismissively.

Pulling up, he smiled and offered her a lift.

The girl brightened. Viking was very brown, his lion's mane bleached. In the last three weeks, he'd got a little more sleep than usual. Such an attractive man, with his arm round such an adorable dog, surely couldn't be an abducter.

'You know,' she consulted a letter, 'the vay to Voodbine Cottage?'

'I go right past the door, hop in. Over you go, Nugent.'

Leaping out, Viking gathered up a pile of scores, paperbacks, CDs and a big bag of duty free and dumped them in the boot, as the big black dog jumped obediently into the back seat.

'He loves kids,' he added, as he opened the back door for the two pale dubious-looking children, and ushered the heavenly blonde into the passenger seat.

Then, raising two fingers at the furiously jealous crescendo of car horns behind him, he drove off with a retaliatory flourish from *Don Juan*.

'My name's Viking.'

'Mine's Astrid.' They gazed at each other in delight.

'Who are you going to see?'

'Boris Levitsky.'

'At Woodbine Cottage?'

Viking was horrified at the idea of Boris hanging round Flora and Abby, exuding Russian machismo.

'He finish *Requiem*,' said Astrid, in her lilting singsong voice. 'He have crisis. Someone called George wanted Boris to pay money back.'

Viking's opinion of George Hungerford rocketed.

'Boris dedicate *Requiem* to me,' went on Astrid happily. 'He say eet almost over. We stay weeth his in-laws, horrible people.' Astrid lowered her voice. 'Marmite sandwich for supper, salad viz no dressing, feenish up every bit, only children's television, bed by eight, so we decided to surprise Boris.'

The two children soon cheered up when Viking stopped and bought them ice-lollies.

Traveller's joy falling in creamy drifts stroked the top of the car, the rain had polished the dusty trees, Viking breathed in a smell of wet earth and moulding leaves as he splashed through the puddles up the rough track.

'Are we nearly there?' asked Astrid, as Nugent began to sniff excitedly.

'Nearly,' said Viking, driving as carefully as possible over the stones to enable Astrid to apply pale pink lipstick to her delicious mouth.

'You look gorgeous,' he added, 'wasted on that Russian.'

'I miss heem so much. Oh what a pretty leetle 'ouse,' exclaimed Astrid as the car drew to a halt.

Getting out, Viking put her hand on Nugent's collar.

'Just hang onto my dog till I see who's in. He's not safe with cats.'

Sauntering up the lichened path, Viking found the pale green front door locked.

'I'll check round the back.'

In the garden, he found Abby and Boris asleep, lying naked in each other's arms. Wonder at Abby's amazing body, rage at what she'd clearly been doing with it, gave way to consternation that Boris's children mustn't catch him like this.

Alas, Marcus's car had conked out on the way home and Flora, meeting a returning Marcus and the cats, had walked back through the woods with them. As they came through the back gate, Mr Nugent had ducked out of his collar and joined his master. Suddenly seeing the two kittens, he hurtled across the lawn, in a frenzy of barking sending both cats scuttling up the horse-chestnut tree.

Rudely awoken, Abby and Boris groped for their clothes. Boris hadn't quite pulled up Marcus's boxer shorts when Astrid appeared round the corner, but a huge smile spread across his face.

'Astrid, oh my Astrid,' he cried running, slipping across the lawn, with arms outstretched. 'You have come to me, 'ow I have meesed you.'

'You 'avent meesed me at all,' screamed Astrid, sizing up the situation. 'You peeg, you absolute peeg.' And she slapped Boris very hard across his face.

'My darling, vy you do that?' Boris clutched his cheek.

'I finish my requiem. Abby and I just embrace for celebration.' Then, turning most unflatteringly to Abby, said, 'Tell Astrid it was nuzzing.'

'Seems to have been a good deal of nuzzling,' observed Flora. 'Oh do shut up, Nugent.'

'You peeg,' repeated Astrid. 'And I don't want requiem dedicate to me.' Bursting into tears she ran back to the car.

'I do see her point,' said Viking coolly. 'I was just returning your kids, Boris, here they are.' As Boris was safely covered now, he drew the two children round onto the lawn. 'And as Astrid hasn't had a day off for a month, I thought I'd take her on a jaunt.'

'No,' roared Boris.

But Viking was too quick for him, whistling to a reluctant Nugent while sprinting back to the car, he jumped in beside a still-sobbing Astrid, and reversed down the lane to the victorious accompaniment of *Don Juan*'s horn call.

Boris was demented.

'Run after my Astrid, tell her it was a moment of euphoria,' he beseeched Abby. 'I love her, and more important I cannot afford to lose a wonderful nanny for keeds.'

'Don't be such a shit, Boris,' said Marcus, putting an arm round Abby's heaving shoulders.

'Everyone ees against me,' said Boris and stormed off to The Bordello.

Abby was livid. What was the point of being the Immortal Beloved if you had to share the honour with a Swedish au pair, and for someone, who delayed for ever when producing music, Boris had proved disappointingly precipitous when it came to making love.

Twenty minutes later, Boris was back, drenched again. Finding The Bordello locked, he had hammered on the door until Astrid had poured a bucket of water over him. He had then hovered in the bushes until Viking

443

emerged to check he had gone and knocked out one of Viking's front teeth.

'I hope he suffer.'

'He won't, it's always being knocked out, it's only crowned,' said Flora.

Boris proceeded to tear up the horn solo of 'Rachel's Lament'.

'Bloody hell, I spent all yesterday copying that out,' grumbled Flora, shuddering at the increase in maggots as she retrieved the page from the bin.

Nor was she very pleased herself. Boris had promised to dedicate the *Requiem* to her, and she'd spent far too much on a pair of new Black-Watch-tartan dungarees for Viking's return, and now he'd shoved off with Astrid. The astrologers had been absolutely right that Jupiter, bringer of jollity, was about to be rammed by a comet.

Boris was now looking helplessly at his children, who were trying to coax down Scriabin and Sibelius.

'Vot would you like for supper?'

'Oh, Marcus'll find them something,' said Abby.

'Marcus will not,' said Flora, catching sight of his stricken face. 'Marcus and I are off to see *Four Veddings and a Funeral.*'

Appassionata

THIRD MOVEMENT

THIRTY-FIVE

The first rehearsal of *Rachel's Requiem* took place on the afternoon of the RSO's first day back at work. Expecting to be bored rigid, the musicians trailed in weighed down by sweets, knitting, magazines, even computer games.

'Ay'd take a good book,' advised Miss Parrott.

'I'd take a library,' said Viking, who had had his front tooth put back, but was secretly incensed that 'Rachel's Lament' had been given to the cor anglais. Carmine was livid that his wife was going to play it and would be around spying on him his first week back.

Simon Painshaw and Peter Plumpton were also livid they hadn't been given the big solo as promised. Eldred had also been promised it, but was too upset to mind. His wife hadn't come back, and after four and a half weeks' respite, he would have to endure Hilary's scorn and sighs once more.

Francis the Good Loser was also fed up. He had mislaid the cup of coffee and the doughnut he'd bought at the buffet, which in fact had been nicked by the First Bassoon, known as 'Jerry the Joker', who was now sitting innocently at his desk.

'Heard the latest viola joke?' he said to Steve, the union rep, who was his Second Bassoon. 'If you're driving down a hill and your brakes fail, who d'you hit, a viola player or a conductor?'

'Dunno,' said Steve.

'The conductor,' said Jerry. 'Business before pleasure.'

'Too right,' said Steve, as Abby marched in looking tight-lipped and embattled.

Immediately, like a great aviary, the RSO launched into a frenzy of tuning up. Determined to stand no nonsense, Abby asked the eternally good-natured Charlton Handsome to move the horns upstage.

'Excuse me, Maestro,' drawled Viking, 'is that a good idea?'

'Why not?' said Abby irritably.

'If we're too far away, you won't be able to follow us.'

Abby's explosion was averted by the librarian running in. 'Here are the parts for the cor anglais and the piccolo, we'll have the rest of the woodwind parts by the break.'

'Why bother?' said Hilary nastily.

Shooting her a withering glance, Abby opened the score. She was relieved that Boris was still too angry with Viking to show up. She could have done with his support, but composers tended to shoot themselves at first rehearsals, because their music, sight-read, sounded so terrible.

'Quiet please.' Abby looked round at the orchestra, spread out like enemy snipers in the forest. Even Miss Parrott's harp reared up like a chess-castle waiting to whizz across the board and take her.

Abby took a deep breath.

'We are about to play the most beautiful piece of music probably of the entire twentieth century. It is a requiem written in memory of Boris's young, incredibly talented wife, who committed suicide.'

'Lucky Boris – what was his secret?' sneered Carmine Jones.

Cathie Jones, who'd gone white as she digested the

importance and extreme complexity of her solo, now flushed scarlet with mortification.

'You basstard, Carmine.' Blue was on his feet – only Cathie's anguished, terrified glance stopped him hitting Carmine across the stage.

'Whose incredibly talented wife committed suicide in 1991,' repeated Abby firmly.

'You must have identified with that,' simpered Hilary.

'Don't be a bitch,' called out Flora. 'This is a master-piece.'

Rank-and-file viola players were not supposed to express opinions. Flora was getting much too uppity. Hilary scowled at her.

'Tell us about your famous mother, Flawless,' said Dixie, putting down his tax returns.

'Why isn't Boris conducting this?' grumbled Juno.

'We used to have Schnapps-breaks every half-hour,' said Nellie wistfully. 'D'you remember the time he gave us miniatures of brandy before we recorded Mahler *One*, and we got through it in an hour with no retakes.'

'I loved Boris,' sighed Juno.

'You'll have to put up with me,' snapped Abby. 'Give us an A, Simon, let's get started.'

After a month off, the orchestra were very rusty, fingers and lips couldn't be trusted. Effing and blinding under their breath they began ploughing through the 'Dies Irae'. Jerry the Joker played 'God Save the Queen' on his bassoon to see if Abby noticed.

'I heard you, get out, Jerry,' she shouted. 'As a section leader you're supposed to set a good example.'

'What a frightful piece of music this is,' sighed Dixie.

'Cheer up,' said Jerry, going out grinning and licking doughnut sugar off his fingers. 'You'll only have to play it once.'

'We're recording it,' Abby, who was battling for at least four performances as well, yelled after him. 'But not till the middle of October to give you the time to digest the complexities.'

'And puke them all up again,' called out Randy.

Abby tried another tack.

'You've got to familiarize yourself with it to love it,' she pleaded. 'In 1915, when they first rehearsed Prokofiev's *Scythian Suite*—'

The orchestra raised their eyes to heaven and started to yawn ostentatiously.

'*Scythian Suite*,' persisted Abby, 'one of the cellists said to the conductor: "Just because I have a wife who is sick and three kids to support, why must I be forced to endure such hell?" Musicians have always resisted innovation, if you know what I mean.'

'That's the trouble,' said Carmine rudely, 'none of us know what you do mean.'

'Musicians don't want to be lectured,' said Davie Buckle, starting another game of patience on top of his drums. 'They want to play the concert, then go out, get pissed and have a curry.'

The orchestra fell about.

It was time for Cathie to play 'Rachel's Lament' for the first time, initially just as an extended echo in the 'Lachrymosa', then leading up to the long final solo in the 'Libera Me'.

Surely they must realize how beautiful it is, prayed Abby. But Cathie was so nervous, so exhausted at the end of the school holidays, and so conscious of Carmine's angry little red brake-light eyes boring into her, that she made a complete hash of it.

'Gee, you screwed up on that one,' said Abby in disappointment after the third botched attempt and leapt down to talk to Cathie. If she fluffed the "Lachrymosa" how the hell was she going to cope with the "Libera Me".

'I thought Boris was giving the big solo to Viking,' whispered Dixie.

'Boris has changed his total lack of tune,' whispered back Randy. 'Evidently Boris is knocking off his au pair and Viking's nicked her, but only after Viking caught

Boris in flagrante with—' a wicked smile spread over Randy's face, as he lowered his voice even more.

'You gotta be joking,' Dixie looked at Abby, his eyes on stalks. Then, immediately turning to his Second Trombone, 'Did you know that Boris is bonking—'

Soon the story was whizzing around the orchestra, like starlings alighting on different trees at dusk.

'What are you reading, Flawless?' asked Viking.

'"Sohrab and Rustram",' snapped Flora, who hadn't forgiven Viking. 'It's about much more heroic men than you lot.'

'Someone should write a poem called "So Bad on Rostrum".'

'That's not funny, if you hadn't jumped on Astrid, you'd be playing that solo.'

As they struggled for another ten minutes, Abby felt utterly superfluous, the orchestra were far too busy sight-reading to look at her.

'Where the fuck are we?' Viking asked Blue, as resounding crashes, twangs and shrieks rent the air.

'Two bars to go. I'll bring you in—'

Abby called a halt. 'That was terrible.'

'It would help if you beat a little more clearly,' called out Juno.

Abby ignored her.

'The next bit is really sad,' Abby attempted a weak joke. 'Could you play it, I guess, as Lionel looks?'

Lionel was furious. Confronted by a series of glissandos and teeth-gritting shrieks achieved by drawing the side of the bow down the strings, he pretended to cry.

'I cannot bear it,' he said, putting his head carefully in his hands so as not to disturb the lustrous blow-dried waves. 'My string players have dedicated their lives to producing a beautiful sound—'

Abby raised an eyebrow.

'And they are forced to make fools of themselves playing this junk.'

Lionel was acting up because over the page he had discovered the long solo Boris had deliberately made difficult for him, which was only accompanied by the basses. Compelled to tackle it, he pretended to be fooling around and deliberately making the most ghastly cock up.

'You're not trying,' raged Abby, beyond any awareness that it was below the belt to bawl out a leader in front of his orchestra.

The RSO brightened at the prospect of a screaming match.

'It's unplayable,' said Lionel flatly.

'Don't be such a goddamn wimp.'

'You only say that, Maestro,' furiously Hilary leapt to the defence of her beloved, 'because there's no way you could ever play it.'

Putting down the *Selected Poems of Matthew Arnold*, Flora said calmly, 'Boris used to play the violin in an orchestra. He's perfectly aware of its limitations and capabilities.'

'You hold your tongue, young lady,' said Hilary furiously.

'It's impossible, unplayable junk,' intoned Lionel.

'It is not,' screamed Abby.

'It fucking well is.'

'Fucking isn't.' Jibbering with rage, Abby leapt from the rostrum, snatched Lionel's fiddle and played the solo absolutely perfectly.

There was a stunned, stunned silence – long enough to play a Bruckner symphony. The musicians looked at Abby in amazement, but not in nearly as much amazement as Abby looked at Lionel's violin. As she handed it back, Flora, roused out of her habitual cool, rushed forward, sending a music-stand and its music flying.

'Oh Abby,' she said in a choked voice. 'Don't you realize what this means? It's come back, you can play again. Oh Abby.'

And the whole orchestra, except Lionel, Hilary, Juno and Carmine, stood up and cheered.

Abby looked utterly shell-shocked.

'Thank you, everyone. That's it for today; we'll start with the Brahms *Violin Concerto* first thing after lunch tomorrow,' she said, ending the rehearsal twenty minutes early and emerging from the dark inferno of Boris Levitsky into the sunshine.

Flora brought a couple of bottles of Muscadet back to Woodbine Cottage, and she and Abby celebrated with Marcus. Abby was still shell-shocked.

'I cannot believe it, I'm sure it was a fluke. Did it really sound OK?' she begged Flora over and over again.

'Course it did,' said Flora. 'And that miraculous blood-curdling wonderful sound couldn't have come from anyone else.'

'Play something now,' pleaded Marcus, picking up Abby's coat and hanging it up in the hall, 'just to convince yourself. I want to hear it, too.'

'I daren't, not yet. I don't want to tempt providence and I don't want any more to drink,' Abby put her hand over her glass. 'I gotta work.'

'I don't know why you bother,' grumbled Flora, topping up her own glass, 'after the way those pigs treat you. Just walk out and go back to reducing the whole world to orgasm on the violin. Come on, let's get pissed.'

But Abby refused. Desperate to be alone, she disappeared to her room to mug up the Brahms concerto. It was the last piece she had done before she had cut her wrist. It would be unendurable not to be playing it tomorrow. Perhaps a miracle had happened and she could return to the violin, but she still hated giving up the RSO without a fight.

She couldn't concentrate. Every note remembered was anguish. Throwing open her bedroom window, which looked on to the front garden, she disturbed a swarm of peacock butterflies gorging themselves on the buddleia. Was it proverbial vanity which made them match their rust-and-purple wings so perfectly to the pale purple flowers?

Thistledown floated through the air; the fields of stubble, platinum-blond in the morning sunshine, were now red-gold after the rain. The white trumpets of the convolvulus rioting along the hedgerow reminded her of her brass section. She could smell frying garlic and onions. Marcus must be cooking supper, banging pans after all that Muscadet. He had been so kind when Boris had humiliated her. She must find him work.

Then everything was forgotten as through the dusk she heard Viking, the ultimate peacock, practising, idling around with 'Rachel's Lament', the sound carrying across the still lake. Oh God, he should be playing the solo. It would be tragic if Lionel persuaded George to drop the *Requiem*. Lionel was also poisoning the orchestra against her. How she longed to follow the path of meadowsweet down the stream and ask Viking's advice.

Maria Kusak, who was playing the Brahms *Violin Concerto*, was yet another Shepherd Denston artist booked at 10 per cent less, because the RSO had employed Abby. A contemporary of Abby's at the Moscow Conservatoire, she was, like Benny, very jealous of Abby's former success. A charming, curvacious, bottled blonde with high cheek-bones and naughty slanting brown eyes, she had been one of Rodney's pets and was upset to find such a dear doting old man had been replaced by her greatest rival.

Lionel, after yesterday's humiliation, was revving up for a showdown. He had already had a word with George.

'I wept for my musicians,' he repeated sententiously, 'and she mocked me. It is an honour to sit in the first chair of a great orchestra, but how can I have any authority as a leader if she constantly undermines me in front of the players.'

'She'd better go back to playing the fiddle,' said George, and had a sharp word with Abby to soft-pedal the histrionics.

'Maria's very popular with the Rutminster audience,' he added brusquely. 'We've nearly sold out this evening – give her her head.'

Maria was also very popular with the orchestra who gave her a round of applause when she arrived the following afternoon, but, although she dimpled and smiled, she was in fact in a furious temper. Having decided that George was as attractively macho as he was rich, she had slipped into Tower Records in Rutminster High Street to buy her own recording of the Saint-Saëns *Third Concerto* in order to sign it for him. She was not pleased to be told by the assistant, who did not recognize her, that she ought to have bought Abigail Rosen's version – it was still easily the best.

On the other hand, Maria had a trump card, which she knew would crucify Abby. She was playing on Abby's old Strad.

Simon Painshaw was also uptight and tearing his red dreadlocks because he had to open the second movement of the concerto with one of the most beautiful solos Brahms or anyone had ever written. All the wood-wind were busy in that movement, but they were still only the Supremes to First Oboe's Diana Ross.

Arriving at the hall, Simon had been accosted by Hilary, bossily ticking him off for not tuning up half an hour earlier so he could play in his quarter-final match in the RSO conker competition. As a result she had re-scheduled his match for this evening in the meal-break before the concert.

Simon had become wildly agitated. He had been making reeds, the thin pipes through which oboists blow, which was a hellishly finickety job, since ten o'clock that morning, he said.

'And I'm not playing any conker match this evening. I've got to psych myself up for my solo.'

'Half the orchestra are in the conker competition,' said Hilary furiously, 'and they're not going to wait around at your convenience. All you think about are your silly reeds.'

Simon had flipped and started screaming about fucking kids' games. Abby, coming out of the conductor's room, had backed him up and told Hilary to eff off.

'Love conkers all,' said a passing Viking in amusement.

Hilary rushed off to tell Lionel who started the rehearsal in an embattled mood.

Bill Thackery, Lionel's co-leader, predictably nicknamed 'Makepeace' because he was kind, equable and always defusing squabbles, had heard the shouting in the passage.

'What's up with L'Appassionata?' he asked as Lionel took his seat beside him, 'P.M.T.?'

'That was yesterday,' said Lionel spitefully. 'She's got the rags up her today.'

Bill winced. He loathed Lionel's coarseness. He glanced up at Abby whose face was a mask to hide her fear.

'Fasten your seat-belts,' murmured Hilary to Juno in front of her. 'Turbulence ahead.'

From the first note it was quite clear that Maria had totally different ideas of interpretation to Abby, and Lionel totally agreed with her. They both completely ignored Abby, as Benny had done.

Abby tried to be accommodating, but she felt as though a great blood-blister was swelling inside her brain and she wanted to snatch back her Strad. She couldn't bear to see it in such insensitive hands.

The second movement was even worse. Sulking because Simon had the good tune, Maria played flatly and lazily when she came in thirty-two bars later. Abby let her scratch away for four or five pages, then aware that

Lionel was deliberately holding back his First Violins, she stopped the orchestra.

'Can we please start this movement again? It was too slow.'

'Why not beat a bit faster,' said Hilary rudely.

Refusing to rise, Abby took Maria aside, suggesting a few changes. Maria snapped back that Rannaldini had warmly praised her interpretation.

'Sure, sure, Maria, if you could just play with a little more passion.'

As Abby stepped back onto the rostrum, Maria made the orchestra laugh by sticking out her tongue at Abby's back.

'OK, from the beginning of the second movement,' Abby gave the up beat, nodding at the bassoons who played A and F followed by an octave from the horns, before Simon came in with the rest of the woodwind. Simon looked as though he were in a trance, sucking his reed like an opium pipe, his fingers tense on the silver keys.

To distract everyone from such a breathtakingly beautiful sound, Maria pointedly rummaged in her violin case for some rosin to give extra grip to the horse-hair in her bow. As she did so, a folded page fell out of her primrose-yellow shirt, fluttering down and landing on the rostrum. But as her panic-stricken hand shot out, Abby's black ankle-boot stamped down on the note. Abby recognized Lionel's flamboyant scrawl.

'Give it to me,' squealed Maria, 'you're not supposed to read other people's letters.'

Ignore the stupid cow and follow me,' read Abby slowly. Then she went ballistic, hurling her score at Lionel's glossy head.

'Quick,' hissed Carmine to Steve Smithson. 'Get Miles and Knickers down to witness this.'

'You son-of-a-bitch,' Abby howled at Lionel. 'You're fired.'

'Maestro, Maestro,' Lionel retrieved her score. 'It was

only a joke. As Maria says you really shouldn't read other people's letters.'

'Go on, get out, get OUT.'

Confronted by such fury, Lionel went, the picture of injured innocence. Steve, who played squash with Lionel, and was feeling well disposed towards him, promptly called out the orchestra, who all filed off into the band room.

'We've got her,' Steve murmured jubilantly to Lionel. 'Don't worry, we'll return a vote of no confidence to the board. George, Miles, Mrs Parker, Ambrose, Canon Airlie, all want her out – they'll be over the moon.'

'At last we've broken her,' said Lionel melodramatically, putting two shaking hands together in prayer. 'And don't you dare go back in there, Flora,' he called out sharply, 'or you're fired.'

As Randy and Dixie started an idle game of ping-pong up at the far end of the room, Viking looked up at Abby's framed photograph, which Charlton Handsome had somewhat provocatively hung over the fireplace.

'She has a lovely face,' he quoted thoughtfully. 'God in His mercy lend her grace.' Then, turning to Lionel, added, 'I don't like conductors used as target-practice, I think we ought to discuss this rationally.'

'We can't go on like this,' said Bill Thackery.

Maria, who was thoroughly overexcited, said she'd never been so insulted in her life and she was very happy to add her weight to the vote against Abby.

Left alone in the empty auditorium, Abby slumped on the rostrum. Slowly all the lights were flicked off except the one over her lectern. She accepted it was the end. She knew she had overreacted, but it would never be any good with Lionel. The thorn in her firm young flesh had proved poisonous. She would leave, not him. The Brahms had jinxed her again. So sweet was ne'er so fatal. For a second she fingered the scar on her wrist.

Sadly she picked up the violin which Francis the Good

Loser had inevitably left behind on his chair, caressing its glossy brown curves. Francis would soon be back to collect it. For a second she put it under her chin; it was still warm. Idly she tuned it.

Then, as if in a dream, she started playing the lovely tune with which the oboe opens the second movement. Somehow, out of the black depths of her despair and the sense of utter failure, the notes came to her, first faltering, many of them wrong, the tempo very shaky, then gradually gaining in strength and beauty.

She played it again, totally immersed in the sound and the sadness, then jumped out of her skin as, through the darkness, she heard a stealthy footstep and then the scraping of a chair. Then miraculous, like the horns of Elfland, she heard the bassoon, luminous and beautiful, echoing round the hall, then the octave on the horns, and then Simon starting the movement again. He didn't need light, he knew it by heart. Like Orpheus, Abby had to steel herself not to look round. Then her heart leapt as she heard more footsteps and scraping chairs and the flute, the clarinet and the Second Bassoon joining in. It couldn't be real, she must be dreaming, but someone was switching on the lights and now there was an arpeggio which could only have come from Viking, and the strings came in, which was the cue for the solo violin. Somehow her trembling hand managed to force her bow back and forth over the strings.

Tears were streaming down her face so fast, she wouldn't have been able to see anyway, but through some mystical inspiration the notes came back to her, as the boards squeaked with more and more footsteps. At the first tutti it was clear that half the orchestra were back in their seats. She jumped as a double bass was knocked over.

Abby had played better technically in her life but never with such passion. As the horns and the woodwind returned to the first subject she had some wicked syncopation, six against four, but she kept her nerve, and then

Viking was accompanying her, swooping divinely alongside, then Peter, sweet and ethereal, then rippling deep arpeggios on the bassoon, and the strings came in like a great flotilla guiding the returning, round-the-world sailor safely into port, until she had soared up to the final A.

Absolutely no-one spoke or moved, as Abby stood trembling, with her head thrown back, her eyes closed as though awaiting a blow.

'Bravo,' said a voice.

Then there was a storm of cheering and out of the corner of her eye Abby saw that the first chair was empty.

Unable to face anyone, she jumped off the rostrum, handed Francis his violin, leapt off the stage, stumbling as she landed, then racing up the gangway, pushed through the swing doors out into the park. Seeing her face deathly pale and still wet with tears as she ran down the High Street, the shoppers parted to let her through. Cars screeched to a halt as she bolted across the road, drawn helplessly towards the lake.

Following her in his car, Viking caught up with her as the town gave way to fields.

'Well done,' he yelled out of the window. 'D'you want a drink?'

But Abby was completely dazed, unable to speak, gazing at him with huge, haunted reddened eyes.

'We all walked out of the union meeting,' he said gently. 'We were glad to get shot of the bastard, none of us liked him. You've won, sweetheart.'

THIRTY-SIX

The next morning, George Hungerford received a letter of no confidence in Lionel as leader, and upheld Abby's decision to sack him. Hilary, Steve Smithson, Carmine, Juno, Militant Moll and Ninion (who was still smarting over Catherine Jones getting the big solo in *Rachel's Requiem*) were the only members of the orchestra who didn't sign.

Although it was RSO policy that its musicians were not allowed to talk to the Press, George caught Cherub on the telephone to the *Evening Standard* diary.

'Yes, we called Lionel the Incredible Sulk,' he was saying in his shrill voice, 'because he sulked all the time. What did he sulk about? Well, people nicking his hair-dryer mostly. Can I think of anything nice about him? That's a tricky one,' Cherub scratched his blond curls and after a long silence, 'not really . . . oh, yes I can.'

'That's enough,' George pressed the cut-off button, then out of curiosity, asked, 'what was the nice thing you remembered about Lionel?'

'That his brother was much worse,' said Cherub, going off into such giggles that George had to join in.

All the same the RSO were left without a leader. The post was hastily advertised and leaders applied from all over the world. Many expected to have their air fares paid. Others crept surreptitiously into auditions hoping no-one would recognize them and sneak to their respective orchestras, or later know they had suffered the humiliation of not being offered the job. It was a laborious, expensive process. Miles and Mrs Parker, who'd lost a powerful ally in Lionel, were all for asking Hugo back. But Abby would have none of it. The sight of Hugo sleekly smirking in the leader's chair at the Albert Hall during the CCO's prom had convinced her she never wanted to work with him again.

Bill Thackery, who'd acted as leader since Lionel left, put himself forward, but was rejected as too stodgily dependable and too lacking in charisma. Rodney had only employed him in the first place because he had once played cricket for Rutshire and scored centuries in the RSO's annual needle-match against the CCO.

Aware that she had hurt Bill, Abby had a restless night. Wandering round the garden at sunrise, leaving foot-prints on the dewy lawn, she realized after the long silence of the summer, a robin was singing again in the old crab-apple tree. Revelling in the sweet liquid notes, Abby was suddenly reminded of Julian Pellafacini, the kind, diplomatic, infinitely charismatic albino leader of Rannaldini's New York Orchestra. She'd kept the letter he'd written her after she'd cut her wrist. Not caring that it was the middle of the night in America she called him at once.

'Did I wake you?'

'No, I have insomnia over Rannaldini. He sack everyone, I never come back from coffee-break to find the same musicians, yesterday he make me play three times alone in front of the orchestra.'

'How obnoxious,' said Abby furiously, adding hastily, 'I'd never do that to you. Please come and lead my orchestra. We're premièring Boris Levitsky's *Requiem* in three weeks and I need you to show the strings how to play it, and in November we're recording Winifred Trapp's *Harp Concertos.*'

'A wonderful composer,' sighed Julian.

'You're the first person who's heard of her,' said Abby joyfully.

'Rannaldini told me you were leaving.'

'Not any more.'

'Then I will come. My wife love England and 'ate New York.'

'We will find you a house. How will you escape?'

'Leave it to me.'

Sweeping onto the platform a week later to conduct a concert version of *Parsifal,* Rannaldini found his orchestra crying with laughter and his leader sitting at the front desk in an emerald-green pleated dress, green high heels, a white pudding-basin hat and full make-up, and sacked him on the spot. By this time, Julian's contract with the RSO had been signed.

Julian arrived at the beginning of October and moved with his wife and children into a beautiful rented house in the Close paid for by the RSO. He was paid twice as much as Lionel, but he was worth every penny.

He was so kind, so respected, so gravely charming, that he had only to clap his hands in rehearsals for everyone to shut up and listen. He agreed that *Rachel's Requiem* was a masterpiece, explaining it to the more inexperienced or resistant players until everyone found themselves singing the tunes.

The young players seemed to absorb his talent by osmosis, and Old Henry at last had someone to appreciate his stories and argue with about which quartet was Beethoven's finest.

Abby was appalled by Julian's appearance when he arrived. His long straight white hair had receded, he was as black under the eyes as his dark glasses, and he had lost over twenty pounds which his thin, stork-like frame could ill afford, but gradually he stopped talking too much about Rannaldini.

Miss Priddock was soon baking him cakes, Miss Parrott knitting him scarves, even Flora picked a lot of sloes intending to make him sloe gin, but they only gathered fluff in the fridge.

'He's terribly attractive,' said Candy.

'But far too nice to be heterosexual,' sighed Clare.

That was before they'd met his lovely bosomy wife, Luisa, whom he adored and who gave uproarious spaghetti-and-red-wine parties at the house in the Close on Sundays to which rank-and-file players were asked with section leaders, so relations within the orchestra improved dramatically.

'To make good music,' said Julian, 'you need to have confidence and people you trust on either side of you.'

'Julian's a mensch,' said Abby. 'That's someone with standards, a good friend, a man you are proud to know.'

She had achieved great kudos for finding him. He also gave her confidence. She could easily have been jealous of his popularity, but he never took decisions without her, and gradually she became less aggressive and tactless, saying please and thank you, and taking people aside for a quiet word in the break rather than humiliating them in front of the entire orchestra.

'I think that's been played better in the past,' she suggested to Jerry the Joker, after he'd made an appalling cock-up of a bassoon solo.

'Yes, but not by me,' said Jerry, to howls of laughter all round.

Morale was so high in Julian's first weeks that everyone was convinced his leadership had been entirely responsible for the New World and Rannaldini sweeping the board at the Gramophone Awards. They didn't even mind that Edith Spink and the CCO had won an early music award for Purcell's *King Arthur*.

* * *

As the date for the première of *Rachel's Requiem* approached, Boris, still minus Astrid, started hanging around H.P. Hall, tearful, apprehensive, aggressive by turns, changing everything.

The rows between him and Abby were pyrotechnic.

'I'm conducting this piece.'

'I wrote zee bloody thing.'

'You didn't even remember you'd introduced a variation of "Rachel's Lament" as a violin solo in the "Agnus Dei".'

After hearing Cathie Jones, still desperately nervous in the 'Libera Me', Boris went into an orgy of self-doubt and threatened to withdraw the lament altogether.

'It sound immaculate in the head. Then you hear orchestra hacking through eet.'

Fortunately, George Hungerford, who'd become a terrifying figure of menace to Boris since threatening to make him pay back his advance, had been listening unnoticed in the stalls and came up and shook Boris's hand.

'Congratulations, it was well worth waiting for.'

Boris was so overcome he burst into tears. Abby then put on the pressure, persuading him that 'Rachel's Lament' would only work if Viking played it. In the interests of art, Boris reluctantly gave in. As a result, Viking nearly got his tooth knocked out again.

Wandering into H.P. Hall after another late-night moon-lighting, and no doubt pleasuring Astrid, he noticed Julian in the leader's room poring over a score. Beside Julian, Viking could see lustrous black curls, and a beautiful lean body in a checked shirt and jeans. Confronted by such a delectable bottom, Viking couldn't resist pinching it. Next moment an enraged Boris had swung round, and Viking was belting down the passage.

'Sorry, sorry Boris,' he pleaded. 'Don't hit me again. I've josst spent five hundred quid at the dentist. You've lost so much weight, I thought you were Abby. Look,' he went on, as Boris kept on coming, 'Astrid wants to come back to you, she's absolutely miserable with me.'

'She is?' Boris lowered his fist. 'Oh my Astrid.'

Terrific news, thought Abby, overhearing the conversation as she came out of the conductor's room. 'And Boris has agreed "Rachel's Lament" sounds better on the French horn, so he's written it back in for you,' she told Viking.

'Sweet of Boris,' said Viking coolly, 'but I'm flying to Glasgow tomorrow to play a Mozart concerto with the Royal Scottish National Orchestra, their First Horn's dislocated a shoulder. I cleared it with George,' he added as Abby's face contorted with fury.

Blue would have killed him, reflected Viking, if he'd stolen Cathie's solo.

Abby could have killed him anyway. 'And that Hugh Grant hairstyle doesn't suit you at all,' she yelled after his departing back view.

The première in fact was a success. All the London critics came down for a number of reasons: Levitsky was still a name; they were curious to see how Abby was making out; but, most of all, they wanted to hear this great new leader who had graced little Rutminster with his lustre. Even the Rutshire Butcher, deliberately invited to the last rehearsal and force-fed lobster thermidor and Moët afterwards by George, wrote that it was good to have some meaty tunes after all those one-note jobs, which had dominated the classical hit-parade for so long.

The two representatives attending from the Arts Council were positively orgasmic about the piece. Nothing got them going like 75 per cent of the audience looking bewildered. By carefully placing round the hall a number of the Friends of the Orchestra to cheer and stamp, George managed to generate a standing ovation for Boris, who looked so mournfully handsome and romantic, that the audience kept on clapping, particularly when he led Cathie Jones forward. Aware that

Blue's good-luck card was hidden in the pocket of her black dress, she had played exquisitely.

Seeing the pink-and-orange chrysanthemums Miss Priddock was bringing on for Abby, Boris thrust them into Cathie's rough red hands. 'I zank you viz all my 'eart. I feel Rachel forgeeve me at last.'

'Well, you must be happy with that,' said Abby, chucking down her baton and the *Requiem* score, as she and Boris finally returned to the conductor's room.

'No-one hackled, no-one booed,' said Boris darkly. 'Maybe I am not avant-garde any more, maybe I'm too predictable.'

'Oh, for Christ's sake.'

But the next moment, predictability and the avant-garde were forgotten, as Astrid, wearing a new lilac suit, no doubt bought with the proceeds of Viking's moon-lighting, barged into the conductor's room without bothering to knock, straight into Boris's arms.

THIRTY-SEVEN

After the première, George took a party out to dinner at the Old Bell. His guests included Abby, Julian and his lovely bosomy wife Luisa, Serena Westwood, head of Artists and Repertoire at Megagram who were recording the *Requiem* at the end of the month, Jack Rodway, the evening's sponsor, who was a specialist in receiverships in a leading firm of accountants, and, representing the Arts Council, a caring beard called Gilbert Greenford and his 'partner', a folk-weave biddy called Gwynneth.

Having laid on limos to the Old Bell, George was extremely irritated to be lectured by Gwynneth all the way on the evils of air-conditioning in large petrol-swilling cars.

'You ought to get a cycle,' she stared beadily at George's straining waistband, 'Gilbert and I cycle everywhere, indeed Gilbert has had his cycle, Clara (after Clara Schumann, of course), since he was at Keble.'

It was clearly going to be difficult reconciling the middle-of-the road tastes of Serena Westwood, a single parent whose calm beautiful face was belied by a rapacious body, with those of Gilbert and Gwynneth from the Arts Council, who only liked the obscure and discordant, and of Jack Rodway, who had a penchant for *Boléro* because 'it makes me feel right randy'.

To George's further irritation, he arrived at the hotel to find a joyfully drunk Boris, who'd been on the red wine all day, had rolled up not only with Astrid, but also Marcus and Flora who was totally unsuitably dressed in sawn-off Black-Watch-tartan dungarees. George hadn't spoken to Flora since she'd brought Marcus over to be impossibly rude to Peggy Parker at the sixtieth-birthday concert, but he had noticed her cool deadpan face among the violas, or more often the top of her red-gold head because her freckled nose was always in a book. He knew she was trouble.

Once the waiter had added another table, Boris, Marcus, Astrid and the Pallafacinis commandeered it, wanting to mull over the concert and talk musical shop. They had kept a place for Flora.

But determined Flora shouldn't cause any more trouble and to keep her away from Gilbert and Gwynneth, George frogmarched her down the table into the seat nearest the window, with Jack Rodway next to her, hissing: 'He's paid for this evening, so bloody well be nice to him.'

Planning to put himself opposite her to keep an eye on her and at the same time talk business with Jack Rodway, George held out a seat for Serena Westwood, intending her to sit next to him, so they could discuss recordings for the RSO. But alas, a second later, ghastly Gwynneth had landed on the seat like a wet lump of potter's clay.

'I feel you and I should get to know each other, Mr Hungerford, and you sit on my left, Mr Brian-Knowles,' she added archly to Miles, nearly giving him a black eye with one of her huge silver earrings, hanging like gongs on either side of her round, smug, pasty face.

Gwynneth had buck teeth, beady little dark eyes, a pepper-and-salt bun, and was also a great lard-mountain of self-importance as she was constantly fawned on by men who ran orchestras and ballet and opera companies who knew she had the power to slash their grants.

Seeing Flora gazing at Gwynneth in horror, George snapped at her not to stare. So Flora looked out of the window at the yellow willow spears falling into the dark river, and at the lights on the bridge silhouetted against the russet glow of the Rutminster sky.

On all sides, at other tables, ancient residents were ekeing out slices of cheddar and half-bottles of red, nudging each other because they recognized Abby. Some of them also recognized George from the local papers, because of the row he was having with the council over planning permission for the fifty acres on Cowslip Hill.

George certainly had a terrific effect on waiters, who had all converged on the table, handing over red velvet, tasselled menus, gabbling about Plats du Jour, and filling glasses, particularly Boris's, whenever they were empty.

'Penny for your forts,' asked Jack Rodway, who'd been admiring Flora's profile.

'I was thinking,' replied Flora with a sweet smile, 'what an ugly cow that is opposite.'

'Her "partner" Gilbert is worse,' murmured Jack. 'I sat next to 'im on the drive down. Stinks like a pole cat.'

Flora giggled. 'Obviously thinks avant-garde is more important than Right Guard.'

Jack looked blank for a second, then roared with laughter.

'That's right, Flora.'

Jack Rodway had dissipated blue eyes in a ruddy expensive face, wore a sharp navy-blue suit, and was such an alley cat that Flora expected to see furry pointed ears protruding through his thatch of blond hair.

'I suppose,' she observed, 'receivers and divorce lawyers are the only people making any money these days.'

'Too right, Flora, with twenty thousand firms going

belly up every year, it's a growf industry, nime of the gime.'

'Must be awfully depressing, like being an undertaker or a nurse in a vivisection clinic,' Flora shivered. 'All those poor employees losing their jobs.'

'We try and mike it as pineless as possible for the personnel involved. No fanks,' Jack rejected a wholemeal roll. Over forty, a flat stomach required sacrifices.

'Moules are nice, Flora, just come in,' suggested the head waiter, who was a great pal of Flora's mother.

'Lovely, I'll have those,' Flora beamed back at him. 'I'm so hopeless at decisions.'

'I'll have smoked salmon, followed by steak and French fries,' said Jack Rodway.

Suddenly Flora twigged.

'You must be an invaluable contact for George. Presumably when companies go into receivership they often have huge crumbling old buildings that no longer qualify as listed, if you knock off a few cornices, but are ripe for development as office blocks or supermarkets.'

'What a very astute young lidy you are, Flora,' said Jack Rodway, filling up her glass. 'Wasted on the violas.'

George, from his bootfaced expression, had obviously heard every word, but was being monopolized by Gwynneth.

'I shall not let my sword sleep in my hand,' she was saying affectedly, 'until I have routed out sexual apartheid in British orchestras and until 50 per cent of the repertoire is by women composers.'

George choked on his glass of wine. Gwynneth turned greedily to the menu. As Megagram and the RSO were splitting the bill, she and Goaty Gilbert, who had granny specs and green teeth, surrounded by a straggly ginger beard, chose all the most expensive things on the menu.

'Disgusting pigs,' muttered Flora, receiving another glare from George. But nothing could dim her happiness.

In the pocket of her Black-Watch-tartan dungarees was a postcard left in her pigeon hole:

Darling Flora,
Astrid is moving out, thank God. The pillow talk was
very limited. Will you have a drink with me the second
I get back from Glasgow?
All love,
Viking.

Viking was another alley cat, reflected Flora, but she felt he was the only person who could get her over Rannaldini. For the moment, she could practise on Jack.

'D'you know Fatima Singh, Mr Hungerford?' Across the table Gwynneth was returning the attack.

'Does she?' asked Flora.

'What?' said Gwynneth impatiently.

'Sing?' giggled Flora.

'No, no, she composes. You must be familiar with her *Elegy for Oppressed Lesbians in the Harem.*'

'Best place for them,' said Jack. 'All girls togevver.'

'She makes lovely use of the sitar,' went on Gwynneth, totally ignoring them. 'Gilbert and I note you have no Asian music in your repertoire, Mr Hungerford.'

Down the table, Boris was gazing into Astrid's eyes and murmuring Pushkin in his deep husky voice. Abby, on an *après*-concert high, was bending Gilbert's dirty ear about the wonders of Winifred Trapp and Fanny Mendelssohn.

'We have a terrific harpist, Miss Parrott, who's mad about the Trapp solos.'

The Pellafacinis were talking about children with Serena Westwood.

'I'm not an achiever,' Luisa was saying apologetically. 'I look after Julian and the kids.'

Abandoning George for a second, Gwynneth was now discussing madrigals with Miles.

'The musicians sing them on the coach on the way to concerts,' he was saying.

'How joyful,' Gwynneth brought her hands together with a clash of bangles. 'When I come down on my three-day assessment of the orchestra, I hope I may be permitted to join in. We could sing motets as well – they are the religious equivalent of the domestic madrigal.' And she went off into a flurry of fa, la, las, in a quavering soprano.

If she got locked into the coffin-shaped lavatory with Viking, decided Flora, there wouldn't be room for Hilary and Militant Moll as well.

Marcus sat in a daze, his fingers playing idly on the white table cloth, still coming down after the *Requiem*, unable to say a word on the noisy journey to the hotel, when everyone else was going beserk expressing their approval.

Suddenly he turned to Boris and blurted out: 'That was one of the most beautiful pieces of music I've ever heard, like discovering America or walking round Chartres Cathedral for the first time.'

There was a pause as everyone suddenly remembered the *Requiem* was why they were there.

Serena Westwood, who believed that a bonk a day kept the doldrums away, and who had high hopes of George, turned and looked at Marcus for the first time. What a beauty, such a sweet, sensitive yet strong face, and he was the only man she'd met whom the Hugh Grant hairstyle really suited.

'Marcus is why *Requiem* happen,' said Boris excitedly. 'Ee copy, ee transcribe, ee listen, ee encourage, is super pianist, you must give him a contract,' he added to Serena. 'Let's all dreenk to Marcus.' Having drained his glass, he smashed it in the fireplace.

The other diners looked wildly excited. The waiters came running in in alarm, until George waved to them to forget it and to bring Boris another glass.

'What have you done recently?' Serena asked a desperately blushing Marcus.

'T-teaching mostly. I had a recital in Bradford last week.'

'Good?'

'Not brilliant, a string broke in the middle of Bartók's *Allegro Barbaro*. It sounded like a bomb going off, all the audience tore out, not many of them bothered to come back.' Marcus smiled deprecatingly.

'You must send me a tape,' said Serena enthusiastically. 'Perhaps you should have a crack at a piano competition. It's good experience and the best way of getting known.'

'It's a lousy idea,' snapped Abby, abandoning Gilbert in mid-flow. 'Marcus doesn't need gladiatorial contests. He's gotta develop at his own pace.'

Marcus opened his mouth and shut it again

'Well, at least get an agent,' urged Serena. 'I could suggest—'

'If he needs an agent,' snapped Abby, 'he can go to Howie Denston.'

'Oh Abby,' sighed Flora, 'when will you learn not to be a bitch in the manger?'

'Thank you.' Gwynneth's small mouth was watering like a waste pipe as a great vat of caviar was placed in front of her. 'Did you mention Bradford?' she called out to Marcus.

Marcus nodded, mortified still to be the centre of attention.

'Did you have time to visit the Early Music Shop?' asked Gwynneth. 'What a pity, Gilbert brought a portative organ set from there and made it up for my birthday. He's thinking of tackling a crumhorn or even timbrels next.'

'What wild ecstasy,' murmured Flora, contemplating a black, shiny mountain of mussels and wondering how hungry she felt.

'Did you listen to the CCO at the proms?' asked Gilbert, forking up lobster at great speed. 'There is no doubt, they are the best orchestra in the South of England and played as such.'

'That's rubbish,' called Flora down the table. 'We can play just as well as the CCO. Ow, ow, ow.' She glanced reproachfully at George. 'Why d'you kick me like that? Just as well, particularly now we've got Julian.'

'Zat is true,' Boris dragged his eyes away from Astrid. 'Zank you for your support, Julian, and welcome to England. Let us drink to Julian.' Another glass smashed in the fireplace.

Flora turned giggling to Jack, who had demolished his smoked salmon in a trice, and was now helping himself to her mussels.

'We've had Boris living with us on and off for the last two months. He's exactly like a two year old, smashing everything and getting his words muddled up.'

Boris grinned down the table at them.

'Always Flora take the puss out of me, but she is good friend who help me. To Flora!' Crash went a third glass.

'Cheaper to hire them by the two dozen,' suggested Julian.

But Gwynneth had put on a soppy, artists-will-be-artists smile. 'And what is your next opus, Mr Levitsky?'

'He's going to write a moonlighting sonata for Viking,' announced Flora.

Gwynneth raised a reproving hand with another crash of bangles. 'I asked Mr Levitsky.'

'I'm going to write opera of *King Lear*.'

'That could be very fine,' mused Gwynneth. 'Good women's roles, and you could make an important statement about paternal oppression.'

'Oh get real,' muttered Flora.

'Will you use a Russian translation or tackle iambic pentameter?' asked Gilbert earnestly.

'Dactyl and Sponsor,' grinned Flora, raising her glass to Jack Rodway, who promptly put his arm round her shoulders.

'I 'ave to say, George, I'll only sponsor concerts in the future if I can have Flora sitting next to me afterwards.'

'George ordered me to be nice to you,' said Flora. 'And it hasn't been difficult at all,' she added, kissing Jack on the cheek.

George was clearly hopping, but, trapped by the need to behave well in front of Gwynneth, he was powerless.

'You've no idea the fun I've had playing on Gilbert's small organ,' she was now telling him. 'Of course today's musicians need an organ that will fit into an estate car or in Gilbert's case to fold up in a briefcase. Were you aware, Mr Hungerford, that small organs were neither usual nor common until recent times?'

'I've always said they had more fun in the Middle Ages,' interrupted Flora. 'Ow, ow, why d'you keep kicking me?'

'Just shut up,' whispered George with a flash of clenched teeth.

Finishing up the juice under her moules, Flora missed her mouth with the spoon and realized how drunk she was. She looked at George through her eyelashes. Why did they all think he was so attractive? He almost had a treble chin from so many sponsors' dinners, and the big horn-rimmed spectacles emphasized the tired, belligerent eyes. He also had the restlessness of the emotionally involved elsewhere. For such a macho man, it must have been a terrible blow when his wife walked out.

Gwynneth was obviously thinking along the same lines. 'D'you have a partner, Mr Hungerford?'

'I'm separated,' said George curtly.

'Did you both try relationship counselling?'

'I don't hold with that sort of thing.' George was fed up with being nice to her.

'Don't be so on the defensive,' teased Gwynneth. 'Even Gilbert and I are counselled every six months, a sort of spiritual MOT.'

Her mouth was watering again as a waiter *flambéed* her *tournedos au foie gras* on a side-table.

'I am not a meat-eater normally, but "when in Rome",' Gwynneth smiled round as if she were making a colossal concession.

'My mother went to a marriage-guidance counsellor,' said Flora. 'She said they were useless and had more problems than she did.'

Gwynneth ignored Flora, but persisted with George. 'You want to get in touch with your feelings.'

Flora decided George needed rescuing. She *must* be drunk.

'What I'd like to ask,' she said to Gwynneth, 'is why the London Met – yes, I read it in *The Times* – are allowed to push off for three months every summer, so their hall can be used for jazz, pop concerts, gospel, cajun music and other relative garbage, and you pay them a massive thirteen million a year, which is more than the RSO grant for the next forty years. Meanwhile we play all the year round except for a month in the summer. We travel fifty thousand miles in coaches, providing music for nine counties and we pay more back to the Government in VAT than you give us in rotten subsidy. So actually we're a net earner.'

'That's enoof, Flora,' said George who entirely agreed with her, but couldn't be seen to support her in public.

'I cannot reveal the reasons we give subsidies to other institutions,' said Gwynneth primly.

'Why not?' demanded Flora. 'You receive government money, therefore the public (and that's me) has the right to know. Everyone needs rises down here.'

'Hear, hear,' agreed Jack, ignoring a glare from George and filling Flora's glass. 'Too much bloody fudgin'.'

Gwynneth's little brown eyes were suddenly as dead

and opaque as sheeps' droppings, her furious face twitching.

'I adore that top, Gwynnie,' said Miles hastily. 'You look marvellous in indigo.'

'It comes from a planet-friendly range,' said Gwynneth, looking most unfriendly towards Flora. 'Even the buttons are biodegradable. I'll give you their card for your partner.'

Marcus could feel Serena's ankle rubbing against his leg like Scriabin, making him incapable of eating his Dover sole. He'd given eight piano lessons earlier in the day, he ought to practise for a couple of hours when he got home, but he'd do anything for a fat record contract, and Serena looked rather like Grace Kelly in *High Society*.

Across the table, Abby and Julian had hardly touched their food.

'It was a wonderful concert,' Julian was saying.

'I'm really looking forward to conducting Winifred Trapp next week,' said Abby.

'Must have a slash,' said Jack getting up.

'As long as no-one slashes our grant any more,' Flora shouted after him.

Relieved to see that Gwynneth was still nose to nose with Miles, George looked across at Flora.

'Pleased with Julian?'

'Oh yes,' sighed Flora, 'he's given us such confidence, and he's so approachable after Lionel. No problem's too small for him, not even Gilbert's organ.'

George shook his head. 'You're a minx.'

'I'm a cunning little vixen.'

'Your doggy bags, Mr Hungerford,' the waiter put two foil-wrapped packets beside George's plate.

'You've got dogs?' said Flora in surprise.

'Three Rottweilers.'

'Four, counting you,' said Flora. 'I like Rottweilers,' she added, remembering wistfully how she used to romp with Rannaldini's.

'You haven't eaten much,' George glanced up at the pudding trolley rumbling towards them. 'You better have an ice, kids like ices.'

Flora shook her head, her red hair splaying out like a marigold. 'No, no, I don't like anything that gets in touch with my fillings.'

Then George did smile, lifting his heavy face like a sudden shaft of sunlight on a limestone cliff.

'Everyone's having a ball,' said Flora. 'Thank you – it's been a terrific evening.'

But she had reckoned without Gwynneth, whose ethnic crimson skirt was about to pop, and thick pepper-and-salt hair about to escape from its bun, as she washed down her final mouthful of *tournedos au foie gras*, with her fourth glass of Pouilly-Fumé.

'You are driving, Gilbert.'

Gilbert looked livid, but his mouth was too crammed with monkfish to refuse.

Gwynneth then turned her shiny off-white face to George.

'Isn't it bizarre the way you hear a name for the first time and then hear it again and again. Miles has just mentioned Winifred Trapp. Did you know that Rannaldini has just recorded all Winifred Trapp's *Harp Concertos* with American Bravo?'

There was a stunned, horrified pause.

'Lovely shimmering music,' went on Gwynneth, delighted at the consternation she had caused. 'An advance copy arrived on my desk this morning. Although Rannaldini, or rather Sir Roberto, tells me he recorded it in Prague very cheaply, the quality is superb. I thought he'd lost his fire, after his last wife left him, but his new partner has regenerated him.'

Watching the colour drain out of Flora's flushed, happy face, Miles wondered if she'd had anything to do with passing on the information.

'Of course Rannaldini's always been innovative,' went on Gwynneth smugly. 'And what is more, he and Dame

Hermione have just recorded all Fanny Mendelssohn's songs with Winifrid Trapp's orchestration. Quite marvellous, don't you agree, Gilbert?'

'Indeed,' said Gilbert, who was trying to scrape hollandaise sauce out of his straggly ginger beard. 'I think if Fanny and Felix had lived, she would have been the more significant composer, although I agree with the Mendelssohn Society that had Felix lived he would have been greater than Richard Wagner.'

George's face was limestone again.

'When did Rannaldini record this?' he asked bleakly.

'In September,' said Gwynneth, who was now leering at the pudding trolley. 'That gateau does look tasty. They get these things out so quickly these days, but Rannaldini'll want to give Winifred, it's pronounced Vinifred actually, a real push, so I doubt if they'll release it before January or February. Such a slap in the face for folk who say there are no great women composers.'

'I knew nothing about this,' said Julian, appalled.

'Nor did I,' said Serena Westwood grimly. American Bravo were Megagram's biggest rivals.

Abby was frantically trying to work out how Rannaldini could have pre-empted her. The brochures, already late because of so many changes, had only been sent out in September. Who else could have told him – Hugo? Lionel? Perhaps unthinkingly Marcus could have said something to Helen. She'd heard Rannaldini was enraged that the RSO had snapped Julian up, but that wouldn't have given him enough time. Either way she'd been left with Egmont on her face.

THIRTY-EIGHT

As a result of Gwynneth's revelations, Megagram pulled the plug on Abby. Serena Westwood had been singularly uncharmed by her peremptory behaviour throughout dinner and she and Megagram had no desire to record obscure repertoire they had been led to believe was exclusive, in competition with the mighty Rannaldini and Harefield.

George and Miles were equally uncharmed to be lumbered with a Fanny Mendelssohn and Winifred Trapp series with no recordings to back it up. Viking's new nickname, 'Poverty Trapp', proved to be prophetic. At the first concert, there were more people on the platform than in the audience.

Having worked flat out in September and October, Abby was due for a break in November, and flew to America to see her mother. She spent most of the vacation locked in her bedroom familiarizing herself with the remaining Trapp-Mendelssohn repertoire and *Rachel's Requiem* (which was now being recorded in December) – anything to avoid her mother's constant moaning that Abby would never get off the shelf and provide her with grandchildren.

'There must be some guy in your life, Abigail.'

For a second Abby's thoughts flickered towards Viking, then sadly she admitted there was no-one.

November had been so mild, that as she was driven back from the airport, she noticed palest green hazel catkins already blending with the amber leaves still hanging from willow and blackthorn. It was a beautiful day. Reaching the H.P. Hall in the lunch-hour, she found Viking asleep under a horse-chestnut tree. He'd probably been up all night, moonlighting. Like some Victorian personification of autumn, his gold hair was spread out on the bleached grass, and his slumped yet still graceful body was almost entirely covered in kite-shaped orange leaves.

Happy days for him, thought Abby wistfully. Seeing an unusually angelic smile on his face, she was about to wake him. Then she noticed a piece of cardboard, cut in the shape of a tombstone, propped against his feet. On it someone had written:

Here lies Viking,
Very much to all our liking,
Who fucked himself to death.

With a howl of misery, Abby turned and ran inside.

Her mood was not improved when she learnt that George had axed the last two Trapp-Mendelssohn concerts and replaced them with lollipops, and that Megagram were now having cold feet about putting up the money for *Rachel's Requiem*. This would be catastrophic for Boris, who had already spent all the advance.

At an emergency board meeting, Peggy Parker said she might bankroll the *Requiem*, but only if Sonny's just completed *Interruption Serenade* could be used as a filler on the CD with a little picture of balding parrot-faced Sonny beside shaggy Boris on the sleeve. The plan was that the *Requiem* would be recorded in a studio, but the

Interruption Serenade would be recorded live at its première just before Christmas, then Sonny could include as many interruptions as possible. Peggy Parker was not at all happy about Abby conducting either work, and after a few telephone calls to Serena Westwood at Megagram, who would still be marketing and distributing the record, felt she had discovered an ally and was biding her time.

Abby felt her authority ebbing away. Worse was to come. The RSO were due to play *Messiah* at the Cotchester Festival in December. At the last moment, Jason, the rackety owner of Macho Motors, ratted on his agreement to sponsor the performance. This was because he'd failed to get Abby into bed, and because the BBC wouldn't allow one of his flash cars to be parked in the nave during the concert.

'I can't see why not,' grumbled Flora. 'Triumphal cars are always turning up in Milton's religious poems.'

'It's a Ferrari, not a Triumph,' said Marcus.

Abby was in no mood for jokes. As the concert was to be transmitted on Christmas Eve, it would be a ghastly humiliation if the RSO had to pull out through lack of funding.

They had only been invited to take part in the festival because Dame Edith, impressed by Abby's début concert, had nagged the organizers. If they weren't careful, their bitter rivals, the CCO, locked in mortal combat with the RSO for the same audiences, sponsors and subsidies from the Arts Council, would step into the breach.

As a final straw, that even more famous Dame, Hermione Harefield, whose single of 'I Know that my Redeemer Liveth' had sold over a million copies, had been booked as one of the soloists and would 'Rejoice Greatly' (which was on the flip side of the single) to see Abby so discomfited.

Abby was determined not to be beaten. As she had just received a large royalty cheque from the reissue of her early records, she blew the lot on a hefty insurance policy with Honesty Insurance in Rutminster High Street on condition that they sponsored *Messiah*.

Honesty Insurance drove a hard bargain. They wanted their slogan, 'Honesty is the Best Policy' on posters all over the cathedral as well as their name on the credits. The BBC refused. The deadlock was only broken when the Bishop of Cotchester, a pompous old fossil on the Venturer Board, agreed to mention the company and the slogan in his interval address.

Abby was livid George wasn't more impressed by her White Knight gesture when she barged into his office to tell him the good news.

'Honesty Insurance are a bunch of crooks,' he said, only giving her half his attention because he was trying to sign his letters around a weaving, purring John Drummond.

'They've given me this,' Abby waved a cheque under George's nose.

'We better bank it at once. Jack Rodway says they're about to go belly-oop. I hope you don't lose out on that policy. You'd have done better to sponsor the concert yourself.'

Like most successful property developers, George believed only in using other people's money. When he took over the RSO he had vowed never to give them a penny. He did, however, have a long-term crush on Dame Hermione. She was thirty-nine like him. He and Ruth, also an avid fan, had enjoyed many of her concerts, and worn out her famous LP of the *Verdi Requiem*. Hermione, like Ruth, was someone George thought of as a 'real lady'. He would therefore have been prepared to bankroll *Messiah* and pay Hermione her vast fee, her first-class air fare and her bill at the Cotchester Hilton. Now, thank God, Abby had saved him the trouble.

To avoid her nagging him about rain pouring

through the hall roof, he had swanned off for a lunch-time meeting with Rutminster District Council.

'Perhaps one of Mr Hungerford's builders could put in a cheap tender,' suggested Miss Priddock.

Abby laughed without humour: 'There is nothing cheap nor tender about Mr Hungerford.'

After a long and obviously successful lunch, George was back wafting brandy fumes, chewing on a huge cigar, and making a nuisance of himself at the afternoon's rehearsal.

'You've got to keep *Messiah* moving,' he told the orchestra. 'Particularly in part two when there aren't many good tunes, before the "Hallelujah Chorus" wakes the audience up, and you've got to really belt it out to be heard in a big cathedral.'

Abby lost her temper. 'Just because you come from Huddersfield, it doesn't mean you own the work.'

'Nor do you,' shouted Carmine, who was anxious to put Abby down and to ingratiate himself with George. 'I don't know what you're doing conducting *Messiah* when it was your lot who crucified the poor sod in the first place.'

'That's out of order, Carmine,' snapped Julian.

'It was Handel's descendants,' yelled back Abby, 'who sent six million of our lot to the gas chambers.'

'Please, everyone,' Julian broke the horrified silence. 'George is right – Abby, Luisa and I visited the cathedral last week, it's huge. I know you all know *Messiah* backwards, but the audience knows it backwards too, so we can't afford to make mistakes.'

'Aint it rarver like takin' coals to Newcastle,' said Barry, who was hugging his double bass to keep warm. 'I fort it was the CCO who'd cornered the baroque market. They're the ones always winnin' prizes.'

'That's why our reputation's on the line,' said George.

* * *

Messiah requires a very small orchestra, just strings, bassoons, oboes, two trumpets, timps and a harpsichord. So it was a depleted and resentful bunch who boarded the coach in the bitter cold under a lowering mustard-yellow sky the following afternoon. They had all been refused rises and resented having to trail over to Cotchester for no extra money.

With no Eldred and Peter Plumpton, the bridge four was incomplete. With no Hilary and Lionel gone, Ninion and Militant Moll couldn't sing madrigals on their own. Without Miss Parrott, Dimitri gloomily shared a back seat with his cello.

All the pretty girls, nervous of appearing on television, drooped because there was no Celtic Mafia, except Randy, who was now an item with Candy, to jolly things along. The only cheerful note was Flora running on at the last moment, clean hair flopping, handing out tabloids like an air hostess. All the orchestra, except Hilary, who pretended to despise gossip, were obsessed with the collapse of the Prince of Wales's marriage and had divided themselves into pro-Charles and pro-Diana factions.

Now they fell on the latest update in ecstasy.

'I fancy the Brigadier, such piercing blue eyes,' sighed Nellie. 'And that's a lovely new hold-all, Flora,' she added, glancing up from the *Daily Express* for a second, 'Louis Vuitton, isn't it?'

'Clever you,' Flora stroked the dark green leather proudly. 'Abby was so ashamed of me turning up at gigs weighed down by carrier bags of knickers that she gave it me as an early Christmas present. I can hang my black dresses up in it, and there's room for Foxie, sponge bags, books and things.'

'Here, let me.' To everyone's amazement, Carmine leapt to his feet and put the hold-all and Flora's viola case up on the rack.

'Come and sit here,' he ushered her into the window-seat beside him.

'Gosh thanks,' stammered Flora. 'Have a Kit-Kat.' Then because Carmine had to play 'The Trumpet Shall Sound' towards the end of the evening, asked 'Aren't you terrified about your solo?'

Carmine shrugged.

'Just because it's TV I'm bound to crack a note in an embarrassing close-up, but this is a doddle compared with the solo in the *B minor Mass*. At the end of that, you really see stars.' And he went on to be fascinating about trumpet music.

Carmine, in fact, was not in a good mood. He had given Cathie hell, because he actually was nervous about the solo, and because Alan Cardew, the planning officer, suddenly appeared to have won the pools, and had just whipped his wife Lindy off to the Seychelles for three weeks; then they were off again, skiing over Christmas.

Denied his mistress and uninhibited today by the endless mockery of the Celtic Mafia, Carmine decided to have a crack at Flora. He'd always fancied the snooty, upmarket little bitch.

Once the tabloids were exhausted, everyone started grumbling about foul letters from their bank manager. Barry the Bass had had to pawn his rings and medallions to get his telephone reconnected. Mary, darning socks, was fretting about paying for Christmas presents. Noriko had sold her little car and nearly died of cold walking to the coach. Old Henry couldn't afford to get his stereo mended – life without music in a tiny bedsit was very bleak.

'After the première of *Messiah*, Handel gave all the profits to the poor, which meant one hundred and forty-two people were released from the debtors prison,' announced Simon Painshaw.

'Can't see Sonny Parker doing that for us,' sighed Candy.

'And the hall was so packed,' went on Simon, 'that men were asked to leave off their swords and the ladies their hoops.'

'Oh look,' said Flora, 'it's started to snow.'

At first it didn't settle on the roads, only laying clean sheets over the fields and crawling like a white leopard along the branches of the trees. But gradually, as the light faded, sky and snow merged, becoming the same stinging sapphire, only divided by evergreens, black trunks, branches and hedgerows that became walls as they crossed over into Gloucestershire. The coach started crackling over frozen puddles and sliding all over the place in the steep narrow lanes.

Flora wished Viking were on the coach. She'd been so upset by Rannaldini's poaching of the RSO repertoire. Then she'd read the inscription on Viking's cardboard tombstone. Not able to bear being hurt again, she had refused all Viking's invitations but she still caught him smiling at her appraisingly, which always made her heart beat faster.

The snow was blanking out signposts and roadsigns. The coach drivers were all for turning back; Knickers, in a serious twist, was more terrified of George's wrath if they didn't arrive, and urged them on. Twenty miles from Cotchester, the snow started drifting, and they ran into blizzards. Trees reared up out of the diminishing visibility like ghosts. Climbing to the top of a hill the coach skidded into the verge and ground to a halt. Wheels whirred impotently, raising fountains of snow.

'What do we do now?' asked Knickers. As he put his long nose outside, his spectacles filled up with white flakes. The wind was blowing straight from Siberia.

'You all get out and push,' said Abby, who'd been in a car just behind them. 'I'm not going to be beaten by that bastard Hugo.'

'*How beautiful are the feet with chilblains,*' sang Flora, wincing as she landed on iron runnels of frozen mud. As she righted herself, she was amazed to feel a coat round her shoulders, and even grateful to be offered a pair of awful driving gloves.

'Can't have you catching cold,' said Carmine and, as

swearing and panting they all pushed the coach, she felt his hand over hers.

'I may be gone some time,' said Randy, sliding off to have a pee.

Two hours and eight miles later, the coach descended into Cotchester to find completely clear roads, starry skies, and the great cathedral floodlit.

'They'd never have believed us if we hadn't got through,' said Abby who'd abandoned her car.

Her orchestra, in various states of hypothermia and mutiny, gazed at her stonily. They hadn't even the heart to boo as they passed a window in the High Street, entirely devoted to Dame Edith and the CCO's latest recording of the *Christmas Oratorio*, or at huge posters everywhere advertising 'Dame Hermione Sings *Messiah*', in huge letters, with the other soloists and the RSO in tiny print underneath. Inside the packed cathedral, lit by hundreds of candles, a huge Christmas tree and television lights, the four soloists, choir, crews and audience were raring to go.

There was no time for a rehearsal. Abby went straight up onto the rostrum to explain what had happened.

'We came through a white hell, OK? The orchestra are frozen. They're just having something hot to eat, I hope you'll bear with us.'

The audience were more than happy to do so, but not Dame Hermione. *She* was the one who kept people waiting. As the harpsichordist had already arrived from London, Hermione had been about to offer the audience an impromptu concert of her latest album, *Soothe the Sad Heart*, which with the television coverage would have sold an extra fifty thousand copies over Christmas.

She had upset the other three soloists by her histrionics about catching cold and her demands. Poor Alphonso, the twenty-five-stone Italian tenor, was forced to have blue drops put in his eyes, and his bald patch blacked out by the make-up girls in a howling draught because Dame Hermione had commandeered the entire vestry as a dressing-room.

Fortunately George Hungerford had missed all these hysterics because he had arrived only five minutes before the orchestra, so the first thing he heard was Dame Hermione's deep voice saying. 'Take me to the fans.'

The first thing Dame Hermione heard was George telling Miles that he'd have his 'goots for garters' if the orchestra didn't turn up.

Surrounded by twenty blow heaters, Dame Hermione shivered from excitement rather than cold. She adored masterful men.

Meanwhile Steve Smithson charged around with his thermometer, complaining the cathedral was too cold, and that there was no proper band room, since Dame Hermione had hogged all the space.

Fortified by a glass of red wine each, paid for by Abby, and pizzas in the Bar Sinister opposite, the orchestra had perked up enough to engage in the usual argy-bargy with the television crews. There was simply not enough room on the stage to accommodate Fat Isobel and Fat Alphonso and the harpsichord, let alone having cables to trip over, mikes up your nose, lights shining in your eyes, and cameramen bossily shoving chairs and music-stands aside to give them a clear camera angle on Dame Hermione.

A BBC minion, in a fake fur coat and strawberry-pink trousers, who looked as though he ate choirboys for breakfast, sidled up to handsome Randy as he blew a few testing blasts on his trumpet.

'Hi, Clark Gable, you playing the big solo?'

'No, him,' Randy jerked his sleek sandy head in Carmine's direction.

'Shame, you're so much more –' the BBC minion ran his eyes over Randy's body – 'photogenic, particularly when you smile.'

'Carmine wouldn't like it very much.'

'We'll have to use green face powder to take his colour down. What are you doing after the show?'

'Your admirer's got an admirer,' giggled Clare.

'Yes, I've lucked out there,' sighed Candy, tightening her G-string.

'There's absolutely no way I'm swapping seats with Moll –' Flora was now telling the BBC minion – 'even to appear on television. Moll would kill me.'

On cue, Moll rushed up in a state of chunter.

'There are no ladies' toilets, so I had to squat in the gents, and someone's written: *"RSO stands for Really Shitty Orchestra"* on the wall. It's not funny, Flora. You're to cross it out in the interval,' she shouted to a cringing Ninion.

On came Julian, smiling broadly, fiddle aloft to relieved applause, and some barracking from the gallery.

'Take off those dark glasses, deary,' urged the BBC minion. 'Looks a bit camp.' Then, as Julian lowered them a fraction showing his red-albino eyes, said, 'well, perhaps not.'

'Jesus, it's cold,' said Bill Thackery looking at the hundreds of candles flickering in the draught.

A rustle of excitement and some cheering greeted Abby and the soloists. Dame Hermione, diamonds sparkling in the camera lights, was clad from top to toe in Rannaldini's sleek, dark Christmas mink.

'Ring up Animal Rights at once,' snarled Flora.

Hermione had no competition from the contralto who looked and sang like a sheep and was eight months' pregnant.

Having bowed to the audience, Abby thanked them once more for being so patient.

'And I just wanna tell you guys,' she hissed at the orchestra, 'that the entire CCO including Hugo, are up in the gallery, waiting to boo, so flaming well play out of your boots, and don't let the soloists drag.'

This had the desired effect. The RSO played with that brilliance and attack often engendered by rage and irritation, and, even without a rehearsal, the Cotchester Choir were infinitely superior to Peggy Parker's screeching seagulls. Despite the icy cold of the cathedral, the sopranos led by Dame Edith's helpmate, Monica Baddingham, had absolutely no difficulty in hitting Top A as they romped through the 'Glory of the Lord'.

Not wanting to bump into any of his father's friends, Marcus crept into the concert after the overture. Returning to Cotchester, which was only a few miles from his home in Penscombe, made him feel desperately homesick.

The great cathedral was as filled with memories as shadows. His father had always read the lesson at Midnight Mass, and despite being divorced had managed to have his second marriage to Taggie there, much to the rage of the bishop. It had snowed that day too, and Marcus remembered his desolation as a young boy as his father and his ravishing new stepmother took off by helicopter into the blizzard.

Alphonso, the hugely fat tenor, seemed to be singing. *'Comfort ye, comfort ye,'* directly to him.

Marcus also noticed, because of a shortage of basses, George Hungerford had joined the choir and could be heard belting out, *'Oonto Oos a Boy is Born'* in true Hoodersfield fashion. Marcus thought how attractive George was, so aggressively macho, compared to the bobbing Adam's apples and waggling beards around him.

George, in fact, was very happy. That very afternoon the Ministry of the Environment had overturned Rutminster District Council's decision and given him planning permission to cover Cowslip Hill with houses. Now he wouldn't have to revert to his contingency plan of letting New Age Travellers onto the site at the dead of night, which normally melted any opposition.

His orchestra were also playing champion, he

couldn't have borne it if they'd let him down in front of Dame Hermione, who'd been all he'd ever dreamt of and had asked him up for a night-cap in the Rupert of the Rhine Suite at the Cotchester Hilton after the *après*-concert party.

The dazzling overhead lights gave a blond halo to Hermione's glossy brown curls. Monocles glinted in the eyes of a thousand colonels and George caught his breath as she slithered out of her sleek, dark fur to reveal shoulders as smooth and white as sand dunes, rising out of a deep purple velvet dress. Looking up at the monitor, George longed to kiss the blue hollows made by her collar bones, the hairs rose at the back of his neck at the unbearable purity of her voice: *'There were shepherds abiding in the fields.'*

Because of the late start and the shortage of lavatories, it was decided to dispense with the first interval which had many of the RSO and the elderly audience crossing their legs in agony. Not so the Cotchester Chamber Orchestra in the gallery, who'd all been to a Christmas party before the concert and who kept slipping in and out with a great banging of doors throughout the second half. In delight, they also counted the number of people reading their programmes or plaques on the wall, or gently snoozing, until the 'Hallelujah Chorus' and a good shout woke everyone up.

Moving her body like a rock star in her dark blue suit, Abby abandoned her stick and directed the orchestra and choir with clenched fists and power salutes. Backed up by Davie going berserk on his drums and by Barry and his basses, all of whom knew how to swing it, her interpretation was gloriously exhilarating, and made the lovely descending chorale of 'The Kingdom of this World' all the more moving, leaving the audience reeling.

Now it was time for the Bishop of Cotchester to give his little sermon, working in Honesty Insurance, whose staff had been waving banners of the logo like football supporters every time the cameras panned to the audience.

'Awfully chic to match his ring to Dame Hermione's dress,' whispered Nellie, as exuding gravitas and pomposity the Bishop mounted the rostrum.

'If we behave ourselves on this earth,' he thundered, glaring at the CCO up in the gallery, who were guilty of even higher jinks than their Rutminster rivals, 'it is an insurance against our going to hell.'

He then carried on, to the rippling snoring counterpoint of some drunk in the gallery, to say people should be honest in their deeds and in their words, and repeated that Honesty was the best Policy, so many times that Randy, handing his hip-flask down to Jerry the Joker, muttered that the old bugger must be getting a bloody good whack of free pension for his services. Glancing round apprehensively to see if George had overheard, Jerry was glad to see George's anger was entirely focused on Flora, who had unearthed Foxie from under her chair and was sending Clare and Candy into fits by putting his paws over his furry ears to blot out the Bishop's jawing.

The drunk was snoring even louder.

'Dunno whether to put a pillow over his face or shoot him,' said Randy, passing his hip-flask to Davie Buckle who was still recovering from his frenzied activity in the 'Hallelujah Chorus'.

'Shoot him *and* the Bishop,' said Davie.

In fact the Bishop rabbited on for so long that Abby nodded to Julian to start tuning up. This was the moment the audience had been waiting for: the re-run of the single that had topped the pop charts, and sold over a million copies: 'Hermione Sings Redeemer'.

Off slithered the dark fur again as Hermione rose to her feet. What a trim waist beneath those wonderful knockers, thought George, his brain misting over.

Aware that the Bishop had made them even later, Abby kept the strings and the bassoons moving on in the opening bars. But there was no way Hermione was going to be hurried.

Eyes widened, hands clasped, she smiled angelically at her swooning public.

'*I know that my Redeemer leeveth,*' rang out joyfully on the arctic, uncentrally heated air, and the audience burst into a round of applause as if they were listening to Frank Sinatra.

Hermione put up a white hand to hush them: 'Thank you, thank you, good people of Cotchester. I'm so happy to be in your lovely city again. From the beginning, Abigail.'

Abby gritted her teeth.

Hermione's voice could crack glasses. Unfortunately this second time around it woke up the drunk in the gallery, who, taking a swig from his bottle of Southern Comfort decided to sing along.

'*I know that moy Redeemer leeeeeveth,*' he caterwauled, wickedly mimicking Hermione, as he clasped his hands, composed his slack mouth in a perfect O, lengthened all his Es, and opened his bloodshot little eyes as far as they would go.

'Oh bliss, there is a God,' muttered Flora.

'*And though worms deestroy theese body,*' sang Hermione, who'd gone bright red from embarrassment and trying to drown him.

'*And though worms deestroy theeese bod-ee,*' quavered the drunk, to a crescendo of furious hissing from a thousand apoplectic colonels. (Gentlemen should have been allowed to wear swords.)

Unfortunately Hermione had many bars of rest in the aria for the drunk to fill in.

'*I know,*' he began again, missing top E with a mighty screech.

Monica Baddingham, in the choir, strained her eyes

to see if – horrors – he was one of Dame Edith's musicians in disguise.

Looking down, Abby saw that the RSO had corpsed. Neither Jerry the Joker, nor Solemn Steve could keep their lips round their reeds. The strings, even Julian, were hunched over their music, to hide their frantically shaking shoulders. Randy, Carmine and Davie were going even redder in the face trying not to laugh, Flora wasn't even trying. Foxie was conducting again, with gracious sweeps and bows to Candy and Clare who were stuffing handkerchiefs into their mouths, and to Fat Isobel who was clutching her massive sides.

I'll kill that drunk and that minx after the concert, raged George. Hemmed in by beards and Adam's apples he was in anguish.

'In my flesh shall I see God,' screeched the drunk, taking another swig. Up in the gallery the CCO were in ecstasy.

'Throw him out,' shouted their First Bassoon.

'Yesh, throw him out,' agreed the Second Horn.

'No,' yelled the First Trumpet, who'd drunk even more whisky. 'Throw him down, he might kill a fiddler.'

A gale of laughter swept the gallery.

Hugo, however, was watching Abby's rigid shoulders and her clenched fist on her baton.

'Look at L'Appassionata,' he murmured to his First Horn, 'she's going to flip.'

As Hermione hit top G with an almighty squawk, George left his seat, punching fellow basses out of the way, and Abby stopped the orchestra and swung round.

The fury in her blazing yellow eyes was so palpable, many of the audience felt they had been burnt by lightning and afterwards swore that all the candles round the cathedral dimmed before flickering back into life.

'Just pack it in, right,' yelled Abby.

'And though worms deestroy theese body,' warbled the drunk, waving his bottle at her.

Abby's voice rose: 'I said pack it in. We've driven through snow and blizzard this evening to play to you, and Dame Hermione and the other soloists have flown thousands of miles to sing. If you don't get that asshole out of here we won't play another note.'

There was a stunned, appalled pause, as a thousand deaf-aids were switched up to discover if they had heard right.

Then the lurking Press went beserk, simultaneously trying to photograph Abby and Hermione and the drunk as he was noisily evicted.

Dame Hermione, who knew how to milk a situation, cast down her eyes. Abby reached across the pregnant alto and put a comforting hand on her white shaking shoulder.

'I'm sorry, let's do it again. We'll skip the introduction, five bars after eleven, and one—'

Hermione rose to the occasion, a woman of sorrows, eyes brimming with tears, moved for once by genuine grief at her own humiliation. At the end the audience cheered her to the shadowy rafters.

As she lumbered off the stage down into the side-aisle, one of her high heels fell down the soi-disant central-heating grill, depositing her into the waiting arms of George Hungerford. Her breasts were so soft, it was like catching a giant pillow.

'Dame Hermione, I'm bluddy proud of you,' said George, offering her the remains of Randy's hip-flask.

THIRTY-NINE

The concert was followed by a splendid party at Dame Edith's house in the Close. Normally the musicians would have been excluded from such a bash, but Dame Edith, who'd always voted Labour, felt that after such a polar trek, they deserved a treat. The coaches would leave in half an hour, which gave everyone time for a bite and several drinks. A route avoiding snow had been charted. They'd be home by two.

Dame Edith lived in a shabbily beautiful Jacobean house on lots of floors, using all her awards as door-stops. The dark William Morris walls were covered with sixty years of musical mementoes. Monica Baddingham had added her Stubbs, her Herrings, her sporting prints, her embroidered cushions to the household, and three yellow labrador bitches who had greatly enhanced the life of Tippett, Dame Edith's pug.

Tippett now sat snuffling beside Dame Edith, who had changed into a burgundy-red smoking-jacket to welcome her guests with a slap on the back.

'Well done, splendid concert, great success. Coats upstairs, booze to the left, *coq au vin* and *bombe surprise* in the kitchen. Monica made them – ' she smiled fondly at

Lady Baddingham, who was brandishing champagne bottles – 'so they must be bloody good.'

'Do you think they both sleep in here?' panted Flora as she plonked her viola case and her new Louis Vuitton on Edith's massive four-poster.

'I guess so,' Marcus blushed slightly. 'The four dog-baskets are all in here.'

'Golly,' giggled Flora, 'we are seeing life. That Augustus John must be of Edith when she was a young boy. D'you think Abby's going to be in awful trouble over that drunk?'

'I thought she was wonderful,' said Marcus. 'Christ knows where it would have ended if she hadn't gone ballistic.'

Downstairs Dame Edith was entirely in agreement.

'Can't think why everyone's making such a fuss,' she was telling a tight-lipped Miles, the Bishop and a hovering Gwynneth and Gilbert, who were already filling their faces from overloaded plates.

'Done just the same myself,' continued Edith, flicking cigar ash into the fire. 'Anyway, what's wrong with the word "asshole"?'

Miles blanched.

'In a House of God, Edith?' asked the Bishop plaintively.

'Very appropriate,' said Edith with a guffaw. 'Assholes seem to be the only thing you bishops are interested in these days, judging by the papers.'

The Bishop turned as purple as the ring on his cherished white hand, but being a very greedy man, he was not prepared to storm out until he'd dined, so merely satisfied himself with: 'You go too far, Edith.'

'It wasn't Abby's church,' said Flora, joining the group to Miles's fury. 'She's Jewish, and people use the word "asshole" all the time in America – it just means idiot. Anyway,' she ploughed on ignoring the shocked faces,

'Abby's in excellent company. Handel used to swear in four languages at anyone, even royalty, who chatted in rehearsals, and he used to throw tiresome singers out of the window, although he'd have been pushed to evict Alphonso.'

'Well said,' Dame Edith gave a shout of laughter, then linking her arm through Flora's led her towards the kitchen. 'Come and have some grub. Like your flowered leggings, just like the Prima Vera.' Then, lowering her voice, whispered, 'How's Marcus? Monica and I are awfully worried about the rift with Rupert and Taggie; poor boy feels things so deeply.'

'The best thing you could do,' said Flora, 'is to get him some work.'

As soon as Dame Edith was out of earshot, Miles, guzzling Gwynneth and Gilbert, and the Bishop drew together for an indignation meeting.

'Abigail's got to be stopped, she can't go on behaving like a yobbo. The "Hallelujah Chorus" sounded like rock music,' said Miles fastidiously.

'And that young woman Flora's just as bad,' sniffed Gwynneth.

Oblivious of the furore she had triggered off, Abby was thrilled to have been sought out by Monica Baddingham and the great Declan O'Hara, who was just to die for, to say how well she had done. She was livid, however, when she overheard several CCO players saying how tremendously the RSO had been improved by Julian.

'It's the great leader, of course, that makes a great orchestra,' said Hugo, smiling coldly at Abby.

He was obviously still festering over his yellow cords. Then he turned to Gwynneth, who looked as though she had a couple of used cars hanging from her ears.

'Lovely earrings, Gwynneth. Can I get you some *bombe surprise*? I know how you like desserts.'

'I thought I'd have seconds of the *coq* first,' simpered Gwynneth.

'Nearest she'll get to cock in this house,' murmured Randy to Candy. 'I'm surprised they're not serving vibrator *au vin.*'

Hugo, who, unlike most of the RSO, realized how crucial it was to suck up to the Arts Council, took Gwynneth's plate.

'You're so caring, Hugo,' Gwynneth edged towards him. 'What did you really think of Rosen's performance?'

Hugo shrugged. 'Not a lot. The jazzing up of the "Hallelujah Chorus" was terribly vulgar. George Frederick would have loathed it, and she's such a drama queen.'

'My sentiments entirely. How far exactly is Rutminster from Cotchester?'

'Two score miles and ten,' said Hugo. 'And the RSO nearly didn't get there by candlelight.'

'One wonders,' mused Gwynneth, 'whether we really need two orchestras in the area.'

'My sentiments even more entirely,' said Hugo.

There was only warmth and sincerity in Hugo's eyes as he forced himself to gaze into her lard-like face. Without flinching he accepted the pressure of her shapeless body. 'I'll get you some more *coq*, Gwynnie.'

Turning, he tripped over a large labrador and nearly deposited Gwynneth's chicken bones into Alphonso's capacious lap.

Alphonso, who was taking up seven-eights of the window-seat, didn't flinch either.

'I hop,' he was telling Nellie, 'that you will come to my suite for a night-hat.'

George, who'd been buttonholed for far too long, grabbed Abby as she passed.

'Have a word with Gilbert, I know he wants to discuss the concert.'

Shoving them together to their mutual distaste, he

belted off to find Dame Hermione. In his car on the way over, she had sung: 'I'm a little lamb that's lost in the wood'. George had never looked forward to a night-cap more in his life.

The heroine of the evening was now holding court on a frayed *chaise-longue* to a circle of admirers, many of them Press.

'I just thought, poor fellow, poor fellow, he must be so terribly unhappy. Anyone that dependent on drink needs help.'

'You're so compassionate, Dame Hermione,' gushed Gwynneth.

'Have some fizz,' said Monica Baddingham, waving a bottle.

Everyone put their hands over their glasses to demonstrate their lack of dependency.

'I just wanted to congratulate you on your *Fanny Cycle*,' went on Gwynneth reverently, 'and Rannaldini has never conducted better.'

'How is Rannaldini?' asked a man from *The Times* idly.

Flora, on her way to the loo, stopped in her tracks.

'Oh, full of beans,' said Hermione heartily, her small hand creeping surreptitiously into George's big one.

'How's his new marriage?' asked the *Guardian*.

'Excellent,' said Hermione, her eyes suddenly twinkling. 'I sometimes think he married her for her packing.'

Flora groaned and ran upstairs. She was desperately tired and near to tears. After admiring the famous musicians, including Rannaldini in arctic profile framed on the wall of Edith's bathroom, she unlocked the door and came out slap into Carmine.

'You played brilliantly tonight,' she stammered, conscious of the lurking menace of the man. 'I wish all the brass section had been at the concert to hear you.'

Edging along the wall towards the stairs, she was stopped by the iron bar of his arm.

'Give us a kiss, then.'

Avoiding a vile sour waft of vinous breath which must have corked inside him, Flora pecked him on the cheek. The next moment, Carmine had grabbed her hair, yanking her head back, forcing his sneering mouth on hers with a clash of teeth, scratching her with his horrible moustache. As she writhed with the strength of utter revulsion, his other hand dived under her dark blue jersey, pinching her breasts till she screamed.

'You bloody little bra-less prick-tease.'

'Lemme go.' Flora was desperately trying to knee him in the balls, when a voice said: 'Ahem. I spy a strugglin' musician.'

'Fuck off,' snarled Carmine, but his grip eased.

Wriggling away, Flora went slap into the scented, medallion-hung bulk of Jack Rodway the receiver.

'Oh, thank God.'

'You OK?'

Flora nodded. 'No fool like a bold fool,' she said shakily.

Jack turned on Carmine.

'If you ever lay a finger on this young lidy again, I'll get George's boys on you, before he fires you.'

Swearing, snarling, Carmine lurched off upstairs.

Flora was shaking uncontrollably.

'Poor li-el fing.' Jack's arms closed around her. 'Come and have a jar at the Bar Sinister.'

Out of the landing window, Flora could see musicians streaming out to the waiting coach.

'I gotta go.'

'I'll run you home later, it's no distance at night. I've thought a lot about you, Flora.'

'My things are still on Edith's bed.' Flora shivered, Carmine was still up there somewhere. 'There's my leather jacket, and a viola case with my name on, and a green Louis Vuitton bag.'

'I'll get them,' said Jackie.

'And you might torch Dim Hermione's fur coat at the same time.'

In the hall, Flora met a happier-looking Marcus.

'Dame Edith's just introduced me to George, he was really nice this time.'

Flora looked old-fashioned. 'Must want something. Look, I'm not coming on the coach – can you or Abby feed the cats if you get home before me?'

'I shouldn't be doing this,' grumbled Flora as Jack aimed the remote control to open huge electric gates. 'What happens if your wife rolls up?'

'She's in Italy,' said Jack.

They seemed to get upstairs to the bedroom awfully quickly.

'I'm glad you turned up at the party,' gabbled Flora. 'Things were a little flat, before Carmine tried to rape me.'

'I'll set you up in a little flat,' Jack guided her into a bedroom out of a Laura Ashley catalogue.

'I ought to clean my teeth,' said Flora, as she collapsed onto a daisy-strewn counterpane. 'I better fetch my smart new bag to match such a smart bedroom.'

'Use my toothbrush,' said Jack, pulling her to her feet. 'Use anyfing in the bathroom, most of all, use me.'

Flora was woken by Jack marching in with black coffee, croissants and a large jug of Buck's Fizz.

'You're a seriously nice man.'

Jack smirked.

'And that is a really pretty view.' Flora reared up in bed to admire a wood and white houses nesting in skewbald hills. People were already tobogganing. 'And a lovely little village.'

'Shame the bloody bells wike us up at twenty to eleven every Sunday morning.'

'Help. Is that the time?'

'You were very tired. I wish I could still crash out like that.'

Jack was wearing a white towelling dressing-gown and was obviously poised for a replay. He looked much older in daylight with his thatched hair pushed off his lined forehead.

'Coincidence you going to Verona,' he went on. 'Have a Crusoe.'

Croissant's the one word that always trips them up, Flora was appalled to find herself thinking, and said hastily, 'I've never been to Verona.'

'Come on, the label's on your smart 'old-all.'

Flora was downstairs in a flash. In the Louis Vuitton bag with the Verona label, she found several toots of cocaine, two very hard-porn mags, a year's supply of condoms, ten grand in cash, some grey silk pyjamas, voluminous enough to make a parachute, Alphonso's tails, his passport and his tickets to Verona on a plane that had left at eight o'clock that morning.

Flora went beserk.

'He's got Foxie,' she sobbed. 'I can't move without Foxie, he's been with me since I was a baby.'

She was on to Woodbine Cottage in even more of a flash.

'Dirty stop-out,' were Abby's first words.

'I've lost Foxie, and my lovely new case.'

It was several seconds before Abby could make herself heard.

'It's OK, Nellie's got them.'

'How on earth?'

'She went back to the Cotchester Hilton with Alphonso.'

'Omigod.'

Abby couldn't stop laughing.

'Nellie said Alphonso burrowed in his case for a line and a condom and discovered Foxie.'

'Condomingo,' said Flora, who was reeling with relief. 'Poor Foxie, where's he now?'

'Alphonso gave him and your case to George.'

'Oh de-ah,' said Flora wearily, 'he's not going to be very happy. I've got Alphonso's case here.'

George had not been able to keep his rendezvous with Dame Hermione. A man of sorrows, acquainted with a whole load of grief, he had instead spent the night with an increasingly hysterical Alphonso, who refused to let him call the police, because of the contents of the case, but insisted George ring every member of the orchestra, which was difficult when the snow had brought down so many telephone lines, to try and locate its whereabouts.

George really roared down the telephone at Flora.

'Where the fuck have you been? Alphonso's threatening to sue the orchestra, unless we get his case back and him on the evening plane. He's got to fly to the States in the morning. I'll send the helicopter for the case at once. Where are you?'

'I can't tell you.'

'Then you're fired.'

Flora put a sweating hand over the receiver.

'Can you lend me the money for a taxi back to Rutminster?'

Grim-faced, Jack seized the telephone.

'George, it's Jack, Jack Rodway, Flora's wiv me.' Then, interrupting the torrent of abuse, snapped, 'I don't want the fuzz involved, Janice'd do her nut, and having seen the contents of Alphonso's case, I can see why he don't either. I'll shunt Flora over to you as quick as possible.'

All Jack's *bonhomie* had evaporated. He couldn't wait to get Flora out of the house.

Beside Foxie, George had found a black dress, a pair of shoes, a sponge bag and the *Selected Poems of Robert Browning*, which he was flipping through, when Flora, very pale but defiant, arrived at his office.

'*How sad and bad and mad it was –*

But then, how it was sweet,' quoted George, throwing

the book across the huge polished table. 'Pretty sad, bad and mad, for a girl of your age to go to bed with a middle-aged roué like Jack Rodway.'

Watching Flora dive on Foxie, kissing him thankfully, he reflected bitterly on his missed night-cap with Hermione, who was off round the world already, who might have soothed his sad heart. He didn't know if he would ever meet her again.

'You'll have to pay for Alphonso's air ticket,' he said harshly.

Flora was gathering up the rest of her belongings and chucking them into her case.

'I'll have to consult my lawyer,' she said haughtily. 'George Carman's a friend of my mother's.'

'I'll dock it off your salary then.'

'I must have picked up Alphonso's bag in the cathedral. It was all your fault – there was no band room for safe keeping, everything was jumbled together. I'm going to talk to Steve.'

Appealed to, the union decided management was in the wrong and Flora didn't have to pay up, but Steve shook his head.

'George hates anyone getting the better of him, Flora. I'm afraid you're a marked woman from now on.'

FORTY

The RSO were highly amused by the annexing both of Jack Rodway and Alphonso's case, and sang, *'Pack up your troubles in a new kit bag,'* each time an increasingly irritated Flora came into the hall.

Although secretly delighted that Flora had got off with someone other than Viking, Abby was currently far more preoccupied with the recording of *Rachel's Requiem*. It was her first CD as a conductor and for the RSO, and she was determined to trounce the CCO in next October's Gramophone Awards if it killed her. Thank God, Boris was too immersed in *King Lear* to come down and interfere.

'I leave it in your capable fingers,' he told Abby. 'Today I write vonderful aria: "Blow vind and crack your chicks."'

Both, however, reckoned without the wrath of Piggy Porker. She was not going to put one hundred thousand pounds into the RSO centenary year, starting on 1 January, and provide half the money for the *Requiem* and Sonny's *Interruption* if a blasphemer was at the helm. Miles, Canon Airlie and Serena Woodward, now known as 'Princess Grace of Megagram', who was producing the record, all backed her up, and so did George, when he saw the cash sum involved. Boris must conduct the *Requiem* he had written. He was also cheap because he liked to keep the adrenalin going by recording pieces straight through without any retakes as though they were live, so there were never any overtime problems.

They had, however, all reckoned without Julian who, in a midnight meeting, threatened to resign if Abby were supplanted, and without Boris, who flatly refused to co-operate.

'Fuck off Parson from Portlock,' he shouted when Miles rang, 'Eef I break off now, I will lose *Lear*; all the characters, all the music vill slip away, it is best theeng I ever write. I try to forget Rachel and *Requiem*. Anyway I can't do this to Abby who is a good friend.'

Nor did he want hassle from Astrid, who was wildly jealous of Abby, Rachel and anything to do with Rutminster.

'Are you prepared to pay back your advance, if the record is pulled?' asked Miles coldly.

Boris, who had just bought a little Polo for Astrid, and had the cheque bounced on him, said he was not.

'You've got two days to mug up on the *Requiem*,' ordered Miles. 'And please catch a train on Sunday night, so you'll be on time on Monday morning.'

Instead Boris caught an early train on Monday morning. It was a tedious union rule that no more than twenty minutes of music could be recorded in a three-hour session. But if he could finish the *Requiem* which lasted an hour in a day, the RSO would still get paid for a three-hour session tomorrow morning, and could go Christmas shopping or have a lie-in instead, and he could belt back to Astrid on a fast train this evening.

Passengers on the 7.05 to Rutminster were amazed to

see the romantic-looking man with the upended Beethoven hair singing along to his frantic scribbling, covering an entire table for four with his papers.

'*With a Hey Ho, the vind and the rain,*' sang Boris.

He hadn't bothered to look at the *Requiem*, and became so immersed in a possible baritone aria: '*As flies to vanton boys, are we to the gods,*' that he forgot to get off at Rutminster, and only arrived at the recording studios, situated in a basement in the High Street, at quarter-past eleven.

Miles, who had to pay for the taxi, was hopping.

'Who produce *Requiem?*' Boris asked him sulkily.

'Serena Westwood. She's been waiting for you since half-past nine.'

Miles might well have poured petrol all over a smouldering Boris, who loathed being bossed about by women. Serena was as smilingly serene as her name, but Boris was convinced a barracuda lurked beneath her steel-grey wool dress. Abby at least was on the side of music and she and Boris could swear at each other in Russian.

Serena, who was now sitting in the control-room, had been immersed in the score all weekend. She had taken the precaution of providing paper cups in case Boris started smashing things. In front of her, at a mixing desk like a vast switchboard and being paid a fortune by the hour, sat Sammy, the recording engineer. Through a glass panel, they could both see a forest of microphones like silver-birch saplings. Around these were grouped the RSO, swelled today by numerous extras, who also had to be paid. Except for Hilary who was ostentatiously reading *Villette*, they had all done the crossword and read the latest instalment in the Royal Soap in their own and each other's papers.

To irritate Flora, the Celtic Mafia were now exchanging viola jokes.

'What's the definition of a lady?'

'Go on, Viking.'

'A woman who can play the viola but doesn't.'

'Ha, ha, ha, ha.'

'Once upon a time, Princess Diana met a frog,' went on Viking. 'The frog said, "If you give me a big kiss, ma'am, I'll turn into a handsome viola player." So Princess Diana put him in her pocket. "Whaddja do that for," protested the frog. "You'll be more use to me as a talking frog," said Princess Diana.'

'Oh, shut up,' snarled Flora, over the howls of mirth. Everything irritated her at the moment.

Over her right shoulder she was constantly aware of Viking's coldness since she'd slept with Jack, and over her left she was equally conscious of Carmine's venomous animosity.

It was also such a long time since the RSO had made a record, that for many of the players: Candy, Clare, Lincoln, Viking's Fifth Horn, Jenny, Cherub, Flora and Noriko, this was a first experience, and they were all terrified. Recordings were for ever. Every wrong note, dropped mouthpiece or rustled page would be picked up.

The long wait was telling on everyone's nerves, particularly as Julian, good as his word, had refused to participate without Abby, and had swept Luisa and the children off to a pantomime in London. Bill Thackery, although thrilled to have this big chance to lead the orchestra, couldn't, as Viking pointed out, lead the winning dog up to get the obedience championship at Cruft's.

Wandering into the studio, Boris apologized for being late, paused to change a couple of bars of 'Blow Vind', opened the score of the *Requiem*, then remembering he hadn't called Astrid picked up the telephone on the rostrum and found himself connected to Serena.

'We're all waiting, Mr Levitsky,' she said icily.

'Vun moment,' Boris shot out to the call-box in the passage.

He'd fix the RSO management for dragging him

away in the middle of *Lear*, and there was his old enemy Viking reading the *Racing Post* and ringing his bookmaker. Thank God he'd given 'Rachel's Lament' to Cathie Jones, although she wouldn't be needed until tomorrow.

The red light was on, shining through the mist of cigarette smoke like a setting September sun.

'The tape's started, Boris,' said Serena, on the talkback that could be heard by the whole studio. She would only use the telephone on the rostrum for private abuse.

Raising his stick, Boris noticed how many bows and instruments were trembling and smiled reassuringly.

'You are nervous, don't be, forget the microphones, we are making music. Eef we make few mistakes it doesn't matter.'

'No-one will notice anyway,' muttered Old Henry who loathed contemporary music.

How lovely to have Boris back, after Abby's relentless exactitude, thought the RSO fondly. Boris always kept them on their toes; they never knew what he would do next.

Unfortunately this time Boris didn't know either. He had totally underestimated the terrifying complexities of a work that suddenly seemed to have been written long ago by someone else. The first tutti was completely haywire, followed by two bars of silence, when the orchestra didn't come in at all, except for a great tummy-rumble from Candy who'd been too nervous to have any breakfast, and who went bright scarlet, which sent all the rank-and-file viola players into fits of giggles.

This was followed by a dreadful crunch when Boris by mistake cued the horns into head-on collision with the trombones totally drowning a flute duet.

'I don't know what happened then,' said Juno in a flustered voice, 'I looked up at Boris.'

'That was your first mistake,' said Peter Plumpton grimly.

Serena glared down at the black tangle of notes like a front on the weather map, and picked up the telephone.

'Let's start again.'

But it was no better. Boris didn't know when to bring anyone in, seemed unaware of colour, dynamics or tempo and was constantly behind the beat.

As his gestures grew wilder and more panicky, the level metres in the control-room kept bouncing off the top, leaving nothing in reserve for any big crescendo coming up.

Without Abby to hold it together or, at least, Julian to bring in other section leaders with great nods, the piece collapsed. Useless take followed utterly useless take.

'Despite what anyone says,' murmured Simon Painshaw to Ninion, 'there is a difference between intended and unintended cacophony.'

The telephone rang constantly.

'Serena's trying to make a date with you, Boris,' shouted Dixie, 'very soft beds in the Old Bell.'

Boris growled back in Russian and retreated to the Old Bell for succour. He was very drunk when he returned after the break, but because the RSO had been taught the *Requiem* painstakingly by Abby, they struggled on to the end of 'Dies Irae'.

'Why isn't Abby conducting this?' grumbled Viking. 'At this rate, we'll be here till Boxing Day.'

Glumly the musicians watched the recording engineer dart in and shift a microphone towards Bill Thackery for the solo with which Julian had reduced everyone to tears at the première. It had been much too difficult for Lionel, and should have completely defeated Bill Thackery. But smilingly aware of opportunity knocking, he ploughed on, sublimely unaware that he sounded as though he was chainsawing through his grandmother's wardrobe with Granny shrieking inside. Boris, however, was too drunk to notice.

* * *

In the lunch-hour, Francis the Good Loser, who had moved up to co-leader for the day and who had the sweetest nature in the orchestra, for once lost his temper.

'How dare that tone-deaf nerd butcher such a beautiful solo?' he stormed to Eldred, who cautiously agreed that Bill could have done with a drop of oil.

Alas the 'tone-deaf nerd' overheard them, retreated to the leader's room in high dudgeon, and had to be coaxed out by Miles and Hilary. 'Take no notice, Bill.'

'Don't listen to two such disgusting slobs.'

'They've upset Bill, the nicest man in the orchestra,' said Hilary as she flounced back to her seat.

'And the worst bloody player,' said Randy.

Serena was going up the wall, too. She had spent the lunch-hour in despair and on her mobile. She had a hundred other projects to look after and a small daughter, whom she'd been hoping to take to *Toad of Toad Hall* on Wednesday. Serena was ambitious. Apart from the cost of paying the musicians for extra sessions, she couldn't afford to make a lousy record. They'd be lucky if they got five minutes in the can today.

Boris, drinking brandy out of a paper cup, was now slumped on one of the sleep-inducing squashy leather sofas at the back of the control-room. Damp patches met across the back of his dark red shirt. He was Lear on the blasted heath being 'pussy-vipped' by the elements.

'I think because of Rachel's death I block out *Requiem*.'

'Nonsense,' said Serena crossly, 'you haven't bothered to learn it. Now get back and finish this session.'

Miles was shuddering with disapproval. Knickers was very, very down. It would totally knock his budget on the head if he had to call in all those extras for additional sessions. How would they ever again be able to afford exciting projects like *Fidelio* and Mahler's *Symphony of a Thousand* to fire the public's imagination.

*   *   *

Half an hour from the end of the afternoon, the RSO limped to the end of the 'Benedictus', and the section leaders crowded wearily into the control-room to listen to the play-back. Eldred, already suicidal at the prospect of a wifeless Christmas, was white and shaking because he hated rows. Dimitri, Simon and Peter Plumpton sat listening with heads bowed because they hated bad playing. Dixie and Carmine just hated each other. Jerry the Joker looked at Serena's legs. Davie Buckle and Barry the Bass who had played jazz all night were asleep.

El Creepo edged along the squashy sofa, so his right-hand fingers folded round his upper arm could rub against the more exciting squashiness of Mary's pretty right breast. A totally oblivious Mary was worrying what food shops would still be open, and if she sold her pearls would she get enough to pay the telephone bill and buy a tricycle for Justin for Christmas. Bill Thackery, radiating decency and solidarity, had quite recovered from his mini-tantrum. Blissful to be centre stage for once, he thought nothing had ever sounded more lovely than his dreadful solo.

'Bill's all right in the higher register where only bats can hear him,' muttered Viking to Tommy Stainforth, Principal Percussion.

Slumped against the parquet wall, reading a rave review in *Gramophone* of his Strauss concerto, Viking looked shattered, his blond mane lank and separating. He had to drive to Bristol to play Mozart's *Fourth Horn Concerto* that evening. Through the glass panel he could see Flora. Having boasted he would pick her off, he had been enraged to be pipped by Jack Rodway. Look at her now, flipping through Clare's copy of *Tatler*, yacking away to Cherub, Noriko and Candy, making them all laugh, always the focus of bloody attention.

Serena was making notes at her desk.

'I'll buy that if you will, Boris,' she said, more out of despair.

Boris, who was sobering up, shook his head. '"Benedictus" is too pretty, too charming.'

'Could have fooled me,' muttered Dixie.

'Those crochets are too long,' agreed Dimitri. 'The melody seduce me.'

'I screw up this tape,' said Boris grandiosely, 'we vill do it again, have this von on me.'

'Well, step on it,' said Serena. 'We've got fifteen minutes to go before we're into overtime.'

Serena was passionately relieved when George stalked in just back from Manchester. Having been briefed by Miles, he immediately asked for a score. His face grew grimmer as once again Boris and the 'Benedictus' drew to its utterly biteless conclusion. Not a chord or a scale was together.

'Good thing this glass is bulletproof,' said Serena bleakly, 'We should have stuck with L'Appassionata.'

'Don't tell her, she'll be even more impossible.'

'At this rate, we'll go into a second week. If he doesn't get his act together tomorrow, we'll have to reschedule or pull the whole thing.'

For a second they gazed at each other; they had planned a leisurely dinner leading to other things.

George sighed. 'I'll take him home and force-feed him the score.' He put a rough hand on hers, 'There'll be oother occasions.'

'Not if the RSO go on playing like this. See you all tomorrow at nine forty-five,' she called over the talk-back.

Like prisoners in the dungeons of *Fidelio* the musicians shambled out, frustrated, tired and blaming Boris.

'Poor Boris,' protested Noriko. 'He is very sad to be dragged away from *King Rear*.'

'Viking's King Rear', said Nellie wistfully, 'always forcing that gorgeous ass into the tightest jeans.'

A swaying Boris was hijacked on the way out. After initial pleasantries, George asked him where he was staying.

'Voodbine Cottage, Abby and Flora invite me.'

'Uh-uh,' George grabbed Boris's arm, 'you're cooming home with me. You're going to sober oop, and spend the night with the score instead of one of those two scroobers.'

Unfortunately he hadn't seen Flora who was lurking in the shadows. She was in total despair, as she remembered the excitement with which they had all worked to finish the *Requiem* in the summer.

'I'm not a scrubber,' she said furiously. 'If you hadn't junked Abby, none of this would have happened,' and fled into the icy night.

Having been forced to drink four Alka-Seltzers before being put straight to bed, Boris slept for nine hours. George woke him at five, giving him black coffee and four hours on the *Requiem*.

By this time Boris was ready for a huge fry-up, including fried bread spread with Oxford Marmalade.

'Public-school habit I peek up from Flora.'

'My cross,' said George bleakly.

'Is excellent girl,' protested Boris.

'You've been seduced by a not particularly pretty face,' snapped George.

'Is Cordelia in *Lear*, *"so young, my lord, and true"*. My God – ' Boris clapped his hand to his forehead in horror – 'vere is my *Lear* manuscript, three month's vork, I am ruined.'

'Sit down.' George poured Boris another cup of coffee. 'I put it in the office safe.'

Boris slumped back in his chair.

'You are horrible, but very good guy. You save vork of art.'

*   *   *

George made sure Boris arrived at the studios in good time. They were greeted by a smirking shifty-eyed Carmine. Cathie had flu, and couldn't play 'Rachel's Lament' in the 'Libera Me'. Knickers was tearing the remains of his red hair out. Where would he find a cor anglais player in Christmas week at five minutes' notice?

'Cathie could have bloody rung.'

Miss Parrott leapt to Cathie's defence.

'That bug going round knocks you for six.'

'So does that bugger,' said an anguished Blue, who hadn't slept for two nights with excitement at the prospect of seeing Cathie and who had turned up in his best blue shirt. 'I know he's blacked Cathie's eye or worse. I'm going round there.'

'Don't,' hissed Viking, 'the bastard will notice you're missing. Lindy Cardew has just returned brown as a berry from the Seychelles, courtesy no doubt of George Hungerford. On Friday she and the planning officer are off again to Gstaad. Carmine doesn't want Cathie around cramping his style.'

Nicholas, Miles, George, Serena and Boris were in a despairing huddle around the rostrum

'We'll have to record the "Libera Me" at a later date,' said Boris.

'The only solution,' said Flora strolling up to them, 'is for Viking to play the solo.'

'The hell I will,' Viking didn't look up from *Classical Music*, 'Boris didn't want me in the first place.'

'That is untrue,' said Boris outraged, 'I offer it to heem once.'

'Oh, for Christ's sake, bury your pride, both of you,' said Flora. 'You bloody well owe it to us, Boris, for wasting all our times yesterday.'

'Ahem,' George cleared his throat, 'I would like to remind you,' he told Flora tartly, 'that until otherwise stated I am nominally in charge of this orchestra.'

'Well, tell them not to be so pigheaded.'

'I don't 'ave French 'orn version,' said Boris sullenly.

'I do,' said Flora, 'I kept it in my locker. One never knows when these things might come in useless, as you're obviously all opposed to the idea.'

'Go and get it,' said George.

'It's only got a bass accompaniment,' said Serena, as they all pored over the Sellotaped-together page. 'You and Barry can practise it in the lunch-hour, Viking.'

'I'm busy,' said Viking haughtily, 'I'll sight-read it.'

Flora's pleasure in having secured him the solo evaporated at his lack of enthusiasm. Battling with an icy wind in the High Street on her way to send flowers to Cathie Jones, she felt even worse. A BMW screamed to a halt and Viking leapt out. He had put on a tie and had brushed his hair. For a blissful moment, Flora thought he was stopping to thank her; instead he belted into the florists, bought every freesia in the place and belted out again.

Flora started to cry. She ached all over. No-one ever said, 'Well done, violas'. She was fed up and lonely. She hated George for calling her a scrubber and Viking for bombarding beauties with freesias. Even worse was the thought of Christmas, with all its jollity and loving kindness. She would have to go home to warring parents and a place that reminded her only of Rannaldini.

The rest of the RSO had a much better day. Boris was back on form conducting with his old fire and inspiration. They worked fast polishing off the 'Agnus Dei', the 'Lux Aeterna' and a vastly improved 'Benedictus'.

It was time for 'Rachel's Lament'.

'Aren't you nervous?' said Cherub admiringly.

Viking shook his head. He had the big-match temperament, that needed adrenalin pumping through his veins to make him perform at his best. Throwing his paper cup of coffee at the waste-paper basket and missing, he picked up his horn. He had removed his tie and jacket. His casket of earth glinted in the V of his dark blue shirt which had escaped from his jeans. Two days in an airless, ill-lit studio had taken their toll. The pale skin fell away from his high cheek-bones, the lines were deeply etched round the bruised mouth, the slitty eyes had disappeared into black shadows.

Too much sex at lunch-time, thought Flora sourly.

I must sign him up, sighed Serena. He'd just have to stand there and smoulder.

Cathie's version of 'Rachel's Lament' had been poignant, haunting, coming from the depth of her sadness, the last cry of the dying swan. Viking curdled the blood, the rising fourths and fifths singing out, probing, incessant, insistent, almost unbearably raw and primitive. One great player saluting the departure of another.

Miles, Nicholas, George, Miss Priddock holding John Drummond, even Harry Hopcraft, the financial director, crowded into the control-room to listen. All sat spellbound. Only Viking and Julian had that ability at five o'clock on a mean, grey afternoon to bring tears spurting out of the weariest eyes.

Boris, whose eyes were completely misted over, pointed vaguely in Carmine's direction to bring in the fanfare of trumpets sounding for Rachel on the other side, before the final majestic tutti.

The instant the red light went out, everyone burst out cheering. Boris had pinched Bill's red-spotted handkerchief to wipe his eyes and was just about to congratulate Viking when the telephone rang. Snatching it up, Boris listened for a second.

'You tell him. Vy do I always do your dirty vurk?' he slammed down the receiver and took a deep breath.

'Viking, that was fantastic, absolutely vonderful, perfect, out of these vorld, but we have technical fault. Could you possibly do exactly the same thing again?'

The orchestra winced collectively, waiting for the explosion.

'I know women just like that,' drawled Viking.

Everyone in the studio and the control-room collapsed in relieved and helpless laughter. And Viking did it again - even better.

The next moment he and Boris were hugging each other.

'Let's go and get vasted.'

FORTY-ONE

After getting plastered with Boris, Viking was woken at noon by his cleaner, Mrs Diggory, banging noisily against the skirting-boards as she hoovered outside his room. She was due to leave at one o'clock. She hadn't been paid for three weeks, and was more hopeful of a Christmas bonus if she woke up Viking, who, when he was in funds, was the most generous of the Celtic Mafia. Picking his way through piles of dropped clothes, dog bowls and curry trays, carrying his head gingerly downstairs as if he were trying not to spill it, Viking begged Mrs Diggory to make him a cup of coffee.

'I can't do the bedrooms, they're all occupied,' she sniffed.

'You can do mine,' said Viking, 'and change the sheets, please.'

'Expecting company?' Mrs Diggory had to slant the kettle to fill it above the mountain of soaking plates and mugs.

'Probably,' Viking peered gloomily at his reflection in the dingy hall mirror. His hair was so long on top, he'd soon have a middle parting like Nugent.

As he let Nugent out to see off any lurking duck, he

noticed the shadow of Woodbine Cottage, across the lake through the bare trees above a fading red carpet of beech leaves.

Picking up the telephone, he called Giuseppe, Parker and Parker's most sought-after hairdresser.

'Of course, I'll fit you in, Viking love, but why must you always call at the last minute?'

'Going to get your hair done?' said Mrs Diggory cosily, as she put three spoonfuls of sugar into night-black coffee.

'I don't have my hair done, I have it cot,' said Viking haughtily, then, picking up Mrs Diggory's copy of the *Sun*, and turning to the back page, exclaimed, 'Glory Hallelujah!'

Seizing Mrs Diggory, he waltzed her round the kitchen.

'Flora's Pride won by three lengths at 40-1, I've just won two hundred quid.'

'Most of that owed to me.'

'Indeed it is.' Viking retrieved a betting-slip before chucking his jeans into the washing-machine, and gave it to Mrs Diggory.

'Hand it in to Ladbrokes in the High Street and keep the change for a Christmas bonus.'

'You sure?' squawked Mrs Diggory in delight.

'Otterly.'

'You won't recognize your room when you get back.'

'Leave the heating on, lock it, and leave the key in there – ' Viking tapped the willow-pattern teapot on the dresser – 'to stop the other basstards using it.'

'Don't get too whistled, and forget where I've left it.'

Viking glanced at his watch, and reached for the last wine bottle in the rack.

'We've got time for a quick glass, then I mosst dash.'

'You better wrap up warm, snow's forecast.'

Searching for her cheque book in the chaos of the

drawing-room, Flora discovered an Advent calendar Cherub had given Abby for Christmas, and in an orgy of misery wolfed all the chocolates behind the doors.

Still feeling sick, she wandered listlessly through Parker's, mostly because it was the only warm place in the High Street. In the record department, she noticed how little music had been written for the viola. She must start singing again. What the hell could she buy her parents? A pair of boxing gloves? On her salary she could hardly afford the wrapping paper.

'*In the Bleak Midwinter,*' sang Hermione over the loudspeaker.

Flora had no difficulty recognizing the orchestra; she'd know that razor-sharp precision anywhere. Looking up, she saw a Rannaldini poster glaring down at her, an inch of white cuff showing off the only hands that had ever really given her pleasure, she had been cold, ever since his arms had left her.

Oh bloody hell, thought Flora, I'm not putting up with any more frozen nights at Woodbine Cottage.

Running downstairs to the Household Emporium, she was just paying for a very expensive electric blanket, when the cheque was removed from her hands and torn into tiny pieces.

Whipping round, Flora found herself looking at dark gold stubble, surrounding the widest, wickedest smile.

'You're not going to need that tonight, darling.'

'I've just made out the bill,' squawked the shop assistant, furious to be robbed of the tiny commission, 'and dogs are not allowed in here.'

But Flora was gazing up into Viking's face, the colour staining her pale cheeks. Suddenly they were interrupted by an old lady tapping on Viking's shoulders.

'That was a lovely concert, Victor, we enjoyed it so much.'

'Thanks, darling,' Viking had to bend right down to kiss her wrinkled cheek. 'Happy Christmas, see you in the spring. And I'll see you later,' he added to Flora, then he and Nugent were gone, haring off to catch the lift for Giuseppe and the hairdressing salon.

'Such a nice young man,' quavered the old lady to Flora and the assistant, who clearly didn't think so at all.

'He played at the centre yesterday: Scott Joplin, "Bye, Bye Blackbird", "We'll Meet Again" – got us all on our feet dancing, even Mrs Bilson and she's over ninety, and he bought a big box of chocolates and everyone a little bunch of flowers.'

'Viking played to you at lunch-time yesterday?' squeaked Flora.

The old lady nodded. 'He often plays to us, and at the hospital. Other people come from the orchestra, but Victor's our pin-up. I love his cheeky grin.'

'Oh, so do I,' said Flora. 'Thank you for telling me, and Happy Christmas. I'm really sorry,' she added to the assistant, 'but I'll spend the money somewhere else in the store. Can you possibly direct me to party dresses?'

Back at Woodbine Cottage, Marcus had finally got rid of his last pupil of the day.

Smothered in *Opium*, wearing the tightest bottle-green cashmere jersey, she had edged her stool up the keyboard, until Marcus was sitting on the window-sill.

Then, when he had showed her some fingering, she had put her other hand over his, imprisoning it and murmuring: 'My mother used to know your father. She said he was seriously wicked.'

'I'm just seriously boring,' said Marcus apologetically, turning his head so her kiss fell on his jawbone.

As she was leaving, she gave him a biography of Rachmaninov and a bottle of Moët.

'See you next term. I'm going to get a terrific suntan skiing.'

He hadn't the heart to tell her that her scent gave him asthma. Why hadn't he kissed her back? She'd been so pretty. What would it have mattered?

Yesterday he had given a Chopin and Liszt recital at an up-market girls' day-school, and afterwards signed two hundred autographs.

'You wouldn't like a job teaching music, Mr Black?' the headmistress had asked skittishly. 'I'm sure you'd cure our truancy problem overnight.'

Then she had given him a fee of seventy-five pounds.

There was no way he could pay the rent or for the Steinway, and buy presents for Abby and Flora. The cottage bills were horrific; Flora left lights and fires on all the time, and neither she nor Abby thought anything of ringing long distance for hours.

Marcus's studio was freezing, but except when he had pupils, he tried to put on four jerseys instead of the heating. As if to save him electricity, the falling snow was lighting the room, thickening branch and twig, filling up the winter jasmine curling inside the lank skeins of traveller's joy. He put the biography of Rachmaninov in the bookshelf, above the rows of CDs, tapes and scores.

The most charitable way you could describe the studio inside was minimalist: as little clutter as possible to attract the dust mites that caused his asthma. There were no carpets on the bare boards. The only furniture was the Steinway, two piano-stools and the bed. On the walls, apart from the bookshelf, hung only the Munnings of Pylon Peggoty, his grandfather's grey, given to him by Rupert.

His asthma had been particularly bad since *The Messiah*. After spending the night with Monica and Edith, his homesickness had been so great that he had driven out to Penscombe, and from the top road had watched Rupert, who used to bobsleigh, hurtling down the fields on a toboggan. In front of him sat Xavier, squealing with joy. A pack of excited dogs followed them, the yelling and barking echoing round the white valley as everything sparkled in the sunshine beneath a delphinium-blue sky.

Then Rupert had taken Xav's hand, and led him and the toboggan back up the hill to help Taggie and Bianca, a dash of colour in a scarlet skiing suit, make a snowman on the lawn in front of the house. Marcus had slumped against the steering-wheel – 'I've failed him, I've failed him,' – and, in utter despair, had driven home.

Now he was going to fail Rupert again by selling the Munnings. He could imagine the letter arriving from Sotheby's. *'We've just got in a painting that might interest you,'* and his father's lip curling when he saw the polaroid.

But the only thing in the pipeline was a concert at Ilkley which would cost him as much in petrol as the fee. Oh God, when would he get a break? He was trying to learn one of Liszt's *Mephisto Waltzes*, but as he sat down at the piano, his fingers were too stiff and frozen to master the diabolical twists and turns, which reminded him of Rannaldini. Helen was pressuring him to join them both for Christmas. Marcus would rather stay in bed without food or heating.

It was half a minute before he realized the telephone was ringing; he only just got there.

'This is Miles Brian-Knowles,' said a prim, fastidious voice.

'Sorry, I was miles away,' stammered Marcus, which wasn't a good start. Miles probably needed a babysitter.

Instead he said the RSO had been badly let down by Benny Basanovich.

'Says he's got flu, diplomatic, I imagine. It's a short piece, only six minutes and quite honestly there's so much din going on, the odd wrong note won't matter. It's Sonny Parker's *Interruption Suite*. We're recording it live. I wondered if you'd be interested?'

'I'll do it,' Marcus was desperate to accept before Miles

changed his mind, or remembered Marcus had once been so rude to Peggy Parker.

'Is a thousand pounds enough?'

'More than.' In passionate relief, Marcus's head dropped onto the top of the piano. 'You've saved my life.'

'I'm afraid there's no time for an orchestral rehearsal, but if you make your way over to the hall, I can give you the score and a practice room.'

'Oh thank you, thank you, Father Christmas has arrived a week early.'

Miles was touched.

'It's a pleasure. I wish all transactions were as easy.'

In her pigeon hole that evening, Flora found a bunch of white roses.

Darling Flora, said the accompanying note. *Just apologizing in advance for my appalling behaviour later on this evening, Love Viking.*

Flora gave a whoop of ecstasy. Dancing down the passage singing *Boléro,* she went slap into George Hungerford.

'Why the bloody hell don't you look where you're going?'

'Dum de-de-de. De-de, de-de, de-de dum, de-de-de,' sang Flora, weaving round him into the women's changing-room, where, to Clare, Candy, Nellie, Mary, Hilary and Juno's irritation, she fought for once just as fiercely, as they did, for a space in front of the communal mirror.

'You don't normally wear make-up,' said Juno accusingly.

'You look really, really pretty,' said Clare in amazement.

Flora broke open the cellophane with her teeth and handed her new eye-liner to Nellie.

'Can you paint it on – my hands are shaking too much.'

'Why are you suddenly so nervous?' demanded Hilary.

'Because my mate, Marcus, is making his début.'

'That is one hell of a sassy dress,' said Candy in wonder, as Flora slithered into a knee-length satin shift, only held up by two ribbon straps.

'You can't wear that, or those,' spluttered Hilary, as Flora tucked her hair into a black velvet toggle and slotted in two of Viking's white roses.

'*Mais, bien sûr,*' Flora wrapped a black silky mantilla round her shoulders, 'particularly as we're playing *Boléro.*' And clacking her fingers like castanets, she danced out into the passage.

'What *has* got into her?' asked a shocked Juno.

Sonny's *Interruption*, a grisly one-note job for orchestra, piano, burglar-alarm, fax, telephone bleeper, railway train, back-firing car, pneumatic drill, coughing, snoring, rustling and lavatory chain, was to be recorded after the interval and before *Boléro* and the singing of carols. Sonny had diverted most of the brass section to the Ladies' lavatory to provide a flushing chorus. Cherub and the percussion section had gone beserk in rehearsal, imitating the various sounds.

Having plink-plonked his way through the piano part several times in his dressing-room, Marcus decided he couldn't be nervous about something quite so silly – particularly when Sonny strutted in to give last-minute advice, wearing a collarless scarlet tunic, white silk trousers, red satin slippers and a white-and-red scarf round his pony-tail.

'Hallo, Marcus Black,' he said in his reedy voice. 'You must not be daunted by the complexities. Mozart appeared complex, too. Like my work, the beauty, richness and depth bewildered his first listeners.'

He then suggested Marcus ran through the solo, paddling away with suggested fingering, and shoving his bony pelvis so hard into Marcus's back, Marcus nearly elbowed him in the groin.

Fortunately Flora barged in to wish Marcus luck.

Sonny was livid.

'I told Miles – *no* interruptions.'

'But the work is all about interruptions. Shall I go out, and come in and interrupt again to get you both in the mood?'

Marcus laughed. Sonny flounced off.

'No-one looks prettier in tails than you do,' said Flora in delight.

'Or in black than you.'

There was a sparkle in her eyes that Marcus hadn't seen for years.

As he tugged the maidenhair fern from behind a white carnation, graciously presented to him by Peggy Parker, he added: 'Someone will have to turn the pages for me.'

'I shall be hidden among the violas, thank God, and if the audience pelts us with tomatoes I hope they put basil on them.'

As Sonny had written in no trombone parts, Dixie volunteered for the job as page-turner, but, having been boozing all day, he couldn't take it seriously.

'Exciting having off-stage cow-bells,' murmured Marcus, as they hovered in the wings.

'Particularly when it's conducted by an on-stage cow,' said Dixie, as Sonny minced out of the conductor's room and swept him and Marcus onto an exceedingly crowded platform.

There were overhead mikes for Marcus and each section, and bigger mikes dotted around the auditorium for general ambience. Sonny gave a little fluting speech, reminding the audience they were taking part in an experience as creatively significant as the first performance of Beethoven's *Ninth Symphony* or Schoenberg's *Gurrelieder*.

'Remember your clap or cough will be recorded for posterity, so make it loud, and wait for the red light.'

Dixie proceeded to belch loudly into Marcus's microphone.

'That's the spirit,' cried Sonny, who loved big butch Glaswegians, 'but save it for the red light.'

The audience looked frightfully excited, delighted to have something as beautiful as Marcus to gaze at if the music became too demanding.

On came the red light, up started the atrocious din. Dixie couldn't stop laughing particularly when the lavatory chains wouldn't pull in time, and the audience, having been exhorted by Sonny to cough as much as possible, found they couldn't stop. Viking and Barry the Bass rang each other up on their mobiles and chatted throughout.

Marcus was thumping away, trying to be heard over the uproar, when Little Cherub, racing back from xylophone to cow-bells, took a flying leap and fell flat on his face. Dixie was in such hysterics, he knocked Marcus's score onto the floor, and picking it up, shoved it back upside-down by mistake.

Flora had also chosen that moment to wriggle out of her black mantilla. Viking was not the only musician to be distracted by the beauty of her shoulders. Dixie was so mesmerized, there was no way Marcus could attract his attention to put his music the right way up. The only answer was to ad lib, plink-plonking away to the end. Immediately the audience leapt to their feet applauding wildly so that their clap could be recorded for posterity.

'Only getting up to relieve their piles,' said Dixie scornfully.

But Marcus had slunk off the stage, petrified the wrath of Parker was going to descend on him for playing the wrong ending. Instead, after taking three bows, an ecstatic Sonny rushed into Marcus's dressing-room, saying his work had never been so movingly interpreted.

'I wept. I could not understand how I could write such beautiful music. Mumsy, Mumsy,' cried Sonny, as Peggy swept in in a mauve satin marquee, 'I am going to write a concerto for Marcus Black.'

Marcus cringed behind the upright piano.

But Peggy was prepared to let bygones be byge-owns, and presented Marcus with a large Christmas hamper.

'You've done my Sonny proud, we look forward to receiving you at Rutminster Towers.'

Cherub also received a smaller hamper for being wounded in action, and the brass section were each given a bottle of champagne for pulling the chain so meaningfully.

Gilbert and Gwynneth were also in raptures. They had never seen a Rutminster audience enjoy themselves so much. At last music was being brought to the people. They made a point of seeking Marcus out and commending his sensitive playing.

'We're staying in the Close with Canon Airlie,' whispered Gwynneth, 'please drop in for carols and wassail later.'

'You're terribly kind,' Marcus ducked to avoid a flying earring.

'We're going to hear a good deal more of Black,' said Gilbert as he drifted out.

That boy's done well, thought George, he made a diabolical piece of music sound almost good.

'Could I have a word?' he asked Marcus.

Ravel had once confessed sadly that *Boléro* was his only masterpiece and it contained no music. But after Sonny's self-indulgent, mindless, ear-murdering junk, *Boléro* sounded glorious. Tommy Stainforth, Principal Percussion, joined later by Cherub, his nose bleed staining his white shirt like a boy soldier in battle, kept up the relentless hypnotic beat on their silver snare-drums, while sections and soloists took it in turns to snake languorously in and out of the one disturbingly beautiful tune.

'The viola player's problem in *Boléro* is keeping awake,' Candy had warned Flora.

But instead, as the entire string section put down their bows and plucked their instruments like flamenco guitars, the sound made Flora burst with pride. She suddenly felt part of the great heartbeat of the orchestra as the music slowly swelled to a stupendous climax with the last clashing discord from the brass.

'That's definitely coitus non-interruptus,' shouted Clare over the delirious torrent of applause. 'I wish sex was as good as that.'

It will be with Viking, thought Flora, but when she glanced round, the First Horn's chair was empty.

Faint with disappointment, suddenly exhausted, Flora could hardly lift her bow during the carols; and, as the last notes of 'Adeste Fideles' died away and the audience, now in party mood, called for encore, Viking was still missing.

'Buggered off on some date,' sighed Candy.

Meanwhile, outside the conductor's room, Miles was having a row with Abby, Julian and a large black-and-white pantomime cow.

'We rehearsed "The Shepherd's Farewell" as an encore,' Miles was saying angrily.

'The audience expect Rodney's cow,' said Abby firmly. 'She's a Christmas fixture.'

The cow nodded in agreement and rubbed its furry head against Abby's arm.

'You can't lower the tone,' ordered Miles, 'not with the Arts Council present.'

'Bugger the Arts Council,' said the back of the cow, doing a high kick. The front of the cow let out a high-pitched giggle, leaving no doubt as to its identity.

'Shut up,' hissed Miles glancing round in terror.

'Gilbert and Gwynneth were backstage earlier. If you don't play "The Shepherd's Farewell", Abby, heads will roll.'

The shouts of encore and the stamp of feet were growing in volume.

'Come on, you guys,' said Abby defiantly, waltzing off towards the stage.

'Miserable old bugger,' said the back legs, as the cow lumbered after her.

'I'll have you know, I'm still here,' said Miles furiously.

Such screams of joy greeted the arrival of the cow on stage, that it was a few minutes before Abby could make herself heard.

'Sir Rodney is really disappointed not to be here to wish you all a merry Christmas – ' the audience gave a great cheer – 'but he's a lot better, right? And he hopes to be back on the rostrum some time next year.'

'Bravo,' shouted everyone.

'Meanwhile, he's sent you a very special soloist.'

The cow did a soft-shoe shuffle to more deafening cheers.

'Good evening, Mrs Cow,' continued Abby, 'are you going to play us a tune?'

Slowly the cow nodded, batting her long black eyelashes.

'What about some Mozart or perhaps some Beethoven?'

The cow shook her head.

'Or some Schoenberg.'

For a second the front of the cow deliberated, wondering whether to drop the back legs in it, then slowly she shook her head again.

'I know,' said Abby over the howls of laughter, 'can you play us some Tchaikovsky?'

The cow nodded frantically, and next moment the back half launched into the beautiful French horn solo from the second movement of the *Fifth Symphony* leaving absolutely no doubt as to his identity either, and the audience went beserk.

But when Flora finally escaped from the platform, she couldn't find Viking anywhere. Aching all over but most of all in her heart, she trailed off to congratulate Marcus.

She found him in a daze; the last well-wisher had only just left.

'The good news is,' he told her, 'that George Hungerford has decided to junk Benny and book me for Rachmaninov's *Third Piano Concerto* at the end of February.'

As Flora whooped and hugged him, an inner voice chided her that both Abby and Marcus were getting on with their careers and she was getting nowhere, not even to first base with Viking. Bitterly ashamed of being mean spirited, she was doing a war dance round Marcus, when he continued: 'And the bad news is that Sonny is a serious bum-bandit and wants me to have dinner with him.'

'Omigod, you'll never cope with Peggy as a mother-in-law. Let's rush off and have an Indian,' said Flora.

Viking had obviously been playing games, she thought despairingly.

FORTY-TWO

Flora's fears were confirmed as she and Marcus ran towards the car-park, and rounding a corner, stumbled on Viking and Serena Westwood in a huddle.

Seeing Flora, Mr Nugent bounded forward joyfully. Viking had his back to her, but, catching sight of her red hair reflected in the window, he reached behind him and grabbed her hand.

'Serena, you haven't met Flora, she's a dote.'

'A dote?' Serena looked puzzled and not very pleased.

Sliding his arm round Flora's shoulders, Viking drew her against his long hard body. His hair was still wet from the shower – he had shaved off this morning's stubble.

'A little dote,' he added caressingly. 'Dotey's the adjective, it's an Irish word,' he curled a warm palm round Flora's neck, 'means that everyone dotes on her.'

'How nice for Flora,' said Serena crisply. She'd heard differently from others. 'Hallo, Marcus,' she added with considerably more warmth. 'You played beautifully.'

'And Hatchet Hungerford's just booked him to do Rach *Three* in Feb,' beamed Flora. It was incredible that Viking's hand on her neck could cure all her aches and tiredness in a second. 'So we must celebrate.'

'We certainly mosst, that's tremendous,' Viking

clapped Marcus on the shoulder. Then, turning to Serena, added, 'Have a good Christmas, darling, let me know what you decide.'

As he led Flora and Marcus towards the car-park, he explained.

'The playback of the *Requiem* was *so* dire, Serena and George have decided to reschedule it with L'Appassionata conducting.'

'Abby'll be knocked out,' said Marcus in delight.

'And with Julian back as leader so he can play the big violin solo.'

'Bill Thackery will shoot himself,' said Flora.

'Save everyone else doing the job.'

Outside, six inches of snow had blanketed everything: cars, houses, railings, lamp-posts, each blade of grass. To this, a heavy hoar frost had added a *diamanté* sparkle, so the great horse-chestnuts in the park seemed like glittering white clouds beneath a clear starry sky. Cyril's bird-table had become a wedding-cake awaiting decoration and across the town, the cathedral gleamed like a vast lurking iceberg.

Nugent went beserk, tunnelling his snapping snout through the snow, leaping in ecstasy, emerging with a white-powdered wig on his furry black head. Having sent him hurtling across the park after a snowball, Viking scooped up more snow, hardened it into another ball and closed Flora's hands round it.

'Josst feel it melting like my heart,' he whispered, then turning to Marcus, said, 'Sorry, mate, I can't control myself any longer.'

Looking up, Flora was amazed to see the amused tenderness softening his thin face and narrowed eyes. His hair gleamed as gold as Mars in the moonlight. As he took her hot flushed face in his long Jack Frost fingers, she could smell the faint apple blossom of Giuseppe's shampoo, taste toothpaste and feel the snowball clutched in her hands melting like her entrails.

Then he kissed her, first very slowly, his tongue flickering over hers, then harder and harder, a mixture of deliberation and such passion that Flora, arching against him, felt like a bonfire bursting into sudden spontaneous flame in the middle of the Antarctic.

Not having the superior breath control of a brass player, she had to pull away first but kept her eyes shut.

'Is it really you?'

'Really.'

'Oh Viking.'

'I am otterly, otterly hooked,' he murmured into her hair.

Flora jumped as, like a rug suddenly laid over her knees, she felt Nugent leaning against her, gazing up with shining eyes, his tail sweeping out a black fan on the white path.

'I'm enjoying watching *Gone with the Wind*,' called out Marcus through blue lips, 'but I'm about to freeze to death.'

'Oh Jesus, I'm sorry,' said Viking.

As his BMW slid round the Close, icicles were glittering from the red roofs of the Queen Anne houses, magnolias and ceanothus in the front gardens buckled under their burdens of snow.

'God knows how they got a licence for this place,' said Viking, as he pulled up beside a club called Close Encounters which was pounding out reggae music. 'Someone must have greased Planning Officer Cardew's palm again.'

Inside, through the gloom, the Celtic Mafia, Cherub, Noriko, Clare, Candy and Nellie could be seen getting plastered, drinking half-pints of wine out of little jugs, coughing in unison and collapsing in laughter at their own jokes.

Once Viking and Marcus had sat down beside them, Dixie started acting up; he had taken a great shine to Marcus, and had them all in stitches offering to turn the pages of his menu for him, then handing it to him upside-down.

'*He's Sonny's Valentine, sweet Sonny's Valentine,*' sang Randy.

Everyone howled again.

'We have got some catching up to do,' sighed Viking, looking sympathetically at Marcus.

Returning from the Ladies, Flora took a slug of wine and nearly spat it out.

'Ugh, it's corked.'

'That's because you've just cleaned your te-heeth,' said Clare slyly. 'Even Krug tastes vile after Colgate.'

'We ought to invent a drink mixing them,' said Marcus, 'and call it Buck Teeth.'

'And Gwynneth could do the ads,' said Flora.

So everyone stuck out their teeth like Gwynneth and giggled hysterically.

'To stop arguments, I've ordered lasagne for everyone,' said Blue.

When the band took a break, the RSO, to the other diners' amazement, took over. Randy seized a trumpet, Nellie and Noriko picked up guitars, Cherub sat down at the drums, Marcus was persuaded to play the piano, as they swung into *Boléro*.

Blue didn't want to dance, so Dixie got up with Candy and Clare, Viking and Flora followed them.

Viking was a wonderful dancer, he had the endless legs, and narrow rubber hips that slide into any rhythm.

'*Dum, de-de, dum, de-de, de-de, de-de, dum de-de-dum,*' sang Flora, writhing like a charmed snake in front of him, her hips occasionally grazing his body, her black skirt and red hair flying.

'Marvellous beat to fock to,' Viking drew her against him, rotating his pelvis against hers.

'OK, Marcus?' gasped Flora as she emerged from his embrace two minutes later with buckling knees.

What would she have done if I'd said I wasn't, wondered Marcus, as he idly picked out the first subject of Rachmaninov's *Third Piano Concerto* – moody, mysterious, impossibly difficult music. He wished he could go home and look at the score, which he had only two months to learn. It would be like taming a dragon.

He'd prayed for a break like this for so long, but looking across at Viking and Flora, he felt hollow with loneliness and would have given every note of the concerto to be able to wipe Abby out with the same white-hot passion. Marcus sighed. Viking had a terrible reputation. He did hope Flora wouldn't be hurt again, and Abby was going to be insane with jealousy when she found out. What an awful lot of pieces to pick up.

The band and the lasagne arrived at the same time. Neither Viking nor Flora wanted theirs, so Nugent ate both.

'It's such years since anyone put me off my food,' said Flora happily.

Turning towards her on the bench-seat, blocking out the others' view with his broad back, Viking removed her mantilla from her left shoulder, examining a row of long scratches.

'Jack Rodway do that?'

'No Scriabin – he thinks he's a witch's cat, and takes flying leaps onto my bare shoulders.'

'Locky Scriabin,' Viking kissed the longest scratch. 'Why'd d'you go to bed with Jack?'

'I needed a practice fence.'

'I was so opset.'

'You're so glamorous,' Flora ran a finger along his jutting lower lip. 'One can't imagine you upset about anything except playing badly or not uniting Ireland.'

'I've dreamt for a long time of being united with Flora.' As insistent as the *Boléro* beat, his hand was stroking the inside of her arm, her jawline, her earlobes.

Then she told him about Carmine trying to rape her. 'Jack was the escape route, he had a green Exit sign on his forehead, and a pushbar at his waist.'

Viking laughed. Only by his hand tightening on her shoulder did he show his fury.

'The basstard,' he said slowly, 'and he keeps his wife in a veal crate. Cathie didn't have flu, he broke her jaw.'

'Omigod, is that why Blue's so down? They ought to elope, she's so good, she could easily support herself.'

'Carmine's ripped away every thread of her self-esteem.'

The waiters were back with menus offering puddings.

Viking shook his head. 'I'm having a pause.'

'You're going through the male menu-pause,' said Flora, falling about at her own joke.

'I'm sorry,' Viking pulled her to her feet, 'I have to fock you.'

Outside it had snowed and frozen again.

'D'you think I'm too dronk to drive?'

'Frankly yes,' said Flora swinging round a lamp-post. 'If you even looked at a Breathalyser it would play "The Drinking Song."'

'Why don't we try one of these bikes?'

Hearing a loud bang outside, the others, who'd started trashing the place, rushed out swinging lavatory chains, to find Nugent barking, Flora giggling in the snow, Viking sitting beside her rubbing her laddered knees and an ancient blue bike on its side with its wheels going round and round.

After that everyone had a go on it, drink insulating them against the cold, their shouts of laughter sending windows shooting up all round the Close. Any grizzled head foolish enough to emerge was pelted with snow-balls. Cherub was so drunk he kept climbing into the engine of Dixie's car. Clare kept patting a black litter-bin, mistaking it for Mr Nugent. As Flora had another go, the seat shot upwards, nearly depositing her on the ground.

'It's a Fanny cycle,' she shrieked, narrowly avoiding a pillar-box. 'Oh Gilbert, Gilbert, oh fa la, la, la.'

'Stop that noise,' said a ringing voice from above.

'Oh fuck off,' said Randy. 'It's my turn now, Flora.'

Vaguely Marcus remembered he had been invited to a wassail party in the Close.

Clambering on board, Randy set off guiding the bike with one hand, swinging a Close Encounter lavatory chain with the other. Shooting across the grass in the centre of the square, straight through a bed of sleeping wallflowers, he hit the fountain where Charles I had refreshed himself during the Civil War with an almighty bang.

The bicycle was a crumpled heap, the fountain in intensive care, the imprint of Randy's huge body lay etched in the snow, but remounting, the intrepid trumpeter shot off down the path, falling off again, so the bike carried on up a ramp, and disappeared through the door of some ecclesiastical building. This was followed by another loud bang to the accompaniment of police sirens.

'Quick,' Viking seized Flora's hand. 'They segregate the sexes in police cells.'

Very slowly Viking drove back down the middle of the road. Snow on top of hoar frost had fluffed up the trees on either side like cherry orchards in bloom. Huge flakes drifted down soft as butterflies.

'Your place or mine?' asked Viking.

'Oh yours,' said Flora, remembering the compost heap of her bedroom and that Abby would be home.

Viking kissed one of her hands.

'So young and soft,' he said mockingly.

'Hands that don't do dishes, I'm afraid. I'm an awful slut.'

'But the nails are bitten – I noticed that at your audition. You smiled, pretty as a daffodil. You played *In the South* to tear the heartstrings. But I knew you were sad.'

'I'm OK,' squeaked Flora, jumping as the top of the car scraped against some bowed-down branches.

'Who hurt you?'

'Oh Christ, a guy called Rannaldini. I was terribly young – I can't talk about it.'

'I'll kill anyone who hurts you.' Somehow Viking manoeuvred the car into the lane down to the lake, skidding most of the way.

'I'll exorcize Carmine, I'll exorcize Rannaldini,' he added dismissively.

'Better buy me an exorcize bicycle,' said Flora.

Between towering beeches, like ice cliffs, the lake glittered in the moonlight, arctic white along the frozen edges, but with a dark badger stripe of flowing water down the centre.

'I've always wondered what this house looks like inside,' said Flora, getting out of the car.

The ground floor of The Bordello trebled up as a kitchen, dining-room and drawing-room. Shabby, different coloured armchairs and a dark blue sofa were grouped around an open fireplace with a huge television set on the right. Chucked into a corner were golf clubs, tennis rackets, cricket bats, an old saddle, football and cricket boots. A not-often-scrubbed table by the oven was weighed down with old newspapers, *Racing Posts*, *Sporting Lifes*, Clare's *Tatlers*, scores, books, shoulder pads, unopened bills.

Flora's eyes, however, were drawn up to an old-fashioned clothes-horse, from which hung white evening shirts and a rainbow riot of clothes, no doubt belonging to the women in Viking's life.

'Why are you so bloody promiscuous?' She was appalled to hear the petulance in her voice.

Viking, who was getting a key out of a blue teapot, smiled sweetly.

'Like Marlon Brando, I have to have at least three women a day to prove I'm not gay. I've only had two this evening, come here.'

But, overwhelmed with shyness and longing, Flora had fled upstairs to the bathroom to find more dripping tights and exotic underwear. She had seen those French knickers on Candy, and the camisole top trimmed with blue ribbon on Clare, but whose was the black lacey 34D cup bra and the black suspender belt and the fishnet stockings.

Oh hell, hell, hell.

Furiously she cleaned her teeth again, then ripped off her laddered tights and knickers, washing between her legs, then splashing herself over and over again with cold water, in case, as Rannaldini had once grumbled, she tasted of soap. She was just nicking Clare's body lotion when Nugent barged in, rounded her up and led her back to Viking's bedroom, curling up on his bean bag with a long sigh.

Flora looked at the huge brass four-poster hiding in its dark red rose-patterned curtains and shivered. The curtains on either side of the window overlooking the lake were drawn, but Viking had opened the ones overlooking the white wilderness of garden so the moonlight flooded the room.

'Oh please, Nugent,' begged Flora, 'give me a few tips, so I can be more exciting than the others.'

Whipping off her dress, she was about to dive under the dark green duvet, when she was distracted by the squares of moonlight on the bare floorboards.

Unzipping his jeans, as he came through the door, Viking found Flora, silver-white as a unicorn, hair and small breasts flying, as she hopscotched back and forth on the moonlit squares.

Her skin was as cool and satiny as new beech leaves, she tasted so sweet and fresh as he kissed her before gathering her up and laying her out on the clean white sheets. Without any hurry, he began to stroke her. Flora tried to be cool as the leisurely caresses crept down her increasingly excited body, but couldn't help gasping with pleasure as his fingers slid inside her. Viking gasped too.

'Jesus, sweetheart, you really want me.'

He was still wearing boxer shorts covered in Golden Retrievers carrying the *Irish Times*.

As he peeled them off, his cock shot upwards.

'Oh wow cubed,' Flora stretched out a hand, 'and you truly want me. Now I know why Yeats kept banging on about Irish towers.'

'Shot op,' Viking's big grinning mouth stopped hers, and his infinitely delicate caresses continued until Flora was squirming with ecstasy. She was dying to come, yet some tension, some passionate desire not to bore him, prevented her, so she wriggled out of his grasp, down the bed to go down on him.

Instantly he pulled her back, burying his head between her legs, a blond haystack at the end of her white sweep of belly, his fingers stroking her nipples.

'Go on, angel,' he mumbled, 'go for it – we've got for ever. I've never tasted anything so delicious.' His tongue rotated languorously.

Flora took several quick breaths and came.

'God, you sweet little girl,' Viking bounded up the bed, pressing his mouth on hers.

'That was bliss,' sighed Flora. 'Let me give you pleasure, please.'

'You are,' Viking slid his cock inside her and began to move.

'Aaaaaah,' moaned Flora, 'God, that's wonderful. Clare was quite wrong about *Boléro* being better than the real thing.'

They made love all night, wallowing in pleasure, constantly changing position. Around quarter to five,

Flora discovered why Viking had been nervous of her going down on him. As she parted his legs, and bent her head to kiss her way up the inside of one of his wonderfully hard muscular thighs, she discovered in the moonlight a tattoo saying, 'I love Juno', and burst out laughing.

'That's a bit arbitrary.'

'I was pissed,' said Viking sheepishly.

'What on earth did Juno think?'

'She was terrified I'd start flashing it around like an engagement ring.'

'She's amazingly pretty, but what made you fall in love with her?'

Viking shrugged.

'She's small minded, suburban and terribly cross, but when I held that tiny waist between my hands and watched her ride me, I guess a standing cock has no taste.'

'Yours tastes lovely,' Flora crouched over him, her tongue was snaking round the rim, searching out pleasure points, probing the top.

Groaning with pleasure, Viking let her continue until he was about to explode. Then he wriggled out from under her, pointing a long finger at the clock beside the bed, whose red numbers said it was five o'clock.

'That was one of Rodney's great sayings.'

'What?'

'No sea too rough, no muff too tough, we dive at five.'

She could feel his shoulders shaking with laughter.

'Please come back and fuck me.'

Viking slid back inside her, gently stroking her face with the back of his fingers. 'You are so lovely.'

'And you,' sighed Flora, 'are a midwinter night's dream come true.'

At eight, Flora staggered out of bed.

'I ought to go home, I've got to change and have a bath.'

'Have one here – I'm not letting you out of my sight.'

As she opened the curtains overlooking the lake, a faint band of orange lay along the horizon. Above, out of a pearly grey sky, shone Venus like a huge glittering snowflake.

'Oh look, the planet of love is smiling at us. Oh Christ!'

At the crunch of passing car wheels, Flora shut the curtains with a snap. 'It's Abby, going to work. She's not going to be very pleased with us.'

FORTY-THREE

Three hours later George barged into the middle of a rehearsal and bawled his musicians out for behaving like hooligans. His fury was fuelled by the sight of Flora, still in last night's black dress, cowering behind Fat Isobel.

'You're a bluddy disgrace,' he thundered. 'And I want everyone who was in Close Encounters last night to write a personal letter of apology to Gilbert Greenford from the Arts Council whose push-bike you totalled last night. Gilbert has had that bike, Clara, since he was at university.'

'Back in the fifteenth century,' piped up Cherub.

'Shut ooop,' roared George, as various musicians started to laugh. Couldn't the stupid fuckers realize the influence the Arts Council had on their future, and how near the edge they were?

'The cost of a new bike and seven toilet chains will be docked off your salaries.'

'Flora will have to consult her lawyer,' shouted Randy. 'Whoops, sorry,' he added as he received a death-ray scowl from George.

Abby was also furious. Any delight that she'd been

vindicated by the rescheduling of *Rachel's Requiem* was wiped out by her misery and excruciating jealousy that Flora had finally got off with Viking.

Refusing to admit this publicly, she later worked off her rage bellyaching about the state of the cottage and Flora's tip of a room in particular, until even Marcus told her to shut up.

'Bloody judgemental home,' grumbled Flora, and promptly moved in with Viking for the weekend, neither emerging from the bedroom except to let Nugent out.

Every time Abby drove into Rutminster she was sent flying by delivery vans from *Oddbins*, the *Pizza House* or the *Star of India* belting the other way.

George just managed to forgive the rest of the RSO in time for the staff Christmas party, which also ushered in Centenary Year.

Miss Priddock supervised the food including a chocolate birthday cake with a hundred candles. The brass players blew up the balloons. Hilary was furious because Randy had taken a photograph of her surreptitiously reading *The Scorpion* and pinned it on the notice-board – life had been very hard since Lionel left – but with a martyred air she joined forces with Juno in decorating the band room.

Romance watchers also were aware that every time Juno put up pale blue paper-chains, George Hungerford seemed to materialize from the fifth floor to hold the ladder and admire her delicate ankles.

Flora, nervous her job might be in jeopardy, as a peace offering bought George a pair of musical socks decorated with santas and reindeers which played 'Jingle Bells' whenever you pulled them up. As George made no comment, he obviously thought Flora was sending him up.

Hilary tartly refused her offer of help with the decorations so Flora retreated to the park to make a snow-woman waving a stick with Cherub. She didn't know why she was feeling depressed, tiredness and post-too-many-coituses probably. Underneath she was miserable about hurting Abby and persuaded Dixie to ask Abby to take part in the Christmas party cabaret.

Abby was touchingly grateful.

'What would you like me to do?'

'What you do best. Play your violin and get young Marcus to accompany you. We'll put you on late in the evening, give him time to get a bit oiled.'

The cabaret kicked off with Randy in a dark curly wig, with two melons stuck into the front of Clare's black dress, coming on as Dame Hermione and screeching: *'I know that my Redeemer liveth.'*

Francis the Good Loser, who didn't have to dress up at all came on as the drunken tramp who tried to out-sing her.

Both were caterwauling away and the audience were holding their sides, when in stumped Blue in one of Miss Priddock's tweed suits, wearing thick tights, brogues, a monocle and a pork-pie hat as Dame Edith. Having driven the tramp off with a hunting-whip she started chatting up Hermione.

'You're a lovely little filly, what does your DBE stand for?'

'Dame of the Bottom Enormous,' simpered Hermione. *'I know that my Redeemer—'*

'Oh, cut that crap,' boomed Edith. 'I hear the shit's hit the Fanny Cycle over the RSO. They'll never get their Arts Council grant now.'

'I'd rather have Hugh Grant,' sighed Hermione. *'I know that my—'*

'Shut up,' repeated Edith. 'Goodo, here come Gilbert and Sillyone to give us the low-down.'

Bellows of laughter, screams of joy and even tighter lips from Miles and Hilary, who was taking a lot of photographs, greeted the entrance of Viking. He was wearing a mauve-and-orange caftan, a grey wig with a lopsided bun, an even more lopsided bosom, sticking-out teeth from the joke shop and earrings made from school band cymbals which he crashed whenever he was making a point. He also kept greedily taking bites out of an enormous Christmas pudding.

'I must have desserts,' he announced, exactly capturing Gwynneth's refined North London whine. 'A *bombe surprise* a day keeps Hungerford away.'

Viking was followed by Dixie, in an identical caftan as goaty Gilbert. He was carrying an urn with the words 'Clara' on the side and wiping his eyes with a long ginger beard.

'Hallo Sillyone,' demanded Edith. 'What's in that urn?'

'Don't upset Gilbert,' whispered Gwynneth. 'His cycle, Clara, passed away last Wednesday. We're off to scatter her ashes on Vinifred Trapp's grave.'

'I know that my Redeemer—' squawked Hermione.

'Actually not quite all Clara's ashes,' confided Gwynneth, as Gilbert gave a great sob. 'Gilbert has donated her handlebars to a co-operative for battered push-bikes, so she can be recycled as intristing earrings to enable me to black a few more people's eyes.' Viking put down his pudding, stuck out his teeth and gave his cymbal earrings a great crash. Peering from the wings Flora saw that George was crying with laughter.

'He *is* human, after all,' she hissed to Abby.

'What happened to Clara?' enquired Dame Edith.

'Battered to death by the Celtic Mafia,' sobbed Gilbert. 'They must be punished.'

'Surely the Celtic Mafia are an ethnic minority and therefore exonerated from all blame,' asked Hermione.

'Certainly not,' Gwynneth crashed her cymbals. 'They are white, male and heterosexual, so it doesn't count.'

'Gimme their address,' squealed Hermione.

'Ah, here comes our favourite patron of the arts, Piggy Porker. Good evening to you, Piggy.'

'This has gone too far,' hissed Miles, to a crescendo of cheering and hysterical laughter, as a heavily padded grotesquely over made-up Flora, teetered on in blue stilettos and a sick-green spangled dress, snorting loudly, and waving a Parker's carrier bag.

'I quite agree,' George wiped his eyes, 'but it is bluddy funny.'

Somehow Flora achieved a wobbly curtsy.

'Good evening, your dameships,' she snorted. 'Ay would so laike to create new looks for you both. Any face is improved by subtle make-up.' And, reaching into her Parker's bag, she slammed custard pies in Edith's and Hermione's faces.

'*I know that my Redeemer—*' screeched Hermione, spitting out cream and pastry.

'Have you got a mirror? I don't carry one,' said Dame Edith.

'You both look much younger,' went on Piggy Parker. 'I've come to invite you all to a brown tre-ouser event at Parker's next week. My Sonny is . . . oh, here's Sonny to tell you himself.'

Despite the yells of approval and laughter, no-one at first recognized the concave fop who minced in in a red tunic and floppy white trousers, because the face was almost entirely concealed by curtains of straggly hair.

'I am the RSO's composer-in-undesirable residence,' fluted Sonny, crashing Viking's earrings, 'but it's getting me nowhere because I've fallen madly in love with Marcus Black and he won't return my calls.'

Marcus gave a gasp of horror and delight.

'Abby, you bitch,' he said.

'It's Abby,' screamed Nellie. 'That's brilliant.'

'I want him to play on my portable organ,' Abby tried to make herself heard over the whistling, stamping and yells of approval.

But George was on his feet, sprinting out through the exit, round onto the stage, stopping the performance before Jerry could video anything more or Hilary take any more photographs.

'I'm sorry that's enoof,' he shouted from the rostrum to equal boos and cheers. 'Mrs Parker, Sonny, Gilbert and Gwynneth all said they might look in later and I for one don't want the RSO committing pooblic suicide joost yet. I joost wish all you boogers would put as much creative energy into your music-making. But I have to admit it was bluddy foony.'

Packing the cast off to seats in the auditorium, he then congratulated the orchestra on some good concerts, but said it was high time they stopped behaving like hooligans.

'We moost capitalize on Centenary Year to put the RSO in the black again.'

As was customary he then asked them to drink to their musical director.

Abby had pulled off her wig and her beard and ruffled her dark curls. A week of sleepless nights over Viking and Flora made her look pale and vulnerable.

'You are a great orchestra,' she said in a choked voice when the drunken cheers had died down. 'And we've always programmed great composers, so if we've managed to make great music, I have only been the catalyst. Thank you for putting up with me.'

'God, I feel a cow,' said Flora, as Viking slid an arm round her shoulders. 'Abby's so lovely.'

'She may not be so lovely when we go back to the cottage together later,' murmured Viking.

Randy's wife and his mother-in-law had descended unexpectedly to Christmas shop and intended to spend the night in The Bordello. Great armfuls of female underwear had been hastily chucked in the cellar. Viking had agreed to vacate his bedroom for Randy's mother-in-law and planned an away fixture. Flora was extremely twitchy about Abby.

On rolled Miss Priddock's cake on its trolley. The

hundred candles were lit which set off the smoke alarm so five butch firemen suddenly appeared. Everyone was convinced they were a stripagram so they stayed on for the party to Nellie's delight.

Rodney had sent six crates of Moët over as a Christmas present so everyone had plenty to drink. Very generously under the circumstances, Peggy Parker had given each member of the orchestra a turkey. Blue didn't get a chance to speak to Cathie because Carmine was watching her, but he did manage to slip a little sapphire ring into the pocket of her coat hanging up in the Ladies and prayed she'd find it.

By eleven o'clock Marcus, slightly drunk and happy because he'd felt he'd comforted Abby a little in the last week, had lost his nerves enough to play the piano.

Not realizing how many people had stopped to listen and started to dance, he meandered through Gershwin and Cole Porter, then launched into a Seventies hit called 'Madly in Love' with Abby accompanying him swooningly on the violin.

What he didn't realize was that Abby had persuaded Charlton Handsome to slip a recording mike in front of him which also picked up the ecstatic cheering and shouts for more at the end.

'That recording'll be worth a fortune one day,' murmured Julian.

'Boy plays like an angel,' George said proudly to Miles, 'I'm right glad we booked him.'

Abby and Marcus left soon afterwards because she was flying back to Philadelphia first thing the following morning. As Flora and Viking tottered out arm in arm several hours later, they found Eldred on the H. P. Hall steps, weeping at the prospect of a wifeless Christmas.

'I'm coming back to Woodbine Cottage on Boxing Day,' Flora comforted him. 'I'll ring you, you must come and try our erratic cooking and Marcus, you and I can play chamber music. We could start off with the Mozart Trio.'

Flora only stopped crying over Eldred as Viking drove over Rutminster Bridge and pointed out a very drunk Davie Buckle hurling his turkey into the River Fleet, yelling: 'Go on, you bastard, fly.'

Trying to creep in without turning on any lights, Flora and Viking knocked over an umbrella stand and fell over Abby's cases already out on the landing. Abby pulled a pillow over her head in anguish. Would she ever sleep again?

It seemed only seconds later that she was woken up by horrifying screams. Wrapping her naked body in a towel, tiptoeing onto the landing, she could hear Viking saying, 'It's OK, sweetheart, I'm here, it's OK.'

He sounded so tender and loving. Almost deranged with misery, Abby could hardly read her watch. Five-thirty. She had to leave for Heathrow in an hour, she might as well get up.

Tottering wearily downstairs, she found it was still dark. Rain was rattling against the windows, pounding away the last patches of snow on the lawn. As she filled up the kettle, she heard piteous mewing. Frightened away earlier by Nugent, but seeing a light on, Sibelius had jumped onto the ledge and was squashing his drenched fur against the window-pane.

'Oh, poor baby.' Abby opened the window and, whipping off her towel, began to dry him, crooning how much she was going to miss him, patting his piebald face, squeezing water out of his furry tail.

Only when he was purring and almost dry did she hear a wolf-whistle and whipped round. To her horror, lounging in the doorway, wearing only jeans and a highly amused smirk on his evil, debauched face was Viking. She had no idea how long he'd been there.

'What in hell are you doing?' she howled. 'Ouch!' she screamed as a terrified Sibelius dug his claws into her breasts.

'I've just come down to make a cup of tea, Flora had a nightmare,' said Viking.

'Called Viking O'Neill,' sobbed Abby.

Seizing her towel, crashing against the door to avoid touching him, she fled upstairs.

Poor Sibelius was mewing again, hoping for an early breakfast. Switching on the kettle, Viking picked him up. His face was expressionless, as burying it in the cat's fur, he breathed in Abby's scent.

Depressed that Abby seemed almost suicidal when he got up to wave her off, Marcus was cheered when the post brought a Christmas card from Taggie, containing three hundred pounds, smuggled out of her private account. But it didn't make up for not hearing from Rupert, and Marcus was so cast down by an enchanting photograph in the *Daily Express* of Rupert, Taggie, Xav and Bianca arriving in Monhaut for a skiing Christmas, that Flora persuaded him to come home to Paradise and stay with her parents.

'I shall be playing the referee's whistle, so you can accompany me. We must drop off a bottle of whisky on the way for poor Eldred.'

Despite Viking ringing every day from Dublin, Flora was ashamed how thrilled she was to hear that Helen's Christmas with Rannaldini's ex-wives and brat-pack had been a disaster. She had never been gregarious, and Rannaldini's endless sexual games had absolutely horrified her.

'I could have told you Helen of Troilism wasn't a viable proposition,' quipped Flora.

Marcus was demented.

'I should have gone out there to protect her.'

What Helen hadn't told him was that for Christmas Rannaldini had given her a blank cheque to have her face, breasts and bottom lifted.

'But you said in Prague you loved me as I am,' sobbed Helen.

'I did, and I know it will hurt dreadfully,' purred Rannaldini, 'but I want you to be even more beautiful.'

Also if Helen was confined to barracks recovering from surgery, it would give him more free time.

'I did,' said I knew it with hurt dreadfully,' purred Raimundini, 'but I saw you in the evening once beautiful. After it, Hilo was condemned to bad lack he wouldn't from supper, it would give him right-five time.'

FORTY-FOUR

After their fortnight off the RSO sank into deep gloom. Life seemed to be summed up by Francis's turkey which he had forgotten to take home and which was found in the band room under Nellie's camisole top belching forth maggots.

Francis had other things on his mind. His house had been repossessed and he had moved into a council flat.

'My children are on free dinners,' he said wearily. 'My milkman earns more than I do.'

Mary-the-mother-of-Justin was horrified to find she was pregnant. Her husband had lost his smart job in television, and was at home looking after Justin and giving Mary a lot of grief.

Everyone except Carmine, Hilary and Juno had overspent at Christmas, couldn't pay their bills and were chasing after fewer teaching jobs as the education departments slashed the music grants to colleges and schools.

Flora was delighted to have a letter from Eldred thanking her for the Christmas bottle of whisky, but worried that she got no answer when she kept ringing to invite him to supper. Finally police broke in on 4 January and found Eldred had been dead for a week from an overdose.

The empty bottle of whisky was at his feet, he was clutching his clarinet and the Mozart *Trio,* which he had obviously been planning to play with Flora and Marcus, was on the music-stand. The gramophone was still on – he had been listening to one of his old records.

'If he hadn't had his coffee black, people would have known from the milk bottles,' sobbed Flora. 'If I'd rung earlier I might have saved him.'

Everyone was too stunned and ashamed to oppose Hilary when she immediately applied for Eldred's job of First Clarinet. She was soon busy auditioning candidates for Second Clarinet.

'One should intercept them at the H.P. Hall gate,' said Viking, 'hissing: "escape while you can, don't work with that bitch."'

With her step-up to section leader, Hilary's bossiness increased a thousand-fold. She was singing madrigals regularly with Miles, Gwynneth and Gilbert. Jogging round the Close with Miles kept her in good shape for running to him if there was any trouble.

The only good thing about Eldred's death was that Abby and Flora made it up, united in their distress. Abby had already brought Flora some rosin, mixed with meteor dust, back from America as a Christmas present. Flora, more generous and much more guilty, had given Abby a scarlet cashmere polo-neck. She also tried to play down her raging and continuing *affaire* with Viking. Viking, as part of his 'exorcize' campaign, had given Flora a toy black sheep for Christmas called Rannaldini.

'You've got to meet it head on, darling.'

Abby pretended she was no longer interested in Viking but, as a post-Christmas fitness regime, took to jogging round the lake. On her first Thursday back, her progress was impeded by the dustcart outside The Bordello. She nearly fell down a rabbit hole, as Viking hurtled out barefoot and just in jeans, his eyes swollen and practically closed with sleep, waving a twenty-pound note to persuade the dustmen to remove the battalions of empties.

As she jogged home, Abby could see Viking, Mr Nugent and all the dustmen across the lake, still standing outside The Bordello clutching beer cans and laughing uproariously. As a result Woodbine Cottage's dustbins weren't emptied until midday.

'Viking's teaching my lad the 'orn,' boasted one of the dustmen. 'He finks the world of Viking.'

'His hobby seems to be ornithology,' said Abby sourly.

The orchestra's black gloom was not improved by increasingly sinister rumours of an intended merger between the CCO and the RSO flying around like seagulls above a plough. Cotchester Ballet Company, accompanied by the CCO, had been staging popular classics during the school-holidays and had pinched a large chunk of the RSO's audience.

One Tuesday in the middle of January, George summoned Abby to his office. He was in a bad mood anyway. An ancient sitting tenant was frustrating his attempts to convert four adjacent freeholds in Park Lane into a splendid office block which would retain the early nineteenth-century façade. When the old biddy rejected a cash offer, George moved the heavies in to frighten her, whereupon she had called up the *Daily Mirror*, who had chewed George out in a double-page spread that morning.

George pulled no punches therefore when he told Abby the orchestra's deficit was the largest ever. To win the audiences back they must 'cross over' which meant programming Gershwin, Rodgers and Hammerstein and other non-classical music in the second half.

Abby was appalled.

'We're a symphony orchestra, for Chrissake.'

'Not for much longer. It's the only way we might survive. And I'm planning a huge gala centenary concert in May. I've already got feelers out for Dancer Maitland and Georgie Maguire.'

'They'll break the bank for starters. You know Georgie's Flora's mother?'

If George didn't, he wasn't going to admit it.

'Can't hold that against the poor woman,' he said nastily. 'Come in, Miles.'

Looking sanctimonious and disapproving, Miles sat down on a high-backed chair with his knees rammed together, and handed George some faxes. The first was a blank page from the Arts Council.

'Is this supposed to be our next year's grant?' demanded George.

Miles smiled thinly.

'The first page didn't print out.'

The second page did and turned out to be a furious letter from Gilbert plus a photostat of a newspaper photograph of himself, Gwynneth, Peggy Parker and Sonny as portrayed by Dixie, Viking, Flora and Abby in the Christmas cabaret. Someone had obviously leaked it to the *Rutminster Echo*. The urn Viking was brandishing with 'Clara' written clearly on the side, had particularly offended Gilbert.

Just for a second George's lips twitched, then he read on.

Now we know what your musicians think both of the Arts Council and their most generous patron. And when am I going to receive compensation for my cycle?

'It was a bit of harmless fun,' protested Abby.

'Not harmless with next year's grant about to be handed out,' snapped George.

'That bitch Hilary must have leaked it; she was taking photographs the whole time.'

'Hilly wouldn't do a thing like that,' spluttered Miles. 'Hilly only thinks of the good of the RSO, unlike some.'

'Hilly' now, thought Abby, they are getting thick.

Fortunately John Drummond chose that moment to seriously endanger a fifty-thousand-pound Perspex model of a neo-Tudor shopping precinct as he weaved round it. Landing with a thud on George's knee, he started shredding Gilbert's fax with his paws.

Abby burst out laughing, but was brought sharply back to earth by Miles, accusing her of taking no interest in the orchestra's educational projects.

'We must make musical excellence available to the widest possible audience,' he added pompously .

'As the last major educational project the RSO got involved in,' snapped Abby, 'was a search for Respighi's Birds in the Forest of Dean, and Randy and Dixie and four schoolgirls vanished for over a week, I don't figure this is feasible in January. They'd all die of hypothermia.'

'Don't be silly,' said George, wincing as Drummond's claws punctured his pin-striped thighs.

'Anyway I haven't got the time,' countered Abby, 'I've got far too much repertoire to learn.'

'If we switched to more popular fare,' Miles cracked his fingers, 'you'd know it already.'

'And you could start,' George added curtly, 'by wasting less time with Flora Seymour – she's a pernicious influence.'

George had not forgiven Flora for Alphonso's case, Gilbert's bike or the musical socks which had played 'Jingle Bells' when he'd absent-mindedly tugged them up during a crucial meeting with the Department of the Environment.

'She's not your greatest fan either,' said Abby disloyally.

'Well, she better watch her back.'

'Rather hard,' said Miles bitchily, 'when she spends so much time on it. Nor did she help matters by suggesting in her letter of apology to Gilbert Greenford that he should replace Clara with a Harley Davidson.'

Abby laughed.

'It is *not* funny,' said Miles primly. 'And as Musical Director you ought to be seen to do more for charity.'

Abby lost her temper.

'All my spare cash, OK, goes to the Cats Protection League, and I don't mean old tabby cats either,' Abby glared pointedly at Miles. 'Get off my back both of you.'

All the Perspex models trembled and John Drummond shot up the brushed suede wall as she walked out slamming the door.

Cooling down, she wandered into the general office and learnt from the notice-board that the RSO were currently doing a project at St Clement's Primary School. As there was no rehearsal that morning she decided to pop in on the way home.

She was not cheered, switching on the car radio, to hear Hugo playing the violin solo in Mozart's *Sinfonia Concertante*.

'That was the CCO, one of our great little orchestras,' said Henry Kelly.

'Oh, shut up,' said Abby.

It had been raining for days. The River Fleet had flooded its banks, St Clement's playing-fields were under water, inhibiting outdoor activity, which probably explained the unholy din issuing from the building.

When the secretary directed her to a far-off classroom, however, Abby was flabbergasted to find Viking perched on the edge of a desk telling a group of enraptured eight year olds about the French horn. They were engaged in a project on Rutminster in the seventeenth century.

'Charles, the King of England, spent a lot of time fighting,' Viking was saying. 'And in the end he had his head chopped off, probably because his hair was longer than mine.'

The children laughed.

'But, on his day off, he often enjoyed a day's hunting in the Blackmere Woods and used a horn to sommon his hounds.'

Picking up his horn, Viking blew pa, pa, pa, pa on it.

'This was a sound that the dogs could hear all over the forest.'

Nugent, who was sitting beside a little boy in a wheelchair, put his head on one side.

Seeing Abby, Viking gave a brief nod.

'You can play the horn on anything,' he went on, producing a piece of hose pipe from a Gap carrier bag.

Coiling it up, he handed one end to the little boy in the wheelchair and then played 'God Save the Queen' on the other.

Finally he made the children shriek with laughter by opening the teacher's big handbag, which she'd left on top of the piano, and magicking out a red suspender belt, a pair of black lace knickers, a banana, a fluffy toy monkey, who pretended to eat the banana, and finally a huge bag of toffees which he handed round the class.

The teacher, who had a lot of freckles and a sweet open face, was clearly bats about him, too.

'Viking's a natural with kids,' she told Abby. 'Joey in the wheelchair's really come out of himself since he's been visiting us. These are the pictures they've been drawing.' Proudly she pointed to a mural of Cavaliers, horses, jolly hounds, trees, wild flowers and a deer miles away with no chance of getting caught.

'When that bully Carmine Jones came to teach an older class about the trumpet,' the teacher lowered her voice, 'they gave him such a rough ride, he came out nearly in tears.'

'Could they give me their secret?' sighed Abby.

As the bell went, Viking told the children they'd all got to make a valentine for their teacher.

'Bye, sweetheart,' he added, kissing her, 'I'll call you.'

Outside it was still raining and Viking tipped a black wool cap over his nose. It was a Christmas present from Rodney, who knew how Viking hated getting his hair wet because it kinked so unbecomingly. There had been rows in the past because Viking kept pinching

Miss Priddock's flowered sou'wester to go to the pub.

'Let's go and have a drink,' he said, putting his arm through Abby's.

The pub garden was filled with aconites and snowdrops. A hazel tree draping its sulphur-yellow catkins over the gate, like Zeus in a shower of gold waiting for Danaë, reminded Abby of Viking.

The pub was warm and dark. As she took refuge on a corner seat, she was glad she was wearing her new red cashmere polo-neck, but she was determined not in any way to betray to Viking how desperately she fancied him.

'Thanks,' she accepted a large glass of white wine, deliberately not allowing their fingers to touch.

Having downed a third of a pint of beer and wiped the froth off his lips with the back of his hand, Viking sat down at right angles to her, long legs so wide apart his knee nearly grazed hers, staring her out in amusement.

'Well?'

'That was kinda impressive,' stammered Abby. 'I never saw you as a Pied Piper.'

'Music's being left to die on its feet in schools,' said Viking suddenly angry. 'There's no band any more, no singing, no hymns at compulsory Assembly. Kids can't learn an instrument any longer unless their parents can afford the extra fees for lessons. Gradually the orchestras will die because there'll no longer be a pool of bright young musicians to draw from.'

He shook his head, 'Sorry, I'm getting heavy.'

'No, it's great,' Abby was thrilled to glimpse a more serious Viking. 'No thanks,' she shook her head as he offered her a packet of crisps. 'I'm also glad of a chance to talk. I wanted to discuss your section.'

'You do?'

'I just adore Cyril,' went on Abby, 'he was obviously a great musician once, but his lips have gone and he's always drunk.'

'That's an exaggeration,' said Viking coldly.

'Well, he reeks of booze.'

'He retires in four years' time.'

'Why can't he teach?'

'Too shy. Those kids today would make dog-meat out of him.'

Abby took a gulp of wine to strengthen her resolve.

'He's pulling back the orchestra.'

'The orchestra'll have to pull a bit harder then. I don't want to discuss it.'

The most delectable smells were wafting in from the kitchen. Abby proceeded to lecture him and Viking to disagree with her, until a barmaid in a tight gentian-blue sweater and an emerald-green mini skirt came over with the menu.

'D'you want to order, Viking?'

'I'm not sure. That's a fantastic sweater.' Then, turning to Abby, asked, 'Do you want some lunch?'

Abby shook her head irritably.

'I've got *far* too much work.'

Viking smiled up at the waitress. 'Can I have my bill?'

'Irish stew's delicious. I could do you a take-away.'

Viking eyed her up. 'There are things I'd rather take away.'

The waitress giggled. 'I'll get you your bill.'

'Can't you pass anything up?' snapped Abby.

She was still lecturing him about his profligate lifestyle as they reached the car-park. Viking took her car keys and opened her door.

'I'm sorry to get heavy,' muttered Abby, 'but I don't want you to hurt Flora, she was absolutely blown away by Rannaldini.'

Viking looked at Abby in that amused wicked testing way until she had turned as red as her jersey.

'I won't hurt Flora,' he said softly. 'I adore her, she's a soul mate; stonningly gorgeous and amazingly loyal to you,' he added sharply.

'Then why do you do a number on every woman you meet?'

'Don't you think my numbers add up to the sum of

human happiness?' Turning, Viking waved to two of the barmaids who were still gazing at him out of the pub window.

'I don't know,' said Abby crossly, 'I guess you're just a womanizer.'

'I'm not a womanizer,' said Viking, 'I'm a charmer!'

Grabbing her, he kissed her on the mouth, sticking his tongue down her throat. Putting up absolutely no resistance Abby kissed him back until her pulses were thundering like the nearby mill-stream and she could hardly stand up.

But, as she pulled away to draw breath, Viking let her go.

'Only way to shot you up, darling.' Laughing, he sauntered off towards his car.

Back at the cottage, Marcus was listening to Pablo Gonzales playing Rachmaninov's *Third Piano Concerto*.

'How perfect, how effortless, how beautiful. Oh Christ,' he was saying.

He was slowly getting to grips with the concerto and only occasionally allowed himself to listen to recordings, terrified of being over-influenced.

'It's a bit quick,' said Flora, who was combing tangles out of a protesting Scriabin, 'I prefer Kissin – more languorous and tender.'

'I like Kissin's applause at the end,' sighed Marcus.

'What can we do this afternoon to stop me eating?' pleaded Flora, who was on a diet. Whichever way she'd put her knickers on that morning they had felt back to front.

She suspected she was stuffing her face because Rannaldini had just won the coveted Conductor of the Year Award. Under his direction, the New World had won Orchestra of the Year, and Winifred Trapp's *Harp Concertos*, newly released, were receiving ecstatic reviews. Flora couldn't open a paper without Rannaldini's face glaring out at her.

She didn't feel any better when Abby floated in.

'Just been having a drink with Viking.'

'Where did you meet him?' asked Flora.

'He was teaching at St Clement's – good to see him occupying his time profitably for a change, I cannot understand people who are super-talented and lazy.'

'I can,' said Flora, taking a tub of ice-cream out of the freezer.

'And don't you get mad at the way he chats up every woman he meets?'

'No-oh,' said Flora, seizing a spoon.

'Viking's attractive, I'll grant you that. George chewed me out earlier this morning, but I guess underneath his animosity, he's kinda attracted to me, like Viking is, or he wouldn't bully me so much.'

'That's a false argument,' said Flora with her mouth full. 'Carmine bullies Cathie.'

'I figure George would be a better bet than Viking,' reflected Abby.

'Georgie, Porgie, Black Pudding and Pie,' Flora took another large spoonful. 'If it was a choice between Mr Wrong but Romantic O'Neill and Mr Right but Repulsive Hungerford, I know who I'd choose.'

'It's weird; George doesn't like you either,' said the ever-tactful Abby.

Marcus winced. He wished Abby's almost pathological jealousy of Flora didn't make her so bitchy. He knew that she'd regret this conversation later.

'Oh hell,' said Flora, miserably, looking down at the empty ice-cream tub and chucking it into the sink. The telephone rang.

'It's Mr Wrong but Romantic,' a returning Marcus gave a faint smirk, 'for Flora.'

'I've just kissed Abby,' were Viking's first words.

'I guessed,' said Flora.

'She was listing my shortcomings.'

'Your comings are never short.' Flora was happy to hear Viking's relieved laughter.

'I love you and need you,' he begged, 'come over at once. I'd come and collect you, but I don't want any more lectures.'

Abby couldn't hide her exasperation.

'Tell Viking to keep that damn dog under control. He's always round here upending dustbins, just like his master.'

Appassionata

FOURTH MOVEMENT

FORTY-FIVE

Cash crisis followed cash crisis throughout the winter. Bad weather kept audiences away in droves. George told the orchestra they might even have to take cuts in salaries. Two more players had their houses repossessed and moved into awful rented rooms where people banged on the wall if they practised. A bass player, a cellist and one of the Second Violins left and were not replaced.

Even Julian was downcast. 'We'll be a string quartet at this rate,' he said gloomily.

Flora's answer to her bank manager was to tell Miles she had an appointment with the dentist in Harley Street and to go busking on the South Bank. One of Viking's mates at the London Philharmonic Orchestra had arranged for her to have a slot.

She chose a horribly cold grey morning and had great difficulty in getting out of bed. Returning to earth after making love, slumped on her back, fingers resting on her forehead, she glanced sideways at the watch on her wrist, worried about missing the train, and saw that instead of figures and hands the dial was filled with roses reflected from the curtains of Viking's four-poster

'Time ceases to exist when I'm with you,' she said in a

choked voice. 'It's turned to roses. You've made me terribly happy,' she added, kissing him, 'I'm so grateful.'

Viking drove her to Rutminster Station. Then, casually as the train was moving out, he said: 'How about you and me getting our own place together?'

'D'you think Nugent could learn to love Scriabin?'

'Will you ever be serious?'

'I'd like it, love it,' stammered Flora. 'It's just such a surprise. As long as I can pay my way – I don't want to be a kept woman.'

'You can be a capped woman then.' Removing Rodney's cap, Viking plonked it on her head. 'Be careful, if anyone asks you for a drink, say no.'

'I love you,' said Flora and, despite the cold, stayed watching him until he was out of sight.

London was much colder than Rutminster. Flora felt so sorry for the shivering sweeps of purply-blue crocuses in the parks and the almond trees whose pink blossom, forced out by a mild January, was already being scattered by a vicious wind.

The newsagents' windows, scarlet with Valentine Day displays, provided the only cheerful note. She must buy a really gorgeous card for Viking, and a big jokey one for Mr Nugent from Scriabin. She couldn't believe he'd asked her to move in with him, but allowed her thoughts to wander happily. He was so good with kids, he'd make a brilliant father and Flora O'Neill sounded so much more romantic than Flora Seymour. Oh God, let her not be too presumptuous.

She took up her position in Concert Hall Approach under Hungerford Bridge in a little paved garden with boxes full of trailing ivy and laurel bushes. At first she tried to put up a stand but the wind blew her music all over the place so she played by ear. Soon concert-goers on their way to the Festival Hall and office workers setting off to lunch were enjoying her exquisite sound, feeling sorry for her playing on such a cold day and chucking coins and even notes into her tin.

It was hard to say thank you when you were playing the viola, so Flora made do with smiles and massive nods. After *In the South,* an old man asked her if she'd made any records and between 'The Pink Panther' and 'Panis Angelicus' a blushing couple asked if she'd play at their wedding. Flora said she'd adore to and gave them her telephone number.

Then she nearly dropped her viola in the middle of 'Where E'er You Walk' as she saw George Hungerford (perhaps he'd come to admire his bridge) jump out of a taxi and dive into the Archduke Wine Bar opposite. He was probably in London for a meeting of the Association of British Orchestras. She'd be sacked if he saw her. Flora pulled Viking's cap over her nose. The next moment her bow really did skid all over the strings as a sleek dark blue Mercedes drew up, a black-leather-clad chauffeur jumped out and opened the door for Rannaldini. Hearing such discords, Rannaldini immediately swung round, but Flora had dived behind a concrete pillar. Rannaldini was wearing his black overcoat with the Astrakhan collar and looked as fatally glamorous as ever. Flora wanted to race through the traffic, fall at his feet and plead with him to take her back; she wasn't cured in the slightest.

In horror, she watched him walk quickly towards the Archduke and the manager fling open the door to welcome him, congratulating him no doubt on being the greatest conductor of the year and of all time.

For a second, a 77 bus blotted out her view. A minute later, through a jungle of glossy dark green plants, Flora could see him and George sitting down at a table on the first floor. Rannaldini was unfolding his napkin and laying it across those iron-hard thighs that had gripped her once with such lust. Now he was picking up the wine list. God, he was wearing a wedding-ring. Helen must have far more influence on him than poor Kitty. Please make him look at me, please make him not, prayed Flora launching into 'Dido's Lament'. And what the hell was he doing with George?

Frozen but oblivious to the cold because the pain in her heart was so terrible, she watched George and Rannaldini coming out forty minutes later both looking much more cheerful. They stood talking for half a minute, until Rannaldini's Merc glided up and whisked them both away.

Flora walked off in deep shock forgetting to take her tin of money. What could they be up to? No good, if Rannaldini had anything to do with it. But the RSO was far too small-fry for him.

It was only when she got back to Rutminster, and passed the newsagent on the platform, that she realized there was no point getting a valentine card for Viking. Then she started to cry.

Viking was utterly angelic.

'So, you're not over Rannaldini?'

'No, no, not at all. I'm so sorry, Viking. It's like thinking you've zapped cancer, then discovering you're only in remission. You've been so lovely to me.'

'Let me go on being lovely, josst give it time, sweetheart.' It was the nearest he got to begging.

'We can't, not if I'm still in love with Rannaldini. You're too, well, decent to put up with half-measures.'

'So young, and so untender' said Viking bitterly.

'So young, my lord, and true.'

Just to test Flora's total immunity, Viking tried another tack. Why didn't he mix business with pleasure by making a play for Jessica, George's thick but stunning secretary?

'Then I can lure her back to The Bordello for long lunches when George is away and you can raid the files and see what the dirty duo are really op to.'

Viking winced when Flora agreed listlessly, but

without any display of jealousy, that this would be a very good idea.

'*But one man loved the pilgrim soul in you,*' he said sadly, taking Flora's hand.

He then went out and got drunk. He was far too proud to show it, but he was desperately unhappy for the first time in his life.

Valentine's Day temporarily distracted the RSO from their gloom. Suddenly red envelopes were nesting like robins in pigeon holes. Still shell-shocked by her sighting of Rannaldini, Flora hardly noticed how many she received. Blue reeled round the band room in ecstasy, because he recognized Cathie's writing on the envelope sending him a chocolate heart. Militant Moll ordered Ninion to put a valentine message in the *Independent* and left it lying around. Poor Fat Isobel sent three cards to herself to avoid humiliation. All Cyril's week's wages went on two dozen red roses for Miss Priddock. Miles smirked to get an unsigned jokey card from Brittlecombe, the village in which Hilary lived. Noriko was thrilled to have a valentine teddy bear holding a single red rose from Cherub. Dixie and Clare, Randy and Candy, Dimitri and Miss Parrott all went out to individual valentine dinners.

George Hungerford was distracted for ten minutes from the deficit while he opened his cards. All the management's secretaries (including Miss Priddock, who had to think of John Drummond's future) and most of the women musicians still harboured hopes of becoming the second Mrs Hungerford. Viking, who got twice as many cards, didn't bother to open them. Jessica, George's lovely secretary, however, was overwhelmed at lunch-time to receive a balloon in the shape of a pink heart bearing the words, 'Hiya sexy', rising out of two dozen pale pink roses accompanied by a card saying: '*Love from Viking.*'

Earlier in the day Jessica had been feeling a bit low. George had called her a blithering idiot for booking a pianist to play Bartók's *Second Piano Concerto* rather than his *First*, which had been rehearsed by the orchestra – a mistake only discovered on the afternoon of the concert.

Viking reassured her it was the easiest of mistakes. He was so comforting the following day, after Jessica had another bollocking from George for passing *'Drunks 6 p.m.'*, on an invitation when it should have been *'Drinks'*, that she accepted a dinner invitation. During the evening Viking learnt that the confidential files were stored on microfilm in George's office and handled by George's London secretary who usually came down one day a week.

Acting dumb, Viking told Jessica he was only bog Irish and had never seen a really sophisticated computer system before. Over a bottle of Moët in Jessica's office on the second date, he managed to persuade her, since she was so brilliant, to initiate him into its mysteries. Jessica was feeling low that day because George had bawled her out for typing *'Piggy Porker'* on a place card.

Immensely flattered by Viking's admiration, Jessica showed him how to find the Index which was called the file menu, how to locate the individual file one wanted and then how to print it out.

'Of course, I've never looked at any of these files,' she said. 'They are far too secret, George would sack me.'

At a fleeting glance at the file menu, Viking couldn't see any reference to Rannaldini, but during a steamy session, after Jessica had drunk seven-eighths of the Moët, he managed to elicit the password *'Georgetown'* needed to enter the system.

'But you must promish, promish not to tell anyone,' whispered the delectable Jessica.

'Georgetown,' cried Viking in elation, as he entered her system.

Having stopped himself coming too soon, by studying the photographs of Mel Gibson and kittens and a poster calling for the banning of veal crates, Viking lay back afterwards playing 'She loves me, she loves me not', with the chewing-gum parked under Jessica's desk. It came out: 'She loves me not.' Jessica was far prettier and had a far more beautiful body, but Viking was missing Flora so much it killed him. Somehow she had to be freed from Rannaldini's evil spell.

In late February George went skiing. 'No doubt to put another million in his Swiss bank account,' said Flora sourly.

By coincidence, it was noticed Juno Meadows had taken the same week off. George was due back late Wednesday afternoon. In anticipation Miss Priddock took herself off to the hairdresser in her lunch-hour and Viking lured Jessica back to The Bordello for a long lunch leaving Flora free to raid the files.

Shaking with terror that she would trigger off an alarm or someone would come in, Flora locked herself into George's office. It was rather like a sweet little village, with all those Perspex models with their balconies, loofah bay trees and Dinky cars outside the front door. Somehow, their cosiness blinded one to the tragedies behind their realization: the terrified old ladies, the threats of knee-capping, the flooded basements, the doors knocked out in the middle of the night.

The only jolly note was John Drummond fatly asleep in George's out-tray and a bunch of Cyril's yellow crocuses like a little gold sun on the big desk. Realizing what an ugly customer she was dealing with, Flora quailed. But, after all Viking's hard work, she must be brave.

Turning on the computer, she was confronted with a screen as blank as Rannaldini's face until the words *Enter Password* came up. Her hands were trembling so much she had three goes before she managed to type in *'Georgetown'*.

Eureka! There was the main menu. Running hastily

down through the files: *'Office Accounts'*, *'Foreign tours'*, *'Salaries'*, she came to the word *'Private.'*

Locating the *'Private'* file menu she found far more exciting fare. She was tempted to stop and read the private detective's report on George's wife's adultery or the details of various property fiddles: the Cotchester bypass, for example, was scheduled to go slap through Rupert's estate. Serve him right for being such a sod to Marcus. Even more interesting would be the assessments on members of the RSO. Bloody hell, she couldn't go through every file. She jumped nervously as John Drummond gave a great snore in his out-tray.

Looking back at the list of files she noted the innocuous words *'Orchestra South'*, scrolled the cursor down the page and double clicked to get into the file. Got it in one! With increasing moans of horror, she realized she had unearthed a fiendish plot to merge the Cotchester Chamber Orchestra with the RSO and form a new Southern Super Orchestra. Rannaldini had always been wildly jealous of Simon Rattle and longed for the same sort of set-up as the Vienna Philharmonic and the Vienna State Opera where the musical director had control of a pool of crack musicans who could be called on to play for either company.

As soon as Edith Spink retired later in the year, Rannaldini would take over as musical director of the CCO, Abby's contract wouldn't be renewed after March, nor would those of most of the RSO.

'This is the only way we can hack out the dead wood,' Rannaldini had written to George. The date was 5 January. Had Hermione introduced George to Rannaldini after *Messiah*?

Julian would be fired because he had defied Rannaldini in New York. Viking, Blue, Simon, Dimitri and Peter were among the few players who would join the new Super Orchestra. Between them George and Rannaldini would build it back to double strength with virtuoso players in every department. Running her eye down the list Flora saw that surprisingly George had put a question mark beside her name. Then she gave a wail of misery discovering Rannaldini's next E-mail.

Definitely not, he had written crushingly, *Flora is unstable, vindictive and a pernicious influence.*

The crumbling H.P. Hall and its surrounding twenty acres were the RSO's only assets. This was where George came in. He would buy the property for a pittance in a white-knight gesture to get the orchestra out of debt, then lease it back to them. As soon as the orchestra folded he would build a supermarket.

The plot was horribly ingenious. Instead of putting horrid little houses all over Cowslip Hill, which no-one wanted, he would build a festival centre, a megaplex with twenty-four drive-in cinemas, golf-courses, food halls, virtual-reality centres and bouncy castles which would bring employment, tourists, fun and prosperity to Rutminster. In return all he asked was planning permission to knock down the highly dangerous, collapsing Victorian monstrosity, the Herbert Parker Hall and build a supermarket with a new roundabout to hive off traffic. No wonder George had been so reluctant to repair the roof. Cotchester already had a beautiful hall, no distance from Valhalla by helicopter in which the new Super Orchestra would be housed. The only sticking point seemed to be Rannaldini's insistence on absolute hiring and firing rights.

Flora was about to print out the whole file when she nearly died of heart failure because there was a great hammering on the door.

'Anyone at home? Come oot, come oot,' called Dixie's voice.

'Priddock must be having a ziz,' said Randy.

'Or Jessica a bonk.'

But after a bit more hammering they got bored and wandered off.

Sweat was trickling down Flora's body. She'd never make a burglar; her hand was shaking so violently she was petrified of pressing the wrong button and wiping all the evidence. But somehow she managed to switch back to the file menu and type in *'Print'* beside *'Orchestra South'*. Slowly but miraculously fifteen pages rolled out. She had just managed to shove them up her jersey and unlock the door when Jessica staggered in. It would have been hard to decide who looked the more guilty. Jessica's hair was sopping from the shower. Flora felt sick with misery. Viking had obviously screwed her.

Hearing a thud behind her, she jumped out of her skin but it was only John Drummond crash landing on the carpet, weaving round Jessica's buckling legs. Flora hoped to God he didn't speak English.

'He's asking for his dinner.' said Jessica. 'George is having a black-tie do at home this evening and he wants everything perfect. I'll have to go out shopping again later, I wasted my entire lunch-hour trying to find scallops. If only there was a Waitrose in Rutminster.'

'There may be one sooner than you think,' said Flora grimly as she sidled out.

What the hell was she to do? Viking would have left for London by now to record the Brahms *Horn Trio*. The only answer, if she were to save Abby and the rest of the orchestra, was to tackle George at once.

Driving down the High Street, she saw a newspaper hoarding: MEGAPLEX FOR COWSLIP HILL.

Screeching to a halt she picked up a paper but it only reported the delighted reaction of councillors and residents.

Alan Cardew, the planning officer, was quoted as saying, 'This really puts Rutminster on the map.'

It was a bitterly cold evening. After a boiling bath to remove the sweat and a couple of stiff vodkas, Flora slid all over the road as she drove round to George's splendid house which was situated on the other side of Rutminster as far as possible from both Cowslip Hill and H.P. Hall. George wouldn't want to spoil his own green hills with megaplexes and supermarkets, thought Flora savagely as her wheel tracks ruined his perfect lawn.

The whole place, she could see, was speedily being wrecked by George's fearful taste, a man on his own who had no truck with interior designers.

'Bet he knocked her arms off,' she muttered, as she passed a huge replica of the *Venus de Milo* glittering with frost.

The butler told her to hop it. So Flora asked him to tell Mr Hungerford that it was Flora Seymour and he better get rid of his dinner party, because she wanted to talk about Orchestra South.

After two minutes, by which time Flora had practically frozen to the doorstep, she was shown into George's study.

The room was lit by a large chandelier which the butler promptly dimmed. The autumnal-leaf-patterned carpet was so new, he had great difficulty tugging the door shut over it. Brown leather sofas and armchairs hung about awkwardly, like buffaloes. Repro-Georgian bookshelves on either side of the gas log fire were filled with book-club editions, videos and reference books including *Encyclopaedia Britannica* by the yard.

One wall was covered by a vast television screen and a stereo, a second by thousands of LPs, tapes and CDs. The third, which faced George's imposing, incredibly tidy desk, was dominated by a Green Park railing portrait of a beautiful woman with short pale yellow hair and cold hare-bell-blue eyes, whose brilliance was accentuated by the huge sapphires round her neck. She had the disdainful perfection of women behind the beauty counters of big department stores, who want to shame you into spending a fortune on make-up and skin care. This must be Ruth whom George refused to divorce. She didn't look a bundle of laughs. You could see why George had the hots for Juno. She and Ruth were the same type, ice rather than nice maidens.

Flora's teeth were rattling like Cherub's castanets, a

glance in the ornate, white gold framed mirror over the fire showed her nose bright red as a clown's. Ruth would no doubt have recommended green foundation. Flora jumped as she heard voices. Obviously guests were being hastily ejected.

Opening the heavy rust dralon curtains a fraction, she could see Alan and Lindy Cardew (very done up in diamonds and a new full-length mink), two other men she recognized as high-profile local councillors, two bankers from the RSO board and their wives and goodness, the Steel Elf, wrapping herself in a long blue velvet cloak, all going towards their cars.

Then she heard George apologizing for some cock-up in the kitchen.

'See you in the Hoogry Hoonter in ten minutes.'

'You'll be lucky,' snarled Flora.

Enticing smells of wine, herbs and scallops wafting from the kitchen, belying any cock-up, reminded her she hadn't eaten all day. Feeling dizzy, she leant against the marble mantelpiece.

A week's skiing, even if the mobile had gone up the mountain with him, had almost ironed out the bags under George's eyes. His dark brown shiny face matched his leather sofas and armchairs. The black and white of his dinner jacket softened the rough, rocky features. White teeth chewing a cigar, big suntanned hand clamped round a glass of whisky, obviously trying to bluff it out, he looked almost genial as he shoved open the door:

'Well, what's all this about? I haven't got much time.'

'You better make it,' snapped Flora.

Except for her red nose, her face was whiter than the marble fireplace. With the collar of her long black overcoat turned up, she looked like a Victorian waif in the last stages of consumption. George was about to offer her a drink when she said: 'I know exactly what you're up to, you bastard. I was busking outside the Archduke in Concert Hall Approach two weeks ago. I saw you and Rannaldini going in and coming out. You must both have needed really long spoons to sup with one another.'

George took a slug of brandy.

'I was in London for a meeting of the Association of British Orchestras,' he said flatly. 'Rannaldini and I were discoosing him guest conducting the orchestra on the occasional date. He does happen to live in the area.'

'Bollocks,' shouted Flora, 'you were discussing his taking over the RSO and firing 90 per cent of the orchestra.'

Then, at George's look of amused incredulity, she added, 'And if you don't renew Abby's contract for starters, I'm going straight to the Press. My mother has contacts with every newspaper editor in Fleet Street and New York.'

'This is blackmail,' said George bleakly and reached for the telephone.

'The blackest possible,' said Flora. 'It's the only way to cope with shits like you. Buying the hall cheaply in a white-knight gesture, then building supermarkets on the site the moment the orchestra folds. You bloody Waitrosencavalier!'

Jolted at last George dropped the telephone back on the hook: 'How d'you know about that?'

'You shouldn't give your stupid secretary, who gets paid twice as much as a rank-and-file viola player, such long-lunch hours. I raided your computer today and printed out the entire "*Orchestra South*" file.'

George gave a long sigh. 'It's the only way to save the orchestra – at least the good people get to keep their jobs.'

'Abby doesn't and she flaming well deserves to. Have you any idea how hard she works, poring over the wretched scores day in day out, till two or three in the morning.'

'She's an hysteric.'

'So – she's an artist. The orchestra's getting better and better.'

'I wish the houses were. We're haemorrhaging to death, can't you understand that?'

'Give her time, look how long it took Simon Rattle to turn the CBSO around.'

'And now they've got a bluddy great deficit,' said George brutally.

'Anyway,' Flora briskly disregarded a point against herself, 'the RSO doesn't want to live in Cotchester and play in some horrible opera pit under a little Hitler. It's like sending ponies down the mine.'

'You overdramatize everything. They'd be well paid and they'd make great music.'

'No, they wouldn't, super orchestras don't work. There are too many chiefs and not enough Indians for them to boss around. The mix is too rich. Anyway, they'd get sacked if they split a note.

'Rannaldini's evil,' Flora's voice was rising, 'He lives near my parents and poisons the air like pesticide and I bet you told him we were about to record Winifred Trapp and Fanny Mendelssohn.'

'Don't be fatuous,' roared George, losing his temper. 'If you think I want to be landed with the bills for soloists you must be joking.'

Somehow he managed to control himself and sitting down at his desk, got out a cheque book.

'OK, how much will it take?'

'I don't want money,' said Flora in outrage. 'I want everyone's contracts renewed – except Hilary's, Carmine and the Steel Elf,' she added as an afterthought.

'Who?'

'Juno Meadows. I saw her poncing out of here with her Gstaad tan. How you have the gall to tell Abby she's losing caste living with me – yes, you did – when you've been guzzling *glühwein* off piste with Juno.'

'Don't by bluddy childish, Juno was making oop the noombers.'

'And doing a number of you, *soixante-neuf*, I suppose, although she'd be a bit refined for that. I'm surprised you haven't built a horrid little chalet on her.'

Flora was beginning to feel faint; somehow she reached the door, half-expecting to slip on those autumn leaves. She must keep talking to shut him up: 'I'll only tear up that print-out when I've got proof everyone's contracts have been renewed. Rannaldini's a fiend, remember, he'll double-cross you the moment he gets the chance.' And she was out of the door running towards her car.

Fortunately the roads were empty. She felt so lonely she longed to drop off at The Bordello, curl up in Viking's bed with Nugent and wait for him to come home. Since they split up, however, the rest of the Celtic Mafia, not knowing the reason and sensing Viking's unhappiness, had become wildly antagonistic.

After a sleepless night and a long unrewarding day of rehearsal with a stupid guest conductor whose beat was impossible to follow, Flora returned to Woodbine Cottage and an equally shattered Marcus. She had refrained from telling him about George's and Rannaldini's skulduggery. He didn't need upsetting. Tomorrow evening he was playing the Rachmaninov. Flora was terrified he'd peaked. He had practically worn out the keys of the Steinway. He had lived the piece, crawled inside it, knew every note, not only his own part, but also the orchestra's by heart. But would he have enough heart to do it justice?

He and Flora were just commiserating over a cup of tea and slices of cherry cake when Abby floated in brandishing a magnum of champagne.

'We have got to celebrate, right? George has just summoned me and said the board are going to renew my contract for another year. I'm not sure how pleased Howie will be – he figures I oughta move on, but I expect George will be able to persuade him.

'And I've persuaded George not to cut salaries at the moment to zap all those rumours about a merger between us and the CCO. He and I are going to assess the merits of everyone in the orchestra over the next few weeks and renew as many contracts as possible.'

And George thinks that'll keep me quiet, fumed Flora.

Abby looked wonderful, the cold weather always whipped up colour in her sallow cheeks.

'And,' she went on scrabbling at the gold paper round the top of the bottle, 'at last I can get rid of El Squeeko and Cyril.'

'You can't,' said Flora appalled. 'Viking'll never let you.'

'And Juno.'

'You may have lucked out there.'

But Abby was on a roll; she had totally misjudged George.

'He's not the philistine I figured he was. It's kinda gratifying when all one's hard grind pays off. Now we can build the orchestra together. I guess he is attracted to me,' she announced happily.

Flora was upset to see the hurt in Marcus's eyes; she herself was enraged – after all she'd done to save Abby, particularly when Abby smugly announced that Flora's was one of the contracts George was iffy about renewing.

'He didn't know you were only on six months' trial. He figures you're not pulling your weight. Says you've got an attitude problem.'

'And he's got a platitude problem,' snarled Flora.

'That is monstrously unfair,' protested Marcus.

'Tell him to go and jump in the cement mixer.'

'I'm just reporting what he said.' The flying champagne cork sent the cats racing from the kitchen. 'But I figure I've managed to persuade him you're a worthwhile member of the orchestra.'

Flora suddenly realized she'd eaten the rest of the cherry cake and had to undo her jeans.

Bloody Abby, if only she knew. Flora was tempted to tell her the truth but again didn't want a scene before Marcus's concert.

Abby should have spent the evening studying the Rachmaninov but, convinced she knew it, because she'd heard Marcus playing it so often, she got tight instead.

FORTY-SIX

On the wall of Marcus's dressing-room was a photograph of Clifton Suspension Bridge. He wished he could jump off it. How could he possibly play the most difficult piano concerto ever written when his violently trembling hands wouldn't tie his white tie or slot in the gold cuff-links bearing the Campbell-Black crest. The rehearsal had been disastrous. Abby had faffed around telling the orchestra Rachmaninov was born on April Fool's Day, and had lived on Lake Lucerne like Rodney, and that Mahler had conducted the second performance of the concerto in the States, until Dixie had yelled, 'Come back, Gustav, all is forgiven.'

Marcus had never dreamt the orchestral sound would be so dense, loud and so distracting or that desperately trying to keep up with Abby's beat he would play so many wrong notes and at one point stop altogether.

The orchestra, totally indifferent to such calamities, only raised the odd eyebrow and carried on reading their newspapers, filling in tax forms and applying for other jobs.

Abby wouldn't even give him time to rehearse the cadenza.

'That's your baby, you know it backwards.'

And instead of going back over the places where he'd screwed up so he could correct his mistakes she then moved on to Hilary's and Simon's solos, and one or two of the more complicated tuttis. She then spent the rest of the rehearsal perfecting the timing of Carmine Jones's off-stage trumpet solo in the *Third Leonora* overture.

'It's exactly eight minutes before you come in, Carmine, so don't fall asleep.'

'Not bloody likely.'

Carmine, in a new butch lumberjack shirt, winked at Lindy Cardew, who, in a tight shocking-pink sweater, was jabbing huge scented pink lilies, no doubt paid for by her husband's massive backhanders from George, into vases along the front of the stage.

Any flowers or blossom played havoc with Marcus's asthma. Flora, in a rare act of domesticity, had brushed and washed down his tails to save fumes from dry cleaning. But even worse chemicals were now wafting from the walls of his dressing-room, newly painted a restful green gloss to calm soloists.

Glancing in the mirror, he noticed his face had a sinister blue tinge. In case of any emergency attack he had brought a pre-loaded syringe but he was terrified of letting down Abby, the orchestra and George, who'd engaged him and been so particularly kind. Worried that Marcus was too thin and probably hadn't eaten all day, George had arranged for lentil soup, grilled plaice and fruit salad to be sent in from the Old Bell, and Marcus had just thrown up the lot, panicking all the while that he might choke. The more he fretted the harder it was to breathe. It was as though someone had held a pillow to his face.

But the greatest terror was the Rachmaninov lurking ahead: dark, fierce, explosive, mysterious as the Russian continent, a huge monster waiting to be captured and tamed by his bare hands.

Passionate relief battled with bitter disappointment

that neither Rupert nor Taggie had bothered to come or even send him a good-luck card. Helen, on the other hand, had rolled up an hour before the off and hung around reading his cards and moaning about Rannaldini who was taking a masterclass in Rome, until George barged in and bluntly told her to pack it in, because 'the lad needs to distance himself'.

George then whisked Helen off to wow the sponsors in the VIP lounge. Lady Rannaldini was looking particularly fetching in a Lindka Cierach suit of ivory silk with a short fitted jacket emphasizing her tiny waist and her newly lifted and remodelled breasts and bottom.

Was Helen in on George's and Rannaldini's plan for a super orchestra and market? wondered Flora. She couldn't see Helen frolicking on a bouncy castle. At least Helen and George can have a good bitch about me, she thought wryly.

Still hubristic over yesterday's renewal of her contract and her *rapprochement* with George, Abby had also nipped into Bath that morning and bought a wildly fashionable, very ostentatious orange satin bomber jacket, which she teamed with matching orange satin drainpipes and a black bra. With her wild, shaggy, dark curls, drug pallid face and snake hips she looked like a rock star.

'Ladies and Gentlemen, please take your places on the platform,' Knickers was shouting along the passage at the musicians.

'Christ, here comes Sunset Boulevard,' said Dixie, as Abby came out of the conductor's room and popped next door to show herself off to Marcus, who was frantically flipping through his score. He could hardly see it for pencil marks.

'Don't look any more, right? You'll confuse yourself.'

'I'm going to throw up again.'

'No, you're not. I'll take care of you. You've got a good twenty minutes. *Leonora* takes about fourteen, then they've got to get the piano on.'

'Don't take it too fast,' pleaded Marcus, 'It says allegro but ma non tanto.'

'Trust me, d'you think George'll like this pant suit?'

'Fantastic, he'll pant with lust.'

'You reckon.' Abby fluffed her hair in the mirror and sauntered off towards the stage.

Marcus felt that his hammering heart would soon leave internal bruising on his ribs. The only benefit of panic attacks was that they dulled the pain of Abby lusting after other men.

He picked up his mascot, the copy of *The Tempest* she had given him which he took everywhere.

'*Merrily, merrily shall I live now,*' he read

'*Under the blossom that hangs on the bough.*'

Ariel couldn't have been an asthmatic.

Viking and Flora should have already been on stage, but Viking had only just got back from recording the Brahms *Horn Trio* and Flora was giving him a whispered update on her raiding of the files, her confrontation of George and George's new alliance with Abby.

'The bastard,' said Viking outraged.

'We must tell the orchestra,' pleaded Flora. 'If they were prepared to strike to get rid of Abby, they'd certainly come out against a merger.'

Viking shook his head.

'No-one loses strikes except musicians. They'd just close us down without any redundancy. Let's see what George does next, he won't want you shopping him to the Press or he might not get planning permission to pull down the hall. At least this gives us room to manoeuvre.'

'I don't trust him.'

'I quite like the guy,' admitted Viking.

'Only because he's offering you a job in the new orchestra. He's just swanned off with Lady Rannaldini.'

'Is Sir Roberto here?'

'He's in Rome,' said Flora bitterly. 'Taking a mistress-class.'

Unable to stop himself, Viking pulled her into his arms.

'I know how this hurts you, sweetheart.'

'What the fuck are you two doing?' screamed Abby, jealousy surging up as uncontrollable as vomit, at finding them together when she was convinced the *affaire* was over.

Flora nearly dropped her viola.

'You both should have been on stage five minutes ago,' yelled Abby. 'Julian is waiting to go on, Knickers is going ballistic looking for you.'

'Great outfit, Maestro.' Totally unabashed, Viking wandered towards the stage. 'Onotterably chic to match it to your soloist's hair.'

'Have you got some sort of death-wish?' Abby turned her fury on Flora. 'I told you last night, OK? Your job's on the line.'

Once again, not wanting to rattle Abby with the merger plot in case she flipped and unnerved Marcus, Flora blurted out that Viking was boasting that he'd just pulled Jessica.

'It's called liaising with the management,' she muttered and fled.

Abby, who still went weak at the knees, every time she remembered Viking kissing her outside St Clement's, was totally thrown. Somehow she got through the overture because the orchestra could play it in their sleep. She didn't even notice that Carmine was late on his off-stage entrance because he'd been kissing Lindy Cardew in the instrument room.

But arrogantly thinking she knew the Rachmaninov well enough and opting to conduct without a score she got hopelessly lost in the first movement.

Flora was bowing away furiously among the violas, worrying about Marcus's set white face and his faltering sound. Looking up for reference, she found Abby's beat wasn't there, lost confidence and started to panic and make mistakes. Soon the rest of the orchestra, who had also been hopelessly under-rehearsed, were all over the place, half of them coming in, half of them not, unravelling and about to stop dead.

'Fucking brown-trouser job,' muttered Dixie to Randy.

Ironically this was Marcus's salvation. He had nearly fainted with terrror when he first saw the size of the audience. Fighting for breath, his smile sellotaped to his face, his fingers, when he began playing, had been impossibly stiff and wouldn't do anything he told them.

But, realizing his darling Abby was in desperate trouble, he forgot himself, concentrating on saving her. Steady as a Welsh cob, he kept going, hammering away repeatedly at the first subject, *Dum, di-di, dum di-di, dum, dum*, nodding until the orchestra found their place.

Abby, with no score for reference, however, was still floundering, her gaudy orange suit making her all the more conspicuous. Towards the end of the movement she got completely lost again so Marcus, with amazing assurance, skipped a page, plunging straight in to the cadenza, so everyone knew where they were and could have some breathing space.

He had chosen Rachmaninov's second cadenza which was far more demanding. Gradually, as he relaxed and the music he adored took over, he forgot everything else. His pale tortured face grew happy and peaceful. Listening to the melancholy torrents of sound, glittering like a waterfall in the moonlight, Flora ached at the beauty of it. Glancing round, she caught Viking looking straight at her, although he smiled, his eyes were as wet as her own.

Marcus held his breath as the cadenza drew to a close. Not having rehearsed it at all, would Abby know when to cue in the orchestra? He had to accompany brief, beautiful echoes from Peter Plumpton on the flute, then Simon, then Hilary and finally Viking and Quinton, but they all came in on the dot, and the movement finished more or less together.

In the intermezzo where Marcus interpreted the word pianissimo in a multitude of different ways, and in the heroic splendid finale, he grew and grew in stature. Beneath his racing fingers, the great dark Russian monster had become suddenly biddable, and was carrying him home as joyfully as Arion's dolphin.

But it was a close-run thing. Marcus got an ecstatic reception, in part because he'd looked so vulnerable and terrified at the beginning and so handsome and touchingly amazed at the applause at the end. Most of the audience hadn't a clue anything had gone wrong. But the orchestra had, and they cheered him to the leaking rooftops, rattling their bows, beating out a tantivy of approval on the shoulders of their cellos and basses.

Utterly distraught, Abby fled to her dressing-room refusing to return, so none of the soloists within the orchestra were raised to their feet for a special clap, which enraged Hilary.

'Abby should have brought the wind up,' she kept saying.

Marcus took five curtain calls and was just collapsing thankfully in his dressing-room when Noriko banged on the door.

'Quick, quick, quick, Mr Brack,' she cried enthusiastically, 'come and pray again, the pubric are still crapping.'

Marcus was still laughing when he reached the middle of the stage and shook hands with a beaming Julian yet again.

'You'll have to give them an encore.'

'But I haven't practised anything.'

It would have seemed so presumptuous.

'Just busk it,' shouted Bill Thackery.

For a second, Marcus gazed at the ecstatic pink faces, their clapping hands growing pinker by the minute, luxuriating in the sound like waves rolling down the shingle. Then he sat down and played Schumann's *Dreaming*, which had everyone in floods and elicited even louder roars of applause.

Meanwhile George had had a wearying two days justifying his volte-face over Abby's contract to various enraged members of the board including Miles, Mrs Parker, Canon Airlie, not to mention Gwynneth and Gilbert. Aware he would receive even more flak after tonight's near débâcle he went grimly into the conductor's room to find Flora yelling at a sobbing Abby.

'You're just jealous because he's got more talent than you, that's what, and you can't bear anyone to get ahead. After all Marcus has done for you. All that transcribing and simplifying and explaining those bloody great scores. Think of the times he's lugged your clothes to the cleaners and cooked and cleaned up after you and fed your cats and polished your shoes and let you pinch his jerseys.'

'You pinch his jerseys,' wailed Abby,

'I've known him longer, I'm allowed to. You wouldn't have got a second foot on the rostrum without him, you stupid bitch, and you're so fucking vain you had to jeopardize his big break conducting without a score.'

'I know, I know.'

Alarmed he might not have a second half, George told Flora to pack it in and Abby to wash her face and pull herself together.

He then dragged Flora outside.

'Nice to see someone else getting it in the neck,' he said drily. 'And that's the "stupid bitch" you're so determined to save.'

Flora blushed, then hastily changed the subject. 'Didn't Marcus play brilliantly?'

'He had absolutely no choice,' said George bleakly.

Somehow Abby managed to limp through Schubert's *Fourth Symphony*.

Then, speaking to no-one, cutting the sponsor's reception again, she hurtled home to a deserted Woodbine Cottage.

Flora had gone out boozing with Cherub, Noriko and Davie Buckle. Marcus had been swept out to dinner by George, Miles and a manic Helen.

FORTY-SEVEN

Sitting next to Marcus at dinner, George fired off endless questions about Abby's, Flora's and Marcus's plans for the future, then insisted that his chauffeur, known as Harve the Heavy, took him back to Woodbine Cottage.

'You're not driving with all that drink inside you. It's not as if we've had to fork out for your room at the Old Bell.' Then, affectionately ruffling Marcus's hair, said, 'You did bluddy well, lad, we'd have been right in it if you hadn't come to Abby's rescue.'

Marcus fought an insane drunken urge to collapse into George's arms. He was so strong and solid and he had the same brusque gentleness, the almost patriarchal kindness that Marcus missed so much since Malise's death. He couldn't imagine why Flora and, until recently Abby, kept slagging him off.

Perhaps George was in love with Helen, Marcus thought wistfully. From Jake Lovell onwards, men had been particularly kind to him for just that reason. Marcus hoped not. George had promised to look at the RSO calendar and try and find him another date.

Slumped happily in the front of the Rolls, Marcus gabbled most uncharacteristically to Harve that Piggy

Parker had booked him for a soirée in June, playing tunes like '*After Henry*' and '*Lady be Good*'. Marcus beat them out on the dashboard until Harve started singing along.

'And Gwendolyn Chisledon wanted to know where Mr Hungerford was going to build his ghastly multiplex,' went on Marcus. 'When she heard it was on Cowslip Hill, she heaved a sigh of relief. "Oh, that's all right, I thought it was *our* side of Rutminster."'

Harve grinned.

'And Howie Denston rang me on George's mobile in the middle of dinner and wants me to get into bed with him.' Marcus giggled. 'I do hope he means financially not sexually.'

'Either way, if I may say so,' said Harve, in his grave-digger's drawl, 'you're going to be screwed.'

It was a beautiful clear night. Although the great beeches along the lake glittered with frost, the moonlight was bright enough to pick out the first pale primroses nestling in their roots.

Singing and laughter was coming from The Bordello; Marcus wished he could have dropped in. One of his best moments of the concerto had been Viking's little horn solo in the middle movement; he'd just liked to have talked the concerto through with someone.

As he stumbled out of the car, Orion, his favourite constellation, was free falling into the poplar copse at the top of the wild-flower meadow. Mars, a gold butterfly, was being chased by Leo the Lion. The outside lamp was still on, transforming the leafless clematis over the front door into a scrunch-dried blond; but the cottage was in darkness.

'Thank you so much,' said Marcus.

'Pleasure sir, I am not a great lover of classical music but may I trouble you for your autograph. One day it will be something to show my grandchildren.'

'*Dum di-di dum di-di dum dum,*' sang Marcus.

His shadow was squat and black at his heels, reminiscent of one of Malise's labradors. Had his stepfather from beyond the grave sent the dog to guard him on such a special evening?

Only after several fumbling attempts did he realize the door wasn't locked.

'I did it, I fucking did it.' As he punched the air he nearly fell over Abby's music case in the hall. Then he heard the sound of desperate sobbing and stumbled upstairs where, watched by two worried cats, Abby lay slumped on her four-poster. She was dressed in jeans and Marcus's old black sweater with two holes in the elbows. She was utterly distraught to have let him down.

'Flora's right – I have always taken you for granted. I haven't cleaned a pair of shoes since I moved in.'

'But I l-like looking after you.'

Collapsing on the patchwork counterpane, he found himself stroking her hair, drenched with tears rather than sweat now, as thick and coarse as a pony's mane. Outside he could see the lake gleaming silver and mysterious. Trailing his hand downwards, he patted her shuddering shoulders, which were hard and muscular from so many hours conducting. Her long legs reached to the bottom of the bed. She hadn't bothered to shower after the concert and smelled disturbingly of dried sweat and *Amarige*. From their moonlit reflection in the long mirror opposite, they could have been two boys. Marcus took her in his arms.

'Oh Christ, Abby, I've always loved you. From the moment you came loping up to the stage at the Academy.'

Her mouth tasted acid from fear, but as he kissed her he thought she would suck the tongue out of his mouth and was amazed by the leaping wolf-like passion of her response.

Apart from an ill-fated scuffle on the lawn with Boris she had been celibate since the trauma of Christopher three years ago. She had Marcus's clothes off him in a trice, ripping off several shirt buttons, nearly garrotting

601

him with his tie and jamming his zip in the process. Like quick silver she was all over him, blowing in his ears, running her fingers through his hair, nuzzling his neck. Then she moved downwards, slowly kissing each bumpy rib, burying her face in his taut belly, exclaiming in wonder at the greyhound grace of his body.

There was only one drawback. Marcus couldn't get it up. Even when his cock was sucked into the warm dark wet cavern of Abby's throat, it remained as soft and as innocent as a lamb's tail.

Marcus was even more contrite than Abby had been about the Rachmaninov. Abby, however, was surprisingly understanding.

'It doesn't matter, you've had a skinful, OK, and you're pooped. You know what Luisa Pellafacini says: "Before a concert Julian won't, after the concert he can't."'

'I feel such a wimp.'

'You can still make me come.' Abby put his hand between her legs.

'I'm seriously sorry,' Marcus muttered into her shoulder, 'but I don't know which doorbell to press.'

Raising his head, prising his face round towards hers, Abby could see him blushing the same blood-red in the moonlight as his hair.

'But I thought you and Flora – surely at school? The way she wanders into the studio half-naked.'

Marcus shook his head.

'We snogged once or twice but we know each other too well and always started to laugh. Oh Abby, darling, I don't know how to tell you this, but I'm a virgin.'

'You gotta be joking, with a father like Rupert.'

'That's the trouble,' Marcus rolled over and buried his face in the pillow. 'Everyone expects me to be a great macho super-stud like Dad, and I just bottle out.'

Then stammering frantically, almost crying, he told her about the night of Basil Baddingham's stag-party. 'Edith was there. She drunk everyone under the table,' and his disastrous encounter with the tart, and the near-fatal asthma attack.

'Every time I try and make it with a girl I see contempt in Dad's face.'

Holding his shuddering rigid body in her arms, Abby was overwhelmed with tenderness.

'That's enough to put anyone off sex,' she said indignantly, 'and on top of that it's a knee-jerk reaction to think you'll choke again. What a son of a bitch, what a damn fool insensitive preppy asshole.'

'He wants an heir,' said Marcus wearily.

'Now listen to me, right.' Abby pulled the duvet up tucking it round his shivering body. 'For starters you're the prettiest guy I ever saw, sure you are, and tonight you were the most shit-scared. I never saw stage-fright like that. I know what guts it took even to get onto the platform, OK? But in the end you showed everyone you're made of steel. You were the superman, you saved us.

'I love you, Marcus,' her voice broke. 'It's just hit me like one of George's bulldozers, and if we love each other we only need time. I'll get you going, there are so many tricks.'

Marcus's shivering became a quiver of pleasure as she ran her fingers lingeringly along the cleft between his buttocks.

'All women,' she went on half-mockingly, 'want to marry a virgin so they can mould him exactly the way they want.'

'Perhaps Barbara Cartland will make me the hero of one of her novels.'

'You're my hero anyway. George never stops nagging me to get involved in educational projects. Teaching you about sex is far more rewarding than relating Respighi's *Birds* to the Blackmere Woods.'

As Marcus started to laugh, Abby took his hand, first moving it over her acorn-hard nipples, then burying it in her wiry dark pubic hair.

'Under the fold you can feel a little nipple, that's the clit, now lick your middle finger and stroke it, very gently, a mild pizzicato, right? Now slide a finger down and inside me in and out, deeper and deeper, testing for wetness, that's lovely, now back to the clit again.'

It was rather like being taught fingering by his old music mistress, thought Marcus hazily. Any minute he expected Abby to tell him to use the long fingers for the black notes, and not to turn his whole hand, when he moved the thumb under.

'Oh, wow,' murmured Abby happily, 'long fingers aren't just good for tenths, I'm nearly there.'

He expected her to scream, shout and thrash about, and was alarmed he'd done something wrong when her body suddenly arched, stiffened, trembled violently all over and seemed to stop breathing.

'Abby, are you OK?'

'Heavenly.' Her body slumped, but inside he could feel her melting and throbbing. 'You're a genius. You made me come.'

'Truly – I thought it would be so noisy.'

'When it's real, it's the quietest thing on earth. I love you.'

She fell asleep at once. Marcus lay awake stunned by the evening's developments, reliving all the mistakes he'd made, particularly at the beginning of the Rachmaninov, luxuriating in the memory of the applause, and the kind things people had said. He hardly dared think how miraculously it would sort out his problems if he got it together with Abby.

I'm straight, I'm straight, he made a thumbs-up sign to his reflection in the mirror. All the same, like some lovely little restaurant you stumble on in the Dordogne when you're pissed, he wondered if he'd ever be able to find the clitoris again. Perhaps Abby would let him bring a magnifying glass into lessons.

The next day, he had great difficulty keeping his newly straight face when he went back to H.P. Hall to collect his car, and was greeted by an overjoyed Noriko, waving a newspaper.

'Mr Black, Mr Black.' At last she'd got her 'L's' right. 'Have you seen your wonderful clit in *Lutminster Echo*?'

The Rutshire Butcher had reviewed the encore not the concerto, and written of '*Marcus Black's exquisite control and beauty of tone, unhindered by orchestra or conductor.*'

his picture was greeted by howls of joy from Marcus, reducing
the tension.

'He likes Mr Eldred,' Abby said once both her dogs split.
Flora was suddenly wonderful to Marcus because Abby's
time together. But her hard covered the chance yes
his concern, and secure of Marcus, felt A's impulsing
anger and felt up to joke, endeavour to make up to
wistful dog.

FORTY-EIGHT

The next day Flora felt very flat after her sighting of
Rannaldini, her rows with George and an inexplicable
feeling of something going on between Abby and
Marcus. She needed a male in her life.

Having bought an electric blanket she went off to
the nearest NCDL kennels. The desperate barking, the
pleading faces, the scrabbling paws saddened her
immeasurably. Like the Anouilh heroine, how could
she ever be happy while there was a single stray dog in
the world? But in the end she chose the smallest,
ugliest black-and-tan mongrel and called him Trevor.
Trevor had been so bored in the kennels, he'd spent all
day playing with his own shadow. Realizing his luck, he
settled in immediately. Abby was livid when he treed
both Scriabin and Sibelius, two chattering magpies up
in the chestnut tree again, and then wolfed all their
food.

'He'll be a partner in crime for that bloody Nugent.'

'He'll be a terrific guard dog,' beamed Flora. 'Lady
Chisleden had a break-in while she was at the concert last
night.'

Trevor was all of nine inches high and sulked dreadfully when Flora forgot to put on the electric blanket.

Although he immediately found his way out through the cat door and went hunting, he howled if Flora left him behind, so she smuggled him into rehearsals and he guarded her coat and her viola case in the women's changing-room.

George was not amused by the arrival of Trevor, particularly when he noisily chased John Drummond between two Perspex models on his first morning. Fortunately for Flora, George had been instantly distracted by devastating news: the Cotchester Chamber Orchestra blithely announcing they would be staging their own Opera Gala in the grounds of Cotchester Cathedral starring Rannaldini and Harefield. The main problem was they had picked the same Sunday in early May that the RSO were mounting their All-Star Centenary Gala.

This would wipe out the RSO's audience. Georgie Maguire and an increasingly doubtful Dancer Maitland singing Rodgers and Hammerstein could hardly compete with the rerun of the most successful classical record of all time.

George made out he was furious. Flora, who still had the print-outs under her mattress, suspected he had tipped Rannaldini off about the date of the gala, in order to run the RSO into the ground. The Arts Council, increasingly dismayed by the popularizing of the RSO repertoire, were muttering openly about closing down one orchestra.

At the beginning of March, El Creepo and Simon Painshaw came to the end of their two-year term as orchestral members of the board. Few players were interested in replacing them, as hatred of the management had reached an all-time high. In the end Hilary and Bill Thackery put themselves forward. Hilary, the orchestra decided, wanted the chance to exchange meaningful glances with Miles. She was a dangerous bitch but Bill would balance her out. Bill was such a nice guy and he'd behaved so well over the re-recording in

January of *Rachel's Requiem* and Julian repossessing his violin solo, that everyone felt he deserved to be on the board. Bill would see them right.

Meanwhile as a thank you and twenty-second birthday present, Abby took Marcus to Covent Garden, where the Cossak-Russe, the most dazzling ballet company in the world, were dancing *Le Corsair*. Tickets had sold out months ago and more touts were hanging round the opera house than pigeons. But the principal soloist, the great Alexei Nemerovsky, known in the Press as 'The Treat from Moscow' was both an old friend of Boris's and a long-time collector of Abby's records and had sent her two tickets.

It was heaven to escape from the RSO and all its problems for an evening, thought Abby, as she and Marcus wandered hand in hand through the packed foyer. Marcus had retrieved her orange satin trouser suit from the waste-paper basket and persuaded her to wear it. She was gratified how many people recognized her and nudged their companions, but she noticed the eyes of both sexes then swivelled to Marcus and stayed there in admiration.

He was wearing a dark suit that had been made for him two years ago by Rupert's tailor and a lilac-and-white striped shirt and a purple tie, which Flora had given him for his birthday. Success in the Rachmaninov had given him new confidence, he seemed to walk taller. He is a beauty, thought Abby proudly. They had made love constantly since that first night, and although Marcus still hadn't got it up, he had given her a lot of pleasure, and was about to graduate (B.Clit) in the geography of female sexual anatomy.

'It'll happen,' Abby kept telling him, 'you mustn't have a hang-up.'

'More of a hang down,' grumbled Marcus.

At least they could laugh about it and after a couple of glasses of champagne in the bar, they sat very close together in the dark warmth of the theatre, opening their scarlet programmes, watching the lit-up bald head and waving arms of the conductor, aware that the vast audience could hardly wait for the overture to be over so they could catch a first glimpse of their god.

Nemerovsky was also known as the third 'N', because with Nijinsky and Nureyev he made up the triumvirate of greatest male dancers of all time. His leonine dark head, with the sliding black eyes, the cheek-bones at forty-five degrees and the huge pouting mouth, glared haughtily out from poster and programme.

Back swept the dark red velvet curtains, like labia minor, thought Marcus in his new knowledge. In delight the audience clapped the brilliant set, in which a heaving sailing ship filled with long-legged, wild-haired pirates was wrecked on a rocky shore. The tallest of the pirates, who was wearing a floppy white shirt, black knickerbockers and a red scarf round his forehead, was clearly hurt and was carried ashore by two of his comrades as the ship broke up in a mass of spray and crashing waves.

'That's Nemerovsky,' whispered Abby, as the pirates took refuge behind a rock and a lot of scantily dressed maidens swarmed on and jumped about.

I'm not sure I like ballet, thought Marcus.

Then Nemerovsky recovered from his concussion and suddenly erupted on to the centre of the stage as glitteringly dominant and beautiful as Orion in the winter sky.

Nemerovsky's leaps were legendary – gasp followed collective gasp as the Corsair seemed to fly through the air, to whirl like a dervish to rise and fizzle like a fire cracker, yet his stillness seemed to freeze audience and orchestra as long as he wanted – so that any spontaneous applause, that could have interrupted the action, also froze on people's hands.

And watching him, Marcus was lost, totally shipwrecked. He even felt himself groan with despair as the cold, poisoned steel of Cupid's arrow plunged deep into his heart, routing out any hope of heterosexuality. He realized he was only in love with Abby emotionally and had never really desired a human being before. He looked at Nemerovsky, remembering that Browning poem Flora was always quoting.

> *'As one who awakes.*
> *The past was a sleep*
> *And his life began.'*

Abby was in raptures, half in wonder for the conductor, who must be having a coronary controlling the orchestra in the face of such unpredictability, half-identifying with Nemerovsky's star quality. She had once held audiences captive, had been the only one on stage they had looked at. She must, must go back to the violin.

'He's got a butt almost as beautiful as Viking's,' she whispered to Marcus.

Boris, who was still wrestling with *King Lear*, only made the last act. It seemed sacrilegious to leave a seat empty for so long.

Afterwards Abby, Marcus and Boris went on to dinner at the Ivy, where they were later joined by Alexei and Evgenia, his stunningly pretty, principal ballerina. The whole restaurant rose and cheered them as they came in, and it was immediately champagne on the dacha.

Boris and Alexei fell on each other's necks. When, demanded Alexei, was Boris going to write a ballet for him? Marcus was in a complete daze which went unnoticed as the other four gabbled away in Russian. Alexei seemed far more taken with Abby than Evgenia. Occasionally his black eyes slid speculatively over Marcus, and when Marcus couldn't eat a thing, Alexei calmly forked up his potatoes announcing he was starving.

'I cannot eat before dancing, I am much too exciting.'

He reminded Marcus terrifyingly of Rupert. He had the same cool arrogance, the same predatory ability to pick off anything he chose. He was now having a terrrific Russian row with Evgenia, because she'd ordered him a Dover sole, rather than *Tournedos Rossini*, and when Boris tried to defuse things, turned on him as well. Then Alexei emptied a glass of red wine over Boris, Boris emptied one over Alexei and they both smashed their glasses against the wall. The management were just moving in to break the whole thing up when they saw the two dripping men were laughing uproariously and left them to it.

Then as instantly they stopped laughing, because Boris asked Alexei about Russia.

'There is no money,' Alexei's voice was deeper than the Corsair's ocean, a thrilling, husky, basso profundo, 'we are crippled by bureaucracy, the Mafia and chaos. There is no hope internally, eet must come from outside. I am OK, I come and go as I please, because I am beeg star. Everyone else is starving. Democracy does not feed people. So I owe eet to geeve my country spiritual uplift. You must come back, Boris, at least make visit.'

Boris, mopping his eyes with his table napkin, was so moved he drained both his own and Evgenia's glass.

'As Chekhov say,' he sighed, '*Freedom is destiny we may never reach, but we must squeeze slavery out of ourselves drop by drop,*' which reminded him his glass was empty, so he waved at the waiter to bring more bottles.

Trying to include Marcus, Abby told the others that he'd just played the Rachmaninov and Howie was trying to wangle him a date with the Royal Scottish National Orchestra playing Prokofiev's *Third Piano Concerto*.

'My father was friend of Prokofiev,' said Alexei, his glittering eyes trailing round the table.

'Just then a beeg grey wolf did come out of the forest,' he said softly, and threw back his head and laughed showing off long flaring nostrils and the stubble darkening his beautiful strong neck, which had left make-up on the collar of his white shirt.

Oh Christ, thought Marcus, what the hell's going to become of me? He felt dizzy with longing. Misinterpreting his distress, Evgenia said sympathetically that it was very difficult to make it as a pianist.

'Marcus is very shy, too,' Abby told her in Russian.

'Is he?' drawled Alexei in English, raising a jet-black eyebrow and staring at Marcus until he went scarlet.

'Then he must make record in Prague. Until you have record you are nuzzing. To managers, engagers, musical directors, record is all.'

'Serena at Megagram liked you a lot, Marcus,' said Boris encouragingly. 'She vill pick up production cost of record. I vill conduct for free, you will only need a few grand to pay the orchestra.'

'Great, I'll help out,' said Abby eagerly.

Sensing Marcus would like to get off the subject, Evgenia asked Abby about her orchestra. In no time Abby was telling her about the RSO's financial plight and Rannaldini's latest act of vandalism, programming an Opera Gala on the same day as their centenary celebrations.

'Rannaldini is very bad man,' said Alexei. 'He conduct in Moscow. Never again, eet was so fast, *Swan Lake* become Swan Rapids.'

Abby took a deep breath.

'Oh Alexei, you're not possibly free on Sunday 7 May to dance at our gala - only for ten minutes or so? It would honestly save us from going belly-up.'

In order to maintain his glitzy lifestyle, Alexei had been known to dance on a pin if the money was good enough but suddenly he agreed to appear at the gala for next to nothing. He and Evgenia would be in Paris at the time. As the gala was on a Sunday they could just nip over for the evening.

'I would like that,' smiled Evgenia, 'I love Vest Country.'

'You always need vest in Eengland,' mocked Alexei.

A manic Abby hugged them both.

'Oh thank you. That'll zap Rannaldini and Harefield at Cotchester. People'll fly in from all over the world to watch you two. What would you like to dance?'

'Prokofiev,' said Alexei, shooting a mocking glance at Marcus. '*Romeo and Juliet.* Stony leemits cannot keep love out.'

The waiters, trying not to yawn, were laying tables for the morrow. As they were leaving, Boris gave Alexei a score of *Rachel's Requiem*, which had just been published.

'Who did you dedicate it to, Flora or me or Marcus?' asked Abby turning the pages. 'To Astrid,' she read in outrage.

Boris shrugged: 'Someone 'as to babyseet.'

The bridges along the Embankment glittered like necklaces on the night, buds thickened against a dun-coloured sky, the park was full of daffodils.

'An 'orse guard, an 'orse guard, my keengdom for an 'orse guard,' yelled Alexei, as the taxi swung into St James's Street, dropping off him and Evgenia at the Stafford.

Abby and Marcus were staying at the Ritz. In the lift up, Abby put an idle hand on Marcus's cock.

'Oh my God.' She gave a whoop of joy. Perhaps Marcus was suddenly relaxed because Howie was getting him work, and she and Boris were going to make a record with him. Potency was so allied to success.

They were hardly inside the door when Abby turned to him, putting her hands on his shoulders, drawing him towards her, not daring to breathe as she felt him rising against her.

There was no time to wash. She unzipped both their flies and left him to wriggle out of his trousers and boxer shorts as she ripped off the orange trousers of her suit. The next moment they were on the floor and he was inside her.

'Aaah,' moaned Abby, 'that feels so good.'

The sex after that was fantastic. Marcus was so turned on by the thought of Alexei that with eyes shut and in desperate hunger he made love to Abby all night.

'I knew it would come right, if we gave it time,' sobbed a joyful Abby.

Marcus was so exhausted he forgot to take his asthma pills and had a bad attack in the morning. Driving back in the afternoon, they agreed not to tell anyone for the moment. Abby, however, couldn't resist confiding in Flora, who was surprisingly unenthusiastic.

Abby construed this as jealousy because Flora hadn't got a man at the moment. But Flora, who'd always suspected Marcus was gay, thought the whole thing would end in tears, and in turn couldn't resist confiding in Viking, who was equally unenthusiastic and drove Abby crackers referring to the Centenary Concert as the 'Gayla' because Dancer Maitland and Alexei were taking part.

'Alexei is not gay,' yelled Abby, 'He has a beautiful "partner" called Evgenia.'

Privately Abby was convinced Alexei had only agreed to dance because he fancied her. At any rate she had scored colossal brownie points with the board for providing Alexei, particularly when Declan O'Hara declared himself horrified by Rannaldini's and the CCO's attempts to sabotage Rutminster's centenary celebration.

'I'm afraid Edith's lost any real interest in the orchestra since she shacked up with Monica,' he told George over the telephone and then offered to read *Peter and the Wolf* at the gala.

Marcus was still reeling from meeting Alexei. He longed to talk to Flora, but felt it would be disloyal to Abby. If only he could have confided in Taggie. As an olive branch he sent her a Mother's Day card, but heard nothing back.

FORTY-NINE

Once it became known that Nemerovsky and Ilanova would be dancing, the gala became a total sell-out. Miles was panicking how to pack a tenth of the audience into the H.P. Hall when a gilt fig leaf obligingly fell off one of the cherubs adorning the front of the dress circle, just missing the Lady Mayoress. Restoring the cherub's modesty the following morning one of George's sharp builders noticed a huge crack in the ceiling over the stalls. Repairs would be lengthy and cost millions.

GALA IN JEOPARDY, trumpeted the *Rutminster Echo*.

Overnight George came neatly to the rescue, offering, as an alternative, his beautiful park. The previous owner had been a polo fanatic and had levelled a field behind the house. Here the multitudes could stretch out and be charged a hundred pounds a car. George's builders were soon at work, knocking up a splendid stage and a pit for the orchestra. Venturer Television were covering the gala because their own chief executive was reading *Peter and the Wolf* and Classic FM would record it. Stands on either side of the stage would seat a thousand people and, in front of the stage, fold-up chairs stretched back for forty rows to join the masses on the polo field.

With tickets ranging from five hundred to fifty pounds and freebies for anyone George wanted to woo, he and the RSO stood to make a killing. George's white-knight gesture was much applauded by the nationals and the *Rutminster Echo*. Readers' letters, no doubt penned by the recipients of George's backhanders, poured in condemning the H.P. Hall as a potential death-trap, urging that another smaller venue be found for the RSO.

'Preferably in Cotchester,' raged Flora to Viking.

'George has turned the whole thing to his advantage. I bet his builders made that crack so he can pick up H. P. Hall even cheaper. I hope it pisses with rain on the day.'

But the luck of the devil held. After a beastly cold grey, dry blustery April, a heatwave hit England in the week running up to the gala.

The only thing that cheered Flora up was George's memo on the notice-board typed by Jessica.

'As the gala takes place on the eve of the Fiftieth Anniversary of VE Day, please note "God Save the Queer", will be played .'

On the great day Rutminster Hall was patriotically decked with red, white and blue bunting. In deference to the soloists, Irish and Russian flags also hung motionless in the burning air alongside the Union Jack.

As a sweating, grumbling RSO settled down to an afternoon rehearsal under a white hot sun, caterers in red, white and blue striped marquees tried to keep flies off the food, Venturer Television checked camera angles and George's minions touched up the balcony, already on stage for *Romeo and Juliet*.

'Trust George to use overwrought iron,' said Flora sourly, 'that balcony's more suited to a Weybridge hacienda. Where are the carriage lamps and the window-boxes of petunias?'

At least George's taste hadn't ruined the park which was lit by white hawthorn exploding like grenades, clumps of white lilac, foaming cow parsley and the candles of the towering horse chestnuts, whose round curves were echoed by plump sheep and their lambs grazing among the buttercups and big white clouds massing on the horizon. Through a gap in the trees, on the banks of the River Fleet, stood a temple of Flora.

'Just think he owns all this, like Mr Darcy,' sighed Candy.

'Mr Nazi,' snapped Flora. 'I'm surprised he hasn't introduced peacocks yet.'

'Why bother with our First Horn around?' said Clare.

Viking, already bronzed and wearing only fraying denim shorts, was squeezing a lemon onto his hair to lighten it in the sun.

Marcus slumped in the stalls. A huge field of yellow rape on the horizon was wafting noxious pollen like chloroform towards him. Willow, birch and oak in the park, as well as all the blossom, were making it almost impossible to breathe. Only the desire to see Alexei had induced him to brave the rehearsal. He was bitterly ashamed that he had been so distracted yesterday, he'd forgotten to play at a wedding and the poor bride had come down the aisle to no music.

He had brought Flora's *Collected Byron* with him, and found the original poem of 'The Corsair'.

'There was a laughing devil in his sneer,' read Marcus.

He should have been at home working on Prokofiev's *Third* but Abby had slid into her old trick of enlisting his help with the repertoire. The running order today was the *Roman Carnival* overture which had a beautiful solo for Cathie Jones; Georgie Maguire singing everything from Gluck to Gershwin; Declan reading *Peter and the Wolf*; the slow movement of Tchaikovsky's *Fifth* because it had a beautiful solo for Viking, more songs from Georgie because Dancer Maitland had tonsilitis and finally *Romeo and Juliet*.

Abby was in a panic about conducting ballet. Rodney had been pragmatic when she called him.

'They're never in time, darling. Nemerovsky's a frightful show-off, he'll spin everything out as long as possible. Give him a fright occasionally by speeding things up but on the whole it's best to wait till they land.'

Men were always showing off, thought Abby furiously, look at Viking sitting half-naked on the edge of the stage, making slitty eyes at every passing pretty caterer or waitress.

No-one could work out whether he was acting up because he was going to be hidden in the pit all evening or whether it was the creeping closeness of George and Juno.

Yesterday Abby had bawled him out for cracking three notes in the Tchaikovsky. Viking had proceeded to wake her up at the cottage at four o'clock in the morning to tell her he'd just finished practising, which was belied by howls of drunken laughter in the background. Then to top it, bloody Trevor, the mongrel, had chewed up her new black T-strap sandals bought to wear at the *après*-gala party and Flora had hardly apologized. She didn't know what had got into Flora either. She was *so* ratty. Thank God for Marcus, who was always so sweet.

Declan hadn't arrived and, as Marcus only had his nose in a book, Abby dragged him unwillingly onto the stage to act as the narrator in *Peter and the Wolf*.

'"*What kind of bird are you, if you can't fly?*" *said the little bird*,' read Marcus sulkily, activating a joyous flurry on the flute from Peter Plumpton.

' "*What kind of bird are you if you can't swim?*" *said the duck, and dived into the pond*' and in came Simon with a ripple of notes on the oboe.

'You're flat, Simon,' said Abby.

'It's the bloody reed,' said Simon shrilly.

'Very appropriate,' giggled Cherub who was wearing a Christopher Robin sunhat. 'Ducks live in reeds.'

As Abby moved on to another tricky bit, Marcus felt

his blue-denim shirt clinging wetly to his body. He wished he could take it off but the sun would torch his fair skin in seconds.

'*No matter how hard the duck tried to run,*' read Marcus, '*the wolf was getting nearer and nearer and nearer.*'

'And then he caught 'er,' said an unmistakable bitchy, deep, husky, foreign voice, 'an' weeth one gulp, swallow 'er.'

Marcus dropped the score, for there piratically grinning up at him, 'a laughing devil in his sneer' stood Alexei, smothered in a great wolf-coat, despite the punishing heat. With him were Evgenia, ravishing in a green sleeveless mini dress, with a white shawl slung round her hips and George looking big and suntanned after a week outside organizing things and as proud as hell.

The orchestra put down their instruments and gave them a clap. Abby jumped down falling on their necks, somewhat ostentatiously gabbling away in Russian, introducing Julian and Dimitri who would translate if they needed him.

'Hi Marcus, how's Prokofiev *Three* going?' shouted Evgenia, holding up a little white hand.

Marcus blushed furiously to be singled out, particularly when Dixie shouted: 'Go for it Marcus, you might get lucky,' and even more so when Alexei reached up, squeezed the back of his leg, and with a sly smile handed him back the score, murmuring: 'Hi, baby boy.'

Saying he and Evgenia would rehearse when they'd warmed up, George was about to whisk them off to their dressing-rooms which had been built under the beech trees when Miles bustled up.

'I've got your schedule here, Mr Nemerovsky.' Then he added unctuously, 'After the rehearsal we know you'd like a steak and French fries, and then a rest but at six I've arranged for the *The Times*, the *Independent*, the *Guardian* and the *Telegraph* to have half an hour each with you.'

'*Niet,*' said Alexi firmly. 'Thees is private visit.'

'But you've got loads of time, you won't be on before half-past ten.'

'I have to lose fifteen year at least to become Romeo, I need till ten-thirty to prepare myself.'

'It's taken weeks to arrange,' spluttered Miles.

'Unarrange eet then.'

'They may write very uncomplimentary things.'

'Ees any different?' shrugged Alexei and stalked off to his dressing-room.

'Disgusting yob,' said Hilary furiously.

'What a star,' sighed Flora.

'He's brought a portable barre,' said Tommy Stainforth knowledgeably.

'I didn't know he was a boozer,' said Cherub.

'No, to practise ballet on, dickhead.'

Leaving poor Jessica to cancel the Press, Miles turned his officiousness on the musicians. Mounting the stage with a large cardboard box, he handed over brilliant crimson silk jackets to the women in the orchestra. They were to wear them with black midi skirts to standardize their appearance, to match the RSO lorry, which had been newly painted crimson, and to curb such excesses as Nellie's plunges and Flora's ribbon straps.

'That colour will clash with my sunburn,' said Candy in outrage.

'Silk's so hot,' moaned poor Mary, who was not enjoying pregnancy in such stifling heat.

'And it's got a polyester lining,' said Clare in horror. 'I can't wear man-made fibres.'

'I'm not wearing it at all,' said Flora, 'I'll look like a blood orange.'

'Not the most becomin' shade for overheated orchestral complexions,' observed Miss Parrott, retrieving a dropped stitch.

'Well, I think they're lovely,' protested Juno, who never flushed pinker than a wild rose.

'So do I, thank you, Miles,' said Hilary, who was pale with dark hair and had also chosen the colour.

'They'll give the orchestra an identity,' fluted Miles. 'And look most dramatic beside the white-dinner jackets and while I've got you I want a word about protocol. Tonight's as good a time to start as any when we're anticipating a huge crowd of first-time concert goers. I want you all to come onto the stage together, five mintues before the off and not all straggle on in your own time, and more important, I want you to look cheerful.'

'On our salary?' scoffed Randy

Despite the heat the musicians laughed.

'And to smile – ' Miles glared at Randy – 'both at the audience and each other. You are performers, not just musicians and at the end of a piece or in a lull, it would be rather nice if you exchanged little smiling conversations like newsreaders.'

'Cuckoo, cuckoo,' the angelic third floated out from the saffron depths of an oak tree.

'You're right, birdie, he is cuckoo,' shouted Dixie in disgust. 'What's the point of smiling if you're hidden in the pit.'

'Can we get on with *Romeo and Juliet*, Miles?' demanded Abby, who was getting increasingly jumpy at the prospect of conducting Alexei.

'What d'you want us to be today, too fast or too loud?' drawled Viking sarcastically.

Abby's lips tightened.

'As you know,' she began, 'Juliet on the night of the ball, from being an under-aged schoolgirl, who wants to stay home and play with her dolls, changes into a young woman swept by deepest passion. This is the greatest love scene ever written in literature or music and tonight it is to be danced by the greatest dancer. As someone said of Nureyev, he only had to walk onto the stage, raise his arm, and the lake would be filled with swans. With Nemerovsky, he has—'

'Only to raise a stand and the polo field will be

swarming with under-aged schoolboys,' shouted Viking. 'God Save the Queer.'

'Will you shut up?' screamed Abby to more guffaws. 'You're just jealous because Alexei's a big star and you're nothing but a big fish in a very small polluted pool.'

'In this country they pronounce it p'lyooted,' said Viking.

The row was only postponed because George returned with Evgenia, pretty as a lily in a white unitard, and Alexei, flaunting everything in clinging black Lycra shorts. Most dancers are well past their prime at thirty-seven, but Alexei's golden body, oiled and rippling with muscle seemed to glow like old ivory in the white hot sun.

'Look at that huge bulge,' said Cherub in awe.

'He's got two pairs of legwarmers shoved down there,' said Viking dismissively.

The Russians like their *Romeo and Juliet* majestic and imposing. Alexei was soon jackbooting around, changing tempi and criticizing the set.

'That's wrong,' said Viking disapprovingly, as the music grew more and more funereal. 'Romeo and Juliet aren't dead yet and who wrote this music anyway, Prokofiev or Nemerovksy?'

Now Alexei was complaining about the pillar, behind which he had to await Juliet and the height of the balcony.

'The balcony is fine, Alexei,' said Evgenia running down the steps, 'last time I dance Juliet, it nearly collapse beneath me.'

'Up two three four, down two three four,' called out Alexei, hoisting her into the air as if she was no heavier than a kitten. 'Eet's still too quick, Abby.'

'Eef we could have *pas de chat* a bit slower too, Abby,' begged Evgenia.

Knowing every man in the place was lusting after Evgenia, Alexei seemed to take a perverse pleasure in playing the scene for real but such was his presence that the bright burning afternoon became as filled with passion and dark lurking menace as night-time Verona.

Marcus was bitterly disappointed to miss Alexei's rehearsal but quite relieved to be dragged inside because Georgie Maguire, with whom he'd spent Christmas, wanted a piano rehearsal. Like Flora, she had rolled up weighed down with presents, a copy of her latest album for Abby, a huge bottle of *Joy* for Flora, chewstiks for Trevor the mongrel, a biography of Pablo Gonzales for Marcus and a huge box of Belgian chocolates for George.

'Miss Priddock said you had a sweet tooth.'

'George'll have to ration them to one a day,' muttered Juno.

Juno was not the only one enraged. How could her mother treat with the enemy, thought Flora furiously, when George's only aim was to build supermarkets and sack 95 per cent of the RSO.

Georgie had also brought several crates of iced beer for the orchestra and was so warm and friendly that Marcus longed to pour all his troubles out to her.

Singing half-voice because she didn't want to tire her vocal cords, Georgie whizzed through Mozart, Puccini, Gershwin, Rodgers and Hammerstein, some VE Day songs and finally two of Strauss's *Four Last Songs* because she wanted to raise two fingers to Dame Hermione who regarded them as her speciality.

Georgie then decided she and Marcus needed a drink but they found there wasn't a maid in the house nor a waiter in the hospitality tent because they'd all sloped off to gaze at Nemerovsky. Over the hawthorn and lilac-scented air drifted the sweet doomed notes of the balcony scene.

'Too slow,' said Marcus with a frown. 'Abby'll have to divide.'

'Lovely,' sighed Georgie. 'Let's raid the fridge, I'm starving.'

The fridge, however, under Juno's influence was disappointingly full of plain yoghurt, undressed lettuce, bean sprouts, carrots cut into strips to fend off George's hunger pangs and plates of cold chicken and beef covered with cling film and marked 'Lunch' and 'Dinner'.

Worse still, there was absolutely no drink so they had to do with Perrier. Georgie lit a cigarette and wanted to gossip.

'Are you OK, Marcus? You look dreadfully pale. I suppose the pollen count's gone through the ozone layer in this heat. You ought to get some concealer for those dark rings.'

Ought to get concealer for my feelings, thought Marcus wearily.

'I saw Nemerovsky in New York.' It was as though Georgie had read his thoughts. 'He's so cool you burn yourself, like ice trays out of the freezer. Is Flora OK? She's been so off-hand, and she wasn't a bit pleased with the bottle of *Joy*. I hoped it might prove symbolic. And she's put on weight.'

'That's because she's given up smoking, very nobly, because it gives me asthma.'

'God, I wish I could. What happened to that nice Irish man who kept ringing her over Christmas?'

'It petered out. He's a seriously good bloke, he's playing your horn solo in the Strauss.'

'I guess she's still hooked on Rannaldini,' sighed Georgie. 'He's such a shit. Oh sorry, I forgot he was your stepfather.'

Opening the fridge again Georgie removed a cling-filmed plate of cold beef.

'Shall we take that for Trevor? He's such a duck. My elder daughter Melanie's having a baby in November – I do hope I like it as much as Trevor.'

As the temperature rose so did tempers. Abby got even angrier with Viking. Not only had he stood on his chair when he was playing so he could watch Evgenia and later Georgie, who, being Irish, of course, took to him immediately, but now she'd caught him coming out of Evgenia's dressing-room, ostentatiously wiping off lipstick.

'Why must you always rock boats?' stormed Abby. 'Alexei's antsy enough without you jumping on his girl-friend.'

'Grow up, sweetheart. Alexei is about as straight as Shirley Temple's curls.'

'You're just jealous. Don't you dare upset him.'

'Not nearly as much as Gwynneth and Gilbert have. That two broomstick family barged in onannounced as Alexei was slapping on his tenth layer of *Max Factor* to bring him greetings from the Arts Council of Great Britain. Alexei threw a queenie fit and started stoning them with pots of cold cream. You have to applaud the guy's style.'

'They have no understanding of the artistic temperament,' raged Abby. 'And I hope you and Flora are going to keep your dogs under control this evening.'

'Of course, here's one of them now,' said Viking as Fat Isobel waddled up with a pile of evening-shirts and a white DJ on a coat-hanger.

'I managed to get the mark out,' she said adoringly.

'That's a darling girl, I'll buy you a beer later,' Viking pecked Isobel's big blushing cheek.

'You are so arrogant and lazy,' said Abby furiously. 'Why don't you get someone to pull your toilet paper for you.'

FIFTY

Not a blade of grass could be seen on George's polo field as loud speakers and huge screens waited to relay the concert to an audience any rock star would have killed for. Many of them waved Union Jacks in anticipation of the VE Day celebrations starting at midnight. In the distance Rutminster Cathedral, its spire rising out of the billowing green woods like a wizard's hat, struck eight o'clock. Over the stage and pit hung a huge canopy like a nun's head-dress, dark blue inside and dotted with stars to create Romeo and Juliet's night-time Verona.

Into the pit through a side-door trouped the RSO in their white DJs and new crimson jackets, which were already uniformly darkened by damp patches under the armpits. The younger girls had rolled back their sleeves. Nellie had undone her top three buttons. Aware that her lower half was totally hidden in the pit, Flora had undone all but the top button. Everyone's toothpaste smiles on Miles's instructions were totally obscured by Peggy Parker's massive flower arrangements.

Huddled in the front of the stalls, Marcus wished Abby had given him a less public seat. He was terrified Declan, his father's great friend, would notice him and seek him out later. Even worse, on his right in a white shirt already covered with chocolate, a bow-tie and shorts of bottle-green velvet, wriggled two-and-half-year-old Justin propped up by three cushions so he could see Mary, his mother, at the front desk of the Second Violins. Marcus liked children but reduced to jelly at the prospect of meeting Alexei at the party later, he was driven demented by Justin's incessant and often incomprehensible prattle. Johnno, his father, demoralized by four months out of work, wearing a crumpled light-weight suit which Mary hadn't had time to iron, didn't seem much of a disciplinarian.

'So good to see little ones brought early to the sacred fountain,' said Gwynneth, who clearly didn't believe in deodorants, and who, to Marcus's horror, was sitting on his left.

She was wearing vast silver earrings in the shape of ballet shoes in deference to Alexei, but was now furious because he'd hit her on the nipple with a jar of moisturizer and a large pot of cleansing cream had landed on Gilbert's sandalled toe.

'Gilbert's bound to lose the nail.'

And half a ton of Rutminster dirt beneath it will be homeless, thought Marcus with a shudder.

'I'd sue. Nemerovsky can afford it,' said Peggy Parker who was massive in maroon on Gilbert's left.

She was livid because Sonny hadn't been given a slot in the gala, and her flowers on the platform hadn't got a large enough plug in the programme.

To tumultuous applause Abby swept on looking dramatic, but definitely OTT in a purple tunic and floppy trousers. Influenced by Byron in the Old Bell, she had added a white turban secured with an amethyst pin.

'Abby just wash her hair,' piped up Justin.

'Where's Jemima, Imran?' shouted the husband of one of Rutminster's new Labour councillors, who'd never been to a concert before, and who was already plastered on George's champagne.

The audience tittered. Abby gritted her teeth. She'd

have had no problem carrying off the turban if Viking hadn't called her Ghandi Pandy in the wings.

Checking that Venturer Television and Classic FM were rolling, she brought down her stick.

Cathie Jones, still ashen with fear despite the punishing heat of the pit, played the solo quite exquisitely in *Roman Carnival.* In fact everything was fizzing along splendidly until Abby discovered Flora's goddamned dog had chewed up the last pages of the score, so she had to pretend to be turning earlier pages not to unnerve the orchestra. Not that she could see anything anyway because of the sweat cascading down from under her turban.

She couldn't even yell at Flora for Trevor's misdemeanour because Flora's mother was on next. Ravishing in plunging coffee coloured lace, her red curls half piled up, half trailing down her freckled suntanned back, Georgie was soon belting out Mozart and Puccini as effortlessly as Gershwin. After years of smoking and far from light drinking, her voice was not perfect but it had exuberance and enormous charm.

'*Some day he'll come along, the man I love,*' sang Georgie.

He already has, thought Marcus helplessly.

'You have to admit my mother is a total star,' muttered Flora to Fat Isobel.

It was time for *Peter and the Wolf* and Declan O'Hara, shaggy, noble and streaming with sweat like a Newfoundland dog just emerged from the sea. Being a true pro, he had spent hours perfecting the timing and, being Declan, he cried in all the sad bits and milked every dramatic effect for the television cameras.

Entranced, hypnotized, Marcus listened to the dark reverberating Irish voice: '*Brave boys like he are not afraid of wolves.*'

Oh but I am, sighed Marcus.

'*Just then a big grey wolf* did *come out of the forest*' went on Declan, narrowing his eyes and dramatically echoing Alexei in the Ivy.

Who else but Viking could play the wicked wolf? thought Abby furiously as she cued in the three horns.

Finally after the catching of the wolf and the triumphant procession, Declan came to the dreadful ending.

'And if you were to listen carefully you could hear the duck quacking in the wolf's belly because the wolf in his hurry had swallowed her alive.'

Even when the orchestra had pelted up the scale in the final tutti, the audience were totally silent for a few shocked seconds before they erupted into a storm of applause.

Justin, who'd been listening enraptured, broke into noisy sobs.

'What happened to the duck, what happened to the poor duck?'

'Of course, the whole thing's political,' said Gilbert sententiously. 'The duck is meant to represent the dissident Russian artists imprisoned by Stalin.'

'If they all behaved as badly as Boris and Nemerovsky,' said Peggy Parker, with a sniff, 'Ay think Stalin had a point.'

Hurriedly, Marcus wiped away the tears. Couldn't everyone detect his longing for Alexei, quacking like the duck inside him, even though he was nightly enveloped by Abby's passion?

He was glad when the birds started singing in the pale green trees during the interval, restoring normality. From the sloping woods on either side rose tier on tier of starry, wild garlic, its pungent smell mingling with lilac and soapy hawthorn making it increasingly difficult for him to breathe.

Glancing into the audience as she and Declan took a final call, Abby was touched to see Marcus's face still wet with tears. He loved her so much and felt things so deeply. After the gala they would have more time.

In fact the only blot on a perfect evening for Abby continued to be Viking. Incensed to be confined to a pit where he couldn't be gazed at or ogle every girl in the stalls, he had rigged up a driving mirror on the front of his music-stand so he could watch Georgie and Declan and no doubt later gaze up Evgenia's skirt.

Worse was to come. After Tchaikovsky's *Fifth*, Georgie returned to sing two of Strauss's *Four Last Songs*, before starting the VE Day numbers.

Locked in Georgie's dressing-room, Trevor stopped howling and decided if he took a Nemerovsky leap he could land on a chair and then take another leap onto the table underneath the open window.

Mr Nugent, on the other hand, had been allowed to wait in the wings, front paws together, gazing lovingly down at his master in the pit, trying not to interrupt his beautiful horn solo by panting. Suddenly Nugent stiffened and gave a muffled growl. His enemy Trevor was jauntily approaching from the other side of the stage, only pausing to lift his leg on one of Peggy Parker's flower arrangements, fox-brown eyes searching everywhere for Flora. The audience nudged each other in ecstasy. Recognizing Flora's mother, who'd given him chewstiks and cold beef, Trevor bounded forward, wagging his curly tail.

'Long by the roses,' sang Georgie with clasped hands, 'she lingers yearning for peace.'

No-one was going to get any peace with Trevor around. Suddenly he clocked another enemy, Abby, waving a stick at eye-level, and proceeded to yap noisily, increasing in volume when Abby refused to throw the stick and even hissed at him to eff off.

All this was too much for Nugent. Shuffling out onto the stage on his belly, he attempted to round Trevor up and off the stage. Affronted, Trevor flew at Nugent's throat, catching mostly shaggy black fur. Nugent was normally the most pacific of dogs, but dignity offended, he weighed in, and furious growling was relayed by speakers all over the ground as though every hound in hell had been unleashed.

In fits of laughter and with great presence of mind, Georgie grabbed Peggy Parker's nearest flower vase and emptied three hundred pounds' worth of lilies over Trevor and Nugent, who took absolutely no notice. There was no alternative but for a cringing Viking to clamber onto the stage and separate them. The crowd, already in stitches, were then treated to the edifying sight of the hero of the RSO in a beautifully pressed cream dinner-jacket and snow-white evening-shirt and, because he hadn't expected his lower half to be seen in the pit, torn espadrilles and boxer shorts covered in fornicating frogs. What really upset Viking was that he hadn't had time to brown his white legs. To a chorus of jeers and wolf-whistles he grabbed both dogs.

'Come off it, ye basstards.' And then, because Trevor was appropriately hanging on like a pit bull, Viking kicked him sharply in the ribs.

'Don't you hurt my dog, you fucking bully.'

The next moment Flora, who also hadn't expected anyone to see her lower half, wearing only her crimson jacket flapping loose from its top button, and a patriotic pair of Union Jack knickers, had joined him on stage to more screams of laughter and roars of applause.

'Talk about the black hole of *"Oh Calcutta,"*' yelled Dixie.

'Drop, Trevor, drop,' screamed Flora, kicking Nugent as hard as she could with her bare feet.

'Who's the great fucking bully now?' shouted Viking.

Only when Georgie, who was now even more hysterical with laughter than the audience, emptied the contents of another flower vase over both dogs *and* their owners, did Trevor release his grip. Whereupon Flora, clutching her dog like a furiously yapping handbag, and Viking frantically examining Nugent's face and shoulders for gashes, continued to hurl abuse at each other, until George Hungerford marched on hissing: 'Get those fooking dogs off stage at once,' and seized the microphone to deafening cheers. He tried to diffuse the situation quickly by apologizing both to Georgie and the crowd.

'I'm afraid everyone, including pooches, gets over-wrought in this heat.'

In agreement Trevor peered round Flora's arm and growled furiously at Nugent. Another great cheer went up:

'What a dreadful, dreadful circus,' said Gilbert appalled.

'Thank goodness Sonny's out of it, Peggy,' said Gwynneth patting Peggy Parker's hand.

Georgie seized the microphone.

'It's all my fault,' she told the audience, 'Trevor belongs to Flora, my daughter, who plays in the orchestra.'

'Oh Mum.' Departing Flora clutched her head with the hand that wasn't clutching Trevor.

'He's a rescued dog, and clearly felt insecure locked up in my dressing-room,' went on Georgie, 'but he rescued me, I was having hellish problems with that Strauss song, so let's get on with VE Day.'

Trevor and Nugent were soon forgotten. The sun set in a ball of flame. The polo field became a mass of waving Union Jacks as Georgie started belting out: 'Roll out the Barrel', 'We'll Meet Again' and 'There'll be Blue Birds Over The White Cliffs of Dover' until Declan joined her on stage, taking it in turns to dry each other's eyes.

'We really ought to be singing "The Rising of the Moon" to strike a balance,' murmured Declan. Finally they brought the house down with 'The Lambeth Walk'.

After a dressing down from George that neither of them would ever forget, Viking and Flora slunk back into the pit. Trevor and Nugent were now in the care of Harve the Heavy.

'And if I get any more trouble out of you,' George

roared at Flora, 'he'll feed that bloody little dog of yours to my Rottweilers.'

Great jubilation resulted when it was relayed over the loud speakers that Rannaldini and Hermione had netted only half the RSO's audience that night. The moment the Opera Gala was over, members of the audience had raced over from Cotchester and were already climbing trees, or crushing the wild garlic as they crept down through the woods, to catch a glimpse of the great Nemerovsky.

George, however, had a huge problem on his hands. Evgenia made up and ravishing in old rose chiffon, her dark hair embroidered with pearls and gold ribbon, had been ready for an hour. But Alexei was refusing to come out of his dressing-room. Not only had he insulted Gilbert and Gwynneth and blacked the eye of a *Scorpion* reporter who'd tried, through his dressing-room window, to do a Trevor in reverse, but he'd taken a passionate dislike to Miles.

'Are you ready to dance, Mr Nemerovsky?'

'No, I am not ready to dance, fuck off.'

'Of course he's not ready,' said Viking scornfully, 'fake tan takes at least eight hours to work.'

'You should know,' hissed Abby.

Convinced she was the only person who could coax Alexei out, she had been bitterly humiliated when he'd dispatched her as summarily as everyone else.

The concert was already running an hour late, which so far had only increased the bar takings and the anticipation. But Abby's head would be on the block if Alexei didn't deliver.

Outside Alexei's dressing-room, George's resolve was stiffened by the sight of Evgenia next door. Slumped on the floor in her beautiful dress, stretching and leaning forward to keep herself supple, smoking too many cigarettes, then cleaning her teeth till her gums bled because Alexei hated the smell of smoke, attacking increasing beads of sweat with a huge powder puff, she had been driven ragged by the delay and by Alexei's monumental selfishness. The longer the wait, the greater the entrance.

Knocking on Alexei's door, ignoring the snarl to fuck off, George went in.

'We need to start, Alexei.'

Alexei's belongings: track-suit bottoms, towels, books, tapes, shoes spilled out of suitcases all over the floor. Fully made up, wearing his wolf-coat over his Romeo costume of white tights and floppy green transparent shirt, Alexei shivered convulsively as he listened to Britten's *War Requiem* on his walkman for the fifth time that day.

And George was suddenly reminded of a ram who'd strayed off the moors into his nan's parlour, during a bitterly cold winter, who had knocked over all the furniture and the knick-knacks, reducing the room to a shambles before leaping straight out through the big sash-window.

George had never forgotten the combined terror and ferocity of that ram and looking at Alexei, he realized he wasn't bloody minded, just shit-scared.

'Always eet is same, why do I put ass on the line? No-one who doesn't dance, understand the cold sweat, the fear.'

'You haven't faced the RSO in a bad mood or Rutminster Council when you're trying to pull a fast one,' George tried to lighten the conversation.

'Is not comparable.' Haughtily Alexei glared at George as if he was the village idiot. 'Will I remember the steps? Will I bore the audience? Am I too old to play Romeo?'

In the still face, the black eyes rolled like marbles.

'You're the best in the world.'

Alexei shrugged. 'Is millstone, eef you are best you must always be bettair.'

Plonking himself in the second armchair, George lit a cigar.

'Please don't smoke.'

George hastily put it out.

'When I was first married,' he said, 'we had no money. We saved and saved either to hear Harefield sing—'

Alexei looked outraged. 'That screeching beech.'

'Or to see you dance. We saw you in *Giselle* at Covent Garden. We couldn't afford a meal out afterwards, didn't matter, we couldn't have eaten anything we were so excited, we could hardly speak on the way home. It was truly the best evening of my marriage.'

'That was fifteen years ago, I am old now.' Sulkily Alexei turned to the mirror, picking up a cotton bud to tidy up a smudged eye-line. George admired the long eyelashes sweeping the slanting cheek-bones.

'You've got a body any twenty year old would die for,' he said humbly, patting his gut, which Juno's diet didn't seem to be having much effect on. He must stop sending Jessica out for Toblerone in the middle of the afternoon.

'What 'appen to your marriage?' asked Alexei.

'My wife left me.'

'Silly cow.'

Getting to his feet, Alexei put a hand on the portable barre, raised his leg till his calf brushed his ear, stretching and turning, then he wandered over to the window. Floating down from George's silver-pillared beech trees was the first pale green foliage. Alexei broke off a twig, caressing the shiny satin leaves.

'Tender as young flesh,' he sighed. 'Tomorrow, perhaps the day after, the leaves darken and harden and coarsen and they will never be that young again. Did you know Prokofiev was lousy ballroom dancer? He write these great ballets, but when he ask pretty young girls to dance with him, they ran away.'

Dropping the twig in his glass of Perrier, stealing a last

glance in the mirror, Alexei touched George's square blushing face with the back of a careless finger.

'You are good guy, I will dance for you.'

Evgenia was waiting outside, bent over, arms flopping loosely, as graceful as one of George's willows.

He's on his way, a rumble of excitement went round the vast crowd, who were really squashed now as more and more people flowed in from Cotchester. Flood-lighting added splendour to the towering trees and the battlements of the house.

Dropping his wolf-coat in the wings as if he were shedding the years, Alexei strutted on, nostrils flaring, dark head thrown back to show off the wondrous slav bone-structure, half-smile playing over the jutting lips, thrust-out chest beneath the floating shirt descending to the flattest belly, above long strong white legs, rippling with muscle. Alexei had no need of the older dancer's disguise of black tights. There was strength and arrogance in every inch of his lithe youthful body.

'Oh Christ, help me,' murmured Marcus.

Never had the RSO strings played with such swooning lyricism. Alexei crept behind the pillar, the lurking lover quivering with anticipation.

Justin woken by the applause, however, had other ideas.

'Dad, Dad, why isn't that man wearing any trousers?'

There was a horrified pause.

'That man's got no trousers on, Dad.'

'Expect he's been playing in the pit,' said the Labour councillor's husband with a guffaw.

'Shut up!' hissed an anguished Marcus.

'Dad, Dad, why's that man got a big willy?'

'It's called a codpiece, Justin,' said Gilbert, who believed in reason.

'Shut up, you little fucker,' hissed Marcus, who didn't.

'More like an 'ole cod in there,' said the Labour councillor's husband. 'They cover that bulge in foam padding so you can't see the meat and two veg.'

A rumble of embarrassed laughter was already sweeping the stalls. Marcus wanted to die. Alexei swung round glaring directly in his direction. The laughter died. Alas Gwynneth had been far too busy chuntering over the dog fight and Alexei's bad behaviour in the interval to eat anything. In her greed, she had emptied a plate of canapés into her Red Riding Hood basket to eat during *Romeo and Juliet.* Choking on a Scotch egg, she couldn't stop coughing.

Alexei waited, then, when Gwynneth, puce as an aubergine, carried on, raised a regal hand and halted both orchestra and Evgenia, who by this time was floating down the staircase, skirts swirling.

'Weel the old lady who ees bent on destroying thees concert,' Alexei's acid drawl echoed round the whole park, 'please either cough everytheeng up now, or get out.'

The dreadful pause seemed to last for ever as Gwynneth stumbled out, then Alexei turned to Abby: 'We are ready to dance, Maestro.'

Briefly he looked drained and middle-aged under the spotlight, then as the doom-laden, swooningly romantic music swept through the park, the years disappeared again. Evgenia danced angelically, but it was Alexei's passion that took the breath away. He didn't just dance, he became the young lover, awkward, shy, bewildered, reverent, deliriously happy by turns, holding Evgenia so tenderly, then releasing her to dance as if he'd opened a window for a trapped butterfly. Then he would leap into the air, showing off with wild grace. Look what I can do. Watch me touch the stars for love.

Wait till he lands, Abby told herself grimly, but time and again as Alexei hovered over the stage, it seemed he would never come down and the poor strings would run out of bow, and the woodwind and brass out of puff.

But as they danced on through the darkening night until the moon rose huge and pink over Rutminster

Cathedral, everyone forgave him the delay and the tantrums.

Oh God, sighed Marcus, if only I were Juliet.

The applause went on for twenty minutes. Stepping over the flowers carpeting the stage, Alexei and Evgenia returned again and again. Pale and drawn, but with eyes glittering with elation, Alexei took up his position on Juliet's balcony and, with princely wave after princely wave, raised each section of the orchestra to their feet, giving the longest stand-up to the strings, which was much appreciated as they were so often taken for granted.

'Look at the old queen on the balcony,' scoffed Viking.

'He's not a queen,' protested Blue. 'He was really French kissing Evgenia.'

'I think he's wonderful. Bravo, bravo, Alexei,' cried Cherub excitedly.

Indignantly Abby noticed Viking was back on his chair squeezing Evgenia's little hand every time she passed. But all her indignation was forgotten because of the deafening cheers when Abby joined the others on the platform and Declan kissed one hand and Alexei the other.

I'm with my peers, thought Abby joyfully, as they bowed again and again to the sea of happy ecstatic faces.

Stamp, stamp, stamp, thundered the feet.

Choking from the dust, Marcus thought how boyish Abby looked. She had thrown away her turban and slicked back her hair like Valentino to show off the amazing yellow eyes. Alexei was burying his big mouth in the palm of her hand again. Christ, things were complicated.

'Encore, encore,' the great rumble grew louder.

'I 'ave idea,' whispered Alexei, sending Abby back to the rostrum.

Once again, he only lifted a hand for a hush to fall.

'It ees nearly meednight, we must all celebrate the

most beautiful words in the twentieth century –' his voice thrillingly deepened and broke slightly – 'Veectory in Europe.'

The next moment he and Evgenia had broken into 'The Lambeth Walk', up and down the stage they danced so merrily and charmingly, followed like two baby elephants by Georgie and Declan, and the crowd bellowed their approval, and all over the polo field and in the aisles between the seats people jumped to their feet singing and joining in. Even Marcus found himself clamped to Peggy Parker's maroon bustier.

'We must finalize a date for my soirée, Sonny's hard at work on your concerto,' she shouted over the din, completely disproving the myth that fat women are light on their feet.

At midnight the fireworks went off, red, white and blue soaring into the sooty sky, writing VE Day across the stars.

Seeing Flora crying, Viking leant across and put a hand on her shoulder.

'Cheer up, darling, you know what VE stands for?'

'W-w-w-what?'

'Viola Extinction Day, of course.'

FIFTY-ONE

It was a measure of George's heavies that they dispersed the multitudes at amazing speed and soon only three hundred guests were left to enjoy Dom Perignon, asparagus, lobster Nemerovsky, cold roast beef, loganberry ice-cream and meringue Evgenia under the stars.

Everyone was desperate to meet Alexei. But, as if to protect himself from boring conversation, he had retreated with a vodka bottle through the cow parsley to a pale green semicircular bench under a big clump of white lilac and proceeded to flirt outrageously in Russian with Abby. Also in the same rowdy over-excited group were Georgie, Declan and Viking, who were all getting plastered and arguing about the peace process, and Evgenia, who seemed content to sit quietly retracing her steps in her head, sipping orange juice and relishing the taut warmth of Viking's body and his hand on the seat behind her occasionally stroking her hair. Nugent sat beside them, pink tongue hanging out from the great heat and to pull in the pieces of roast beef everyone was giving him.

Watching them from the shadow of a weeping ash, Marcus was once more reminded of *Peter and the Wolf.*

The cat (Viking) was sitting on one branch, the bird (Abby) on another, not *too* close to the cat, and the wicked wolf (Alexei) walked round and round the tree looking up at them with greedy eyes.

God, he'd shoot himself if Abby got off with Alexei, and, if she didn't, how could Alexei not fancy Viking? thought Marcus in additional anguish.

Viking was wearing just his denim shorts and his white evening shirt with all the buttons undone, gold hair ruffled, lazy smile showing the chipped very white teeth. His eyes, however, were cool and calculating, a beach-bum on the hunt for a sugar mummy to bankroll him through a long hot summer.

'The lads are coming out all over Europe,' he was telling Declan, as he glared at Nemerovsky 'I'm so sick of being propositioned by gays in the music business, I'm getting an "I love Pussy" T-shirt printed.'

Then he put Abby's turban on Mr Nugent which Nugent adored.

'He's going to open an Indian restaurant the Celtic Mafia won't get thrown out of,' Viking told everyone.

Abby tried to be a good sport about the turban and join in the roars of laughter, but underneath Marcus could see she felt hurt and foolish, which was no doubt Viking's intention.

He daren't go over and protect her in case Declan collared him. The ash pollen was tightening the band round his chest, he longed to slope off home but couldn't tear himself away.

If anyone was unhappier than Marcus that evening it was Flora. From the safety of a little summer-house, she could see her mother getting plastered with Declan.

'I'm just not trying any more,' Georgie was yelling, 'I'm on a permanent fault-finding mission, which doesn't help my poor husband.'

Declan would make a nice stepfather, decided Flora, but Georgie, looking so good at the moment, made her feel fatter and frumpier than ever. She also knew that she would have been fired if her mother hadn't diffused the dog fight.

All around her people were crowing about the gala pulling in a bigger crowd than Rannaldini and Harefield. If only people would stop talking about him.

A lamb was bleating persistently for its mother in a nearby field, which made her eyes fill with tears. God, the smell of wild garlic was strong. To stop a bristling Trevor wriggling out of her arms and attacking Nugent, who was still getting too much attention in his turban, Flora retreated to the shelter of a great oak tree, and watched George relentlessly working the room.

She also noticed the Steel Elf had piled up her golden hair and changed into a ravishing sea-green dress, Grecian in style and leaving one shoulder bare. Whenever George came across a restless pocket of bored men, he'd feed her in to bat her long blonde eyelashes and charm them. Watching them drool, Flora realized what an asset Juno was to him.

'What a little cracker,' said one of new Labour councillors, as she moved away from them. 'Wouldn't mind giving her one. Trust George.'

'There's no doubt,' said his Liberal Democrat friend, 'if George can mount a do like tonight, he can produce a megaplex with one hand tied behind his back. I think we should back him on that supermarket.'

Seeing Flora, they paused.

'Lovely show, well done.'

Going through the french windows in search of more beef for Trevor, Flora surprised George eating illicit potato salad. He made some attempt at geniality.

'How d'you enjoy playing in the pit?'

'Good training for when we're a super orchestra.'

George's face hardened.

'Hallo, George, great party. God, it's hot.' It was Lord Leatherhead mopping his very low brow and in search of strawberries.

'Moost be nearly in the eighties,' said George. 'Look at that butter, it's completely melted.'

'Makes it easier for you to grease the palms of all those incoming socialist councillors,' spat Flora.

'That is no way to talk to your boss,' said Lord Leatherhead with unusual sharpness.

'One wonders how such a lovely warm, beautiful woman as Georgie Maguire can have such a bitch for a daughter,' said George curtly and stalked out into the garden.

Shaken, Flora went in the opposite direction into the hall where she found Miles, Hilary, Juno, Gwynneth and Gilbert in a huddle with Mrs Parker.

'She spoilt our concert,' Hilary was saying, 'wearing those dreadful Union Jack panties and letting that horrid little dog loose.'

Marcus trailed miserably through the park. The white hawthorn bushes were so like fluffy white sheep and their lambs that Marcus half-expected the smaller bushes to run bleating up to the larger ones as he approached.

Declan cornered him in the summer-house.

'Darling boy, I'm onotterably sorry about the rift with your father. Are you OK?'

The boy didn't look it; he was wheezing terribly and was far whiter than the cherry trees which were steadily snowing down their petals.

'I hear you had a great triumph with Rachmaninov.'

'It was OK.'

'Taggie sent special, if surreptitious, love.'

Marcus looked up.

'She did? D'you think Dad will ever forgive me?'

Declan shrugged his massive shoulders.

'He blames you for Tabitha's defection. She's still in the Rannaldini camp, riding wonderful horses in America. He also thinks Rannaldini masterminded your Rachmaninov concert.'

'But that was George's doing,' stammered Marcus, really agitated, fighting desperately for breath. 'I haven't spoken to Rannaldini since he married my mother. He's destroying her.'

'Let me talk to Rupert.'

'No, no,' Marcus shook his head frantically. 'It wouldn't do any good.'

What would Rupert do with a gay son? Marcus thought despairingly.

Cathie Jones leant against a wall, empty glass hidden in the folds of her skirt. Blue stood beside her close enough for the hairs on their arms to touch, neither able to speak. For once she didn't mind that Carmine was in the bushes with Lindy Cardew. Half a dozen people had drifted over in the last half-hour and praised her solo, giving Blue the perfect opportunity to escape, but he was still there.

As the last person moved on, he said: 'I ought to get you another drink, but I'm terrified you'll vanish. I'm going to make sure the programme needs a cor anglais when we go on tour in October, then you can come, too.'

A limousine had arrived to take Georgie home.

'Thank you for a heavenly evening – can I come back soon?' she asked George and Miles as, swaying on her high heels, she fell back into the car.

'Of course you can.'

'And we're going to lunch.' She waved at Declan.

'Indeed we are.'

Then, seeing Marcus, she called out wistfully: 'Will you say goodbye to Flora for me? I haven't seen her all night.' For a second her face crumpled. 'I'm afraid I embarrass her,' then pulling herself together, said, 'Well, thanks everyone.'

But, as the chauffeur moved forward to close the door, he was knocked sideways by Flora hurtling across the gravel.

'Oh Mum,' she sobbed, 'I'm sorry I've been such a bitch.'

Grabbing Trevor, plonking him down on the seat beside her, Georgie pulled Flora into the car, and took her in her arms.

'It's OK baby, it's all right.'

I've got no-one to run to, thought Marcus despairingly as the limo bore them away.

To cap it, Howie, having paid court to Hermione in Cotchester, had beetled over to Rutminster to cash in on Abby's great triumph. Seeing his newest client, he took Marcus's arm.

'How's Prokofiev *Five*?'

'It's *Three* actually. I've got to go, Howie.'

'Abby asked me to find you.'

Abby was still on the semicircular seat. Alexei was stretched out, his dark head in her lap, smoking a joint while Evgenia massaged his bony calloused feet.

Howie rushed forward. 'Hi there, Alexei, I'm your greatest fan. Wonderful concert.'

'Vonderful,' said Alexei sarcastically. 'The public, they clap even when it's good.' Then, peering round Howie at Marcus, murmured, 'Hallo, little peasant.'

'Hardly a peasant,' laughed Abby. 'Marcus's father owns most of Gloucestershire.'

Marcus stared at them unable to move, his eyes huge and shadowed, his dinner-jacket slung over his shoulders.

'He's the one who should play Romeo,' mocked Alexei.

'*Theese love is too rash, too unadvised, too sudden;*
Too like the lightning, which does cease to be
'Ere one can say it lightens.'

Howie, who wasn't interested in Shakespeare, broke the silence.

'I want Marcus to enter the Appleton, Alexei,' he said. 'Help me persuade him.'

'Piano competitions are sheet,' Alexei took a drag on his joint. 'Rachmaninov greatest pianist ever, Clara Schumann, Liszt, Schnabel, Horowitz, Gilels, Pablo Gonzales, none of them went een for competitions.'

'John Ogdon did and John Lill and Murray Perahia,' protested Marcus.

'Ees media circus,' said Alexei. 'If someone ees good he come through anyway. Competition is queek passport. Your priority should be long-term aspect of music.'

'Marcus has to pay the rent,' protested Abby.

'Eef you lose competition,' Alexei took a slug of vodka from the bottle, 'you are finished.'

'Not true,' said Howie, 'and if you win, OK, you're made. Here's my card, Alexei, let's lunch anywhere in the world, you name it, what's your favourite restaurant?'

Alexei glanced up at Howie's waxy sweating face.

'One een which you are not.'

Tearing Howie's card into little pieces, he dropped it on the grass.

'Don't be so bloody rude,' said Marcus furiously and stumbled off into the night.

Abby caught up with him by the car-park:

'What's gotten into you? You're not mad because Alexei's doing a number? I do believe you're jealous. Oh Markie, you must know you're the one I love.'

FIFTY-TWO

In the weeks that followed, as Alexei kept ringing up Woodbine Cottage from all over the world, Abby grew more uppity and convinced he had fallen in love with her. Horrified by the conflict inside him, Marcus lavished even more attention on Abby, but suffered fearful guilt. He could still only get it up when he made love by thinking about Alexei.

By day he concentrated on work. Having dispatched Prokifiev's *Third* with credit in Glasgow, he now had another concert playing Bartók's *Second Concerto* with the Rutminster Youth Orchestra in the pipeline. Persuaded by Abby, Helen and Howie, deliberately ignoring Alexei's advice at the gala, he had also entered for the Appleton Piano Competition in October. As competitors came from all over the world seeking the twenty-thousand-pound prize, Marcus didn't even expect to qualify. But if he did, it would be good experience of playing under pressure.

In a Rutminster jeweller, Abby pointed out a ruby ring in the shape of a heart. Knowing Marcus couldn't afford it, she suggested she bought it instead. But Marcus was adamant. Any engagement ring would be paid for by him.

On the morning after the gala, Flora found a note from
Julian in her pigeon hole, summoning her to the
leader's room at five-fifteen, which meant she had to
sweat her way through six hours of rehearsals and a
lunch-break before she knew her fate.

'Has Julian said anything to you?' she asked Abby.

'Nothing, I guess he's going to carpet you for the dog
fight, flashing those Union Jack panties, and generally
having a bad attitude, rubbishing George, and so on.'

'George is a bastard.'

'Just because he lent his house to us, and saved the
RSO yet again? I don't understand you, Flora.'

Flora didn't understand herself at the moment. 'I just
hate playing for this bloody orchestra,' she said crossly.
'Perhaps I should switch to singing.' She had promised
her mother last night that she would start taking lessons
again.

When she went quaking into the leader's room, however, and was faced not just with Julian, but Old Henry,
Dimitri and Peter, his grizzled desk partner: the firing
squad, the RSO suddenly seemed very, very dear to her.

'I'm sorry,' she bleated, 'I didn't mean to act up.'

'Sit down,' said Julian, pouring her a glass of red wine.
'We wanted to talk to you; we don't feel you're very
happy.'

It's the sack, thought Flora in panic, being held open
for me to jump into, then they'll tie it up and drop me at
the bottom of the River Fleet.

'Sally Briggs is getting married next month,' Old
Henry was saying, 'so she wants her evenings free.'

Sally Briggs sat on the front desk of the violas beside
El Creepo. She was a beautiful player who over the years
had somehow withstood his wandering hands. Why's
Old Henry beating about the bush? thought Flora
miserably.

'Megagram vant us to record Schubert's *C Major Quintet*,' said Dimitri.

'So we wondered if you'd like to join our chamber-music group,' said Julian diffidently.

Flora choked on her wine.

'Might seem a bit fuddy-duddy,' said Old Henry apologetically, 'probably got better things to do with your evenings.'

Flora gazed at them in bewilderment, fighting back the tears, colour flooding her grey cheeks.

'You're asking me? I could try,' she mumbled 'Oh, my God, it's the nicest thing. I'll have to make time to fit in my singing lessons as well.'

'Of course,' said Julian. 'Just think about it.'

'I don't have to, I can't think of anything I'd like better. But you're all such wonderful players, I'm not nearly good enough.'

'We're the best judges of that.' said Barry.

'And we need some muffin for the record sleeve,' smiled Dimitri.

'He means crumpet,' said Julian. 'If you can get to my place tomorrow evening around six. Luisa will provide some kind of supper around half-eight.'

Flora reeled out of the leader's room, slap into Viking who'd been hovering outside, also terrified she was going to get the sack. He now bore her off to the Old Bell for a drink. They travelled in convoy, Nugent glaring furiously out of the back window of Viking's car, and Trevor, with his front paws on the dash board, hysterically yapping on the front seat beside Flora.

'We are divided by our dogs like Montague and Capulet,' sighed Viking as, abandoning both animals in their respective vehicles, they went into the pub.

Viking was touchingly pleased at her news.

'It's no more than you deserve, darling. Think how it's going to put the toffee-noses of all those bitches, Hilary,

Moll – and even Juno,' he added as an afterthought, 'out of joint.'

'I don't think Abby's going to be very pleased, either,' Flora said nervously.

'Might get her off her ass and make her start playing the fiddle again,' said Viking.

Viking was right. Abby tried to be generous, but raging inwardly with jealousy, she did start practising again, constantly dragging in poor Marcus to accompany her.

In June, however, she received the splendid accolade of being asked to conduct the London Met in a Sunday-afternoon concert because their principal guest conductor had been rushed to hospital with appendicitis. Abby was in raptures. Rannaldini's old orchestra was still regarded as one of the greatest in Europe, and this invitation would certainly keep George and the RSO board on their toes. She was slightly miffed that Marcus refused to come up to London to witness her triumph because he wanted to work on the Bartók, but at least he could look after the cats.

Marcus was exceedingly twitchy. The night before Abby's concert he had had a terrible dream about Alexei, and his beautiful oiled naked body dancing away from him. He woke pouring with sweat, sobbing his heart out.

'I dreamt I lost my car keys,' he lied.

'That means frustration,' reproached Abby.

Marcus hadn't made love to her for three days. Being uptight about Bartók's *Second Concerto* wasn't a sufficient excuse.

As she was leaving the telephone rang. Smirking, buckling the aerial on the top of the back door, Abby waltzed the cordless into the garden, then returned three minutes later still chattering.

'I guess I've broken through the gender gap, right, people no longer see me as the first woman to do this or that, but want to know what kind of artist I am. No, poor

Markie's battling with Bartók *Two*. I can't entice him away. Well, if I see you, OK, I see you. Come backstage afterwards.'

'That was Alexei.' Smugly Abby switched off the telephone and then scooped up Scriabin, covering him with kisses, then spitting out his fur. 'He's stopping at the Ritz. He wanted to know what I, I mean, we were up to. Oh, there's the car.'

A large black BMW had skilfully made its way up to the splashing stream scattering elderflower petals to right and left.

'I must go.' Kissing Marcus lightly, Abby climbed into the back of the limo so she could spread out the afternoon's scores. A week ago she would have blown kisses and waved until she was out of sight.

It was such a beautiful day. Although the trees had lost the bright, shiny green of early summer, the field sloping upwards from the gate was streaked silver and gold with ox-eye daisies and buttercups, the limes were in flower luring the bees with their sweet, lemony scent. In a frenzy of jealousy and despair, Marcus washed up Abby's breakfast and last night's dinner, hoovered the drawing-room, choking on the dust, watered the pink geraniums falling out of the front windows, loaded the washing-up machine, changed the sheets on his and Abby's bed. He then made a cup of coffee and, wondering why it tasted so disgusting, realized in his disarray he had added a teabag as well. But anything was better than the loneliness of wrestling with Bartók *Two*. He'd played the concerto his first year at the Academy, but half-forgotten, it was like dragging up an ancient wreck from the bottom of the sea. He must find his own voice but he had to master the notes first.

Oh God, like scrubbing off a tattoo, he tried to wipe out the indelible horror of Abby in Alexei's arms, the *après*-concert euphoria leading on to something more. He loved Abby and she seemed his only hope of keeping out of the quicksand. As he wandered distracted into the garden he noticed the little stream shaking the ferns hanging over its bank as it hurtled towards the lake. Hart's tongues, the ferns were called – like the tongues that would frantically wag if he were outed. 'RUPERT'S SON A POOFTER,' he could imagine the headlines. The papers would have a field-day. Sweating, he imagined his mother's horror, Rupert's lip curling in scorn – what else could any father have expected from such a wimp?

He wished Flora were here. He had so wanted to tell her about Alexei, but each time he'd bottled out. She was so busy playing chamber music with Julian and Old Henry and taking singing lessons that he never saw her.

By the front gate he noticed a white scented branch of philadelphus had been bashed down by last night's downpour. As he broke it off to give it a few more days of life, he heard the telephone ring. Frantic with excitement, slipping on the mossy flagstones, he raced into the house. But it was only Helen, pumping him about Abby. Wasn't it fascinating that she was conducting Rannaldini's old orchestra? Rannaldini was kinda put out, said Helen laughing without amusement, but she thought she'd go along anyway.

Rannaldini was in Rome, she went on, expected back tomorrow. How was Marcus's asthma? She rattled out the questions. Was he practising too little? Too much? Had he heard whether he'd qualified for the Appleton? She didn't listen to any of his answers.

She sounded uptight when Marcus said Flora was away, then relieved when he added that she and Trevor were staying with her parents. Was Helen frightened of all Rannaldini's exes? wondered Marcus, as he studied the Bartók, pencilling in reminders, as he listened to her.

Outside he could see Scriabin stalking a mouse, teetering along the fence, plumy tail aloft, like the sail of The Corsair's pirate ship. Stealthily she crept towards him, on her velvet paws, thought Marcus.

He could bear it no longer. The moment Helen rang off he dialled the Ritz only to be told that Mr Nemerovsky had checked out, gone straight to Abby, no doubt. Marcus banged his burning forehead against the window-pane.

Work was the only salvation.

'Always practise as though you were playing in front of an audience, even if it's only the cat,' Marcus remembered his old teacher's words, so now he played for Scriabin, nearly breaking the keys in the fireworks of the last movement, working off his anguish until he was wringing wet. The sun had also appeared round the brow of the hill, blazing into his studio.

As he flung open the window, he could hear shouting and a time bomb tick. He must be hallucinating, for there, getting out of a taxi, smothered in the same grey wolf-coat that he had been wearing at the gala, was Alexei.

As he tore across the lawn into the darkness of the cottage, Marcus realized he had forgotten to put the branch of philadelphus in water. Brandishing it like a white hot, scented sword to defend himself, he opened the door.

'I 'ave no money,' said Alexei simply. 'Can you pay the taxi? He will take cheque.'

'I've got the cash,' Marcus tried to curb his elation. 'It's only a fiver from the station.'

'I come from the Reeetz.'

By the time Marcus had settled the bill, with a cheque which would probably bounce, Alexei had made himself at home, dipping chunks of brown bread into taramasalata and pouring Abby's vodka neat into two ice-filled glasses.

'For you,' Alexei chucked a little grey bag at Marcus,

which clinked as he caught it. 'Roubles for when you come to Moscow.'

Alexei tossed back one entire glass of vodka and handed the other to Marcus, who shook his head.

'I've got to work. I've got a concert on Saturday. I don't know the piece yet, anyway,' he stammered, his blushing crimson cheeks clashing with his dark red hair, 'Abby isn't here.'

'Of course, zat is vy I am here.'

Marcus's heart was beating so fast, only Alexei's flying feet could have kept up with it. Grabbing a rolling-pin, he bashed the stem of the philadelphus ferociously, before ramming it into a pale green Wedgwood jug. The heady sweet scent was overpowering.

'I ought to work,' he said obstinately.

'I ought to walk,' mocked Alexei. 'I need country air in my lungs.'

He refused to remove his wolf-coat.

'In Eengland, I am always cold.'

Outside, the sun highlighted his night-owl pallor, the flecks of grey in the thick straight black hair.

Last evening's eye-liner still ringed eyes that were just slits of amused malice beneath the heavy lids. A half-smile played over the rubber-tyre mouth. A cocksucker's mouth, his father would call it, thought Marcus, Oh God, help me.

Alexei walked, as he danced, with a springy step leaning backwards, chin raised, head thrown back proudly, idly whistling tunes from *Romeo and Juliet* as he went. As they reached the wider path along the edge of the lake, he took Marcus's arm – it was like walking with a bear. Marcus prayed they didn't bump into any of the Celtic Mafia. He was having great difficulty breathing, and longed to collapse on the bank amid the meadowsweet and watch the dark blue dragonflies dive-bombing the water lilies.

But Alexei was gazing at the mayflies endlessly

dancing above the still dark water, making the most of their one day of life.

'They are like me,' observed Alexei bitterly, 'you 'ave sixty, perhaps seventy more years to play the piano. I have ten to dance, eef I'm lucky. I'm not going to drag myself on like a wounded eagle like Rudi.'

'You could always direct or teach.'

Alexei shrugged. 'No more bravos, no more centre of attention.'

Reaching the end of the lake, they turned back up a rough track into the wood, going deeper and deeper until only the occasional sunbeam pierced the darkness, throwing ingots of gold light on the carpet of dark moss. It was wonderfully cool after the blazing heat. The birds were silent beneath their green-baize cloth of leaves. Marcus kept his distance.

'What d'you call this 'ere?' Alexei was shaking a great acid green shawl slung over the branch of a towering sycamore tree.

'Old man's beard,' muttered Marcus. 'Some people call it traveller's joy.'

'A nicer name, I am a traveller, who will bring you joy,' announced Alexei, then, when Marcus didn't respond, asked, 'How ees anyone as beautiful as you so frightened, leetle Marcus? You should be enjoying your beauty. Brave boys like you should not be afraid of wolves,' he added mockingly.

Marcus started, opened his mouth and shut it again. They had been joined by Mr Nugent and Mrs Diggory's spaniel, who often escaped together on illicit hunting sprees.

Now the two dogs were crashing round trampling the last green seed-heads and yellow leaves of the wild garlic. The smell reminded Marcus of Taggie's cooking and the gentle intimacy of long chats with her in the kitchen, until these had been ruined by the return of disdainful, disruptive Rupert, who was even jealous of a son he despised.

Once again Marcus thought how alike were Rupert and Alexei. Did all gays fall for men like their father?

Alexei walked very fast splashing through the puddles, while the dogs tiptoed round the edge. Marcus was getting breathless – he wished he'd remembered his inhaler.

'You should take more exercise,' said Alexei reprovingly.

'I have asthma. It's hard to breathe, the pollen and things.'

'Foo to the pollen! Ees difficult to breathe because I am 'ere, and you know it.' As Alexei raised his hand to touch Marcus's cheek, the boy jumped away in panic, his eyes enormous.

Alexei laughed. 'Just then a beeg grey wolf *did* come out of the forest.'

'I can't, Alexei,' gabbled Marcus, 'I can't do it to Abby, the last time a man cheated on her, she slashed her wrists.'

'Hopefully she do eet proper theese time.'

'Shut up, I love her; anyway I've got to marry and have kids, my father's got to have an heir. I've let him down so much already being a wimp, being shit-scared of horses, being terrified of him, not even succeeding as a pianist.'

'It would feenish him off altogether eef he knew you were in love with a ballet dancer, hey?'

In terror, Marcus gazed into the still but curiously speculative face.

'Am I?' he muttered. 'I'm supposed to be marrying Abby.'

'You will make her terribly unhappy.'

'Oh Christ, are you sure?'

This time when Marcus tried to jump away, Alexei held onto his hand with a boa-constrictor grip, drawing him close.

'No matter how 'ard the wolf try to escape, he only

pulled the rope round his tail tightair,' he whispered in Marcus's ear.

The path ahead was really churned up – like walking on turkey fat. Brambles clawed Marcus's legs as if trying to hold him back. Twice he slipped, twice Alexei caught him.

Then Alexei halted, idly pulling aside the curtains of ivy hanging from the roots of a massive beech tree to reveal a little cave. Marcus had to duck his head as Alexei pulled him inside, down onto a bed of mossy yellow stone strewn with ancient beech leaves.

'You're so beautiful,' Alexei took the boy's flushed, freckled face between his hands, gently smoothing his cheek-bones to wipe out the dark brown circles beneath the haunted apprehensive eyes.

'Ees stupid to fight, it is so strong.' The hard, haughty face was suddenly miraculously gentle and kindly. 'First time I see you, I want you. You are the only reason I dance at Rutminster for pittance. You make me believe it would be possible to geeve the 'eart.'

Marcus could hear the manic rustling of the dogs after a rabbit, the gruff drone of a helicopter. Through the ivy curtain, he could see the brilliant blue sky thrusting between soaring grey limbs of a beech tree, then Alexei's big mouth came down on his and Alexei's body on top of him was as hard and elemental as the mossy Cotswold stone beneath.

A minute later, unable to breathe, Marcus wriggled away, but Alexei was too strong for him.

'Look at me, silly boy, you 'ave pretty eyelashes, but it would be nice to see your eyes. Doesn't this make your 'eart pound like nothing before?'

'Nothing,' gasped Marcus. 'You know I love you. It was the same for me, I was utterly lost from the moment you bounded onto the stage like Nimrod.'

'Neemrod?' demanded Alexei in outraged jealousy.

'My father's lurcher, he's got killer eyes,' Marcus gave

a half laugh, that became a sob. 'You're a cross between Nimrod and my father. I love you, but I can't do this to Abby.'

''Ush, 'ush, look into my eyes. I am real, you are home where you belong. No more pretending, let eet happen.'

He was mumbling endearments in Russian now, which sounded so marvellous in his husky basso profundo voice. 'You will always remember thees, because it ees the first time. Anyway,' he added wickedly, 'I must get out of these boots, I bought them to eempress you and they kill me.'

Back at the cottage dizzy with exhaustion and happiness, Marcus cooked burnt sausages and lumpy mash for Alexei which was mostly polished off by Mr Nugent and Mrs Diggory's spaniel. The dogs didn't stay, however, to hear Marcus play Schumann's *Dreaming* in the fading light. He wasn't nervous any more. Alexei had ironed all the tension out of his body.

At the end, Alexei got up and put his arms round him.

'You cannot marry Abby.'

'I must, it would destroy her.'

'Not so much as eet would destroy her eef you do. Break it off now. She would be devastated, but only for a month or two. Far better an end with horror, than horror without end. You cannot afford to be tied. You and I are artists, like stars een the sky, we seem close in the night, but we are light year apart. We are pellegrino – eet means orphan and wanderer. We belong to the world, not each other. We are married to Art. Art is far more important than love.'

Not any more, thought Marcus, as Alexei slid two hands deep down inside his shirt.

He wanted to drive Alexei to Birmingham Airport to catch a late flight to Berlin, but Alexei insisted on taking a taxi.

'Eef you are feet to drive, you should not be. My agent weel pay the other end.'

Alexei wouldn't leave until Marcus had promised to join him wherever he was in the world, the moment he'd dispatched the Bartók. He also insisted they swapped watches. Strapping his Rolex, which reeked of *Givenchy for Men* round Marcus's wrist, he proudly carried off Marcus's schoolboy Swatch, as though it were made of diamonds.

Marcus was only too happy to be left alone in the dusk, stunned by the enormity of the afternoon's events. A thrush was singing in the garden, repeating each exquisite phrase.

As he wandered down to the lake, it started to pour, huge raindrops dive-bombing unwary moths, clattering on the leaves, thrashing the lake, creating rings which spread and ran into each other. Marcus thought, watching them, how everyone's actions affected everyone else's in life.

'Nemerovsky loves me,' he shouted over and over again to the blue-black sky, his belly churning and caving in to meet his backbone as he shivered at the memory.

Waltzing home in the deluge, he was running a scalding bath, about to dream of Alexei before crashing out, when the front door flew open, and in burst Abby and Helen in a state of euphoria. Abby had had a wonderful success with the London Met.

'It's extraordinary,' she told Marcus earnestly. 'After four years, they still retain Rannaldini's precision and special timbre.'

I don't give a shit, thought Marcus as they rabbited on. Why are they telling me this?

Now Helen was explaining how she had gone back-stage after the concert, and while she and Abby had supper together, Abby had confided that she and Marcus were getting married. Helen had been delirious with joy, not only was Abby a great and respected artist, but an American like herself.

'She'll help you in your career, and Rupert is bound to come round when he hears you're getting married, and then you and he and Rannaldini can all be reconciled at the wedding.'

Helen, like Rupert, had always suppressed a deep-rooted dread that Marcus might be gay.

Marcus listened incredulously, watching their mouths moving like rapacious baby birds, as they planned his future. He must give up 'all the horrible pupils with their awful mothers that drained him so dreadfully,' and Rupert must give him a decent allowance. But they agreed that Rupert would only rate Marcus when he won a big piano competition, so all his sights must be set on the Appleton.

I'm on the wrong train hurtling towards a cliff and I can't find the communication cord, thought Marcus in panic.

'And what is more,' crowed Abby, 'I saw Lady Appleton, who runs the Appleton this evening, and she said you've qualified, but we're not to tell anyone. You walked it. We must have a drink to celebrate.'

Neither she nor Helen realized that Marcus hadn't moved, still on the bottom step of the stairs slumped against the wall, watching them.

Rootling around in the cupboard, Abby swore she had had some vodka. Flora must have drunk it, they'd have to make do with brandy.

'And best of all,' she said happily, filling up three glasses, 'Lady Appleton is so fed up with the orchestra who normally play at the finals overcharging, that she's chucked them, and she wants me and the RSO to accompany the finalists instead, which means two days of prime-time TV. Wow, what a day.'

Marcus's mind was racing like a cornered rat.

'I can't go in for the Appleton if you're conducting the orchestra,' he stammered.

'Only in the finals,' said Abby soothingly. 'There are two preliminary rounds before that. Let's cross that bridge when we come to it.'

Then suddenly she had a feeling of *déjà vu*, as water

started dripping on her head reminiscent of the H.P. Hall, only this time it was hot.

'Christ, Marcus, you've left the bath running.'

Racing upstairs, Marcus found it a relief to plunge his hand into the scalding water to find the plug. Anything to offset the agony of not seeing Alexei again.

When he came down, noticing how shivering and pale he was, except for one bright red arm, Helen and Abby decided he'd been overworking and packed him off to bed.

'We'll have to get your morning-coat out of moth-balls,' teased Helen, as she kissed him good night. 'I'm so happy for you darling.'

A mourning-coat, thought Marcus, as he tossed and turned all night in agony.

The next day, as a gesture of defiance, he sold Rupert's Munnings and bought Abby the ruby heart as an engage-ment ring. Abby, however, decided to wear it on her right hand until after the Appleton, in case she was accused of favouring Marcus.

Later in the day, while she was out shopping, Marcus wrote a brief letter of renunciation to Alexei, quoting Coventry Patmore:

> *Love wakes men, once in a lifetime each;*
> *They lift their heavy lids, and look;*
> *And lo, what one sweet page can teach,*
> *They read with joy, then shut the book.*

Then he thanked Alexei for the most wonderful few hours of his life, past, present and future, but insisted that they must never see each other again.

Alexei's only reply was a white feather in an airmail envelope.

The leaves of the rescued branch of philadelphus were now shrivelled, its petals fallen. Ramming the branch in the dustbin, Marcus reflected bitterly that at least he had given it the same brief chance to blossom as Alexei had given him. Freedom was clearly a destiny he was not going to reach.

Flora was horrified, but didn't show it, when Abby confided over lunch that she and Marcus were getting married.

FIFTY-THREE

The long summer ground on, with all the inhabitants of Woodbine Cottage working flat out. As well as playing for the RSO, Flora was studying *The Creation* with her singing teacher because the Academy had invited her to sing the soprano part in a student production in September. She had most fun playing chamber music, as part of Julian's quintet. It taught her to listen to herself, and she soon lost her shyness, joining in the furious arguments about tempo, and merrily added to the wrong notes which increased dramatically as the red wine flowed, until Canon Airlie who lived next door banged plaintively on the walls.

Flora grew so fond of Luisa and the Pellafacini children that she could not bear the thought of such a happy family being ousted by a *putsch*. Late one hot night, when she and Julian were polishing off a bottle together in the garden, she told him about George's and Rannaldini's merger plot. Julian's bony face was impassive, but, as he drained his glass, his trembling hand spilled red wine dark as blood in the moonlight on his white shirt.

'George is a great guy,' he said slowly. 'He's done a helluva lot for the orchestra and he speaks his mind.'

'About a quarter of his mind,' snapped Flora, 'the rest is working out dirty deals, he's utterly Machiavellian beneath that bluff northern exterior.'

'I somehow trust the guy,' persisted Julian. 'Rannaldini's different, inflicting pain is the only other way he gets his rocks off.'

'If he takes over, we're both for the high jump,' said Flora.

Julian, however, agreed with Viking that the whole truth would only panic a dreadfully demoralized orchestra,

'Let me do some digging. I'll have a word with Bill Thackery, he's so discreet and now he's on the board he may have inside information.'

Flora was also worried about Marcus, trapped at Woodbine Cottage slogging away at pieces for the Appleton, and endlessly accompanying Abby on the violin. Flora, having been invited to join the Pellafacini Quintet, had indeed been the spur to make Abby practise seriously again. The sound was amazing; there was no doubt she would be up to concert standard by the autumn.

Marcus, however, was listless and losing weight. Helen, encouraged by Rannaldini, had struck up a terrific friendship with Abby and had taken to dropping in, getting on Marcus's nerves, constantly harping on her delight at his secret engagement.

Meanwhile George and Miles were busy finalizing details for the tour of Spain at the beginning of October. The orchestra would be playing *Rachel's Requiem* with Tchaikovsky's *Romeo and Juliet* overture and Rachmaninov's *Paganini Rhapsody*, to pull in the punters, and on alternate nights, Beethoven's *Ninth Symphony* with a Spanish chorus. The highlight of the tour, however, would be Barcelona, where a sufficiently recovered Rodney would fly in to conduct his old orchestra in an eightieth-birthday concert.

Megagram were chipping in because the tour was a splendid opportunity to launch *Rachel's Requiem* in Europe. But the RSO were still desperately short of cash. London orchestras charged large fees on tour, but payments to regional orchestras didn't ever cover their costs. Additional funding therefore had to be found.

During the summer break, George had taken to dropping in on Woodbine Cottage to discuss the orchestra with Abby who automatically assumed he was after her. She hoped he would act as a spur to Marcus, who seemed increasingly detached. She also continually harped on about Flora's antagonism.

'Marcus and I want to have you and Juno over to dinner, but we'll have to choose an evening when Flora's playing chamber music, as I know Juno, you and she don't get along.'

This was borne out by Flora vanishing like smoke whenever George rolled up. Then, on the first Saturday in August, Trevor went missing. Flora, Abby and Marcus had been watching the CCO at the proms on television. Dame Edith was due to retire in the autumn, and, as this would probably be her last prom, had camped it up like mad in white tie and tails. In the middle the cameras had panned to Gilbert and Gwynneth looking odiously enthusiastic in the stalls. This had produced so much barracking that Trevor, who only liked noise if he made it himself, bolted out of the cat door.

Absolutely demented, Flora combed the woods for twenty-four hours trying to find him.

'I know he's trapped down a rabbit hole or been kidnapped by vivisectionists,' she sobbed.

As a final straw, having been stung, scratched and pricked to bits by nettles, thistles and brambles, her mobile had run out early on Sunday evening. Returning home, filthy, tearful, exhausted and hoarse from shouting, to check if anyone had rung the cottage with news, she was greeted at the back gate by Trevor. Trying to pretend he had been searching for her with equal fervour all day, he scrabbled at her so ecstatically that he pulled her boob tube down to her waist. He had in fact been languishing after one of George's Rotweillers, who was on heat. Arriving home from Zurich, George had returned the lovelorn suitor and was now downing a large Pimm's with Abby in the garden.

Flora, out of relief and gratitude, was forced to join them. Blushing because George must have had a good look at her breasts, she adjusted her boob tube, pulled down the green baseball cap, covering her dirty hair and prayed there were enough cuts and nettle stings on her legs to hide the fact that they had not been shaved for a fortnight.

What a ghastly contrast she must be to beautifully groomed Juno, or Abby, sleek and replete in a scarlet sarong.

'I'll just see if Trev's hungry,' Flora sidled towards the kitchen.

'He isn't, George and I tried to tempt him, he must be love sick,' Abby handed Flora a glass of Pimm's. 'Try it, George and I made it with Kiwi fruit and mangoes.'

She couldn't help feeling glad that Flora was being seen at such a disadvantage. Conversation was very stilted.

'How's the chamber music going?' asked George.

'Fine.'

'Flora's also learning *The Creation*,' said Abby.

Convolvulus trumpets weaving in and out of the blackthorn hedge, blushed pink in the setting sun; George also blushed as he announced that there was a coincidence.

'Having given the CCO a boost earlier this year, Dame Hermione feels she would like to redress the balance and award a similar favour to the RSO on her birthday on 31 August.'

'Hermione's a Virgo,' gasped Abby.

'Not for many years,' giggled Flora.

'I'm not having that bitch over the RSO threshold,' snapped Abby flatly.

'Stop being a drama queen,' said George crushingly. 'We need the cash. So we're planning a huge spectacular of *The Creation*, and because it's a religious work, the Bishop is allowing us to use the grounds of Rutminster Cathedral. We'll bill it,' his voice thickened slightly, 'as Dame Hermione in Birthday Concert.'

'If she's singing Eve,' pointed out Flora, 'it ought to be Dame Hermione in Birthday Suit.'

'Don't be fatuous.'

Flora lifted Trevor onto her knee.

'I'm so pleased to see you,' she said, covering his little face with kisses. 'Goaty Gilbert has such a crush on Hermione,' she went on unrepentantly, knowing George had one, too. 'Perhaps he'll deliver her on the pillion of his new bike.'

'She arrived by Land Rover at Cotchester,' said Abby.

'We're aiming for a helicopter, more impact,' said George briskly.

'Ah! So she's got a choice of your Chopper or Rannaldini's,' murmured Flora into Trevor's rough fur. 'I tort a taw a *coup d'état* a-creeping up on me.'

'Shut up,' hissed George, shooting a wary glance at Abby, who was far too upset to notice.

'I am not going to work with that bitch after the way she and Rannaldini tried to scupper the gala.'

'Pink, pink, pink, pink,' cried an agitated blackbird, unnerved by the proximity of Scriabin and Sibelius who were chasing each other and big moths through the soft blue dusk.

'With any luck, it'll rain,' said Flora.

'Even if it chucks it down it won't shrink Hermione's monstrous ego,' stormed Abby.

The *coup de grâce* for Abby was when Hermione announced a week before the concert, that she would need an extra ticket for her agent, Christopher Shepherd, who would be jetting in from New York.

Abby downed sticks and refused to conduct.

'That man screwed my career,' she screamed at George.

'Not from what Marcus was telling me, he says you're back playing chumpion.'

'I don't care, right? I am not conducting in front of Christopher.'

'Best revenge – to show him how good you've got.'

But Abby was adamant. At such short notice she expected George would bring in the Fat Controller or one of the RSO regular guest conductors. But to her horror and Hermione's delight, within an hour, Rannaldini, who was after all a local boy living in nearby Paradise, had found a rare window in his diary and agreed to take over.

Flora went ballistic. The whole thing was a set-up, a plot to infiltrate Rannaldini into the RSO. George had invited Christopher over deliberately, knowing Abby would back down.

'I'm not going to be conducted by Rannaldini either,' she told Viking, 'I'm going off sick.'

The rehearsals for 'Dim Hermione's creating,' as it became known, were incredibly acrimonious. The lecherous tenor, Alphonso, last seen adding a profane note to *The Messiah* when he swapped Louis Vuitton cases with Flora, was back, singing the archangel Uriel and jumping on everyone. He had got so much fatter that Miles, who met him at the station, couldn't change gear and when they arrived at the cathedral, and George leapt forward to open the door, Alphonso tumbled out. Later when he fell over lurching forward to pinch Nellie's bottom, he couldn't get up but lay like a turtle and George had to rustle up the entire chorus to right him.

Adam and Raphael were both played by Walter, a

charming bearlike bearded German, who detested Hermione.

'Last time, I sing vith her and take a bow, she step in front and kick me in the shin,' he told Flora.

Walter was very taken by Marcus, who accompanied him in a piano rehearsal. The boy, he said, was a natural accompanist and should take it up as a career as there was such a shortage of good ones. And why was Marcus so unhappy? When Flora mumbled about Marcus wanting to marry a beautiful girl and worrying about not being able to support her, Walter gave her an old-fashioned look.

'You are sad too, my child.'

Flora confessed she couldn't face Rannaldini and the moment his big black helicopter blotted out the sun, when he flew in to take a full choral rehearsal on the afternoon of the performance, she pushed off, claiming she'd got the flu. Abby, traumatized at the thought of Christopher's arrival, had dragged Marcus off to Paris for the weekend. Flora would have joined them if she hadn't promised to cat and dog sit.

In his pretty house in the Close, Julian had also seen the helicopter land. Knowing that Rannaldini would spend at least ten minutes primping in his dressing-room, he picked up the score of *The Creation*. He loved the joyful tunes, the celebration of nature, the exuberant orchestration full of ravishing woodwind solos, which enhanced but never overwhelmed the singing. Every day during its composition, Haydn had knelt down and prayed to God to 'strengthen me for my work'. God had answered his prayers.

The last time Rannaldini and Julian had met, Julian had been sitting in the leader's chair in drag. Aware that his job, and the house in which he and his family had been so blissfully happy, might at any moment be taken away from him, Julian fell to his knees, praying that he might keep his cool and have the courage to protect his orchestra.

Out of the window as he rose to his feet, he could see the RSO warming up, nervous yet thrilled at the prospect of playing under such a great conductor. The stage had been set up on the yellow, drought-dried water meadows in the shadow of the cathedral and sheltered by two huge limes, whose gold leaves trailed on the ground as if they were already in long dresses for tonight's performance.

Twenty minutes later, the wilting musicians, still waiting for Rannaldini, were running through the recitative in which God created the animal kingdom.

Loudly and briskly Julian led his First Violins up the scale, followed by a fortissimo bellow from the bassoons and trombones. '*With cheerful roaring, there stands the Lion,*' sang a smiling Walter.

The strings then scampered up another scale, followed by loud staccato pounces.

'*The Tiger comes bouncing in leaps from his lair,*' sang Walter.

Exactly on cue, more feline and explosively unpredictable than any tiger, Rannaldini bounded on to the rostrum. He looked magnificent, lean, fit and dark brown, as though he'd spent a month in linseed oil rather than Sardinia. Both his tan and his swept-back thick pewter-grey hair were enhanced by a polo shirt, the clear scarlet of a runner-bean flower, which was tucked into pale grey trousers. Despite his outward sophistication, all the primaeval darkness that had once covered the earth seemed concentrated in his malevolent black eyes. But as they swept disdainfully over choir and orchestra, every woman except Militant Moll, was glad she'd spent all morning, frantically pulling on different clothes, scenting, bathing, shaving legs, washing hair and putting on waterproof mascara, because Rannaldini always made women cry.

Rannaldini didn't miss a beat when he saw Julian.

'They told me you had come here, Mr Pellafacini,' he said softly.

Seeing their revered leader white and shaking, fear ran through the RSO. Cyril put away his bulb catalogue, Davie Buckle his pack of cards.

Rannaldini knew every note of the score and demanded fanatical precision. His personality was so strong that musicians responded to the slightest move of a suntanned finger, the lift of a thick ebony eyebrow. A flared nostril had been known to bring entire flute sections out in a rash.

Not by a flicker of a muscle, did he now show how jolted he was by how much the RSO had improved. When it came to attack, emotion and beauty of tone they were streets ahead of the CCO.

So, as was his wont, Rannaldini tore them apart, instantly identifying the weakest musicians, ordering them to play on their own, making his beat so small, and his instructions so piano, that it was also impossible at the back to interpret them.

'Could you possibly beat a little more distinctly, Maestro, and speak up a little,' quavered Old Henry.

'I speak quietly,' hissed Rannaldini, 'so you will concentrate more. Get a hearing-aid, old man, eef you can't interpret my beat, how will you ever read that telegram from the Queen when eet arrives.'

Seeing Militant Moll's pursed lips, he rounded on her.

'And you can stop faking,' he screamed. 'You're not lying underneath your weemp of a boyfriend now.'

The orchestra gave a nervous guffaw.

'Say something, Nin,' hissed Moll.

Ninion gazed fixedly at his oboe.

Rannaldini's cruellest jibes were reserved for Old Cyril, who had got plastered at lunch-time. In one aria, in which God created the flowers and fruits, the horns had beautiful drifting bars of triplets.

Realizing Cyril's trembling lip couldn't produce a pure note, Rannaldini made him play over and over again on his own, finally suggesting Cyril replaced his French horn part with his P45. Cyril burst into tears. Mortified, the orchestra gazed at the floor. Julian clenched his fists, willing himself to speak out.

Viking was already in a bad temper. He hated the chorus resting their scores on his head, and ramming their big knees into his back. Seeing him lean over and pat Cyril's heaving shoulders, Rannaldini realized there was a member of the orchestra still to torture.

'Seven bars after ten, on your own, First Horn.'

Flawlessly the notes floated round the water meadows.

'Again,' yelled Rannaldini, 'I want no hint of brassiness. You are not weeth the Black Dykes Band now.'

Viking played it again: perfectly.

'You no understand.' Rannaldini jumped down from the rostrum and picked up Julian's fiddle. 'Theese is how I want it.' And he proceeded to play the phrase beautifully but with a slightly different emphasis.

Viking put down his horn and, strolling towards the rostrum, picked up Mary's violin and repeated the phrase even more beautifully.

'Now you play it on the horn, Maestro,' he said insolently.

The orchestra grinned.

Rannaldini lost his temper.

'Your section sound like donkey gelded with sceesors,' he screamed.

On cue the sun had crept round the cathedral spire, gilding Viking's blond mane.

'With cheerful roaring, there stands the lion,' muttered Clare to Candy. 'Oh, go on, Viking.'

'Are you speaking to me?' drawled Viking.

'What does eet look like?' Tigerish, Rannaldini was poised to lash out.

'Eeet looks awfully rude. Please don't slag off my section like that, we are quite prepared to do anything you want, but only if you ask us nicely. Secondly the orchestra have now played for an hour and a half, I suggest you thank them and give them a break. Finally Cyril used to play in a horn section that was known as God's Own Quartet. Frankly, you're not fit to lick his boots.'

With Rannaldini's screams ringing in his ears, Viking strolled off to Close Encounters which by special licence was open all day.

On his return, Rannaldini was still yelling in his dressing-room.

'How dare you insult Maestro Rannaldini,' spluttered Miles. 'He says he never been spoken to like that in his life.'

'What a good thing I was here to teach the little shit some manners.'

'I didn't know you played the violin,' said Knickers reproachfully thinking of the times he had been short of a fiddler.

'Indeed I do, Knickers, I'm Irish.'

By this time Hermione had arrived and was savaging her poor dresser. She had just been the subject of *This is Your Life* (who'd had an awful time finding people to be nice about her) and was also *Artist of the Week* on Radio Three, so you couldn't escape the old bat, particularly if you were George. He had been excited and wildly flattered when Dame Hermione had asked if she could deal with him directly. He had never dreamt it would involve endless reversed-charged calls at four o'clock in the morning.

'I've just remembered something else you can put in the programme about me, George. I've sung Susannah forty-eight times not forty-seven.'

And George had had to go back to the printers again because after 'God Save the Queer', he didn't trust Jessica.

But Hermione still had numerous admirers. All the occupants of the Close had their binoculars trained on her heaving bosom as they pretended to do *The Times* crossword.

A besotted Gilbert had even shipped Gwynneth off to a crumhorn workshop in Bath for the afternoon and rolled up with her Red Riding Hood basket filled with aubergine rissoles and a bottle of parsnip wine. Hermione accepted a glass graciously, but unfortunately Gilbert had been pre-emptied. Always on the prowl for likely lads, Hermione had taken a shine to Viking. The shine was not reciprocated. For a start, Viking didn't like her dismissive remarks about Abby.

'Look how happy these musicians are to be playing once more under a great conductor,' Hermione told him, as the entire RSO, who'd all felt the need for several strong drinks, filed grinning back from Close Encounters after the break.

Hermione then started bitching about her fellow soloists.

'I don't know why I'm working with such people.'

'To make money, presumably,' said Viking, emptying the last of Gilbert's parsnip wine into her glass.

Seeing his mistress coffee-housing with Viking as he returned to the rostrum, the 'great conductor' decided not to appreciate her next aria.

'Why you make a pausa on Top E.'

'I always make a pausa there, Rannaldini.'

'Eef Haydn had wanted a pausa, he would have written. He didn't write, so we do not make.'

The screaming match that ensued shocked even moony Gilbert.

'You seeng like a strangulated parrot.'

'I won't sing at all if you speak to me like that,' squawked Hermione, certainly sounding like one, and stormed off the set.

'Menopausa,' grinned Viking and, as Rannaldini was yelling at the cellos, carried on an argument he and Blue were having about who had bonked the oldest women.

'I've had lots in their seventies,' said Viking airly. 'And their daughters at the same time.'

'Bet you can't bonk Dim Hermione on her birthday.'

'Indeed I can.'

'How will you prove it?'

'You can watch from the wardrobe. Just bring some rope.'

After the rehearsal, Viking sidled up to Hermione who was still foaming over the pausa, and suggested a drink at her hotel before the concert.

Orchestras and managements all over the world had discovered if you gave Hermione a less than perfect hotel on which to vent her spleen, she was less likely to be histrionic before a performance. The Rutminster Royale was a new and fearfully expensive high-rise barracks, half a mile outside Rutminster. When asked by Hermione to collect her key, Viking, with great aplomb, asked the dopey receptionist for the key to the room above, which even better, turned out to be unoccupied.

Having kissed Hermione with Celtic fervour in the lift up (during which time she had to clench her buttocks because Gilbert's parsnip wine was making her fart like a drayhorse), Viking thrust her into the empty bedroom.

Enraptured by such youthful vigour, Hermione murmured she must freshen up. Telling Viking to open a bottle of 'bubbly' she disappeared into the bathroom giving him time to smuggle Blue and an old bell rope he'd found in the vestry into the wardrobe.

When Hermione emerged, grumbling she couldn't find her sponge bag, Viking threw her on the bed, and produced Blue's rope.

'I thought you might like a spot of bondage.'

Hermione's brown eyes glittered with excitement as he tied her to the bed post. Blue was laughing so much he fell out of the wardrobe.

'A threesome,' cried Hermione in excitement.

To Blue's regret, Viking then stuffed a handkerchief

into Hermione's mouth, no-one was allowed to slag off
Abby except himself, and hanging a 'Do not Disturb'
sign on the door, he locked it, handing in the key as he
and Blue left the building.

FIFTY-FOUR

No-one could find Hermione. There was no answer from her hotel room. Christopher Shepherd, her agent, supposedly on his way down from London, wasn't answering his mobile. Fears grew that the great diva had actually carried out her threat and walked out.

'Perhaps she's playing Haydn-seek,' giggled Clare.

'Perhaps she's been kidnapped,' said Miles in alarm.

'Chance would be a fine thing,' muttered George. He was fed up with both Hermione and Rannaldini, neither of whom had stopped complaining. In the inside pocket of his blue-and-white striped seersucker jacket, bulky as a hidden gun, was one hundred thousand pounds in cash to be handed over to them before they emerged from their dressing-rooms tonight.

All the same, he was faced with a mega crisis. Fans in their thousands waving banners and wearing 'I love Hermione' T-shirts were pouring into the water meadows, unpacking lavish picnics. Close Encounters was doing a roaring trade in bottles of chilled champagne. Every seat in the stands was sold. Everyone living in the Close had turned their chairs round to watch from the windows.

Starlings making a din overhead scattered as the cathedral clock tolled seven. It was an hour to blast off.

'Flora's been studying the part with her singing teacher,' said Julian. 'She knows it backwards.'

'And she's got a beautiful voice,' said Viking, who'd just rolled up looking innocent.

'Flora has flu,' said Miles beadily.

'Came on very fast,' said Hilary bitchily. 'She was in the pub at lunch-time.'

Getting no answer on his mobile, George drove over to the cottage. The drought was in its fourth week. He had got the baking hot evening he'd prayed for.

The tractors raised clouds of dust as they chugged back and forth over the bleached fields. Collapsed goosegrass lay like brown dust sheets over bramble and nettles. As he turned the Mercedes up the rough track to Woodbine Cottage, George's view was obscured by giant hogweed disappearing into the thick cloak of traveller's joy. Next moment he'd gone slap into Flora and Trevor driving the other way. Flora was tear-stained and eating a Mars bar. Neither car was damaged badly. Grabbing Trevor, Flora tore back to the cottage. She was locking George out, when he put his foot in the door.

Expecting a bollocking, she was amazed when he asked her to go on in Hermione's place.

'Don't be fatuous.'

'Viking says you have a beautiful voice.'

'Viking lied before he could talk.'

George shouted, then pleaded. She couldn't let the RSO down.

'Don't pull that boy-scout number on me. Anyway I can't go on. I look ghastly.' Flora glared at herself in the hall mirror.

'The make-up girls'll patch you up,' George was inside the cottage now.

'And I've got nothing to wear. Although as I keep saying nothing's very appropriate for Eve, why not provide fig leaves for me and Walter? Alphonso would need a rhubarb leaf,' Flora was edging across the kitchen. 'No prizes for guessing who's going to play Satan.' And with that she disappeared out through the back door.

George, who had once played wing forward for the West Riding, caught up with her, bringing her down with a fine tackle on the parched yellow lawn. For a second as they struggled he realized how thin she had become, and she discovered he was far less fat now than solid muscle.

'Stop playing Jeremy Guscott,' she hissed up into his battered Rotweiller face. 'You're not pretty enough.'

'Ouch,' yelled George as Trevor bit his ankle.

'Well done Trev,' Flora was temporarily ecstatic.

Looking down, George could see her eyes were the same smoky green as ash leaves on the turn.

'Please, Flora, please,' he rubbed his ankle.

For a second Flora pressed her head against his shoulder, then the tears spilled over.

'Rannaldini won't let me onto the platform.'

'He's got no option, come on, luv, we'll all be behind you.'

'You're on top of me,' grumbled Flora.

Her last defence was that she'd lost Foxie.

'I'll find him, go and get dressed.'

Abby's cream silk shirt was miles too big and fell to just above Flora's knees. She looked like a shepherd boy.

'What about a skirt.'

'I've only got minis.'

'OK forget it.'

'Why don't you ramraid Parker's, and get me a little spangled number?'

'You look chumpion.' George thrust Foxie into her arms.

Only the child lock stopped Flora jumping ship, first into the lake whose surface was suddenly darkened as a black cloud moved over the sun, then onto the burnt verges, particularly when she saw the huge crowds.

Overhead drifted a lilac-and-shocking-pink striped air balloon.

'I've always longed to go up in one of them,' moaned Flora, 'particularly now.'

But the waiting make-up girls had fallen on her like vultures, drawing her into the cathedral chapter.

'What kind of base would you like?'

'Preferably one that sings in tune,' said Flora.

She couldn't study the score, because they were putting blue drops in her reddened eyes, and then making them up. She couldn't reply to Walter's and Alphonso's rather hearty assurances of support because her lips were being painted. Passionately relieved they didn't have to compete with Hermione, they were clearly apprehensive about being landed with an absolute lemon. Sweat was flowing in rivulets down Flora's ribs, she was shaking violently, she knew Rannaldini would screw her up, not giving her time to breathe.

'There, you look lovely, good luck, there's so much goodwill for an understudy,' chorused the make-up girls.

Outside George's fingers closed on her wrist like a handcuff.

'You look beautiful,' he said in surprise.

'I look like a tart in all this slap, Eve would have no need of an apple.'

'How are zee buttieflowers?' asked Alphonso, whose girth was winning the battle against his white waistcoat.

Leaving her in the warder care of Miles and Walter, George steeled himself to make an announcement. Christ, the crowd was enormous, all those excited faces suddenly becoming an ugly black sea of hostility.

'I have to apologize for the ubsence of Dame Hermione, who I'm afraid is indisposed,' George shouted over a rising surge of disapproval. 'But I am happy to announce that a local lass has gallantly taken her place, Miss Flora Seymour, who is the daughter—'

'Oh no, poor Mum,' groaned Flora, appalled.

'Is the daughter of Rutshire's very own Georgie Maguire.'

The crowd wasn't remotely mollified. There was a lot of booing and shouts of 'Give us our money back'.

Miles knocked cautiously on Rannaldini's door. He didn't want a repeat of Alexei and the gala.

I'm going to faint, thought Flora.

Her heart was pounding her ribs, the inside of her knees were black and blue from knocking, her throat as dry as Miles's drinks cupboard, she'd never be able to sing.

Out swept Rannaldini, his musky cloying scent nearly anaesthetizing her. She noticed his teeth were whiter than the gardenia in his buttonhole, as he smiled and clapped friendly hands on the shoulders of Alphonso and Walter.

'Good luck, my friends, not that either of you need it,' followed by little jokey asides in Italian and in German.

'This is Flora Seymour,' George propelled her forward like a reluctant dog towards the vet. 'Who is very courageously standing in. I know you'll give her every assistance, Maestro.'

'We know each other,' said Rannaldini flatly. Only Flora could read the implacable hatred in the midnight-black eyes.

'Rannaldini was once with me in Paradise,' she said sadly.

The orchestra gave her a great cheer when she came on, but a rictus animal grin was frozen on her face.

As his chief executive collapsed into the seat beside him, Lord Leatherhead noticed that George hadn't changed and his seersucker jacket was covered in grass stains.

'Hope you know what you're doing, George.'

Only then did George pause and realize what he had done in his desperation for the concert to go ahead.

There was the poor child looking frightened out of her wits and absolutely tiny beside Walter. How could he have bullied her into it? Suddenly despite the now-stifling heat of the evening he, too, was drenched in icy sweat. As he opened his programme, Hermione's serene and lovely face smiled up at him. Getting out a biro, George drew a moustache on it. Along the front of the stage, huge regale lilies were scenting the hot evening air.

'I would never have wasted my best blooms if I'd known that trollop was going to sing,' hissed Peggy Parker.

Rannaldini had deliberately chosen to wear black tails braided with satin, so he would stand out more dramatically against the white DJs and shocking pink jackets of the RSO. Down whisked his stick introducing Chaos which was portrayed by deafening discordant crashes, interspersed with sweet pianissimo murmurs on the strings followed by woodwind calling to each other across the dark void.

Flora was dimly aware behind her of Rannaldini's beautifully manicured hands controlling the orchestra, hands that had once explored every inch of her body and brought her to the ultimate corrupt pleasure.

Perched on a gold chair, glared at by a vast crowd, she had a fifteen minutes' wait before her first aria, and what terrible words to start with.

'*Astonished Heaven's happy host gazes upon the wondrous work.*'

Words and notes were a jumble of black. Alphonso and Walter had already sung. The audience were looking slightly less hostile. Here we go. Flora stood up. No-one could miss her frantically trembling legs – that must be why singers wore long dresses. Rannaldini gave her a curt nod.

'*Astonished haven's hippy host,*' sang Flora, her voice coming out breathy and squeaky, '*gazes on the wondrous wok.*'

Someone laughed, someone booed.

'*And from their throats rings out praise,*' croaked Flora.

As the booing grew to a crescendo, she dropped her red score with a clatter and put her hands over her face.

'I'm sorry, I can't go on,' she sobbed.

The ground fell silent. A police horse neighed.

George leapt to his feet, trying to climb along the row.

'Sid-down,' yelled the rows behind, who didn't want to miss a thing.

Anyway George had been forestalled. Rannaldini had jumped down from the rostrum putting his arms round Flora, whipping the arctic-white handkerchief from his breast pocket, gently tugging down her hands, so he could dry her eyes.

'Of course she can do eet,' he shouted to the crowd. 'She ees verra brave girl.' Then turning to Flora, smiling at her with such encouragement. 'We know you 'ave most beautiful voice in the world, carissima,' he murmured 'Do you want to go off for a moment?' he added as Charlton Handsome belted on with a glass of water.

Flora shook her head. It was all over in a minute, Rannaldini gave her another hug, ruffled her hair causing a collective wince among the make-up girls, and climbed back onto the rostrum.

Then, on second thoughts, he leapt down handing her back his handkerchief sending a benign rumble of amusement through the crowd.

Back on the rostrum he raised his stick, turning, smiling dazzlingly: 'Okkay, Flora?'

Flora nodded, and the crowd gave a great roar of applause until Rannaldini silenced them.

'How charming,' hissed Peggy Parker to Gwynneth. 'Abigail could never have handled that.'

Even Gilbert came out of mourning for Hermione. Flora Seymour had rather interesting breasts in that silk thingy, he must send her a bottle of parsnip wine.

Flora's voice was a little choked and ragged to begin with, but grew in strength and sweetness by the minute.

Throughout her first aria, Walter held her small hand. As Alphonso got up to sing he smiled across lovingly. The vast audience felt they were part of some family drama.

Flora's next recitative began: '*And God said let the earth bring forth grass.*' And legalize it, too, thought Flora which made her smile, and the aria that followed about the gentle jewelled charm of the wild flowers and golden fruit was so beautiful, that she suddenly realized the audience were smiling as well.

Rannaldini still wants me, she thought in rapture, I'm being given another chance. Her next entry was the trio with Alphonso and Walter. Both of them unselfishly held back so that her clear piercing voice could soar lark-like above theirs. There was a deafening applause at the end of part two and once the audience had accepted the fact that there was no interval and they'd have to cross their legs for another hour, they relaxed and enjoyed themselves watching the stars come out, and the houses in the Close light up like Hallowe'en pumpkins.

Pictures were now coming up on the huge television screens on either side of the platform, first the glitter of a trumpet, the gold of Viking's mane, the hair on Julian's bow drawn out like chewing-gum, Rannaldini's left hand dancing like a blown leaf to the music, but mostly the cameras concentrated on Flora.

Watching her face growing more distinct as the light faded, George wanted to put her under his arm and warm her into clarity like a polaroid. By comparison, the ladies of the chorus looked like the witches in *Macbeth*.

He was increasingly uneasy about the undeniable chemistry between her and Rannaldini. Like one of Dracula's bats, he could see the shadow of the television microphone on her freckled breast bone. Nor was Viking happy. The last thing he wanted either was for Rannaldini to get off with Flora again. He was extremely curious to see the man for whom Abby had cut her wrist, but noticed in extreme indignation that the seat beside

Miles was still empty. Christopher Shepherd hadn't even bothered to show. Bloody hell! So Abby needn't have pushed off, after all, and Rannaldini needn't have taken over and Viking had to admit that the bastard gave off such electricity that the orchestra were playing out of their boots and Abby couldn't fail to show up unfavourably by comparison. He also had to confess that without Abby's histrionics the RSO seemed very dull.

God was now creating Eve.

'*Adam's lovely gracious wife in happy innocence she smiles,*' sang Alphonso.

Such was his swelling emotion that his waistcoat button gave up the unequal struggle and flew through the air nearly blacking Goaty Gilbert's eye. Flora fought the giggles and only sobered up when she caught a glimpse of Helen looking blasted with misery in the fourth row.

The orchestra had played miraculously for nearly two hours, the strings' bow-ties were under their ears. But at last they reached the final chorus with soloists.

'*To the glory of God, let song with song compete,*' sang Flora joyfully, '*The glory of the Lord shall last forever, Amen.*'

There was total silence, a dog barked, a car backfired, followed by hysterical screaming applause. The orchestra were all cheering for Flora.

'Well done, darling,' she could hear Viking yelling.

At first, very shy, not knowing how to accept such applause, she gradually began to smile and even blow kisses to the rapturous stamping, clapping, shouting throng.

And how could she not, with Rannaldini beside her lifting her hand to his lips, covering it with kisses, pouring sweet everythings into her ear.

'My little star, my angel child, I knew you could do it. I distance myself, I know suffering produce great art.'

Flora had wanted to make him crawl, but she couldn't help herself.

'I love you,' she whispered, clutching a huge bunch of copper roses to her breast.

Helen was distraught. That bloody girl, she'd always been after Rannaldini.

George who had read *Paradise Lost* at school suddenly remembered Satan like a toad squatting beside Eve, whispering words of temptation into her ear. He'd got to rescue Flora, he was convinced now that something had gone on between her and Rannaldini. But when he fought his way to her dressing-room, she had already been spirited away by Miles and Lord Leatherhead to the big celebration dinner for sponsors, soloists and the management at the Rutminster Royale who were giving the RSO a discount. He wasn't even cheered that he'd saved forty thousand pounds on Hermione's fee.

Christopher Shepherd, who'd been delayed at the Barbican signing up a very pretty thirteen-year-old Chinese cellist, was not pleased to find a strange redhead singing the final chorus in Hermione's place, and Shepherd Denston ten thousand pounds the lighter. He proceeded to jackboot about.

'Where's Dame Hermione?'

'Never showed up,' said George.

'Dame Hermione has never been late in her life,' thundered Christopher, quite untruthfully. 'What in hell's happened to her? She may have been kidnapped, right? Why didn't you provide a body guard. Shepherd Denston will expect full compensation.'

Arriving at the Royale, however, Christopher and the other guests were relieved but somewhat startled to see Dame Hermione swinging like Guy the Gorilla from a rope of knotted sheets and duvet covers trying to find a foothold on the floodlit balcony of the Bridal Suite.

Unwilling to admit she'd been tied up and left by Viking and Blue, she had to fabricate a tale about being so upset about the 'pausa' row that she had locked herself into the wrong room without a telephone.

'I couldn't make anyone hear,' she sobbed into Christopher's manly chest.

'Don't worry, we'll sue the hotel, and Rannaldini and the orchestra,' Christopher glared at George, 'for booking you into such a crumby joint.'

'Bollocks,' exploded George. 'There's absolutely no way we're responsible. Every attempt was made to trace Dame Hermione.'

What a pompous prat, he decided.

Although Dame Hermione was hastily reassured by Christopher that she was insured against accident, her squawks increased when she discovered that Flora had stood in for her so triumphantly and, even more so, when she learnt Rannaldini and the little tramp had vanished.

Even more upset than either Hermione, Helen or Christopher, who was furious not to be able to sign Flora up, or Alphonso, who wanted to jump on her, or Walter, who wanted Marcus's telephone number, was George. Totally abandoning his duties as host to an ever-willing Miles, in increasing despair he commuted between Rannaldini's house in Paradise and Woodbine Cottage but both remained in darkness.

On a third visit to the cottage, which Flora in her haste had left unlocked, George collected a hysterical Trevor and took him back home.

At two o'clock the storm broke, the first clap of thunder sending the little dog shuddering into George's arms.

George was still drinking whisky, stubbing out the umpteenth cigarette, listening to the thunder grumbling in the distance as though it had been evicted from the pub, when the doorbell jangled frantically and Flora staggered in.

There was an ugly bruise on her cheek. She was soaked to the skin. Abby's shirt, ripped down the front, was almost transparent. She was clutching Foxie and shaking convulsively.

'I can't go back to the cottage in case Rannaldini follows me. Oh thank God, you've got Trev. You are kind.' She gathered up the screaming excited little dog, whose scrabbling claws ripped Abby's shirt even further. 'Oh Angel, how could I have left you in this storm. Rannaldini has this horrible effect on me.' Then she glanced up at George. 'Please please don't be cross with me. Can I have a bath?'

She must have slept with Rannaldini, thought George. The pain was horrifying, but he said of course, and poured her a large brandy.

When she came down wrapped in his huge green-and-blue striped dressing-gown, he gave her another brandy and put her in a leather armchair and turned on the gas logs.

'I'm sorry,' she sobbed, 'I can't talk about it,' and then proceeded to do so for nearly two hours without stopping, telling him how Rannaldini had destroyed her.

'He pursued me and pursued me and when I was sixteen, I didn't fancy him at all, I was much keener on his son Wolfie, but finally I gave in and got totally hooked. Then he binned me like a mail-order shot because I said Boris was a brilliant conductor, and he promptly seduced Boris's wife Rachel to punish Boris and me.'

'I've behaved dreadfully badly,' she went on in a whisper, 'but I wanted to sleep with him one more time tonight, just so he could see how I'd improved – like the RSO –' tears were streaming down her blanched cheeks – 'and I was so cross with you and Viking for forcing me to go on.'

'I'm sorry,' George shook his head, 'but you were funtastic, ubsolutely woonderful. You saved the orchestra. None of us will ever be able to thank you enoof.'

'I was lucky. Rannaldini was on my side for most of the evening. Anyway I thought you getting him in to conduct was all part of your plot to oust Abby, and infiltrate Rannaldini into the RSO.'

'Happen it was,' George looked faintly sheepish, 'but

not any more. Working with him at close range, I've realized what a shit he is.'

'Bed wasn't any good tonight.' Dolefully Flora wiped her nose on the sleeve of George's dressing-gown. 'Now I feel empty, I've wanted him back for so long. But when he made love to me, I just felt dirty. We were in his tower.'

George touched the bruise on her cheek.

'He do this.'

Flora nodded. 'Because I didn't want to make a night of it. But the scratches on my legs, those are brambles. I ran out on him through the wood, when I reached the road I hitched a lift.'

'Christ, in that dress.'

'I know it was crazy, I just felt if I got to you I'd be safe.'

A pale grey triangle between the curtains showed dawn was breaking, so George put her and Trevor to bed in a spare room with a hot-water bottle and a night-light.

Looking up at his tired turned-down eyes and squashed face, Flora decided he was more like a mastiff than a Rottweiler.

'Why don't you wear your glasses any more?'

'They were only plain glass to intimidate people.'

Flora laughed drowsily. 'Sorry, I screwed up your evening. I misjudged you – you're a sweet guy.'

Closing the biggest deal had never given George such a lurch of happiness. He left her to fall asleep counting glow stars, but when he went in with a cup of tea at nine-thirty, she had fled again. The net curtains were flapping in the open window like a Dracula film. Perhaps Rannaldini had spirited her away. George was shocked at the wave of desolation that overwhelmed him.

FIFTY-FIVE

Flora didn't become a star overnight, because she didn't want to. She had seen what stardom had done to her parents' marriage. Instead she told the journalists who clamoured for a story that she preferred to build her singing career slowly and stay with her friends in the orchestra.

'What orchestra?' snarled Dixie brandishing the *Telegraph* Appointment page. 'We'll be lucky if we're still in business at Christmas.'

The Arts Council, meanwhile, with predictable pusillanimity, had set up an independent review body to study the two orchestras. The Rutshire Butcher had not helped by giving *The Creation* a rave review, saying it showed what a lazy, lacklustre orchestra could do under a great conductor.

'*The sooner the CCO and the RSO are closed down and merged into a Super Orchestra,*' he had added, '*presided over by Rannaldini the better.*'

The review was picked up by all the nationals.

Rodney was outraged and weighed in from Lucerne in a letter to *The Times*. Independent review bodies, he wrote, consisted of a lot of old tabby cats and failed politicians guzzling digestive biscuits and exhausting entire rain forests, to produce reports that no-one read, for a sum of money that would keep both orchestras going for the next ten years. The Arts Council, he went on, ought to have their legs and hands tied together and be merged with the biggest tidal wave in history.

A fuming Miles rang Rodney and bollocked him for muddying the waters. Gilbert and Gwynneth had to be kept sweet.

'Nothing could keep those guzzling pigs sweet except *bombe surprise*,' replied Rodney sharply. 'And don't you speak to me like that, you little twerp, I'm nearly eighty and I can do exactly what I like.'

Feelings therefore ran high at the annual cricket match between the two orchestras, which this year was held at Cotchester. Everyone remembered why Rodney had employed Bill Thackery in the first place when he made an opening partnership of one hundred and fifty with Davie Buckle. The RSO were all out for two hundred and twenty-five and, justifiably certain of victory, got stuck into the beer in the tea-interval, only pausing to cross themselves as a shadow moved over a watery sun and Rannaldini's helicopter landed on the pitch. To everyone's horror Gwynneth and Gilbert were with him. As Gwynneth jumped down, the wind from the helicopter blades blew her natural-dyed skirt above her head to reveal hairy legs and a hugh black bush.

'As though John Drommond had hitched a lift,' said Viking.

Gwynneth promptly charged up to Miles and Hilary.

'Just had luncheon in Paradise. Sir Roberto was so caring and remembered my weakness for caviar and *bombe surprise*. He picked us up in the heli, but I said he'd have to let Gilbert and I come home with you on the coach, because we want to sing madrigals.'

'How wonderful,' Hilary clapped her hands.

'I sang "The Silver Swan" to Sir Roberto on the way here, he says my voice is remarkable,' said Gwynneth complacently.

Rannaldini had had to do a lot of leg work with Gwynneth to make up for disappearing with Flora after *The Creation*, but had now completely won her over.

RSO spirits rose even higher when Hugo, very pleased with himself after a dazzling *Lark Ascending* at the proms was bowled for a duck, followed by the rest of the CCO losing eight wickets for one hundred and ten.

'That'll teach you to programme vegetarian crap,' sneered Barry the Bass rubbing the ball on his long hard thigh, as Dame Edith strode in swinging her bat like Botham. Having captained Cheltenham Ladies before the war, she proceeded to play like Botham, making a hundred and twenty and breaking two Cotchester Town Hall windows.

'Good thing those weren't H.P. Hall windows,' barracked the CCO from the pavilion. 'You couldn't afford to get them mended.'

Rannaldini who'd been pressing the flesh of local councillors then presented the cup to a puce and dripping Dame Edith, but left kissing her on both cheeks to a very uptight Lady Rannaldini.

Feelings ran so high, that after the shortest *après*-match drinks in the history of the fixture, a punch-up broke out in which Hugo's eye was blacked and Viking lost his front tooth again, which had most of the RSO on their knees in the dusk looking for it. Miles was relieved to get Gilbert, Gwynneth and Hilary safely onto the Pond Life coach, leaving poor harassed Knickers to get the others and Viking's tooth into Moulin Rouge before further mishap occurred. Or so he thought.

Five miles from Rutminster, as the madrigal group were soulfully carolling, suddenly Moulin Rouge overtook Pond Life, and 'The Silver Swan' died on Gwynneth's lips as the entire Celtic Mafia, plus Cherub, Davie and Barry the Bass, flashed by doing a moonie.

*   *   *

'What the fuck were you playing at?' roared George, when he summoned Viking, Dixie and Barry as section and ring leaders into his office next day.

'Giving Gwynneth a bum surprise,' said Viking.

For a second George fought laughter, then he shouted: 'It's not funny, have you guys got some kind of death wish? I am trying to save this orchestra.'

'Are you?' snapped Viking who had not forgotten Orchestra South.

'I bloody well am,' snapped back George, who had just paid Mary-the-Mother-of-Justin's telephone bill. 'Even your pretty face isn't enough to pull in the punters these days. An audience of twenty-eight in Stroud last week is not going to get us out of the wood.'

The one cheery note was that as a result of *The Creation* there was just enough money to go on tour. The hotels, the chartered flights, the coaches and train fares had all been paid for in advance.

Enough money had been set aside for the pianist in Rachmaninov's *Paganini Rhapsody,* and the four soloists in Beethoven's *Ninth Symphony,* when the soprano pulled out with shingles. Flora was consequently persuaded by Miles and Julian to take her place, which would save the orchestra a further ten thousand. The highlight of the tour, however, was still Rodney's birthday concert. Knowing she would feel upstaged by his return, Rodney had telephoned Abby.

'The birthday treat that would make me most happy, darling, would be our double come-back, and for you to play one of the Mozart concertos.'

To his amazement Abby had agreed. She'd have to take the plunge some time, and she couldn't bear Flora to be the only one saving the orchestra money. She was annoyed that even when she promised to provide pianos in every city Marcus had refused to accompany her to Spain.

'All anyone can think about around here is money,' said Abby crossly.

But at least all the horrors of bills, repossessions, overdrafts and looming redundancy were forgotten as the tour approached.

Eighty-six musicians make up a sexually volatile mix. Tours abroad were regarded as bonking bonanzas. Davie Buckle, for example, was terrified by and totally faithful to his hefty wife Brünnhilde at home, but went berserk on tour. Players started stepping round each other, setting up liaisons weeks before. Dimitri brushed his wild hair for the first time in years in the hope of advancing beyond tea and cakes with Miss Parrott. Dirty Harry, an ancient bass player who never washed, was actually seen cleaning his teeth in the Gents. Even stingy Carmine bought a round in the pub.

Among the women, there was much highlighting of hair, bad temper over crash diets and waxing of legs. Despite Miles's strictures that no-one might bring more than twenty kilos of luggage, everyone spent money they hadn't got on new clothes.

It would be warm in Spain, announced Miles, shorts and a cardigan for the evening. Aware that she would be the prettiest girl on tour, Juno saw no point in buying anything but a chastity belt. She wished George were coming to protect her from lecherous Latins, but the poor darling was working too hard to get away.

Hilary had bought a copy of *Don Quixote* and several guidebooks, but felt mantillas would be cheaper when she got out there; she and Miles were looking forward to praying in several cathedrals.

On a management level, parsimony wrestled with morality. To save money, Miles wanted as many musicians to share rooms as possible, but he wanted blokes to share with blokes. Everyone refused to share with Dirty Harry or El Creepo.

There was consequently an unofficial list and an official one. Randy officially shared with Dixie, Candy with Clare. Once on tour, Candy would move in with Randy, Clare with Dixie. Everyone intended to play musical beds. Nellie had philanthropically promised herself to a different brass player each night, except for Blue and Lincoln, Viking's Fifth Horn, a handsome willowy youth, who was in love with Little Jenny. Cherub was dying to make a pass at Noriko and had bought some black silk pyjamas which Miss Parrott had turned up for him.

The main push of the tour, however, was who was going to finally bed Abby. All interested parties had chipped in fifty pounds, the winner getting two thousand. Proof of the bonking had to be a picture of the winner and Abby in bed.

As a result Polaroid cameras sold out in Rutminster High Street. As an alternative, the event could be witnessed by telephoning Dixie who, since his success as Gwynneth in the Christmas concert, had taken to occasional cross dressing. Dixie would then barge into the room, disguised as a waitress, pretending to be delivering room service to the happy couple.

Randy had taken a book on the winner. Viking was favourite, Blue 5–1, himself 8–1 and handsome Barry the Bass 10–1, right up to Cherub 50–1, Peter Plumpton and Simon Painshaw, who were both gay, 100–1, and El Creepo, Carmine Jones and Dirty Harry 1000–1. This had all to be kept secret from the women of the orchestra, who might sneak to Abby, and particularly from Flora and Julian, who would both violently disapprove.

Most of the men would have liked to have a crack at Flora. They had originally backed off because they felt Viking had claimed *droit de seigneur*. But since *The Creation* Flora seemed to be putting out fewer signals than ever.

Flora didn't want to go on tour one bit. She loathed the idea of leaving Trevor, whom she kept finding shuddering under the clothes in her suitcase, and although she scuttled away like an embarrassed daddy-long-legs every time George appeared in the building, she hated the thought of not seeing him for ten days either.

Blue had made no progress with Cathie Jones, but he knew she was in a bad way, because he'd seen her, grey as the fluffing willow herb, sitting down by the railway line which she always did when she was feeling suicidal. But good as his word at the gala, he had persuaded Knickers to take Cathie on tour as an extra.

At first Cathie refused because her only black dress stank under the armpits, and Carmine refused her the money for a new one. Blue got round this by buying her a crushed velvet midi from Next. He then tore out the label and persuaded a friend who worked for the Oxfam shop in Rutminster to make out a fifty-pence bill to show Carmine.

Carmine was furious, but he didn't intend Cathie's presence to cramp his style, he and El Creepo intended changing bedrooms several times.

Viking liked going on tour. Being blond like Juno, he was always mobbed in Latin countries. Not trusting the barbers of Seville, he had his hair cut and streaked by Giuseppe of Parker's the week before. Dropping in at the solarium afterwards, he found the entire brass section stretched out on sun beds.

Returning in 'disgosst' to H.P. Hall, he was summoned to the top floor, where George, Miles, Digby, Quinton, his Third Horn, and an unhappy Julian awaited him. A very over-excited Miss Priddock was hovering in the doorway.

George then told Viking that Old Cyril must go. He was drinking far too heavily, he couldn't centre the notes any more, and last week during Shostakovich's *Fifth Symphony* he had fallen off the stage and carried on playing a different tune.

'And on Saturday Cyril passed water on stage,' said Miles with a shudder.

'He did not,' snapped Viking.

'Ay saw the steam raysing,' chipped in Miss Priddock.

Viking looked at Cyril's scarlet dahlias on George's desk.

'That steam was coming out of Blue's ears, because Abby was wearing a silver flying suit,' he said, but he knew he was fighting a losing battle.

'He's got to go,' George said gently. 'You can't protect him for ever.'

'Best before the tour,' said Miles. 'I'll speak to him at once.'

'We're leaving on Monday,' said Viking in outrage.

'Well, he's certainly not up to the Fourth Horn Solo in Beethoven's *Ninth* – it goes on for pages,' protested Quinton.

'It's really too high for Fourth Horn,' said Julian reasonably. 'Quinton had better play it.'

'I'll tell Cyril,' said Viking icily, 'and he can go at Christmas, give him time to adjosst.' Then, looking round at their several dubious and disapproving faces, threatened, 'If he goes before then, I go too.'

Viking found Cyril at home, downing his second bottle of red of the day and looking at the delphinium catalogue. They had such beautiful names, Faustus, Pericles, Othello, which was dark crimson, and Cassius, a rich dark blue. He could order some Cassius, and watch them merging into the deepening blue dusk next summer, as he sat out in the garden, listening to his old records and getting through the odd bottle before tottering off to bed.

He was delighted to see Viking, but surprised he wouldn't have a drink. Viking did it so kindly.

'I'm sorry, Cyril, we all adore you, but you're not cutting it any more. You're the best guy I've ever played with, I'll still need your advice, so stay to the end of the year, and after that you must come and see us.'

Cyril would have preferred to have gone straight away, but he needed the money.

'What will you do?' asked Viking

'I expect I'll go and live with my sister.'

After Viking had left, Cyril tore up the catalogue – he couldn't afford delphiniums now and there wouldn't be room for them in his sister's window-boxes.

Mrs Rawlings who lived next door could have sworn she heard pitiful sobbing later in the evening, but Cyril was such a cheery soul, it must have been the wireless.

Viking had gone out and got absolutely plastered.

On the eve of the tour, over in the Close, a disconsolate Julian, watched Luisa pack for him. He loathed touring, he couldn't bear being parted from his dear wife for even a night.

'Poor old Cyril,' he sighed, 'I'm not sure it isn't kinder to put musicians down than to retire them. The RSO is all the family he's got.'

Julian looked at the 'Save the RSO' sticker in the window – somehow he had to save his orchestra.

Appassionata
FIFTH MOVEMENT

FIFTY-SIX

Finally on a cold grey morning at the beginning of October, the orchestra were waved off by a disconsolate troop of wives, girlfriends, a few martyred-looking husbands weighed down by baby slings, Brünnhilde Buckle towering over everyone and Marcus waving the paw of a swallowing Trevor.

But just like *Cosi Fan Tutte*, the moment the buses were out of eyeshot, everyone swapped places particularly on Moulin Rouge and out came the drink and the fags.

'I've got some freshly squeezed orange juice for you,' said Hilary as she sat down beside Miles, who had just rolled up in an uncharacteristically smart off-white linen suit and an open-necked navy-blue shirt.

'Doesn't Miles look nice in stone?' said Clare, as she collapsed beside Dixie.

'Nicer still if he were turned to it.'

'At least that colour won't show up the scurf.'

'*We're all going on a workaholiday*,' sang Flora to Viking as they sailed past Parker's, displaying frightful autumn fashions, in burgundy, rust and snuff-brown.

Out in the country, autumn was busy daubing the woods in orange and yellow. Rooks and gulls argued over newly ploughed fields. Behind veils of little cobwebs, the hedgerows blushed with berries. An ironic cheer went up as the buses approached Heathrow and were overtaken by a sleek black limo with Abby immersed in Beethoven's *Ninth* in the back. Maestros usually travelled separately, going first class on plane and train and sometimes staying with the soloists in more expensive hotels than the orchestra, which would tax the ingenuity of Abby's would-be seducers even further.

'Our fright will last two hours,' said Noriko consulting the schedule as they queued to check in.

Totally ignoring Miles's twenty-kilo limit, Clare rocked up with four suitcases and three tennis rackets weighing one hundred and twenty kilos, confidently expecting brawny Dixie to hump it all around for her. Being her first tour, she hadn't appreciated that musicians never carry anyone else's stuff, or that Dixie would be far too busy competing with the other men to carry Abby's six suitcases of scores (Beethoven's *Ninth* was larger than the Chinese telephone book) and clothes for each concert, plus a second change for dinner with the ambassador later.

'Did you pack your suitcase yourself?' the check-in girl asked Randy.

'Of course.'

'He did not,' said Candy indignantly.

Militant Moll went puce in the face when a customs man insisted she carried her vibrator in her hand luggage.

'What's wrong with Ninion?' chorused the Celtic Mafia.

Miss Parrott scuttled through the passport check; she didn't want Dimitri or anyone else to discover her real age.

Abby was touched when every man in the orchestra converged to lift her hand luggage into the lockers and sit next to her on the flight.

Francis bought her a copy of the *Independent,* Old Henry, some glacier mints. Randy, who was intending to spend the two thousand on a new set of golf clubs, to Clare's irritation, upstaged everyone by buying Abby some *Amarige* body lotion in duty free, and murmuring that he hoped he might have the privilege to rub it in during the next week.

Poor Cathie Jones, always airsick, and green before take-off, was cringing at the back of the plane. Putting as much distance between her and himself as possible, Carmine shot up the front to ask Abby's view on his solo in the trumpet fanfare in *Rachel's Requiem.* Watching him, Blue slid in beside Cathie with a bag of barley sugars.

'Talk to me, and you won't have time to throw op.'

Hilary and Juno were infuriated. Having bought *Hello!* and *Tatler* they found endless pictures of Clare and her father on 12 August.

'I've always made shooting lunches for Daddy,' explained Clare apologetically. 'If I'd objected he'd have shot me as well.'

'Isn't that Dixie peering out of the bracken?' hissed Juno.

'No, it's a herd of Daddy's Highland cattle,' said Clare airily, in all senses of the word, because they'd taken off.

Even before the first drinks trolley started rumbling down the aisle, Miles was on his feet.

'This is an important tour. Please remember you are an English,' (loud boos) 'I mean British,' (more boos) 'orchestra and behave like ambassadors for your country and exercise decorum on all occasions.'

Exactly on cue, Randy and Candy emerged from the lavatory, straightening their clothes and Miles's exhortation that they must rout out hooliganism was drowned in howls and catcalls.

'An important tour,' ploughed on Miles.

'Particularly as we're going to witness the return of L'Appassionata as a soloist,' quavered Old Henry, who wanted the two thousand for a new bow, to loud cheers all round.

'What the hell's going on?' wondered Flora, as different players queued up to ask Abby if, after the concert, she'd like a personally guided tour of the lovely old city of Seville, which, after all, had been the setting for Don Giovanni's ill-fated scrap with the Commandatore.

Meanwhile, beside Julian, Mary, eight months pregnant, was embroidering a sampler for the new baby.

'D'you think she's going to explode?' whispered Cherub nervously to Noriko.

'I have just seen a pig fly past the window,' Viking muttered to Blue, as they waited for their luggage in Seville. 'Carmine has just forked out a hundred pesetas for a trolley for Abby's cases. This is going to be a fight to the death.'

The Seville sky was the palest blue, as though it had been through the washing-machine a thousand times. As they chugged past ancient tawny houses, and streets lined with glossy green trees, Viking leant out of the bus and picked an orange. It was much hotter than Rutminster. This time everyone was housed in the same hotel. Before the rehearsal, Abby had a quick swim in the hotel pool. Every man in the RSO seemed to have the same idea, showing off with high dives and flashy crawls.

Old Henry, dreaming of his new bow, dog-paddled eagerly around Abby. Carmine kept vanishing under the water, only deterred from groping her by Viking, who wouldn't have dreamt of crinkling his hair by swimming before a concert, but who prowled round the edge of the pool keeping an eye on his quarry.

At six o'clock there was a panic instead of a rehearsal, because the cherry-red RSO van hadn't arrived with the instruments and all the music. The real heroes of the tour, Charlton Handsome and his humpers and roadies, had been driving from Rutminster since Saturday morning. They had been held up at the border, where Customs, assuming they were a rock band, upended the entire van for drugs.

As the van finally drew up outside the Seville concert hall, frenzied musicians fell on it, terrified their precious instruments might have gone astray. Charlton was rolling the big bass drum down the ramp, when he was pushed aside by Dimitri, frantic to find his Guarnieri, vowing they'd never be parted again.

'Just fuck off, Knickers,' Charlton was now saying to an hysterical Nicholas, 'or I'll drive the 'ole lot into the river.

'Fanks, love,' he added to Flora, who'd brought out a six-pack of iced beer.

'I will not have drinking during working hours,' spluttered Miles, rolling up in a dinner-jacket.

'I'll 'ave you remember, Mister Brian-Knowles,' snapped back Charlton, 'that while you was shacked up all cosy last night wiv Lady 'Ilary, me and the boys,' he pointed to an ice pick and shovel attached to the inside of the lorry, 'was digging our way outa the Pyrenees.'

Miles went purple, particularly when Flora burst out laughing.

'What's in that box?' she asked, as Charlton relieved her of another can of beer.

'Viola players – you get more in if you slice them thinly.'

The concert was a massive success. John Lill, the soloist, played the Rachmaninov so beautifully he had the very formal, straight-backed audience yelling their dark sleek heads off.

Abby was nervous how they'd react to *Rachel's Requiem*, but they listened enraptured, and when Viking launched into 'Rachel's Lament', they all started to clap as though he were Pavarotti singing 'Nessun Dorma', so

Viking played it again, and the applause at the end went on for ten minutes.

As the roadies loaded up again for the drive to Granada, Charlton told Julian he'd heard that 'triffic tune' twice on the bar radio during the concert. Francis the Good Loser, climbing up a lamp-post in the main square to get a better reception on the World Service, nearly got arrested later in the evening.

'Listen,' he thrust out his radio.

'Ah, "Rachel's Lament", very good tune,' chorused the ring of policemen, giving him a round of applause when he played it on his fiddle.

As Abby came into the hotel around one o'clock after an official dinner with John Lill and the Mayor of Seville, the foyer was suddenly full of male musicians. Jerry and Quinton both wanted words about their solos in Beethoven's *Ninth*, and individually wondered if they could run through them in Abby's suite.

'No, you fucking can't,' Viking was at Abby's elbow, waving her key. 'You pinched that solo from Cyril, Quinton, you bloody sort it out.'

'What about a drink?' he murmured to Abby, two minutes later as he opened her door.

Abby havered, then said wistfully, 'I ought to get an early night, and I've gotta practise the Mozart – it's more difficult than I figured, I'm terrified of letting Rodney down.'

Or yourself, thought Viking.

He wasn't going to push it. Instead he gave her the orange he'd picked from the bus, and made her promise to have dinner with him later in the week.

On tours, as on away fixtures, the orchestra tended to split into two groups. Pond Life was epitomized by Peter Plumpton, Simon, Hilary, Militant Moll (and a reluctant Ninion), along with others who were either desperately broke or tight with money. This group, because breakfast was the only meal provided, came down, stuffed themselves, then loaded rolls, cheese, ham, yoghurt, apples, even cartons of decanted prunes into carrier bags, and lived off that for the rest of the day. This meant they could go home with enough totted-up lunch and dinner allowance to pay the gas bill or buy a microwave. They never went out boozing.

In utter contrast, Moulin Rouge led by the Celtic Mafia were hell bent on whooping it up.

'If you make breakfast,' as Dixie was fond of saying, 'you're not regarded as one of the lads.'

It would be hard to decide which group disapproved more strongly of the other. With the making of Abby on the agenda, however, the two groups became blurred with Ninion realizing he could buy an inferno of microwaves with the two thousand, and Francis appreciating he'd be able to pay for a hip operation for his wife, instead of waiting a year for one on the NHS. Peter Plumpton had already earmarked a button-backed sofa in an antique shop in Eldercombe.

To add to the tension as the days passed, the schedule was absolutely punishing. Seville, Granada, Santiago, Corunna, in four days, with Madrid, Barcelona and Toledo to come, which meant rising at dawn to catch the coach to get to the airport or station followed by a long journey, no time to unpack before a rehearsal in a strange hall, with hardly any more time to change, tart up or snatch something to eat before the concert. After which it was natural to have a few drinks and let off steam. Staggering into bed around three o'clock in the morning, they all had to be up at crack of dawn to get on the coach to the next town the following day.

The tour was an even worse nightmare for Miles and Nicholas, who not only had to keep Moulin Rouge in order, but also had to hand out and retrieve all the hotel-room keys at every stop, get suitcases into the right rooms, and drag musicians out of their beds into the coaches as alarm calls were increasingly ignored.

No matter how many signs Knickers put up at each concert hall, the buggers still wandered round bleating: 'Where's the stage? Where's the changing-room? Where's the bog?' which was odd when they never had any difficulty finding a pub or restaurant the instant the concert was over. There was a frightful row in Corunna because breakfast consisted only of croissants, coffee and orange juice. Pond Life, with nothing to live on for the rest of the day, nearly refused to get on the coach taking them to the station.

Abby's suitors got very excited in Santiago, when Viking started a rumour that she'd gone up the cathedral spire with Blue. Having panted to the top, with Old Henry and El Creepo nearly dying of heart attacks in the process, they found only Militant Moll bawling out Ninion, because she'd caught him peering into the women's changing-room. With the coast clear, meanwhile, Viking had belted round to Abby's hotel, only to find she'd gone out shopping.

Her seducers had principally drawn a blank in the past few days because after the first night Abby'd been staying in different hotels.

Tonight, however, they'd all be together in the Picasso Grand in Madrid. So many people were trying to bed her, in fact, that Abby-baiting had been suspended as the chief orchestra pastime and mobbing-up Miles had taken its place.

In Corunna, a pedal had fallen off the piano and Miles had managed to put it back.

'First time you've lain between a pair of legs and been able to find the right aperture,' shouted Dixie to cheers all round.

On the express to Madrid, which looked like a long grey electric shaver, Cherub charmed the guard into letting him use the Tannoy.

'I'm afraid,' he announced in his shrill voice, 'that this train has run out of bog paper. Anyone in need – particularly anyone who had Squid Corunna in the Sir

John Moore Wine Bar last night – is advised to apply to Miles Brian-Knowles for RSO contracts which are probably worth considerably less.'

Roused by guffaws, Miles stopped telling Hilly how much he was looking forward to showing her Guernica and the other Picassos in the Prado.

Julian, halfway through *War and Peace*, was sitting next to Mary who had nearly finished her sampler.

'*Dear Little One*,' read Flora over Mary's shoulder, '*I wish to give you two things: roots and wings*. Oh, that's lovely.'

Flora's eyes filled with tears. Roots and wings should be the basis for any happy relationship. She suddenly wondered how George was getting on in England and hoped Trevor was OK.

Her reverie was interrupted by Cherub's shrill voice over the Tannoy again, interspersed with fits of giggles.

'This is a special message for all members of the RSO. Tonight's rehearsal has been cancelled.'

An enraged Miles then had to hurtle up and down the train, denying this and thrusting aside garlic-reeking peasants, sleek businessmen, and Randy and Candy, once again straightening their clothes as they emerged from the loo.

As the train stopped at a station Miles saw Cherub belting down the platform in the other direction.

'This is your last life, Wilson,' he yelled out of the window.

'Look at Thrilary, mouth vanished altogether,' murmured Viking to Blue. 'She is being screwed by Miles.'

As reddy-brown fields and orange, pink and green rock like vegetable pâté flashed by, Steve was waving the rule book at poor Knickers. 'An orchestra marches on its stomach,' he was shouting. 'That breakfast was a diabolical travesty.'

'Foxie is so hungry,' piped up Flora, making her

puppet fox clutch his furry tummy, 'that he's going to eat Miles in a minute.'

'Gimme that fox.' Dixie, still plastered from the night before, snatched and threw Foxie to Randy, who threw him down the open compartment to Davie who threw him to Barry, who threw him to Carmine, who threw him out of the window, whereupon a screaming Flora pulled the communication cord, and the orchestra never made the Madrid rehearsal at all. Hilary was absolutely hopping because she was not going to see Guernica.

'Why bother?' said Viking. 'It's all around you.'

The result was a duff Beethoven's *Ninth Symphony*. The only thing which excited the fur-coated Madrid audience was Davie Buckle, his fluffy white drum heads frenziedly dancing on the surface of his kettle drums, going beserk in the scherzo.

'Apart from Beethoven *Nine* and *The Rite of Spring*, all music is piffle,' Davie told anyone who would listen, as he got legless afterwards in the bar of the Picasso Grand.

It looked as though Abby's suitors thronging the foyer just after midnight were going to be disappointed again. Returning from dinner with King Carlos, she had escaped to her suite up the back stairs.

'No-one is going to get L'Appassionata into bed this evening either,' announced Viking firmly. 'She's got to practise the Mozart concerto for tomorrow night.'

'We'll see about that,' muttered Davie.

As the week progressed, Abby in fact had hardly noticed her suitors, even Viking, because she was increasingly terrified about playing again in public. She was now so engrossed in perfecting the langorous trills of the adagio, she didn't even notice the bulky figure on the balcony outside. Davie, having downed twelve pints of beer, and dropped his mobile down the lavatory trying to ring Brünnhilde in England, had intrepidly climbed across from the next-door balcony, and settled down to wait for Abby to finish practising.

Three hours later, she wandered next door into her bedroom. Finding Old Henry sitting up in her bed, wearing only pyjama bottoms and reading *Murder on the Nile*, she was so bombed that she thought she'd strayed into the wrong room.

'Oh Henry, just the person I wanted to see. I'm so sorry to barge in, but could you possibly help me with the dynamics in the rondo? Mozart puts in so few marks.'

'It's the same with his later piano concertos,' Henry put a book mark in *Murder on the Nile*. 'He leaves it up to you.'

Even when they'd sorted out the problem and Abby asked Henry to rub tiger balm into her aching neck and shoulders, he made no pass.

'She's playing better than ever,' he sighed to a lurking band of suitors when he finally left her room.

'That two thousand could have bought you a bow *and* paid your gas bill,' said Barry reprovingly.

'Some things are more important than gas bills,' said Old Henry.

Abby took a long time to go to sleep. She was worried that every time she called the cottage to ask after the cats, she got her own voice on the answering-machine. Where the hell was Marcus? And although she doted on Rodney, she was depressed that the RSO were so longing to see him in Barcelona tomorrow. All the old anecdotes and catch phrases were coming out.

'Why are we so happy, boys and girls? Because Uncle Rodney's in charge. Where's Dixie? When he arrives tell him he's much too loud.'

Programmes of Rodney's concerts before the war; photographs of him looking dashing in the Navy or with great musicians: Solomon, Kreisler, Rubinstein, Callas and Gigli had been collected and framed. Messages of love were pouring in from the living: Domingo, Pavarotti, Kiri, Alfred Brendel, Simon Rattle, Pablo Gonzales, and Menuhin. They all loved Rodney. He had brought enormous fun to music.

Forget the Bennies, the Maria Kusaks, the Bill Thackeries, and the Junos, thought Abby bitterly, Rodney in all his life never worked as hard as I do.

Restlessly she picked up a fax from George that had just been shoved under the door. *Rachel's Requiem* was Number Twenty in the classical charts, people were playing it on pop channels as well, and even more amazing, Sonny Parker's *Interruption Suite* for lavatory chain, coughing, etc., had been nominated for a *Gramophone* award. The *Observer* had also got wind of her come-back and done a big piece headed: OUR OWN ABBY ROSEN.

Abby felt happier and she fell into such a deep sleep, she didn't even wake when dozing Davie fell off the balcony and sprained his ankle.

FIFTY-SEVEN

No-one was more on the ball than George Hungerford. He understood balance sheets, had an instant grasp of any financial problem, never missed a crooked picture nor an appointment. He also drove the hardest bargains. The deal had been all. His first marriage had collapsed because he was a workaholic. To survive the pain, he had worked even harder.

But now the RSO had gone like Bonnie Lesley to spread their conquests further, it was time for him to take stock of their future. Could they possibly survive even until Christmas? The latest estimate for the repairs and revamp of H.P. Hall was five million pounds. It was also essential that he devoted some time to his other companies, which, after all, brought in the dosh. Ten acres in central Manchester couldn't run themselves.

But George, who had never had a daydream in his life, found himself hopelessly inattentive. Only this morning he had found a file he had accused Jessica of losing in the office fridge, and his boxer shorts in the pedal dustbin at home instead of in the washing-machine.

He had even started reading horoscopes and poetry and gazing at the clump of beeches in the park whose leaves were turning the same red-gold as Flora's hair. He ought to be looking for companies to buy and properties to snap up, but his mind, like Scarlatti's *Adonis*, had turned from hunting to love. Frequently he was cast into an abyss of self-doubt. How could such a bright, beautiful young lady possibly fancy an uncouth, working-class, middle-aged, North-Country lout?

All that he had to go on was that she had once called him a really sweet guy, but since then she'd scuttled away from him, and he'd been far too shy to ring her up.

He should at least have been working out how they could cut costs on the orchestra's trip up north for the Appleton Piano Competition; instead he sent for the holiday lists, and chose the weeks his Principal Viola, El Creepo, was away to programme *Harold in Italy* and Elgar's *In the South* overture, both of which had wonderful solos for Flora.

'*Oh, she does teach the torches to burn bright,*' murmured George.

Then Miss Priddock had barged in and announced that the soprano who was singing in *The Messiah* next month had decided to cry off because she was expecting triplets.

'That's a shame,' said George, 'I was just brooshing oop on my obstetrical skills. Still she might have suspended belief when she sang, "A Virgin Shall Conceive". Oh well . . . Flora can take her place. We'll have to pay her extra though.'

'Judgin' by the way she's been behavin' on tour, Ay would have thought Flora would find it even more difficult to portray a virgin,' said Miss Priddock with a sniff.

'That was quite uncalled for,' snapped George. 'Get out.'

Miss Priddock flounced off, squawking like a wet hen. George picked up *The Times*.

'*Venus is a morning object,*' he read in the monthly astronomy round-up of the stars.

How could the Goddess of Love be so prosaically

strait-jacketed? In George's heaven, she was on twenty-four-hour duty.

Back came Miss Priddock, ten minutes later, exuding smugness and reproach in equal proportions, as she ushered in Gilbert and Gwynneth, whom George had clearly forgotten were coming. By this time, he was drinking a large Scotch, with his feet on the table, feeding strips of smoked salmon to a purring John Drummond, and watching a video of Flora singing *The Creation*.

Gwynneth and Gilbert promptly went into raptures over the way Rannaldini had held the orchestra together after Hermione's disappearance – surely the mark of a great conductor.

'The orchestra played great,' said George icily. 'They saved the performance because they luv Flora and their pride is sooch they wouldn't allow themselves to produce anything less than a rare defiant performance.'

Gilbert and Gwynneth, who'd come to discuss the merger, or even dropping one orchestra altogether, which would save them even more money, were very disappointed. Rannaldini had given them to understand that George would co-operate in every way.

'Man's only interested in money,' he had told them.

Listening to Gilbert droning on and Gwynneth smacking her pale fat lips over Miss Priddock's ginger bread, George started fidgetting with his right hand drawer, which opened to show a photograph of Ruth. George gazed at her perfect face for a long time. Underneath was his passport.

Gilbert and Gwynneth were even more put out, when George announced he'd have to break up the meeting because he was off to Barcelona to give the orchestra moral support.

'They're playing chumpion,' he went on. '*Rachel's Requiem*'s in the Top Twenty in its first week – that's because Abby's photograph's on the sleeve, and I want to wish Rodney a happy birthday.'

'Oh, I wish I'd sent him a card,' said Gwynneth looking caring, and deciding to forgive Rodney for his disparaging remarks about the Arts Council. 'I draw them myself,' she went on. 'People often frame my cards.'

'Who will hold the fort while you're away?' chuntered Gilbert.

'I'll be sending Miles back,' said George, grabbing his briefcase and car keys. 'After all, it's the fort what counts.' Good God, he was even making jokes like Flora now. 'If it's urgent,' he handed a piece of paper to Miss Priddock, 'you'll find me on this number.'

Gilbert and Gwynneth exchanged glances. They found Miles much easier to deal with.

'Don't forget the board meeting on Friday,' Miss Priddock called after him.

'I'd no idea he was going,' said Jessica, when she returned from the dentist – then she whistled as far as her frozen jaws would allow. 'Golly, that's Ruth's number he's left. I'd forgotten she has a house near Marbella. Perhaps they're getting back together again. He's been ever so distracted recently. He didn't even shout at me when I forgot to buy his lottery tickets.'

Eyes were getting smaller with tiredness as the R.S.O. landed at Barcelona Airport, waists growing bigger. The musicians were sleepwalking, nodding off on any available sofa, armchair or bench.

'I had warbling singers on either side of me last night,' grumbled Simon. 'Wonder if they sell sleeping-pills off prescription?'

'Wish I could buy some homesick pills,' sighed Julian.

'I cut myself shaving this morning,' said Randy, who was still drunk from last night. 'My red eyes have nearly gone white again.'

'Baa, baa, baa,' bleated Dixie, as the entire orchestra, like zombies, followed him blindly into the airport Gents.

Despite Knickers racing round like a collie nipping everyone's ankles, it was half an hour before they all meandered out to the waiting coaches, eating chocolate, reading newspapers, putting new film in their cameras. Miles was absolutely fed up with them. Half of them had overslept and nearly missed the plane that morning.

'If anyone loses their boarding passes or their hotel keys, or forgets to pay their bar bills once more, their pay will be docked,' he yelled to each coach-load in turn. 'And tomorrow morning I want you all to line up outside the hotel at six-thirty so we can take a roll-call.'

'What about a roll-in-the-hay call?' shouted Randy from the back of Moulin Rouge. As they drove past battlements and palm trees along the seafront, Dixie yelled, 'Don't forget to declare Hilly.'

'*Sneaks and lechers, come away, come away, come, come, come away,*' sang Cherub, going into fits of giggles which set the whole coach off.

Hilary stopped writing postcards about the cathedral in Madrid.

'Why d'you all reduce everything to your own disgusting level?' she hissed.

You'll pay for this, thought Miles furiously. Every single one of you.

He was even crosser three-quarters of an hour later. As Flora was struggling up the steep, narrow cobbled street to the hotel, weighed down by a heavy suitcase, her viola and a large bottle of Fundador, presented to her by a waiter last night, she felt a hand taking her suitcase and turned in amazement. No musician ever carried anyone else's stuff. Then she dropped the Fundador with an almighty crash, for there stood George, sweating in a pin-striped suit, and blushing as much as she was.

'I thought you were in Rutminster?'

'I was. I thought I'd come and wish Rodney many happy returns.'

For a moment they gazed at each other as brandy streamed down the street.

'Sorry about the bottle,' said George, clicking his fingers at the hotel porter to come and sweep it up.

'Oh, it's just good, clean Fundador,' said Flora, belting into the hotel.

'Fucking hell,' said Viking, Dixie, Blue and Randy, who'd been following Flora up the hill.

'That's going to cut down our fun and games,' said Blue, dropping to his knees and pretending to lick up the Fundador.

'Why the hell isn't he at home running the orchestra?' said Dixie.

'Into the ground,' said Randy.

Disloyally, they forgot that if it hadn't been for George's indefatigable fund-raising efforts they would never have been able to go on tour.

'Perhaps he's after Abby,' said Dixie.

'Well, he's not going to win the two grand,' snapped Viking.

'No, he's after the Steel Elf,' said Randy.

As Hilary handed her postcards to the hotel receptionist Viking noticed the top one was to Rannaldini in Czechoslovakia.

'Our shit has reached Bohemia,' he muttered to Blue. 'I reckon Gilbert, Gwynneth, Rannaldini and Miles are all in cahoots. I better have a serious word with Rodney.'

Miles was absolutely livid to be dispatched home by George. Telling Hilary to keep an eye on things and chronicle every misdemeanour, he flew northwards to Rutminster freezing like an iceberg as he went.

Tiredness was forgotten as the orchestra dumped their bags and surged off in great expectations to meet Rodney.

The beautiful little palace of music could have been designed especially for Rodney's birthday. Stucco horses with rolling eyes romped high above the stage. Seats rose in tiers fantastically decorated with different coloured sugar tulips. From a ceiling, embossed with scarlet-and-white roses, hung a vast Tiffany lamp, glittering with amber, emerald and kingfisher-blue glass. On the faded terracotta mural, curving round behind the stage, garlanded nymphs in long flowery dresses played flutes and harps, violins and triangles, their eyes closed in deepest trance, bewitched by their music.

'*What maidens loth? What mad pursuit? . . . What pipes and timbrels? What wild ecstasy?*' murmured Flora, trying to tighten her strings with a trembling hand. What the hell was George doing here?

Rodney's dressing-room was already piled high with coloured envelopes and brightly wrapped presents. The RSO had clubbed together and given him a Victorian station-master's cap and a new midnight-blue velvet cloak with a cherry-red lining. A huge iced cake in the shape of a train carrying eighty candles would be wheeled on after the concert. A florist was busy weaving dark red roses and white jasmine in and out of the rostrum.

'It's unlucky to use red-and-white flowers,' said Miss Parrott in alarm.

But her concern was drowned in a deafening cheer as Rodney shuffled on, Beatle cap over one eye, leaning heavily on George's arm. The musicians who'd worked with him in the past were shocked how he'd aged, particularly when they saw what an effort it was for him to climb onto the rostrum and collapse into his chair.

But as they launched into 'Happy Birthday', specially orchestrated by Peter Plumpton, Rodney struggled up from his chair, stretched out his arms, putting his head on one side, and smiling with such sweetness and roguish delight, they were all reassured.

'Oh my dear children – ' wafting *English Fern*, he mopped his eyes with a lemon-yellow silk handkerchief

– 'you have no idea how excited I am to see you all again, and some, too, I haven't met before: great artists.' He beamed down at Julian and Dimitri. 'Learning the cello myself has taught me how clever all you string players are.' Then, glancing at the back of the First Violins, continued, 'and you, pretty child, must be Noriko, and that lovely little redhead must be Flora.'

Aware of George watching from the stalls, Flora cringed into the violas with a weak smile.

Then, to even louder cheers, Rodney whipped out a 'Save the RSO' banner, waving it above his head.

'We'll have no more talk of mergers. I have written to my friend, John Merger –' the orchestra giggled in delight – 'telling him it's simply not on. What are they going to call this merged orchestra? The RSCCO? – stands for Royal Society for the Continued Cruelty to Orchestras – sums up that gruesome twosome, Gilbert and Gwynneth. I hope their ears are burning because I'm flying back to Rutminster to box·them next week.

'You are a symphony orchestra,' he went on, fierce for a second, 'and will remain so. As an encore tonight we will play the beginning of the second movement of Tchaik *Five*, one of the greatest symphonies ever written, with a great horn solo from a great player.' He blew a kiss at Viking.

'But as you all know that, and the other pieces, *Romeo and Juliet* and *Don Quixote* backwards, let's play the Mozart. Not a day goes by,' he added in a stage-whisper as Abby strolled in with her fiddle under her arm to a chorus of wolf-whistles, 'that I don't envy you having such a gorgeous popsy as musical director. Isn't she lovely?'

'She certainly is,' bellowed Abby's suitors.

As if she were shrugging off her role as conductor, Abby had abandoned her severe, often deliberately desexing gear, for a clinging orange vest and the shortest, tightest, brown suede skirt, just acquired in a Barcelona boutique. Her newly washed black gypsy curls danced loose down her shoulders. Terror and excitement simultaneously lit her glowing face: the heaven and hell of performance.

'My dear,' sighed Rodney, 'what a time to bring those legs out of hiding. I'll never concentrate. That was a wonderful century you made against the CCO last week, Bill,' he went on, keeping up the patter, 'tiddle, om, pom, pom. Did you know carthorse was an anagram of orchestra? Tiddle, om, pom, pom, ready darling?'

Abby nodded. Surreptitiously, mysteriously, always when a great star is playing, the hall fills up. Stage hands, doormen, cleaners with mops, admin staff were already gathering in the red velvet boxes and creeping into the stalls.

Rodney raised his baton a couple of inches and brought it down. There was an explosion of sound. Playing the lovely but comparatively undemanding horn accompaniment, Viking listened in wonder. No composer but Mozart, no musician except Abby, could express such sweetness, such caressing tenderness, such extremes of sadness and joy. He watched her breasts and golden arms quivering as her bow darted across the strings, the voluptuous swing of her suede hips, her tossing shining hair, and the rapacious absorption on her proud, hawklike face, and was filled with lust as well as admiration.

Abby was a good conductor, but her heart constantly fought her head, like a swan struggling across land to some destination. But when she played she flew, all heart, totally committed, as bewitched as the nymphs on the wall.

'We'll be looking for a new musical director,' sighed Old Henry, tapping his bow against Francis's chair-back. 'Can't deprive the world of a sound like that.'

As he joined in the rapturous applause, George was shocked to see how Rodney was sweating, and how much brown make-up came off on the lemon-yellow silk handkerchief when he mopped his brow. He was a ghastly colour, but outwardly full of pride and joy for his protégée.

'I can die happy now,' he told Abby. 'The sorrow of that middle movement was almost unbearable. And if I hadn't known you were the RSO, boys and girls, I could have sworn you were the Berlin Phil.'

'It's because you're back, Sir Rod,' shouted Dixie, then remembering he was trying to pull Abby, 'and because we've got a great soloist.'

George stepped forward. 'You must rest, Maestro.'

'Think I'd better, journey took it out of me. Got a lovely chambermaid as siesta-fodder back at the hotel. Got to be as fresh as a daisy for the party later. Lots of champagne, lovely grub: I can open all my presents, and we'll all behave as badly as possible, toodle-oo everyone.'

Waving his flag, he adjusted his Beatle cap at a more rakish angle. As he was helped down from the rostrum, the musicians surged forward to shake his hand and show how happy they were he was back.

Clutching the door leading to the stage, he patted the head of his pantomime cow, whose furry black-and-white body was slumped over the rail waiting to take part in the encore.

'Nice to see my old girl again. Got her a Swiss bell to wear tonight. *Connaissez-vous Schoenberg, Madame Vache*? No, that's French, must remember to speak Spanish. Must stop this merger, dear boy, Rannaldini's such a shit,' he added, clapping a hand on George's shoulder, but using it more as a support.

Abby ran after them.

'I love you, Rodney,' she stammered.

'And I you, darling.'

'Was I really OK?'

'Better than ever. Utterly breathtaking. Oh, there's Charlton, how are you?'

'Great, and great to see you, Sir Rod. Fanks for the Scotch, biggest fucking bottle I've ever seen.'

'You deserve it, dear boy, after flogging all those miles.'

'Oh, damn you,' sighed Abby, as a departing Rodney wriggled like an old badger into the back of the waiting limo. 'Why d'you always have to show me up by being so nice to everyone?'

She never saw him again.

In the men's changing-room, musicians were combing hair over bald patches, running electric razors over their faces, spraying deodorant on earlier layers, cleaning teeth, fighting for the mirror to tie their ties. Those with good bodies wandered round in their underpants. Those already dressed were warming up in the passage outside the conductor's room. Viking was playing 'The Teddy Bears Picnic' when George arrived, looking grim and very shaken, and dragged him into an empty-dressing room. Just as he was leaving the hotel, Rodney had died of a massive heart attack.

'He was so excited,' George's voice cracked, 'his last words were, "I moosn't be late for my dear children."'

The colour drained from Viking's face; for a second he clung onto a chair, his eyes closed, fighting back the tears.

'Oh Jesus, I don't believe it. Thank God we saw him one last time. This is terrible.' Then he pulled himself together. 'Poor little Abby.'

'I better go and tell her.'

'I'll tell her. You tell the orchestra.'

'Ought we to cancel the concert?'

'Certainly not, Rodney's worst thing was disappointing people.'

The orchestra were devastated – most of them in tears.

Steve abandoned his noisy row with Knickers about the musicians not having had long enough between rehearsal and concert.

Abby had just emerged from the shower and was

wrapped in a very inadequate olive-green towel, when Viking walked in. At first she didn't believe him.

'It's just another of your obnoxious jokes.'

Then she went into such raving, screaming hysterics that Viking was very reluctantly forced to slap her face before she collapsed sobbing wildly in his arms.

'I know how you loved him, sweetheart, I know, I know, I'll look after you.'

Gradually he calmed her down, pouring her a large brandy from Rodney's cupboard, then saying he hoped he wouldn't get sacked for hitting the conductor.

'Cut it out,' sobbed Abby. 'Trust you to make jokes.'

'I loved him, too, sweetheart. What are you doing?' he demanded as Abby reached for her new suede skirt.

'Going to Lucerne to take care of Gisela. She's worked for him for forty years, for chrissake.'

'You can't, not yet. You've got to go on tonight.'

'Don't be insane, George must cancel.'

'Rodney would expect it.'

'What about my solo?'

'Mozart played it and conducted at the same time. If you prefer, Julian could play your solo.'

'Like hell he will. Oh Viking, I can't believe it.' She broke down again.

Hearing weeping coming from the conductor's room, Hilary turned to Juno.

'She must have been Rodney's mistress to be so upset.'

'Who's in there?' asked Carmine.

'Viking,' said Hilary.

'Trust Viking to cash in on some poor guy's death to win his bloody bet.'

The next moment Blue had Carmine against the wall.

'You dirty basstard,' he hissed.

Deathly pale in her short pink chiffon dress, Abby looked like a lost masquerader. She left the rose-and-jasmine-woven rostrum empty and conducted from the soloist's position, from which she could see the shock and deep distress on the faces in the audience, many of whom had flown in from all over the world.

Cathie Jones brought all her sadness to the solo in *Romeo and Juliet*. Abby didn't play the Mozart that followed with as much dash as she had in rehearsal, but even though she had to conduct it at the same time, there was an added depth and sorrow.

She's playing a requiem, thought Viking. It was so private, so other worldly, that for a second he was so moved he felt he was going to lose it.

Everyone was so distraught about Rodney that few people appreciated that this was Abby's first time playing in public again.

Mozart was followed by *Don Quixote*. Tears streamed unashamedly down Dimitri's face, as he played the part of the Don, Abby nearly broke down, too, as she introduced the piece:

'In the words of your greatest novel,' she told the audience in Spanish, "*I have battled, I have made mistakes, but I have lived my life the best I can, according to the world as I see it.*" That sums up the Rodney we all knew and loved.'

Neither Viking nor Cherub had the heart to get inside the pantomime cow, so the orchestra played 'Nimrod', Rodney's favourite tune. He had always chided the RSO for playing it too slowly.

'It's an ode to a mighty hunter, he's not dead yet, for goodness' sake.'

Finally, as a mark of respect, the vast audience filed out in silence.

The usual crowd of well-wishers and ghouls were queuing outside Abby's dressing-room. The Press were massing outside. Nicholas was having great difficulty keeping them at bay. Viking caused chuntering and a lot of raised eyebrows when he barged to the front of the queue. Inside he found Abby in tears again.

'Oh Viking, I can't believe it,' she wailed, as he put his

arms round her. 'D'you think the orchestra'll ever love me as much as him?'

This made Viking laugh.

'Not till you leave them, sweetheart. Let's go and get wasted,' then when Abby hesitated, 'we were his favourites, he'd have wanted it.'

'Give me five minutes to have a shower,' said Abby, asking as he went towards the door, 'Was my solo OK?'

'Brilliant, *and* the conducting.'

'I guess I was just the catalyst.'

'In that case,' Viking smiled slightly, 'I'm a member of the Catalyst's Protection League.'

Abby was shocked she looked so beautiful and as she smothered herself in *Amarige*, turning herself on by her caresses, she could already feel Rodney's ghost egging her on.

'Go on, darling, it's worth a try.'

'I love you, Rodney,' she pleaded, 'and I love Viking, please forgive me, you always said as long as we played well, you didn't mind what we got up to below the waist.'

Tiredness hit Flora in the form of the blackest depression. Having bolted in embarrassment when George arrived, she hadn't seen him to talk to since, because he'd been so busy looking after Rodney and then sorting out the ramifications of his death. All she had to listen to was pesky members of the orchestra speculating as to why he'd come out in the first place. On the coach home from the concert, she found out. Slumped in a seat clutching Foxie, and her black dress, she overheard Hilary and Miss Parrott whispering behind her about Rodney's death being 'a merciful release'.

'Ay will miss him,' sighed Miss Parrott. 'Even George seemed upset, and he hardly knew him. Is he stayin' at our hotel?'

'No, riveting news.' Hilary paused, aware of Flora, who pointedly lolled her head on one side and pretended to snore. 'You'll never guess –' Hilary went on – 'he's staying with his wife, Ruth. She's got a hacienda,' Hilary prided herself on her pronunciation, 'near Marbella.'

'I thought they were divorced.'

'No, only separated, and only by her choice. He's mad about her, Miles says, got pictures of her all over his home.'

'How romantic if they've got together again,' sighed Miss Parrott.

'Bit of a smack in the eye for Juno,' said Hilary with satisfaction, 'she was so certain George was about to pop the question.'

Jumping at the sound of tearing, Flora looked down at the ripped-open bodice of her only black dress. She'd need it, if she was going to spend the rest of her life in mourning.

'Of course Juno was much too young for him,' observed Miss Parrott. 'In his position he'd want someone older and more sophisticated, like that nice Serena who works at Megagram.'

As the coach doors clanged open, Flora leapt up, out of the coach, up the steps of the hotel. Reprieve awaited her. As she collected her key, the receptionist handed her a telephone number and a message to ring George. She couldn't bear to wait for the lift and could have won the One Thousand Guineas, at the speed she belted up five flights. She then misdialled the number three times only to get through to her mother, Georgie, who was also on tour, in America.

'Darling, how are you?'

'Fine, absolutely fine.' Fighting back the tears, Flora slumped on the bed. 'Did you ring earlier?'

'About twenty minutes ago. I'm amazed you got the message. I had to repeat the number about four times. I just wanted to know how it's all going.'

Flora couldn't inject a flicker of animation into her voice.

'I'm OK, Mum. You know tours, up and down, we're

all a bit tired.' She couldn't face her mother's torrent of sympathy if she told her about Rodney. 'But it's going well.'

'How are you enjoying Spain?'

'Haven't seen much of it really. There's so much going on within the orchestra. How was the concert?'

'Oh terrific, packed out.'

But her mother didn't want to talk about that. Like Abby, she'd rung home several times in the middle of the night in the last week, but only got herself on the answering-machine.

Flora felt a great weariness.

'Dad's probably asleep, Mum, or pulled out the telephone. You know what he's like.'

I can't face it, she thought in panic, when her mother finally rang off. There must be someone, good, true, safe and constant in the world. I'm a basket case, she thought, as she gazed at her wan, white face in the mirror. I've just transferred the agony of being in love with Rannaldini to the even worse pain of being in love with George.

But a man 'in his position' was not likely to be interested in a twenty-one-year-old slut.

When the telephone rang again, she pounced on it in hope, but it was only Nellie saying there was one helluva party going on in Abigail's suite, the Don Juan, and why didn't Flora come up.

'I've got a migraine,' said Flora, and hung up.

FIFTY-EIGHT

It was one helluva party. In death we are in life. The RSO had played their hearts out. Knowing that Rodney would have wanted it, they now felt an hysterical need to hell-raise.

Back and forth, back and forth went the waiters with room service. Carmine, orgasmic at the prospect of drink paid for by someone else, kept ordering his own bottles of Krug.

A splendid sub-party was going on inside Abby's wardrobe. At least three people, including Simon Painshaw, Ninion and Fat Isobel, had been seen going in. Every so often a hand holding an empty glass would shoot out of the wardrobe. Once it was filled, the door would snap shut again.

In different rooms of the Don Juan Suite, different wirelesses were blaring. Every time 'Rachel's Lament' was played, everyone stopped drinking or dancing and cheered. Cherub kept turning the lights out.

Davie, whose sprained ankle was as puffy as a sumo wrestler's, was using Abby's telephone. He was desperately trying to clock in with Brünnhilde to explain he'd fallen off the platform when sober, rather than Abby's balcony when drunk, before any of the orchestra wives at home told her otherwise. But he was so plastered, he kept dialling wrong numbers and was now through to Australia.

'Whatsh the wevver like out there?'

Cries of admiration greeted the arrival of Viking in a beautiful sky-blue shirt.

'Enough to make a sailor's trousers,' sighed Miss Parrott.

'I'd settle for a sailor,' said Candy sourly. 'We're not going to get any joy out of this lot tonight.'

'That's my shirt,' hissed Blue, 'Cathie saved up months to buy it for me.'

'My need is greater than yours,' murmured Viking. 'You're not even trying to pull Abby.'

To egg on Abby's suitors, a mural showed Don Juan plucking guitars under moonlit windows, being admonished by large ladies, and chasing peasant girls round double beds. Getting into the spirit, Chloë, the comely alto soloist in Beethoven's *Ninth* was trying to pull Julian, kneeling at his feet, pressing her pretty bosom against his locked knees.

'As my wife, Luisa, is always complaining –' apologetically Julian lifted Chloë's hand from his groin – 'after a concert, I simply can't.'

'No such word as *can't*,' said Miss Parrott, delicately picking bits of onion out of a Spanish omelette. Then dropping her fork with a clatter, she started to cry: 'Rodney always loved the harp.'

'Well, he's gone to the right place,' said Viking, filling up her glass. 'By now he'll be knocking back Holy Spirit and goosing his first angel. Don Quixote was magic, Dimitri, would your Guarneri like a top up?'

In the centre of the living-room, rapidly colouring the green carpet with spilt drink, a raucous game of strip poker was in progress. Abby's suitors, realizing they had only two more nights to win the two thousand, had decided this would be as good a way as any to get her clothes off. But Abby had turned out to be an ace player, who was still fully clad in her orange vest, suede mini and high-heeled black sandals.

Among the ring of musicians who surrounded her, on the other hand, Dixie was down to Bugs Bunny boxer shorts, Randy to one sock, Barry to his gold medallions, El Squeako to grey long-johns, and El Creepo to a corn plaster. Nellie had somehow retained her cut-out bra and mauve crotchless knickers. Cherub was wearing just Abby's sunhat and giggling non-stop. A fully dressed Noriko crouched behind trying to cheat for him.

'Abby's got a furr house and Dixie a straight frush,' she whispered.

'There's the straight frush,' cried Cherub, who was far too drunk to make use of any information. 'Sings his song twice over, without a repeat mark.'

Everyone shouted with laughter and re-filled their glasses.

'Just like *Dejeuner sur l'Herbe*,' mused Henry, putting on his glasses to examine the poker groups on the green carpet.

Candy and Clare, who'd eaten too much paella over the past few days to have any desire to strip off, were absolutely hopping. Randy and Dixie totally ignored them by day, then expected to move into their beds at night. Having drunk a bottle apiece, they had retired to a distant sofa.

'I'm going for brains in future,' said Candy. 'If there's a body thrown in, that's a bonus.'

'I'm going for breeding,' said Clare. 'They never ran after Abby until she took up the violin again. Bloody gold diggers.'

'I fancy Julian, only decent bloke in the orchestra.'

'Let's go and rescue him from Alto Sex. Who were you talking to?' added Clare disapprovingly, as Davie came off the telephone to Texas.

'Wrong number, she shounded very nicesh. Got two liel girls.'

'And you told her you were six foot two and twenty-six,' said Candy in outrage.

'Thatsh my inside leg, musht get 'old of Brun'ilde.'

Despite continuous whoops, howls and blaring music, Chloë had finally fallen asleep across Julian's thighs. Gently, like a violin case, he laid her on the floor. On the sofa beside him sat Francis and Bill Thackery, both very drunk.

'We've gotta zap this merger the moment we get home,' urged Julian. 'We lost a great ally in Rodney.'

'I loved the man,' Bill Thackery's eyes were very red.

'Only conductor I've ever met who brought the word "you" into his conversation,' sighed Francis.

'How's your wife's hip, Francis?' called out Abby, who'd been eavesdropping while shuffling the cards.

Francis flushed. 'Oh, much the same.'

'I do hope you'll get her into the hospital soon.'

'Sooner than you think if Francis gets his leg over,' murmured a now naked Dixie, as he lobbed shiny black olives at Nellie's nipples.

Abby, who still hadn't shed a garment, dealt again. The men in the orchestra had all been so complimentary about her solo and her handling of the concert. But she was utterly unmoved that most of them were now stripped for action because of a certainty that she and Viking were finally going to make it. Drink had anaesthetized the pain of Rodney's death. She could only remember the heaven of Viking's arms around her, even the very reluctant slap had been oddly comforting. In a matter of seconds, she had exchanged one father figure for another.

Even now Viking was detached from the party, leaning against the wall in that heavenly blue shirt, sweating out a weak Scotch, swapping Rodney stories with a stunned, tearful Cyril. But all the time, his eyes never left Abby's face, a little smile flickering over his beautiful, stubborn mouth. Totally forgetting Marcus, liberated from a disapproving Flora's chaperonage, Abby felt a pulse as insistent as a snare drum throbbing between her legs. It was going to happen.

A drunken shout greeted another extract from *Rachel's Requiem*, this time on the violin.

'That was a glorious solo, Julian,' shouted Cherub, then seeing the uncontrollable jealousy on Bill Thackery's face, added, 'but your century against the CCO was even better, Bill.'

Always the good sport, Bill joined in the roars of laughter.

Julian was glad he had confided to Bill his worries about Rannaldini and the closing-down of the RSO. Bill would fight their corner with the board.

A hand was sticking out of the wardrobe again so Julian gave it a bottle this time. Tarzan howls greeted the removal of Nellie's crotchless knickers. Carmine, who'd been discussing an expedition to a bull-fight tomorrow with Quinton, glanced over at Nellie and winked.

'Must have a tinkle,' said Nellie ten seconds later, and tottered after Carmine into Abby's spare bathroom.

A hovering Blue, hearing the lock snap, looked round for Cathie, who was wearily listening to Little Jenny droning on about the Celtic Mafia.

'They are all pigs, Cathie.'

Everyone was too far gone to begin behaving when Hilary marched in, demanded a Perrier and started photographing the more advanced forms of debauchery, which included Dimitri drinking Famous Grouse whisky out of an ashtray.

'Didn't you see the "No Moles" sign on the door,' shouted Randy.

Ignoring him, Hilary announced she must go and spend a penny. Viking watched her go towards Abby's spare bathroom, which contained Nellie and Carmine, then surreptitiously turn left into Abby's bedroom. Equally surreptitiously, Viking stole after her.

He found her trying on a diamond necklace, before regretfully turning to Abby's briefcase, systematically opening envelopes, reading letters, flicking through Abby's diary and her address book.

Padding up behind her, Viking closed his hands round her neck.

'What the hell do you think you're doing?'

Hilary shrieked and dropped the briefcase with a clatter.

Under his fingers, Viking watched an ugly red blush rise out of her pie-frill collar.

'I was looking for a copy of tomorrow's schedule,' stammered Hilary, 'to – er – see what time we're leaving for Toledo.'

'Bollocks, as if you didn't know, since your poxy lover called a special inspection at six-thirty outside the hotel.'

He let his hands fall.

'You were snooping, darling. Just how much is Rannaldini paying you to shop Abby?'

It was a complete shot in the dark. But Hilary's jump of horror, like a suddenly buggered maiden aunt, said it all.

'Get out, you meddling bitch, or I'll call the police,' said Viking.

Alone in the room, still shaking with fury, he picked up a periwinkle-blue silk scarf, breathing in *Amarige*. How trusting Abby was – with most of her orchestra in the next room – leaving the unlocked briefcase, the rubies, sapphires, diamonds, the platinum Amex card all spilling wantonly out of her jewel case. Amidst them, like a golden egg, with its leaves shrivelling, was the orange he'd picked her from the coach.

Viking had never been in any doubt that he would win the two thousand pounds. He had already earmarked the money, and told his Wexford grandmother that he would be sending her to America for her seventieth birthday. She hadn't seen her elder sons and their families who lived in New York and Philadelphia for twenty years.

Viking knew that Abby adored him. He had not

forgotten how she had trembled in his arms outside the pub at Christmas. It had been the same this evening. It would require less effort than picking that orange. She would fall into his hands like a sleek ripe yellow pear.

Flora had told him about the secret engagement to Marcus and her grave doubts about the whole thing. Viking felt it was almost his duty to break it up.

'Sorry, mate,' he turned Marcus's photograph to the wall. 'You've lucked out on this one.'

As he wandered back into the living-room, he was pleased to see the silhouettes of his Second Horn and Cathie Jones become one under the stars on the balcony. It would make up for nicking Blue's shirt.

Peter Plumpton, totally naked, was now mincing around with an upended bread basket on his head.

'D'you thenk it's suitable for Escot?' he was asking, to howls of drunken laughter.

Abby's other suitors, having failed to beat her at poker, were getting desperate. El Creepo, who wanted the two thousand for a big screen for his porn videos, was clumsily trying to chat her up.

'What brassière size d'you take Abby?'

'Don't insollt my woman,' howled Viking, grabbing El Creepo by his food-stained lapels.

'Don't, Viking, your tooth,' screamed Abby, as El Creepo raised a nervous fist.

Diversion was provided by a mighty splash from next door as the brass section threw a fully dressed Dirty Harry into the jacuzzi because they thought he needed a bath.

All the other revellers surged into the bathroom, with El Creepo sidling hastily after them, leaving Viking and Abby gazing at each other.

'Am I?' she whispered.

'What?'

'Your woman?'

'Sure you are.'

Unnerved by his nearness, Abby reached for her champagne, but Viking caught her wrist and emptied the glass into a vase of chrysanthemums.

'No more,' he said softly. 'It dolls the senses, you don't need Dottch courage with me.'

Abby was always banging on about the importance of bonding. Next door, it was more a case of James Bonding, as the rest of the party stripped off with squeals of glee to see how many of them could jump into the jacuzzi so the water spilled over, turning the blue shag-pile into a soggy pond.

'I've always longed to go skinny-dipping,' yelled Ninion.

'And I've always wanted to go fatty-dipping,' screamed Isobel, erupting from the wardrobe, breasts flying like duffle-bags, landing amid the heaving flesh, dispatching the last of the water.

'Quite extraordinary, pure Rubens,' said Old Henry, putting on his spectacles to walk round the jacuzzi.

'Who killed Cock Rubens?' shouted Dixie, active at the back of the scrum, to more cackles of laughter.

Davie Buckle sat beside them on the loo with the seat down swigging from a bottle of Dubonnet and tele-phoning Japan. Everyone jumped as Militant Moll stomped in, dressed for bed in men's wool striped pyjamas and leather slippers.

'Anyone seen Ninion?'

'No,' chorused the heaving flesh.

Burying his face gratefully in Isobel's massive breasts, Ninion prayed Moll wouldn't recognize his skinny flanks.

'He said he was going to Mass in one of the cathedrals,' called out Miss Parrott.

'Plenty of steeples round here,' giggled Clare.

'You're despicable,' thundered Moll, marching out to rousing cheers. 'Can't you see how this degrades women?'

'Get us some more hooch, Davie, love,' asked Randy

who was busy degrading Candy. 'Just give room service a bell.'

'Got to cock in with Brün'ilde,' mumbled Davie, redialling.

'Tum, ta, ta, tum, tum, tum, ta, ta, tum, tum,' yelled the RSO to *The Ride of the Valkyries*.

'You get the booze, Lincoln, you're the youngest,' Dixie ordered the Fifth Horn, who was sitting on the edge of the jacuzzi, in his Y-fronts, sadly gazing into space.

Opening the wardrobe and finding Simon Painshaw and Peter Plumpton passed out in each other's arms, Lincoln hastily shut the door, and staggered into Abby's bedroom where he found Little Jenny in tears on the bed.

'I thought you loved me.'

'I do, I do.' Lincoln collapsed on the bed beside her.

Viking would throttle him, but he couldn't keep the secret any longer.

'Two thousand pounds would have paid off my overdraft,' he admitted finally, 'paid a deposit on a flat, and bought you an engagement ring, because, oh Jenny, I want to marry you.'

'Did you say engagement ring?' yelped Jenny, blowing her nose on Abby's scarf. 'Oh please, oh yes please.'

Having kissed her at length, Lincoln staggered to his feet.

'Let's go to my room, Cherub won't be back for hours. I'll go and find the key.'

Looking for stray bottles of drink in Abby's bedroom, Candy found Jenny, gargling with Abby's mouthwash and spraying *Amarige* on her bush.

'You'll never guess why they've all been chasing Abby,' she whispered. 'Promise you won't tell anyone?'

Candy promised.

'Randy wanted some new golf clubs,' Jenny was still explaining two minutes later.

'I'll club him,' screeched Candy, storming back to the jacuzzi.

'Found it,' cried Lincoln, waving his room key.

'Why are you carrying Cherub's clothes?' asked Jenny.

'It'll take him longer to get back to our room,' said Lincoln.

As none of the sorties for more booze had been successful, Francis was dispatched on yet another recce.

'*Lady in buff, Lady in buff,*' said the RSO, swaying to the tune of 'Lady in Red'.

Going into the sitting-room to round up any spare drink, Francis discovered Abby and Viking kissing the life out of each other. They looked so beautiful. Viking was stroking Abby's cheek as though he was rubbing the earth away from some long-buried Grecian urn. The blaze of triumph on his face made Francis reach for his dark glasses.

Oh fuck, groaned Francis. Bang went poor darling Janey's hip operation. Never had he found it harder to be a good loser.

When he returned, the revellers fell on his armful of bottles.

'Viking's won the two grand,' he murmured sadly to Old Henry.

For a second, Isobel stopped French kissing Ninion.

'Viking's always been too grand,' she said dismissively.

'It was Catch 25 situation,' sighed Dimitri, emptying a whole bottle of *Amarige* into the steadily overflowing jacuzzi. 'I vanted to take you to Petersburg, but I love you too much to vin sweepstake.'

'You can take me to Paradise instead,' cried Miss Parrott. 'Oh my wonderful, wonderful Whayte Russian.'

FIFTY-NINE

Viking was not happy about the contrast between Abby's seven-room suite, and the cupboard he was sharing with Blue which was stuffy, airless, shaken with stamping music from the Flamenco night-club opposite and already littered with his discarded possessions.

He felt as though he was shoving a beautiful bird of paradise into a bantam coop. But he had no time to fret. The pack, in their last-ditch scramble for their prize money, would be soon on his trail.

'You have the choice of two ironing boards,' he said, unbuttoning his heavenly blue shirt.

Abby shoved the beds together.

'We can make love across them.'

'A woman of experience.'

'Only of hotel bedrooms. I toured for four years. They provided French champagne and baskets of fruit but nothing as appealing as—' the words died on her lips. The fastest undresser in the world, Viking kicked off his shorts with one foot and caught them on his upright cock.

'That's awful neat,' said Abby in admiration.

'It was a trick of Rodney's.'

Oh shit, what a time to remind her.

Abby collapsed on the bed, her face crumpling.

'Perhaps we shouldn't with Rodney just—'

She gazed up, her eyes huge, enflamed, anguished.

'Rodney's ondyng wish,' Viking crossed his fingers behind his back, 'was for us to end op together. I expect the old dote's already installed a two-way mirror in the floor of heaven so he can watch us.'

'He wanted us to be together? Are you sure?'

'Quite.' Ducking Jove's thunderbolts, Viking peeled off Abby's orange vest. 'Jesus, you're lovely, darling.' Tipping back the yellow bedside lamp, he lifted one warm gold breast wonderingly, then let it drop.

But, as he unzipped her suede skirt, Abby hung her head, uncharacteristically shy and terrified, the giraffe finally cornered by poachers.

'You need a tranquillizing dart, my darling,' Viking stroked her quivering shoulders, talking to her softly. 'You have no idea how stonning you look, or how beautiful it's going to be.'

Thank Christ he'd beaten the others to it, the thought of them groping and fumbling her was unbearable. He reckoned that Abby was far too tall often to have been carried by a man, and probably never in a bedroom. So, to make her feel precious and fragile, Viking gathered her up, telling her her mouth was like a dark red rose, before he buried his lips in it, kissing her so passionately and for so long, that it was Abby who pulled away gasping for breath.

Then, with the ecstasy of an art dealer unrolling a previously undiscovered Modigliani, he laid her across the two beds, sliding his hands in wonder over the sleek satiny scented contours.

'Oh, my beauty.'

'Am I OK?' Fazed by the intensity of his gaze, Abby's hands fluttered to shield her breasts and her pubic hair.

'*Oh my American, my newfound land,*' murmured Viking.

Normally, he would have progressed with infinite slowness, talking her through it, making her so relaxed she glided into her first orgasm almost without realizing it, but he had no time. He could feel her long eyelashes fluttering against his cheek, and then her gasp, as his finger tested her slipperiness.

'Oh, please say you love me.'

'I've never lossted after anyone so much,' said Viking diplomatically, as he guided his cock deep inside her, letting it rest for a moment.

'Isn't that great?' he whispered. 'Lie still, my darling, josst feel what's happening inside you, now go for it, my angel.'

Viking had had many women, but none had ever wanted him so much, nor made love with such utter conviction and desire to please. With most girls, you made them come, then they made you come. Abby, with a conductor's ability to do many things at once, could give and take at the same time.

'L'Appassionata,' Viking glanced down at her reddening cheeks, her eyes cloudy and drugged with desire, 'who would have thought it, but who wouldn't, having heard you play.'

Abby didn't even miss a beat when she noticed the 'I Love Juno' tattoo.

'Lasers'll zap that.'

'If you carry on sucking me,' groaned Viking in ecstasy, 'it'll soon be covered in correcting fluid anyway. No, no, don't bite my dick, I won't take the piss any more.'

Arching himself out of her like a great golden cat, he slid downwards until his mouth was level with hers.

'The first time I come,' he listened to her breathing getting faster and faster, 'it's going to be inside you.'

Afterwards Abby buried her face in the smooth ivory curve of his sweating shoulder.

'Definitely *Guinness Book of Records*,' she mumbled.

'Good, tell all your friends about it.'

'You're a rat.'

'You're a revelation. How come you've got lava in your veins?'

'Not lava, love. I lova you.'

Down below in the night-club, a lone guitar was playing Rodrigo's *Concierto de Aranjuez*.

Reaching for the bottle of Evian by the bed, Abby hazily noticed how right Viking's blue shirt looked entangled with her suede skirt. On the side-table, his casket and St Christopher lay in a glittering heap with her gold bracelet and Marcus's ruby ring.

'Omigod,' she sat bolt upright, 'what about Marcus?'

'He's a darling boy,' Viking kissed the soft flesh above Abby's hip-bones, then working up her ribs, reached her breast. 'But he's too young and too onforceful. You need a man.'

'I figure I've just had one.' Then, as Viking slowly licked her nipple, she pushed his thick yellow hair out of his eyes and said, 'I love you, Viking.'

When he didn't answer straightaway, she asked hastily, 'How come, when you've pulled everyone else in the RSO—?'

'I have not,' interrupted Viking with some hauteur. 'I have not pulled Cathie Jones, nor Miss Parrott, nor Isobel, nor Moll, thank the Lord, nor Hilary, nor Mary-the-mother-of-Josstin.'

'—that you never tried it with me?'

'Did you mind?'

'Sure I did, it was like being frantic for a taxi and one with its "For Hire" sign blazing driving round and round and round me, refusing to stop.'

Viking laughed.

'Didn't you want to?' asked Abby indignantly.

'Indeed I did,' then, half-joking, 'I'm shit-scared of being emasculated by powerful women.'

'But you're the most powerful person in the orchestra.'

'Josst a minute, listen.' Gently Viking tugged at her earlobe. 'It was also respect and not wanting to rossh things, as my Granny Wexford's always saying. There's a time for loving.'

Longing for Viking to introduce her to his family, Abby said she'd just adore to meet Granny Wexford. Had she ever visited the States?

'Not yet.' Like Francis earlier, Viking had the grace to blush.

To distract Abby, he slid his thumb in and out of her, the knuckle gently grazing her clitoris, his long fingers caressing the tender underside of her bottom.

'Oh wow,' Abby drew in her breath. 'Oh please, can we make love again?'

'Don't be greedy. As Bruno Walter said, "*In every truly great work there is only one climax.*"'

'Can't you ever be serious?'

Not when I'm this jolted, thought Viking.

There was a long pause.

'Was I better than Juno?' asked Abby in a small voice.

'Onotterably. She used to slide table mats onder my elbows in case I burnt the sheets.'

As Abby burst out laughing, Viking reached under his bed.

'Here's a present for you.' He handed her his latest CD of the Brahms *Horn Trio*.

'Oh wow,' said Abby in excitement. 'Will you sign it for me, please write something lovely.'

As she ran a hand down his cheek, she could have grated Parmesan on the hard, emerging stubble.

'I can't help it, I just love you.'

He was about to kiss her, when there was a terrific hammering on the door.

'Go away,' shouted Abby.

'Shot op,' hissed Viking, putting fingers reeking of sex and *Amarige* over her mouth. 'Don't answer it.'

The hammering increased.

'Must be Blue trying to get in – it is his room,' protested Abby.

'Who is it?' she shouted.

'Room shervish,' said a voice.

'We didn't order anything, leave it,' snarled Viking, tense as a roused Dobermann.

'I could do with some more Dottch courage,' teased Abby, 'since you watered those flowers with my last lot.' And wriggling out of his grasp, she wrapped herself in the blue shirt and fumbled with the door handle.

'Don't, for Chrissake,' begged Viking, but it was too late.

At first she thought it was the Press, as the flashes of a dozen cameras blinded her. Then, in horror, she took in the muscular hairy legs below the straining black skirt of the waitress who was carrying the sliding magnum of Moët aloft. Behind her, leering and cheering in varying degrees of drunkenness, were most of the male members of her orchestra.

'Who's a clever Viking, then?' shouted Randy.

'Hooray for the lucky winner,' cried Peter Plumpton, who was still wearing his upended bread basket.

'Too much molestar – hic, too much molesta ar,' cried a dripping Dirty Harry.

'I've won more than you, Viking.' An exuberant Dixie smugly patted his strawberry-blond wig. 'I had a grand on you at three to one.'

'Fock off the lot of you,' howled Viking, yanking Abby back inside, 'and leave os alone.'

A moment later, the crowd dispersed as a yelling regiment of policemen and soldiers, brandishing guns, stormed the landing.

Another moment later, there was a crack like a pistol shot as Abby drove her high heel through Brahms's *Horn Trio*.

Davie Buckle, having passed out behind the jacuzzi, had missed the arrival of the forces of law and order, but waking, had dragged a pair of underpants on over his trousers, and was now progressing noisily along the third floor.

Julian caught up with him outside Number 387.

'Hallo there,' he was saying to an enraged Spanish bureaucrat in a hairnet.

'Come on, Davie.' As Julian took his arm, Davie started walking away from him in little circles. 'You've got to stop disturbing people.'

'Got to find Abby.'

'Not at four o'clock in the morning.'

Julian decided his own room was the nearest.

Once he'd thrown Davie on the bed, however, Davie started to fight.

'Got to find Abby.'

'I shall telephone Brünnhilde,' said Julian sternly.

Davie looked owlish. He was terrified of Brünnhilde.

'She's in Rutminshter,' he said sulkily, then brightening, added, 'then I'll telephone Luisa.'

'Luisa doesn't mind, she trusts me,' said Julian, dropping five Redoxins into a tooth mug, and handing them to Davie.

'You've got Beethoven *Nine* again tomorrow, no it's tonight now, drink it.'

'This isn't Scotch,' Davie looked into the tooth mug in outrage. 'Someone's pissed in this glass.'

Limping towards the window, he was about to chuck it into the street.

'Drink it,' ordered Julian.

A shattered George fell into bed at four o'clock in the morning after trying to unravel the endless red tape of flying Rodney's body back to Lucerne. Having switched off his mobile, he was roused a few minutes later by his wife.

'It's Nicholas someone, he sounds put out,' she added, as George took the house telephone from her.

Knickers was apoplectic. The orchestra were completely out of control, orgying and rioting in Abby's jacuzzi which had overflowed and flooded the bridal suite below, where the President of some African state was having an illicit unbridal bonk. His bodyguards had gone beserk and called the troops out. Twenty members of the orchestra had been arrested and were now cooling their heels in Barcelona gaol.

'Which members of the orchestra?' asked George icily.

'Dixie, Randy, Blue, Nellie, Ninion, Dimitri, Candy and Clare. Cherub escaped I think, Flora, I can't remember exactly.'

The arrested players had never seen anything equal to the rage George had worked up by the time he'd driven the forty miles to Barcelona gaol.

He found most of his orchestra still plastered. Dimitri was crying because he couldn't remember where he'd left his cello; Miss Parrott was hiccupping with her rhubarb-pink beehive askew and singing 'Land of Hope and Glory'; Dixie, still in his black-and-white maid's outfit, was being leered at by the guard; and Ninion, still necking ferociously, looked as though he was going to be sucked inside Fat Isobel like a minnow at any second.

Only by handing over hoards and hoards and hoards of greenbacks did George manage to spring them. The one saving grace was that none of them had got round – yet – to taking drugs.

'Where's Flora?' snarled George, as the motley bunch swayed in front of him.

'Oh, Flora wasn't with us,' said Nellie, who was wearing a Spanish policeman's hat, 'the poor thing had a migraine. She was crying with pain when I popped in around midnight.'

Only Blue, who had his hand in Cathie's and was soberer than most, noticed that George suddenly cheered up, and the great thundercloud threatening to drench them all suddenly rolled away.

'You better go back to the hotel and pack,' he told them unsympathetically. 'And get your baggage outside your doors. The coach leaves in an hour.'

*　　*　　*

Ignoring two wake-up calls, Barry the Bass was finally roused by a call from the leader of the orchestra who'd spent the rest of the night in an armchair.

'It's about Davie,' said Julian apologetically.

'Where did he end up?'

'My room, eventually. He's snoring so loudly, Brünnhilde will hear him in Rutminster, and I can't wake him. He's going to miss this goddamn roll-call.'

'Give me five minutes.'

Barry the Bass, who was highly experienced in these matters, from his days in a rock band, kicked Davie in the ribs.

'Get up, you drunken bastard.'

Davie groaned, but didn't stir.

Deodorant sprayed into his face had no effect.

It was only when Barry seized the foot with the sprained ankle and twisted it round and round that Davie finally woke up.

The three made it outside just in time.

In the absence of Miles, Knickers begged George to inspect the troops. 'And please, please chew them out. I simply can't control them any more.'

Dawn was making flamingo-pink in-roads on the East as George walked slowly down the row. The Spaniards, he decided, could not have seen so many wrecks since the Armada. Flora looked frightful, her face chalk-white, her eyes through crying as red as a white rat's. Slumped against the coach, slitty eyes gazing into space, Viking looked even whiter than she did. Of the whole lot, only the Steel Elf, who didn't drink, looked beautiful, the violet shadows under her eyes increasing her look of fragility.

'Where's Cherub?' intoned Knickers, checking his list.

'It's not his fort,' piped up Noriko. 'Poor Cherub's lost all his crows.'

On cue, Cherub shot through the swing doors,

holding a tambourine over his cock and totally naked except for his shoes.

Scuttling down the steps, he slid into the line-up just as George reached him. The players, despite hangovers, were in total hysterics – waiting for a blistering undressing down. But George's eyes merely ran over Cherub for a second.

'Shoes need cleaning, Wilson,' he said coldly and moved on.

The next moment, Noriko had hurtled down the row and wrapped Cherub in her long pink cardigan.

George returned to the middle of the row, climbing back up three of the hotel steps so he could talk to his orchestra. In his haste to reach the gaol, he had put his dark blue poloshirt on inside out – lucky for him, thought Flora wistfully.

'You're all an absolute disgrace,' he roared, then, like the turned-up corner of a page, a faint smile lifted his square face. 'We'll be in Toledo by ten o'clock. Beethoven *Nine* is appropriately scheduled to start at nine. As you can play it in your sleep, I suggest a short rehearsal at eight after your meal-break, but only on condition that you spend the afternoon in bed, alone and you play out of your boots this evening.'

And he strode off towards the car-park.

'He's in a jovial mood,' said Miss Parrott in surprise.

Out of masochistic yearning, Flora stationed herself in front of Hilary and the Steel Elf, but they both slept all the way to Toledo. A rowdy party carried on at the back of the coach, but they couldn't persuade Flora to join them.

'*Milesie loves me, yes I know,*
Cos my pay cheque tells me so,' sang Cherub to the tune of 'Jesus Loves Me'.

Viking sat by himself. The sky clouded over as they drove into Toledo. Viking could see a red traffic-light reflected in the bus window like a setting sun. If only he could have turned back the clock twelve hours. He was in the kind of eruptive, jungle-cat mood where everyone avoided him.

But, as they surged into the hotel reception which was appropriately filled with glossy dark jungle plants, to collect their new keys from Knickers, Randy shouted 'Lunch on Viking, everyone.'

'I'm crashing out,' Viking shot a warning glance in Flora's direction.

'Dom Perignon all round,' went on Randy evilly.

A mocking Dixie put his arm round Flora's shoulders. 'You missed all the fun last night.'

'Shot your face,' howled Viking.

'What *are* you talking about?'

Flora didn't believe Dixie at first. Then he waved a polaroid under her nose, and she flipped. All her pent-up misery over George going back to his wife and the thieving bloody randiness and fecklessness of men in general, poured out of her, as she screamed at all of them.

'How could you do that to Abby, you bastards, BASTARDS. You swore you'd break her, and now you bloody well have.'

Locking herself in her room she threw herself down on the bed, sobbing her heart out, ignoring the bombardment on the door until they all got bored and wandered off. Then the telephone went. It was Viking.

'It wasn't like you think,' he begged. 'Please put in a good word to Abby.'

'Oh, fuck off. I am just writing a stinking letter to St Patrick, telling him there was one utterly poisonous snake he didn't drive out of Ireland. Haven't you any idea either how this will hurt Marcus?'

The moment she slammed the telephone down, it rang again.

'Fuck off, fuck off,' shrieked Flora.

'Is thut Room 854?'

'How do I know?'

'It's George.'

'Whadja want?' She mustn't start crying again.

'You once said you wanted to go oop in an air balloon.'

'I've got a headache.'

'Fresh air'll do you good – a car'll pick you up at two o'clock.'

SIXTY

Remembering the coiffured, manicured Ruth, Flora decided two could play at that game. Systematically, she worked her way through the little bottles in her bathroom, washing her hair, then lying in a bubble bath, in a shower cap as transparent as her motives, as she scrubbed her body with a tiny oblong of soap. Then she rubbed in all the available moisturizer and gargled away all the pink mouthwash. She would have scrubbed her entrails if she could have got at them. She put on a dove-grey sundress, thrown out by her mother as being too young, and left her hair loose so it shone and swung like a copper bell. With a desperately trembling hand, she just managed to draw two thick lines round her eyes until they dominated her face like a bush baby's, and painted her lips the glowing coral of japonica in spring. The gentle dove-grey was wonderfully becoming. Jumping with nerves, she went downstairs to find various members of the orchestra passed out on chairs and sofas in the foyer. The bar was propping up a green-faced Davie. Others were setting out on jaunts with guide books.

'I've got to see something of Spain other than concert halls and ceilings,' announced Nellie.

In a nearby booth, Randy's big checked shoulders were hunched over the telephone as he called home for the first time in six days. The next moment he was crying so much he could hardly tell his wife he'd see her tomorrow.

'What on earth's the matter?' asked Flora.

'Kirsty put each of the children on to speak to me,' sobbed Randy, 'I miss them all so much.'

'Then why play around so much, when you've got such a lovely family?'

'I don't know,' Randy blew his nose, then caught sight of Flora. 'God, you look sexy, come 'ere.'

But Flora had bounded away. Calm down, she kept telling herself, it's daft to get so excited.

'You car's here, Mees Seymour,' announced a hot-eyed chauffeur sweating in black uniform.

'How d'you know it's me?' squeaked Flora.

'I was told you was gorgeous with red 'air.'

'Oh goodness.' Flora bolted down the steps.

But all her happiness drained away as inside the car she found Juno looking so bloody beautiful in a pale pink shirt and shorts, showing off tiny suntanned thighs half the width of Flora's. It was no comfort that Juno was as cross to see her, or that they were soon joined by Simon (perhaps George was after him, too) and Hilary. Flora slumped in the back; she might as well have got drunk on Viking's ill-gotten champagne with all those other bastards.

They drove past ploughed fields and rocks the colour of lobster bisque through beautiful white villages, up an avenue of yellowing, peeling plane trees to a ravishing castle about five miles out of town.

A crowd of people in light trousers and rather well-pressed shirts, dressed up with nattily tied silk scarves, were making a din on the terrace. On the unblemished and blatantly sprinkled lawn below, a panting Spaniard in blue dungarees was wrestling with a purple-and-emerald-green dragon's skin spewing out of a vast basket.

'What a lovely spot,' said the Steel Elf.

George came straight up. The rings under his eyes were heavier than his eyebrows. He had turned his navy-blue polo shirt the right way round, but tucked into his white trousers, it showed he had completely lost his spare tyre. His feet looked vulnerably pale in loafers. Flora suppressed an insane urge to drop to her feet and kiss them. She must get a grip on herself.

'What does anyone want to drink?'

'Perrier, please,' said Juno.

'And me, too,' simpered Hilary.

'I'll have an orange pressé if it's feasible,' said Simon.

'I'll have a quadruple vodka and tonic,' said Flora.

'You won't be able to play,' reproved Hilary.

'I've got to sing,' said Flora. 'It's so hard, I'll never get onto the platform if I'm sober.'

Having taken Flora at her word, and persuaded the others to accept a glass of champagne each, George introduced Ruth, who was much too done-up, in a frilly white shirt and shocking-pink trousers with gold high heels, for lunch-time in the campa.

Having given Flora a not-altogether friendly look she introduced her 'partner' Trevor.

Flora giggled. 'I've got a partner called Trevor, too,' she said. 'Only in my Trevor's case, he has black eyes, and a tight skin and a very curly tail, and a squeaky bark, and I rescued him.' She rattled on. 'You don't look as though *you* need rescuing.'

Trevor II smirked, gave Flora slightly too hot a glance for Ruth's liking, and asked her if she'd ever been up in an air balloon before.

Flora shook her head. Suddenly she was too shy to say anything in George's presence.

'We're coming along to the concert this evening to

look at George's latest toy,' said Ruth with a slight edge. 'I love Beethoven's *Choral Symphony*. To think the wonderful old man wrote the whole thing when he was deaf.'

She beckoned the maid to bring over the bottle.

'Have some more shampoo.'

'I shouldn't,' giggled Juno, 'it makes my nose tickle.' She smiled roguishly at George, who had also fallen oddly silent.

'Just a half,' said Hilary. 'I expect we'll be in the balloon soon.'

'Oh no, Pedro-Maria takes at least half an hour to get it up,' said Ruth.

'Poor Mrs Pedro-Maria,' murmured Flora. Just for a second her eyes met George's and, to stop herself laughing, she sloped off and gazed at a hideous bed of red gladioli and purple asters. Ruth was hell. George was the one who needed rescuing.

Only George and the four musicians from the RSO, and Pedro-Maria to steer the thing, went up in the balloon. Extraordinary, reflected Flora, as they took off into the blue, that a slain dragon could swell up into something so huge and beautiful with the orange flame belching up into the purple-and-emerald-green dome. Turning, she saw George's waving wife getting smaller and smaller.

It was literally heavenly. This is how God must feel, thought Flora, as she gazed down on the turning, tawny woods and the gold and green fields, as the darkness of the balloon's shadow fell over the face of the earth. Below them flocks of sheep and herds of cows scattered in temporary terror.

Flora had deliberately positioned herself at the front of the basket as far away from George as possible, giving him the chance if he wanted to stand behind the Steel Elf. Everyone was oohing and aahing as they floated over a little village, driving dogs to hysterical barking and bringing children screaming with excitement into the streets.

Then a sudden gust tipped the basket forward and she felt a body, solid as a Rottweiler, thrown against hers, and knew instantly with a thumping heart that it was George's.

'Sorry,' she gasped, ramming herself even harder against the front of the basket, putting half an inch between them, but a second later, the wind tossed the basket backwards, throwing her against him. As she leapt away, his big hands closed on her hip bones, steadying her, and he was right behind her giving her absolutely no room for manoeuvre. With St George *and* the dragon pitted against one poor damsel – what chance of escape did she have?

I must be dreaming, thought Flora in bewilderment, but she could have sworn George dropped a kiss on her bare shoulder and now his thumbs were softly stroking her ribcage, as the flames surged upwards with another dragon roar.

For a second, he took his right hand away, resting a muscular arm on her shoulder, the soft dark down tickling her cheek, as he pointed out hares racing up and down the rows of stubble.

'What a wonderful view,' gushed Hilary.

'Mine's much better,' murmured George into Flora's hair.

His right hand was back but higher up her ribs this time, and oh my God, his thumb was slowly caressing her right breast outside her dress, and now, oh heavens, it had crept inside – there was no mistaking it. Her nipples were pushing out the dove-grey sundress as proof, and it was the most blissfully erotic thing that had ever happened to her. It knocked any of Rannaldini's caresses into a cocked cock. She was so faint with desire her insides were churning and disintegrating like peaches in a liquidizer.

She couldn't bear it, gradually they were losing

height, drifting down over a sage-green poplar copse. The lovely balloon of her happiness was going to subside.

'That's very good timing, George,' said Simon.

In despair, Flora noticed two chauffeurs leaning against two hearse-like limos waiting at the edge of the big yellow field below them. She glanced sideways and realized that Hilary was gazing at George's still-wandering right hand in absolute horror. Then another greater gust of wind caught the balloon. The next moment Hilary and Juno were screaming as they crashed and bumped to the ground like cats in a basket chucked out of a car, with everyone falling higgledy-piggledy on top of each other.

'Get me out of here,' shrieked Hilary, outraged to find herself trapped beneath an excited Pedro-Maria, who was in turn beneath an even more excited Simon.

'You OK, Flora, luv?' George's accent was even broader with anxiety.

'Gone to heaven,' sighed Flora, squirming blissfully under the weight of his body.

A second later George had pulled her to her feet, lifted her out of the basket and dragged her across the stubble into the first limo.

Jumping into the driving seat, he screeched off in a cloud of dust, leaving behind the two drivers and the rest of the party waving and shouting impotently.

'Plenty of room for the rest of them,' he said, nearly removing a gatepost as he swung into the road. 'Do oop your seat belt,' then, after a long pause, 'I luv you, I luv you, I bluddy luv you to distraction.'

'What?' squeaked Flora, 'I thought you still loved Ruth.'

'I came here last night to ask her for a divorce.'

'I thought it was you who refused to give *her* one.'

'You know a lot about my life, don't you?' said George, murdering unfamiliar gears as he swung onto the main road, and rammed his foot on the accelerator.

'I hated Trevor,' he said. 'He was one of my competitors and he took my wife off me. Now I know he's done me a good deed. I didn't hate him any more today. Anyway, I want to be free to marry someone else.'

Flora was speechless, and reached for the strap above her window as the needle hit 100 m.p.h.

'But I don't understand, I mean – ' then, as the car only just missed a bank – 'Jesus!'

'Yes, you better shoot up, and let me concentrate on driving.'

Reaching Ruth's hacienda, he grabbed Flora's hand again and, ignoring the party that was still roaring on the terrace, dragged her up three flights of stairs into his bedroom, and locking the door took her in his arms. For a second he gazed into her face, so sweet and apprehensive and striped by the sunlight streaming through the shutters, and then he kissed her.

Flora had never experienced such tenderness, nor passionate enthusiasm nor clumsiness all at once. Then he ripped off her sundress, and kissed her breasts, before tearing off her knickers and throwing her on the bed.

'I'm not on the p-p-pill,' Flora hated herself for stammering.

'Doesn't matter. I want to fook you more than anything in the world,' George stammered even more as he fumbled with his belt, 'but I want you to know I luv you and want to marry you as well.'

Flora helped him with his zip and boxer shorts.

'Oh my,' she said in a choked voice, 'you are well Hungerford.'

'Don't take the piss,' pleaded George. 'I can't 'andle it. Let's take things very slowly.'

''Andel's Largo,' began Flora, until George stopped her nervous prattle by kissing her.

Having exhausted the bed, they moved into the bathroom. Lying on the shag-pile, Flora admired the gleaming undersides of the lavatory bowl, and thought she must remember to clean under the loo at the cottage. Then she thought of nothing else except George.

Finally ending up on a pile of duvets on the bedroom floor, she staggered to her feet.

'I have to sing "Ode to Joy", in a few hours,' she sighed, 'but I'm so happy it'll probably sing itself this evening.'

'I luv you,' repeated George, who was running water into a round cyclamen-pink bath next door. 'I mean it about marrying you.'

'And I mean it, too,' said Flora, bending over to kiss him, 'it's just a bit new and all. The bliss of having a bathroom en suite,' she went on, 'is that you don't have to scuttle across the landing trapping a towel between your legs.'

A shadow flickered across George's face.

'Have you done that lots of times?'

'A few.'

'How many blokes have you been to bed with?'

'I've lost Count,' said Flora, 'as Countess Dracula was always complaining. D'you want a bowdlerized version?'

'No, I want the truth.'

'Right, well,' Flora took a deep breath. 'I had several schoolboys at Bagley Hall, then I had Rannaldini. I wonder if women who've slept with Rannaldini make love in a certain way, like string players who've been to the Juillard.'

'Go on,' George almost snapped, as Flora's body disappeared under the surface then emerged like a seal, the bubbles coating her freckled back.

'Rannaldini obliterated everyone else. Then I tried a few students at the Academy to exorcize him, but it didn't work. Then no-one till Jack, but I only went to bed with him because he rescued me from Carmine – rather like accepting a large brandy from a St Bernard when you're stuck halfway up the Matterhorn.'

Unable to suppress a smile, George started to rub

Pears soap, the colour of Flora's wet hair, down her arm.

'That's all, except Viking,' she said.

Dropping the soap, George's hand did a Chinese burn on her wrist. He really minds, thought Flora, gazing at the red mark in wonder.

'W-w-was it foontastic?' asked George wistfully.

'Yes and no, we were both a bit too expert like Torvill and Dean. Anyway, I honestly think Viking went to bed with me to get at Abby. He can't leave her alone, he's always bitching at her.

'That's about it. Truly. I'm at my journey's end.' Putting both arms up, feeling George as warm, wide and solid as an Aga against her, Flora pulled him into the bath with a huge splash. 'You are the loveliest hunk.'

But George was still fretting.

'Will I be exciting enough for you?'

'Exciting,' Flora's eyes flooded with tears. 'I can't begin to tell you, like that great balloon soaring into the sky out of that limp rubber, what it's like suddenly to be happy again, wildly, ecstatically happy with the most adorable man in the world. That's exciting, I have to joke, I have to, I'm just so terrified it's going to end.'

'In my end is my beginning,' said George, kissing her soapy hand. 'I'm going to marry you the second my divorce is through.'

'Oh goodness.'

'And I want to say, Floora –' (she loved the way he pronounced it with a long first syllable)– 'I've had a change of heart because of you. I know I've been greedy in the past, I've ridden roof-shod over folk, been a bastard. Knocking down houses, in-filling, leaning on old ladies, I've thought about it a lot. I've totally given oop the idea of buying H.P. Hall and turning it into a supermarket.'

'I know someone who could do with a bit of in-filling at the moment,' said Flora slyly.

Rising up in the bath, she started to kiss her way down

his body, plunging into the water until his cock came up to meet her. Then she looked up, quickly gasping for breath, eyelashes like star fish.

'Abby's always telling me to play with every inch of my beau.'

George ruffled her hair.

'You're utterly deranged.'

'Let's have a deranged marriage then.'

'When can I start telling everyone?'

'Not until I tell Abby,' said Flora. 'I'm not sure how pleased she'll be.'

SIXTY-ONE

Abby was in a murderous mood and shouted at Flora as she slid in late to the rehearsal and took her place beside the other three soloists.

'She's in a terrific paddy,' whispered Clare in awe.

'Correction,' whispered Candy, 'a terrific Paddy's been inside her.'

Poor Abby, in fact, had just had a hideous session with Hilary. Oozing spurious concern like a lanced boil, Hilary had come into the conductor's room, and begged Abby not to take Viking's seduction too seriously.

'The sweepstake was just a bit of fun, Abby. And you must remember the musicians aren't wealthy like you. That two thousand would have got most of them out of debt, saved the repossession of Barry's barn, paid for Janey's hip, cushioned Cyril's retirement, bought Randy some new clubs.'

'And a new prayer-mat for Miles.'

'Oh, Miles would never involve himself with anything so tacky.'

'Unlike fucking Viking.'

Hilary sighed deeply.

'I'm afraid Viking's too lazy to get anywhere in life. He'd never have scraped together enough money to send Granny Wexford to America, if he hadn't won it. They'll think he's such a hero in Dublin, and of course he has to keep up his reputation as the orchestra stud.'

'The son-of-a-bitch,' hissed Abby, 'I'll get him for sexual harassment.'

'I'm afraid the orchestra will say the boot was on the other foot – they'll swear black's white for Viking.'

'I've been made a complete fool of, right?'

'Where's your sense of humour, Abby?' Hilary was loving this. 'Get things in proportion. If you need some counselling when you get back to England, Miles will arrange it.'

'Can he arrange for Viking to be Bobbitted as well?'

Hilary sighed. 'Miles and I are praying for you.'

Certainly during the rehearsal Abby's wrath was reserved for Viking.

They were only running through the last movement from where the chorus and soloists come in, but she wasted everyone's time singling out any intervening horn passages, and pulling them to pieces, particularly Viking's contribution.

'More pianissimo, First Horn,' she screamed until Viking wasn't making any sound at all. 'Play it again.'

'Why? It was perfect.'

'Don't smart-ass me, leave your brains in your trousers where they belong.'

The minute she said that, Abby could have kicked herself.

'You should know,' chorused the Celtic Mafia.

'I said, on your own, First Horn.'

And Viking, who'd never been called First Horn in his life except by Rannaldini, retaliated by playing the solo from *Ein Heldenleben* which had so bewitched her on her first day at the RSO. Abby promptly burst into tears and stormed out.

Julian ran after her, but she wouldn't talk to him. After last night she didn't know who to trust, not even Flora, who'd been grinning like a jackass throughout the rehearsal.

Somehow, by the evening, fortified by a couple of beta-blockers, Abby had pulled herself together, and the applause, as always, even for a run-of-the-mill Beethoven's *Ninth*, was tumultuous because it was such a happy piece, and because so many of the chorus's relations were swelling the audience.

George sat in a box high above the orchestra. It was hard to tell who looked more frozen with misery, Viking or Cyril, for whom it was his last concert abroad, and who had been denied the great horn solo in the third movement.

But George couldn't be bothered with other people's problems tonight. And the moment Flora filed on with the other soloists, he never took his eyes off her, rejoicing in every note, as her piercing exquisite voice soared above everyone else's, even when she joined in the chorus. Several times she smiled up at him and even made Foxie give him a wave. She has brought radiance to my life, thought George. Thank you, God, for giving me a second chance.

Having given her all to the ecstatic Toledo audience, Abby was on her knees. There had been too much going on to take in Rodney's death. Now the shock was wearing off, and the pain beginning to hurt. Only to Rodney could she have confessed the agony and utter humiliation of having offered herself to Viking so totally and so trustingly, when all he was after was the macho gratification of winning some bet. She could imagine the guffaws, the sniggering, the slaps on the back.

'What was the snooty cow like, Viking? What was she really like?'

And it had been so beautiful, so perfect, that was the pity of it.

She wanted to creep into bed and die, but George had

to fly back for tomorrow's RSO board meeting, so she had to take his place at dinner with the Toledo organizers.

Viking, probably for the first time in his career, didn't go out on an end-of-tour razzle. He was utterly bewildered how depressed and ashamed of himself he felt. Abby had got under his skin and irritated him more than any woman he'd ever met. He had dreamt for so long of wiping the haughty expression off her face and reducing her to grovelling, pleading, adoring submission, and now he had, he loathed himself.

As leader of the pack, his street cred would have been utterly destroyed if he hadn't won the bet. He also owed it to his backers. As the favourite, there had been a lot of money on him. Now he desperately wanted to explain to Abby that winning the bet had only been part of the incentive, and the actuality had been miraculous. He was certain if he and Abby had spent a week or so together unwatched by the lascivious or disapproving eyes of the orchestra, he could have fucked her out of his system and remained friends. Guilt was not a familiar emotion to Viking, and he didn't think this time he'd be able to rid himself of it with a few Hail Maries.

He was also miserably aware that the three other people he loved and trusted – Flora, Julian and Blue – were absolutely furious with him.

'You behaved abominably, Viking,' Julian had shouted. 'Rodney was just saying yesterday how you'd swung the RSO behind Abby. Now you've let him down. You're as repulsive as Anatole in *War and Peace*. Rake Magdalene, he loved much, so much will be forgiven him. You're nothing but a fucking havoc-maker.'

Blue was even more upset. Cathie, having learnt about the bet, was refusing to have anything to do with him.

'How could you men all hurt that lovely warm girl?'

* * *

Wandering wearily down the hotel landing, Viking could hear the sound of hair-dryers. Orchestra wives washing their hair to be pretty for their husbands tomorrow, leaving doors open so they could chat to one another. Mary, her hair in rollers, was finishing her sampler. One thing Viking hadn't given Abby was 'roots and wings'. God, he felt awful. Davie was asleep on a *chaise-longue*, a plastered Cyril was declaiming 'Ulysses' to a large yucca plant:

> *'Old age has yet his honour and his toil;*
> *Death closes all, but something 'ere the end*
> *Some work of noble note, may yet be done.'*

Viking had only just collapsed into bed wondering whether to ward off suicide or encourage sleep with a large whisky from the mini-bar, when Blue arrived and whispered that he'd finally persuaded Cathie to come back to the room with him.

'I trapped her in the revolving doors so she couldn't escape.'

'Where's Carmine?'

'Enjoying a bonk with Nellie, since you bottled out. He left Cathie fast asleep in bed, having taken a Mogadon, or so he thinks.'

'Bloody risky.'

'Sure it is, we won't have long, just bogger off and leave the coast clear.'

'I won't watch I promise,' pleaded Viking, 'I josst want to crash out.'

'I don't believe you,' hissed Blue, 'it's my only chance. Please Viking, or Cathie'll do a runner – she's furious with you as it is.'

Wearily, Viking staggered upstairs, wrapped only in a towel, and dragging his duvet and a pillow. He was just banging on the Steel Elf's door when the lift opened and out stepped Lord and Lady Leatherhead, Knickers and Hilary, all jolly from the official dinner. Trailing after them was a haunted, ghostly-pale Abby.

'Abby, sweetheart, we mosst talk.' Viking bounded forward, his only thought to comfort her.

Abby, who'd been on the Fundador on an utterly empty stomach, went beserk.

'Get out of my life, you fucking son-of-a-bitch,' she screamed, and slapped him really hard across the face.

With fatal timing, the door behind Viking opened to show the Steel Elf with her hair tied up in a pink bow and wearing a pretty rose-patterned nightgown.

'Go back to your little prick-teaser, right?' yelled Abby. 'Let her put some more beer mats under your elbows, two grand'll keep up her mortgage for at least six months.' And with that she lashed her other hand back across Viking's cheek, cutting it open with Marcus's ruby.

Lord and Lady Leatherhead and Knickers looked on in horror; Hilary in delight, as Abby ran off down the landing to her suite, slamming the door behind her.

During the sex which took place between Blue and Cathie, which Cathie was far too frightened and ashamed of her body to enjoy, her make-up rubbed off to reveal a dark bruise below her left cheek-bone. She tried to cover up two more on her ribs.

Blue struggled to control his fury.

'For poorer and poorer, for battered and even more battered, you've got to leave him, Cath.'

'I can't, I don't believe in divorce.'

'I wouldn't believe in it either if you were married to me.'

Blue tried to kiss her but she jerked her head away. Only that morning Carmine had untruthfully told her her breath smelt, her bottom had dropped and her breasts were like drooping poached eggs.

'I must go,' she whispered, but, as she dived for her clothes, so he shouldn't see her ugly body, Blue caught her wrist pulling her back.

'I want to tell you a story.'

For a second, Cathie thought he was joking, but his clear blue eyes, the kindest in the world, were completely serious.

'Once upon a time, there was a beautiful woman, married to a wicked philanderer who constantly diminished her and beat her op. But because she was a good Catholic, who wanted to go to Heaven, she stayed with him for fifty dreadful years.'

Cathie gave a sob.

'In the end the philanderer died a week before his wife did, and, free of him at last, she arrived on the other side.

'"Here for all eternity," said God, welcoming her with open arms, "there's someone here you know already," and there on the first fluffy white cloud was her husband shafting an angel.'

There was a long pause. Glancing sideways, Blue saw the bruise getting darker and darker as tears washed away the last vestiges of make-up.

'Cathie darling, I didn't mean to hurt you, but you've got to leave him. No-one will punish you. I'll look after you, I promise.'

'I can't. He'd come after me and he'd kill us both.'

'I'll never turn my mobile off,' Blue was in tears, too. 'If ever you want me, just ring and I'll come and get you.'

Imagining the rest of the orchestra and especially Flora trailing home the following morning with no-one to carry her case, George found it impossible to concentrate on his board meeting. He hoped none of the bitches in the orchestra nor those brutes in the brass section nor any section for that matter were pricking Flora's bubble or wising her up about his thousand and one deficiencies. God, he missed her.

The board meeting had begun with regrets and a minute's silence for Rodney's death. Miss Priddock had sobbed all over her shorthand notebook, which made it difficult for her to use her biro, but she had been cheered up by yet another miniature from one of the brewers. Everyone expressed delight that Sonny's *Interruption* had been nominated. Peggy Parker bowed graciously.

Then followed the usual moans about poor houses, insufficient sponsors and the rocketing cost of the latest marketing operations which George had introduced.

At least the cat-nip matador he'd brought back from Toledo had been a huge success, thought George. As if to avenge generations of brave bulls, John Drummond was now tossing it up in the air, and pouncing on it.

'How did the tour go?' demanded Peggy Parker, noticing George's total inattention.

'You better ask Miles – he was there longer than me.'

George was incensed when Miles, after pouring a glass of Lord Leatherhead's spring water from the silver carafe Hilly had given him for his birthday, rose to his feet and deplored the hooliganism that had poisoned the tour.

'Although there are still players who know how to act as worthy ambassadors for Rutminster, a crackdown is imperative before the Appleton Piano Competition in ten days' time,' emphasized Miles, 'when the RSO will be scrutinized under the microscope, not only by the music world, but by the international media and the general public.

'In a word,' Miles cracked his knuckles, 'I feel Abigail has lost control of the orchestra.'

'That was a great many more than one word,' said George furiously, 'and your description of the tour is joost as inaccurate. The orchestra played brilliant, made many friends all over Spain and really put Rootminster on the map. They only screwed up on Saturday night because they were choked about Rodney, and that was only after they'd cobbled together the best memorial concert I've ever heard. There wasn't a dry eye in the house when they played *Nimrod*,' George's voice shook slightly. 'Abby did chumpion. It was the first time she'd played in pooblic and she had to conduct as well. She and Rodney were very close.'

'How close, one wonders,' said Mrs Parker sourly, 'I gather Sir Rodney left her his home on Lake Lucerne.'

'That's out of order,' snapped George.

Mrs Parker went puce.

'And who's going to foot the bill for the jacuzzi flooding the Don Hoo-an Suite?' she spluttered.

'I am,' said George.

'And what about Flora Seymour pulling the communication cord on the train to Madrid?' chuntered Lady Chisleden.

'Over the defenestration of some cuddly toy,' said Canon Airlie. George started to laugh.'Perhaps some latterday Zola will leap to our defence in the *Rootminster Echo*,' he suggested, 'and start his letter, "J'acuzzi".'

Everyone looked at him as though he'd gone off his head.

'Oh forget it,' said George, then added grimly, 'you've been sneaking, Miles. The reviews were bloody good. Abby's emerging as a first class conductor. *Rachel's Requiem*'s Number Ten in the charts. We've got a big hit on our hands.'

'What news of the merger?' asked Canon Airlie earnestly. 'What was the outcome of your discussions with the Arts Council on Wednesday? Did they provide any guidance?'

'That lot are about as capable of guidance as a droonken guide-dog.'

Canon Airlie pursed his lips.

'Lousy for morale,' said a banker, 'with so many conflicting rumours flying around.'

'The RSO need a strong leader who can set a good example,' Mrs Parker glared at George.

'Why did the jacuzzi flood?' asked Lady Chisleden.

'Not really a matter for ladies,' said Lord Leatherhead hastily, casting an eye at Miss Priddock who was stolidly taking the minutes.

Abandoning his cat-nip matador, John Drummond jumped onto the window-ledge to chatter angrily at two pigeons copulating on the roof. Cat's television was much better in the summer, when the house martins and swallows flew in and out of the eaves.

They've all gone to warmer climes *In the South*, thought George. That was the tune Flora had played so beautifully at her audition. He looked at his watch. Her plane would be taking off any minute. If he hurried he could meet her at Heathrow. It had been the longest twelve hours of his life.

'I agree that leadership must come from the top,' Miles was saying. 'If there were a merger, I think Rannaldini is the only man who could pull the orchestra together and save us from financial disaster.'

'Where is Rannaldini?' enquired Peggy Parker reverently.

'Recording in Prague with some brilliant young Czech pianist. He always noses out the talent.'

George stubbed out his cigar and rose to his feet. Flora must have told Abby by now.

'I'm afraid the only merger I'm remotely interested in at the moment is my own,' he announced. 'I'd like the board's permission to take a three-month sabbatical.'

'But you never take holidays,' said Miss Priddock aghast. 'Even durin' that week's skiing you worked in the evenings.'

'Not this time,' said George proudly. 'I'm going to take Miss Flora Seymour, the most wonderful young lady round the world, and as soon as I get a divorce, she's going to marry me.'

There was an absolutely appalled silence.

'But she's a member of the orchestra, and about half your age,' exploded Mrs Parker.

'And a baggage,' chuntered Miles.

'Well, I certainly didn't put her outside my door at six o'clock,' said George with a broad grin.

'I hope you didn't abuse your position, Hungerford,' snorted Canon Airlie.

'Ooterly,' said George happily. 'So would you if you'd been me, you old goat.'

'But who is going to do your job?' protested Lord Leatherhead. 'Have left us in rather a hole yer know.'

'As Miles is so frantic to run the orchestra, let him have a go. Now, if you'll excuse me, I've got a plane to meet.'

After he'd left and the uproar had subsided, Miles moved into George's chair at the head of the table.

'It was hard to talk when George was here, but I think it's important that you all hear exactly how bad things were on tour and why we ought to replace Abigail as soon as possible.'

Flora's happiness faded like a conker out of its husk as she struggled off the plane weighed down with presents for George, Trevor and Marcus. Having been briefed about the afternoon in the hot air balloon by Hilary and Juno, the orchestra had been mobbing her up about George all the way home. Some of the remarks had been very bitchy, until Flora had lost her temper and snapped that George loved her and was taking her round the world.

Guffaws greeted this.

As they all shuffled through Customs, Nellie turned to Carmine, who had been behaving in a very smug proprietorial way after two nights on the trot, and said: 'D'you mind if we don't walk out into the airport together, Carmine, because my husband's meeting me,' which caused even louder guffaws.

Carmine was incensed. As the orchestra mothers charged the barrier to hug their children, and Julian fell into Luisa's arms, Flora's eyes filled with tears.

'I see your grand friend hasn't come to meet you,' said Carmine nastily, as they made their way out to the coaches. 'The only reason he'd want to take you round the world would be to have a bit of free crumpet while he was avoiding tax.'

'I must not cry,' said Flora through gritted teeth. But her eyes had misted over so much that when the airport doors opened automatically for Viking and Dixie, who were walking out in front of her, and she caught a glimpse of Trevor the mongrel outside, she knew she was imagining things.

All the same, she ran forward. Then the doors opened again and stayed open like her mouth, for there holding an ecstatically wriggling Trevor, blushing like an autumn sunset, stood George.

Dropping her luggage, and her presents, Flora rushed towards them, and George took his rank-and-file viola player in his arms and kissed her on and on in front of his entire orchestra.

'Oh George,' gasped Flora.

'I'm not taking you round the world, I've got a better idea,' said George.

That evening a delirious Flora telephoned her mother from George's double bed.

'Mum, Mum, I'm getting married.'

'You're far too young,' wailed Georgie. 'Who is he? Where did you meet him? Has he got a job?'

'He works for the RSO.'

'I'm not having you throwing yourself away on some penniless musician. I know too many of them.'

'Mu-um, it's George Hungerford.'

There was a long pause.

'*The* George Hungerford?'

'None other.' Giggling, Flora handed the receiver to George so he could hear her mother's screech of amazement down the telephone.

'Oh darling, he'll be able to keep us all in our old age. How lovely, such a sweet man, too. When will you bring him to see us? I suppose he ought to ask Daddy for your hand.'

'Not until I've stopped biting my nails. Actually we thought we'd push off for a holiday first. George wanted to take me round the world, but I said we couldn't leave Trevor.'

Trevor, who was lying across George's feet, wiggled his tail.

'Oh Mum, you'll never guess what George has done.'

'What?'

'You know they don't allow dogs on beaches any more because of "fouling". Well, George has bought Trevor a beach all of his own with a sweet little cottage for us thrown in.'

'Oh, how wonderful,' said Georgie. 'Anyone that nice to dogs will make a wonderful husband.'

SIXTY-TWO

The Pellafacini Quintet were very sad to lose their young viola player, but the person totally unhinged by Flora's whirlwind romance was Abby. Not only was she terribly jealous of Flora's and George's almost incandescent happiness, but also how dare Flora land a real man and such a rich, attractive one? How could her singing career not soar with such a back-up? On the other hand, how lucky she was to be able to settle down and play house and have babies. Worst of all, with Rodney dying and George's departure, Abby felt utterly defenceless.

'You can't quit now. There's the Appleton coming up,' she railed at George. 'And I've had an enquiry today about taking the orchestra to the States.'

George found he couldn't give a stuff.

'Miles will cope, he's very capable.'

'He's no good at zapping mergers. Can't you wait till after the Appleton?'

'Flora's my noomber one priority, now,' said George firmly. 'I'm not going to let that slip through my fingers. Work ruined my last marriage. It's only for three months.'

Abby felt the peacekeeping forces had left the orchestra. Even worse with Flora gone, she and Marcus were thrown into each other's company. Abby felt increasingly bad about betraying him with Viking. How long would it be before one of those rogues in the orchestra tipped him off – probably in the middle of the Appleton.

When she finally got home, having made a detour via Lucerne for Rodney's funeral, she couldn't meet Marcus's eyes and became even more aggressive through guilt.

'Where the hell have you been? I've been calling for days. Oh, there you are, baby,' as a mewing Scriabin came running down the stairs, 'I was so worried about you.'

'Mrs Diggory's been looking after them,' stammered Marcus, 'and George came and collected Trevor. Isn't it amazing about him and Flora?'

'Don't change the subject. How could you push off and leave them?' Abby looked lovingly down at Scriabin, who was now purring in her arms, sucking at her jersey like a baby.

'My asthma got so bad,' mumbled Marcus, 'and the cats missed you and kept coming into the studio and Howie isn't getting me any work so I flew over to Prague and tried to set up a cheap record deal.'

He didn't add that Boris's and Abby's promises back in March of conducting and bankrolling him had never materialized.

'Any luck?' asked Abby.

'I'm waiting to hear.'

Even Abby in her state of preoccupation noticed he looked awful, dreadfully thin and pale but with an unnatural hectic flush on his cheeks, and the rash of too many steroids speckling his mouth. By the time he'd carried her cases upstairs, he could hardly breathe and collapsed wheezing onto the bed.

'How was the tour?'

'So so, great houses, great performances, but Rodney

died.' Abby was angrily crashing coat-hangers along rails to make more room.

'I know – I'm desperately sorry.'

'Whatever for? You only met him once.'

'I knew what he meant to you.'

'I don't want to talk about it. I'm exhausted.' Then, knowing she was being vile, added, 'You look wiped out, too.'

'I've been working on stuff for the Appleton.'

'What have you chosen?'

'A Bach prelude, Liszt's *B Minor Sonata*, a little suite of Boris's. Great that he's gone to Number Ten in the Charts.'

'Great that the orchestra's gone to Number Ten,' corrected Abby sharply, crashing pots and bottles down on her dressing-table.

'What are you doing in the second round?'

'Chopin *Études*, the *Grande Polonaise*, a couple of Debussy *Preludes* and the *Waldstein*.'

'Not the *Appassionata*?'

Marcus blushed. 'I made such a cock-up at Cotchester.'

That was what he'd decided to play today, but such was his panic and indecision, nothing sounded any good and he kept changing his mind. There was music all over the floor of his normally tidy studio.

Helen, who hadn't recovered from Rannaldini disappearing with Flora after *The Creation*, hadn't helped by ringing at all hours.

'I thought she'd cheer up when she heard about Flora and George. But she seems curiously pissed off that Flora's landed such an ace bloke. She's already channelled her suspicions in another direction, some Czech pianist, called Natalia, who's entered for the Appleton, and evidently Rannaldini's seeing a lot of Hermione.'

'Helen shouldn't hassle you,' fumed Abby, finding a

genuine excuse for fury. 'How can you concentrate when she's on your back all the time?'

'It's OK. She's got to dump somewhere.'

Abby was frantic for Marcus to make love to her, but when he almost shrank away, she manufactured a row, seized the nearest Barbour and stormed out for a walk.

There were lights on in The Bordello, but finding herself helplessly drawn towards them, she realized it was only the setting sun shining across the lake, turning both water and window-panes to gold. She had never physically ached for someone so much in her life as Viking.

By the time she had reached the end of the lake, the sun had deepened to blazing vermilion, its reflection now cooling its burning body in the lake. Oh God, if only it were as easy to extinguish desire.

Delving in the Barbour pocket for a tissue to wipe her eyes she found, amid the debris of leaves and wild flowers, a torn-up letter in Marcus's handwriting. Piecing it together with trembling hands she read:

> *My darling, darling, darling A,*
> *I am dying for you, I can't go on. I never believed it was possible to miss anyone so much or so impossible to suppress my desperate, desperate longing.*

Then there was a quote from Pushkin, ending: '*What can my heart do but burn, it has no choice.*'

How darling of Marcus to leave the poem in Russian, knowing she understood the language. Abby felt ashamed but happier. *Two loves have I of comfort and despair*, and she must concentrate on the love that comforted her.

Going into H.P. Hall after a sleepless night worrying how many of the musicians would know by now about her and Viking, she was cheered by a wonderfully funny piece of news.

On the notice-board next to details for the Appleton where tails and black dresses would be worn was an announcement that Sonny Parker's *Interruption* had won a *Gramophone* Award for the best CD of contemporary music.

That would mean another hundred thousand pounds from Mother Parker.

Forgetting George was on sabbatical, Abby barged into his office for a giggle to find Miles heavily ensconced. George's squashy leather sofas, his high-tech toys, his models of tower blocks and Regency façades, the fridge full of drink, the Edward Burra and the Keith Vaughan, all had been replaced by a functional oatmeal hessian sofa, a totally empty desk and some very uncomfortable chairs. The decorators had obviously been at work, slapping beige emulsion over the shredded ginger suede walls.

'I thought George had only gone for three months,' said Abby aghast.

'Everything's very much in the air at the moment,' said Miles coolly. 'Please don't let that cat in and I'd prefer it if you knocked.'

'Very minimalist,' Abby looked round the room, then attempting a joke, because she suddenly felt so nervous, 'to match Jessica's minis.'

Miles ignored John Drummond's piteous mewings.

'Jessica's left,' he said curtly.

'Whatever for? She really cheered us up with those typing errors.'

'Important for morale,' Miles smiled thinly, 'for the orchestra to realize we're prepared to make cuts on the admin side as well.'

'But the sponsors just adored her.'

'Actually she left of her own accord. She realized she would be expected, now George isn't around, to do a little more than pour champagne and forget to hand in lottery tickets.

'Far more interestingly,' Miles cracked his knuckles

joyfully, 'Rannaldini has just been appointed musical director of the CCO,' then, at Abby's look of horror, continued, 'He'll still retain his directorships in New York, Berlin and Tokyo, of course.'

'Then he won't have time to look after the CCO,' snapped Abby. 'They'll be short-changed like everyone else.'

'Course they won't. Don't be so needlessly spiteful. The Arts Council are delighted,' said Miles looking equally pleased, 'and having someone of Sir Roberto's calibre near by should put you all on your mettle.'

Miles certainly hadn't purchased any kid gloves in Spain.

'So Rannaldini's now in a prime position to merge us and the CCO,' blurted out Abby. Oh why couldn't she keep her trap shut?

'Rannaldini's a wonderful musician –' for a second Miles's eyes contained a flicker of genuine warmth – 'and a natural disciplinarian.'

'Viking wouldn't stand for that.'

'Viking's left us, too,' said Miles silkily.

'W-w-what?' whispered Abby, bruising her spine as she collapsed onto one of the uncomfortable chairs. 'Where? When? How?'

'He resigned this morning.'

'But why?'

'To be quite honest, I think he's bored. He's been here eight years. Nothing to keep him. Should have gone to London years ago.'

'But he's the best player we've got and he's under contract.'

'We thought he was, too, and that we could hold him at least until after the Appleton, but when we checked, it ran out last month. There was nothing we could do.'

'But all the contracts have been renewed.'

'It seems they haven't. George has been a shade lax.'

'But this is awful. Viking lifted the orchestra with every note.'

As if in agreement, John Drummond's black paw appeared supplicatingly under the door.

'Viking is a dangerous influence,' said Miles briskly. 'Quinton is far less erratic, more responsible and can't wait to sort out the section; Rannaldini agrees.'

'What's he got to do with it?' hissed Abby.

'When he did *The Creation* he thought Viking was very overrated. *Big fish in a small polluted pond*, to quote yourself, and didn't he know it.' Miles rose to his feet. 'I'm disappointed in you, Abby, after your little tantrum in Toledo in front of the chairman and his wife, not to mention Nicholas and Hilly,' his voice thickened lasciviously as he mentioned her name, 'I thought you would be delighted he's left us. Now, if you'll excuse me,' he said chillingly.

As he moved forward to open the door for her, Abby thought for a second he was going to stamp on Drummond's twitching paw. Prufrock had become Robespierre overnight.

Outside she found Miss Priddock in tears.

'Mr Hungerford loved cats, he's left some money so I can go on buying Drummond a lottery ticket every week.'

Utterly stunned, Abby sought out the Celtic Mafia, who looked bleak and said Viking had flown back to Ireland. None of them would elaborate.

'Didn't he leave me any message?' pleaded Abby.

'He left you this,' said Blue.

It was a cheque for two thousand pounds for the Cats' Protection League.

Poor Abby had to go straight into rehearsal. They were playing *The Fairy's Kiss* which had a fiendishly difficult horn solo. Quinton played it well enough, but there was no halo round the interpretation. The rest of the horn section looked suicidal. Even the prospect of his marriage to Jenny couldn't raise Lincoln's spirits. Cyril was wearing a black armband.

'I reckon Viking was greater than Dennis Brain,' he kept saying.

And now that George and Viking have gone, Miles will have you out by the end of the week, thought Abby.

Suddenly Noriko started crying and rushed off the stage. Cherub dropped his drumsticks and rushed off to comfort her. Abby felt the implicit blame of the entire orchestra. It was monstrously unfair. Viking had been in the wrong, he'd made the bet.

In the afternoon they rehearsed Mahler's *First Symphony*, which had three trumpets playing off stage. Believing Carmine and Randy were deliberately bitching her up, coming in at the wrong moment and much too loud, Abby screamed at them to put socks in it. The next time the passage was so quiet, no-one could hear it. Abby was left flailing in space. Knickers discovered the trumpeters playing darts in the band room.

'She insisted we play pianissimo, she can't have heard us,' protested Randy innocently.

So Abby made them do it again. And Randy played it from his car; everyone could hear him revving up and started to laugh.

Storming out to the car-park, Abby noticed Viking's empty parking place had been taken by Quinton's very clean Rover and burst into tears. Desolate, she drove home to find Marcus had lit a fire and left her some melon, chicken Kiev and a note saying he loved her.

Marcus is the one true thing in my life, Abby told herself numbly, I must cling on to him.

She was roused by the doorbell. Standing outside was a raddled but very sexy-looking blonde. Her name was Beatrice, she said, and she was a freelance who fed copy to most of the papers, particularly the music magazines.

'I only talk to the media if it's authorized by the RSO press office.' Abby was about to slam the door.

'I only wanted to give you this,' Beatrice smiled winningly. 'I was in Megagram's press office and asked what was hot, and guess what they produced?'

A gust of wind seemed to blow her and a shower of leaves into the house. Abby gave a crow of delight as Beatrice handed her a galley of 'Madly in Love', the pop tune she and Marcus had recorded without Marcus knowing at the Christmas party. On the sleeve was a picture of Marcus looking wildly romantic at the piano, Abby had her arm round him, her cheek against his, her fiddle in her left hand.

'I didn't think Megagram were going to release it till January,' squeaked Abby in excitment.

'They've brought it forward and they're very high on it. They want to cash in on the success of *Rachel's Requiem.*'

'How does it sound?'

'Great,' said Beatrice, 'all the clapping and cheering in the background adds to the fun. He's a fantastic pianist. You sound wonderful, too. Even better than you did in the old days.' Then, very carefully, she added: 'Is it true he's Rupert Campbell-Black's son?'

'Oh Christ,' Abby glanced at the sleeve. 'Have they put in the "Campbell"? Marcus will go ballistic. He's crazy to get to the top on his own.'

'Sell more records,' said Beatrice cosily, 'better publicity for the orchestra, *and* for him.'

After they had played the single, which had colossal charm, Beatrice produced a bottle of champagne.

'We must toast the new Richard Clayderman.'

'I ought to give *you* a drink,' said Abby.

'I can put it on expenses.'

Oh why not, thought Abby, Marcus always shied away from publicity, but he wouldn't be back for hours, and she would at last have a chance to push his career and the record. Unbeknownst to Howie she had made her share of the royalties over to the orchestra.

Nor did Beatrice know that the RSO had been chosen to accompany the finalists in the Appleton, and was so thrilled for Abby. She really was a delightful woman, despite her rather tarty looks, decided Abby, and it was such a relief to meet someone enthusiastic about success. The Brits were generally so carping.

'D'you mind if I switch on my tape-recorder? I hate not getting the facts right?' asked Beatrice.

After three-quarters of a bottle and no food all day, Abby forgot to emphasize what was *off* the record and what *on*.

'This is the *record* that matters,' said Beatrice, picking up the sleeve of 'Madly in Love'. 'I must say Marcus is almost as devasting as his famous father.'

'More so,' said Abby, clumsily trying to tug open a drawer in a nearby desk which had expanded because of the damp. Then it gave, and she pulled it out altogether, scattering photographs all over the floor.

'My God,' Beatrice dropped to her knees leafing through everything. 'Pretty girl, who's that?'

'Flora Seymour, she shared the cottage with Marcus and me until last week.'

'And my goodness, look at that.' It was a topless Abby stretched out on the grass. Marcus, stripped to the waist, lay beside her, his head on her shoulder, his hand trailing across her ribs.

'What a beautiful picture, pure Calvin Klein,' Beatrice examined it in rapture.

'Flora took it one afternoon. Great, isn't it?'

'Certainly is and he *is* gorgeous. What a profile and that gentle passionate mouth. No wonder he wows them on the platform. No wonder Megagram are thrilled to bits.'

She emptied the rest of the champagne into Abby's glass. 'How does he get on with Rupert?'

'When are you hoping to get married?' Beatrice asked finally. She was now kneeling on the floor with her scarlet dress rucked up, and her thighs wide apart so you could see her black lace panties. Her blond bob fell over her hot brown eyes and she displayed a rift of cleavage where the three top buttons were undone.

Viking would have had her upstairs in five seconds flat, thought Abby in sudden anguish.

'He only has to say, "Hi, sweetheart" in that peat-soft voice and he's got them horizontal in the car-park.' She could hear Hugo's envious disgruntled voice as though it were only yesterday.

'You OK?' said Beatrice.

'Fine,' mumbled Abby. 'Must go to the john. Fine,' she repeated, cannoning off the doorway. Out in the garden she collapsed against an old apple tree, sobbing her heart out. When would she even see Viking again? By the time she'd splashed her face and wiped away the streaked mascara and pulled herself together, Beatrice had her coat on.

'Mustn't take up any more of your time. I'm such a fan, you're so much prettier in the flesh and look so much younger! I hope to get up to the Appleton. Perhaps you and Marcus would have dinner with me. At least, can I have your autograph on my notebook?'

Abby didn't tell Marcus about Beatrice's visit. He had inherited Rupert's pathological loathing of the Press, and she couldn't remember which papers Beatrice had said she worked for, but the piece was bound to be friendly. She'd been so excited for Abby. Anyway Abby wanted to surprise Marcus with a lovely boost to his career.

SIXTY-THREE

Beatrice's story broke in *The Scorpion* two days before the Appleton. CHIP OFF THE OLD BLACK said the headline.

The photograph taken by Flora had been blown up and cropped just above the waist so Abby and Marcus looked naked in each other's arms. 'L'Appassionata's Madly in Love', said the caption.

Abby was quoted as saying that she and Marcus were secretly engaged and planning to make the announcement after the Appleton, so people wouldn't accuse Abby of favouring Marcus if her orchestra had to accompany him in the finals.

> *'I sure hope he's going to win, but naturally we'll treat all the contestants the same.'*

The copy then switched to the record itself which Abby had had secretly made at Christmas as a surprise present for Marcus.

> *' "Everyone thinks Marcus is wealthy, but he hasn't spoken to his snooty dad in two years." Rupert cut him off after a family tiff and he is too proud to take any money from his multi-millionaire stepdad, Sir Roberto*

Rannaldini (family motto: I will dump from a great height).

"I admire Marcus more than any boy I know," enthuses Abby. *"He sold the twenty-thousand-pound painting by horse artist Alf Munnings his dad gave him for his twenty-first to buy me a ruby engagement ring and he is a wonderful, caring and tender lover. But I hope one day that he, Rupert and Sir Roberto will be reconciled, perhaps at our wedding."'*

There was a lot of guff about Abby having slashed her wrist four years ago:

'When she caught her agent and married lover cheating on her with his secretary: but Abby's certainly turned her career around. Just back from a wildly successful tour of Spain, next week it's the Appleton, and she still dreams of taking her orchestra on tour to the US. "But Marcus comes first," sighs L'Appassionata. "His career is more important because we're madly in love."'

Abby had never seen Marcus really angry before.

'How could you, Abby, how fucking could you?' he yelled. 'You know I never wanted to get anywhere on Dad's back, and how could you say I flogged the Munnings? How d'you think Dad's going to feel, and Mum? And you've totally buggered any chance I might have had in the Appleton. Even if I get through the first round they'll say you pulled strings, or Rannaldini has, and finally that fucking record, you know how I feel about pop music.'

He was blue in the face, gasping for breath, clinging onto the kitchen table.

'Don't you remember me warning you. Beattie Johnson was Dad's mistress between marriages, and his nemesis,' he went on furiously. 'She's been trying to bring him down ever since.'

'She stitched me up too, right?' screamed Abby, 'She never let on she was from *The Scorpion*, it was all off the record. I thought she was a legit music critic, or Megagram wouldn't have given her an advance copy. It's their fault for telling her where I live.'

'It's your bloody fault; why d'you always blame everyone else?'

'I wanted people to know how good you are. Someone's got to blow your own trumpet. You won't.'

'By putting out some fucking pop record. Why the hell didn't you ask me? Because you knew I'd say no.'

'Because I knew you needed the money.' Abby was now hurling insults as if they were crockery. 'I'm sick of having to pay for everything. I'm sick of you wasting your energy on stupid pupils. I'd quite like to be taken somewhere nice occasionally, get a few flowers and chocolates, the odd pin. If it becomes a hit you'll make a bomb.'

'Bombs bloody maim and destroy people. Anyway, why the hell did you give them that photograph?'

'She stole it without asking. I only wanted to show her how beautiful you were. There must be *some* reason I'm throwing myself away on a penniless wimp.'

The telephone rang. Abby ran out of the room. Marcus picked it up, so short of breath he could only croak, 'Hallo.'

It was Helen. Marcus steeled himself. But his mother was surprisingly chipper. Abby had given her a very good press, and had been quoted as saying:

> *'Marcus gets his looks from his beautiful mother, she's very supportive of him and is the only member of his family he can relate to.'*

'After all,' protested Helen, 'Abby hasn't said anything that isn't true. You and she *are* madly in love. Rupert has been fiendish to you all his life, and given you no encouragement at all. And everyone will buy the record now.

Abby only meant it as a surprise. Everyone will understand it was just a bit of fun at the office Christmas party. And it's wonderful publicity for both you and the RSO.'

'I don't want to be a fucking pop star.'

'Kiri and Placido cross over – didn't do them any harm. You're overreacting – don't excite yourself before the competition. At least you and Abby really love each other.' Helen's voice broke. 'I'm sure Rannaldini's got someone else. He was checking his Interflora bill, but when I came into the room yesterday, his hand shot down over it like a guillotine.'

'You shouldn't bloody well have married him,' howled Marcus, slamming down the telephone.

What was happening to him?

Immediately it rang again. It was the *Sun* and then the *Mail*, then the *Express* and then the whole of Fleet Street, and soon the cars were crunching over the conker husks, splashing up the path to Woodbine Cottage.

'The only time I escape fucking tension is when I walk out onto the platform,' Marcus yelled at a flabbergasted Abby.

The RSO the next day were almost as hostile. Management, i.e. Miles revved up by Hilly, were horrified by the picture in *The Scorpion*.

'Ghastly vulgar publicity,' he told Abby furiously, 'musical directors should not emulate Page Three girls. Any sense of gravitas is totally destroyed and Miss Priddock's been fielding calls from the tabloids all day.'

'Then buy her some gloves and a baseball cap,' snarled Abby.

The Arts Council were also appalled. Gwynneth was particularly disapproving because Gilbert, having bought his own copy of *The Scorpion*, seemed to spend an unconscionable time reading the headline, the caption and the few lines of text flanking Abby's naked boobs.

Peggy Parker and Canon Airlie had collective coronaries.

The rehearsals that day were even more acrimonious. When Abby came in to conduct Tchaikovsky's *Sixth* every single player except Hilary was hidden behind a copy of *The Scorpion*, and all started singing 'Madly in Love'. Abby started yelling at them and things went from bad to worse.

'If you don't get your act together after the break I'm walking out,' shouted Abby.

'Good,' said Old Henry to everyone's amazement.

'Whaddid you say?'

'He said, "good",' shouted Nellie. 'Can't you get it into your thick head, Abby, that without Viking the *Pathétique* is absolutely pathetic.'

Nor did Abby get any help at home. For a few days the Press hung around like starlings settling noisily on a tree, then just as suddenly they all flew off leaving the tree bare and bereft. Marcus retreated into his studio, practising for ten or eleven hours a day until the pieces held no surprises for him. He found it impossible to relax and kept a score beside him at mealtimes as a wall between him and Abby. Unable to sleep since she'd returned, he had retreated at nights to the studio, but was also getting up at first light to intercept the post in case a letter arrived from Alexei.

The morning after the Press took their departure he had heard Dixie's springer spaniel barking down at The Bordello, and knew the postman would reach Woodbine Cottage in a couple of minutes.

Leaping out of bed, he had hurtled across the lawn, round the corner of the cottage, slap into Abby, wrapped in a towel, hoping for the miracle of a letter from Viking. Both jumped guiltily.

'I was hoping to hear from Philadelphia,' mumbled Abby.

'I was h-h-hoping to h-h-hear from the record company in Prague,' stammered Marcus.

But all the postman produced was an ecstatic postcard from Flora and the telephone bill, which Marcus pocketed instantly. 'I'll pay that, you've picked up far too many bills recently.' Anything to stop Abby seeing the itemized calls to Moscow.

'Come back to bed, Markie,' pleaded Abby.

Marcus shook his head.

'Ought to have a bath first, I just fell into bed like a polecat last night.'

'Oh OK, if you feel like that.' Abby retreated upstairs banging her bedroom door.

As Marcus soaked in the last of Flora's bath oil, he noticed a pale sun looking at him from the marble tiles on the right of the bath. The tiles were picking up the sun's reflection in the mirror opposite. It gave Marcus the creeps that the sun, hovering unseen and in apparent innocence outside, could watch him naked in the bath. Just like the Press, thought Marcus with a shiver. He kept hearing the collective rattle of himself and skeletons coming out of the closet.

He had made heroic attempts to be faithful to Abby, but five weeks ago Alexei had sent him a pair of emerald cuff-links with just one sentence: *'Here are two green eyes of the monster who is jealous of anyone you even talk to.'*

And Marcus had weakened and written back, and Alexei and he had been ringing up and writing to each other ever since. Finally when the RSO was in Spain, Marcus had flown out to Prague for four days, on the pretext of looking for a record deal, but instead spending every second with Alexei, growing more and more hopelessly in love. It was as though he had found a part of himself that had always been missing.

There had been a performance of the ballet *Don Quixote* on the second night. And although Marcus almost expired with desire and pride as he watched Alexei bringing the Prague audience over and over again cheering to their feet in stupified wonder, he realized he loved the man, not just the great star.

In a few years' time, Alexei would have to give up dancing, probably to become a wonderfully autocratic director, but Marcus wanted to be there to take care of him while he made the adjustment.

Alexei, on the one hand, was still playing word games, insisting art was more important than love and that he and Marcus were owned by the world.

'Ballet devour your whole life.'

But it didn't stop him trying to persuade Marcus to leave Abby.

'It will be perfectly better for you to live in Moscow weeth me.'

But Marcus, wiped out once more by ecstasy and guilt, had returned to England, insisting they must never see each other again and Alexei had stormed off in a fury, accusing Marcus of cowardice and hypocrisy.

It was this guilt that had made Marcus react so strongly to *The Scorpion* piece: Abby trumpeting fortissimo to the world of their passion for one another, when he was totally fogged with love for Alexei.

As he lay in the cooling water, Marcus noticed a bottle on the side for detangling hair. If only it could detangle his life.

When he settled down to practise he was so tired that he kept making stupid mistakes.

Much later as the light faded he went for a walk. Sibelius and Scriabin followed him, pouncing on gold leaves which were tumbling out of the wood. The sun, which had spied on him earlier, was now huge, orange and warming the slim bare limbs of the trees, so beautiful freed of their clothing of leaves, they reminded him of Alexei.

He hadn't heard a word from Rupert or Taggie since *The Scorpion*. They were probably too outraged and saddened to get in touch. How *dare* Abby say Helen was the only person he related to, when Taggie had always given him so much love and understanding.

Ahead Marcus could see the lights of the cottage. Abby must have come home early. He found her still in her overcoat, gazing hopelessly at a burnt-out kettle. Sobbing hysterically, she collapsed against him.

'I'm desperately sorry, Markie. My foot's like a colander I've shot myself in it so often. I've just turned your evening-shirt blue putting it in the same wash as my scarf.'

The Fat Controller was guesting at the RSO for the next week, she continued, so she was pushing off to Philadelphia to clinch the American tour.

'I lied to Miles that I was going to see Mom. He'd be so fucking smug if the tour didn't come off, and if it does I guess it's the only way the orchestra'll forgive me. You'd think it was me sacked Viking. Anyway it'll get me out of your hair and theirs. You all need a break.'

'I need you to tell me what to do in the first round,' protested Marcus, but only to comfort her.

Abby gulped. 'You're the sweetest liar. You'll be far better on your own. I'll fly back on Thursday morning and come straight up to Appleton for the finals the next day.'

'Aren't you cutting it a bit fine?' said Marcus in alarm. Abby was going to have to conduct six concertos. 'It's a hell of a marathon.'

'It won't give me time to be scared. Imagine five million viewers.'

She was so tired it took her ages to pack, dragging out her power suits with shoulder pads to impress the conservative and sometimes stuffy American cultural committees. The cats kept getting into her cases; she loathed the idea of them going to a cattery, but at least they'd be together.

When, at last, she wandered across the moonlit lawn to Marcus's studio, the crowded stars were listening enraptured to the last joyful tumultuous bars of the Schumann concerto.

'You and I are going to play that together in the finals,' said Abby, massaging his shoulders.

'Some hope. It's tempting fate to work on it when I

know I won't get that far. Did you know Benny's entered, and a mass of other seriously good people.'

'You'll zap the lot of them. You know Rodney always sang "To the Life Boats, to the Life Boats", during that bit in the last movement, when every pianist wants to jump ship because it's so difficult to cope with the cross-rhythms. Play it again. I'll be the orchestra.'

'Promise to sing it slowly,' Marcus flipped back the pages.

'I promise. "To the Life Boats, to the Life Boats, to the Life Boats,"' sang Abby, faster and faster, with Marcus frantically scurrying to keep up, until they collapsed in hysterical laughter for the first time in days until Abby's laughter turned once more to tears.

'Make love to me, Marcus. It's been so long, I need it so badly.'

Falling on each other, they tried to eradicate the memories of Viking and Alexei. For Marcus, it was as if he were attempting to quench a frantic thirst with great gulps of sea water. At least he hoped he had satisfied Abby. She fell asleep in his arms immediately. The studio was flooded with moonlight. On her right hand, clutching the pillow, Marcus's ruby glowed like a drop of blood. Burning through the floorboards, under the bed, were Alexei's hidden love letters, his Rolex and the emerald cuff-links.

White in the moon the long road lies

That leads me from my love, thought Marcus despairingly.

As Abby slept, he stole out of the studio and across the dewy lawn, his heart pounding. He didn't even have to memorize the code for Moscow. But there was no answer. Alexei must have found other arms.

Appassionata

SIXTH MOVEMENT

SIXTY-FOUR

Appleton, a dark satanic mill town, lay just west of the Pennines with its grimy houses and factories spilling over the steep hillside as though someone had hurled a pot of black ink against a green wall. The surrounding countryside was dotted with imposing Victorian houses built by the old cotton manufacturers, who found patronizing the arts in the nineteenth century a gratifying way up the social ladder. The most imposing of these houses had belonged to the late Lord Appleton, a great charmer and music lover, who each year had invited a group of friends to play together over a long weekend. On the last day, the musician, who, by popular vote, had pleased his companions the most, was awarded five hundred pounds.

The comely Welsh pianist, Blodwyn Jones, who won the prize at the end of the Fifties, became Lord Appleton's much younger wife, and when he died she joined forces with his inconsolable friends to found the Appleton Piano Competition in his memory. The Appleton had become as prestigious as the Leeds Piano Competition which took place every four years in August. Indeed Fanny Waterman, the founder of the great Leeds Competition was a friend of Blodwyn Appleton and had advised her in the early stages.

Lady Appleton was well named. She had a face as round, rosy and sweet as a Worcester Pearmain, and a nature to match. Although well into her sixties, she was able to charm distinguished musicians to give their services for almost nothing. This year, the very international jury contained several piano teachers, old trouts of both sexes, including a Romanian, a Latvian, a vast Ukrainian and a Chinese who spent his time writing a biography of Schumann from right to left on a laptop computer. Among the judges who still played in public was Marcus's ancient admirer Pablo Gonzales, who had arrived without his blond boyfriend. Others included Bruce Kennedy, a cool laconic American, and Sergei Rostrov, a hot-headed voluble Russian, both great and famous pianists who felt they should put something back into music by sitting on the odd jury, but who detested one another.

Ernesto (an Italian who spoke little English) and Lili (a green-eyed German) were less good pianists. Both in their fifties, they preferred to judge rather than be judged and were making a nice living, thank you, sitting on juries all over the world and bonking each other.

Among the non-piano-playing judges were a svelte French feminist who played the harpsichord, and an Irish Contralto called Deirdre O'Neill, who had a winning cosy exterior, which mostly disguised a pathological loathing of the Brits, no doubt exacerbated by a recent divorce from a Weybridge stockbroker.

Completing the pack were Boris, Hermione and Dame Edith, who, because Monica was in Kenya awaiting her first grandchild, had rolled up with Monica's yellow labrador Jennifer; and surprise, surprise, Rannaldini. All the judges were staying at the Prince of Wales Hotel in Appleton High Street.

The candidates on the other hand were housed at St Theresa's, a local girls' boarding-school, situated about three miles out of town on the edge of the moors. As the pupils had gone home for half-term, each contestant was allotted a tiny study/bedroom. Marcus collapsed in hysterical laughter when he found the walls of his room covered in half-naked posters of James Dean and Mel Gibson. Outside in the park, almost obscuring the view from his window, was a magnificent chestnut tree which still held on to its reddy gold leaves.

Across khaki fields, criss-crossed with stone walls and bobbled with sheep, Marcus could see the lights of Appleton. In case by some miracle he reached the final, he had brought his tails and the dress-shirt which Abby had turned pale blue in the washing-machine.

During a rather strained and stilted drinks party, when the contestants stared at each other like cats, Marcus noticed Benny Basanovich, black hair curly as a Jacob's sheep, surrounded by girls, but paying particular attention to a voluptuous Slav beauty, with long sloe-black eyes, soft, drooping scarlet lips and large breasts. That must be Rannaldini's protégée Natalia Philipova. Marcus felt a surge of pity for his mother. How could all the silicone implants in the world compete with that, he thought savagely.

Over an excellent dinner of steak and kidney pudding, and a huge pie made from dark blue bilberries picked off the moor, served with big jugs of cream, the level of chat and laughter started to rise.

Everyone then drew for position in the competition. With forty-eight contestants to play, the first round would take four days. Mid-morning or mid-afternoon were best. People who played first thing had to warm up the jury and the audience. Immediately after lunch was dodgy, because half the jury would be sleeping it off. By the end of the day everyone was irritable and tired. Marcus drew the very last number, then had a nail-biting, four-day wait.

On the first morning of the competition, however, all the contestants were expected to turn up at the small concert hall belonging to Appleton University, where the first two rounds were taking place, to be officially welcomed by Lady Appleton.

The jury were already in position in the gallery, including Jennifer the labrador, who was leaving blond hairs all over the shiny dark suit of the Ukrainian judge.

Marcus nearly fainted when he saw Boris, Rannaldini and oh God, Pablo Gonzales, who was raising binoculars with a shaky hand to spy out the better-looking male contestants.

Only after the last winner had accepted her little silver piano, had it been discovered that before the competition she had deliberately taken private lessons with most of the jury then further sucked up by writing them sycophantic thank-you letters.

This year Lady Appleton was taking no chances, and kept the names of the judges under wraps to prevent them being got at before the competition.

After welcoming everyone, and thanking the sponsors, Mr Bumpus of Bumpy's Scrumpy, she stressed the importance of the jury not having any contact with the contestants.

'I know many of you know each other, but try and restrict yourselves to a little wave until after the final.'

Monocled and massive in Prince of Wales check, Dame Edith promptly raised Jennifer's fat yellow paw and waved it at Marcus.

'Finally,' went on Lady Appleton charmingly, 'don't be frightened or discouraged if you go no further – remember that every member of the jury was once knocked out in the first round of a competition.'

'I was not,' said a deep voice in outrage.

'Sorry, except Dame Hermione,' laughed Lady Appleton. 'Now let us welcome our first candidate, Miss Han Chai from Korea.'

On went the jurors' spectacles, as the prettiest little raven-haired teenager came dancing onto the stage with her pink skirts swirling and played Debussy, Liszt and

Mozart with such proficiency and delight that she plunged every other candidate into despair.

Bruce Kennedy, the great American pianist, who always voted against the Eastern bloc only gave her five out of ten.

'Technically perfect,' he muttered to Dame Edith, 'but I don't figure she's experienced "Life".'

'If you want to see raw emotion,' whispered back Edith, who'd given her six, 'look at her teacher in the front row. Don't you agree, Boris?'

Boris, who was sitting behind them, gave a sulky grunt, and added another semi-quaver to the clarinet's part in Act Two of *King Lear*. There was manuscript paper all over the floor and the seats on either side of him. He supposed it would be construed as collusion if he enlisted Marcus's help to put in the bar lines.

Boris had only fallen under Lady Appleton's spell and agreed to judge when he was plastered at some reception last year, and was livid to be dragged away from work.

He wasn't remotely gratified that *Rachel's Requiem* had now gone to Number Five, and he was incensed that Rannaldini had been given a suite at the Prince of Wales, with a room next door for Clive, his sinister leather-clad henchman, while he, Boris, had only a dimly lit shoe-box facing a grubby brick wall with no mini-bar.

Hermione was even crosser than Boris. Having promised her his full attention, Rannaldini had rolled up with a beady-eyed Helen, and then spent his time caballing.

For despite Lady Appleton's strictures, corruption was gloriously rife. Everyone, particularly the Eastern bloc, indulged in tactical voting. All the judges had been tempted by massive bribes. Dame Edith was shocked to be offered three Steinways, a diamond necklace and a week's holiday for two by the Black Sea, Dame Hermione less so. The only safe unbugged place for intrigue was the heated pool. Rannaldini, who had the advantage of a magnificent Sardinian suntan and fluency in most languages, soon had wrinkled paws from dog-paddling with large lady judges, their long grey hair swept up on top.

A few of the judges argued the whole time, the rest were too terrified of Rannaldini and making fools of themselves to put forward any forceful opinions. This happened particularly after the Italian contestant, whom Dame Edith had described as 'a fairly good-looking pig who unfortunately sounded as though she was playing with trotters', turned out to be the daughter of Ernesto, the Italian judge. The strain of listening to music from nine in the morning until eight at night was telling on all of them. The old trouts found it impossible to stay awake, particularly after Bumpy's Scrumpy and a large lunch.

As contestant followed contestant, however, stars were beginning to emerge. Most of the judges liked Han Chai, none of them liked Benny, who had only entered because both Howie and Rannaldini had persuaded him certain victory would lift a sagging career. Benny, on the other hand, was very famous, and rather good with judges, claiming not only genuine French-Russian parentage, but also aunts from Latvia, Romania, China and Ireland who, when necessary, became 'my favourite relation'.

Also much fancied was Carl Matheson, a cheery, bouncing Texan with a terrific stage personality, who'd been told by his agent to leave his tails behind. This was an old trick. The contestant would then appear not to have expected to reach the final. If he did and walked onto the platform in his plaid jacket or a too large borrowed DJ, the audience and jury would be touched by his modesty and humility, and the fairy tale element of a rags-to-riches win, and mark him up accordingly.

Dominating the candidates, however, was Natalia Philipova, who'd 'come a long way, baby', since two years ago in Prague when Rannaldini had advised her to give up the piano, then relented and financed her private lessons. Now he was determined to make her a big star. Hence his tickling of all the old trouts in the swimming-pool and his waking them with a cattle-prod when it was Natalia's turn to play.

He had chosen Natalia's first round pieces well. Liszt's piano adaptation of *Tristran,* and a Chopin sonata with a funeral march middle movement reduced everyone to tears. Howie had already signed up Natalia, but he was soft-pedalling the connection, as he and Rannaldini didn't want Benny to go into drunken orbit. A win from Natalia would be that much more impressive and dramatic if she beat an established talent like Benny's.

Finally, there was Anatole, a moody handsome Russian, and a marvellous pianist. He was left handed, which made him very strong in the bass and gave his playing a wonderful thunder. His hair was the browny blond of newly laid parquet, and like most eastern bloc players, he wore cheap clothes: shiny brown trousers, plastic shoes and his freckled back could be seen through his thin nylon shirt. But nothing detracted from his eruptive presence. His deadpan face, deep husky voice and occasional bursts of temper reminded Marcus agonizingly of Alexei. Howie, who was gasping to sign him up, had nicknamed him the 'Prince of Polyester'.

Anatole, like all the other Russians who'd entered, had been playing his first- and second-round repertoire and his chosen concerto in concert halls all round Siberia for the last six months. Although aware he would probably go back to Siberia for good if he didn't win, Anatole was far more interested in winning the local pub talent competition.

All the contestants reacted to pressure in different ways. Some paced before they played, some took deep breaths or did yoga, others stared into space, some shook and sweated. Anatole kept throwing up, then lighting a cigarette immediately afterwards.

Marcus's four-day wait would have been a torment if

every day a fleet of cars hadn't arrived to ferry the contestants either to the concert hall or to big houses in the area, where they were offered a grand piano on which to practise. Marcus was sent to a darling old lady called Mrs Bateson who'd been a friend of Thomas Beecham. Deciding Marcus needed fattening up, she baked wonderful cakes for him. All her family rolled up and listened whenever he played, but when they appeared at the hall to cheer him when his turn finally came, they had great difficulty getting seats. The place was packed with Press, chasing more copy on Rupert's estranged son and Abby's live-in lover.

Driven crackers by Helen's moans about Natalia and Rannaldini, Marcus was almost relieved to get onto the platform, then started the Liszt *B minor Sonata* with an appalling crash of wrong notes.

Helen, Boris, Pablo Gonzales, Edith, Jennifer the labrador, Mrs Bateson and all her family gave a collective groan of dismay. Marcus, on the other hand, thought: sod it. He'd obviously blown it, so he might as well enjoy himself on this wonderful piano, whose tone was as soft and mellow as any burgundy covered in cobwebs in his father's cellar.

Forgetting the audience, he continued to play the Liszt so beautifully that the entire hall was in floods. He then raced with all the insouciance of an Olympic skier, through Balakirev's *Oriental Fantasy*, which because of its racing octaves and chords is supposed to be the hardest piece ever written. He then collapsed in a giggling heap the moment he left the platform.

'I have *never* been so scared in my life.'

By this time, he had brought the hall to their feet. To his amazed delight, he went through to the last twenty-four.

The second round was even more of an ordeal for the judges, consisting of long fifty-minute recitals. If any of the candidates overran Lady Appleton was meant to ring a large bell, but was often too kind to do so. Many of the contestants, however, had complained of the soft muddy tone of the piano in the first round, so it was now replaced by one with a harder, brighter sound.

The first day of the second round was also Pablo Gonzales eightieth birthday. Thinking it was a learned work of discography, the big Ukrainian judge brought him a copy of the *Guinness Book of Records*. Pablo was henceforth so transfixed with interest that he did hardly any judging at all.

All the other jurors fought to sit next to him so they could wile away the tedious hours of Bach and Debussy, reading about the fattest dog, the largest elephant or the heaviest twins in history.

Meanwhile the Irish judge, nicknamed 'Deirdre of the Drowned Sorrows' by Dame Edith, was quietly getting through a good litre of red wine a day. Boris was getting through about the same, but was a little happier, having orchestrated a whole act of *King Lear*. The Chinese judge had reached Schumann's first signs of madness on his laptop. Jennifer had put on half a stone eating digestive biscuits.

The ancient Latvian judge, who had promised to vote for Natalia after caballing in the pool with Rannaldini, had not fared so well, and was now in bed with a head cold, unlikely to make the final. Rannaldini was so enraged to have wasted so much time on her, and even crosser when a grinning Dame Edith suggested Jennifer should take the Latvian's place, that he was reduced to bonking Hermione in the lunch-hour.

Once again Marcus was the last to play. This time his agonizing wait was extended because Natalia had insisted on finishing Liszt's *Dante Sonata*, despite Lady Appleton's bell, and then complained bitterly about the brittle tinny sound of the new piano. A piano tuner was subsequently summoned and, after laboriously checking the piano, announced it was in perfect order.

Marcus bore this out by dispatching the Bach *Busoni*

Chaconne with exquisite clarity and warmth, making the allegedly brittle and tinny piano reverberate like an organ. The jury were entranced, particularly by the accompanying drumroll from a lunchless Hermione's tummy.

'Even such an intellectual piece becomes audience-friendly under his fingers,' murmured Bruce Kennedy.

'No-one looks better in a dark suit than Marcus,' sighed Pablo.

The Bach was followed by Beethoven's *Waldstein Sonata* which was going splendidly until the middle of the slow movement, when Marcus pressed down the soft pedal for the first time to add a little colour. He then discovered to his horror that the pedal had jammed, and as a result only two out of the three strings were being struck in the treble.

He was so thrown he momentarily lost his place and ground to a halt. Throughout the rest of the slow movement, and the ravishing flowing rondo, which was why Marcus had chosen the *Waldstein* in the first place, he had to bash away like Benny in an attempt to be heard at all by the jury in the dress circle.

Convinced the piano had been got at, Marcus came off the platform in a white-hot rage and immediately complained to the waiting officials. This was regarded as dreadfully unsporting. Natalia kicking up about a tinny sound was quite different to accusations of sabotage. Back came the piano tuner huffing and puffing.

'When instruments are out of tune in an orchestra,' he grumbled, 'everyone blames the musician, when a piano's out of tune, everyone blames the tuner,' and having taken the piano apart once more, proved there was nothing wrong with it.

Still utterly unconvinced, Marcus escaped from the uproar and the lurking Press and stormed round the town square until shortness of breath forced him to collapse onto a hard bench. Opposite, against a pinky-yellow evening sky, was the town hall, where he certainly wouldn't be playing on Sunday.

'I'm sorry, Alexei,' he muttered almost in tears, 'I've let you down.'

How could he possibly be a great artist who only belonged to the world, when he couldn't even make the final of a piddling piano competition?

To his right was a statue of the first Lord Appleton, examining a roll of cloth and with bird lime all over his frock coat and top hat. What was the point of becoming famous anyway? The Press dumped on you when you were alive, and pigeons when you were dead.

'Oh fuck, fuck, fuck,' sighed Marcus.

Meanwhile the judges had retreated into the jurors' room to select the last six, unimpeded by parents, teachers, agents and representatives from the various countries. The contestants had retreated to the bar. The consensus of opinion was that Marcus had blown it.

'Although they always have a Brit in the last six to pull in the crowds,' said Benny snidely.

Piano competitions, however, do not end with the presentation of the award and a cheque for twenty thousand pounds. Afterwards the winner is assured a couple of years' engagements in the greatest concert halls of the world. In the past, winners had often had difficulty coping with this pressure. The reputation of the Appleton worldwide depended on choosing a winner who could.

Reliability was therefore considered even more important than talent; someone who would carry out these engagements without letting them down, someone who wouldn't make mistakes in recordings.

Rannaldini was soon at work influencing the jury.

'Regretfully,' he said winningly, 'I must abstain from voting for my dear stepson, Marcus, but speaking totally impartially, although it pains me to do so, I feel the boy did not project enough, particularly in the *Waldstein*, where he gave a very flat two-dimensional performance.'

'Bollocks,' thundered Dame Edith. 'He played exquisitely in the *Chaconne*, and in the first half of the *Waldstein* he had something quite beyond the notes.'

'He had a memory lapse,' snapped Rannaldini, who now that he had Dame Edith's job, didn't need to suck up to her any more.

'Probably just nerves,' snapped back Dame Edith.

She felt Marcus should go through. Pablo and Bruce Kennedy agreed. Pablo said he would resign if Marcus didn't. The Russian, Sergei, deliberately voting against Bruce Kennedy, said he would resign if Marcus did. The *Waldstein* had no passion. He agreed with Rannaldini the boy was a 'veemp'. Two of the old bids from Poland and Yugoslavia, who'd been chatted up by Rannaldini, and accepted promises of help from him for several of their pupils, voted against Marcus as well. So did Hermione, because Rannaldini told her to, and Deirdre O'Neill, because she hated the English. So did the vast Ukrainian because he was voting tactically. The ancient Swedish judge, who had only been kept awake after lunch by Benny's banging, and nodded off afterwards, felt guilty he'd slept through the *Chaconne* and gave Marcus an amazing ten out of ten. The French judge loathed both Rannaldini and Sergei and had a crush on Dame Edith, so she gave him nine.

Lili voted against him because Rannaldini pinched her bottom in the lift and promised her a concert in New York. Ernesto promptly voted for Marcus because he was jealous of Rannaldini, so did Boris, which tied the score and a casting vote was needed.

'Blodwyn,' purred Rannaldini.

Lady Appleton looked up from a long list: *Warm-up piano to be delivered, seven outside broadcast vans to be parked, seven microphones* . . . and thought her name had never been pronounced so seductively.

'Sorry, Maestro?'

'Do you theenk Marcus Campbell-Black should go through?' Surely not said those compelling inquisitorial night-black eyes.

'Yes,' said Lady Appleton.

Her friend, Mrs Bateson, had said the boy was a genius.

Taking Jennifer for a widdle in the town square, Dame Edith passed Marcus gazing into space with such a look of desolation on his face.

'You're through, you chump,' she yelled. 'And I agree – that piano was got at.'

All the favoured candidates – Han Chai, Carl the jokey homespun Texan, Anatole the moody Russian, Natalia and Benny – had made it. Marcus was the only outsider. A few tears were shed by the disappointed contestants. Lord Gargrave, on whose piano a brilliant German candidate had practised, was so upset the poor fellow hadn't gone through that he invited him to stay on for a weekend's shooting.

Euphoric that they had two days off before the finals, Edith, Irish Deirdre, Boris and Pablo Gonzales, who'd never had Lancashire Hot Pot before, dined together at the Dog and Duck on the edge of the moor.

'If I see another pair of crossed hands I go cuckoo,' said Pablo, collapsing into a chair and handing his sticks to the waiter.

'Bloody awful dump that Prince of Wales,' said Edith, splashing red wine into everyone's glasses. 'Lousy grub, piddling rooms and a fax takes two minutes from Kenya and half a day to get upstairs. How's *Lear*?' she asked Boris.

'Nearly finished. Now I wonder what to do next.'

'Wheech is the largest newt in the world?' asked Pablo who refused to be parted from his *Guinness Book of Records*.

'Probably me,' said Deirdre, who was already well away.

'Wheech is the fattest cat?'

'Rannaldini,' said Dame Edith, smothering a roll with butter. 'I'm sure he's rigging the votes. Blodwyn's such an innocent. I voted for that German boy.'

'So deed I,' said Pablo, 'I even stop reading thees wondairful book when he play the Prokofiev.'

'So did Deirdre and I,' said Boris. 'He still didn't make it.'

'At least we all got Marcus through,' said Dame Edith with satisfaction.

'I didn't,' said Deirdre stonily. 'God protect me if I ever vote for a Brit.'

'Don't be unsporting,' boomed Edith, waving to the waiter for some more red.

'You weren't married to one,' snapped Deirdre.

I nearly am, thought Edith.

Even though she and Monica were running up massive bills ringing each other every day, she didn't believe it were possible to miss anyone as much. The fax that had taken so long to get upstairs was Monica's confirmation of their purchase of a cottage with a stretch of river in the west of Scotland. The prospect of Monica in breast waders made Edith's mind mist over, and she herself would be able to compose full time. She hadn't written anything she was really proud of since *The Persuaders* in 1980.

But she felt dreadfully guilty that like George Hungerford she had sold her orchestra down the river for love. Once she had announced her absolute determination to retire, the CCO had been forced to look for a new musical director and had searched no further than Rannaldini. Both orchestra and management had voted him in unanimously.

'He's the only person who could ever take your place, Edith,' said Hugo.

The bastard had seduced the lot of them with his

alarming charm. But if Edith hadn't wanted Monica and out so desperately, she would have tried harder to dissuade them.

She was brought back to earth by Deirdre's grumbling.

'Lancashire Hot Pot is exactly like Irish Stew. Talk about another British rip-off.'

'Very delicious though,' said Pablo with his mouth full. 'Do you know which is most venomous snake in world?'

'Rannaldini,' they all said in unison.

SIXTY-FIVE

Marcus was flabbergasted that he'd got so far. He was also ashamed how much he was enjoying himself. The bracing northern winds seemed to have blown away all his worries and obsessions, and more importantly his asthma. He got on very well with all the other finalists, and they had great fun on their two days off before the final, sightseeing, eating fish and chips, playing ping-pong and cheering Anatole on in the pub talent competition.

Marcus was relieved Helen had temporarily shoved off to London. He was also tremendously touched when the huge Ukrainian judge took him aside. As the contestant from the Ukraine had gone out in the last round, he no longer had a vested interest. The majority of the jury, he felt, despite Rannaldini, were, in reality rooting for Marcus.

'We vant you to vin, but we theenk you must change to heavyweight concerto, Brahms *One* or *Two* or Rachmaninov *Three*, something more explosive, more dramatic. The Schumann may be the graveyard of musicians, but it sound very easy. It ees not theatrical enough to impress jury or bring audience to their foots.'

Marcus's eyes filled with tears. He felt the kind words

had somehow come straight from Alexei. But beyond thanking the big Ukrainian profusely, he explained he'd worked on the Schumann so he'd stay with it.

'If there ees any chance to win, zee English start to feel sorry for other contestants,' sighed the Ukrainian.

The finals would take place on Saturday and Sunday, with Carl, Anatole and Han Chai playing their concertos on the first night, and Benny, Natalia and Marcus playing on the second.

Abby had rung Marcus with a change of plan, saying she'd be leaving the States the next night and flying straight to Manchester, arriving in Appleton first thing on Saturday morning to rehearse with the first three finalists in the afternoon.

America, Abby told him, had been terrific, and it was even more terrific he'd made the final.

'The only problem, I guess, is that Woodbine Cottage has been burglarized. Thank God the cats were in kennels, and they didn't take anything except the TV and the video, although the cops fingerprinted Flora's vibrator.'

'What about my studio?' said Marcus, who'd gone cold thinking of Alexei's letters under the floorboards.

'No, nothing appears to be gone from there.'

Marcus was ashamed how relieved he felt to have another forty-eight hours without Abby. Mrs Bateson, jubilant he had gone through, cooked him roast beef, Yorkshire pudding and apple tart for lunch, and gave him a little jet cat for luck.

'You must really project on Sunday,' she begged him, 'you've no idea how absorbent the good people of Appleton are when they crowd into the town hall.'

On Friday morning there was a press conference, where naturally the attention focused on Marcus.

'I'm so knocked out to make the finals,' he told the journalists, 'that as long as I play well on Sunday, I don't mind too much about winning.'

In the afternoon, the finalists were taken for a drive over the bleak, but ravishing countryside, which now flamed with bracken. They ended up having supper in the Dog and Duck which was a quarter of a mile down the road from St Theresa's.

Marcus, who'd been asked by Lady Appleton to keep an eye on Anatole, was having great difficulty keeping the Russian sober. He must go to bed early if he were to cope with Brahms' mighty *First Concerto* tomorrow. But Anatole had got even deeper into the pub talent competition and wouldn't stop singing "Knees up Muzzer Brown", with the landlord. Han Chai had fallen in love with the homespun Carl, who still couldn't decide whether to play in his plaid jacket or a borrowed DJ. They sat holding hands drinking Coca-Cola in the corner. Benny, who had forty-eight hours to sober up before he played his concerto, was knocking back Bacardi and drunkenly propositioning Natalia, who, looking at her watch, was wondering if Rannaldini was back from London, and would somehow tonight infiltrate himself into her bedroom at St Theresa's like a cat burglar. She quivered with desire. No-one had ever been so marvellous to her.

Before the competition he had also given her some beta-blockers to calm her nerves.

'And do see eef you can persuade Marcus to have one before he plays, but don't say they come from me; sadly my stepson 'ates me, and wouldn't touch them. But I so long for heem to do well.'

How could anyone hate Rannaldini? wondered Natalia.

Marcus sat ekeing out a glass of red, still stunned at reaching the finals, idly playing 'To the Life Boats, to the Life Boats', on the pub table wondering what had happened to the soft pedal on Wednesday, wishing he could feel more enthusiastic about Abby arriving tomorrow. Across the pub he could see Anatole thumping out 'You are My Sunshine', his eyes creased with laughter above the high cheek-bones. Marcus felt hollow with longing for Alexei.

It was several seconds before he realized the barman was shouting, 'Marcus Campbell-Black. Phone for Marcus Campbell-Black'.

Marcus winced. He had insisted on dropping the 'Campbell' for the competition. But hearing his famous name, people nudged and stared as he edged through the tables. He had told Alexei he never wanted to hear from him again but always when the telephone rang he prayed it might be him. Equally irrationally he had prayed all week for a good-luck card. The telephone was in an alcove by the stairs. The walls were covered with numbers.

'Hallo,' he picked up the receiver, 'you'll have to speak up, there's a hell of a din going on here.'

'Hi, Marcus. I gather congratulations are in order on your engagement to Abby Rosen. Lucky sod, when are you getting married?'

Hearing the whining, thin, ingratiating, very common, male voice, Marcus started to tremble.

'Who the hell are you?'

'It's *The Scorpion*.'

'I've nothing to say.' Marcus was drenched in sweat.

'We wanted to run a little story about you getting to the finals of the Appleton. Abby must be knocked out. It'll be hard for her not to favour you.'

Marcus was about to hang up, when the voice thickened and became even oilier, almost lascivious with menace. 'Another thing. We've got in our possession some letters to you written by Alexei Nemerovsky.'

Marcus couldn't breathe, his crashing heart seemed to have filled his lungs and windpipe.

'Hallo, are you there? They make very interesting reading. Things were obviously pretty passionate between you, particularly in Prague when you broke the bed.'

'I don't know what you're taking about,' croaked Marcus. 'I never wrote any letters to Alexei, he never wrote any to me.'

'Oh come, come. Some of them are very poetic: "*My little white dove lying warm and no longer frightened in my hands*".'

'They're fakes,' wheezed Marcus. 'P-please burn them. My father and mother . . . no-one could be interested.'

'I think they could. It's very much in the public interest. Two household names like your dad and Nemerovsky, not to mention L'Appassionata, lovely girl, Abby, tried to top herself last time a man cheated on her. Think you've been quite fair to her?'

'No, yes, it must have been you who broke into the cottage.' Oh Christ, he shouldn't have said that. 'You don't have any right to publish those letters.'

'That's a matter for the lawyers. We're going with the story anyway. We just wanted to give you the chance to put your point of view to us.' The voice became suddenly cosy, the mental nurse about to hand over the valium. 'We're talking six figures, I'm sure you could use the money.'

'No, no,' Marcus was frantic. 'Please burn them. I'm not anyone important.'

'You're Rupert's son, mate,' said Torquemada chillingly. 'Does he know you're gay?'

Marcus gave a sob and dropped the telephone, leaving it clattering against the wall. He was desperately fighting for breath. Perhaps it would be better if he did die.

Choking, sobbing, he stumbled through the night back to St Theresa's. He kept slipping on wet leaves, and fell over twice. Fortunately the foyer was temporarily deserted. Marcus tried to ring Alexei, but there was no answer. Abby would be on the way to the airport by now. Rupert was at the Czech Grand National. Marcus had read it in *The Times* that morning. Penscombe Pride was running in the big race on Sunday, just to prove he wasn't past it.

Where was Helen? Marcus tried to gather his thoughts. Oh Christ, he couldn't tell Helen.

Crawling into bed, pulling the bedclothes over his head, gasping for breath, fighting an advancing tidal wave of panic, he waited for the dawn and the army of reporters who, like a slavering pack of hounds, would tear him to pieces. How was he going to face Abby, Helen and, worst of all, Rupert?

As soon as it was light, he got up, and staggered into Appleton to get the papers. The temperature had dropped, bringing winter. The glowing horse-chestnut tree outside his room had been stripped in a day. Like a burst pipe in a distant room, he could hear the leaves rustling down in the park. As he passed the lake, there was a dull thud, and a figure leapt up in front of him. Marcus cringed, imagining a lurking reporter, but it was only a heron. Rising with flapping wings like a biplane, it carried a wriggling carp in its mouth.

I'm that fish, but without its innocence, thought Marcus in horror. It would be so much easier for everyone if he topped himself. He had to stop every ten yards to get his breath. He was wheezing like the kind of broken-winded old chaser his father would have dispatched to the knackers.

As he reached a newsagents on the edge of town the gutters were full of beech leaves like rivers of blood. In a garden opposite a large magpie strutted across the lawn. Self-satisfied, rapacious in its white tie and tails, it was just like Rannaldini. Bird of ill omen: one for sorrow.

'Oh please, Mr Magpie, where's your friend?' begged Marcus, 'Oh God, let *The Scorpion* not have printed it.'

'You don't want to read that rag,' chided the newsagent, as Marcus picked up a copy. 'It's roobish. Good luck for tomorrow evening.'

'We recognize you from the *Manchester Evening News*,'

said his wife. 'Used to love your Dad when he were show jumping.'

Gasping his thanks, stumbling out of the shop, collapsing against a wall, Marcus fumbled frantically through the pages. There was nothing, thank Christ, maybe it had been some practical joke. Maybe they'd pulled the story . . . no, that reporter had known too much. He was only in remission.

He tried to act normally, but he was shaking and wheezing so badly when he finally reached St Theresa's that Natalia persuaded him to take one of Rannaldini's beta-blockers.

'They're terreefic for zee nerves, I had one before both rounds.'

Carl Matheson was worried by tendonitis.

'I guess I better see a doctor before I rehearse this afternoon.'

Abby had stayed on an extra twenty-four hours in Philadelphia to confirm the American tour, so she could brandish the details as one glorious *fait accompli* in front of Miles, the board and Shepherd Denston. Nor could they winge about money. The wonderfully generous US cultural committee, coupled with American Bravo Records, had agreed to pick up most of the bill.

'We figured we'd lost you to the UK for good, Abby,' the chairman had told her. 'We all feel it's high time you brought your orchestra home.'

Abby's eyes filled with tears every time she repeated his words. Always one track, she had concentrated all her energies on the deal in a desperate attempt to forget Viking. But now it was clinched, surely she could ask him back. The Americans would just adore him.

Appleton looked particularly bleak on such a cold wintery morning, but at least the huge begrimed town hall had been decorated by the flags of the nations in the finals. Abby was delighted an American had made it. She hoped Carl would at least come second.

She reached the Prince of Wales at ten o'clock which would give her a few hours' zizz before rehearsing Beethoven's *Third* with Han Chai at two-thirty.

There was a tray of red poppies for Remembrance Day in reception. Abby couldn't see her pigeon hole for messages. The first asked her to call Marcus at St Theresa's urgently. The second wanted her to call *The Scorpion*. Like hell she would. The third was to call Miles.

The RSO's greatest *coup* for years was to be the orchestra chosen to play in the Appleton. Most of the board had flown up to bask in reflected glory. Looking round the splendid suite, for which the orchestra had forked out to enable her to give interviews, Abby decided she better ring Miles first.

'Where the hell have you been?' It was his Miles-below-zero voice. 'We've got to talk.'

'Can't it wait,' protested Abby. 'I've just checked in.'

'No, I'm coming over.'

Abby kicked off her shoes and unpacked the long slinky purple velvet dress, slit up one side, which she had brought to wear that evening, on the off-chance that among the five million viewers, Viking might be watching. She must get the housekeeper to press it. She'd have to snatch time to wash her hair after the rehearsal. She hoped Miles hadn't organized some elaborate press conference. God, she was tired, but she mustn't show it, although with three different concertos to rehearse and perform, it was going to be one helluva marathon. She rang down for some black coffee – 'at once, please.'

Miles, looking almost svelte in a new beautifully cut pin-stripe suit, was accompanied by a bootfaced Lord Leatherhead. When they both grimly refused breakfast, Abby asked when the orchestra was expected.

'I can't wait to see them,' she crowed. 'I've got such terrific news. I've fixed up the most incredible American tour with record backing, OK? It's gonna put us in the black and on the map,' then, amazed by their still bleak expressions, she continued, 'they're planning to stage a Cotswold fortnight down the East Coast. They're paying accommodation, travel, subsistence, printing and publicity. And all because they want *me*, right?' Abby's voice broke. 'I'm gonna take my orchestra home.'

'You're not taking them anywhere,' said Miles brutally. 'You're fired.'

They all jumped as the telephone rang. Abby snatched it up.

'I can't take any calls.'

But it was Marcus frantically stammering, gasping for breath, on the verge of tears.

'Abby darling, I wanted to tell you to your face but I had to get to you before the Press do.'

Abby could hear the desperate wheezing.

'Whatever's the matter?'

'I'm g-g-gay, Abby, I'm dreadfully sorry. Alexei and I've been having an *affaire. The Scorpion* have got hold of our letters. They're going to print them. They'll probably run it tomorrow. I'm so sorry.'

The colour drained out of Abby's face. Her legs started to shake so violently she had to collapse onto the bed.

'I don't believe it. How long's this been going on?'

'About four months, but we've only seen each other twice, and it's over now, I promise.'

'You son-of-a-bitch,' screamed Abby, banging her fist down on her bedside table scattering ashtrays and message pads. 'Two-timing me exactly like Christopher did, only wanting me for the dough. You fucker! Why didn't you break it off, instead of making a goddamn idiot of me? God, I hate you, hate you, hate you.' Her voice rose to a hysterical scream.

But Marcus couldn't breathe and couldn't answer, so Abby slammed down the telephone, and sat shuddering on the bed, clenching and unclenching her hands, her eyes darting madly round the room.

Lord Leatherhead got a miniature brandy out of the fridge and poured it into a glass. He wasn't enjoying this at all. When the telephone rang again Miles snatched it up. It was *The Scorpion*. 'I'm afraid Miss Rosen has no comment to make,' said Miles, then ordered the switchboard not to put through any more calls.

'*The Scorpion* has already been on to us with the whole story,' he told Abby bleakly. 'It reflects disastrously on the orchestra. First their musical director posing naked with a lover to promote a pop record—'

'Beattie Johnson stitched me up,' whispered Abby. 'She stole that photograph.'

'But you gave her the interview. All that nauseating claptrap about being ma-a-a-dly in love,' Miles lingered lubriciously over the word.

He's loving this, thought Abby numbly.

'Then we learn,' he added silkily, 'that you've both got other people and are only masquerading as lovers to push the record.'

'That's bullshit,' shouted Abby. 'I loved Marcus. I'm supposed to be marrying the guy. I didn't know anything about him being gay.'

'You've hardly been a vestal virgin yourself and *your* orchestra are so nauseatingly avaricious it can't be long before one of them sells the story of you and Viking to *The Scorpion*.'

'I'm *not* having an *affaire* with Viking,' hissed Abby.

Miles gave her a pained look of utter disbelief. 'What about the night Rodney died? There are dozens of witnesses.'

'That was a one-night stand, everyone was plastered. Hilary was there. She probably shopped us to *The Scorpion*. It only happened once, for Chrissake.'

'I find that very hard to believe. Anyway, it's going to be all over *The Evening Scorpion* this afternoon, and all the other papers will carry the story tomorrow, bringing utter disrepute on the orchestra. The one thing the Press hate is being cynically manipulated.'

'I didn't manipulate them, right,' Abby was hysterical. 'I genuinely believed Marcus and I were getting married. Look, he gave me this ring,' she held out her right hand.

'A virtuous woman should have a price above rubies,' said Miles sarcastically, as he selected a Granny Smith from Abby's fruit bowl. Hilly's new diet had done wonders for his spots.

'I was only pushing "Madly in Love",' gibbered Abby, 'because the orchestra got half the royalties.'

'I'm afraid we don't want your – er – ill-gotten gains.'

'We had an emergency board meeting this morning,' said Lord Leatherhead gently. 'There was a unanimous vote demanding your resignation.'

'I can see Hilly voting me out, but not Bill Thackery – Bill's a good friend.'

'Not so you would know it,' Miles bit viciously into the apple. 'He's never forgiven you for not making him leader after Lionel left, nor for giving his solo back to Julian.'

'Oh for Chrissake.'

'You can't expect to conduct the orchestra with such a scandal hanging over you,' added Lord Leatherhead. 'We'll honour your contract and pay you up to the end of February.'

'George is still chief executive. He won't let you fire me.'

'Having seduced a member of the orchestra almost half his age,' said Miles fastidiously, 'I hardly think George, or his opinion, would carry much weight. I doubt either if he'd be very interested. He hasn't even had the manners to leave a telephone number.'

'But I can't let the orchestra down.' Leaping forward, Abby clung to Miles's new lapels. 'Please, *please!*'

'You've let them down enough already.'

'Who's going to conduct them at such short notice?'

But Abby already knew the answer.

'Rannaldini has very kindly agreed to step into the breach,' said Miles triumphantly.

SIXTY-SIX

At St Theresa's, Marcus came off the telephone in total shock, wheezing in short bursts like a frantically panting dog. Oh poor darling Abby, he must get to her and stop her killing herself. He couldn't find his puffer, he'd never make it upstairs to inject himself with steroids. No-one was about to help him. Lurching into the common room he found the score of the Schumann concerto open on the upright piano, with all his instructions pencilled in. But where he'd scribbled 'Ped' for Pedal, someone in emerald-green ink had turned the word to 'Pederast'. Giving a choked sob, frantically battling for the tiniest breath, he stumbled into the hall, out through the front door, slap into a cameraman and a girl reporter.

'It's him,' the reporter proffered her tape-recorder as casually as if it had been a packet of fags. 'How long have you been having an *affaire* with Nemerovsky?'

But Marcus, blue in the face, could only give desperate little whimpers, stretching out pleading hands for help.

'You sure it's him,' said the photographer snapping away like a jackal, 'more like some kind of deaf mute.'

'Probably a ruse to fox us,' said the girl. 'Have you told Abby yet, Marcus?'

'Looks as though he's having an epi. You OK, mate?' the photographer lowered his camera.

Ducking round them, Marcus collapsed with a crash on the stone steps.

'Christ, someone better give him the kiss of life,' said the reporter.

'Don't touch him,' shouted the doctor, who'd arrived to treat Carl's tendonitis, then taking one look at Marcus. 'He's having a massive asthma attack.'

Fortunately in his car he had a portable nebulizer, a breath mask, which delivered the drug Marcus so desperately needed in tiny drops of damp air. In an attempt to rally him, the doctor also gave him a steroid injection, but Marcus was too far gone, the blue had a purple tinge now, his airways had closed up like one of Simon's oboe reeds, and he was too weak and exhausted to draw in air through such minuscule holes.

The doctor had to make a lightning decision. It would take too long to summon an ambulance. Appleton's little cottage hospital only worked skeleton shifts at weekends; Marcus must be rushed the ten miles to Northladen General.

'You drive,' he ordered the cameraman, as they laid Marcus down in the back of his estate car, 'I'll look after him and direct you. You telephone Northladen Intensive Care, and tell them he's going to need a ventilator,' he added to the reporter.

'Who is he anyway?' he asked as the cameraman, used to chasing Princess Di round Gloucestershire, hurtled at a steady 80 m.p.h. between high stone walls.

'Rupert Campbell-Black's son – what d'you give his chances?' the reporter had kept on her tape-recorder.

'Not a lot, he's not responding at all, poor little sod. I wonder if he's been taking beta-blockers, a lot of contestants do to calm the nerves. Fatal with asthma.'

Aware that they had a 'very important patient', Intensive Care was already all stations go. Within seconds of his arrival, to the accompaniment of bells and flashing lights, a lifeless, unconscious Marcus had been laid on a bed, and given an injection to paralyse him totally. This was so that he couldn't resist the transparent tube which had been shoved down his throat, and which was now pumping air and oxygen from a huge black box into his lungs.

'Christ,' muttered the anaesthetist, glancing at the box to judge the extent of the resistance in Marcus's lungs, 'he's up to eighty.'

'Is that bad?' asked the reporter, who, passing herself off as Marcus's sister, had infiltrated herself into the room.

'Let's say a normal person's between ten and twenty.' Then catching a flicker of terror in Marcus's staring eyes, the anaesthetist put on a heartier voice, 'It's all right, lad, we've had to paralyse you, only temporarily, to keep the tube down your throat. This is to sedate you, so you don't fight against it.' And he plunged another injection into Marcus's arm. 'Don't fret yourself, we'll soon have you breathing on your own.'

They're lying to me, thought Marcus in panic, I've had a stroke, or I've broken my back falling over, I'm going to be trapped inside this coffin of a body for the rest of my life. Oh please let me see Alexei once more, and he drifted back into unconsciousness.

Marcus was sinking. Sister Rose, a pretty nurse from Glamorgan sat by his bedside talking to him all the time in case he woke and panicked. Mozart piano concertos were being played to soothe him. They had tried taking him off the ventilator for short spells, but he had showed great distress and no sign of being able to breathe on his own.

'We better alert his next of kin,' said the anaesthetist. 'He doesn't seem to have any will to live, he must have had some terrible shock.'

What this was became evident when the piece on Marcus and Nemerovsky appeared in *The Evening*

Scorpion, as vicious as it was damaging. Spectacles misted up, grey buns stood on end, as every judge in the lounge of the Prince of Wales read *The Scorpion* inside their copies of the *Daily Telegraph* and the *The Times*.

Although Miles had issued a brief emollient statement that Abby had resigned and been replaced by Rannaldini, it soon leaked out that she'd been fired and had vanished without trace. Both the hospital and the hotel were besieged by reporters. Helen, in a state of mounting horror, sat beside Marcus's bed, as drips, tubes, catheters, huge black machines and most of Northladen General appeared to be fighting to save his life.

'I know it's difficult,' kindly Sister Rose gave Helen a cup of tea, 'but try not to show how worried you are, it's crucial that Marcus is subjected to as little stress as possible.'

To complicate matters, Rupert had taken off for a twenty-four-hour break with Taggie before the Czech Grand National and, leaving no telephone number, could not be traced.

The RSO arrived in Appleton, already hot and bothered because Miles in the latest economy drive had insisted they travel on coaches without air-conditioning. As they hung up their tails and black dresses in the town hall dressing-rooms, they learnt from a distraught Charlton Handsome that Marcus was on the critical list, Abby had been sacked and Rannaldini had taken over – news that both outraged and terrified them. In one maestro stroke, Rannaldini had virtually gained control of both the CCO and the RSO.

He was already cleverly infiltrating CCO players into the RSO instead of extras. One of their fiddlers had replaced Bill Thackery on the front desk of the First Violins.

Nicholas, when badgered, mumbled something about Bill being off with a frozen shoulder.

'More likely, been frozen out,' said Dixie. 'Now L'Appassionata's been given the push, Rannaldini doesn't need Bill's vote any more, nor does he have to put up with Bill's terrible sound.'

Quinton had moved up to First Horn, but the entire section was shocked to find the Third Horn seat had been filled by Rowena Godbold, the CCO's charismatic blond First Horn.

'Couldn't you and I just merge with each other and forget about orchestras,' said Quinton with a leer, as he followed Rowena's tight-jeaned bottom up onto the platform.

Blue, on the other hand, was totally unmoved, sunk into despair. His mobile had been switched on since the tour, but Cathie hadn't telephoned.

Little Han Chai couldn't stop crying over Marcus and was almost too upset to rehearse Beethoven's *Third*, her chosen concerto. At first Rannaldini was moderately accommodating, announcing that Northladen General had his mobile number and would ring if there were any change in Marcus's condition. But he was soon picking on individual players, and talking sinister notes into a pocket computer.

'That is a strange sound your instrument ees making,' he sneered at Barry.

'That's because it didn't have any time for lunch,' Barry cuddled the sunburnt Junoesque curves of his double bass defensively.

'What does it eet for lunch?'

'Conductors,' snarled Barry.

But the laughter was nervous and uneasy. Never had the orchestra been more in need of Viking to raise their spirits.

It was during the break that the RSO clapped horrified eyes on *The Evening Scorpion* and realized that poor Abby had not just been the victim of a *coup d'état*, but also, since Marcus had been outed, of a homosexual conspiracy. Like many departed conductors, she had suddenly become very dear to them. They had only needed a rehearsal to remind them how much they loathed Rannaldini.

They were also desperately upset about Marcus, as the bulletins grew increasingly bleak. Nor were they the only ones, even those judges who'd taken bribes and frolicked in the chlorine with Rannaldini were deeply shocked that such an outstanding candidate should have dropped out.

Nor was Benny very happy as the odds shortened on Natalia.

'I want first prize, Rannaldini.'

'Why?' mocked Rannaldini. 'Are the others so bad?'

'I only entered because Howie promised you'd see me right.'

Benny couldn't face the humiliation of being beaten by a girl, particularly one he had failed to pull.

Woken fleetingly by the chorus singing fortissimo on a CD of Mozart's *Requiem*, finding he couldn't move and forgetting he'd been deliberately paralysed, Marcus thought he'd already arrived in hell. Standing at the foot of the bed, wafting *Maestro*, magnificent in white tie and tails, the Prince of Darkness in person, stood Rannaldini.

'Of course he won't die,' he was reassuring a sobbing Helen, but his solicitous air was belied by the implacable hatred twisting his face.

Seeing the panic in Marcus's eyes and the reading on the ventilator rising sharply, Sister Rose, who was for once reluctant to go off duty, hastily ushered Rannaldini from the room.

'I know you're worried, but it's best if he has one visitor at a time.'

Emerging from the hospital on his way to the town hall, just when it would make a maximum impact and the morning papers, Rannaldini paused for a second.

'Of course I am standing by my stepson,' he announced smoothly. 'Eef by some miracle Marcus pull through, what matter eef he is gay. So are many, many of my closest friends. I weesh I could stay longer, but I cannot let down the three young people who play their concertos at the town 'all. Now eef you'll excuse me.'

And as Clive and a huge black basketball player called Nathan, who'd been roped in as an extra bodyguard, held back the ravening paparazzi, Rannaldini slid into his black limo.

Meanwhile, on the steps of the town hall, Dame Hermione was giving an interview to Sky Television. 'As a very close friend of Rupert Campbell-Black, my heart goes out to him at this difficult time.'

Like horses on the tightest bearing rein, Rannaldini drove the RSO through the packed-out evening performance. Anatole played his Brahms concerto magnificently, and was heavily tipped to take the competition from Natalia, although Carl in his plaid coat had brought warmth and almost folksy charm to the Mozart *E Flat Major*.

Far west on the coast of Cornwall in their little cottage under the cliffs, Flora, George and Trevor had taken blissful refuge. They had no telephone, nor television and had read no papers for days. Flora, in the nude, had just sung, 'Where E'er You Walk', to George, but had got no further than the second verse, because Trevor had thrown back his head and howled and George had pulled her back into bed.

Running the three of them up supper of rainbow trout, chips and Dom Perignon, Flora suddenly remembered it was the first night of the finals at Appleton, and turned on the ancient wireless to listen to Abby and her friends in the RSO. She was appalled to learn not only that Abby had been ousted but also, in the news bulletin that followed, that Marcus was sinking fast in Northladen General.

The abandoned chip pan then caught fire and might have burnt down the cottage if George, hearing Flora's wails, hadn't rushed in and put it out.

'Rannaldini's pulled off that merger,' sobbed Flora, 'and Marcus is dying of an asthma attack.'

'We'll fly oop to Appleton at once.' George drew her into his great warm bear-hug.

'But you wanted a rest from the orchestra. This is meant to be our honeymoon.'

'With you, honeymoons last for ever.'

All the papers on Sunday morning ran huge stories about Marcus fighting for his life, Helen keeping an all-night vigil, Rannaldini standing by, and Rupert, Nemerovsky and Abby being untraceable. The reporter who'd caught Marcus on the steps of St Theresa's was delighted with her scoop: CARING *SUNDAY SCORPION* IN MERCY DASH, said the headline.

Back in Rutminster, Cathie Jones couldn't stop crying. Poor sweet Marcus, who'd always been prepared to accompany her, poor Blue so soon out of a job, poor Abby who'd been so kind. Carmine would probably be fired, too. Rannaldini wouldn't tolerate such bolshiness. Cathie trembled at the thought of her husband at home all day with no-one to kick but herself.

As Christmas presents, she was planting some indoor bulbs, laying them out in neat piles on the kitchen floor. White bulbs called Carnegie to remind Julian of Carnegie Hall, pink bulbs for Abby, Blue Delft, of course, for Blue.

The damp bulb fibre squelched in her hands like chocolate cake mix, as she put it into the blue chinese bowls she had bought for fifty pence each at the local market. Tiger the cat had just strolled up to inspect these impromptu earth boxes. Any moment he'd bound through the piles of bulbs mixing up the colours.

Gathering up the Blue Delfts, she hid them beneath the damp fibre, like me burying my love for Blue, she thought despairingly.

There were always things to do in the autumn to make winter bearable. When the bulbs came up, probably not in time for Christmas, their sweet smell would be a reminder of bluebells in the summer. Blue bowls, blue bulbs, bluebells, how would she ever get through the winter without him?

Boris couldn't sleep, desperately worried about his little friend Marcus and kept awake by the lorries still rattling down Appleton High Street. Suddenly he was roused by a terrible crash. It must be burglars trying to steal the finally completed *Lear*. Switching on the light, Boris found that the glass rack had fallen off the wall into the wash basin, smashing everything, including his half-full bottle of whisky and the *Aramis* Marcus had given him for his birthday. He couldn't see *Lear* anywhere, and rushed in panic out into the passage, where he bumped into Deirdre who had also been woken by the crash.

Having located the manuscript under his pillow, Deirdre, who was wearing a red satin nightgown, invited Boris back to her room for a night-cap.

'You know I'd never vote for a Brit,' she told him fiercely, 'but I'm sorry your friend Marcus can't make it.'

For a second Marcus thought he had gone to heaven, when he briefly regained consciousness and found sweet Sister Rose smiling down at him. She'd just returned from the day-shift with a pile of CDs. If anyone could make him heterosexual . . .

'Here's something to cheer you up,' she whispered.

The next moment Prokofiev's introduction to *Romeo and Juliet* poured into the room. Seeing the tears sliding out of Marcus's eyes into his hair, Rose realized her mistake.

'Oh help, I'm sorry, Nemerovsky danced that at Rutminster, didn't he?' Turning off the CD player, she took Marcus's hand. 'I was in the audience. My boyfriend and I took the coach all the way down to Rutminster to watch him. He's such a hero. I understand why you love him.' She gave Marcus's fingers a squeeze. 'There's nothing wrong with being gay, you just need to accept that there isn't only one way to be in life.'

SIXTY-SEVEN

At the start of the afternoon's rehearsal with Benny and Natalia, the orchestra enraged Rannaldini by waving 'Save the RSO' banners and all wearing hastily printed 'Viva L'Appassionata' T-shirts.

Miles rushed up in a frenzy.

'Take those bloody things off.'

To which Nellie promptly obliged, showing off splendid duo-tanned breasts.

'How could you, Nell?' stormed Militant Moll.

'I think Rannaldini's rather sexy,' pouted Nellie.

'If you collaborate, Nellie Nicholson,' hissed Candy, 'we'll shave all your hair off.'

By the time they'd changed into less subversive gear, Blue noticed that Cyril, who'd been knocking back Bumpy's Scrumpy at lunch-time, was missing. Blue was about to send Lincoln to find him, when yet another highly embarrassed French horn player from the CCO slid into the Fourth Horn's place.

'Where's Cyril, Knickers?' shouted Blue.

Knickers was too distraught to answer. If Rannaldini kept feeding in extras, he'd be out of a job.

'Cyril's been sacked,' said Rannaldini coldly.

'For the second day running he was drunk when he arrived at the hall,' said Miles sanctimoniously.

Blue rose to his feet.

'I'm going too, then.'

'Sit,' howled Rannaldini. There were demanding solos for the Second Horn in both the evening's concertos.

'Don't talk to me like Barbara Woodhouse,' snapped Blue, then all the colour ebbed from his face as his mobile rang.

Only Cathie knew the number. With a trembling hand, he switched it on.

'Blue.'

'My darling.'

'I'm leaving Carmine.'

She had piled the children, the ducks, the hens, Tiger the cat, and all the bulb bowls into the car.

'Go to The Bordello. Mrs Diggory's got the key,' said Blue softly. 'There's plenty of whisky and tins in the larder and lots of catfood. The ducks and hens won't hurt in the kitchen till I get there. I'll be as quick as possible. I love you. Yippee!' yelled Blue as he switched off his mobile. 'Yippee!'

Momentarily roused out of their despondency, the RSO looked at him in amazement.

'Where are you going?' screamed Rannaldini.

'Over the hills and as far away as possible,' said Blue. 'I'm not playing your fucking concert.'

'Then you're fired.'

'Good, you can send on my redundancy money.'

'Is Blue drunk, too?' whispered Cherub in awe to Davie Buckle.

'Only with 'appiness,' said Davie.

Rupert's and Taggie's romantic forty-eight-hour break in an ancient castle high up in the Czechoslovakian forests had not been a success. Taggie had had a punishing eighteen months anyway looking after Bianca, and coping with Xav undergoing a final and completely successful operation to straighten his eyes. She had then had to keep him quiet and happy during his convalescence. But she had had a far more difficult task trying to soothe Rupert as he became increasingly outraged and miserable over the defection of both Marcus and Tabitha, although he had been far too proud to approach either of them. Abby's interview with Beattie in *The Scorpion* had destroyed him, although again he wouldn't admit it.

Rupert, on the other hand, was aware that he had been giving his sweet wife a rotten time, and had insisted they went away for a break without Bianca and Xav. He was then appalled how much he missed them.

'They're bloody well coming with us next time,' he told Taggie as the helicopter landed on the racecourse at Pardubika.

'And Marcus and Tabitha, too,' Taggie wanted to plead. But she didn't want to set Rupert off before a big race.

The course itself resembled the park of some great house, with massive beech hedges, yew colonnades, long lakes and banks acting as fences. Goodness – they looked massive.

The off for the Czech Grand National was in an hour and a quarter. Rupert went straight to check on Penscombe Pride, who'd spent the night in his large, luxurious, dark blue lorry. But before he could look at the horse, Dizzy, his head groom, beckoned him up the steps into the living-room area of the lorry.

'Thank God you've come.'

'What's the matter? It's not Pridie?'

'You better see this. I'm sorry, Rupert, but the Press are everywhere.'

Rupert took one look at yesterday's *Evening Scorpion*. On the front page was a startled wide-eyed photograph of Marcus at his most delicately beautiful: RUPERT'S SON IS GAY said the huge headline.

It was as though he'd always known it.

'So?' he turned on Dizzy.

'And Flora Seymour's just rung from Appleton,' stammered Dizzy, quailing in the blast of such ice-cold rage. 'She says Marcus has collapsed with the most dreadful asthma attack. He's in intensive care at Northladen General. Helen didn't want you to be "bothered", but I think he's really, really ill. He's been on a ventilator for twenty-four hours. He's had to pull out of the piano competition,' Dizzy's voice cracked. She had known Marcus since he was three. He'd always been such a kind gentle little boy. 'Flora left a number,' she added.

'Well, get her, for fuck's sake.'

Having taken in the caption 'Nemerovsky's Little White Dove', Rupert skimmed the front-page copy.

'Gay deceiver, Marcus Campbell-Black, pretended to be straight to woo millionaire-maestro Abby Rosen after his super-stud dad, Rupert, cut him off without a penny. But all the time Marcus was cheating on his lovely fiancée with mega-star ballet dancer, Alexei Nemerovsky. (Continued on pages 4-5)'

Ripping the pages in his fury as he found the place, Rupert discovered other headlines:

'THE STATELY HOMO. L'APPASSIONATA FLEES. RED IN HIS BED. A PRINCIPAL WITH NO PRINCIPLES' above huge photographs of himself, Abby and Alexei. There was even a picture of Woodbine Cottage with a caption: 'Fag Cottage'.

Irrationally, Rupert wondered how Nemerovsky felt about getting fourth billing. His eyes seemed to fill with blood. He felt a thrumming in his head.

'Here's Flora for you.' Nervously, Dizzy pulled him back to earth.

'I think he's dying, Rupert.' Flora's voice was shriller than ever with anxiety. 'The hospital are worried stiff, although they're keeping up a pretence that his condition is stabilized. I know you've had a row, but Marcus really, really loves you. He did everything for your sake. All that mattered to him was you not thinking he'd been an utter failure as a son.'

'I hardly think this latest escapade—'

'Oh shut up, let me finish. He never betrayed you with Rannaldini. He tried to stop Helen marrying him, and he's refused ever to speak to Rannaldini since then, he's *too* loyal to you. He's utterly, utterly honourable. Please go to him.'

'I'm not having anyone dictating—'

Flora lost her temper.

'People who live in bloody glass historic houses shouldn't throw stones. If you hadn't carried on like a rabbit when Marcus was a child – causing scandal after scandal – what did you do in the Circulation War, Daddy? – and given him the tiniest bit of support, he wouldn't have needed to search out father-figures like Malise or Nemerovsky.'

'Have you finished?' hissed Rupert.

'Yes . . . but please go to him. It's the one thing that might save him.'

'What the fuck else do you think I was going to do?'

'It's Room Twenty-Five on the second floor,' said Flora, and hung up.

The dearest and most precious horse Rupert had ever owned and trained was about to run in the most treacherous and demanding race in the world. Most people thought Pridie was past his best, and should not be subjected to such an ordeal. Nor had worry about this helped Rupert's and Taggie's romantic break.

Dizzy had told Taggie about Marcus. Rupert was ashen as he came down the steps of the box. Taggie ran to him, holding him in her arms, feeling him rigid with shock.

'Oh darling, poor Marcus, poor you, we must go to him.'

'What else can we do?' said Rupert bleakly, then, turning to Dizzy: 'Tell the pilot to refuel.'

Pridie whickered with relieved delight at the sight of his master and nearly pulled Sandra the stable girl over as he bounded down the ramp. He had been bred at Penscombe and had never run a single race without Rupert. Having given him a couple of Polos, Rupert quickly felt the little horse's legs, praying he could find some swelling or heat to give him an excuse to pull him. But they were perfect, and Pridie's coat gleamed in the soft autumn sunshine, redder and brighter than any of the RSO cellos.

Briefly Rupert hugged his old friend.

'We're going to have to cope without each other. Pray for me, Pridie.'

Taggie felt utterly helpless on the flight home, as Rupert glared unseeingly out of the window, tension flickering like lightning around his jaws. Only once did she try to tempt him with a large whisky, but he shook his head violently.

'It's probably just a one-off with Nemerovsky,' she stammered. 'He's so powerful and glamorous, anyone would find him difficult to resist . . .Lots of people have flings.'

'What the fuck do you know about it?' snarled Rupert, gazing through the dusk down at the white horses flecking the English Channel.

'N-nothing.'

'Well, shut up then.'

'He could be bisexual. One *affaire* doesn't mean he's gay.'

'Course he is . . . always has been.'

Taggie gave up. Oh dear God, she thought, please don't let him be horrible to Marcus.

Back at Appleton Town Hall, the judges, after a jolly rest day visiting Delius's old haunts in nearby Yorkshire, and enjoying a long lunch at the famous Box Tree

Restaurant in Ilkley, were looking forward to a boring, untaxing evening. Although Benny would pull out the stops and wow the audience tonight, most of them had already chosen either Anatole or Natalia as the winner. But with only two contestants this evening, the edge had gone out of the competition. The bleak bulletins from Northladen General had cast a shadow over the proceedings. They all felt poor Marcus had been very shabbily treated. After all, as Dame Edith had pointed out noisily at lunch,

'Everyone knows there are only three types of pianist – Jewish, Gay or Bad.'

The Scorpion and all the rest of the Press, they agreed, were making a ridiculous fuss.

'Lucky, lucky Nemerovsky,' sighed Pablo Gonzales.

'Rather nice for Helen to have a gay son,' said Dame Hermione with her head on one side. 'They're always so devoted to their mothers.'

Seven-fifteen . . . Benny had been to make-up and could be heard by the entire audience warming up in a practice room. The great clock of the town hall had been stopped for two hours to prevent it tolling during performances. Time would stand still, but hopefully the whole contest would be wrapped up by ten o'clock in time for the news.

As Benny left the practice room, Rupert gave his third police car the slip, hurtling a hired Mercedes through the driving rain towards Northladen General. A white-knuckled Taggie nearly bit her lower lip in half trying not to cry out in terror.

Meanwhile in Room Twenty-Five on the second floor, Marcus tried not to exhaust himself as, desperately slowly, he put on black evening trousers and the crumpled blue dress-shirt which he had pulled out of his suitcase which his mother had brought him from St Theresa's.

He had waited, feigning sleep, until she had left for

the town hall. Helen had sat with Marcus through the night and morning until he miraculously regained enough strength in his lungs to come off the ventilator. When the effects of the paralysing drug and sedatives had worn off, and he was able to swallow again, she had even fed him some pale tasteless scrambled eggs. But he was acutely conscious that she couldn't meet his eyes, and was dreadfully embarrassed to be in the same room with him. No-one had let him see the papers, although Helen had told him Rannaldini had replaced Abby, but her face had said it all.

For now her ewe lamb wasn't going to die, the other two nightmares had enveloped her life: her husband was a compulsive womanizer and her son was a homosexual, his career in smithereens. There was also a deep-seated guilt that her obsessive, clinging love might have caused both these things. If only Malise was still alive.

Rannaldini had been sympathetic, but always at Rupert's expense.

'If Rupert had not been a sadist, you wouldn't have had to compensate so much. Marcus never had a father to relate to. You always implied Rupert and Billy Lloyd-Foxe were unnaturally close, and even more so, Rupert and Lysander. It's in the genes, you mustn't torment yourself.'

This situation suited Rannaldini perfectly. Marcus had been the only serious threat to Natalia in the competition and, with Helen cemented to Marcus's sick-bed and unhinged with worry, he had had all the more opportunity to spend time with Natalia.

He had virtuously resisted from making love to her after her rehearsal in case it relaxed her muscles too much before the final. But between chatting to Northern Television and escorting Benny onto the platform, Rannaldini found time to slip into Natalia's dressing-room. How adorable the sweet child looked with her shining hair in rollers.

'Thees is how I warm up,' he said sliding his soft, newly

manicured hands inside her willow-green silk dressing-gown. Oh, the wonder of those large springy young breasts. Helen's silicone replicas were like two buns on a cake rack since she had fretted away so much weight.

'Good luck, my Maestro,' whispered Natalia, resting her spiky head against his starched white shirt-front. 'I am safe when you are 'ere.'

'Tonight,' promised Rannaldini, 'we weel drink champagne together from the Appleton Cup.'

The RSO stopped tuning up and gave a great shout of relieved joy as George walked into the hall with Flora. They both looked very tired from worry about Marcus, but their glow of happiness in each other and in his recovery seemed to light them from inside and set them apart from the black-tied, taffeta and satin audience around them. Neither of them had bothered to pack much when they'd leapt into the helicopter. George was now wearing a blazer, a blue-and-white-striped shirt, and no tie, because Flora had borrowed the only one he had brought to belt in his dark blue shirt which she had also annexed.

'Aren't they glamorous,' sighed Clare.

'I'm sure Flora's pregnant,' hissed Candy. 'Look how her boobs have grown.'

The big smile of pride was wiped off George's face when he saw Miles, Hilary's mother, Gilbert, Gwynneth, Mrs Parker and Lord Leatherhead all huddled together looking wrong-footed in the stalls.

'You've been bluddy busy in my ubsence,' said George not lowering his voice at all. 'I'd like to remind you that I'm only taking a sabbatical and I'm still chief executive of the RSO, and you and your fancy piece, Miles,' Hilary's mother turned purple, 'better hop it, as you're sitting in our seats.'

To the left of the stage, the flags of the five participating finalists soared to the dark blue vaulted ceiling. If only the Union Jack had been up there as well, thought Helen despairingly as she huddled in dark glasses in the middle of the stalls. Behind the orchestra rose a huge, far from portable, red-and-white organ, flanked by two proud unicorns holding up the red rose of Lancashire. Above them two angels held out a scroll saying: 'The Truth is Great and Shall Prevail.'

There were gasps of admiration as Rannaldini in his black-and-white splendour, swept on and mounted a rostrum a foot higher than usual so everyone could see him. The great prevailer, he smiled down at Benny's shock of dark curls. He knew exactly how to wrong-foot the foolish Frenchman to Natalia's advantage.

His two bodyguards, Clive and Nathan, the black basketball player, stood watchful at the back of the hall. Rannaldini was taking no chances.

As the clock started on the monitor, the vast audience went quiet. Five, four, three, two, one. The camera panned in on the little silver piano, which would be awarded to the winner. The last round of the Appleton Piano Competition, live from the town hall, was under way.

SIXTY-EIGHT

The Press swarming round the hospital were thrown into a frenzy by Rupert's totally unexpected arrival, particularly when he screeched to a halt in a muddy puddle, drenching the lot of them.

'What's the latest, Rupe? Is the kid going to be OK? Terrible shock for you,' they closed round him. 'How'd you feel about him being a woofter?'

Wrath gave Rupert superhuman strength as he barged a gangway through for himself and Taggie. He had more trouble fighting his way through the barricade of outraged medics. Helen had left tearful instructions that if, in the unlikely event Rupert rolled up, he mustn't be allowed to see his son.

'It's the one thing that really triggers off Marcus's asthma. Rupert's got a terrible temper. I'll only be gone a couple of hours.'

'He's not allowed visitors, he must be kept quiet. I'm afraid no-one can see him.' The pleas, and then orders, fell on deaf ears as Rupert stalked through the lot of them.

He loathed hospitals, the smell and glaring whiteness instantly brought back poor little Xav's countless operations and Taggie nearly dying twice when she miscarried. It also took him back twenty-two years to Helen also nearly dying, giving birth to Marcus – a sickly, carroty-haired baby, who, from the start, had never endeared himself to Rupert.

Finding the lift blocked by a massive matron, Rupert dodged round her and ran up the stairs with Taggie panting after him.

Three doctors, pretty Sister Rose and two male nurses barred the door to Room Twenty-Five.

'I really must insist you don't go in there.'

'Fuck off.' Once more Rupert parted them – a bowling ball through skittles – then he turned on a panting Taggie.

'Stay outside, I want to see him on my own.'

'I'd like to be with you,' pleaded Taggie.

'This is my problem,' snarled Rupert.

'That is the handsomest Angel of Death I've ever seen,' sighed Sister Rose.

Expecting to find Marcus unconscious and a mass of tubes, Rupert was astounded to see him sitting on the bed buttoning up a blue dress-shirt. His red hair hung lank and darkened by sweat to the colour of a copper beach. His deathly pallor was tinged green by the fluorescent lighting, his huge frightened eyes were black caves as though he could see deep into his own tortured soul.

'D-d-dad, I thought you were at the Pardubika,' Marcus leapt to his feet, cringing against hideous yellow-and-orange curtains, waiting for the firing-squad invective.

For a second Rupert gazed at him, reminded of the only time he'd gone stag hunting. Appalled by the terrified eyes of a little doe trapped against a huge wall, he had been too late to call hounds off before they ripped her to pieces.

'I'm really, really sorry,' gasped Marcus.

Rupert shrugged. 'It's the way you're made. Campbell-Black libido has to come out somewhere, I guess. Sorry I haven't been any help. Been meaning to ring you for months – ever since you sent Tag that Mothering Sunday card.'

'That was just after I'd met. . . . I wanted to see you. Oh Dad,' for a minute, Marcus's lip trembled, then he stumbled forward and, for a brief moment, he and Rupert embraced.

Passionately relieved the boy was all right, Rupert patted his desperately bony shoulder.

'You poor little sod.' Then as Marcus half-laughed, added 'Oh God, that wasn't very tactful. Get back into bed.'

Marcus shook his head. 'I'm going to play.'

'Don't be ridiculous.'

But Marcus stood his ground. 'You won a gold with a trapped nerve. If I don't crack it now, I never will. It's the only way to throw off the stigma of being Abby's walker, Alexei's catamite and Rannaldini's stepson.'

'And my son, too,' said Rupert wryly. 'Look, there'll be other competitions. It's crazy to risk it, when you've just pulled through.'

'That's *why* I pulled through. Would you terribly mind ringing the town hall? I don't think they will let me use the telephone here. Just tell them I want to go on, and I'll be there in half an hour.'

Finding it difficult to breathe and talk, he slumped onto the bed.

'Benny'll just be starting the second movement,' he smiled slightly and cupped his hand round his ear, 'I can hear him now. My tail-coat needs a press and a brush, but someone can do that at the other end. And could you get me a taxi, because I don't think the hospital would do that for me either.'

'I'll take you if you're really set on it.'

Marcus nodded, unable to speak, overwhelmed by Rupert's totally unexpected acceptance. Then he muttered: 'You've missed the Pardubika, I'm terribly sorry.'

'Blood is thicker than water jumps,' said Rupert, getting out his mobile.

All hell broke out as the doctors frantically tried to dissuade Marcus.

'It's insanity,' they berated Rupert. 'The pressure could kill him. He's desperately weak and he needs to go on the nebulizer again in two hours' time.'

'Sometimes the mind reaches out and the body follows.'

'You've pushed him into it.'

'He has *not*,' protested Marcus, unearthing the score of the Schumann from the bedside cupboard, and swaying at the sudden rush of blood to his head as he stood up. 'Someone's got to fight Abby's corner. She should never've been fired.'

'You realize we're not responsible if he insists on discharging himself,' boomed Matron, blocking the entire doorway.

'The discharge of the heavy brigade,' said Rupert, bodily removing her from Marcus's path.

Taggie was hovering in the waiting-room on the way to the lifts with an undrunk cup of tea in her hands. Her eyes were very red. Marcus went straight into her arms.

'It's so lovely to see you,' they cried.

Rupert put his arms round both of them, but just for a second. 'Come on, we mustn't be late.'

The only concession the hospital made was to smuggle them out of a side-door.

Panic gripped Marcus the moment he was installed in the back of the car. As they hurtled through the night, rain lashing and clawing at the windscreen, he took great gulps from his puffer and under a pallid overhead light, desperately riffled through the score which seemed terrifyingly unfamiliar. What were all the pitfalls? He hadn't touched a piano for two days. With Abby, the orchestra would have seemed familiar, but Rannaldini would take everything much slower or much faster, whipping the orchestra up to an unnatural frenzy. Rannaldini also despised Schumann as an over-romantic wimp.

Thank God neither Rupert nor Taggie talked, although Marcus noticed his father's hand sliding over Taggie's whenever he entered a straight piece of road. As they reached the outskirts of Appleton, the reflections of the orange street-lights shivered like carp on the shiny black cobbled streets. Breathing in the conflicting wafts of hamburgers, curry and fish and chips, Marcus retched. Rupert's mobile rang. It was Northern Television.

'Howyer doing? Can you make it by eight-thirty, then Marcus can warm up during the interval. Everyone's knocked out he's coming on.'

Most of the space round the hall had been taken up by the seven OB vans and the cherry-red RSO lorry, but Rupert got them as near the artists' entrance as possible. The only other stumbling-block was a river of damp press who immediately turned into a frenzied whirlpool.

'Christ, it's Rupert,' shouted the *Daily Express*. 'Looks as though he's made it up with the lad.'

'Dangerous bugger,' warned the *Mail*, 'watch out.'

'Spect Rupert forced him to go on,' said the *Mirror*. 'What d'you feel about your son's *affaire* with Nemerovsky, Rupert?'

Rupert looked the reporter up and down, about to tell him to get stuffed, then he changed his mind.

'Shows Nemerovsky's got extremely good taste.'

'You don't mind having a gay son?' asked the *Sun* in amazement.

Briefly, Rupert put an arm round Marcus's shoulders, the rain falling through the rays of the street-lamps, casting a speckled light on his haughty expressionless face.

'I've got a son with enough guts to discharge himself from hospital and face the toughest ordeal of his life,'

he drawled. 'I'm very proud of him. His sexual prefer-
ences, as long as they bring him happiness, are quite
immaterial.'

'What about his engagement to Abby?'

'Much better they both found out before they got
married.'

'Do you know where Abby is?'

'No.'

'Nemerovsky's got a terrible track-record, aren't you
worried about AIDS?' asked an evil-looking blonde.

Rupert's face suddenly betrayed such hatred everyone
shrank back.

'If he'd slept with you, Beattie,' he said icily, 'I'd worry
about something much worse than AIDS.'

The surrounding journalists laughed nervously.

'Are you disappointed about the Czech Grand
National?' asked *The Times*.

Rupert stopped in his tracks – incredible that he'd
forgotten all about it in his race from the hospital.

'It's a Snip won, not Penscombe Pride,' said the
Telegraph, 'Lysander broke a shoulder, Pridie fell at
the last fence.'

For a second, Rupert's face clenched in horror, then
he said lightly, 'But Marcus won't,' and they were
through the swing-doors.

'I said he was a dangerous bugger,' grumbled the
Mail, trying to make his biro work on a rain-sodden page.

'It's his son who's the bugger,' hissed Beattie Johnson.

'Awfully good of you to show up, Martin,' said an earnest
woman in a billowing grey jersey. Brandishing a
clipboard as she scuttled up to them on spindly red-
stockinged legs, she looked like a turkey.

'I'm Chrissie,' she shook Marcus's hand. 'Our
presenter, James Vereker's going to announce you're
participating, just before Natalia Philipova goes on.
Means the competition's wide open. Do you need
anything ironed? I expect you'd like to see your dressing-

room before you warm up, Martin, and then go to make-up, but if James Vereker could have a brief chat first—'

'James can have it afterwards. Martin needs to distance himself,' said Rupert firmly, as he relieved her of the dressing-room key. 'Come on, Martin.'

Marcus's laughter almost turned to tears as he saw the 'Save the RSO' sticker on his door and the hundreds of cards and great banks of flowers waiting for him inside.

'We were going to send them over to the hospital when we had a mo,' said Chrissie apologetically.

Marcus suppressed a flare of hope that one might be from Alexei. But there was no time to look.

'Could you bear to open them?' he asked Taggie.

As he was pouring with sweat, he tugged off his jersey, then turning to Rupert, said, 'I don't mean to be horrible, but could you possibly keep Mum away while I warm up?'

Tripping over cables, climbing round petulant rank-and-file fiddle players, James Vereker, the presenter, reached the rostrum. Having smoothed his streaked blond hair and straightened his peacock-blue tie which exactly matched his eyes, he said he was so very, very pleased to announce that the British contestant, Marcus Campbell-Black, would be taking up his place in the final, after all. Over a burst of applause, he shouted that Marcus would be appearing after a further ten-minute interval, which would take place after Natalia Philipova's concerto. The jury would then try to reach a decision during the *Ten o'clock News*, and the scheduled programme on the male menopause of *Daniel Deronda* would be postponed to a later date.

Like petrol-ignited flames, excitement crackled around the hall. Cherub dropped a cymbal in his excitement, the orchestra gave a great cheer, only half-induced by the fact that this would push them into over-time. Journalists were fighting to use the telephones with members of the audience, frantic to reorganize restaurant bookings and pick-up times, and to check on last buses and trains. The atmosphere had become electric. People were hardly back in their seats when a thunder of applause greeted the arrival of Rannaldini and Natalia on the platform.

With a black-tie audience, an orchestra in their tails and black dresses tend to look less distinctive and blend into one black whole. Nothing therefore could have stood out better than Natalia's poinsettia-red taffeta dress, which emphasized her small waist, her lovely white arms and shoulders, and her shining dark curls. Showing off her glorious cleavage, she proceeded to bow several times to the judges in the gallery and the jam-packed audience, who were now well oiled by drinks in the interval. Benny had impressed but not entirely captivated.

'Bet Rannaldini paid an arm and a legover for that dress,' muttered Dixie.

Marcus and Helen had not been the only people to clock Rannaldini's preference.

It was plain from the start that the NTV cameras were more besotted with Natalia even than Rannaldini. As she delivered Rachmaninov's *Third* with an explosion of romantic passion, the cameras hardly left her beautiful face, whether she was smiling seraphically or whether her big scarlet mouth was drooping and her eyes closing in anguish during the sad bits.

Swinging round fondly, Rannaldini followed her every note, making sure phrases flowed into each other, slowing down if she looked like falling over herself, quietening the orchestra if there was any danger of her being drowned.

'The brass section have at last learnt the meaning of the word pianissimo,' whispered Flora in George's ear. 'Don't you absolutely loathe, loathe, loathe Rannaldini.'

George took her hand. His jealousy instantly doused. He had been thinking how satanically handsome the bastard looked, as his hands languorously cupped and stroked the air, and wondering how Flora could possibly not still carry a torch for him. Gazing at her furious freckled profile only slightly softened by red tendrils still damp from the shower, George marvelled yet again that his love seemed to double by the second.

'And he's making it so bloody easy for that little tart,' hissed Flora. 'We can't let him take over the RSO.'

'Be Kwy-et,' whispered Peggy Parker furiously.

Resplendent in puce velvet to match her face, she was sitting beyond George. She turned even pucer when she saw Trevor's little furry face emerging from Flora's dark blue shirt to lick his mistress on the chin.

Mrs Parker, was however, feeling considerable disquiet. Particularly as Natalia reached the end of the second movement, and the cameras panned lovingly on to the snow-white handkerchief with which she wiped both the damp keys and her sweating fingers.

'More like the Rannaldini and Natalia Show,' chuntered Lord Leatherhead, who was furious with Miles for cancelling the RSO bottled-water account. 'When are we going to see some shots of the orchestra?'

'I agree,' hissed Mrs Parker, 'Clare and Candy, Nellie and Juno, Noriko and Hilly are just as pretty as that Czech.'

'And Cherub's much prettier than Rannaldini,' volunteered Flora.

'Think that chap may be too overbearing for the RSO,' muttered Lord Leatherhead.

In the row behind them, Gwynneth, who was reviewing the competition for the *Guardian*, and Gilbert, for the *Independent*, were busily scribbling. The last time they had heard Rach *Three* was in Rutminster, when only Marcus's tenacity and presence of mind had saved Abby and the RSO from total calamity. How different it was tonight!

'*Not since Toscanini*,' wrote Gwynneth, who had a mega-crush on Rannaldini.

'*Not since Eileen Joyce*,' wrote Gilbert, who had his opera-glasses trained on Natalia's bosom.

They both felt a huge satisfaction that they had been so instrumental in effecting the merger. There would be no more bum surprises on Moulin Rouge.

Canon Airlie, who should have sat next to Gilbert, had flu, so Miles had bagged his seat. Wearing a new DJ specially run up by Rannaldini's tailors, Miles craned round the piano to gaze at Hilly. She looked so lovely in her new diamond brooch, another present from Rannaldini. He was glad Marcus was playing the Schumann, which had a wonderful clarinet solo.

The last movement of the Rachmaninov was a triumph. It seemed impossible that Natalia's little hands could possibly cover all the notes. Playing with hardly a pause, probing the depths of hell in the bass, shaking out shoals of silver coins in the treble, she galloped to a triumphant finale which was followed by an even more triumphant burst of applause.

Rannaldini, looking like a cat who'd swallowed the Canary Isles, made sure she got even more call-backs than Anatole. He was not pleased, hurrying her back for a fourth time, when the applause had almost petered out, to go slap into Julian bringing the orchestra off the stage.

The bars were crowded out, but the consensus was that not even the stormy splendour of yesterday's Russian nor the American who'd played Mozart so heart-warmingly could possibly beat Natalia.

Charlton Handsome and NTV technicians were now reassembling the stage and readjusting microphones for the smaller orchestra needed for the Schumann. Carmine Jones, who wanted to know if he'd won the lottery, was livid not to get Cathie on his mobile.

Marcus had been buoyed up by the sudden miraculous *rapprochement* with Rupert. But alone with the upright piano in the practice room, he was overwhelmed with the impossibility of his task. His fingers were rigid and inflexible, yet slipping all over the keys. Even though

Rupert had made him put his jersey back on again, he couldn't stop shaking, his body encased in icy sweat. Even worse he was having increasing trouble breathing. He looked at the plaster on the back of his hand where the drip had gone in. How terrible if he had held up the competition for forty minutes only to have a memory lapse, or even worse another asthma attack and let everyone down. The piece seemed hideously unfamiliar and on stage he would have no score to help him. He must relax, make his mind blank, take slow, deep breaths. Sometimes the mind can take the body into impossible terrain. Wasn't that what Rupert had promised?

The storm of hurrahs and bravos for Natalia's obviously sensational performance had long since died away. He'd be on soon.

'*Our Father,*' began Marcus, '*Which art in heaven.* What came next? Unable to remember, he started to panic. '*Which art in heaven, forgive us our trespasses* . . . Oh Alexei, Alexei.'

For a second, he banged his head against the top of the piano, wiped out with longing. He must concentrate. Frantically he leafed through the score to the last movement. Singing 'To the Life Boats, to the Life Boats', in a breathless tenor, he tried to match the frantically syncopated piano part. As he groped for a handkerchief to wipe his hands, Mrs Bateson's little jet cat fell out. He mustn't let her down either.

The next moment, he jumped violently as Helen barged in.

'Marcus darling, you mustn't go on. Dr Brewster says it would kill you – it's insanity.'

'Mum, per-lease! I need to be on my own.'

'You mustn't go on.'

'For God's sake, fuck off.' Marcus raised clenched fists to heaven.

'Even you reject me.' Helen burst into tears.

Rupert, who'd been guarding the door, had been

caught temporarily on the hop, as he tried to get through to Czechoslovakia on his mobile to find out if Pridie was all right. But he immediately took Helen away for a large brandy.

For a second they gazed at each other. Helen's eyes were dark with resentment.

'I couldn't help loving him so much. He was all I had when I was married to you.'

'I know, I'm sorry,' said Rupert.

The passage outside his dressing-room was like a herbaceous border. Taggie had lined up all his flowers in vases, so they didn't trigger off another asthma attack. Inside, Marcus couldn't see the shelves for cards, one had been signed by every member of the RSO. Taggie had kept back a white carnation for his buttonhole. Now she was pressing his tails.

'How're Xav and Bianca?' Marcus tried to force his trembling lips into a confident smile.

'OK. I've just rung home. Xav's always asking about his big brother. Oh Marcus, I'm so happy you and Rupert have made it up. He's so pleased and proud of you for going on.'

Marcus's hands were shaking so much that when Rupert returned, he had to tie his tie for him.

'You can use your puffer between movements,' urged Taggie.

'That's the bit when we wait 'til Flora claps,' said Rupert.

'Is Flora here?' asked Marcus in amazed delight.

As he was giving his hands a last wash to remove the sweat, Howie Denston barged in, followed by a chattering retinue of his own sex.

'Markie baby, why didn't you tell me you were gay? You've no idea the doors I can open for you, now.'

'Get out,' said Rupert, slamming the door in all their faces.

A second later Chrissie was knocking discreetly, 'Are

you ready, Martin? You're on now. And *Gay News* has asked especially if they can have a brief interview afterwards.'

'You're not talking to *them*,' snapped Rupert. 'Charity does not begin at homos.'

As they left the dressing-room, Marcus was nearly sent flying by a gorgon in a caftan.

'Got to phone my copy through,' cried Gwynneth bossily. 'Never heard Rach *Three* played so well. How little Philipova's hands stretched that far – must be a clear winner. I'm going to stick my neck out.'

Marcus nearly burst out laughing at the horror on his father's face.

'Beware a pale rider on a dark horse,' hissed Rupert, making a V-sign at Gwynneth's vast back.

'Oh, there's Maestro Rannaldini,' said Chrissie reverently.

Rupert straightened Marcus's tie again.

'Taggie and I better go and find our seats, good luck. Try not to rush things. Remind me to buy you some new evening-shirts.'

Turning, he nearly bumped into Rannaldini. Rupert was six inches taller but, as he glanced down into the cold uncompromising face of his enemy, he dropped his guard.

'Look after him, please.'

'Of course,' Rannaldini smiled like an expectant wolf.

'Come along, Marcus,' then, lowering his voice, added nastily, 'But don't play too slowly or we'll overrun the news.'

Brave boys, thought Marcus irrationally, are not afraid of wolves.

Shaking off Rannaldini's obtrusively guiding hand, he walked out onto the stage. For a second, he halted in panic at the beginning of the First Violins, blinded by the dazzling white camera lights, staggered by the vastness of the audience, an ocean of wary and unsmiling faces. There was a sudden and embarrassed silence.

Perhaps they would all boo him for what he had done to Abby. Then he felt a small, warm hand creeping into his.

'Good ruck, Marcus, good ruck,' whispered Noriko, and a shove from Rannaldini thrust him forward.

Seeing how desperately pale, shadowed and apprehensive he looked, Flora leapt without thinking to her feet.

'Bravo, bravo, Marcus, great to see you,' she yelled, clapping frantically, and a second later the audience had joined in.

Coming down the row, to take up Marcus's two complimentary tickets, were Rupert and Taggie. Sitting down next to Flora, Rupert kissed her on both cheeks.

'You are a star in every possible way. Sorry I chewed you out earlier.'

Glancing beyond her, he encountered a murderous glare from the square-shouldered, square-jawed minder beyond her.

'Rupert, this is my future husband, George Hungerford,' said Flora hastily.

Marcus was amazed to see how many of the orchestra were smiling at him. There was Quinton in Viking's place clutching his golden horn, and Candy and Clare clapping wildly, and Dimitri discreetly waving two crossed fingers, and Randy and Davie Buckle cocking their heads and winking, and Barry and all the basses making thumbs-up signs. Hilary, Simon and Peter were too preoccupied with long difficult solos ahead to do more than nod, but Juno gave him a radiant smile. She was feeling very chipper, because James Vereker, the presenter, had just asked her out to dinner.

'Good on you, Marcus. Go for it.' Julian stood up and pumped Marcus's hand as he passed. Then, lowering his voice, added, 'You've got to win, we've all got so much money on you.'

Rannaldini mounted the rostrum glaring round, instantly wiping the smiles off everyone's faces. George would have difficulty over-turning the decision of an entire board. They knew Rannaldini could put them all out of work next week. Once again they wished Viking was here, if only in the audience.

Having lowered the piano-stool, checked if he could reach the pedals comfortably, given his fingers a last wipe on his black trousers, Marcus put his head back with his eyes shut for a moment to compose himself. Then he placed his hands on the keys and was about to nod to Rannaldini, when the down beat descended like an executioner's axe, and the entire orchestra came in on the first crashing quaver. Caught on the hop, Marcus's first three bars followed like a mad scramble down the steps to a lake, immediately followed by the woodwind taking off like a great swan across the water's surface. This gave him eight bars' respite to catch his breath before echoing the lovely piano expressivo melody, then rippling on in accompaniment to the strings.

But Rannaldini was taking it horrendously fast and Marcus had his work cut out trying to keep up.

It was soon clear that this was a contest not a partnership. With every tutti, Rannaldini whipped up the tempo; with every exquisitely languorous cascade of notes, Marcus tried to slow it down.

He was touched that whenever Simon, Peter and even Hilary had ravishing solos, which he had to accompany, they tried to check their speed, adjusting to his slower tempo. But inevitably this made his performance uneven. Until following a magical andante interchange between woodwind and piano, Rannaldini suddenly accelerated as if he were turning up a mixer to full speed, and Marcus ran away with himself, and came off the rails, and stopped completely.

In the gallery, Dame Edith, Pablo and Boris groaned in despair. But having thoroughly frightened himself, Marcus steadied. Realizing Rannaldini was deliberately bent on sabotage, his terror hardened into cold rage.

At least he looked absolutely beautiful on the

monitor, as though Narcissus had wandered into the hall and was gazing at his reflection in the shiny black piano lid. And, as his confidence grew, so did the depth and lyricism of his playing. There was none of Benny's unrelenting stridency, nor Natalia's sloppy, splashy lushness. Up in the gallery Pablo even stopped grumbling that Lady Appleton had confiscated his *Guinness Book of Records*. All round the hall, people began thinking that perhaps the Schumann was the greatest piano concerto of them all.

Even Rannaldini couldn't rot up the cadenza, although he did his best to distract the audience, adjusting his gardenia, examining his nails and flipping the pages of the score back and forth, and he hardly waited for the final trill to bring the orchestra in at an even faster tempo. But this time Marcus was ready and, like a television camera on top of a car, he somehow managed to keep up with the galloping cheetah right to the end of the movement.

'Bloody marvellous,' muttered Clare, as she and Candy tuned their instruments and adjusted the dusters on their shoulders.

'Even more marvellous,' muttered back Candy, 'is the man on Flora's right. Christ, he's good looking – how the hell does Flora do it?'

'That's Marcus's father,' said Clare, 'I think he once went to bed with Mummy.'

Rupert was tone deaf, but he'd never taken his eyes off Marcus throughout the entire movement.

'Was that all right?' he asked anxiously over the coughing and murmer of chat.

'Sensational,' whispered Flora. 'He kept his nerve, despite chronic aggravation from Rannaldini. And Marcus certainly wins on looks. Because of the red hair, everyone says he's like Helen, but I reckon he's the image of you.'

'That's nice,' Rupert blushed slightly.

'I also think he's up to something,' observed Flora. 'I've seen that look before.'

Marcus reached for his inhaler, had a puff, and glanced up meditatively at Rannaldini's impeccably tailored back, wondering what devilries he was plotting now. He has ridden expensively shod over too many people, thought Marcus.

Rannaldini, in fact, was busy polishing his pewter hair and reflecting that the Steel Elf, despite her squeaky sound, was extraordinarily pretty. He must remember to fuck her before he gave her the sack. Determined to observe the niceties this time, he turned graciously to check if Marcus were ready. Timidly Marcus beckoned him. The picture of concern, Rannaldini leapt youthfully down from his rostrum. Perhaps the little wimp had decided to retire. Beckoning him a fraction closer, Marcus hissed: 'This one's for Abby, you bastard,' and giving a quick nod to Julian, he started playing: ta, ta, ta, tum, ta, ta, ta, tum. The orchestra were so astounded they only just came in time. Rannaldini, however, was totally wrong-footed. Tripping over a cable in his built-up shoes, he nearly fell flat on his face and was reduced to scrambling furiously back to his rostrum, frantically flailing in a desperate attempt to regain the ascendancy over the orchestra, who played on with broad grins on their faces. The jury were divided between outrage, ecstasy and helpless laughter.

As the slow movement was merely a short, sweet intermezzo, with the strings, woodwind and piano mournfully echoing one another, there was nothing Rannaldini could do in retaliation except smoulder. But the allegro vivace, graveyard of pianists, lay ahead. That would be the time to show the little faggot who was maestro.

Without a glance in Marcus's direction, Rannaldini swept the orchestra into the last movement. Marcus had eighty bars of scampering glamorously round the keyboard before the orchestra, like a will-o'-the-wisp leading the unwary traveller into the quicksand, launched into the deceptively simple, jaunty little tune. 'To the Life Boats, To the Life Boats', sung Marcus to himself grimly. It was one hell of a pace. He mustn't panic.

At first the jury and many of the audience thought Julian must be drunk, because he had for once taken off his dark glasses and swayed crazily round his leader's chair, bloodshot eyes rolling, pale lank hair flying.

Then Deirdre twigged.

'He's not dronk,' she whispered to Boris in admiration. 'He's josst making sure that every member of the orchestra can see him.'

Aware that Marcus could never keep up with the terrifying syncopated cross-rhythms if the musicians went at Rannaldini's pace, Julian was utterly ignoring Rannaldini, playing at a slower tempo, and the RSO stayed with him.

After two days of responding with the docility of dressage horses, they were suddenly raising two hooves to Rannaldini. Abby – very dear because she was now departed – had been sacked unfairly. This was their rebellion.

Overjoyed, astounded, Marcus realized they were doing to the mighty Rannaldini what they had done to Abby in the old days. They were following the soloist. He felt a great surge of confidence. Like shoals of goldfish, released from a tiny tank into a great river, like a door opening and sunlight pouring in on the darkness, the notes were flowing gloriously away from his fingers.

Rannaldini was insane with rage. The leader, whom he'd fired in New York and would certainly fire again the moment the concerto was over, was refusing like an overworked barman to let his eye be caught. But, being on camera, Rannaldini couldn't betray his fury. Short of thrashing Julian with his baton he could do nothing.

'I 'ave never seen anything like it,' murmured Pablo to the other judges. 'I 'ave waited many, many years for that sheet to meet his Vaterloo. *C'est magnifique, mais c'est aussi la guerre.*'

To avoid public humiliation, Rannaldini had now readjusted his beat to Marcus's joyfully dancing fingers.

'Nearly there,' murmured Flora to Rupert. 'Only one more fence to jump.'

And perfectly controlled, but racing faster and faster like a winner on the home straight at Cheltenham, the orchestra launched into the final tutti, followed by Marcus's last euphoric helter-skelter up the keyboard leading into the last crashing chords, accompanied by Davie Buckle's tumultuous drumroll, and it was all over.

Marcus bowed his head as if he were in total trance. There was a long, stunned silence, broken by Flora once again leaping to her feet.

'Bravo, bravo,' she screamed bringing her hands together in clap almost as noisy as the final chord: a flash of lightning which was followed by the most deafening thunder of applause, as stamping, cheering, yelling, the entire audience rose to their feet.

For a moment, Marcus gazed at them in bewilderment, the colour stealing into his face. Then he smiled more radiantly than any sunrise, and getting unsteadily to his feet, holding the edge of the piano for support, bowed low as the applause grew more and more delirious. Then, giddy, he straightened up, and fell into Julian's waiting arms.

Unable to speak they hammered each other's backs, listening to an even sweeter sound: a manic rattling of bows on the backs of chairs.

Unfortunately for Rannaldini, Marcus was blocking his exit, and Rannaldini was forced, because he was on camera, to hold out his hand.

Marcus looked at it for a second. Then, deliberately rejecting it, he said quite distinctly: 'That was for screwing up Flora and Abby and cuckolding my mother.'

Then he added as an afterthought, 'And for trying to destroy my father,' and stalked off the platform.

How could Marcus have rejected Rannaldini's olive branch? thought Helen in horror. I'm seeing Rupert all over again.

'That was worth a bloody gold,' crowed Rupert as he and Taggie fought their way out to Marcus's dressing-room. 'Absolutely no doubt who the audience want to win.'

Marcus was waiting for them, smiling apologetically. 'I've probably screwed up my career for ever, but God, I enjoyed that.'

He was so soaked in sweat, yet burning white-hot, that Taggie needed ovengloves to hug him.

'You were wonderful,' she said tearfully.

But what really made Marcus's evening, almost his whole life, was Rupert's face. He'd only seen that blaze of elation when his father had won big races, or major show-jumping classes in the old days.

'You were fucking fantastic,' Rupert told him, then stopped to listen in wonder to the accelerating stamp of feet from the hall. 'I only got applause like that at the Olympics.'

'You've got to go back again, Marcus,' an NTV minion popped his head round the door. 'You took it so fast, we've got a couple of minutes to fill before the break.'

Going out of his dressing-room, Marcus collided with an outraged Howie Denston.

'You've blown it, you stupid fucker. How could you screw Rannaldini like that? He controls everything. The jury won't touch you now – you're blown out of the water, finished.'

Howie was followed by a tearful Helen.

'Oh Marcus, how could you do that to Rannaldini? What must he be feeling at this moment?'

'Natalia's boobs, probably,' said Marcus curtly. 'He's a bastard, Mum, the sooner you chuck him the better.'

And leaving a frantically mouthing Helen, he went

back to face the ecstatic crowds and because Rannaldini had refused to return, bringing the orchestra and then Hilary, Peter and Simon to their feet and even kissing little Noriko's hand.

'Hey, lay off,' yelled Cherub from the gallery and everyone laughed.

'For God's sake, get them off the stage,' an NTV official was yelling to Nicholas, 'or we'll be into another hour's overtime.'

'That's your problem,' said Knickers cheerfully. 'That was absolutely marvellous, Marcus.'

'He was always so sweet and polite,' sobbed Helen.

Taggie put an arm round her shoulders.

'He's been under a terrible strain, so have you. Let's all have a huge drink,' she added to Rupert, who was already opening bottles from a crate of champagne, which he had magically produced.

When Julian at last brought the orchestra off the platform, he was accosted by a maddened Rannaldini, 'D'you realize,' he spat, 'that you have just lost the chance of leading what will become the greatest orchestra in the world.'

'I'd far rather work for the happiest,' said Julian coldly and walked straight past him.

SIXTY-NINE

Up in the jurors' room it was pandemonium.

'He had a memory lapse in the first movement,' intoned the Chinese judge who still had hopes of Han Chai.

'The boy's a genius. I never heard it so well played, he has a delicateness and a strongness the others have not,' said the big Ukrainian.

'The last two movements were impeccable, and so lyrical,' said the French feminist, 'Rannaldini sabotage Marcus the whole time.'

'His manners to Rannaldini were most disrespectful,' snapped Lili, seeing her Steinway, and her promised concert with the new super orchestra sliding away. 'He wouldn't even shake the Maestro's hand.'

'I prefer Natalia,' agreed Ernesto, who had changed sides after Rannaldini offered him a Cartier watch and trials for all his pupils. 'She and Rannaldini interacted so charmingly together.'

'That's because she has beeg teets,' said Pablo, who was still sulkily searching for his *Guinness Book of Records*.

'Can't we have a serious drink, Blodwyn?' grumbled Bruce Kennedy.

'Not till you've finished judging,' said Lady Appleton,

pouring him a glass of Evian. 'What d'you feel, Hermione?'

'I would prefer Natalia,' urged Hermione in her deep voice. 'And it would be more politically correct to give it to a woman.'

This support had been drummed up by Rannaldini. While Natalia had been resting that afternoon, he had found half an hour to administer so much unpolitical correction to Hermione that she could hardly sit down.

Marcus's supporters gazed at her stonily.

'I thought it was jolly funny,' snorted Dame Edith, blowing cigar smoke in Hermione's pained face. 'Rannaldini tried to scupper Marcus, and the boy rose magnificently to the occasion, just like his father always did. Boy's a genius, and brave as a lion, nothing more to be said.'

Lady Appleton, however, had a lot more: the reputation of the competition was at stake.

'Can one rely on Marcus to perform all those concerts?' she asked cautiously.

'Oh well, if you're going for the safe candidate,' boomed Edith, 'we might as well settle on the American and go and get blotto.'

Jennifer, sitting in the next armchair, her mouth full of crisps, wagged in agreement.

The jury, however, bridled. They'd all read a piece in the *Daily Telegraph* by Norman Lebrecht last Monday which accused today's juries of rejecting genius, passion and true individuality in favour of reliability and predictability.

'Marcus 'as a voice all his own, a radiance beyond the notes,' sighed Pablo. 'What emotion, what power, what eenocence, what wiseness, what love.'

'He had a memory lapse,' repeated the Chinese judge, who was busy rewriting the chapter on the Schumann concerto on his laptop.

'I still think Natalia has the – ouch!' screamed Dame

Hermione, as Ernesto surreptitiously pinched her on her pained bottom. 'Just a twinge of neuralgia,' she added hastily.

'I shall resign if Marcus doesn't ween,' said Boris, taking his hand out of Deirdre's, and speaking for the first time.

'I, too,' said Pablo.

'And I shall resign if he does,' said Rannaldini, sweeping in in such icy rage that everyone wilted. The ladies, who'd dog-paddled with him in the deep end, felt their resolve weakening.

'We cannot let soloist deectate,' hissed Rannaldini. 'We must eradicate thees kind of hooliganism. I geeve heem every courtesy, every encouragement, see what he does in the middle movement, see 'ow he reject my proffered hand? Never 'ave I been treated like that. It is all part of grudge match,' he went on. 'Marcus's father 'ate me for marrying his ex-wife. The boy worsheep his mother – like many homosexuals he is wildly jealous of anyone she love. He is seek, he is unbalanced.'

'*Marcus* is unbalanced?' said Boris in amazement.

No-one dared laugh. Rannaldini's rage was so controlled, yet so venomous.

How could I have let that man take over my orchestra? thought Dame Edith in horror.

'Marcus is seek in body, too,' went on Rannaldini. 'Constantly 'e pull out of concert at the last moment because of asthma.'

'We certainly must have a healthy candidate,' said a worried Lady Appleton, 'with all those wonderful engagements lined up.'

'Under that kind of pressure, he will crack,' said Rannaldini dismissively. 'You see him go to pieces in the first movement. How boring he play *Waldstein* in early round. You make terrible mistake.'

Pablo Gonzalez could see the jury sliding away from him.

'Marcus was zee most chivalrous accompanist,' he pleaded. 'Whenever the orchestra 'ave big solo, he just drop gently out of the limelight, that seem balanced to me. He get up from his deathbed, and all that scandal with Nemerovsky.'

'I agree with Pablo. I never see finer example of grace under pressure,' said the burly Ukrainian stubbornly.

'Yes, I thought you found him attractive,' said Rannaldini bitchily. 'I saw you having a clandestine dreenk with him the other night.'

'Gentlemen, gentlemen,' Lady Appleton glanced at the clock. 'The news will be over in a minute or two, we must vote.'

There was a knock on the door of Marcus's dressing-room. Outside stood a grey-faced piano tuner.

'We're busy,' snapped Rupert.

'I must have a private word with Mr Black,' then, as Marcus went outside with him, the tuner stammered: 'I know it's too late to change anything, but I've got to tell you what I did to the piano on Wednesday.'

He then explained how he had slid a ball-bearing on top of the two concealed blocks of wood at the bass end of the keyboard, which divide when the soft pedal is pressed.

'The ball-bearing just slipped down between the blocks, holding them apart,' mumbled the tuner, 'jamming the soft pedal for the rest of the *Waldstein*. When they called me back because you'd kicked up a fuss, all I had to do was roll out the ball-bearing with a long screwdriver when no-one was looking.'

'How very ingenious,' said Marcus, fascinated. 'I couldn't think what had happened. Could you do it to Benny next time?'

The piano tuner was shattered.

'I can't believe you're taking it like this,' he muttered. 'I'm sorry I can't tell you who bribed me, but I'm going to pay back every penny of the money.'

'I wouldn't,' advised Marcus. 'Rannaldini can afford it. Thanks for telling me.'

Marcus couldn't be bothered to say anything when he went back to his dressing-room. The whole confession had been a welcome interruption. He had been interviewed by the frightful James Vereker and now found the strain of waiting in a crowded dressing-room intolerable. People, including half of the orchestra, seemed to have poured in to congratulate him and drink Rupert's drink.

A still furious Howie, and a still tearful Helen, who'd been bawled out by a foaming Rannaldini and banished from the conductor's room, were the only dissenting voices.

Seeing Marcus whitening near to death, the shadows deepening under his eyes, Rupert kicked everyone out.

'You OK?'

Marcus nodded. 'It's crazy. On the drive here, all that mattered was that I got through it,' he blushed. 'Now I seriously want to win.'

'That's my boy, you're learning.'

'Course you'll win, you're a star now,' said Taggie.

Suddenly Marcus remembered Alexei warning him that stars could never belong to each other, that the true artist could only belong to the world, and the pain came roaring back. What did winning matter without Alexei? There was a knock on the door.

Chrissie had put on some crimson lipstick to match her turkey legs.

'Ready, Martin? They are going to tell you the results beforehand in the green room.'

Rupert got to his feet, and straightened Marcus's tie again. Taggie brushed down his tail-coat.

'Good luck,' said Helen in a tight, trembling voice. 'I'll see you later.'

'By the way,' murmured Rupert, then waiting till

Helen had left, he drew a cellophane box containing a white flower out from behind the curtain. The envelope attached to it had been opened.

'Someone chucked this in the bin.' He handed the box to Marcus.

Ripping it open, Marcus nearly fainted, as he breathed in the sweet apple smell of philadelphus, instantly bringing back that baking hot June afternoon. There were only two lines on the card.

'I was wrong. With love all is possible. I am very jealous of the world. Alexei.'

Seeing the incredulous joy on the boy's face, Rupert removed the carnation from Marcus's buttonhole and replaced it with the philadelphus.

'Come on, Martin,' grumbled Chrissie. 'We can't keep the Princess waiting. Although Lady Appleton will have told you the order beforehand do try not to show your disappointment when you file onto the platform as it spoils it for the audience. Anyway,' she added, seeing Marcus's face fall, 'you're way ahead in the NTV viewers' poll.'

As he walked into the Green Room, Anatole greeted him in ecstasy.

'I ween pub competition, I ween thees,' he brandished a huge beer mug. '*Knees up Muzzer Brown.*' He did a little dance.

'Hush,' chorused the NTV minions.

A strip of black velvet had been pinned to one of the Green Room walls. In front was a huge arrangement of lilies and chrysanthemums. On the table was a note saying:

'James Vereker to interview winner in front of black velvet immediately after results.'

'I dropped those flowers three times,' observed a passing technician.

'Hush,' said Chrissie.

Lady Appleton cleared her throat.

'I'll give you the order back to front,' she told the contestants, 'starting with the lowest.'

'Don't forget to curtsy, Marcus, when you shake hands with the Princess,' said Benny nastily.

Natalia was perfectly calm. She knew she had won. Rannaldini had told her so.

'*Knees up Muzzer Brown*,' sang Anatole.

As the six contestants filed onto the platform, sitting high up on the chairs that had earlier been occupied by the brass players, Marcus looked so white and stunned, Rupert knew with a terrible lurch of pity and disappointment he hadn't won.

'I'm so sorry,' whispered Taggie.

'It's OK.'

Rupert took her hand. 'What matters somehow is that for the first time he's miraculously mine. I'm sorry I've been so vile today. I can always be relied upon to be a tower of gelignite in a crisis.'

'I love you.'

'Doesn't Her Royal Highness look dignified?' sighed Peggy Parker, as the Princess, resplendent in Listermint-green taffeta and lots of diamonds, led a trail of local dignitaries in robes and furry burghers' hats slowly up the centre aisle to take their seats on the platform.

'And now our finalists in reverse order,' said James Vereker, batting his dyed eyelashes at the Princess. 'Lady Appleton will announce the winners.'

'We're just waiting for a signal from NTV,' said Lady Appleton, her round pink face glowing like a harvest moon. 'I'd just like to remind everyone that we judge the candidates on all three rounds, not just tonight's nor yesterday's efforts. All right, James,' she smiled into the camera. 'In sixth place, we have Han Chai.'

As the little Korean came dancing down the steps, looking so pretty and happy to be sixth, everyone decided she should have been placed higher and gave her a terrific reception.

'Fifth from France, Mr Benjamin Basanovich,' cried Lady Appleton.

Benny was absolutely livid, but he got an even louder cheer because everyone was so relieved he hadn't won.

'Fourth,' Lady Appleton cleared her throat and rustled her notes, 'our very popular contender from across the Atlantic.'

Still in his plaid jacket, Carl bounded down the steps two at a time, grinning broadly, thrilled to be meeting royalty, taking the Princess's little hand in his two big ones.

'Marcus is third,' whispered an excited Flora to George and Trevor.

Then followed a long pause because the Princess was having such a long chat with Carl.

'Oh, get on with it,' yelled Dixie from the gallery.

'Third prize,' began Lady Appleton.

Here we go, at least he's placed, thought Rupert.

'Is our friend from Russia.'

'*Knees up Muzzer Brown*,' shouted Anatole, waving his beer mug, bouncing up to the Princess and, charming her just as much as he charmed the crowd, he kissed her hand.

Rannaldini glanced across at Natalia. A tear was trickling down her rosy cheek. Little darling, crying with happiness, he thought complacently. Soon he would be drinking champagne out of her and the cup.

The atmosphere in the hall crackled with excitement. Lady Appleton enjoyed her four-yearly moment of glory. George squeezed Flora's hand till she winced.

'I love you, I love you. Oh please God, make it be Marcus,' she begged.

'Second, a very worthy contestant, is our charming friend from Czechoslovakia, Natalia—'

But no-one heard her surname as Lady Appleton was drowned by a demented roar of joy that took the roof off, as the crowd realized the home side had won. On the strength of that they could now afford to feel sorry for Natalia as, battling with disappointment, the picture of desolation, she accepted her silver plate and allowed the kind Princess to mop up her tears.

The atmosphere was now a seething cauldron. A cheer rose and fell. Rupert hugged Taggie until her ribs cracked. The orchestra leaning over the gallery were yelling their heads off.

Boris was kissing Deirdre.

'Zank you, zank you, my darling, you are not bloody bigot after all.'

'He's won,' screamed Flora, holding George even tighter as a somewhat squashed Trevor barked his approval.

Up in the dress circle, a grinning Jennifer barked back.

At last there was silence.

'And the winner of the 1995 Appleton Piano Competition—' Lady Appleton smiled round.

'You don't need to be Inspector Morse to deduce that,' bellowed Randy.

Even Lady Appleton laughed.

'The winner of the 1995 Appleton,' she repeated shakily, 'is our own Marcus Campbell-Black.'

The Princess taking both Marcus's hands had to shout to make herself heard.

'Are you sure you're all right? You've been so terribly ill. It's a wonderful victory. You played so beautifully.'

'And you look so beautiful,' Marcus found himself blurting out.

The Princess was so sweet and after that he couldn't remember anything she said until she handed over the little silver piano, as well as a huge cup.

'Of course queers get on awfully well with women,' sniffed Mrs Parker.

'Oh shut up, you old monster,' snapped Flora.

'Speech,' bellowed the orchestra.

Oh no, thought Taggie in anguish, remembering how

Marcus had dried during a debate in front of the whole of Bagley Hall. He had never been able to string a sentence together in public.

But Marcus had taken the microphone and was waiting for a lull. He was whiter than the piano keys. A lock of damp auburn hair had fallen over his freckled forehead, he looked absurdly young. To speak now was far more terrifying than playing the Schumann, but he had to do it. What a beauty, and our own, thought the audience in raptures.

'Your Royal Highness, Ladies and Gentlemen,' gasped Marcus, fighting for breath, 'I'd like to thank all the judges for giving me this amazing prize –' he waved the silver piano – 'and the organizers, particularly Lady Appleton for – er – organizing such a marvellous competition, and Mrs Bateson for looking after me – and baking such terrific cakes and everyone at Northladen General for saving my life—' There was a burst of cheering.

As he gained in confidence he had a voice just like Rupert's, thought Flora.

'I also want to thank my parents,' Marcus went on steadily, 'my mother and my stepmother, but, most of all, my father, Rupert Campbell-Black,' deliberately he emphasized the 'Campbell'. 'It isn't easy for parents to accept their son is a homosexual. And they've been absolutely terrific,' he glanced in Rupert's direction, 'particularly my father.'

'Oooooooh dear,' mumbled Flora, smearing all her mascara as she wiped her shirtsleeve across her eyes.

Glancing sideways Taggie also saw the wetness of Rupert's lashes. The silence was total.

'And most of all,' Marcus grinned up at the gallery, 'I've got to thank the RSO, for playing so brilliantly today and being such a great orchestra.'

'Tell that to the Arts Council,' roared Dixie.

Marcus joined in the laughter. There was a volley of applause which faded because people wanted to listen.

Aware that the cameras were rolling, unfazed that he was addressing millions of viewers, Marcus went on.

'But this may be the last time you hear the RSO because they are being forced to merge with the Cotchester Chamber Orchestra. This means most of them will lose their jobs.'

'That's enough,' snarled Rannaldini, who was already foaming like a pit bull.

'I agree, Maestro,' Lady Appleton rose to her feet.

The Princess, however, who was looking madly interested, stayed seated.

'I've almost finished,' Marcus raised his hand. 'I only want to say the real heroine of this evening, Abigail Rosen, wasn't allowed to be here.' The orchestra gave another great cheer. 'Because Abby was involved with me, she was sacked and not allowed to conduct her own orchestra today. Although I love her very much, I can't marry her, because I couldn't give her the happiness she deserves. No-one has done more to make the RSO the truly great orchestra you heard today.' Marcus's voice broke, but he just managed to finish. 'I hope the ban will be lifted and Abby will get her job back. Thank you.'

The cheers were still echoing in his ears when he finally fought his way back to his dressing-room. A mad party was spilling out into the passage. Everyone was opening champagne bottles and celebrating. Mrs Bateson hugged him.

'Your little cat really worked,' Marcus told her.

Lord Leatherhead and Mrs Parker and even awful Miles were all there getting in on the act.

'Sonny will write you a concerto, Marcus,' promised Mrs Parker. 'He says no-one can play the *Interruption* like you do.'

'From the first,' Goatie Gilbert was boasting, 'I recognized Marcus Black's talent.'

Rupert couldn't remember feeling so happy or so proud, it was as though a dam, built of years of irritation, contempt and antagonism, had suddenly burst, and he could feel love for Marcus pouring out of him. Sister Angelica had been right about El Dorado being found in the heart. Thank God, it wasn't too late, and he had time ahead to make it up to Marcus.

'I can smell the fatted calf,' said Flora slyly.

Rupert laughed. 'Lousy with cholesterol. At least Taggie knows how to cook it. The downside is I don't get you as a daughter-in-law. I suppose you couldn't wait for Xav to grow up?'

'I'm suited,' said Flora, blushing slightly, 'but thanks all the same.'

Then, as George, who was holding out a town-hall teacup of water for Trevor to drink out of, shot Rupert yet another murderous glance, she added hastily: 'You really must get to know George.'

'I don't think George feels that's strictly necessary,' said Rupert.

Across the room Helen was in raptures over Marcus's victory.

'Oh darling, darling, I'm so proud. Think of all the wonderful concerts ahead. You'll be in work for the next two years and your speech was so lovely, so assured. I hope Abby heard it.'

'More importantly, I hope the board did,' said Marcus glaring at Miles and taking a glass of champagne from Rupert.

'Do you think you ought to drink after all that medication?' reproved Helen.

The next moment Howie Denston rushed in and embraced Marcus.

'Great, kid, great! Always knew you could do it. You've talked to James Vereker, OK. In ten minutes there'll be a press conference. I'll field any tricky questions about Nemerovsky and then there's the party. You'll be sitting near Lady A. and the Princess. Your folks are invited, of course. Tomorrow around ten, we'll sign the contracts. You'll be working your fingers off for the next two years.'

He tapped his mobile. 'I've already had two big record producers on to me.'

But Marcus was re-reading Alexei's note.

'Fine, Howie.' Then he looked up. 'Could you all clear out? I want a word with Mum and Dad.'

Helen's heart swelled. Marcus had grown so authoritative. In a day, he seemed to have turned into a man, and she was feeling much more cheerful having just met Lord Leatherhead, who'd asked her out to lunch next week.

Rupert, meanwhile, was talking to Czechoslovakia on his mobile.

'Pridie's absolutely fine,' Dizzy was telling him. 'You're not to be cross with Lysander. His shoulder's been set and he's really sorry he didn't win.'

'Doesn't matter – Marcus did,' said Rupert jubilantly. 'Christ, he did brilliantly.'

Taggie snatched the telephone from him.

'And guess what?' she told Dizzie, 'Rupert didn't fall asleep once.'

As Taggie joined the rest of the revellers drifting out, saying, 'Absolutely brilliant, see you at the party,' Marcus shut the door and leant against it looking at his parents squarely.

'You ought to be in bed,' chided Helen.

'I'm going to Moscow,' said Marcus.

Helen gave a scream. 'Oh no, you can't, your career! All those engagements!'

Rupert's sigh was almost imperceptible and in no way betrayed his desolation at suddenly discovering El Dorado was disappearing into the mists again.

'Are you sure that's what you want?' he asked slowly.

Marcus nodded.

'Moscow's bloody dangerous at the moment.'

'I know, but I will come back.'

'Then I'll drive you to the airport. We better look up a flight.'

'I know them all backwards.'

Helen burst into tears.

'Please don't go, after all we've worked for. Think what you're throwing away: the Queen Elizabeth, the Festival Hall, the Wigmore, the Barbican. Have you got some sort of death-wish? I wanted Penscombe to be yours *and* your sons,' she sobbed, 'and your sons' sons. Then you'd never have to worry about money. And now you're chucking everything away, just when fate's given you a second chance. You and Abby were so happy. There are counsellors you could talk to.'

'Mum,' said Marcus gently as he hugged his mother, 'you don't understand. I love Alexei. I can't hang around this evening. I've proved to myself I can play the piano. I don't want to get into that circus. I want to develop as a soloist in my own time.'

Gently, he pulled away from her, then briefly he put his arms round Rupert.

'I love you, Dad, I'm sorry it's taken me so long to say it.'

I don't understand, thought Helen in despair, why does Rupert always swan in at the last moment and win out?

SEVENTY

When Marcus didn't show up at the party, it was at first assumed he'd flaked out and gone back to bed. A home win in itself was enough to ensure the most riotous celebrations. Anyway the RSO were too busy getting legless to notice. Cherub, who'd packed in more drinking time because there was no percussion in the Schumann, was absolutely plastered and, by smiling sweetly at Pablo, had joyfully appropriated the *Guinness Book of Records*.

'That's the biggest mole in history,' he pointed at Hilary's rigid back, going off into fits of giggles. 'And here's the prickliest cactus,' he pointed at Militant Moll. 'And he-ah we have the biggest goldfish,' pausing behind Hermione he started making fish faces and mouthing: '*I know that my Redeemer.*'

His fellow musicians were in stitches.

'Who's the biggest rat?' asked Fat Isobel, who had practically obscured Ninion by sitting on his knee.

'Him,' said Cherub, pointing at Carmine who was still trying to reach Cathie on his mobile.

'I am biggest gooseberry,' sighed Pablo, who was sitting at a table with a passionately embracing Boris and Deirdre.

'And there is the coldest fish,' naughty Cherub pointed at Miles, who, up at the end of the room, was being given the biggest flea in his ear by George.

Not having been to bed for forty hours, George was, in fact, suddenly overwhelmed with tiredness. He had called an emergency board meeting for one o'clock in the morning, but he was not optimistic. Rannaldini had probably bribed too many of the board for George to be able to overturn their decision to appoint him musical director. If he did, it wouldn't save the situation. There was no way the RSO could survive even a month longer without a massive injection of cash.

George himself owed twenty million pounds to German banks at the moment, so the money couldn't come from him. Anyway, he wanted to be with Flora, who, with Sister Rose and Miss Parrott, was now noisily teaching Dimitri and Anatole the hokey-cokey. Glancing round, she smiled at him and George felt his heart melting like a Yorkie Bar in the sun.

Meanwhile the largest plague of locusts, discovered over the Red Sea in 1889, was nothing to the way the RSO were demolishing the cold buffet. Only Julian, still violently shaking after his defiance of Rannaldini, couldn't eat or drink a thing. Through the sound of revelry, he could hear the cannon's opening roar of a Rannaldini rabid for vengeance.

The long top table was the only one with a seating plan. Trapped between the Princess and Lady Appleton, Rannaldini was having to be polite, but his darkly tanned face was twitching like treacle toffee coming up to the boil.

Cherub was off again.

'That's the biggest toad in the world,' he said, sticking a pink tongue out at Gilbert.

'And here comes the sexiest man,' squeaked Nellie in excitement.

'Rupert Campbell-Black? He's already taken,' said Clare, not bothering to look round.

'Nope.'

'Sean Bean?'

'Nope.'

Clare swung round irritably.

'Viking,' she screamed.

'Viking!' yelled the RSO, as they joyfully and drunkenly stumbled towards him.

'Cousin Victor,' cried Deirdre in amazement, letting go of Boris.

But Viking, poised in the doorway, looked so tall, thin, pale and quivering with menace, that Deirdre almost crossed herself.

'Hi, kids.' Almost absent-mindedly, Viking pushed the orchestra out of the way, his eyes, narrowed to black thread, never leaving Rannaldini's face.

The next moment, fleeter than any cheetah, he crossed the room to the top table and, reaching over, had grabbed Rannaldini by his suede lapels, dragging him across the white table-cloth, scattering glass, silver, china and flowers, until Rannaldini was standing beside him on the blue carpet.

'How dare you hurt my Abigail?' yelled Viking and, to equal cheers and screams of horror, he smashed his fist into Rannaldini's evil mahogany face, lifting him up in a perfect parabola, so his descent onto the pudding trolley was only cushioned by Gwynneth who was piling her plate with a third helping of *bombe surprise.*

The interminable, stunned silence was finally broken by Dixie.

'That's the only way you'll ever get Sir Roberto to lie on top of you, Gwynnie,' he shouted.

The RSO collapsed with laughter.

'Partners in cream, partners in cream,' they chorused as Rannaldini and Gwynneth floundered in a sea of chocolate, sticky fruit and meringue.

But the laughter died on their lips, as Rannaldini's

minders, Clive and Nathan, moved in with deadly swiftness.

'Look out, Viking,' yelled Julian.

'Run,' shrieked Cousin Deirdre.

It was sage advice.

Viking realized he couldn't take on both Clive and Nathan, particularly as a shiny dark object glinted menacingly in Nathan's huge hand.

'Get him,' hissed Rannaldini, rubbing Black Forest gâteau out of his eyes.

And Viking was off, darting through the little tables, sending a huge vase of bronze chrysanthemums flying, catching Trevor and Jennifer in flagrante behind the carving trolley, out through a side-door, up a flight of stairs.

Shouting voices and footsteps pounding after him sent him hurtling along a corridor. There was no time to catch the lift, the footsteps were getting nearer. At the end of the corridor were stone stairs and, panting down seven flights and sidling across the lounge, Viking found himself in the lobby.

But as he paused to catch his breath, Clive emerged from the lift. Dummying past him, Viking hurled himself into the revolving doors, only to find Nathan leering at him on the other side, still waving the same menacing shiny object.

With huge yuccas to left and right of the door, there was no escape. Wincing as Clive grabbed his arm, Viking turned, looking into the vicious, unpitying face of Death.

'The basstard had it coming,' muttered Viking.

For a second or two, Death stared at him, then suddenly warmed up and smiled almost affectionately.

'Couldn't agree with you more, dear,' lisped Clive. 'Been waiting ten years for someone to give Rannaldini his comeuppance. May I shake you by the hand?'

Then, as Viking's jaw dropped, Nathan bounded in through the revolving doors with a grin as wide as the keys on a Steinway, and thrust the menacing object into Viking's hand.

'You dropped your wallet, man.'

'We'd very much like to buy you a drink,' said Clive.

'It's very generous of you both,' Viking started to shake, not entirely with laughter.

Through the revolving doors, he could see his taxi-driver polishing off a pork pie and a can of lager to sustain him after the first leg of the journey from Holyhead.

'I'm on my way to Heathrow,' said Viking, 'but perhaps I've josst got time for a quick one.'

Rannaldini, swearing vengeance, had disappeared to wash *crème brulée* out of his pewter hair before the emergency board meeting, when the bellboy walked in with a telephone.

'Call for you, Mr Hungerford.'

As George lifted the receiver, everyone around him could hear the frantic squawking as if a hen had just laid a dinosaur's egg.

'Mr Hungerford,' cried Miss Priddock, 'Ay saw you in the audience. Thank goodness you're back. An amazin' thing has happened. I don't know quaite how to tell you.'

'Try,' said George unhelpfully.

But as he listened, his I-don't-want-to-be-bothered-with-paper-clips scowl creased into a huge smile.

'That is amazing, Miss P. Woonderful in fact. Are you at home? I'll call you later. Yes, it was great – Marcus won.'

As he switched off the telephone, he turned to Flora: 'Well done, John Droommond.'

'He's caught the biggest rat in the world?' giggled Flora.

Cherub had reached the prehistoric chapter, his finger moving shakily along the line: 'The largessht exshtinct animal in the world wash the two hundred and fifty ton supersaurus,' he informed his audience.

'And the most extinct ensemble in the world,' said George draining his glass of brandy, 'is Rannaldini's Super Orchestra.'

and the most exquisite; so informed a cadence
And the most exquisite ensemble in the world, said
Cecaré Charton, his glass of brandy... to Rannaldini'
Super Christmas

C O D A

'Happy birthday,' said Gisela, thrusting out a big bunch
of autumn crocuses.

Abby looked round listlessly and put down her violin.

'Thank you, they're lovely,' she examined the delicate
veins on the pale mauve petals. 'In fact they're exquisite.
You're so good to me, Gisela. I'd forgotten it was my
birthday. I guess hitting thirty's kind of painless
compared with losing everything else in my life.'

'The autumn crocus bloom when everything else is
dying,' said the housekeeper gently.

'Oh Gisela,' Abby turned hastily towards the window
to hide her tears. She had already wept enough to fill
Lake Lucerne, which as far as the eye could see sparkled
brilliant blue and utterly unsympathetic in the afternoon sunshine.

In her old rust-red jersey and brown suede skirt, which
was now hopelessly loose on her, she had all the sad
defencelessness of an autumn leaf blown against the
window.

'You must eat, child,' urged Gisela. 'I've just made
onion soup and there's bread fresh from the oven.'

'You're so darling, I'm sorry, I'm just not hungry, and
I can't practise any more. I'll take a walk along the lake.

Can you put the flowers in water? Thank you, I just love them.'

Handing back the crocuses, Abby ran from the room. A crawling restlessness, an inability to settle to anything was part of her malaise.

'Put on a coat,' Gisela shouted after her, but the front door had banged.

Gisela had never seen such despair.

Abby reminded her of a child, whose family had all been killed, huddling in the ruins of a bombed-out city.

It was a beautiful day. The air was misty and silky. The lake, reflecting a big cloud that had drifted overhead, was grey-blue now. Little waves caressed the banks along which autumn blazed. Amid the amber gloom of the woods, the beeches stood out stinging red like huntsmen riding by. Abby could almost hear their horns. Oh Viking, Viking!

Splashing through the puddles from last night's deluge, she battled to come to terms with the anguish of last weekend. After the first dreadful shock of being conned and betrayed, Marcus being outed had been almost a relief. It explained his lack of desire (except for those heady frenzied days when he'd first met Alexei), which had made her feel such a failure as a woman. But she missed him as a best friend, as she missed Flora, who now belonged to George. In addition, her violin wouldn't sing to her, and she was eaten up with guilt and sadness at abandoning her friends in the orchestra to the non-existent mercies of Rannaldini. She had let them down, she had blabbed to the Press. She had loved not wisely.

But it was the loss of Viking that wiped her out. Not only did she frantically crave his love-making, but only now did she appreciate how much she had looked forward to seeing him every day, how his dreadful sexist cracks had warmed her blood.

What d'you call a woman maestro? Mattress. Oh

Viking, she sighed, you can lie on me whenever you want. How she'd enjoyed the sparring, how she missed his kindness, his *louche* elegance, the sun in his arms.

I've grown accustomed to his face, thought Abby, as she watched the leaves drifting down for a last kiss with their reflection on the surface of the lake.

'*It was my thirtieth year to heaven,*' she quoted sadly. '*My birthday began with the waterbirds . . . and I rose in rainy autumn and walked abroad in a shower of all my days.*'

What the hell could she do with the rest of all her days? She couldn't go back to the loneliness of being a soloist. Being the tallest poppy, waiting to be hacked down, the Press pulling out her petals, this week we love her, this week we love her not. She supposed she could try for a job as a leader. But as a soloist, she had her own distinctive sound. She would have to learn to fuse with the rest of the orchestra.

I've never been able to fuse with anything in my life, she thought wearily.

She had the temporary security of Rodney's house on the lake, but that was being contested by his family. She missed Rodney so much, too. Every room was filled with his ghost, a faint waft of lemon cologne and cigars. Every evening, she expected him to bounce in brandishing a bottle of champagne, wearing nothing but his pin-striped apron.

'Oh well, it was worth a try.'

Only now did she realize how much Rodney had given her, letting her stay for so long, putting up with her tantrums, always ready to listen. She was sure his big heart had failed in the end because he had given so much of it away to other people. She wished he could send her a fax just to tell her he was OK.

Ahead Mount Pilatus, already covered in snow, gleamed in the sunshine. Pilate had come to the lake to suffer.

'How did you hack it, Pontius?' pleaded Abby. 'If you

and God have made it up, put in a good word. *It was my thirtieth year to heaven*,' she intoned wearily, as she shuffled through a thick carpet of curling sycamore leaves, 'or rather hell.'

She had drawn level with the little island, about sixty yards from the shore. Willows, alders, and tall ashes, hung with glittering grey pelts of traveller's joy, crowded its banks. Every puff of wind sent a shower of gold leaves drifting into the water, some falling into a little crimson rowing boat, with pale blue oars, which Abby suddenly noticed moored in the rushes.

Halting to listen to the water birds calling, Abby suddenly froze. No, it couldn't be. They didn't have hunting in this part of Switzerland. But there it was again, pa, pa, pa, the faint, sweet, sad sound of the horn drifting across the water.

Abby felt her whole body prickling, her hair rising, her tummy bungy-jumping without the aid of any rope. It must be the ghost of Hans Richter, the greatest conductor of his age, come back to mock her, as one who had failed. I'm going crazy, thought Abby, it must be exhaustion and lack of food.

Pa, pa, pa. There it was again, and not just any horn, no-one played with that dash and raw radiance. Sliding down the bank to the edge of the lake, straining her ears, Abby tried to hush the galloping crescendo of her heart beat, which threatened to blot out all sound.

It *was* coming from the island. Totally unaware of what she was doing, drawn by her longing, Abby crashed through the bull rushes into the icy water. For the horn had stopped tuning up and was now playing the soft infinitely tender love theme from *Ein Heldenleben*, when, after the tantrums, the bitching of the critics, the catalogue of past achievements and the great battle, the hero and his wife are blissfully reunited.

Oh, how beautiful it was. The rich dark notes were calling to her, weaving round her like a great purring panther. Abby stood knee deep and quivering, unable to believe what she was hearing, then she plunged into the water, gasping first at the cold, pushing through a thick gratin of leaves, then when she was out of her depth, swimming faster and faster.

'Viking,' she croaked as she came up for air, then choking and spitting. 'Oh Viking, I'm here, I'm here.'

And he had heard. As if in a dream, she saw him fighting his way through the nearest clump of yellow trees, then pause on the bank, gold conch in his hand with the traveller's joy draping his shoulders like the grey wolf-pelts of some Viking conqueror. His face was deathly white, his slitty eyes, beneath eyelids heavier than thunderclouds, were searching and anguished.

'Oh Abby, I was only bossking.' Then he chucked his gleaming horn in the rushes, and slithering down the bank, fell into her arms. For a second, he glanced down at her dripping face and removed a strand of weed from her hair with a desperately shaking hand. She could feel his heart crashing against hers. Then he buried his lips in hers, kissing her on and on, holding her tighter and tighter. Then as she wriggled free, hiding her face in his black-and-green plaid shirt, he muttered:

'Oh Abby, darling, darling, my darling, I've been such a basstard to you. But I can't live a single second longer without you. I'll die, I'll be cast away on an island of desolation for the rest of my life unless you rescue me.'

Abby looked up in bewilderment, but saw no jokes, no mockery, only tenderness in his face. And he was so pale.

'You're not sick?' Worried, she touched his cheek.

'Only with love.'

'And I love you,' gasped Abby, 'I've been so unhappy.'

Suddenly she was sobbing and shivering so violently that Viking pulled her up the bank, holding back the trees and leading her into a little clearing. Then he put his leather jacket round her and pulled her down onto a mossy log, holding her close and telling her he loved her until she was quiet and still.

'Why did you run away without saying goodbye?' she wailed.

'Because I knew you hated me. I had to win that horrible bet, in case anyone else got you. I went home to Ireland to distance myself, to try and get over you, but I couldn't. It was like a party political broadcast on all four channels telling me how lovvly you were. I didn't want to opset you, so I thought I'd wait till after the Appleton. Blue rang me and said you'd been sacked. I couldn't stay away any more. I just prayed you might need me.'

'Need you?' Abby wriggled even closer to him. 'I've done that from the moment I saw you.'

'Me, too,' Viking shook his head. 'I just took longer to admit it.'

Abby put her hand up to touch the scar where her ring had lashed his cheek.

'I was so horrible to you.'

'Not nearly as horrible as I was to you. And did you know we've been looking everywhere for you? Gisela only confessed you were here last night, because she was so worried.'

'She never told me you'd called,' said Abby indignantly. 'Why didn't you speak to me?'

'I bottled out, I was scared of saying the wrong thing.' Getting up Viking retrieved his horn from the rushes. 'This is the only way I can really express my love for you. Till I met you, my heart was onbreakable like a CD,' he half-smiled. 'That one you stamped on still plays.'

Gathering up her hair at the back, he twisted it round and round squeezing out the water.

'My Rosen d'être, I want to give you the world,' he said falteringly, 'but I being poor have only my dreams. But I won't be poor for long,' he added with a touch of his old swagger, 'I'm going to get my act together, make a bomb as a soloist, keep you in fine style, and stop being a womanizer.'

Abby laughed shakily.

'You're not a womanizer, you're a charmer.'

'Orpheus with his lute. I've come to lead you out of the Onderworld, back to Rotminster. They all miss you.'

'Only because I've left – and what about Rannaldini?'

'He's gone.'

'What!'

'Otterly routed. He hadn't a clay foot to stand on after the way he screwed up Marcus in the finals.' Then, at Abby's look of bewilderment, added, 'Marcus won, you know.'

'He won?' gasped Abby incredulously. 'But that's wonderful.'

'He made a fantastic winner's speech, live and straight to camera, telling everyone he loved you, but he was no good for you because he was gay and that you should be reinstated.'

'That's incredible,' Abby's eyes spilled over with tears. 'Oh, how darling of Marcus. Where is he?'

Viking's arms tightened round her.

'Please don't be sad, sweetheart – he's gone to Moscow.'

'My God! To Alexei.'

'You don't still love him, you're not too opset?' Viking's face was suddenly so fearful and worried, Abby had to kiss him better, entwining her body with his, melting into him until she thought he was going to take her then and there in the leafy clearing.

'God, I'm so lucky,' he murmured. 'And Nugent promises not to eat Sibelius or Scriabin.'

Abby smiled, still unable to take it all in. Then she nearly fell back into the water in amazement as she heard the most glorious cacophony. Leaping to her feet, she was just turning towards the bank, when Viking, who had also jumped up, clamped her to his chest.

'Josst listen,' he whispered.

Now I really am going crazy, thought Abby, as a full orchestra belted out, admittedly somewhat haphazardly, the first bars of *Ein Heldenleben* before switching to 'Happy Birthday'.

Struggling frantically until Viking loosened his grasp, Abby wriggled round, then she gazed and gazed, clutching his hand, leaning against him for support as the tears flowed down her cheeks. For the entire RSO still in their white ties and tails and last night's black dresses were grinning at her from the bank.

They were all standing out of order and obviously in the middle of a splendid party. Randy and Dixie were brandishing champagne bottles as well as their instruments. Dimitri was mopping his eyes, with Miss Parrott fondly beside him, her harp blending into the golden woods behind. Julian and Francis were brandishing a huge streamer, saying 'Happy 30th Birthday, Abby'. Juno – my goodness – was dancing cheek to cheek with Charlton Handsome, and – even more my goodness – there was Lord Leatherhead doing a stately jive with Peggy Parker, while Old Cyril merrily bopped with Old Henry, and a totally unharassed Knickers twisted the day away with Militant Moll.

In the background stood George, happily smoking a huge cigar and hugging a giggling Flora who was trying to play her viola. As Isobel and Ninion let off a great volley of bangers, a little boat struck out from the bank, with Noriko rowing through the yellow leaves, and Cherub frantically pinging his triangle.

'Herro. Abby, Herro,' called out Noriko.

'Actually she's a heroine,' shouted back Viking.

Then everyone cheered and cheered.

'I d-d-don't understand,' whispered Abby.

'They had an emergency board meeting last night after the competition,' said Viking, wiping her eyes, 'and George decided to charter a plane to fly us all out. It's been one helluva bash. We dropped Miles and Hilly in the English Channel.'

'But George shouldn't be wasting money charting planes, when we're bankrupt.'

'We're not any more,' Viking could hardly speak for

laughing. 'John Drommond won the lottery, so even if you programme Winifred Trapp every day, we'll still be solvent in the year 2000.'

'I can't believe it,' muttered Abby.

'Indeed you can, darling. It's the only way they can tell you they love you,' added Viking as 'Happy Birthday' swung very discordantly into the Wedding March.

'Your orchestra has come to take you home.'

Abby burst into tears of joy.

'But they're not together,' she wailed.

'No, but you and I are, and that's all that matters,' said Viking.

THE END

PANDORA
by Jilly Cooper

No picture ever came more beautiful than Raphael's *Pandora*.
Discovered by a dashing young lieutenant, Raymond Belvedon, in
a Normandy Chateau in 1944, she had cast her spell over his
family – all artists and dealers – for fifty years. Hanging in a turret
of their lovely Cotswold house, *Pandora* witnessed Raymond's
tempestuous wife Galena both entertaining a string of lovers, and
giving birth to her four children: Jupiter, Alizarin, Jonathan and
superbrat Sienna. Then an exquisite stranger rolls up, claiming to
be a long-lost daughter of the family, setting the three Belvedon
brothers at each other's throats. Accompanying her is her fatally
glamorous boyfriend, whose very different agenda includes an
unhealthy interest in the Raphael.

During a fireworks party, the painting is stolen. The hunt to
retrieve it takes the reader on a thrilling journey to Vienna,
Geneva, Paris, New York and London. After a nail-biting court case
and a record-smashing Old Masters sale at Sotheby's, passionate
love triumphs and *Pandora* is restored to her rightful home.

'Open the covers of Jilly Cooper's latest novel and you lift the lid
of a Pandora's box. From the pages flies a host of delicious and
deadly vices . . . Her sheer exuberance and energy are contagious'
The Times

'This is Jilly in top form with her most sparkling novel to date'
Evening Standard

'One reads her for her joie de vivre . . . and her razor-sharp sense
of humour. Oh, and the sex'
New Statesman

'She's irresistible . . . she frees you from the daily drudge and
deposits you in an alternative universe where love, sex and
laughter rule'
Independent on Sunday

'The whole thing is a riot – vastly superior to anything else in a
glossy cover'
Daily Telegraph

'A wonderful, romantic spectacular of a novel'
Spectator

9780552156400

CORGI BOOKS

RIDERS
by Jilly Cooper

'Sex and horses: who could ask for more?'
Sunday Telegraph

Offering a heady blend of skulduggery, sexual adventure and hilarious high jinks, Jilly Cooper's Rutshire chronicles include *Rivals, Polo, The Man who made Husbands Jealous* and *Appassionata*.

Riders, the first and steamiest in the series, takes the lid off international show jumping, a world in which the brave horses are almost human, but the humans frequently behave like animals.

Here are the loves, lusts and hatreds of a tight circle of star riders who move from show to show, united only by bitter rivalry and the terror of failure.

Even the hero, gypsy Jake Lovell, under whose magic hands the most difficult horse or woman becomes biddable, is driven by his loathing of the beautiful bounder and darling of the show ring, Rupert Campbell-Black. Having raided each others yards, and fought and fornicated their way round the capitals of Europe, the feud between these two super stars finally erupts with devastating consequences at the Los Angeles Olympics.

'Blockbusting fiction at its best'
David Hughes, *Mail on Sunday*

'I defy anyone not to enjoy her book. It is a delight from start to finish'
Auberon Waugh, *Daily Mail*

9780552156172

CORGI BOOKS